Praise for
The Sky Is Everywhere

"Heart-warming." *The Independent*

"Compelling, funny and heart-warming... I couldn't
put it down." *The Bookseller*

"How grief and love can run side by side is
sensitively and intensely explored in this energetic,
poetic and warm-blooded novel."
The Guardian

Also by Jandy Nelson

I'll Give You the Sun

WALKER
BOOKS

JANDY
NELSON

For my mother

First published in Great Britain 2010 by Walker Books Ltd
87 Vauxhall Walk, London SE11 5HJ

This edition published 2016

2 4 6 8 10 9 7 5 3 1

This book has been typeset in Fairfield

Printed and bound in Great Britain by Clays Ltd, St Ives plc

British Library Cataloguing in Publication Data:
a catalogue record for this book is
available from the British Library

ISBN 978-1-4063-7639-5

www.walker.co.uk

Dear Reader,

I am honored you are going to read Lennie's story, a story very close to my heart. Without warning, she burst into my world one day wielding her clarinet and worn copy of *Wuthering Heights* – the next thing I knew, I was typing at the speed of light. Right on her heels were Gram in her enchanted garden of aphrodisiacal roses, Uncle Big with his wacko pyramids, and a wild sorrow rushing through them all like the Rain River just steps from their home. I knew this sorrow. Years ago, like Lennie, I suffered a devastating loss. I wanted to explore this kind of cataclysmic and deeply transformational life event, but being a devout romantic, I wanted to explore it through a love story … or two – because what's a love story without a little complication? And so, in walked the laconic and seductive Toby Shaw and the charismatic Joe Fontaine. Poor Lennie! In her band-girl world, triangles belong in the percussion section, not her love life!

I so hope you enjoy this book!
Jandy

P.S. A secret: The kookiest elements of this novel are all true: The Spotted Plant, The Bad Luck House Purge, The Forest Bedroom, The Pyramids, and the biggie: A grief-stricken girl who scatters her poems all over town.

Part 1

1

Gram is worried about me. It's not just because my sister Bailey died four weeks ago, or because my mother hasn't contacted me in sixteen years, or even because suddenly all I think about is sex. She is worried about me because one of her houseplants has spots.

Gram has believed for most of my seventeen years that this particular houseplant, which is of the nondescript variety, reflects my emotional, spiritual and physical well-being. I've grown to believe it too.

Across the room from where I sit, Gram – all six feet and floral frock of her, looms over the black-spotted leaves.

"What do you mean it might not get better this time?" She's asking this of Uncle Big: arborist, resident pothead and mad scientist to boot. He knows something about everything, but he knows everything about plants.

To anyone else it might seem strange, even off the wall, that Gram, as she asks this, is staring at me, but it doesn't to Uncle Big, because he's staring at me as well.

"This time it has a very serious condition." Big's voice trumpets as if from stage or pulpit; his words carry weight, even *pass the salt* comes out of his mouth in a thou-shalt-Ten-Commandments kind of way.

Gram raises her hands to her face in distress, and I

go back to scribbling a poem in the margin of *Wuthering Heights*. I'm huddled into a corner of the couch. I've no use for talking, would just as soon store paper clips in my mouth.

"But the plant's always recovered before, Big, like when Lennie broke her arm, for instance."

"That time the leaves had white spots."

"Or just last fall when she auditioned for lead clarinet but had to play second chair again."

"Brown spots."

"Or when—"

"This time it's different."

I glance up. They're still peering at me, a tall duet of sorrow and concern.

Gram is the town of Clover's Garden Guru. She has the most extraordinary flower garden in Northern California. Her roses burst with more color than a year of sunsets, and their fragrance is so intoxicating that town lore claims breathing in their scent can cause you to fall in love on the spot. But despite her nurturing and renowned green thumb, this plant seems to follow the trajectory of my life, independent of her efforts or its own vegetal sensibility.

I put my book and pen down on the table. Gram leans in close to the plant, whispers to it about the importance of *joie de vivre*, then lumbers over to the couch, sitting down next to me.

Then Big joins us, plopping his enormous frame down beside Gram. We three, each with the same unruly hair that sits on our heads like a bustle of shiny black crows, stay like this, staring at nothing, for the rest of the afternoon.

This is us since my sister Bailey collapsed one month ago from a fatal arrhythmia while in rehearsal for a local production of *Romeo & Juliet*. It's as if someone vacuumed up the horizon while we were looking the other way.

2

The morning of the day Bailey died,
she woke me up
by putting her finger in my ear.
I hated when she did this.
She then started trying on shirts, asking me:
Which do you like better, the green or the blue?

The blue.
You didn't even look up, Lennie

Okay, the green. Really, I don't care what shirt you wear...
Then I rolled over in bed and fell back asleep.

I found out later
she wore the blue
and those were the last words I ever spoke to her.

(Found written on a candy wrapper on the trail to the Rain River)

My first day back to school is just as I expect, the hall does a Red Sea part when I come in, conversations hush, eyes swim with nervous sympathy, and everyone stares as if I'm holding Bailey's dead body in my arms, which I guess I am. Her death is all over me, I can feel it and everyone can see it, plain as a big black coat wrapped around me on a beautiful spring day. But what I don't expect is the unprecedented hubbub over some new boy, Joe Fontaine, who arrived in my month-long absence. Everywhere I go it's the same:

"Have you seen him yet?"

"He looks like a Gypsy."

"Like a rock star."

"A pirate."

"I hear he's in a band called Dive."

"That he's a musical genius."

"Someone told me he used to live in Paris."

"That he played music on the streets."

"Have you seen him yet?"

I have seen him, because when I return to my band seat, the one I've occupied for the last year, he's in it. Even in the stun of grief, my eyes roam from the black boots, up the miles of legs covered in denim, over the endless torso, and finally settle on a face so animated I wonder if

13

I've interrupted a conversation between him and my music stand.

"Hi," he says, and jumps up. He's treetop tall. "You must be Lennon." He points to my name on the chair. "I heard about— I'm sorry." I notice the way he holds his clarinet, not precious with it, tight fist around the neck, like a sword.

"Thank you," I say, and every available inch of his face busts into a smile – whoa. Has he blown into our school on a gust of wind from another world? The guy looks un-abashedly jack-o'-lantern happy which couldn't be more foreign to the sullen demeanor most of us strove to per-fect. He has scores of messy brown curls that flop every which way, and eyelashes so spider-leg long and thick that when he blinks he looks like he's batting his bright green eyes right at you. His face is more open than an open book, like a wall of graffiti really. I realize I'm writing *wow* on my thigh with my finger, decide I'd better open my mouth and snap us out of this impromptu staring contest.

"Everyone calls me Lennie," I say. Not very original, but better than *guh,* which was the alternative, and it does the trick. He looks down at his feet for a second and I take a breath and regroup for Round Two.

"Been wondering about that actually, Lennon after John?" he asks, again holding my gaze – it's entirely pos-sible I'm going to faint. Or burst into flames.

I nod. "Mom was a hippie." This is *northern* Northern California after all – the final frontier of freakerdom. Just in the eleventh grade we have a girl named Electricity, a guy

14

named Magic Bus, and countless flowers: Tulip, Begonia and Poppy – all parent-given-on-the-birth-certificate names. Tulip is a two-ton truck of a guy who would be the star of our football team if we were the kind of school that had a football team. We're not. We're the kind of school that has optional morning meditation in the gym.

"Yeah," Joe says. "My mom too, and Dad, as well as aunts, uncles, brothers, cousins … welcome to Commune Fontaine."

I laugh out loud. "Got the picture."

But whoa again – should I be laughing so easily like this? And should it feel this good? Like slipping into cool river water.

I turn around, wondering if anyone is watching us, and see that Sarah has just walked – rather, exploded – into the music room. I've hardly seen her since the funeral, feel a pang of guilt.

"Lennieeeee!" She careens toward us in prime goth-gone-cowgirl form: vintage slinky black dress, shit-kicker cowboy boots, blond hair dyed so black it looks blue, all topped off with a huge Stetson. I note the breakneck pace of her approach, wonder for an instant if she's going to actually jump into my arms right before she tries to, sending us both skidding into Joe, who somehow retains his balance, and ours, so we all don't fly through the window.

This is Sarah, subdued.

"Nice," I whisper in her ear, as she hugs me like a bear even though she's built like a bird. "Way to bowl down the gorgeous new boy." She cracks up, and it feels both

15

amazing and disconcerting to have someone in my arms shaking from laughter rather than heartbreak.

Sarah is the most enthusiastic cynical person on the planet. She'd be the perfect cheerleader if she weren't so disgusted by the notion of school spirit. She's a literature fanatic like me, but reads darker, read Sartre in tenth grade – *Nausea* – which is when she started wearing black (even at the beach), smoking cigarettes (even though she looks like the healthiest girl you've ever seen) and obsessing about her existential crisis (even as she partied to all hours of the night).

"Lennie, welcome back, dear," another voice says. Mr James – also known in my mind as Yoda for both outward appearance and inward musical mojo – has stood up at the piano and is looking over at me with the same expression of bottomless sadness I've gotten so used to seeing from adults. "We're all so very sorry."

"Thank you," I say, for the hundredth time that day. Sarah and Joe are both looking at me too, Sarah with concern and Joe with a grin the size of the continental United States. Does he look at everyone like this? I wonder. Is he a wingnut? Well, whatever he is, or has, it's catching. Before I know it, I've matched his continental USA and raised him Puerto Rico and Hawaii. I must look like The Merry Mourner. Sheesh. And that's not all, because now I'm thinking what it might be like to kiss him, to *really* kiss him – uh-oh. This is a problem, an entirely new un-Lennie-like problem that began (*WTF-edly?!*) at the funeral: I was drowning in darkness and suddenly all these boys in the room were glowing. Guy friends of Bailey's from work or college, most of whom I didn't know, kept coming up to me saying how sorry they were, and I don't know if it's because they thought I looked like Bailey, or because they felt bad for me, but later on, I'd catch some of them staring at me in this charged, urgent way, and I'd find myself staring back at them, like I was someone else, thinking things I hardly ever had before, things I'm mortified to have been thinking in a church, let alone at my sister's funeral.

This boy beaming before me, however, seems to glow in a class all his own. He must be from a very friendly part of the Milky Way, I'm thinking as I try to tone down this nutso smile on my face, but instead almost blurt out to Sarah, "He looks like Heathcliff," because I just realized he does, well, except for the happy smiling part – but then all of a sudden the breath is kicked out of me and I'm shoved onto the cold hard concrete floor that is my life now, because I remember I can't run home after school and tell Bails about a new boy in band.

My sister dies over and over again, all day long.

"Len?" Sarah touches my shoulder. "You okay?"

I nod, willing away the runaway train of grief barreling straight for me.

Someone behind us starts playing "Approaching Shark", aka the *Jaws* theme song. I turn to see Rachel Brazile gliding towards us, hear her mutter, "Very funny," to Luke Jacobus, the saxophonist responsible for the accompaniment. He's just one of many band-kill Rachel's left in her wake, guys duped by the fact that all that haughty horror is stuffed into a spectacular body, and then further deceived by big brown faun eyes and Rapunzel hair. Sarah and I are convinced God was in an ironic mood when he made her.

"See you've met The Maestro," she says to me, casually touching Joe's back as she slips into her chair – first chair clarinet – where I should be sitting.

She opens her case, starts putting together her instrument. "Joe studied at a conservatory in *Fronce*. Did he tell you?" Of course she doesn't say *France* so it rhymes with *dance* like a normal American-speaking human being. I can feel Sarah bristling beside me. She has zero tolerance for Rachel ever since she got first chair over me, but Sarah doesn't know what really happened – no one does.

Rachel's tightening the ligature on her mouthpiece like she's trying to asphyxiate her clarinet. "Joe was a *fabulous* second in your absence," she says, drawing out the word *fabulous* from here to the Eiffel Tower.

I don't fire-breathe at her: "Glad everything worked out for you, Rachel." I don't say a word, just wish I could curl into a ball and roll away. Sarah, on the other hand, looks like she wishes there were a battle-ax handy.

The room has become a clamor of random notes and scales. "Finish up tuning, I want to start at the bell today," Mr James calls from the piano. "And take out your pencils, I've made some changes to the arrangement."

"I'd better go beat on something," Sarah says, throwing Rachel a disgusted look, then huffs off to beat on her timpani.

Rachel shrugs, smiles at Joe – no not smiles: twinkles –

oh brother. "Well, it's true," she says to him. "You were – I mean, are – *fabulous*."

"Not so." He bends down to pack up his clarinet. "I was just keeping the seat warm. Now I can go back to where I belong." He points his clarinet at the horn section.

"You're just being modest," Rachel says, tossing fairy-tale locks over the back of her chair. "You have *so* many colors on your tonal palette."

I look at Joe expecting to see some evidence of an inward groan at these imbecilic words, but see evidence of something else instead. He smiles at Rachel on a geographical scale too. I feel my neck go hot.

"You know I'll miss you," she says, pouting.

"We'll meet again," Joe replies, adding an eye-bat to his repertoire. "Like next period, in history."

I've disappeared, which is good really, because suddenly I don't have a clue what to do with my face or body or smashed-up heart. I take my seat, noting that this grinning, eye-batting fool from Fronce looks nothing like Heathcliff. I was mistaken.

I open my clarinet case, put my reed in my mouth to moisten it and instead bite it in two.

At 4.48PM on a friday in April,
My sister was rehearsing the role of Juliet
and less than one minute later
she was dead.
To my astonishment, time didn't stop
with her heart.
People went to school, to work, to restaurants;
they crushed crackers into their clam chowder,
fretted over exams,
sang in ~~their~~ their cars with the windows up.
For days and days, the rain beat its fists
on the roof of ~~our~~ our house —
evidence of the terrible mistake
God had made.
Each morning, when I woke
I listened for the tireless pounding,
looked at the drear through the window
and was relieved
that at least the sun had the decency
to stay the hell away from us.

(Found on a piece of music paper, spiked on a low branch,
Flying Man's Gulch)

3

The rest of the day blurs by and before the final bell, I sneak out and duck into the woods. I don't want to take the roads home, don't want to risk seeing anyone from school, especially Sarah, who informed me that, while I've been in hiding, she's been reading up on loss and according to all the experts, it's time for me to talk about what I'm going through – but she, and the experts, and Gram, for that matter, don't get it. I can't. I'd need a new alphabet, one made of falling, of tectonic plates shifting, of the deep devouring dark.

As I walk through the redwood trees, my sneakers sopping up days of rain, I wonder why bereaved people even bother with mourning clothes when grief itself provides such an unmistakable wardrobe. The only one who didn't seem to spot it on me today – besides Rachel, who doesn't count – was the new boy. He will only ever know this new sisterless me.

I see a scrap of paper on the ground dry enough to write on, so I sit on a rock, take out the pen that I always keep in my back pocket now, and scribble a conversation I remember having with Bailey on it, then fold it up and bury it in the moist earth.

When I break out of the forest onto the road to our house, I'm flooded with relief. I want to be at home, where

Bailey is most alive, where I can still see her leaning out the window, her wild black hair blowing around her face as she says, "C'mon, Len, let's get to the river pronto."

"Hey you." Toby's voice startles me. Bailey's boyfriend of two years, he's part cowboy, part skate rat, all love slave to my sister, and totally missing in action lately despite Gram's many invitations. "We really need to reach out to him now," she keeps saying.

He's lying on his back in her garden with the neighbor's two red dogs, Lucy and Ethel, sprawled out asleep beside him. This is a common sight in the springtime. When the angel's trumpets and lilacs bloom, Gram's garden is positively soporific. A few moments among the blossoms and even the most energetic find themselves on their backs counting clouds.

"I was, uh, doing some weeding for Gram," he says, obviously embarrassed about his kick-back position.

"Yeah, it happens to the best of us." With his surfer flop of hair and wide face sun-spattered in freckles, Toby is the closest a human can come to lion without jumping species. When Bailey first saw him, she and I were out road-reading (we all road-read; the few people who live on our street know this about our family and inch their way home in their cars just in case one of us is out strolling and particularly rapt). I was reading *Wuthering Heights*, as usual, and she was reading *Like Water for Chocolate*, her favorite, when a magnificent chestnut brown horse trotted past us on the way to the trailhead. *Nice horse*, I thought, and went back to Cathy and Heathcliff, only looking up a few seconds later when I heard the thump of Bailey's book as it hit the ground.

She was no longer by my side but had stopped a few paces back.

"What's wrong with you?" I asked, taking in my suddenly lobotomized sister.

"Did you see that guy, Len?"

"What guy?"

"God, what's wrong with *you*, that gorgeous guy on that horse, it's like he popped out of my novel or something. I can't believe you didn't see him, Lennie." Her exasperation at my disinterest in boys was as perpetual as my exasperation at her preoccupation with them. "He turned around when he passed us and smiled right at me – he was *so* good-looking … just like the Revolutionary in this book." She reached down to pick it up, brushing the dirt off the cover. "You know, the one who whisks Gertrudis onto his horse and steals her away in a fit of passion— "

"Whatever, Bailey." I turned back around, resumed reading, and made my way to the front porch, where I sank into a chair and promptly got lost in the stampeding passion of the two on the English moors. I liked love safe between the covers of my novel, not in my sister's heart, where it made her ignore me for months on end. Every so often though, I'd look up at her, posing on a rock by the trailhead across the road, so obviously feigning reading her book that I couldn't believe she was an actress. She stayed out there for hours waiting for her Revolutionary to come back, which he finally did, but from the other direction,

23

having traded in his horse somewhere for a skateboard. Turns out he didn't pop out of her novel after all, but out of Clover High like the rest of us, only he hung out with the ranch kids and skaters, and because she was exclusively a drama diva, their paths never crossed until that day. But by that point it didn't matter where he came from or what he rode in on because that image of him galloping by had burned into Bailey's psyche and stolen from her the capacity for rational thought.

I've never really been a member of the Toby Shaw fan club. Neither his cowboy bit nor the fact that he could do a 180 Ollie into a Fakie Feeble Grind on his skateboard made up for the fact that he had turned Bailey into a permanent love zombie.

That, and he's always seemed to find me as noteworthy as a baked potato.

"You okay, Len?" he asks from his prone position, bringing me back to the moment.

For some reason, I tell the truth. I shake my head, back and forth, back and forth, from disbelief to despair, and back again.

He sits up. "I know," he says, and I see in his marooned expression that it's true. I want to thank him for not making me say a word, and getting it all the same, but I just remain silent as the sun pours heat and light, as if from a pitcher, all over our bewildered heads.

He pats the grass with his hand for me to join him. I sort of want to but feel hesitant. We've never really hung out before without Bailey.

I motion toward the house. "I need to go upstairs."

This is true. I want to be back in The Sanctum, full name: The Inner Pumpkin Sanctum, newly christened by me, when Bailey, a few months ago, persuaded me the walls of our bedroom just had to be orange, a blaringly un-apologetic orange that had since made our room sunglasses optional. Before I'd left for school this morning, I'd shut the door, purposefully, wishing I could barricade it from Gram and her cardboard boxes. I want The Sanctum the way it is, which means exactly the way it was. Gram seems to think this means: *I'm out of my tree and running loose through the park*, Gramese for *mental*.

"Sweet pea." She's come out onto the porch in a bright purple frock covered in daisies. In her hand is a paintbrush, the first time I've seen her with one since Bailey died. "How was your first day back?"

I walk over to her, breathe in her familiar scent: patchouli, paint, garden dirt.

"It was fine," I say.

She examines my face closely like she does when she's preparing to sketch it. Silence tick-tocks between us, as it does lately. I can feel her frustration, how she wishes she could shake me like she might a book, hoping all the words will just fall out.

"There's a new boy in honor band," I offer.

"Oh yeah? What's he play?"

"Everything, it seems." Before I escaped into the woods at lunch, I saw him walking across the quad with Rachel, a guitar swinging from his hand.

"Lennie, I've been thinking … it might be good for you now, a real comfort…" Uh-oh. I know where this is going. "I mean, when you were studying with Marguerite, I couldn't rip that instrument out of your hands— "

"Things change," I say, interrupting her. I can't have this conversation. Not again. I try to step around her to go inside. I just want to be in Bailey's closet, pressed into her dresses, into the lingering scents of riverside bonfires, coconut suntan lotion, rose perfume – her.

"Listen," she says quietly, reaching her free hand out to straighten my collar. "I invited Toby for dinner. He's quite out of his tree. Go keep him company, help him weed or something."

It occurs to me she probably said something similar to him about me to get him to finally come over. Ugh.

And then without further ado, she dabs my nose with her paintbrush.

"Gram!" I cry out, but to her back as she heads into the house. I try to wipe off the green with my hand. Bails and I spent much of our lives like this, ambushed by Gram's swashbuckling green-tipped paintbrush. Only green, mind you. Gram's paintings line the walls of the house, floor to ceiling, stack behind couches, chairs, under tables, in closets, and each and every one of them is a testament to her undying devotion to the color green. She has every hue from lime to forest and uses them to paint primarily one thing: willowy women who look half mermaid, half Martian. "They're my ladies," she'd tell Bails and me. "Halfway between here and there."

Per her orders, I drop my clarinet case and bag, then plant myself in the warm grass beside a supine Toby and the sleeping dogs to help him "weed".

"Tribal marking," I say, pointing to my nose.

He nods disinterestedly in his flower coma. I'm a green-nosed baked potato. Great.

I turtle up, tucking my knees to my chest and resting my head in the crevice between them. My eyes move from the wisteria cascading down the trellis to the several parties of daffodils gossiping in the breeze to the indisputable fact that springtime has shoved off its raincoat today and is just prancing around – it makes me queasy, like the world has already forgotten what's happened to us.

"I'm not going to pack up her things in cardboard boxes," I say without thinking. "Ever."

Toby rolls on his side, shields his face with his hand, trying to block the sun so he can see me, and to my surprise says, "Of course not."

I nod and he nods back, then I flop down on the grass, cross my arms over my head so he can't see that I'm secretly smiling a little into them.

The next thing I know the sun has moved behind a mountain and that mountain is Uncle Big towering over us. Toby and I must have both crashed out.

"I feel like Glinda the Good Witch," Big says, "looking down on Dorothy, Scarecrow and two Totos in the poppy field outside of Oz." A few narcotic springtime blooms are no match for Big's bugle of a voice. "I guess if you don't wake up, I'm going to have to make it snow on you." I grin groggily up at him with his enormous handlebar mustache poised over his lip like a grand Declaration of Weird. He's carrying a red cool box as if it were a briefcase.

"How's the distribution effort going?" I ask, tapping the cool box with my foot. We are in a ham predicament. After the funeral, there seemed to be a prime directive in Clover that everyone had to stop by our house with a ham. Hams were everywhere; they filled the fridge, the freezer, lined the counters, the stove, sat in the sink, the cold oven. Uncle Big attended to the door as people stopped by to pay their respects. Gram and I could hear his booming voice again and again, "Oh a ham, how thoughtful, thank you, come in." As the days went on Big's reaction to the hams got more dramatic for our benefit. Each time he exclaimed "A ham!" Gram and I found each other's eyes and had to suppress a rush of inappropriate giggles. Now Big is on a mission to make sure everyone in a twenty-mile radius has a ham sandwich a day.

He rests the cool box on the ground and reaches his hand down to help me up. "It's possible we'll be a hamless house in just a few days."

Once I'm standing, Big kisses my head, then reaches down for Toby. When he's on his feet, Big pulls him into his arms, and I watch Toby, who is a big guy himself, disappear in the mountainous embrace. "How you holding up, cowboy?"

"Not too good," he admits.

Big releases him, keeping one hand on his shoulder, and puts the other one on mine. He looks from Toby to me.

28

"No way out of this but through … for any of us." He says it like Moses, so we both nod as if we've been bestowed with a great wisdom. "And let's get you some turpentine." He winks at me. Big's an ace winker – five marriages to his name to prove it. After his beloved fifth wife left him, Gram insisted he move in with us, saying, "Your poor uncle will starve himself if he stays in this lovelorn condition much longer. A sorrowing heart poisons recipes."

This has proven to be true, but for Gram. Everything she cooks now tastes like ashes.

Toby and I follow Big into the house, where he stops before the painting of his sister, my missing mother: Paige Walker. Before she left sixteen years ago, Gram had been painting a portrait of her, which she never got to finish but put up anyway. It hovers over the mantel in the living room, half a mother, with long green hair pooling like water around an incomplete face.

Gram had always told us that our mother would return. "She'll be back," she'd say like Mom had gone to the store for some eggs, or a swim at the river. Gram said it so often and with such certainty that for a long while, before we learned more, we didn't question it, just spent a whole lot of time waiting for the phone to ring, the doorbell to sound, the mail to arrive.

I tap my hand softly against Big, who's staring up at The Half Mom like he's lost in a silent mournful conversation. He sighs, puts an arm around me and one around Toby, and we all plod into the kitchen like a three-headed, six-legged, ten-ton sack of sad.

29

Dinner, unsurprisingly, is a ham and ash casserole that we hardly touch.

After, Toby and I camp out on the living room floor, listening to Bailey's music, poring over countless photo albums, basically blowing our hearts to smithereens.

I keep sneaking looks at him from across the room. I can almost see Bails flouncing around him, coming up from behind and dropping her arms around his neck the way she always did. She'd say sickeningly embarrassing things in his ear, and he'd tease her back, both of them acting like I wasn't there.

"I feel Bailey," I say finally, the sense of her overwhelming me. "In this room, with us."

He looks up from the album on his lap, surprised. "Me too. I've been thinking it this whole time."

"It's *so* nice," I say, relief spilling out of me with the words.

He smiles and it makes his eyes squint like the sun is in his face. "It is, Len." I remember Bailey telling me once that Toby doesn't talk all that much to humans but is able to gentle startled horses at the ranch with just a few words. Like St Francis, I'd said to her, and I believe it – the low slow lull of his voice is soothing, like waves lapping the shore at night.

I return to the photos of Bailey as Wendy in the Clover Elementary production of *Peter Pan*. Neither of us mentions it again, but the comfort of feeling Bailey so close stays with me for the rest of the evening.

Later, Toby and I stand by the garden, saying goodbye.

The dizzy, drunk fragrance of the roses engulfs us.

"It was great hanging out with you, Lennie, made me feel better."

"Me too," I say, plucking a lavender petal. "Much better, really." I say this quietly and to the rosebush, not sure I even want him to hear, but when I peek back up at his face, it's kind, his leonine features less lion, more cub.

"Yeah," he says, looking at me, his dark eyes both shiny and sad. He lifts his arm, and for a second I think he's going to touch my face with his hand, but he just runs his fingers through the tumble of sunshine that is his hair.

We walk the few remaining steps to the road in slow motion. Once there, Lucy and Ethel emerge out of nowhere and start climbing all over Toby, who has dropped to his knees to say goodbye to them. He holds his skateboard in one hand, ruffling and petting the dogs with the other as he whispers unintelligible words into their fur.

"You really are St Francis, huh?" I have a thing for the saints – the miracles, not the mortifications.

"It's been said." A soft smile meanders across the broad planes of his face, landing in his eyes. "Mostly by your sister." For a split second, I want to tell him it was me who thought that, not Bailey.

He finishes his farewell, stands back up, then drops his skateboard to the ground, steadying it with his foot. He doesn't get on. A few years pass.

"I should go," he says, not going.

"Yeah," I say. A few more.

Before he finally hops on his board, he hugs me goodbye

31

and we hold on to each other so tightly under the sad, starless sky that for a moment I feel as if our heartbreak were one instead of two.

But then all of a sudden, I feel a hardness against my hip, him, *that*. *Holy freaking shit!* I pull back quickly, say goodbye, and run back into the house.

I don't know if he knows that I felt him.

I don't know anything.

Someone from Bailey's drama class
yelled BRAVO at the end of the service
and everyone jumped to their feet
and started clapping
I remember thinking the roof would blow
from the thunder in our hands
that grief was a room filled
with hungry desperate light
We clapped for nineteen years
of a world with Bailey in it
did not stop clapping
when the sun set, moon rose
when all the people streamed into our house
with food and frantic sorrow
did not stop clapping
until dawn
when we closed the door

on Toby
who had to make his sad way home
I know we must have moved from that spot
must have washed and slept and ate
but in my mind, Gram, Uncle Big and I
stayed like that for weeks
just staring at the closed door
with nothing between our hands
but air

(Found on a piece of notebook paper blowing down Main Street)

4

This is what happens when Joe Fontaine has his debut trumpet solo in band practice: I'm the first to go, swooning into Rachel, who topples into Cassidy Rosenthal, who tumbles onto Zachary Quittner, who collapses onto Sarah, who reels into Luke Jacobus – until every kid in band is on the floor in a bedazzled heap. Then the roof flies off, the walls collapse, and when I look outside I see that the nearby stand of redwood trees has uprooted and is making its way up the quad to our classroom, a gang of giant wooden men clapping their branches together. Lastly, the Rain River overflows its banks and detours left and right until it finds its way to the Clover High music room, where it sweeps us all away – he is *that* good.

When the rest of us lesser musical mortals have recovered enough to finish the piece, we do, but as we put our instruments away at the end of practice, the room is as quiet and still as an empty church.

Finally, Mr James, who's been staring at Joe like he's an ostrich, regains the power of speech and says, "Well, well. As you all say, that sure sucked." Everyone laughs. I turn around to see what Sarah thought. I can just about make out an eye under a giant Rasta hat. She mouths *unfreakingbelievable*. I look over at Joe. He's wiping his trumpet, blushing from the response or flushed from playing, I'm not sure which. He looks up, catches my eye, then raises his eyebrows expectantly at me almost like the storm that has just come out of his horn has been for me. But why would that be? And why is it I keep catching him watching me play? It's not interest, I mean, *that* kind of interest, I can tell. He watches me clinically, intently, the way Marguerite used to during a lesson when she was trying to figure out what in the world I was doing wrong.

"Don't even think about it," Rachel says as I turn back around. "That trumpet player's accounted for. Anyway, he's like so out of your league, Lennie. I mean, when's the last time you had a boyfriend? Oh yeah, never."

I think about lighting her hair on fire.

I think about medieval torture devices: The Rack, in particular.

I think about telling her what really happened at chair auditions last fall.

Instead I ignore her like I have all year, swab my clarinet, and wish I were indeed preoccupied by Joe Fontaine rather than by what happened with Toby – each time I recall the sensation of him pressing into me, shivers race all through my body – definitely not the appropriate reaction to your sister's boyfriend's hard-on! And what's worse is that in the privacy of my mind, I don't pull away like I actually did but stay wrapped in his arms under the still sky, and that makes me flush with shame.

I shut my clarinet case wishing I could do the same on these thoughts of Toby. I scan the room – the other horn players have gathered around Joe, as if the magic were

35

contagious. Not a word between him and me since my first day back. Hardly a word between me and anyone at school really. Even Sarah.

Mr James claps to get the attention of the class. In his excited, crackly voice, he begins talking about summer band practice because school's out in less than a week. "For those who are around, we will be practicing, starting in July. Who shows up will determine what we play. I'm thinking jazz" – he snaps his fingers like a flamenco dancer – "maybe some hot Spanish jazz, but I'm open to suggestions."

He raises his arms like a priest before a congregation. "Find the beat and keep it, my friends." The way he ends every class. But then after a moment he claps again. "Almost forgot, let me see a show of hands of those who plan on auditioning for All-State band next year." Oh no. I drop my pencil and bend over to avoid any possible eye collision with Mr James. When I emerge from my careful inspection of the floor, my phone vibrates in my pocket. I turn to Sarah, whose visible eye is popping out of her head. I sneak out my phone and read her text.

Y didn't u raise ur hand??? Solo made me think of u – that day! Come over 2nite???

I turn around, mouth: *Can't.*

She picks up one of her sticks and dramatically feigns stabbing it into her stomach with both hands. I know behind the hari-kari is a hurt that's growing, but I don't know what to do about it. For the first time in our lives, I'm somewhere she can't find, and I don't have the map to give her that leads to me.

I gather my things quickly to avoid her, which is going to be easy because Luke Jacobus has cornered her, and as I do, the day she mentioned comes racing back. It was the beginning of freshman year and we had both made honor band. Mr James, particularly frustrated with everyone, had jumped on a chair and shouted, "What's wrong with you people? You think you're musicians? You have to stick your asses in the wind!" Then he said, "C'mon, follow me. Those of you who can, bring your instruments."

We filed out of the room, down the path into the forest where the river rushed and roared. We all stood on the banks, while he climbed up onto a rock to address us.

"Now, listen, learn and then play, just *play*. Make *noise*. Make *something*. Make *muuuuuuuuusic*." Then he began conducting the river, the wind, the birds in the trees like a total loon. After we got over our hysterics and piped down, one by one, those of us who had our instruments started to play. Unbelievably, I was one of the first to go, and after a while, the river and wind and birds and clarinets and flutes and oboes mixed all together in a glorious cacophonous mess and Mr James turned his attention from the forest back to us, his body swaying, his arms flailing left and right, saying, "That's it, that's it. *That's it!*"

And it was.

When we got back to the classroom, Mr James came over to me and handed me Marguerite St Denis's card. "Call her," he said. "Right away."

I think about Joe's virtuoso performance today, can feel it in my fingers. I ball them into fists. Whatever it was, whatever that thing is Mr James took us in the woods that day to find, whether it's abandon or passion, whether it's innovation or simply courage, Joe has it.

His ass is in the wind. Mine is in second chair.

(Lennie?)

Yeah?

You awake?

Yeah.

We did it.

Did what?

Toby and I did it, had sex last night.

I thought you already had, like 10,000 times.

Nope.

Well...

It was incredible.

Congratulations then.

~~that's boy~~

Sheesh, why can't you ever be happy for me about Toby?

I don't know.

What is it, are you jealous?

I don't know... sorry.

It's okay. Forget it, go to sleep.

Talk about it if you want to.

I don't want to anymore.

fine.

fine.

*(Found on a takeaway cup along the banks
of the Rain River)*

I know it's him, and wish I didn't. I wish my first thought was of anyone in the world but Toby when I hear the ping of a pebble on the window. I'm sitting in Bailey's closet, writing a poem on the wall, trying to curb the panic that hurls around inside my body like a trapped comet.

I take off the shirt of Bailey's I'd put on over mine, grab the doorknob, and hoist myself back into The Sanctum. Crossing to the window, my bare feet press into the three flattened blue rugs that scatter the room, pieces of bright sky that Bailey and I pounded down with years of cut-throat dance competitions to out-goofball the other without cracking up. I always lost because Bailey had in her arsenal The Ferret Face, which when combined with her masterful Monkey Moves, was certifiably deadly; if she pulled the combo (which took more unself-consciousness than I could ever muster), I was a goner, reduced to a helpless heap of hysterics, every time.

I lean over the sill, see Toby, as I knew I would, under a near full moon. I've had no luck squelching the mutiny inside me. I take a deep breath, then go downstairs and open the door.

"Hey, what's up?" I say. "Everyone's sleeping." My voice sounds creaky, unused, like bats might fly out of my mouth. I take a good look at him under the porch light. His face is wild with sorrow. It's like looking in a mirror.

"I thought maybe we could hang out," he says. This is what I hear in my mind: *boner, boner, erection, hard-on, woody, boner, boner, boner* – "I have something to tell you, Len, don't know who else to tell." The need in his voice sends a shudder right through me. Over his head, the red warning light could not be flashing brighter, but still I can't seem to say no, don't want to. "C'mon in, sir."

He touches my arm in a friendly, brotherly way as he passes, which sets me at ease, maybe guys get hard-ons all the time, for no reason – I have zero knowledge of boner basics. I've only ever kissed three guys, so I'm totally in-experienced with real-life boys, though quite an expert at the kind in books, especially Heathcliff, who doesn't get erections – wait, now that I'm thinking about it, he must get them *all the time* with Cathy on the moors. Heathcliff must be a total freaking boner boy.

I close the door behind him and motion for him to be quiet as he follows me up the steps to The Sanctum, which is soundproofed so as to protect the rest of the house against years of barky bleating clarinet notes. Gram would have a coronary that he's here visiting me at almost 2 a.m. on a school night. *On any night, Lennie.* This is most definitely not what she had in mind by reaching out to him.

Once the door of The Sanctum is closed, I put on some of the indie-kill-yourself music I've been listening to lately, and sit down next to Toby on the floor, our backs to the

41

wall, legs outstretched. We sit in silence like two stone slabs. Several centuries pass.

When I can't handle it anymore, I joke, "It's possible you've taken this whole strong silent type thing to an extreme."

"Oh, sorry." He shakes his head, embarrassed. "Don't even realize I'm doing it."

"Doing it?"

"Not talking…"

"Really? What is it you think you're doing?"

He tilts his head, smiling squintily, adorably. "I was going for the oak tree in the yard."

I laugh. "Very good then, you do a perfect oak impersonation."

"Thank you … think it drove Bails mad, my silent streak."

"Nah, she liked it, she told me, less chance of disagreements … plus more stage time for her."

"True." He's quiet for a minute, then in a voice ragged with emotion, says, "We were so different."

"Yeah," I say softly. Quintessential opposites, Toby always serene and still (when not on horse or board) while Bailey did everything: walk, talk, think, laugh, party, at the speed of light, and with its gleam.

"*You* remind me of her…" he says.

I want to blurt out: *What?! You've always acted like I was a baked potato!* but instead I say, "No way, don't have the wattage."

"You have plenty … it's me that has the serious shortage," he says, sounding surprisingly like a spud.

42

"Not to her," I say. His eyes warm at that – it kills me. What are we going to do with all this love?

He shakes his head in disbelief. "I got lucky. That chocolate book…"

The image assaults me: Bailey leaping off the rock the day they met when Toby returned on his board. "I knew you'd come back," she'd exclaimed, throwing the book in the air. "Just like in this story. I knew it!"

I have a feeling the same day is playing out in Toby's mind, because our polite levity has screeched to a halt – all the past tense in our words suddenly stacking up as if to crush us.

I can see the despair inching across his face as it must be across mine.

I look around our bedroom, at the singing orange paint we'd slathered over the dozy blue we'd had for years. Bailey had said, "If this doesn't change our lives, I don't know what will – this, Lennie, is *the color of extraordinary*." I remember thinking I didn't want our lives to change and didn't understand why she did. I remember thinking I'd always liked the blue.

I sigh. "I'm really glad you showed up, Toby. I'd been hiding in Bailey's closet freaking out for hours."

"Good. That you're glad, I mean, didn't know if I should bug you, but couldn't sleep either … did some stupid-ass skating that could've killed me, then ended up here, sat under the plum tree for an hour trying to decide…"

The rich timbre of Toby's voice suddenly makes me aware of the other voice in the room, the singer blaring from the speakers who sounds like he's being strangled at best. I get up to put on something more melodic, then when I sit back down, I confide, "No one gets it at school, not really, not even Sarah."

He tips his head back against the wall. "Don't know if it's possible to get it until you're in it like we are. I had no idea…"

"Me neither," I say, and suddenly I want to hug Toby because I'm just so relieved to not have to be in it by myself anymore tonight.

He's looking down at his hands, his brow furrowed, like he's struggling with how to say something. I wait.

And wait.

Still waiting here. How did Bailey brave the radio silence?

When he looks up, his face is all compassion, all cub. The words spill out of him, one on top of the next. "I've never known sisters so close. I feel so bad for you, Lennie, I'm just so sorry. I keep thinking about you without her."

"Thanks," I whisper, meaning it, and all of a sudden wanting to touch him, to run my hand over his, which rests on his thigh just inches from mine.

I glance at him sitting there so close to me that I can smell his shampoo, and I am stuck with a startling, horrifying thought: he is really good-looking, alarmingly so. How is it I never noticed before?

I'll answer that: he's Bailey's boyfriend, Lennie. What's wrong with you?

Dear Mind, I write on my jeans with my finger, *Behave*.

44

I'm sorry, I whisper to Bailey inside my head, I don't mean to think about Toby this way. I assure her it won't happen again.

It's just that he's the only one who understands, I add. *Oh brother*.

After a wordless while, he pulls a bottle of tequila out of his jacket pocket, uncaps it.

"Want some?" he asks. Great, that'll help.

"Sure." I hardly ever drink, but maybe it will help, maybe it'll knock this madness out of me. I reach for the bottle and our fingers graze a moment too long as I take it – I decide I imagined it, put the bottle to my lips, take a healthy sip, and then very daintily spit it out all over us. "Yuck, that's disgusting." I wipe my mouth with my sleeve. "Whoa."

He laughs, holds out his arms to show what a mess I've made of him. "It takes time to get used to it."

"Sorry," I say. "Had no idea it was so nasty."

He cheers the bottle to the air in response and takes a swig. I'm determined to try again and not projectile spew. I reach for the bottle, bring it to my lips, and let the liquid burn down my throat, then take another sip, bigger.

"Easy," Toby says, taking the tequila from me. "I need to tell you something, Len."

"Okay." I'm enjoying the warmth that has settled over me.

"I asked Bailey to marry me…" He says it so quickly it doesn't register at first. He's looking at me, trying to gage my reaction. It's stark, raving WTF!

"Marry you? Are you kidding?" Not the response he wants, I'm sure, but I'm totally blindsided; he could have just as easily told me she'd been secretly planning a career in fire-eating. Both of them were just nineteen, and Bailey a marriage-o-phobe to boot.

"What'd she say?" I'm afraid to hear the answer.

"She said yes." He says it with as much hope as hopelessness, the promise of it still alive in him. *She said yes.* I take the tequila, swig, don't even taste it or feel the burn. I'm stunned that Bailey wanted this, hurt that she wanted it, really hurt that she never told me. I have to know what she'd been thinking. I can't believe I can't ask her. Ever. I look at Toby, see the earnestness in his eyes; it's like a soft, small animal.

"I'm sorry, Toby," I say, trying to bottle my incredulity and hurt feelings, but then I can't help myself. "I don't know why she didn't tell me."

"We were going to tell you guys that very next week. I'd just asked…" His use of *we* jars me; the big *we* has always been Bailey and me, not Bailey and Toby. I suddenly feel left out of a future that isn't even going to happen.

"But what about her acting?" I say instead of: *What about me?*

"She was acting…"

"Yeah, but…" I look at him. "You know what I mean." And then I see by his expression that he doesn't know what I mean at all. Sure some girls dream of weddings, but Bailey dreamt of Juilliard: the Juilliard School in New York City. I once looked up their mission statement on the Web: *To provide the highest caliber of artistic education for gifted musicians, dancers and actors from around the world, so that they may achieve their fullest potential as artists, leaders and global citizens.* It's true after the rejection she enrolled last fall at Clover State, the only other college she applied to, but I'd been certain she'd reapply. I mean, how could she not? It was her dream.

We don't talk about it anymore. The wind's picked up and has begun rattling its way into the house. I feel a chill run through me, grab a throw blanket off the rocking chair, pull it over my legs. The tequila makes me feel like I'm melting into nothing, I want to, want to disappear. I have an impulse to write all over the orange walls – I need an alphabet of endings ripped out of books, of hands pulled off of clocks, of cold stones, of shoes filled with nothing but wind. I drop my head on Toby's shoulder. "We're the saddest people in the world."

"Yup," he says, squeezing my knee for a moment. I ignore the shivers his touch sends through me. *They were getting married.*

"How will we do this?" I say under my breath. "Day after day after day without her…"

"Oh, Len." He turns to me, smoothes the hair around my face with his hand.

I keep waiting for him to move his hand away, to turn back around, but he doesn't. He doesn't take his hand or gaze off of me. Time slows. Something shifts in the room, between us. I look into his sorrowful eyes and he into mine, and I think, *He misses her as much as I do*, and that's when he kisses me – his mouth: soft, hot, so alive, it makes me

47

moan. I wish I could say I pull away, but I don't. I kiss him back and don't want to stop because in that moment I feel like Toby and I together have, somehow, in some way, reached across time, and pulled Bailey back.

He breaks away, springs to his feet. "I don't understand this." He's in an instant-just-add-water panic, pacing the room. "God, I should go, I *really* should go."

But he doesn't go. He sits down on Bailey's bed, looks over at me and then sighs as if giving in to some invisible force. He says my name and his voice is so hoarse and hypnotic it pulls me up onto my feet, pulls me across miles of shame and guilt. I don't want to go to him, but I do want to too. I have no idea what to do, but still I walk across the room, wavering a bit from the tequila, to his side. He takes my hand and tugs on it gently.

"I just want to be near you," he whispers. "It's the only time I don't die missing her."

"Me too." I run my finger along the sprinkle of freckles on his cheek. He starts to well up, then I do too. I sit down next to him and then we lie down on Bailey's bed, spooning. My last thought before falling asleep in his strong, safe arms is that I hope we are not replacing our scents with the last remnants of Bailey's own that still infuse the bedding.

When I wake again, I'm facing him, our bodies pressed together, breath intermingling. He's looking at me. "You're beautiful, Len."

"No," I say. Then choke out one word. "Bailey."

"I know," he says. But he kisses me anyway. "I can't help it." He whispers it right into my mouth. I can't help it either.

I

wish

my

shadow

would

get

up

and

walk

beside

me

(Found on the back of a French exam in a flower bed, Clover High)

There were once two sisters who shared the same room,
the same clothes,
the same thoughts at the same moment.
These two sisters did not have a mother
but they had each other.
The older sister walked ahead of the younger
so the younger one always knew where to go.
The older one took the younger to the river
where they floated on their backs
like dead men.
The older girl would say:
Dunk your head under a few inches then open your eyes and look up at the sun
The younger girl:
I'll get water up my nose
The older:
C'mon, do it
and so the younger girl did it
and her whole world filled with light.

(Found on a piece of notebook paper caught in a fence up on the ridge)

Judas, Brutus, Benedict Arnold and me.

And the worst part is every time I close my eyes I see Toby's lion face again, his lips a breath away from mine, and it makes me shudder head to toe, not with guilt, like it should, but with desire – and then, just as soon as I allow myself the image of us kissing, I see Bailey's face twisting in shock and betrayal as she watches us from above: her boyfriend, her *fiancé* kissing her traitorous little sister *on her own bed*. Ugh. Shame watches me like a dog.

I'm in self-imposed exile, cradled between split branches, in my favorite tree in the woods behind school. I've been coming here every day at lunch, hiding out until the bell rings, whittling words into the branches with my pen, allowing my heart to break in private. I can't hide a thing – everyone in school sees clear to my bones.

I'm reaching into the brown bag Gram packed for me, when I hear twigs crack underneath me. Uh-oh. I look down and see Joe Fontaine. I freeze. I don't want him to see me: Lennie Walker: Mental Patient Eating Lunch in a Tree (it being decidedly out of your tree to hide out in one!). He walks in confused circles under me like he's looking for someone. I'm hardly breathing but he isn't moving on, has settled just to the right of my tree. Then I inadvertently crinkle the bag and he looks up, sees me.

"Hi," I say, like it's the most normal place to be eating lunch.

"Hey, there you are—" He stops, tries to cover. "I was wondering what was back here…" He looks around. "Perfect spot for a gingerbread house or maybe an opium den."

"You already gave yourself away," I say, surprised at my own boldness.

"Okay, guilty as charged. I followed you." He smiles at me – that same smile – wow, no wonder I'd thought—

He continues, "And I'm guessing you want to be alone. Probably don't come all the way out here and then climb a tree because you're starving for conversation." He gives me a hopeful look. He's charming me, even in my pitiful emotional state, my Toby turmoil, even though he's accounted for by Cruella de Vil.

"Want to come up?" I present him a branch and he bounds up the tree in about three seconds, finds a suitable seat right next to me, then bats his eyelashes at me. I'd forgotten about the eyelash endowment. Wow squared.

"What's to eat?" He points to the brown bag.

"You kidding? First you crash my solitude, now you want to scavenge. Where were you raised?"

"Paris," he says. "So I'm a scavenger *raffiné*."

Oh so glad *j'étudie le français*. And jeez, no wonder the school's abuzz about him, no wonder I'd wanted to kiss him. I even momentarily forgive Rachel the idiotic baguette she had sticking out of her backpack today. He goes on, "But I was born in California, lived in San Francisco until I was nine. We moved back there about a year ago and now we're here. Still want to know what's in the bag though."

"You'll never guess," I tell him. "I won't either, actually. My grandmother thinks it's really funny to put all sorts of things in our – my lunch. I never know what'll be inside: e. e. cummings, flower petals, a handful of buttons. She seems to have lost sight of the original purpose of the brown bag."

"Or maybe she thinks other forms of nourishment are more important."

"That's exactly what she thinks," I say, surprised. "Okay, you want to do the honors?" I hold up the bag.

"I'm suddenly afraid, is there ever anything alive in it?" Bat. Bat. Bat. Okay, it might take me a little time to build immunity to the eyelash bat.

"Never know…" I say, trying not to sound as swoony as I feel. And I'm going to just pretend that the sitting-in-a-tree k-i-s-s-i-n-g rhyme did not just pop into my head.

He takes the bag, then reaches in with a grand gesture, and pulls out – an apple.

"An apple? How anti-climactic!" He throws it at me. "Everyone gets apples."

I urge him to continue. He reaches in, pulls out a copy of *Wuthering Heights*.

"That's my favorite book," I say. "It's like a pacifier. I've read it twenty-three times. She's always putting it in."

"*Wuthering Heights* – twenty-three times! Saddest book ever, how do you even function?"

"Do I have to remind you? I'm sitting in a tree at lunch."

"True." He reaches in again, pulls out a stemless purple peony. Its rich scent overtakes us immediately.

"Wow," he says, breathing it in. "Makes me feel like I might levitate." He holds it under my nose. I close my eyes, imagine the fragrance lifting me off my feet too. I can't. But something occurs to me.

"My favorite saint of all time is a Joe," I tell him. "Joseph of Cupertino, he levitated. Whenever he thought of God, he would float into the air in a fit of ecstasy."

He tilts his head, looks at me skeptically, eyebrows raised. "Don't buy it."

I nod. "Tons of witnesses. Happened all the time. Right during Mass."

"Okay, I'm totally jealous. Guess I'm just a wannabe levitator."

"Too bad," I say. "I'd like to see you drifting over Clover playing your horn."

"Hell yeah," he exclaims. "You could come with, grab my foot or something."

We exchange a quick searching glance, both of us wondering about the other, surprised at the easy rapport – it's just a moment, barely perceptible, like a lady bug landing on your arm.

He rests the flower on my leg and I feel the brush of his fingers through my jeans. The brown bag is empty now. He hands it to me, and then we're quiet, just listening to the wind rustle around us and watching the sun filter through the redwoods in impossibly thick foggy rays just like in children's drawings.

Who is this guy? I've talked more to him in this tree than I have to anyone at school since I've been back. But how could he have read *Wuthering Heights* and still fall for Rachel Bitchzilla? Maybe it's because she's been to Fronce. Or because she pretends to like music that no one else has heard of, like the wildly popular Throat Singers of Tuva.

"I saw you the other day," he says, picking up the apple. He tosses it with one hand, catches it with the other. "By The Great Meadow. I was playing my guitar in the field. You were across the way. It looked like you were writing a note or something against a car, but then you just dropped the piece of paper—"

"Are you stalking me?" I ask, trying to keep my sudden delight at that notion out of my voice.

"Maybe a little." He stops tossing the apple. "And maybe I'm curious about something."

"Curious?" I ask. "About what?"

He doesn't answer, starts picking at moss on a branch. I notice his hands, his long fingers full of calluses from guitar strings.

"What?" I say again, dying to know what made him curious enough to follow me up a tree.

"It's the way you play the clarinet…"

The delight drains out of me. "Yeah?"

"Or the way you don't play it, actually."

"What do you mean?" I ask, knowing exactly what he means.

"I mean you've got loads of technique. Your fingering's quick, your tonguing fast, your range of tones, man … but it's like it all stops there. I don't get it." He laughs, seemingly unaware of the bomb he just detonated. "It's like

55

you're sleep-playing or something."

Blood rushes to my cheeks. Sleep-playing! I feel caught, a fish in a net. I wish I'd quit band altogether like I'd wanted to. I look off at the redwoods, each one rising to the sky surrounded only by its loneliness. He's staring at me, I can feel it, waiting for a response, but one is not forthcoming – this is a no trespassing zone.

"Look," he says cautiously, finally getting a clue that his charms have worn off. "I followed you out here because I wanted to see if we could play together."

"Why?" My voice is louder and more upset than I want it to be. A slow familiar panic is taking over my body.

"I want to hear John Lennon play for real, I mean, who wouldn't, right?"

His joke crashes and burns between us.

"I don't think so," I say as the bell rings.

"Look—" he starts, but I don't let him finish.

"I don't want to play with you, okay?"

"Fine." He hurls the apple into the air. Before it hits the ground and before he jumps out of the tree, he says, "It wasn't my idea anyway."

7

I wake to Ennui, Sarah's Jeep, honking down the road – it's an ambush. I roll over, look out the window, see her jump out in her favorite black vintage gown and platform combat boots, back-to-blond hair tweaked into a nest, cigarette hanging from blood red lips in a pancake of ghoulish white. I look at the clock: 7.05 a.m. She looks up at me in the window, waves like a windmill in a hurricane.

I pull the covers over my head, wait for the inevitable.

"I've come to suck your blood," she says a few moments later.

I peek out of the covers. "You really do make a stunning vampire."

"I know." She leans into the mirror over my dresser, wiping some lipstick off her teeth with her black-nail-polished finger. "It's a good look for me… Heidi goes goth." Without the accoutrements, Sarah could play Goldilocks. She's a sun-kissed beach girl who goes goth-grungepunkhippierockeremocoremetalfreakfashionista-braingeekboycrazyhiphoprastagirl to keep it under wraps. She crosses the room, stands over me, then pulls a corner of the covers down and hops into bed with me, boots and all.

"I miss you, Len." Her enormous blue eyes are shining down on me, so sincere and incongruous with her get-up.

"Let's go to breakfast before school. Last day of junior year and all. It's tradition."

"Okay," I say, then add, "I'm sorry I've been so awful."

"Don't say that, I just don't know what to do for you. I can't imagine…" She doesn't finish, looks around The Sanctum. I see the dread overtake her. "It's so unbearable…" She stares at Bailey's bed. "Everything is just as she left it. God, Len."

"Yeah." My life catches in my throat. "I'll get dressed."

She bites her bottom lip, trying not to cry. "I'll wait downstairs. I promised Gram I'd talk with her." She gets out of bed and walks to the door, the leap in her from moments before now a shuffle. I pull the covers back over my head. I know the bedroom is a mausoleum. I know it upsets everyone (except Toby, who didn't even seem to notice), but I want it like this. It makes me feel like Bailey's still here or like she might come back.

On the way to town, Sarah tells me about her latest scheme to bag a babe who can talk to her about her favorite existentialist, Jean-Paul Sartre. The problem is her insane attraction to lumphead surfers who (not to be prejudicial) are not customarily the most well-versed in French literature and philosophy, and therefore must constantly be exempted from Sarah's Must-Know-Who-Sartre-Is-or-at-Least-Have-Read-Some-of-D.H.Lawrence-or-at-the-Minimum-One-of-the-Brontës-Preferably-Emily criteria of going out with her.

"There's an afternoon symposium this summer at the college in French Feminism," she tells me. "I'm going to go. Want to come?"

I laugh. "That sounds like the perfect place to meet guys."

"You'll see," she says. "The coolest guys aren't afraid to be feminists, Lennie."

I look over at her. She's trying to blow smoke rings, but blowing smoke blobs instead.

I'm dreading telling her about Toby, but I have to, don't I? Except I'm too chicken, so I go with less damning news.

"I hung out with Joe Fontaine the other day at lunch."

"You didn't!"

"I did."

"No way."

"Yes way."

"Nah-uh."

"Uh-huh."

"Not possible."

"So possible."

We have an incredibly high tolerance for yes-no.

"You duck! You flying yellow duck! And you took this long to tell me?!" When Sarah gets excited, random animals pop into her speech like she has an Old MacDonald Had a Farm kind of Tourette's syndrome. "Well, what's he like?"

"He's okay," I say distractedly, looking out the window. I can't figure out whose idea it could've been that we play together. Mr James', maybe? But why? And argh, how freaking mortifying.

"Earth to Lennie. Did you just say Joe Fontaine is okay? The guy's holy horses *unfreakingbelievable*! And I heard he has two older brothers: holy horses to the third power, don't you think?"

"Holy horses, Batgirl," I say, which makes Sarah giggle, a sound that doesn't seem quite right coming out of her Batgoth face. She takes a last drag off her cigarette and drops it into a can of soda. I add, "He likes Rachel. What does that say about him?"

"That he has one of those Y chromosomes," Sarah says, shoving a piece of gum into her orally fixated mouth. "But really, I don't see it. I heard all he cares about is music and she plays like a screeching cat. Maybe it's those stupid Throat Singers she's always going on about and he thinks she's in the musical know or something." Great minds ... then suddenly Sarah's jumping in her seat like she's on a pogo stick. "Oh Lennie, do it! Challenge her for first chair. Today! C'mon. It'll be so exciting – probably never happened in the history of honor band, a chair challenged on the last day of school!"

I shake my head. "Not going to happen."

"But why?"

I don't answer her, don't know how to.

An afternoon from last summer pops into my head. I'd just quit my lessons with Marguerite and was hanging out with Bailey and Toby at Flying Man's Gulch. He was telling us that Thoroughbred racing horses have these companion ponies that always stay by their sides, and I remember thinking, *That's me*. I'm a companion pony, and companion ponies don't solo. They don't play first chair or audition for All-State or compete nationally or seriously consider a certain performing arts conservatory in New York City like Marguerite had begun insisting.

They just don't.

Sarah sighs as she swerves into a parking spot. "Oh well, guess I'll have to entertain myself another way on the last day of school."

"Guess so."

We jump out of Ennui, head into Cecilia's Bakery, and order up an obscene amount of pastries that Cecilia gives us for free with that same sorrowful look that follows me everywhere I go now. I think she would give me every last pastry in the store if I asked.

We land on our bench of choice by Maria's Italian Deli, where I've been chief lasagna maker every summer since I was fourteen. I start up again tomorrow. The sun has burst into millions of pieces, which have landed all over Main Street. It's a gorgeous day. Everything shines except my guilty heart.

"Sarah, I have to tell you something."

A worried look comes over her. "Sure."

"Something happened with Toby the other night." Her worry has turned into something else, which is what I was afraid of. Sarah has an ironclad girlfriend code of conduct regarding guys. The policy is sisterhood before all else.

"Something like something? Or something like *something*?" Her eyebrow has landed on Mars.

My stomach churns. "Like *something* ... we kissed." Her eyes go wide and her face twists in disbelief, or perhaps it's horror. This is the face of my shame, I think, looking at her. *How could I have kissed Toby?* I ask myself for the thousandth time.

"Wow," she says, the word falling like a rock to the

ground. She's making no attempt to hold back her disdain. I bury my head in my hands, assume the crash position – I shouldn't have told her.

"It felt right in the moment, we both miss Bails so much, he just gets it, gets me, he's like the only one who does … and I was drunk." I say all this to my jeans.

"Drunk?" She can't contain her surprise. I hardly ever even have a beer at the parties she drags me to. Then in a softer voice, I hear, "Toby's the only one who gets you?"

Uh-oh.

"I didn't mean that," I say, lifting my head to meet her eyes, but it's not true, I did mean it, and I can tell from her expression she knows it. "Sarah."

She swallows, looks away from me, then quickly changes the topic back to my disgrace. "I guess it does happen. Grief sex is kind of a thing. It was in one of those books I read." I still hear the judgment in her voice, and something more now too.

"We didn't have sex," I say. "I'm still the last virgin standing."

She sighs, then puts her arm around me, awkwardly, as if she has to. I feel like I'm in a headlock. Neither of us has a clue how to deal with what's not being said, or what is.

"It's okay, Len. Bailey would understand." She sounds totally unconvincing. "And it's not like it's ever going to happen again, right?"

"Of course not," I say, and hope I'm not lying.

And hope I am.

Everyone has always said I look like Bailey,
but I don't.
I have grey eyes to her green,
an oval face to her heart-shaped one,
I'm shorter, ~~thinner~~ scrawnier, paler,
flatter, plainer, tamer.
All we shared is a madhouse of curls
that I imprison in a pony-tail
while she let hers rave
like madness
around her head.
I don't sing in my sleep
or eat the petals off flowers
or run into the rain instead of out of it.
I'm the unplugged-in one,
the side-kick sister,
tucked into a corner of her shadow.
Boys followed her everywhere;
they filled the booths at ~~the~~ the restaurant
where she waitressed,
herded around her at the river.
One day, I saw a boy come up behind her
and pull a strand of her long hair.
I understood this —
I felt the same way.
In photographs of us together,
she is always looking at the camera,
and I am always looking at her.

*(Found on a folded-up piece of paper half-buried
in pine needles on the trail to the Rain River)*

8

I am sitting at Bailey's desk with St Anthony: Patron of Lost Things.

He doesn't belong here. He belongs on the mantel in front of The Half Mom where I've always kept him, but Bailey must've moved him, and I don't know why. I found him tucked behind the computer in front of an old drawing of hers that's tacked to the wall – the one she made the day Gram told us our mother was an explorer (of the Christopher Columbus variety).

I've drawn the curtains, and though I want to, I won't let myself peek out the window to see if Toby is under the plum tree. I won't let myself imagine his lips lost and half wild on mine either. No. I let myself imagine igloos, nice, frigid, arctic igloos. I've promised Bailey nothing like what happened that night will ever happen again.

It's the first day of summer vacation and everyone from school is at the river. I just got a drunken call from Sarah informing me that not one, not two, but three unfreaking-believable Fontaines are supposed to be arriving momentarily at Flying Man's, that they are going to play outside, that she just found out the two older Fontaines are in a seriously awesome band in LA, where they go to college, and I better get my butt down there to witness the glory. I told her I was staying in and to revel in their Fontainely glory for me,

64

which resurrected the bristle from yesterday: "You're not with Toby, are you, Lennie?"

Ugh.

I look over at my clarinet abandoned in its case on my playing chair. It's in a coffin, I think, then immediately try to unthink it. I walk over to it, unlatch the lid. There never was a question what instrument I'd play. When all the other girls ran to the flutes in fifth grade music class, I beelined for a clarinet. It reminded me of me.

I reach in the pocket where I keep my cloth and reeds and feel around for the folded piece of paper. I don't know why I've kept it (for over a year!), why I fished it out of the garbage later that afternoon, after Bailey had tossed it with a cavalier "Oh well, guess you guys are stuck with me," before throwing herself into Toby's arms like it meant nothing to her. But I knew it did. How could it not? It was Juilliard.

Without reading it a final time, I crumple Bailey's rejection letter into a ball, toss it into the garbage can, and sit back down at her desk.

I'm in the exact spot where I was that night when the phone blasted through the house, through the whole unsuspecting world. I'd been doing chemistry, hating every minute of it like I always do. The thick oregano scent of Gram's chicken fricassee was wafting into our room and all I wanted was Bailey to hurry home already so we could eat because I was starving and hated isotopes. How can that be? How could I have been thinking about fricassee and carbon molecules when across town my sister had just

65

taken her very last breath? What kind of world is this? And what do you do about it? What do you do when the worst thing that can happen actually happens? When you get *that* phone call? When you miss your sister's rollercoaster of a voice so much that you want to take apart the whole house with your fingernails?

This is what I do: I take out my phone and punch in her number. In a blind fog of a moment the other day I called to see when she'd be home and discovered her account hadn't yet been canceled.

Hey, this is Bailey, Juliet for the month, so dudes, what say'st thou? Hast thou not a word of joy? Some comfort...

I hang up at the tone, then call back, again and again, and again, and again, wanting to just pull her out of the phone. Then one time I don't hang up.

"Why didn't you tell me you were getting married?" I whisper, before snapping the phone shut and laying it on her desk. Because I don't understand. Didn't we tell each other everything? *If this doesn't change our lives, Len, I don't know what will*, she'd said when we painted the walls. Is that the change she'd wanted then? I pick up the cheesy plastic St Anthony. And what about him? Why bring him up here? I look more closely at the drawing he was leaning against. It's been up so long that the paper has yellowed and the edges have curled, so long that I haven't taken notice of it for years. Bailey drew it when she was around eleven, the time she started questioning Gram about Mom with an unrelenting ferocity.

She'd been at it for weeks.

"How do you know she'll be back?" Bailey asked for the millionth time. We were in Gram's art room, Bailey and I lay sprawled out on the floor drawing with pastels while Gram painted one of her ladies at a canvas in the corner, her back to us. She'd been skirting Bailey's questions all day, artfully changing the subject, but it wasn't working this time. I watched Gram's arm drop to her side, the brush sending droplets of a hopeful green onto the bespattered floor. She sighed, a big lonely sigh, then turned around to face us.

"I guess you're old enough, girls," she said. We perked up, immediately put down our pastels, and gave her our undivided attention. "Your mother is ... well ... I guess the best way to describe it ... hmmm ... let me think..." Bailey looked at me in shock – we'd never known Gram to be at a loss for words.

"What, Gram?" Bailey asked. "What is she?"

"Hmmm..." Gram bit her lip, then finally, hesitantly, she said, "I guess the best way to say it is ... you know how some people have natural tendencies, how I paint and garden, how Big's an arborist, how you, Bailey, want to grow up and be an actress—"

"I'm going to go to Juilliard," she told us.

Gram smiled. "Yes, we know, Miss Hollywood. Or Miss Broadway, I should say."

"Our mom?" I reminded them before we ended up talking some more about that dumb school. All I'd hoped was that it was in walking distance if Bailey was going there. Or at least close enough so I could ride my bike to

67

see her every day. I'd been too scared to ask.

Gram pursed her lips for a moment. "Okay, well, your mother, she's a little different, she's more like a ... well, like an explorer."

"Like Columbus, you mean?" Bailey asked.

"Yes, like that, except without the *Niña*, *Pinta* and *Santa Maria*. Just a woman, a map, and the world. A solo artist." Then she left the room, her favorite and most effective way of ending a conversation.

Bailey and I stared at each other. In all our persistent musings on where Mom was and why she left, we never ever imagined anything remotely this good. I followed after Gram to try and find out more, but Bailey stayed on the floor and drew this picture.

In it, there's a woman at the top of a mountain looking off into the distance, her back to us. Gram, Big, and I – with our names beneath our feet – are waving up at the lone figure from the base of the mountain. Under the whole drawing, it says in green *Explorer*. For some reason, Bailey did not put herself in the picture.

I bring St Anthony to my chest, hold him tight. I need him now, but why did Bailey? What had she lost?

What was it she needed to find?

I put on her clothes
I button one of her frilly shirts
over my own t-shirt.
Or I wrap one, sometimes two,
sometimes all of her diva scarves around my neck.
Or I strip and slip one of her slinkier dresses over my head,
letting the fabric
fall over my skin like water.
I always feel better then,
like she's holding me.
Then I touch all the things
that haven't moved since she died:
crumpled up dollars
dredged from a ~~sticky~~ sweaty pocket
the three bottles of perfume
always with the same amount of liquid in them now,
the Sam Shepherd play
Fool for Love
where her bookmark will never move forward.
I've read it for her twice now,
always putting the bookmark back
where it was when I finish —
it kills me
she will never find out
what happens
in the end.

(Found on the inside cover of Wuthering Heights,
Clover High library)

9

Gram spends the night
in front of The Half-Mom.
I hear her weeping—
sad
endless
rain.
I sit at the top of the stairs,
know she's touching
Mom's cold flat cheek
as she says: **I'm sorry**
I'm so sorry.
I think a terrible thing.
I think: **You should be.**
I think: **How could you have**
let this happen?
How could you have let both of
them leave me?

(Found written on the wall of the bathroom at Cecilia's Bakery)

School's been out for two weeks. Gram, Big and I are certifiably out of our trees and running loose through the park – all in opposite directions.

Exhibit A: Gram's following me around the house with a teapot. The pot is full. I can see the steam coming out the spout. She has two mugs in her other hand. Tea is what Gram and I used to do together, before. We'd sit around the kitchen table in the late afternoons and drink tea and talk before the others came home. But I don't want to have tea with Gram anymore because I don't feel like talking, which she knows but still hasn't accepted. So she's followed me up the stairs and is now standing in the doorway of The Sanctum, pot in hand.

I flop onto the bed, pick up my book, pretend to read.

"I don't want any tea, Gram," I say, looking up from *Wuthering Heights,* which I note is upside down and hope she doesn't.

Her face falls. Epically.

"Fine." She puts a mug on the ground, fills the one in her hand for herself, takes a sip. I can tell it's burned her tongue, but she pretends it hasn't. "Fine, fine, fine," she chants, taking another sip.

She's been following me around like this since school got out. Normally, summer is her busiest time as Garden

71

Guru, but she's told all her clients she is on hiatus until the fall. So instead of guruing, she happens into Maria's while I'm at the deli, or into the library when I'm on my break, or she tails me to Flying Man's and paces on the path while I float on my back and let my tears spill into the water.

But teatime is the worst.

"Sweet pea, it's not healthy..." Her voice has melted into a familiar river of worry. I think she's talking about my remoteness, but when I glance over at her I realize it's the other thing. She's staring at Bailey's dresser, the gum wrappers strewn about, the hairbrush with a web of her black hair woven through the teeth. I watch her gaze drifting around the room to Bailey's dresses thrown over the back of her desk chair, the towel flung over her bedpost, Bailey's laundry basket still piled over with her dirty clothes... "Let's just pack up a few things."

"I told you, I'll do it," I whisper so I don't scream at the top of my lungs. "I'll do it, Gram, if you stop stalking me and leave me alone."

"Okay, Lennie," she says. I don't have to look up to know I've hurt her.

When I do look up, she's gone. Instantly, I want to run after her, take the teapot from her, pour myself a mug and join her, just spill every thought and feeling I'm having.

But I don't.

I hear the shower turn on. Gram spends an inordinate amount of time in the shower now and I know this is because she thinks she can cry under the spray without Big and me hearing. We hear.

72

Exhibit B: I roll onto my back and before long I'm holding my pillow in my arms and kissing the air with an embarrassing amount of passion. Not again, I think. What's wrong with me? What kind of girl wants to kiss every boy at a funeral, wants to maul a guy in a tree after making out with her sister's boyfriend the previous night? *Speaking of which, what kind of girl makes out with her sister's boyfriend, at all?*

Let me just unsubscribe to my own mind already, because I don't get any of it. I hardly ever thought about sex before, much less did anything about it. Three boys at three parties in four years: Casey Miller, who tasted like hot dogs; Dance Rosencrantz, who dug around in my shirt like he was reaching into a box of popcorn at the movies. And Jasper Stolz in eighth grade because Sarah dragged me into a game of spin the bottle. Total blobfish feeling inside each time. Nothing like Heathcliff and Cathy, like Lady Chatterley and Oliver Mellors, like Mr Darcy and Elizabeth Bennet! Sure, I've always been into the Big Bang theory of passion, but as something theoretical, something that happens in books that you can close and put back on a shelf, something that I might secretly want bad but can't imagine ever happening to me. Something that happens to the heroines like Bailey, to the commotion girls in the leading roles. But now I've gone mental, kissing everything I can get my lips on: my pillow, armchairs, doorframes, mirrors, always imagining the one person I should not be imagining, the person I promised my sister I will never ever kiss again. The one person who makes me feel just a little less afraid.

The front door slams shut, jarring me out of Toby's forbidden arms.

It's Big. Exhibit C: I hear him stomp straight into the dining room, where only two days ago, he unveiled his pyramids. This is always a bad sign. He built them years ago, based on some hidden mathematics in the geometry of the Egyptian pyramids. (Who knows? The guy also talks to trees.) According to Big, his pyramids, like the ones in the Middle East, have extraordinary properties. He's always believed his replicas would be able to prolong the life of cut flowers and fruit, even revive bugs, all of which he would place under them for ongoing study. During his pyramid spells, Big, Bails and I would spend hours searching the house for dead spiders or flies, and then each morning we'd run to the pyramids hoping to witness a resurrection. We never did. But whenever Big's really upset, the necromancer in him comes out, and with it, the pyramids. This time, he's at it with a fervor, sure it will work, certain that he only failed before because he forgot a key element: an electrically charged coil, which he's now placed under each pyramid.

A little while later, a stoned Big drifts past my open door. He's been smoking so much weed that when he's home he seems to hover above Gram and me like an enormous balloon – every time I come upon him, I want to tie him to a chair.

He backtracks, lingers in my doorway for a moment.

"I'm going to add a few dead moths tomorrow," he says, as if picking up on a conversation we'd been having.

I nod. "Good idea."

74

He nods back, then floats off to his room, and most likely, right out the window.

This is us. Two months and counting. Booby Hatch Central.

The next morning, a showered and betoweled Gram is fixing breakfast ashes, Big is sweeping the rafters for dead moths to put under the pyramids, and I am trying not to make out with my spoon, when there's a knock at the door. We freeze, all of us suddenly panicked that someone might witness the silent sideshow of our grief. I walk to the front door on tiptoe, so as not to let on that we are indeed home, and peek through the peephole. It's Joe Fontaine, looking as animated as ever, like the front door is telling him jokes. He has a guitar in his hand.

"Everybody hide," I whisper. I prefer all boys safe in the recesses of my sex-crazed mind, not standing outside the front door of our capsizing house. Especially this minstrel. I haven't even taken my clarinet out of its case since school ended. I have no intention of going to summer band practice.

"Nonsense," Gram says, making her way to the front of the house in her bright purple towel muumuu and pink towel turban ensemble. "Who is it?" she asks me in a whisper hundreds of decibels louder than her normal speaking voice.

"It's that new kid from band, Gram, I can't deal." I swing my arms back and forth trying to shoo her into the kitchen.

I've forgotten how to do anything with my lips but kiss furniture. I have no conversation in me. I haven't seen anyone from school, don't want to, haven't called back Sarah, who's taken to writing me long e-mails (essays) about how she's not judging me at all about what happened with Toby, which just lets me know how much she's judging me about what happened with Toby. I duck into the kitchen, back into a corner, pray for invisibility.

"Well, well, a troubadour," Gram says, opening the door. She has obviously noticed the mesmery that is Joe's face and has already begun flirting. "Here I thought we were in the twenty-first century…" She is starting to purr. I have to save him.

I reluctantly come out of hiding and join swami seductress Gram. I get a good look at him. I've forgotten quite how luminous he is, like another species of human that doesn't have blood but light running through their veins. He's spinning his guitar case like a top while he talks to Gram. He doesn't look like he needs saving, he looks amused.

"Hi, John Lennon." He's beaming at me like our tree spat never happened.

What are you doing here? I think so loudly my head might explode.

"Haven't seen you around," he says. Shyness overtakes his face for a quick moment – it makes my stomach flutter. Uh, I think I need to get a restraining order for all boys until I can get a handle on this newfound body buzz.

"Do come in," Gram says, as if talking to a knight. "I

was just preparing breakfast." He looks at me, asking if it's okay with his eyes. Gram's still talking as she walks back into the kitchen. "You can play us a song, cheer us up a bit." I smile at him, it's impossible not to, and motion a welcome with my arm. As we enter the kitchen, I hear Gram whisper to Big, still in knight parlance, "I daresay, the young gentleman batted his extraordinarily long eyelashes at me."

We haven't had a real visitor since the weeks following the funeral and so don't know how to behave. Uncle Big has seemingly floated to the floor and is leaning on the broom he had been using to sweep up the dead. Gram stands, spatula in hand, in the middle of the kitchen with an enormous smile on her face. I'm certain she's forgotten what she's wearing. And I sit upright in my chair at the table. No one says anything and all of us stare at Joe like he's a television we're hoping will just turn itself on.

It does.

"That garden is wild, never seen flowers like that, thought some of those roses might chop off *my* head and put me in a vase." He shakes his head in amazement and his hair falls too adorably into his eyes. "It's like Eden or something."

"Better be careful in Eden, all that temptation." The thunder of Big's God voice surprises me – he's been my partner in muteness lately, much to Gram's displeasure. "Smelling Gram's flowers has been known to cause all sorts of maladies of the heart."

"Really?" Joe says. "Like what?"

"Many things. For instance, the scent of her roses causes

a mad love to flourish." At that, Joe's gaze ever so subtlety shifts to me – whoa, or did I imagine it? Because now his eyes are back on Big, who's still talking. "I believe this to be the case from personal experience and five marriages." He grins at Joe. "Name's Big, by the way, I'm Lennie's uncle. Guess you're new around here or you'd already know all this."

What he would know is that Big is the town lothario. Rumors have it that at lunchtime women from all over pack a picnic and set out to find which tree that arborist is in, hoping for an invitation to lunch with him in his barrel high in the canopy. The stories go that shortly after they dine, their clothes flutter down like leaves.

I watch Joe taking in my uncle's gigantism, his wacked-out mustache. He must like what he sees, because his smile immediately brightens the room a few shades.

"Yup, we moved here just a couple months ago from the city, before that we were in Paris—" Hmm. He must not have read the warning on the door about saying the word *Paris* within a mile radius of Gram. It's too late. She's already off on a Francophiliac rhapsody, but Joe seems to share her fanaticism.

He laments, "Man, *if only* we still lived—"

"Now, now," she interrupts, wagging her finger like she's scolding him. Oh no. Her hands have found her hips. Here it comes: she singsongs, *"If only* I had wheels on my ass, I'd be a trolley cart." A Gram standard to forestall wallowing. I'm appalled, but Joe cracks up.

Gram's in love. I don't blame her. She's taken him by the hand and is now escorting him on a docent walk through

78

the house, showing off her willowy women, with whom he seems duly and truly impressed, from the exclamations he's making, in French, I might add. This leaves Big to resume his scavenging for bugs and me to replace fantasies of my spoon with Joe Fontaine's mouth. I can hear them in the living room, know they are standing in front of The Half Mom because everyone who comes in the house has the same reaction to it.

"It's so haunting," Joe says.

"Hmm, yes … that's my daughter, Paige. Lennie and Bailey's mom, she's been away for a long, long time…" I'm shocked. Gram hardly ever talks about Mom voluntarily. "One day I'll finish this painting, it's not done…" Gram has always said she'll finish it when Mom comes back and can pose for her.

"Come now, let's eat." I can hear the heartache in Gram's voice through three walls. Mom's absence has grown way more pronounced for her since Bailey's death. I keep catching her and Big staring at The Half Mom with a fresh, almost desperate kind of longing. It's become more pronounced for me too.

Mom was what Bails and I did together before bed when we'd imagine where she was and what she was doing. I don't know how to think about Mom without her.

I'm jotting down a poem on the sole of my shoe when they come back in.

"Run out of paper?" Joe asks.

I put my foot down. Ugh. What's your major, Lennie? Oh yeah: Dorkology.

Joe sits down at the table, all limbs and graceful motion, an octopus.

We are staring at him again, still not certain what to make of the stranger in our midst. The stranger, however, appears quite comfortable with us.

"What's up with the plant?" He points to the despairing Lennie houseplant in the middle of the table. It looks like it has leprosy. We all go silent, because what do we say about my doppelgänger houseplant?

"It's Lennie, it's dying, and frankly, we don't know what to do about it," Big booms with finality. It's as if the room itself takes a long awkward breath, and then at the same moment Gram, Big and I lose it – Big slapping the table and barking laughter like a drunk seal, Gram leaning back against the counter wheezing and gasping for breath, and me doubled over trying to breathe in between my own uncontrolled gasping and snorting, all of us lost in a fit of hysterics the likes of which we haven't had in months.

"Aunt Gooch! Aunt Gooch!" Gram is shrieking in between peals of laughter. Aunt Gooch is the name Bailey and I gave to Gram's laugh because it would arrive without notice like a crazy relative who shows up at the door with pink hair, a suitcase full of balloons, and no intention of leaving.

Gram gasps, "Oh my, oh my, I thought she was gone for good."

Joe seems to be taking the outburst quite well. He's leaned back in his chair, is balancing on its two back legs; he looks entertained, like he's watching, well, like he's watching three heartbroken people lose their marbles. I finally settle enough to explain to Joe, amidst tears and residual giggles, the story of the plant. If he hadn't already thought he'd gained entry to the local loony bin, he was sure to now. To my amazement, he doesn't make an excuse and fly out the door, but takes the predicament quite seriously, like he actually cares about the fate of the plain, sickly plant that will not revive.

After breakfast, Joe and I go onto the porch, which is still eerily cloaked in morning fog. The moment the screen door closes behind us, he says, "One song," as if no time has elapsed since we were in the tree.

I walk over to the railing, lean against it, and cross my arms in front of my chest. "You play. I'll listen."

"I don't get it," he says. "What's the deal?"

"The deal is I don't want to."

"But why? Your pick, I don't care what."

"I told you, I don't—"

He starts to laugh. "God, I feel like I'm pressuring you to have sex or something." Every ounce of blood in a ten-mile radius rushes to my cheeks. "C'mon. I know you want to…" he jokes, raising his eyebrows like a total dork. What I want is to hide under the porch, but his giant loopy grin makes me laugh. "Bet you like Mozart," he says, squatting to open his case. "All clarinettists do. Or maybe you're a Bach's Sacred Music devotee?" He squints up at me. "Nah, don't seem like one of those." He takes the guitar out, then sits on the edge of the coffee table, swinging it over his knee. "I've got it. No clarinet player with blood in her veins can resist Gypsy jazz." He plays a few sizzling chords.

81

"Am I right? Or … I know!" He starts beating a rhythm on his guitar with his hand, his foot pounding the floor. "Dixieland!"

The guy's life-drunk, I think, makes Candide look like a sourpuss. Does he even know that death exists?

"So, whose idea was it?" I ask him.

He stops finger-drumming. "What idea?"

"That we play together. You said—"

"Oh, that. Marguerite St Denis is an old friend of the family – the one I blame actually for my exile up here. She might've mentioned something about how Lennie Walker *joue de la clarinette comme un rêve*." He twirls his hand in the air like Marguerite. *"Elle joue à ravir, de merveille."*

I feel a rush of something, everything, panic, pride, guilt, nausea – it's so strong I have to hold on to the railing. I wonder what else she told him.

"Quelle catastrophe," he continues. "You see, I thought *I* was her only student who played like a dream." I must look confused, because he explains, "In France. She taught at the conservatory, most summers."

As I take in the fact that my Marguerite is also Joe's Marguerite, I see Big barreling past the window, back at it, broom over head, looking for creatures to resurrect. Joe doesn't seem to notice, probably a good thing. He adds, "I'm joking, about me, clarinet's never been my thing."

"Not what I heard," I say. "Heard you were *fabulous*."

"Rachel doesn't have much of an ear," he replies matter-of-factly, without insult. Her name falls too easily from his lips, like he says it all the time, probably right before he

82

kisses her. I feel my face flush again. I look down, start examining my shoes. What's with me? I mean really. He just wants to play music together like normal musicians do.

Then I hear, "I thought about you…"

I don't dare look up for fear I imagined the words, the sweet tentative tone. But if I did, I'm imagining more of them. "I thought about how crazy sad you are, and…"

He's stopped talking. *And what?* I lift my head to see that he's examining my shoes too. "Okay," he says, meeting my gaze. "I had this image of us holding hands, like up at The Great Meadow or somewhere, and then taking off into the air."

Whoa – I wasn't expecting that, but I like it. "*A la* St Joseph?"

He nods. "Got into the idea."

"What kind of launch?" I ask. "Like rockets?"

"No way, an effortless take-off, Superman-style." He raises one arm up and crosses his guitar with the other to demonstrate. "You know."

I do know. I know I'm smiling just to look at him. I know that what he just said is making something unfurl inside. I know that all around the porch, a thick curtain of fog hides us from the world.

I want to tell him.

"It's not that I don't want to play with you," I say quickly so I don't lose my nerve. "It's that, I don't know, it's different, playing is." I force out the rest. "I didn't want to play first chair, didn't want to do the solos, didn't want to do any of it. I blew it, the chair audition … on purpose." It's the first time I've said it aloud, to anyone, and the relief is the size of a planet. I go on. "I hate soloing, not that you'd understand that. It's just so…" I'm waving my arm around, unable to find the words. But then I point my hand in the direction of Flying Man's. "So like jumping from rock to rock in the river, but in this kind of thick fog, and you're all alone, and every single step is…"

"Is what?"

I suddenly realize how ridiculous I must sound. I have no clue what I'm talking about, no clue. "It doesn't matter," I say.

He shrugs. "Tons of musicians are afraid to fall on their faces."

I can hear the steady whoosh of the river as if the fog's parted to let the sound through.

It's not just performance anxiety though. That's what Marguerite thought too. It's why she thought I quit – *You must work on the nerves, Lennie, the nerves* – but it's more than that, way more. When I play, it's like I'm all shoved and crammed and scared inside myself, like a jack-in-the-box, except one without a spring. And it's been like that for over a year now.

Joe bends down and starts flipping through the sheet music in his case; lots of it is handwritten. He says, "Let's just try. Guitar and clarinet's a cool duet, untapped."

He's certainly not taking my big admission too seriously. It's like finally going to confession only to find out the priest has earplugs in.

I tell him, "Maybe sometime," so he'll drop it.

"Wow." He grins. "Encouraging."

And then it's as if I've vanished. He's bent over the strings, tuning his guitar with such passionate attention I almost feel like I should look away, but I can't. In fact, I'm full on gawking, wondering what it would be like to be cool and casual and fearless and passionate and so freaking alive, just like he is – and for a split second, I want to play with him. I want to disturb the birds.

Later, as he plays and plays, as all the fog burns away, I think, he's right. That's exactly it – I am crazy sad and, somewhere deep inside, all I want is to fly.

10

Grief is a house
where the chairs
have forgotten how to hold us
the mirrors how to reflect us
the walls how to contain us
Grief is a house that disappears
each time someone knocks at the door
or rings the bell
a house that blows into the air
at the slightest gust
that buries itself deep in the ground
while everyone is sleeping
Grief is a house where no one can protect you
where the younger sister ~~will~~
will grow older than the older one
where the doors
no longer let you in
or out

(Found under a stone in Gram's garden)

As usual I can't sleep and am sitting at Bailey's desk, holding St Anthony, in a state of dread about packing up her things. Today, when I got home from lasagna duty at the deli, there were cardboard boxes opened by her desk. I've yet to crack a drawer. I can't. Each time I touch the wooden knobs, I think about her never thumbing through her desk for a notebook, an address, a pen, and all the breath races out of my body with one thought: *Bailey's in that airless box—*

No. I shove the image into a closet in my mind, kick the door shut. I close my eyes, take one, two, three breaths, and when I open them, I find myself staring again at the picture of Explorer Mom. I touch the brittle paper, feel the wax of the crayon as I glide my finger across the fading figure. Does her human counterpart have any idea one of her daughters has died at nineteen years old? Did she feel a cold wind or a hot flash or was she just eating breakfast or tying her shoe like it was any other ordinary moment in her extraordinary itinerant life?

Gram told us our mom was an explorer because she didn't know how else to explain to us that Mom had what generations of Walkers call the "restless gene." According to Gram, this restlessness has always plagued our family, mostly the women. Those afflicted keep moving, they go

from town to town, continent to continent, love to love –
this is why, Gram explained, Mom had no idea who either
of our fathers were, and so neither did we – until they wear
themselves out and return home. Gram told us her Aunt
Sylvie and a distant cousin, Virginia, also had the affliction,
and after many years adventuring across the globe, they,
like all the others before them, found their way back. It's
their destiny to leave, she told us, and their destiny to return, as well.

"Don't boys get it?" I asked Gram when I was ten years
old and "the condition" was becoming more understand-
able to me. We were walking to the river for a swim.

"Of course they do, sweet pea." But then, she stopped
in her tracks, took my hands in hers, and spoke in a rare
solemn tone. "I don't know if at your mature age you can
understand this, Len, but this is the way it is: when men
have it, no one seems to notice, they become astronauts
or pilots or cartographers or criminals or poets. They don't
stay around long enough to know if they've fathered children or not. When women get it, well, it's complicated, it's
just different."

"How?" I asked. "How is it different?"

"Well, for instance, it's not customary for a mother to
not see her own girls for this many years, is it?"

She had a point there.

"Your mom was born like this, practically flew out of
my womb and into the world. From day one, she was running, running, running."

"Running away?"

"Nope, sweet pea, never *away*, know that." She squeezed my hand. "She was always running toward."

Toward what? I think, getting up from Bailey's desk. What was my mother running toward then? What is she running toward now? What was Bailey? What am I?

I walk over to the window, open the curtain a crack and see Toby, sitting under the plum tree, under the bright stars, on the green grass, in the world. Lucy and Ethel are draped over his legs – it's amazing how those dogs only come around when he does.

I know I should turn off the light, get into bed, and moon about Joe Fontaine, but that is not what I do.

I meet Toby under the tree and we duck into the woods to the river, wordlessly, as if we've had a plan to do this for days. Lucy and Ethel follow on our heels a few paces, then turn back around and go home after Toby has an indecipherable talk with them.

I'm leading a double life: Lennie Walker by day, Hester Prynne of *The Scarlet Letter* fame by night.

I tell myself, I will not kiss him, no matter what.

It's a warm, windless night and the forest is still and lonely. We walk side by side in the quiet, listening to the fluted song of the thrush. Even in the moonlit stillness, Toby looks sun-drenched and windswept, like he's on a sailboat.

"I know I shouldn't have come, Len."

"Probably not."

"Was worried about you," he says quietly.

"Thanks," I say, and the cloak of being fine that I wear with everyone else slips right off my shoulders.

Sadness pulses out of us as we walk. I almost expect the trees to lower their branches when we pass, the stars to hand down some light. I breathe in the horsy scent of eucalyptus, the thick sugary pine, aware of each breath I take, how each one keeps me in the world a few seconds longer. I taste the sweetness of the summer air on my tongue and want to just gulp and gulp and gulp it into my body – this living, breathing, heart-beating body of mine.

"Toby?"

"Hmm?"

"Do you feel more alive since…" I'm afraid to ask this, like I'm revealing something shameful, but I want to know if he feels it too.

He doesn't hesitate. "I feel more *everything* since."

Yeah, I think, more everything. Like someone flipped on the switch of the world and everything is just on now, including me, and everything in me, bad and good, all cranking up to the max.

He grabs a twig off a branch, snaps it between his fingers. "I keep doing this stupid stuff at night on my board," he says, "gnarly-ass tricks only show-off dip-shits do, and I've been doing it alone … and a couple times totally wasted."

Toby is one of a handful of skaters in town who regularly and spectacularly defy gravity. If *he* thinks he's putting himself in danger he's going full-on kamikaze.

"She wouldn't want that, Toby." I can't keep the pleading out of my voice.

He sighs, frustrated. "I know that, I know." He picks up his pace as if to leave behind what he just told me.

"She'd kill me." He says it so definitively and passionately that I wonder if he's really talking about skating or what happened between us.

"I won't do it anymore," he insists.

"Good," I say, still not totally sure what he's referring to, but if it's us, he doesn't have to worry, right? I've kept the curtains drawn. I've promised Bailey nothing will ever happen again.

Though even as I think this, I find my eyes drinking him in, his broad chest and strong arms, his freckles. I remember his mouth hungrily on mine, his big hands in my hair, the heat coursing through me, how it made me feel—

"It's just so reckless…" he says.

"Yeah." It comes out a little too breathy.

"Len?"

I need smelling salts.

He looks at me funny, but then I think he reads in my eyes what has been going on in my head, because his eyes kind of widen and spark, before he quickly looks away.

GET A GRIP, LENNIE.

We walk in silence then through the woods and it snaps me back into my senses. The stars and moon are mostly hidden over the thick tree cover, and I feel like I'm swimming through darkness, my body breaking the air as if it were water. I can hear the rush of the river getting louder with every step I take, and it reminds me of Bailey, day after day, year after year, the two of us on this path, lost in talk, the plunge into the pool, and then the endless splaying on the rocks in the sun—

I whisper, "I'm left behind."

"Me too..." His voice catches. He doesn't say anything else, doesn't look at me; he just takes my hand and holds it and doesn't let it go as the cover above us gets thicker and we push together farther into the deepening dark.

I say softly, "I feel so guilty," almost hoping the night will suck my words away before Toby hears.

"I do too," he whispers back.

"But about something else too, Toby..."

"What?"

With all the darkness around me, with my hand in Toby's, I feel like I can say it. "I feel guilty that I'm still here..."

"Don't. Please, Len."

"But she was always so much ... more—"

"No." He doesn't let me finish. "She'd hate for you to feel that way."

"I know."

And then I blurt out what I've forbidden myself to think, let alone say: "She's in a coffin, Toby." I say it so loud, practically shriek it – the words make me dizzy, claustrophobic, like I need to leap out of my body.

I hear him suck in air. When he speaks, his voice is so weak I barely hear it over our footsteps. "No, she isn't."

I know this too. I know both things at once.

Toby tightens his grip around my hand.

Once at Flying Man's, the sky floods through the opening in the canopy. We sit on a flat rock and the full moon shines so brightly on the river, the water looks like pure rushing light.

"How can the world continue to shimmer like this?" I say as I lie down under a sky drunk with stars.

Toby doesn't answer, just shakes his head and lies down next to me, close enough for him to put his arm around me, close enough for me to put my head on his chest if he did so. But he doesn't, and I don't.

He starts talking then, his soft words dissipating into the night like smoke. He talks about how Bailey wanted to have the wedding ceremony here at Flying Man's so they could jump into the pool after saying their vows. I lean up on my elbows and can see it as clearly in the moonlight as if I were watching a movie, can see Bailey in a drenched bright orange wedding dress laughing and leading the party down the path back to the house, her careless beauty so huge it had to walk a few paces ahead of her, announcing itself. I see in the movie of Toby's words how happy she would have been, and suddenly, I just don't know where all that happiness, her happiness, and ours, will go now, and I start to cry, and then Toby's face is above mine and his tears are falling onto my cheeks until I don't know whose are whose, just know that all that happiness is gone, and that we are kissing again.

When I'm with him,
there is someone with me
in my house of grief,
someone who knows
its architecture as I do,
who can walk with me,
from room to sorrowful room,
making the whole rambling structure
of wind and emptiness
not quite as scary, as lonely
as it was before.

(Found on a branch of
a tree outside Clover High)

11

J oe Fontaine's knocking. I'm lying awake in bed, thinking about moving to Antarctica to get away from this mess with Toby. I prop myself up on an elbow to look out the window at the early, bony light.

Joe's our rooster. Each morning since his first visit, a week and a half ago, he arrives at dawn with his guitar, a bag of chocolate croissants from the bakery and a few dead bugs for Big. If we aren't up, he lets himself in, makes a pot of coffee thick as tar and sits at the kitchen table strumming melancholy chords on his guitar. Every so often he asks me if I feel like playing, to which I reply *no*, to which he replies *fine*. A polite stand-off. He hasn't mentioned Rachel again, which is okay by me.

The strangest part about all this is that it's not strange at all, for any of us. Even Big, who is not a morning person, pads down the stairs in his slippers, greets Joe with a boisterous back slap, and after checking the pyramids (which Joe has already checked), he jumps right back into their conversation from the previous morning about his obsession *du jour*: exploding cakes.

Big heard that a woman in Idaho was making a birthday cake for her husband when the flour ignited. They were having a dry spell, so there was lots of static electricity in the air. A cloud of flour dust surrounded her and due to a spark from a static charge in her hand, it exploded: an inadvertent flour bomb. Now Big is trying to enlist Joe to re-enact the event with him for the sake of science. Gram and I have been adamantly opposed to this for obvious reasons. "We've had enough catastrophe, Big," Gram said yesterday, putting her foot down. I think the amount of pot Big's been smoking has made the idea of the exploding cake much funnier and more fascinating than it really is, but somehow Joe is equally enthralled with the concept.

It's Sunday and I have to be at the deli in a few hours. The kitchen's bustling when I stumble in.

"Morning, John Lennon," Joe says, looking up from his guitar strings and throwing me a jaw-dropping grin – what am I doing making out with Toby, *Bailey's* Toby, I think as I smile back at the holy horses unfreakingbelievable Joe Fontaine, who has seemingly moved into our kitchen. Things are so mixed up – the boy who should kiss me acts like a brother and the boy who should act like a brother keeps kissing me. Sheesh.

"Hey, John Lennon," Gram echoes.

Unbelievable. This can't be catching on. "Only Joe's allowed to call me that," I grumble at her.

"John Lennon!" Big whisks into the kitchen and me into his arms, dancing me around the room. "How's my girl today?"

"Why's everyone in such a good mood?" I feel like Scrooge.

"I'm not in a good mood," Gram says, beaming ear to ear, looking akin to Joe. I notice her hair is dry too. No grief-shower this morning. A first. "I just got an idea last night. It's a surprise." Joe and Big glance at me and shrug. Gram's ideas often rival Big's on the bizarre scale, but I doubt this one involves explosions or necromancy.

"We don't know what it is either, honey," Big bellows in a baritone unfit for 8 a.m. "In other breaking news, Joe had an epiphany this morning: He put the Lennie houseplant under one of the pyramids – I can't believe I never thought of that." Big can't contain his excitement, he's smiling down on Joe like a proud father. I wonder how Joe slipped in like this, wonder if it's somehow because he never knew her, doesn't have one single memory of her, he's like the world without our heartbreak—

My cell phone goes off. I glance at the screen. It's Toby. I let it go to voicemail, feeling like the worst person in the world because just seeing his name recalls last night, and my stomach flies into a sequence of contortions. How could I have let this happen?

I look up, all eyes are on me, wondering why I didn't pick up the phone. I have to get out of the kitchen.

"Want to play, Joe?" I say, heading upstairs for my clarinet.

"Holy shit," I hear, then apologies to Gram and Big.

Back on the porch, I say, "You start, I'll follow."

He nods and starts playing some sweet soft chords in G minor. But I feel too unnerved for sweet, too unnerved for soft. I can't shake off Toby's call, his kisses. I can't shake off cardboard boxes, perfume that never gets used, bookmarks that don't move, St Anthony statues that do. I can't shake off the fact that Bailey at eleven years old did not put herself in the drawing of our family, and suddenly, I am so upset I forget I'm playing music, forget Joe's even there beside me.

I start to think about all the things I haven't said since Bailey died, all the words stowed deep in my heart, in our orange bedroom, all the words in the whole world that aren't said after someone dies because they are too sad, too enraged, too devastated, too guilty to come out – all of them begin to course inside me like a lunatic river. I suck in all the air I can, until there's probably no air left in Clover for anyone else, and then I blast it all out my clarinet in one mad bleating typhoon of a note. I don't know if a clarinet has ever made such a terrible sound, but I can't stop, all the years come tumbling out now – Bailey and me in the river, the ocean, tucked so snug into our room, the backseat of cars, bathtubs, running through the trees, through days and nights and months and years without Mom – I am breaking windows, busting through walls, burning up the past, pushing Toby off me, taking the dumb-ass Lennie houseplant and hurling it into the sea—

I open my eyes. Joe's staring at me, astonished. The dogs next door are barking.

"Wow, I think I'll follow next time," he says.

I'd been making decisions for days.
I picked out the dress Bailey would wear *forever*—
a black slinky one—inappropriate—that she loved.
I chose a sweater to go over it, earrings, bracelet, necklace,
her most beloved strappy sandals.
I collected her make-up to give to the funeral director
with a recent photo—
I thought it would be me that would dress her;
I didn't think a strange man should see her naked
touch her body
shave her legs
apply her lipstick
but that's what happened all the same.
I helped Gram pick out the casket, the plot at the cemetery
I changed a few lines in the obituary that Big composed.
I wrote on a piece of paper what I thought
should go on the headstone.

I did all this without uttering a word.
Not one word, for days,
until I saw Bailey before the funeral
and lost my mind.
I hadn't realized that when people say so-and-so
snapped
that's actually what happens—
I started shaking her—
I thought I could wake her up
and get her the hell out of that box.
When she didn't wake,
I screamed: **TALK TO ME.**
Big swooped me up into his arms,
carried me out of the room, the church,
into the slamming rain,
and down to the creek
where we sobbed together
under the black coat he held over our heads
to protect us from the weather.

(Found on a piece of music paper crumpled up by the trailhead)

12

I wish I had my clarinet, I think as I walk home from the deli. If I did, I'd head straight into the woods where no one could hear me and fall on my face like I did on the porch this morning. *Play the music, not the instrument*, Marguerite always said. And Mr James: *Let the instrument play you*. I never got either instruction until today. I always imagined music trapped inside my clarinet, not trapped inside of me. But what if music is what escapes when a heart breaks?

I turn onto our street and see Uncle Big road-reading, tripping over his massive feet, greeting his favorite trees as he passes them. Nothing too unusual, but for the flying fruit. There are a few weeks every year when if circumstances permit, like the winds are just so and the plums particularly heavy, the plum trees around our house become hostile to humans and begin using us for target practice.

Big waves his arm east to west in enthusiastic greeting, narrowly escaping a plum to the head.

I salute him, then when he's close enough, I give a hello twirl to his mustache, which is waxed and styled to the hilt, the fanciest (i.e. freakiest) I've seen it in some time.

"Your friend is over," he says, winking at me. Then he puts his nose back into his book and resumes his

101

promenade. I know he means Joe, but I think of Sarah and my stomach twists a little. She sent me a text today: *Sending out a search party for our friendship.* I haven't responded. I don't know where it is either.

A moment later, I hear Big say, "Oh, Len, Toby called for you, wants you to ring him right away."

He called me on my cell again too while I was at work. I didn't listen to the voicemail. I reiterate the oath I've been swearing all day, that I will never see Toby Shaw again, then I beg my sister for a sign of forgiveness – *no need for subtlety either, Bails, an earthquake will do.*

As I get closer, I see that the house is inside out – in the front yard are stacks of books, furniture, masks, pots and pans, boxes, antiques, paintings, dishes, knick-knacks – then I see Joe and someone who looks just like him but broader and even taller coming out of the house with our sofa.

"Where do you want this, Gram?" Joe says, like it's the most natural thing in the world to be moving the couch outside. This must be Gram's surprise. We're moving into the yard. Great.

"Anywhere's fine, boys," Gram says, then sees me. "Lennie." She glides over. "I'm going to figure out what's causing the terrible luck," she says. "This is what came to me in the middle of the night. We'll move anything suspicious out of the house, do a ritual, burn sage, then make sure not to put anything unlucky back inside. Joe was nice enough to go get his brother to help."

"Hmmm," I say, not knowing what else to say, wishing I

could've seen Joe's face as Gram very sanely explained this INSANE idea to him. When I break away from her, Joe practically gallops over. He's such a downer.

"Just another day at the psych ward, huh?" I say.

"What's quite perplexing..." he says, pointing a finger professorially at his brow, "is just how Gram is making the lucky or unlucky determination. I've yet to crack the code." I'm impressed at how quickly he's caught on that there is nothing to do but grab a wing when Gram's aflight with fancy.

His brother comes up then, rests his hand carelessly on Joe's shoulder, and it instantly transforms Joe into a little brother – the slice into my heart is sharp and sudden – *I'm no longer a little sister*. No longer a sister, period.

Joe can barely mask his adulation and it topples me. I was just the same – when I introduced Bailey I felt like I was presenting the world's most badass work of art.

"Marcus is here for the summer, goes to UCLA. He and my oldest brother are in a band down there." Brothers and brothers and brothers.

"Hi," I say to another beaming guy. Definitely no need for lightbulbs Chez Fontaine.

"I heard you play a mean clarinet," Marcus says. This makes me blush, which makes Joe blush, which makes Marcus laugh and punch his brother's arm. I hear him whisper, "Oh Joe, you've got it so bad." Then Joe blushes even more, if that's possible, and heads into the house for a lamp.

I wonder why though if Joe's got it so bad he doesn't

make a move, even a suggestion of one. I know, I know, I'm a feminist, I could make a move, but a) I've never made a move on anyone in my life and therefore have no moves to make, b) I've been a wee bit preoccupied with the bat in my belfry who doesn't belong there, and c) Rachel – I mean, I know he spends mornings at our house, but how do I know he doesn't spend evenings at hers?

Gram's taken a shine to the Fontaine boys. She's flitting around the yard, telling them over and over again how handsome they are, asking if their parents ever thought about selling them. "Bet they'd make a bundle on you boys. Shame to give boys eyelashes like yours. Don't you think so, Lennie? Wouldn't you kill for eyelashes like that?" God, I'm embarrassed, though she's right about the eyelashes. Marcus doesn't blink either, they both bat.

She sends Joe and Marcus home to get their third brother, convinced that all Fontaine brothers have to be here for the ritual. It's clear both Marcus and Joe have fallen under her spell. She probably could get them to rob a bank for her.

"Bring your instruments," she yells after them. "You too, Lennie."

I do as I'm told and get my clarinet from the tree it's resting in with an assortment of my worldly possessions. Then Gram and I take some of the pots and pans she has deemed lucky back into the kitchen to cook dinner. She prepares the chicken while I quarter the potatoes and spice them with garlic and rosemary. When everything is roasting in the oven, we go outside to gather some strewn plums to make a tart. She is rolling out the dough for the crust while I slice tomatoes and avocados for the salad. Every time she passes me, she pats my head or squeezes my arm.

"This is nice, cooking together again, isn't it, sweet pea?"

I smile at her. "It is, Gram." Well, it was, because now she's looking at me in her talk-to-me-Lennie way. The Gramouncements are about to begin.

"Lennie, I'm worried about you." Here goes.

"I'm all right."

"It's really time. At the least, tidy up, do her laundry or allow me to. I can do it while you're at work."

"I'll do it," I say, like always. And I will, I just don't know when.

She slumps her shoulders dramatically. "I was thinking you and I could go to the city for the day next week, go to lunch—"

"That's okay."

I drop my eyes back to my task. I don't want to see her disappointment.

She sighs in her big, loud, lonely way and goes back to the crust. Telepathically, I tell her I'm sorry. I tell her I just can't confide in her right now, tell her the three feet between us feels like three light-years to me and I don't know how to bridge it.

Telepathically, she tells me back that I'm breaking her broken heart.

When the boys come back they introduce the oldest Fontaine, who is also in town for the summer from LA.

"This is Doug," Marcus says just as Joe says, "This is Fred."

"Parents couldn't make up their mind," the newest Fontaine offers. This one looks positively deranged with glee. Gram's right, we should sell them.

"He's lying," Marcus pipes in. "In high school, Fred wanted to be sophisticated so he could hook up with lots of French girls. He thought Fred was way too uncivilized and Flintstoneish so decided to use his middle name, Doug. But Joe and I couldn't get used to it."

"So now everyone calls him DougFred on two continents." Joe hand-butts his brother's chest, which provokes a counter-attack of several jabs to the ribs. The Fontaine boys are like a litter of enormous puppies, rushing and swiping at each other, stumbling all around, a whirl of perpetual motion and violent affection.

I know it's ungenerous, but watching them, their camaraderie, makes me feel lonely as the moon. I think about Toby and me holding hands in the dark last night, kissing by the river, how with him, I'd felt like my sadness had a place to be.

We eat sprawled out on what is now our lawn furniture. The wind has died down a bit, so we can sit without being pelted by fruit. The chicken tastes like chicken, the plum tart like plum tart. It's too soon for there not to be one bite of ash.

Dusk splatters pink and orange across the sky, beginning its languorous summer stroll. I hear the river through the trees sounding like possibility—

She will never know the Fontaines.

She will never hear about this dinner on a walk to the river.

She will not come back in the morning or Tuesday or in three months.

She will not come back ever.

She's gone and the world is ambling on without her—

I can't breathe or think or sit for another minute.

I try to say "I'll be right back," but nothing comes out, so I just turn my back on the yard full of concerned faces and hurry toward the tree line. When I get to the path, I take off, trying to outrun the heartache that is chasing me down.

I'm certain Gram or Big will follow me, but they don't, Joe does. I'm out of breath and writing on a piece of paper I found on the path when he comes up to me. I ditch the note behind a rock, try to brush away my tears.

This is the first time I've seen him without a smile hidden somewhere on his face.

"You okay?" he asks.

"You didn't even know her." It's out of my mouth, sharp and accusatory, before I can stop it. I see the surprise cross his face.

"No."

He doesn't say anything more, but I can't seem to shut my insane self up. "And you have all these brothers." As if it were a crime, I say this.

"I do."

"I just don't know why you're hanging out with us all

the time." I feel my face get hot as embarrassment snakes its way through my body – the real question is why I am persisting like a full-fledged maniac.

"You don't?" His eyes rove my face, then the corners of his mouth begin to curl upward. "I like you, Lennie, duh." He looks at me incredulously. "I think you're amazing…" Why would he think this? Bailey is amazing and Gram and Big, and of course Mom, but not me, I am the two-dimensional one in a 3-D family.

He's grinning now. "Also I think you're really pretty and I'm incredibly shallow."

I have a horrible thought: *He only thinks I'm pretty, only thinks I'm amazing, because he never met Bailey*, followed by a really terrible, horrible thought: *I'm glad he never met her*. I shake my head, try to erase my mind, like an Etch A Sketch.

"What?" He reaches his hand to my face, brushes his thumb slowly across my cheek. His touch is so tender, it startles me. No one has ever touched me like this before, looked at me the way he's looking at me right now, deep into me. I want to hide from him and kiss him all at the same time.

And then: Bat. Bat. Bat.

I'm sunk.

I think his acting-like-a-brother stint is over.

"Can I?" he says, reaching for the rubber band on my ponytail.

I nod. Very slowly, he slides it off, the whole time holding my eyes in his. I'm hypnotized. It's like he's unbuttoning my shirt. When he's done, I shake my head a little and my hair springs into its habitual frenzy.

"Wow," he says softly. "I've wanted to do that…"

I can hear our breathing. I think they can hear it in New York.

"What about Rachel?" I say.

"What about her?"

"You and her?"

"You," he answers. Me!

I say, "I'm sorry I said all that, before…"

He shakes his head like it doesn't matter, and then to my surprise he doesn't kiss me but wraps his arms around me instead. For a moment, in his arms, with my mind so close to his heart, I listen to the wind pick up and think it just might lift us off our feet and take us with it.

13

The dry trunks of the old growth redwoods creak and squeak eerily over our heads.

"Whoa. What is *that*?" Joe asks, all of a sudden pulling away as he glances up, then over his shoulder.

"What?" I ask, embarrassed how much I still want his arms around me. I try to joke it off. "Sheesh, how to ruin a moment. Don't you remember? I'm having a crisis?"

"I think you've had enough freak-outs for one day," he says, smiling now, and twirling his finger by his ear to signify what a wack-job I am. This makes me laugh out loud. He's looking all around again in a mild panic. "Seriously, what was that?"

"Are you scared of the deep dark forest, city boy?"

"Of course I am, like most sane people, remember lions and tigers and bears, oh my?" He curls his finger around my belt loop, starts veering me back to the house, then stops suddenly. "That, right then. That creepy horror movie noise that happens right before the ax murderer jumps out and gets us."

"It's the old growths creaking. When it's really windy, it sounds like hundreds of doors squeaking open and shut back here, all at the same time, it's beyond spooky. Don't think you could handle it."

He puts his arm around me. "A dare? Next windy day

then." He points to himself – "Hansel" – then at me – "Gretel."

Right before we break from the trees, I say, "Thanks, for following me, and..." I want to thank him for spending all day moving furniture for Gram, for coming every morning with dead bugs for Big, for somehow being there for them when I can't be. Instead, I say, "I really love the way you play." Also true.

"Likewise."

"C'mon," I say. "That wasn't playing. It was honking. Total face-plant."

He laughs. "No way. Worth the wait. Testament to why if given the choice I'd rather lose the ability to talk than play. By far the superior communication."

This I agree with, face-plant or not. Playing today was like finding an alphabet – it was like being sprung. He pulls me even closer to him and something starts to swell inside, something that feels quite a bit like joy.

I try to ignore the insistent voice inside: *How dare you, Lennie? How dare you feel joy this soon?*

When we emerge from the woods, I see Toby's truck parked in front of the house and it has an immediate bone-liquefying effect on my body. I slow my pace, disengage from Joe, who looks quizzically over at me. Gram must have invited Toby to be part of her ritual. I consider staging another freak-out and running back into the woods so I don't have to be in a room with Toby and Joe, but I am not the actress and know I couldn't pull it off. My stomach churns as we walk up the steps, past Lucy and Ethel, who are, of course, sprawled out on the porch awaiting Toby's exit, and who, of course, don't move a muscle as we pass. We push through the door and then cross the hall into the living room. The room is aglow with candles, the air thick with the sweet scent of sage.

DougFred and Marcus sit on two of the remaining chairs in the center of the room playing flamenco guitar. The Half Mom hovers above them as if she's listening to the course, fiery chords that are overtaking the house. Uncle Big towers over the mantel clapping his hand on his thigh to the feverish beat. And Toby stands on the other side of the room, apart from everyone, looking as lonely as I felt earlier – my heart immediately lurches toward him. He leans against the window, his golden hair and skin gleaming in the flickery light. He watches us enter the room with an inappropriate hawkish intensity that is not lost on Joe and sends shivers through me. I can feel Joe's bewilderment without even looking to my side.

Meanwhile, I am now imagining roots growing out of my feet so I don't fly across the room into Toby's arms because I have a big problem: even in this house, on this night, with all these people, with Joe Fabulous Fontaine, who is no longer acting like my brother, right beside me, I still feel this invisible rope pulling me across the room toward Toby and there doesn't seem to be anything I can do about it.

I turn to Joe, who looks like I've never seen him: unhappy, his body stiff with confusion, his gaze shifting from Toby to me and back again. It's as if all the moments between Toby and me that never should have happened are spilling out of us in front of Joe.

"Who's that guy?" Joe asks, with none of his usual equanimity.

"Toby." It comes out oddly robotic.

Joe looks at me like: *Well, who's Toby, retard?*

"I'll introduce you," I say, because I have no choice and cannot just keep standing here like I've had a stroke.

There's no other way to put it: THIS BLOWS.

And on top of everything, the flamenco has begun to crescendo all around us, whipping fire and sex and passion every which way. Perfect. Couldn't they have chosen some sleepy sonata? Waltzes are lovely too, boys. With me on his heels, Joe crosses the room toward Toby: the sun on a collision course with the moon.

The dusky sky pours through the window, framing Toby. Joe and I stop a few paces in front of him, all of us now caught in the uncertainty between day and night. The music continues its fiery revolution all around us and there is a girl inside of me that wants to give in to the fanatical beat – she wants to dance wild and free all around the thumping room, but unfortunately, that girl's in me, not me. Me would like an invisibility cloak to get the hell out of this mess.

I look over at Joe and am relieved to see that the fevered chords have momentarily hijacked his attention. His one hand plays his thigh, his foot drums the ground, and his head bobs around, which flops his hair into his eyes. He can't stop smiling at his brothers, who are pounding

113

their guitars into notes so ferocious they probably could overthrow the government. I realize I'm smiling like a Fontaine as I watch the music riot through Joe. I can feel how intensely he wants his guitar, just as, all of a sudden, I can feel how intensely Toby wants me. I steal a glance at him, and as I suspected, he's watching me watch Joe, his eyes clamped on me. How did we get ourselves into this? It doesn't feel like solace in this moment at all, but something else. I look down, write *help* on my jeans with my finger, and when I look back up I see that Toby's and Joe's eyes have locked. Something passes silently between them that has everything to do with me, because as if on cue they look from each other to me, both saying with their eyes: *What's going on, Lennie?*

Every organ in my body switches places.

Joe puts his hand gently on my arm as if it will remind me to open my mouth and form words. At the contact, Toby's eyes flare. What's going on with him tonight? He's acting like my boyfriend, not my sister's, not someone I made out with twice under very extenuating circumstances. And what about me and this inexplicable and seemingly inescapable pull to him despite everything?

I say, "Joe just moved to town." Toby nods civilly and I sound human, a good start. I'm about to say "Toby was Bailey's boyfriend," which I loathe saying for the *was* and for how it will make me feel like the traitorous person that I am.

But then Toby looks right at me and says, "Your hair, it's down." Hello? This is not the right thing to say. The

114

right thing to say is "Oh, where'd you move from, dude?" or "Clover's pretty cool." Or "Do you skate?" Or basically anything but "Your hair, it's down."

Joe seems unperturbed by the comment. He's smiling at me like he's proud that he was the one that let my hair out of its bondage.

Just then, I notice Gram in the doorway, looking at us. She blows over, holding her burning stick of sage like a magic wand. She gives me a quick once-over, seems to decide I've recovered, then points her wand at Toby and says, "Let me introduce you boys. Joe Fontaine, this is Toby Shaw, Bailey's boyfriend."

Whoosh – I see it: a waterfall of relief pours over Joe. I see the case close in his mind, as he probably thinks there couldn't be anything going on – because what kind of sister would ever cross that kind of line?

"Hey, I'm so sorry," he tells Toby.

"Thanks." Toby tries to smile, but it comes out all wrong and homicidal. Joe, however, so unburdened by Gram's revelation, doesn't even notice, just turns around buoyant as ever, and goes to join his brothers, followed by Gram.

"I'm going to go, Lennie." Toby's voice is barely audible over the music. I turn around, see that Joe is now bent over his guitar, oblivious to everything but the sound his fingers are making.

"I'll walk you out," I say.

Toby says goodbye to Gram, Big and the Fontaines, all of whom are surprised he's leaving so soon, especially Gram, who I can tell is adding some things up.

I follow him to his truck – Lucy, Ethel and I, all yapping at his feet. He opens the door, doesn't get in, leans against the cab. We are facing each other and there's not a trace of the calm or gentleness I've become so accustomed to seeing in his expression, but something fierce and unhinged in its place. He's in total tough-skater-dude mode, and though I don't want to, I'm finding it arresting. I feel a current coursing between us, feel it begin to rip out of control inside of me. *What is it?* I think as he looks into my eyes, then at my mouth, then sweeps his gaze slowly, proprietarily over my body. *Why can't we stop this?* I feel so reckless – like I'm reeling with him into the air on his board with no regard for safety or consequence, with no regard for anything but speed and daring and being hungrily, greedily alive – but I tell him, "No. Not now."

"When?"

"Tomorrow. After work," I say, against my better judgment, against any judgment.

What do you girls want for dinner?
What do you girls think about my new painting?
What do the girls want to do this weekend?
Did the girls leave for school yet?
I haven't seen the girls yet today.
I told those girls to hurry up!
Where are those girls?
Girls, don't forget your lunches.
Girls, be home by 11 PM.
Girls, don't even think of swimming — it's freezing out.
Are the Walker Girls coming to the party?
The Walker Girls were at the river last night.
Let's see if the Walker Girls are home.

(Found written on the wall of Bailey's closet)

14

I find Gram, who is twirling around the living room with her sage wand like an overgrown fairy. I tell her that I'm sorry, but I don't feel well and need to go upstairs.

She stops mid-whirl. I know she senses trouble, but she says, "Okay, sweet pea." I apologize to everyone and say good night as nonchalantly as possible.

Joe follows me out of the room, and I decide it might be time to join a convent, just cloister up with the Sisters for a while.

He touches my shoulder and I turn around to face him. "I hope what I said in the woods didn't freak you out or something … hope that's not why you're crashing…"

"No, no." His eyes are wide with worry. I add, "It made me pretty happy, actually." Which of course is true except for the slight problem that immediately after hearing his declaration, I made a date with my dead sister's boyfriend to do *God knows what*!

"Good." He brushes his thumb on my cheek, and again his tenderness startles me. "Because I'm going crazy, Lennie." Bat. Bat. Bat. And just like that, I'm going crazy too because I'm thinking Joe Fontaine is about to kiss me. Finally.

Forget the convent.

Let's get this out of the way: my previously non-existent floozy-factor is blowing right off the charts.

"I didn't know you knew my name," I say.

"So much you don't know about me, *Lennie*." He smiles and takes his index finger and presses it to my lips, leaves it there until my heart lands on Jupiter: three seconds, then removes it, turns around, and heads back into the living room. Whoa – well, that was either the dorkiest or sexiest moment of my life, and I'm voting for sexy on account of my standing here dumbstruck and giddy, wondering if he did kiss me after all.

I am totally out of control.

I do not think this is how normal people mourn.

When I can move my legs one in front of the other, I make my way up to The Sanctum. Thankfully, it has been deemed fairly lucky by Gram so is mostly untouched, especially Bailey's things, which she mercifully didn't touch at all. I go straight over to her desk and start talking to the explorer picture like we sometimes talk to The Half Mom.

Tonight, the woman on the mountaintop will have to be Bailey.

I sit down and tell her how sorry I am, that I don't know what's wrong with me and that I'll call Toby and cancel the date first thing in the morning. I also tell her I didn't mean to think what I thought in the woods and I would do anything for her to be able to meet Joe Fontaine. Anything. And then I ask her again to please give me a sign that she forgives me before the list of unpardonable things I think and do gets too long and I become a lost cause.

I look over at the boxes. I know I'm going to have to start eventually. I take a deep breath, banish all morbid thoughts from my mind, and put my hands on the wooden knobs of the top desk drawer. Only to immediately think about Bailey and my anti-snooping pact. I never broke it, not once, despite a natural propensity for nosing around. At people's houses, I open medicine cabinets, peek behind shower curtains, open drawers and closet doors whenever possible. But with Bailey, I adhered to the pact—

Pacts. So many between us, breaking now. And what about the unspoken ones, those entered into without words, without pinky swears, without even realizing it? A squall of emotion lands in my chest. Forget talking to the picture, I take out my phone, punch in Bailey's number, listen impatiently to her as Juliet, heat filling my head, then over the tone, I hear myself say, "What happens to a stupid companion pony when the racehorse dies?" There's both anger and despair in my voice and immediately and illogically I wish I could erase the message so she won't hear it.

I slowly open the desk drawer, afraid of what I might find, afraid of what else she might not have told me, afraid of this rollicking bananas pact-breaking me. But there are just things, inconsequential things of hers, some pens, a few playbills from shows at Clover Repertory, concert tickets, an address book, an old cell phone, a couple of business cards, one from our dentist reminding her of her next appointment, and one from Paul Booth, Private Investigator with a San Francisco address.

WTF?

I pick it up. On the back in Bailey's writing it says *April 25 4 p.m., Suite 2B*. The only reason I can think of that she would go see a private investigator would be to find Mom. But why would she do that? We both knew that Big already tried, just a few years ago in fact, and that the PI had said it would be impossible to find her.

The day Big told us about the detective, Bailey had been furious, torpedoing around the kitchen while Gram and I snapped peas from the garden for dinner.

Bailey said, "I know you know where she is, Gram."

"How could I know, Bails?" Gram replied.

"Yeah, how could she know, Bails?" I repeated. I hated when Gram and Bailey fought, and sensed things were about to blow.

Bailey said, "I could go after her. I could find her. I could bring her back." She grabbed a pod, putting the whole thing, shell and all, into her mouth.

"You couldn't find her, and you couldn't bring her back either." Big stood in the doorway, his words filled the room like gospel. I had no idea how long he'd been listening.

Bailey went to him. "How do you know that?"

"Because I've tried, Bailey."

Gram and I stopped snapping and looked up at Big. He hulked over to the table and sat in a kitchen chair, looking like a giant in a kindergarten classroom. "I hired a detective a few years back, a good one, figured I would tell you all if he came up with something, but he didn't. He said it's the easiest thing to be lost if you don't want to be

121

found. He thinks Paige changed her name and probably changes her social security number if she moves…" Big strummed his fingers on the table – it sounded like little claps of thunder.

"How do we even know she's alive?" Big said under his breath, but we all heard it as if he hollered it from the mountaintop. Strangely, this had never occurred to me and I don't think it had ever occurred to Bailey either. We were always told she would be back and we believed it, deeply.

"She's alive, she's most certainly alive," Gram said to Big. "And she will be back."

I saw suspicion dawn again on Bailey's face.

"How do you know, Gram? You must know something if you're so sure."

"A mother knows, okay? She just does." With that, Gram left the room.

I put the card back in the desk drawer, take St Anthony with me, and get into bed. I put him on the nightstand. Why was she keeping so many secrets from me? And how in the world can I possibly be mad at her about it now? About anything. Even for a moment.

Bailey and I didnt talk too much
about Gram's spells,
What she called her Private Times
days spent in the art room
without break.
It was just a part of things,
like green summer leaves,
burning up in fall.
I'd peek through the crack in the door,
see her surrounded by easels
of green women, half-formed—
the paint still wet and hungry.
She'd work on them all at once,
and soon, she'd begin
to look like one of them, too,
all that green spattered on her clothes,
her hands, her face.
Bails and I would pack
our own brown bags those days,
would pull out our sandwiches at noon,
hating the disappointment of a world
where polka dotted scarves,
sheets of music, blue feathers,
didnt surprise us at lunch.
After school, we'd bring her tea
or a sliced apple with cheese,
but it'd just sit on the table, untouched.
Big would tell us to ride it out—
that everyone needs a break
from the routine now and then.
So we did—
it was like Gram would go
on vacation with her ladies
and like them
would get caught somewhere
between here and there.

(Found on a piece of paper in Lennie's clarinet case)

15

Len, you awake?

Yeah, Mom.

Let's do Mom.

Okay, I'll start. She's in Rome —

She's always in Rome lately —

Well, now she's a famous Roman pizza chef and it's late at night, the restaurant just closed and she's drinking a glass of wine with —

With Luigi, the drop dead gorgeous waiter, they just grabbed the bottle of wine and are walking through the moonlit streets, it's hot, and when they come to a fountain she takes off her shoes and jumps in ...

Luigi doesn't even take off his shoes, just jumps in and splashes her, they're laughing....

But standing in the fountain under the big, bright moon makes her think of Flying Man's, how she used to swim at night with (Big....

You really think she's in a fountain in Rome on a hot summer night with gorgeous Luigi and thinking about us? About Big?

Sure.

No way.

We're thinking about her.

That's different.

Why?

Because we're not in a fountain in Rome on a hot summer night with gorgeous Luigi.

True.

Night, Bails.

(Found on a piece of notebook paper
balled up in a shoe in Lennie's closet)

The day everything happens begins like all others lately with Joe's soft knock. I roll over, peek out the window, and see only the lawn through the morning fog. Everything must have been moved back into the house after I'd gone to sleep.

I go downstairs, find Gram sitting at her seat at the kitchen table, her hair wrapped in a towel. She has her hands around a mug of coffee and is staring at Bailey's chair. I sit down next to her. "I'm really sorry about last night," I say. "I know how much you wanted to do a ritual for Bailey, for us."

"It's okay, Len, we'll do one. We have plenty of time." She takes my hand with one of hers, rubs it absentmindedly with the other. "And anyway, I think I figured out what was causing the bad luck."

"Yeah?" I say. "What?"

"You know that mask Big brought back from South America when he was studying those trees. I think that it might have a curse on it."

I've always hated that mask. It has fake hair all over it, eyebrows that arch in astonishment, and a mouth baring shiny, wolfish teeth. "It always gave me the creeps," I tell her. "Bailey too."

Gram nods but she seems distracted. I don't think she's

125

really listening to me, which couldn't be more unlike her lately.

"Lennie," she says tentatively. "Is everything okay between you and Toby?"

My stomach clenches. "Of course," I say, swallowing hard, trying to make my voice sound casual. "Why?"

She owl-eyes me. "Don't know, you both seemed funny last night around each other." Ugh. Ugh. Ugh.

"And I keep wondering why Sarah isn't coming around. Did you get in a fight?" she says to further send me into a guilt spiral.

Just then, Big and Joe come in, saving me. Big says, "We thought we saw life in spider number six today."

Joe says, "I swear I saw a flutter."

"Almost had a heart attack, Joe here, practically launched through the roof, but it must have been a breeze, little guy's still dead as a doornail. The Lennie plant's still languishing too. I might have to rethink things, maybe add a UV light."

"Hey," Joe says, coming behind me, dropping a hand to my shoulder. I look up at the warmth in his face and smile at him. I think he could make me smile even while I was hanging at the gallows, which I'm quite certain I'm headed for. I put my hand over his for a second, see Gram notice this as she gets up to make us breakfast.

I feel somehow responsible for the scrambled ashes that we are all shoveling into our mouths, as if I've somehow derailed the path to healing that our household was on yesterday morning. Joe and Big banter on about resurrecting bugs and exploding cakes – the conversation that would not die – while I actively avoid Gram's suspicious gaze.

"I need to get to work early today, we're catering the Dwyers' party tonight." I say this to my plate but can see Gram nodding in my periphery. She knows because she's been asked to help with the flower arrangements. She's asked all the time to oversee flower arrangements for parties and weddings but rarely says yes because she hates cut flowers. We all knew not to prune her bushes or cut her blooms under penalty of death. She probably said yes this time just to get out of the house for an afternoon. Sometimes I imagine the poor gardeners all over town this summer without Gram, standing in their yards, scratching their heads at their listless wisteria, their forlorn fuchsias.

Joe says, "I'll walk you to work. I need to go to the music store anyway." All the Fontaine boys are supposedly working for their parents this summer, who've converted a barn into a workshop where his dad makes specialty guitars, but I get the impression they spend all day working on new songs for their band Dive.

We embark on the seven-block walk to town, which looks like it's going to take two hours because Joe comes to a standstill every time he has something to say, which is every three seconds.

"You can't walk and talk at the same time, can you?" I ask.

He stops in his tracks, says "Nope." Then continues on for a minute in silence until he can't take it anymore and stops, turns to me, takes my arm, forcing me to stop,

127

while he tells me how I have to go to Paris, how we'll play music in the metro, make tons of money, eat only chocolate croissants, drink red wine, and stay up all night every night because no one ever sleeps in Paris. I can hear his heart beating the whole time and I'm thinking, *Why not?* I could step out of this sad life like it's an old sorry dress, and go to Paris with Joe – we could get on a plane and fly over the ocean and land in *France*. We could do it today even. I have money saved. I have a beret. A hot black bra. I know how to say *Je t'aime*. I love coffee and chocolate and Baudelaire. And I've watched Bailey enough to know how to wrap a scarf. We could really do it, and the possibility makes me feel so giddy I think I might catapult into the air. I tell him so. He takes my hand and puts his other arm up Superman-style.

"You see, I was right," he says with a smile that could power the state of California.

"God, you're gorgeous," I blurt out and want to die because I can't believe I said it aloud and neither can he – his smile, so huge now, he can't even get any words past it.

He stops again. I think he's going to go on about Paris some more – but he doesn't. I look up at him. His face is serious like it was last night in the woods.

"Lennie," he whispers.

I look into his sorrowless eyes and a door in my heart blows open.

And when we kiss, I see that on the other side of that door is sky.

16

I CAN'T SHOVE THE DARK OUT OF MY WAY

(Found scrawled on the bench outside Maria's Italian Deli)

I make a million lasagnas in the window at the deli, listening to Maria gossip with customer after customer, then come home to find Toby lying on my bed. The house is still as stone with Gram at the Dwyers' and Big at work. I punched Toby's number into my phone ten times today, but stopped each time before pressing send. I was going to tell him I couldn't see him. Not after promising Bailey. Not after kissing Joe. Not after Gram's inquisition. Not after reaching into myself and finding some semblance of conscience. I was going to tell him that we had to stop this, had to think how it would make Bailey feel, how bad it makes us feel. I was going to tell him all these things, but didn't because each time I was about to complete the call, I got transported back to the moment by his truck last night and that same inexplicable recklessness and hunger would overtake me until the phone was closed and lying silent on the counter before me.

"Hi, you." His voice is deep and dark and unglues me instantly.

I'm moving toward him, unable not to, the pull, unavoidable, tidal. He gets up quickly, meets me halfway across the room. For one split second we face each other; it's like diving into a mirror. And then I feel his mouth crushing into mine, teeth and tongue and lips and all his raging sorrow crashing right into mine, all our raging sorrow together now crashing into the world that did this to us. I'm frantic as my fingers unbutton his shirt, slip it off his shoulders, then my hands are on his chest, his back, his neck, and I think he must have eight hands because one is taking off my shirt, another two are holding my face while he kisses me, one is running through my hair, another two are on my breasts, a few are pulling my hips to his and then the last undoes the button on my jeans, unzips the fly and we are on the bed, his hand edging its way between my legs, and that is when I hear the front door slam shut—

We freeze and our eyes meet – a mid-air collision of shame: all the wreckage explodes inside me. I can't bear it. I cover my face with my hands, hear myself groan. What am I doing? What did we almost do? I want to press the rewind button. Press it and press it and press it. But I can't think about that now, can only think about not getting caught in this bed with Toby.

"Hurry," I say, and it unfreezes and de-panics both of us.

He springs to his feet and I scramble across the floor like a crazed crab, put on my shirt, throw Toby his. We're both dressing at warp speed—

"No more," I say, fumbling with the buttons on my shirt, feeling criminal and wrong, full of ick and shame. "Please."

He's straightening the bedding, frenetically puffing pillows, his face flushed and wild, blond hair flying in every direction. "I'm sorry, Len—"

"It doesn't make me miss her less, not anymore." I

131

sound half resolute, half frantic. "It makes it worse."

He stops what he's doing, nods, his face a wrestling match of competing emotions, but it looks like hurt is winning out. God, I don't want to hurt him, but I don't want to do this anymore either. I can't. And what is *this* anyway? Being with him just now didn't feel like the safe harbor it did before – it was different, desperate, like two people struggling for breath.

"John Lennon," I hear from downstairs. "You home?"

This can't be happening, it can't. Nothing used to happen to me, nothing at all for seventeen years and now everything at once. Joe is practically singing my name, he sounds so elated, probably still riding high from that kiss, that sublime kiss that could make stars fall into your open hands, a kiss like Cathy and Heathcliff must have had on the moors with the sun beating on their backs and the world streaming with wind and possibility. A kiss so unlike the fearsome tornado that moments before ripped through Toby and me.

Toby is dressed and sitting on my bed, his shirt hanging over his lap. I wonder why he doesn't tuck it in, then realize he's trying to cover a freaking hard-on – oh God, who am I? How could I have let this get so out of hand? And why doesn't my family do anything normal like carry house keys and lock front doors?

I make sure I'm buttoned and zipped. I smooth my hair and wipe my lips before I swing open the bedroom door and stick my head out just as Joe is barreling down the hallway. He smiles wildly, looks like love itself stuffed into a pair of jeans, black T-shirt, and backward baseball cap.

"Come over tonight. They're all going to the city for some jazz show." He's out of breath – I bet he ran all the way here. "Couldn't wait…" He reaches for my hand, takes it in his, then sees Toby sitting on the bed behind me. First he drops my hand, and then the impossible happens: Joe Fontaine's face shuts like a door.

"Hey," he says to Toby, but his voice is pinched and wary.

"Toby and I were just going through some of Bailey's things," I blurt out. I can't believe I'm using Bailey to lie to Joe to cover up fooling around with her boyfriend. A new low even for the immoral girl I've become. I'm a Gila monster of a girl. Loch Ness Lennie. No convent would even take me.

Joe nods, mollified by that, but he's still looking at me and Toby and back again with suspicion. It's as if someone hit the dimmer switch and turned down his whole being.

Toby stands up. "I need to get home." He crosses the room, his carriage slumped, his gait awkward, uncertain. "Good seeing you again," he mumbles at Joe. "I'll see you soon, Len." He slips past us, sad as rain, and I feel terrible. My heart follows after him a few paces, but then it ricochets back to Joe, who stands before me without a trace of death anywhere on him.

"Lennie, is there—"

I have a pretty good idea what Joe is about to ask and so I do the only thing I can think of to stop the question from coming out of his mouth: I kiss him. I mean *really* kiss him, like I've wanted to do since that very first day in band. No sweet soft peck about it. With the same lips that just kissed someone else, I kiss away his question, his suspicion, and after a while, I kiss away the someone else too, the something else that almost just happened, until it is only the two of us, Joe and me, in the room, in the world, in my crazy swelling heart.

Holy horses.

I put aside for a moment the fact that I've turned into a total strumpet-harlot-trollop-wench-jezebel-tart-harridan-chippy-nymphet because I've just realized something incredible. *This is it* – what all the hoopla is about, what *Wuthering Heights* is about – it all boils down to this feeling rushing through me in this moment with Joe as our mouths refuse to part. Who knew all this time I was one kiss away from being Cathy and Juliet and Elizabeth Bennet and Lady Chatterley?!

Years ago, I was crashed in Gram's garden and Big asked me what I was doing. I told him I was looking up at the sky. He said, "That's a misconception, Lennie, the sky is everywhere, it begins at your feet."

Kissing Joe, I believe this, for the first time in my life.

I feel delirious, Joelirious, I think as I pull away for a moment, and open my eyes to see that the Joe Fontaine dimmer switch has been cranked back up again and that he is Joelirious too.

"That was—" I can hardly form words.

"Incredible," he interrupts. "Totally *incroyable*."

We're staring at each other, stunned.

134

"Sure," I say, suddenly remembering he invited me over tonight.

"Sure what?" He looks at me like I'm speaking Swahili, then smiles and puts his arms around me, says, "Ready?" He lifts me off my feet and spins me around and I am suddenly in the dorkiest movie ever, laughing and feeling a happiness so huge I am ashamed to be feeling it in a world without my sister.

"Sure, I'll come over tonight," I say as everything stops spinning and I land back on my own two feet.

17

What's wrong, Lennie?

Nothing.

Tell me.

No.

C'mon, spill it.

Okay. It's just that you're
            different now.

How?

Like Zombieville.

I'm in love, Len — I've never
        felt like this before.

Like what?

Like forever.

Forever?

Yeah. This is it. He's it.

How do you know?

My toes told me. The toes knows

(Found on a napkin stuffed in a mug, Cecilia's Bakery)

"I'm going over to Joe's," I say to Gram and Big, who are both home now, camped out in the kitchen, listening to a baseball game on the radio, circa 1930.

"That sounds like a plan," Gram says. She's taken the still despairing Lennie houseplant out from under the pyramid and is sitting beside it at the table, singing to it softly, something about greener pastures. "I'll just freshen up and get my bag, sweet pea."

She can't be serious.

"I'll go too," says Big, who is hunched over a crossword puzzle. He's the fastest puzzler in all Christendom. I look over and note, however, that this time he's putting numbers in the boxes instead of letters. "As soon as I finish this, we can all head up to the Fontaines'."

"Uh, I don't think so," I say.

They both look up at me, incredulous.

Big says, "What do you mean, Len, he's here every single morning, it's only fair that—"

And then he can't keep it up anymore and bursts out laughing, as does Gram. I'm relieved. I had actually started to imagine trucking up the hill with Gram and Big in tow: the Munsters follow Marilyn on a date.

"Why, Big, she's all dressed up. And her hair's down. Look at her." This is a problem. I was going for the short flowery dress and heels and lipstick and wild hair look that no one would notice is any different from the jeans, ponytail, and no makeup look I've mastered every other day of my life. I know I'm blushing, also know I better get out of the house before I run back upstairs and challenge Bailey's Guinness-Book-of-Changing-Clothes-Before-a-Date record of thirty-seven outfits. This was only my eighteenth, but clothes-changing is an exponential activity, the frenzy only builds, it's a law of nature. Even St Anthony peering at me from the nightstand, reminding me of what I'd found in the drawer last night, couldn't snap me out of it. I'd remembered something about him though. He was like Bailey, charismatic as anything. He had to give his sermons in marketplaces because he overflowed even the largest of churches. When he died all the church bells in Padua rang of their own accord. Everyone thought angels had come to earth.

"Goodbye, you guys," I say to Gram and Big, and head for the door.

"Have fun, Len … and not too late, okay?"

I nod, and am off on the first real date of my life. The other nights I've had with boys don't count, not the ones with Toby I'm actively trying not to think about, and definitely not the parties, after which I'd spent the next day, week, month, year thinking of ways to get my kisses back. Nothing has been like this, nothing has made me feel like I do right now walking up the hill to Joe's, like I have a window in my chest where sunlight is pouring in.

when
Joe
plays
his
horn
I
fall
out
of
my
chair
and
onto
my
knees
when
he
plays
all
the
flowers
swap
colors
and
years
and
decades
and
centuries
of
rain
pour
back
into
the
sky

18

(Found on the bathroom wall,
music room, Clover High)

The feeling I had earlier today with Joe in The Sanctum overwhelms me the moment I see him sitting on the stoop of the big white house playing his guitar. He's bent over it, singing softly, and the wind is carrying his words through the air like fluttering leaves.

"Hey, John Lennon," he says, putting aside his guitar, standing up and jumping off the front step. "Uh-oh. You look *vachement* amazing. Too good to be alone with me all night long."

He's practically leaping over. His delight quotient mesmerizes me. At the human factory, someone must have messed up and just slipped him more than the rest of us. "I've been thinking about a duet we could do. I just need to rearrange—"

I'm not listening anymore. I hope he just keeps talking up a storm, because I can't utter a word. I know the expression *love bloomed* is metaphorical, but in my heart in this moment, there is one badass flower, captured in time-lapse photography, going from bud to wild radiant blossom in ten seconds flat.

"You okay?" he asks. His hands are on either side of my arms and he's peering into my face.

"Yes." I'm wondering how people breathe in these situations. "I'm fine."

"You are *fine*," he says, looking me over like a major dork, which immediately snaps me out of my love spell.

"Ugh, *quel dork*," I say, pushing him away.

He laughs and slips his arm around my shoulders. "C'mon, you enter Maison Fontaine at your own risk."

The first thing I notice about Maison Fontaine is that the phone is ringing and Joe doesn't seem to notice. I hear a girl's voice on an answering machine far away in another room and think for a minute it sounds like Rachel before deciding it doesn't. The second thing I notice is how opposite this house is to Maison Walker. Our house looks like Hobbits live there. The ceilings are low, the wood is dark and gnarly, colorful rag rugs line the floors, paintings, the walls, whereas Joe's house floats high in the sky with the clouds. There are windows everywhere that reveal sunburned fields swimming in the wind, dark green woods that cloister the river and the river itself as it wends from town to town in the distance. There are no tables piled with weeks of mail, shoes kicked around under furniture, books open on every surface. Joe lives in a museum. Hanging all over the walls are gorgeous guitars of every color, shape and size. They look so animate, like they could make music all by themselves.

"Pretty cool, huh? My dad makes amazing instruments. Not just guitars either. Mandolins, lutes, dulcimers," he says as I ogle one and then the next.

And now for something completely different: Joe's room. The physical manifestation of chaos theory. It's overflowing with instruments I've never seen before and can't

141

even imagine what kind of sound they'd make, CDs, music magazines, library books in French and English, concert posters of French bands I've never heard of, comic books, notebooks with tiny boxlike weirdo boy writing in them, sheets of music, stereo equipment unplugged and plugged, broken-open amps and other sound equipment I don't recognize, odd rubber animals, bowls of blue marbles, decks of cards, piles of clothes as high as my knee, not to mention the dishes, bottles, glasses … and over his desk a small poster of John Lennon.

"Hmm," I say, pointing to the poster. I look around, taking it all in. "I think your room is giving me new insight into Joe Fontaine aka freaking madman."

"Yeah, thought it best to wait to show you the bomb-room until…"

"Until what?"

"I don't know, until you realized…"

"Realized what?"

"I don't know, Lennie." I can see he's embarrassed. Somehow things have turned uncomfortable.

"Tell me," I say. "Wait until I realized what?"

"Nothing, it's stupid." He looks down at his feet, then back up at me. Bat. Bat. Bat.

"I want to know," I say.

"Okay, I'll say it: wait until you realized that maybe you liked me too."

The flower is blooming again in my chest, this time three seconds from bud to showstopper.

"I do," I say, and then without thinking, add, "A lot."

142

What's gotten into me? Now I really can't breathe. A situation made worse by the lips that are suddenly pressing into mine.

Our tongues have fallen madly in love and gotten married and moved to Paris.

After I'm sure I've made up for all my former years of kisslessness, I say, "I think if we don't stop kissing, the world is going to explode."

"Seems like it," he whispers. He's staring dreamily into my eyes. Heathcliff and Cathy have nothing on us. "We can do something else for a while," he says. "If you want…" He smiles. And then: Bat. Bat. Bat. I wonder if I am going to survive the night.

"Want to play?" he asks.

"I do," I tell him, "but I didn't bring my instrument."

"I'll get one." He leaves the room, which gives me a chance to recover, and unfortunately, to think about what happened with Toby earlier. How scary and out of control it was today, like we were trying to break each other apart. But why? To find Bailey? To wrench her from the other's heart? The other's body? Or was it something worse? Were we trying to forget her, to wipe out her memory for one passionate moment? But no, it's not that, it can't be, can it? When we're together, Bailey's all around us like air we can breathe; that's been the comfort until today, until it got so out of hand. I don't know. The only thing I do know is that it's all about her, because even now if I imagine Toby alone with his heartache while I am here with Joe obliterating my own,

143

I feel guilty, like I've abandoned him, and with him, my grief, and with my grief, my sister.

The phone rings again and it mercifully ejects me from these thoughts, and crash-lands me back into the bomb-room – this room where Joe sleeps in this unmade bed and reads these books strewn everywhere and drinks out of these five hundred half-full glasses seemingly at once. I feel giddy with the intimacy of being where he thinks and dreams, where he changes his clothes and flings them abso-lutely all over the place, where he's naked. *Joe, naked*. The thought of it, him, all of him – *guh*. I've never even seen a real live guy totally naked, ever. Only some Internet porn Sarah and I devoured for a while. That's it. I've always been scared of seeing all, seeing *it*. The first time Sarah saw one hard, she said more animal names came flying out of her mouth in that one moment than all other moments in her life combined. Not animals you'd think either. No pythons and eels. According to her it was a full-on menagerie: hip-pos, elephants, orang-utans, tapirs, gazelles, etc.

All of a sudden I'm walloped with missing her. How could I be in Joe Fontaine's freaking bedroom without her knowing? How could I have blown her off like this? I take out my phone, text: *Call back the search party. Please. Forgive.*

I look around again, curbing all impulses to go through drawers, peek under the bed, read the notebook lying open at my feet. Okay, I curb two out of three of those impulses. It's been a bad day for morality. And it's not really reading someone's journal if it's open and you can glance down and make out your name, well, your name to him, in a sentence that says…

I bend my knees, and without touching the notebook in any way, read just the bit around the initials JL. *I've never met anyone as heartbroken as JL, I want to make her feel better, want to be around her all the time, it's crazy, it's like she's on full blast, and everyone else is just on mute, and she's honest, so honest, nothing like Genevieve, nothing at all like Genevieve…* I hear his steps in the hall, stand up. The phone is ringing yet again.

He comes back with two clarinets, a B flat and a bass, holds them up. I go for the soprano like I'm used to.

"What's the deal with the phone?" I say, instead of saying *Who's Genevieve?* Instead of falling to my knees and confessing that I'm anything but honest, that I'm probably just exactly like Genevieve, whoever she is, but without the exotic French part.

He shrugs. "We get a lot of calls," he says, then begins his tuning ritual that makes everything in the world but him and a handful of chords disappear.

The untapped duet of guitar and clarinet is awkward at first. We stumble around in sound, fall over each other, look up embarrassed, try again. But after a while, we begin to click and when we don't know where the other is going, we lock eyes and listen so intently that for fleeting moments it's like our souls are talking. One time after I improvise alone for a while, he exclaims, "Your tone is awesome, so, so lonely, like, I don't know, a day without birds or something," but I don't feel lonely at all. I feel like Bailey is listening.

* * *

"Well, you're no different late at night, exactly the same John Lennon." We're sitting on the grass, drinking some wine Joe swiped from his father. The front door is open and a French chanteuse is blasting out of it into the warm night. We're swigging out of the bottle and eating cheese and a baguette. I'm finally in France with Joe, I think, and it makes me smile.

"What?" he asks.

"I don't know. This is nice. I've never drunk wine before."

"I have my whole life. My dad mixed it with water for us when we were little."

"Really? Drunken little Fontaine boys running into walls?"

He laughs. "Yup, exactly. That's my theory of why French children are so well behaved. They're drunk off their *petits mignons* asses most of the time." He tips the bottle and takes a sip, passes it to me.

"Are both your parents French?"

"Dad is, born and raised in Paris. My mom's from around here originally. But Dad makes up for it, he's Central Casting French." There's a bitterness in his voice, but I don't pursue it. I've only just recovered from the consequences of my snooping, have almost forgotten about Genevieve and the importance of honesty to Joe, when he says, "Ever been in love?" He's lying on his back, looking up at a sky reeling with stars.

I don't holler, *Yes, right now, with you, stupid*, like I

146

suddenly want to, but say, "No. I've never been anything."

He gets up on one elbow, looks over at me. "What do you mean?"

I sit, hugging my knees, looking out at the spattering of lights down in the valley.

"It's like I was sleeping or something, happy, but sleeping, for seventeen years, and then Bailey died…" The wine has made it easier to talk but I don't know if I'm making any sense. I look over at Joe. He's listening to me so carefully, like he wants to catch my words in his hands as they fall from my lips.

"And now?"

"Well, now I don't know. I feel so different." I pick up a pebble and toss it into the darkness. I think how things used to be: predictable, sensible. How I used to be the same. I think how there is no inevitability, how there never was, I just didn't know it then. "I'm awake, I guess, and maybe that's good, but it's more complicated than that because now I'm someone who knows the worst thing can happen at any time."

Joe's nodding like I'm making sense, which is good, because I have no idea what I just said. I know what I meant though. I meant that I know now how close death is. How it lurks. And who wants to know that? Who wants to know we are just one carefree breath away from the end? Who wants to know that the person you love and need the most can just vanish forever?

He says, "But if you're someone who knows the worst thing can happen at any time, aren't you also someone who

147

knows the best thing can happen at any time too?"

I think about this and instantly feel elated. "Yeah, that's right," I say. "Like right now with you, actually…" It's out of my mouth before I can stop it, and I see the delight wash across his face.

"Are we drunk?" I ask.

He takes another swig. "Quite possibly."

"Anyway, have you ever…"

"I've never experienced anything like what you're going through."

"No, I mean, have you ever been in love?" My stomach clenches. I want him to say no so badly, but I know he won't, and he doesn't.

"Yeah, I was. I guess." He shakes his head. "I think so anyway."

"What happened?"

A siren sounds in the distance. Joe sits up. "During the summers, I boarded at school. I walked in on her and my roommate, killed me. I mean really killed me. I never talked to her again, or him, threw myself into music in kind of an insane way, swore off girls, well, until now, I guess…" He smiles, but not like usual. There's a vulnerability in it, a hesitancy; it's all over his face, swimming around in his beautiful green eyes too. I shut my eyes to not have to see it, because all I can think about is how he almost walked in on Toby and me today.

Joe grabs the bottle of wine and drinks. "Moral of the story: violinists are insane. I think it's that crazy-ass bow." Genevieve, the gorgeous French violinist. Ugh.

"Yeah? What about clarinettists?"

He smiles. "The most soulful." He trails his finger across my face, forehead to cheek to chin, then down my neck. "And so beautiful." Oh my, I totally get why King Edward VIII abdicated his throne for love. If I had a throne, I'd abdicate it just to relive the last three seconds.

"And horn players?" I ask, intertwining my fingers with his.

He shakes his head. "Crazy hellions, steer clear. All-or-nothing types, no middle ground for the blowhards." Uh-oh. "Never want to cross a horn player," he adds flippantly, but I don't hear it flippantly. I can't believe I lied to him today. I have to stay away from Toby. Far away.

A pair of coyotes howl in the distance, sending a shiver up my spine. Nice timing, dogs.

"Didn't know you horn guys were so scary," I say, letting go of his hand and taking a swig off the bottle. "And guitarists?"

"You tell me."

"Hmm, let me think…" I trail my finger over his face this time. "Homely and boring, and of course, talentless—" He cracks up. "I'm not done. But they make up for all that because they are so, so passionate—"

"Oh, God," he whispers, reaching his hand behind my neck and bringing my lips to his. "Let's let the whole fucking world explode this time."

And we do.

19

I'm lying in bed, hearing voices.

"What do you think is wrong with her?"

"Not sure. Could be the orange walls getting to her." A pause, then I hear: "Let's think about it logically. Symptoms: still in bed at noon on a sunny Saturday, goofy grin on her face, stains on her lips likely from red wine, a beverage she's not allowed to drink, which we will address later, and the giveaway, still in her clothes, a dress I might add, with flowers on it."

"Well, my expert opinion, which I draw from vast experience and five glorious, albeit flawed marriages, is that Lennie Walker aka John Lennon is out of her mind in love."

Big and Gram are smiling down at me. I feel like Dorothy waking in her bed, surrounded by her Kansans after having been over the rainbow.

"Do you think you're ever going to get up again?" Gram is sitting on the bed now, patting my hand, which is in hers.

"I don't know." I roll over to face her. "I just want to lie here forever and think about him." I haven't decided which is better: experiencing last night, or the blissed-out replay in my mind where I can hit pause and turn ecstatic seconds into whole hours, where I can loop certain moments until the sweet grassy taste of Joe is again in my mouth, the clove scent of his skin is in the air, until I can feel his hands running through my hair, all over my dress, just one thin, thin layer between us, until the moment when he slipped his hands under the fabric and I felt his fingers on my skin like music – all of it sending me again and again right off the cliff that is my heart.

This morning, for the first time, Bailey wasn't my first thought on waking and it had made me feel guilty. But the guilt didn't have much of a chance against the dawning realization that I was falling in love. I had stared out the window at the early-morning fog, wondering for a moment if she had sent Joe to me so I would know that in the same world where she could die, this could happen.

Big says, "Would you look at her. We've got to cut down those damn rosebushes." His hair is particularly coiled and springy today, and his mustache is unwaxed, so it looks like a squirrel is running across his face. In any fairy tale, Big plays the king.

Gram chides him, "Hush now, you don't even believe in that." She doesn't like anyone to perpetuate the rumor about the aphrodisiacal nature of her roses, because there was a time when desperate lovers would come and steal them to try to change the hearts of their beloveds. It made her crazy. There is not much Gram takes more seriously than proper pruning.

Big won't let it go though. "I follow the proof-is-in-the-pudding scientific method: Please examine the empirical evidence in this bed. She's worse than me."

"No one is worse than you, you're the town swain." Gram rolls her eyes.

"You say swain, but imply swine," Big retorts, twisting his squirrel for effect.

I sit up in bed, lean my back against the sill to better enjoy their verbal tennis match. I can feel the summery day through the window, deliciously warming my back. But when I look over at Bailey's bed, I'm leveled. How can something this momentous be happening to me without her? And what about all the momentous things to come? How will I go through each and every one of them without her? I don't care that she was keeping things from me – I want to tell her absolutely everything about last night, about everything that will ever happen to me! I'm crying before I even realize it, but I don't want us all to tailspin, so I swallow and swallow it all down, and try to focus on last night, on falling in love. I spot my clarinet across the room, half covered with the paisley scarf of Bailey's I recently started wearing.

"Joe didn't come by this morning?" I ask, wanting to play again, wanting to blow all this everything I'm feeling out my clarinet.

Big replies, "No, bet a million dollars he's exactly where you are, though he probably has his guitar with him. Have you asked him if he sleeps with it yet?"

"He's a musical genius," I say, feeling my earlier giddiness returning. Without a doubt, I've gone bipolar.

"Oh, jeez. C'mon Gram, she's a lost cause." Big winks at me, then heads for the door.

Gram stays seated next to me, ruffling my hair like I'm a little kid. She's looking at me closely and a little too long.

Oh no. I've been in such a trance, I forget that I haven't really been talking to Gram lately, that we've hardly been alone like this in weeks.

"Len." This is definitely her Gramouncement tone, but I don't think it's going to be about Bailey. About expressing my feelings. About packing up Bailey's things. About going to the city for lunch. About resuming my lessons. About all the things I haven't wanted to do.

"Yeah?"

"We talked about birth control, diseases and all that…" Phew. This one's harmless.

"Yeah, like a million times."

"Okay, just as long as you haven't suddenly forgotten it all."

"Nope."

"Good." She's patting my hand again.

"Gram, there's no need yet, okay?" I feel the requisite blush from revealing this, but better to not have her freaking out about it and constantly questioning me.

"Even better, even better," she says, the relief evident in her voice, and it makes me think. Things with Joe last night were intense, but they were paced to savor. Not so with Toby. I worry what might've happened if we weren't interrupted. Would I have had the sense to stop us? Would he have? All I know is that everything was happening really quickly, I was totally out of control, and condoms were the furthest thing from my mind. God. How did that happen? How did Toby Shaw's hands ever end up on my breasts? Toby's! And only hours before

Joe's. I want to dive under the bed, make it my permanent residence. How did I go from bookworm and band geek to two-guys-in-the-same-day hussy?

Gram smiles, oblivious of the sudden bile rising in my throat, the twisting in my guts. She ruffles my hair again. "In the middle of all this tragedy, you're growing up, sweet pea, and that is such a wonderful thing."

Groan.

20

"Lennie! Lennie! Lennnnnnnnnnie! God, I've missed you!" I pull the cell phone away from my ear. Sarah hadn't texted me back, so I assumed she was really pissed. I cut in to say so, and she responds, "I *am* furious! And I'm *not* speaking to you!" then she launches into all the summer gossip I've missed. I soak it up but can tell there was some true vitriol in her words. I'm lying on my bed, wiped after practicing Cavallini's Adagio and Tarantella for two straight hours – it was incredible, like turning the air into colors. It made me think of the Charlie Parker quote Mr James liked to repeat: *If you don't live it, it can't come out of your horn*. It also made me think I might go to summer band practice after all.

Sarah and I make a plan to meet at Flying Man's. I'm dying to tell her about Joe. Not about Toby. I'm thinking if I don't talk about it, I can just pretend it didn't happen.

She's lying on a rock in the sun reading Simone de Beauvoir's *The Second Sex* – in preparation, I'm sure, for her very promising guy-poaching expedition to State's Women's Studies Department feminism symposium. She springs to her feet when she sees me, and hugs me like crazy despite the fact that she's completely naked. We have our own secret pool and mini-falls behind Flying Man's that we've been coming to for years. We've declared it clothing

155

optional and we opt not. "God, it's been forever," she says.

"I'm so sorry, Sarah," I say, hugging her back.

"It's okay, really," she says. "I know I need to give you a free pass right now. So that's…" She pulls away for a second, studies my face. "Wait a minute? What's wrong with you? You look weird. I mean *really* weird."

I can't stop smiling. I must look like a Fontaine.

"What, Lennie? What happened?"

"I think I'm falling in love." The moment the words are out of my mouth, I feel my face go hot with shame. I'm supposed to be grieving, not falling in love. Not to mention everything else I've been doing.

"Whaaaaaaaaaaaaaaaaaaaaaaaat! That is so unfreaking-freakingfreakingfreakingbelieveable! Cows on the moon, Len! Cows. On. The. Moon!" Well, so much for my shame. Sarah is in full on cheerleader mode, arms flailing, hopping up and down. Then she stops abruptly. "Wait, with whom? NOT Toby, I hope."

"No, no, of course not," I say as a speeding eighteen-wheeler of guilt flattens me.

"Whew," Sarah, says, sweeping her hand off her brow dramatically. "Who then? Who could you be in love with? You haven't gone anywhere, at least that I know of, and this town is beyond Loserville, so where'd you find him?"

"Sarah, it's Joe."

"It's not."

"Yeah, it is."

"No!"

"Yup."

"Not true."

"Is true."

"Nah-uh, nah-uh, nah-uh."

"Uh-huh, uh-huh, uh-huh."

Etc.

Her previous display of enthusiasm was nothing compared to the one that is going on now. She's doing circles around me, saying, "Oh my God. I am soooooooooooooo jealous. Every girl in Clover is after one Fontaine or another. No wonder you've been a shut-in. I would be too, if I could shut-in with one of them. God, let me live vicariously through you. Tell me every freaking detail. That beautiful, beautiful boy, those eyes, those *eyelashes*, that unfreakingbelievable smile, that trumpet playing, wow, Lennnnnnnnnie." She's pacing now, has lit another cigarette, is chain smoking in glee – a naked smokestack maniac. I'm so happy to be hanging out with the marvel that is my best friend Sarah. And I'm so happy to be happy about it.

I tell her every detail. How he came over every morning with croissants, how we played music together, how he made Gram and Big so happy just by being in the house, how we drank wine last night and kissed until I was sure I had walked right into the sky. I told her how I think I can hear his heart beating even when he's not there, how I feel like flowers – Gramgantuan ones – are blooming in my chest, how I'm sure I feel just the way Heathcliff did for Cathy before—

"Okay, stop for a second." She's still smiling but she

looks a bit worried and surprised too. "Lennie, you're not in love, you're demented. I've never heard anyone talk about a guy like this."

I shrug. "Then I'm demented."

"Wow, I want to be demented too." She sits down next to me on the rock. "It's like you've hardly kissed three guys in your whole life and now this. Guess you were saving it up or something…"

I tell her my Rip Van Lennie theory of having slept my whole life until recently.

"I don't know, Len. You always seemed awake to me."

"Yeah, I don't know either. It was a wine-induced theory." Sarah picks up a stone, tosses it into the water with a little too much force. "What?" I ask.

She doesn't answer right away, picks up another stone and hurls it too. "I am mad at you, but I'm not allowed to be, you know?"

It's exactly how I feel toward Bailey sometimes lately.

"You've just been keeping so much from me, Lennie. I thought … I don't know."

It's as if she were speaking my lines in a play.

"I'm sorry," I say again feebly. I want to say more, give her an explanation, but the truth is I don't know why I've felt so closed off to her since Bailey died.

"It's okay," she says again quietly.

"It'll be different now," I say, hoping it's true. "Promise."

I look out at the sun courting the river's surface, the green leaves, the wet rocks behind the falls. "Want to go swimming?"

"Not yet," she says. "I have news too. Not breaking news, but still." It's a clear dig and I deserve it. I didn't even ask how she was.

She's smirking at me, quite dementedly, actually. "I hooked up with Luke Jacobus last night."

"Luke?" I'm surprised. Besides for his recent lapse in judgment, which resulted in his band-kill status, he's been devotedly, unrequitedly in love with Sarah since second grade. King of the Nerdiverse, she used to call him. "Didn't you make out with him in seventh grade and then drop him when that idiot surfer glistened at you?"

"Yeah, it's probably dumb," she says. "I agreed to do lyrics for this incredible music he wrote, and we were hanging out, and it just happened."

"What about the Jean-Paul Sartre rule?"

"Sense of humor trumps literacy, I've decided – and jumping giraffes, Len – growth geyser! The guy's like the Hulk these days."

"He is funny," I agree. "And green."

She laughs, just as my phone signals a text. I rifle through my bag and take it out hoping for a message from Joe.

Sarah's singing, "Lennie got a love note from a Fontaine," as she tries to read over my shoulder. "C'mon let me see it." She grabs the phone from me. I pull it out of her hands, but it's too late. It says: *I need to talk to you. T.*

"As in Toby?" she asks. "But I thought … I mean, you just said … Lennie, what're you doing?"

"Nothing," I tell her, shoving the phone back in my bag,

already breaking my promise. "Really. Nothing."

"Why don't I believe you?" she says, shaking her head. "I have a bad feeling about this."

"Don't," I say, swallowing my own atrocious feeling. "Really. I'm demented, remember?" I touch her arm. "Let's go swimming."

We float on our backs in the pool for over an hour. I make her tell me everything about her night with Luke so I don't have to think about Toby's text, what might be so urgent. Then we climb up to the falls and get under them, screaming over and over into the roar like we've done since we were little.

I scream bloody murder.

21

There were once two sisters
who were not afraid of the dark
because the dark was full of the other's voice
across the room,
because even when the night was thick
and starless
they walked home together from the river
seeing who could last the longest
without turning on her flashlight,
not afraid
because sometimes in the pitch of night
~~they'd lie on their backs~~
~~in the middle of the path~~

they'd lie on their backs
in the middle of the path
~~and look up until the stars came back~~
and look up until the stars came back
and when they did,
they'd reach their arms up to touch them
and did.

(Found on an envelope stuck under the tire of a car on Main Street)

By the time I walk home from the river through the woods, I've decided Toby, like me, feels terrible about what happened, hence the urgency of the text. He probably just wants to make sure it will never happen again. Well, agreed. No argument from demented ol' *moi*.

Clouds have gathered and the air feels thick with the possibility of a rare summer rain. I see a takeaway cup on the ground, so I sit down, write a few lines on it, and then bury it under a mound of pine needles. Then I lie down on my back on the spongy forest floor. I love doing this – giving it all up to the enormity of the sky, or to the ceiling if the need arises while I'm indoors. As I reach my hands out and press my fingers into the loamy soil, I start wondering what I'd be doing right now, what I'd be feeling right this minute if Bailey were still alive. I realize something that scares me: I'd be happy, but in a mild kind of way, nothing demented about it. I'd be turtling along, like I always turtled, huddled in my shell, safe and sound.

But what if I'm a shell-less turtle now, demented and devastated in equal measure, an unfreakingbelievable mess of a girl, who wants to turn the air into colors with her clarinet, and what if somewhere inside I prefer this? What if as much as I fear having death as a shadow, I'm beginning to like how it quickens the pulse, not only mine, but the pulse of the whole world. I doubt Joe would even have noticed me if I'd still been in that hard shell of mild happiness. He wrote in his journal that he thinks I'm on full blast, me, and maybe I am now, but I never was before. How can the cost of this change in me be so great? It doesn't seem right that anything good should come out of Bailey's death. It doesn't seem right to even have these thoughts.

But then I think about my sister and what a shell-less turtle she was and how she wanted me to be one too. *C'mon, Lennie*, she used to say to me at least ten times a day. *C'mon, Len.* And that makes me feel better, like it's her life rather than her death that is now teaching me how to be, who to be.

I know Toby's there even before I go inside, because Lucy and Ethel are camped out on the porch. When I walk into the kitchen, I see him and Gram sitting at the table talking in hushed voices.

"Hi," I say, dumbfounded. Doesn't he realize he can't be here?

"Lucky me," Gram says. "I was walking home with armfuls of groceries and Toby came whizzing by on his skateboard." Gram hasn't driven since the 1900s. She walks everywhere in Clover, which is how she became Garden Guru. She couldn't help herself, started carrying her shears on her trips to town and people would come home and find her pruning their bushes to perfection: ironic yes, because of her hands-off policy with her own garden.

"Lucky," I say to Gram as I take in Toby. Fresh scrapes cover his arms, probably from wiping out on his board. He looks wild-eyed and disheveled, totally unmoored. I know two things in this moment: I was wrong about the text and I don't want to be unmoored with him anymore.

What I really want is to go up to The Sanctum and play my clarinet.

Gram looks at me, smiles. "You swam. Your hair looks like a cyclone. I'd like to paint it." She reaches her hand up and touches my cyclone. "Toby's going to have dinner with us."

I can't believe this. "I'm not hungry," I say. "I'm going upstairs."

Gram gasps at my rudeness, but I don't care. Under no circumstances am I sitting through dinner with Toby, *who touched my breasts*, and Gram and Big. What is he thinking?

I go up to The Sanctum, unpack and assemble my clarinet, then take out the Edith Piaf sheet music that I borrowed from a certain *garçon*, turn to "La Vie en Rose," and start playing. It's the song we listened to last night while the world exploded. I'm hoping I can just stay lost in a state of Joeliriousness, and I won't hear a knock at my door after they eat, but of course, I do.

Toby, *who touched my breasts and, let's not forget, put his hand down my jeans too*, opens the door, walks tentatively across the room, and sits on Bailey's bed. I stop playing, rest my clarinet on my stand. Go away, I think heartlessly, just go away. Let's pretend it didn't happen, none of it.

Neither of us says a word. He's rubbing his thighs so

intently, I bet the friction is generating heat. His gaze is drifting all around the room. It finally locks on a photograph of Bailey and him on her dresser. He takes a breath, looks over at me. His gaze lingers.

"Her shirt…"

I look down. I forgot I had it on. "Yeah." I've been wearing Bailey's clothes more and more outside The Sanctum as well as in it. I find myself going through my own drawers and thinking, Who was the girl who wore these things? I'm sure a shrink would love this, all of it, I think, looking over at Toby. She'd probably tell me I was trying to take Bailey's place. Or worse, competing with her in a way I never could when she was alive.

But is that it? It doesn't feel like it. When I wear her clothes, I just feel safer, like she's whispering in my ear.

I'm lost in thought, so it startles me when Toby says in an uncharacteristic shaky voice, "Len, I'm sorry. About everything." I glance at him. He looks so vulnerable, frightened. "I got way out of control, feel so bad." Is this what he needed to tell me? Relief tumbles out of my chest.

"Me too," I say, thawing immediately. We're in this together.

"Me more, trust me," he says, rubbing his thighs again. He's so distraught. Does he think it's all his fault or something?

"We both did it, Toby," I say. "Each time. We're both horrible."

He looks at me, his dark eyes warm. "You're not horrible, Lennie." His voice is gentle, intimate. I can tell he wants to reach out to me. I'm glad he's across the room. I wish he were across the equator. Do our bodies now think whenever they're together they get to touch? I tell mine that is most definitely not the case, no matter that I feel it again. No matter.

And then a renegade asteroid breaks through the earth's atmosphere and hurtles into The Sanctum: "It's just that I can't stop thinking about you," he says. "I can't. I just…" He's balling up Bailey's bedspread in his fists. "I want—"

"Please don't say more." I cross the room to my dresser, open the middle drawer, reach in and pull out a shirt, my shirt. I have to take Bailey's off. Because I'm suddenly thinking that imaginary shrink is spot on.

"It's not me," I say quietly as I open the closet door and slip inside. "I'm not her."

I stay in the dark quiet getting my breathing under control, my life under control, getting my own shirt on my own body. It's like there's a river under my feet tumbling me toward him, still, even with everything that's happened with Joe, a roaring, passionate, despairing river, but I don't want to go this time. I want to stay on the shore. We can't keep wrapping our arms around a ghost.

When I come out of the closet, he's gone.

"I'm so sorry," I say aloud to the empty orange room.

As if in response, thousands of hands begin tapping on the roof. I walk over to my bed, climb up to the window ledge and stick my hands out. Because we only get one or two storms a summer, rain is an event. I lean far over the ledge, palms to the sky, letting it all slip through my fingers,

166

remembering what Big told Toby and me that afternoon. *No way out of this but through.* Who knew what through would be?

I see someone rushing down the road in the downpour. When the figure gets near the lit-up garden I realize it's Joe and am instantly uplifted. My life raft.

"Hey," I yell out and wave like a maniac.

He looks up at the window, smiles, and I can't get down the stairs, out the front door, into the rain and by his side fast enough.

"I missed you," I say, reaching up and touching his cheek with my fingers. Raindrops drip from his eyelashes, stream in rivulets all down his face.

"God, me too." Then his hands are on my cheeks and we are kissing and the rain is pouring all over our crazy heads and once again my whole being is aflame with joy.

I didn't know love felt like this, like turning into brightness.

"What are you doing?" I say, when I can finally bring myself to pull away for a moment.

"I saw it was raining – I snuck out, wanted to see you, just like this."

"Why'd you have to sneak out?" The rain's drenching us, my shirt clings to me, and Joe's hands to it, rubbing up and down my sides.

"I'm in prison," he says. "Got busted big-time, that wine we drank was like a four-hundred-dollar bottle. I had no idea. I wanted to impress you so took it from downstairs. My dad went ape-shit when he saw the empty bottle – he's

167

making me sort wood all day and night in the workshop while he talks to his girlfriend on the phone the whole time. I think he forgets I speak French."

I'm not sure whether to address the four-hundred-dollar bottle of wine we drank or the girlfriend, decide on the latter. "His girlfriend?"

"Never mind. I had to see you, but now I have to go back, and I wanted to give you this." He pulls a piece of paper out of his pocket, stuffs it quickly into mine before it can get soaked.

He kisses me again. "Okay, I'm leaving." He doesn't move. "I don't want to leave you."

"I don't want you to," I say. His hair's black and snaky all around his glistening face. It's like being in the shower with him. Wow – to be in the shower with him.

He turns to go for real then and I notice his eyes narrow as he peers over my shoulder. "Why's he always here?"

I turn around. Toby's in the doorframe, *watching us* – he looks like he's been hit by a wrecking ball. God. He must not have left, must have been in the art room with Gram or something. He pushes open the door, grabs his skateboard, and rushes past without a word, huddled against the downpour.

"What's going on?" Joe asks, X-raying me with his stare. His whole body has stiffened.

"Nothing. Really," I answer, just as I did with Sarah. "He's upset about Bailey." What else can I tell him? If I tell him what's going on, what went on even after he kissed me, I'll lose him.

168

So when he says, "I'm being stupid and paranoid?" I just say, "Yeah." And hear in my head: *Never cross a horn player.*

He smiles wide and open as a meadow. "Okay." Then he kisses me hard one last time and we are again drinking the rain off each other's lips. "Bye, John Lennon."

And he's off.

I hurry inside, worrying about what Toby said to me and what I didn't say to Joe, as the rain washes all those beautiful kisses off of me.

22

I'm lying down on my bed, holding in my hands the antidote to worrying about anything. It's a sheet of music, still damp from the rain. At the top, it says in Joe's boxlike weirdo boy handwriting: *For a soulful, beautiful clarinettist, from a homely, boring, talentless though passionate guitarist. Part 1, Part 2 to come.*

I try to hear it in my head, but my facility to hear without playing is terrible. I get up, find my clarinet, and moments later the melody spills into the room. I remember as I play what he said about my tone being so lonely, like a day without birds, but it's as if the melody he wrote is nothing but birds and they are flying out of the end of my clarinet and filling the air of a still summer day, filling the trees and sky – it's exquisite. I play it over and over again, until I know it by heart.

It's 2 a.m. and if I play the song one more time, my fingers will fall off, but I'm too Joelirious to sleep. I go downstairs to get something to eat, and when I come back into The Sanctum, I'm blindsided by a want so urgent I have to cover my mouth to stifle a shriek. I want Bails to be sprawled out on her bed reading. I want to talk to her about Joe, want to play her this song.

I want my sister.

I want to hurl a building at God.

I take a breath and exhale with enough force to blow the orange paint right off the walls.

It's no longer raining – the scrubbed newness of the night rolls in through the open window. I don't know what to do, so I walk over to Bailey's desk and sit down like usual. I look at the detective's business card again. I thought about calling him but haven't yet, haven't packed up a thing either. I pull over a carton, decide to do one or two drawers. I hate looking at the empty boxes almost more than I hate the idea of packing up her things.

The bottom drawer's full of school notebooks, years of work, now useless. I take one out, glide my fingers over the cover, hold it to my chest, and then put it in the carton. All her knowledge is gone now. Everything she ever learned, or heard, or saw. Her particular way of looking at *Hamlet* or daisies or thinking about love, all her private intricate thoughts, her inconsequential secret musings – they're gone too. I heard this expression once: Each time someone dies, a library burns. I'm watching it burn right to the ground.

I stack the rest of the notebooks on top of the first, close the drawer, and do the same with the one above it. I close the carton and start a new one. There are more school notebooks in this drawer, some journals, which I will not read. I flip through the stack, putting them, one by one, into the box. At the very bottom of the drawer, there is an open one. It has Bailey's chicken scrawl handwriting all over it; columns of words cover the whole page, with lines crossing out most of them. I take it out, feel a pang of guilt,

171

but then my guilt turns to surprise, then fear, when I see what the words are.

They're all combinations of our mother's name combined with other names and things. There is a whole section of the name Paige combined with people and things related to John Lennon, my namesake, and we assume her favorite musician because of it. We know practically nothing about Mom. It's like when she left, she took all traces of her life with her, leaving only a story behind. Gram rarely talks about anything but her amazing wanderlust, and Big isn't much better.

"At five years old," Gram would tell us over and over again, holding up her fingers for emphasis, "your mother snuck out of her bed one night and I found her halfway to town, with her little blue backpack and a walking stick. She said she was on an adventure – at five years old, girls!"

So that was all we had, except for a box of belongings we kept in The Sanctum. It's full of books we foraged over the years from the shelves downstairs, ones that had her name in them: *Oliver Twist, On the Road, Siddhartha, The Collected Poems of William Blake*, and some Harlequins, which threw us for a loop, book snobs that we are. None of them are dog-eared or annotated. We have some yearbooks, but there are no scribbles from friends in them. There's a copy of *The Joy of Cooking* with food spattered all over it. (Gram did once tell us that Mom was magical in the kitchen and that she suspects she makes her living on the road by cooking.)

But mostly, what we have are maps, lots and lots of them: road maps, topographic maps, maps of Clover, of California, of the forty-nine other states, of country after country, continent after continent. There are also several atlases, each of which look as read and reread as my copy of *Wuthering Heights*. The maps and atlases reveal the most about her: a girl for whom the world beckoned. When we were younger, Bailey and I would spend countless hours poring over the atlases imagining routes and adventures for her.

I start leafing through the notebook. There are pages and pages of these combinations: Paige/Lennon/Walker, Paige/Lennon/Yoko, Paige/Lennon/Imagine, Paige/Dakota/Ono, and on and on. Sometimes there are notes under a name combination. For instance, scribbled under the words Paige/Dakota is an address in North Hampton, Massachusetts. But then that's crossed out and the words *too young* are scrawled in.

I'm shocked. We'd both put our mother's name into search engines many times to no avail, and we would sometimes try to think of pseudonyms she might have chosen and search them to no avail as well, but never like this, never methodically, never with this kind of thoroughness and persistence. The notebook is practically full. Bailey must have been doing this in every free moment, every moment I wasn't around, because I so rarely saw her at the computer. But now that I'm thinking about it, I did see her in front of The Half Mom an awful lot before she died, studying it, intently, almost like she was waiting for it to speak to her.

I turn to the first page of the notebook. It's dated February 27, less than two months before she died. How could she have done all this in that amount of time? No wonder she needed St Anthony's help. I wish she'd asked for mine.

I put the notebook back in the drawer, walk back over to my bed, take my clarinet out of the case again, and play Joe's song. I want to be in that summer day again, I want to be there with my sister.

At night,
when we were little,
we tented Bailey's covers,
crawled underneath with our flashlights
and played cards: Hearts,
Whist, Crazy Eights,
and our favorite: Bloody Knuckles.
The competition was vicious.
All day, every day,
we were the Walker Girls —
two peas in a pod
thick as thieves—
but when Gram closed the door
for the night,
we bared our teeth.
We played for chores,
for slave duty,
for truths and ~~dares~~ dares and money.
~~We played for~~
We played to be better, brighter,
to be more beautiful,
more,
just more.
But it was all a ruse —
we played
so we could fall asleep ~~in the same bed~~
in the same bed
without having to ask,
so we could wrap together
like a braid,
so while we slept
our dreams could switch bodies

*(Found written on the inside cover
of* Wuthering Heights, *Lennie's room)*

23

I used to talk to The Half Mom a lot,
but I'd wait until no one else was home
and then I'd say:
I imagine you
up there
not like a cloud or a bird or a star
but like a mother,
except one who lives in the sky
who doesn't make a fuss
about gravity
who just goes about her business
drifting around with the wind.

(Found on a piece of newspaper under the Walkers' porch)

When I come down to the kitchen the next morning, Gram is at the stove cooking sausages, her shoulders hunched into a broad frown. Big slouches over his coffee at the table. Behind them the morning fog shrouds the window, like the house is hovering inside a cloud. Standing in the doorway I'm filled with the same scared, hollow feeling I get when I see abandoned houses, ones with weeds growing through the front steps, paint cracked and dirty, windows broken and boarded up.

"Where's Joe?" Big asks. I realize then why the despair is so naked this morning: Joe's not here.

"In prison," I say.

Big looks up, smirks. "What'd he do?" Instantly, the mood is lifted. Wow. I guess he's not only my life raft.

"Took a four-hundred-dollar bottle of wine from his father and drank it one night with a girl named John Lennon."

At the same time, Gram and Big gasp, then exclaim, "Four hundred dollars?!"

"He had no idea."

"Lennie, I don't like you drinking." Gram waves her spatula at me. The sausages sizzle and sputter in the pan behind her.

"I don't drink, well, hardly. Don't worry."

"Damn, Len. Was it good?" Big's face is a study of wonder.

"I don't know. I've never had red wine before, guess so." I'm pouring a cup of coffee that is thin as tea. I've gotten used to the mud Joe makes.

"Damn," Big repeats, taking a sip of his coffee and making a disgusted face. I guess he now prefers Joe's sludge too. "Don't suppose you will drink it again either, with the bar set that high."

I'm wondering if Joe will be at the first band practice to-day – I've decided to go – when suddenly he walks through the door with croissants, dead bugs for Big, and a smile as big as God for me…

"Hey!" I say.

"They let you out," says Big. "That's terrific. Is it a con-jugal visit or is your sentence over?"

"Big!" Gram chastises. "Please."

Joe laughs. "It's over. My father is a very romantic man, it's his best and worst trait, when I explained to him how I was feeling—" Joe looks at me, proceeds to turn red, which of course makes me go full-on tomato. It surely must be against the rules to feel like this when your sister is dead!

Gram shakes her head. "Who would have thought Lennie such a romantic?"

"Are you kidding?" Joe exclaims. "Her reading *Wuthering Heights* twenty-three times didn't give it away?" I look down. I'm embarrassed at how moved I am by this. *He knows me.* Somehow better than they do.

"Touché, Mr Fontaine," Gram says, hiding her grin as she goes back to the stove. Joe comes up behind me, wraps his arms around my waist. I close my eyes, think about his body, naked under his clothes, pressing into me, naked under mine. I turn my head to look up at him. "The melody you wrote is so beautiful. I want to play it for you." Before the last word is out of my mouth, he kisses me. I twist around in his arms so that we are facing each other, then throw my arms around his neck while his find the small of my back, and sweep me into him. Oh God, I don't care if this is wrong of me, if I'm breaking every rule in the Western World, I don't care about freaking anything, because our mouths, which momentarily separated, have met again and anything but that ecstatic fact ceases to matter.

How do people function when they're feeling like this?

How do they tie their shoes?

Or drive cars?

Or operate heavy machinery?

How does civilization continue when this is going on?

A voice, ten decibels quieter than its normal register, stutters out of Uncle Big. "Uh, kids. Might want to, I don't know, mmmm…" Everything screeches to a halt in my mind. Is Big stammering? Uh, Lennie? Probably not cool to make out like this in the middle of the kitchen in front of your grandmother and uncle. I pull away from Joe; it's like breaking suction. I look at Gram and Big, who are standing there fiddly and sheepish while the sausages burn. Is it possible that we've succeeded in embarrassing

179

the Emperor and Empress of Weird?

I glance back at Joe. He looks totally cartoon-dopey, like he's been bonked on the head with a club. The whole scene strikes me as hysterical, and I collapse into a chair laughing. Joe smiles an embarrassed half smile at Gram and Big, leans against the counter, his trumpet case now strategically held over his crotch. Thank God I don't have one of those. Who'd want a lust-o-meter sticking out the middle of their body?

"You're going to rehearsal, right?" he asks.

Bat. Bat. Bat.

Yes, if we make it.

We do make it, though in my case, in body only. I'm surprised my fingers can find the keys as I glide through the pieces Mr James has chosen for us to play at the upcoming River Festival. Even with Rachel sending me death-darts about Joe and repeatedly turning the stand so I can't see it, I'm lost in the music, feel like I'm playing with Joe alone, improvising, reveling in not knowing what is going to happen note to note ... but mid-practice, mid-song, mid-note, a feeling of dread sweeps over me as I start thinking about Toby, how he looked when he left last night. What he said in The Sanctum. He has to know we need to stay away from each other now. He has to. I tuck the panic away but spend the rest of rehearsal painfully alert, following the arrangement without the slightest deviation.

After practice, Joe and I have the whole afternoon together because he's out of prison and I'm off work. We're walking back to my house, the wind whipping us around like leaves.

"I know what we should do," I say.

"Didn't you want to play me the song?"

"I do, but I want to play it for you somewhere else. Remember I dared you in the woods that night to brave the forest with me on a really windy day? Today is it."

We veer off the road and hike in, bushwhacking through thickets of brush until we find the trail I'm looking for. The sun filters sporadically through the trees, casting a dim and shadowy light over the forest floor. Because of the wind, the trees are creaking symphonically – it's a veritable philharmonic of squeaking doors. Perfect.

After a while, he says, "I think I'm holding up remarkably well, considering, don't you?"

"Considering what?"

"Considering we're hiking to the soundtrack of the creepiest horror movie ever made and all the world's tree trolls have gathered above us to open and close their front doors."

"It's broad daylight, you can't be scared."

"I can be, actually, but I'm trying not to be a wuss. I have a very low eerie threshold."

"You're going to love where I'm taking you, I promise."

"I'm going to love it if you take off all your clothes there, I promise, or at least some of them, maybe even just a sock." He comes over to me, drops his horn, and swings me around so we are facing each other.

I say, "You're very repressed, you know? It's maddening."

181

"Can't help it. I'm half French, *joie de vivre* and all. In all seriousness though, I haven't yet seen you in any state of undress, and it's been three whole days since our first kiss, *quelle catastrophe*, you know?" He tries to get my wind-blown hair out of my face, then kisses me until my heart busts out of my chest like a wild horse. "Though I do have a very good imagination…"

"*Quel dork*," I say, pulling him forward.

"You know, I only act like a dork so you'll say *quel dork*," he replies.

The trail climbs to where the old growth redwoods rocket into the sky and turn the forest into their private cathedral. The wind has died down and the woods have grown unearthly still and peaceful. Leaves flicker all around us like tiny pieces of light.

"So, what about your mom?" Joe asks all of a sudden.

"What?" My head couldn't have been further away from thoughts of my mother.

"The first day I came over, Gram said she'd finish the portrait when your mother comes back. Where is she?"

"I don't know." Usually I leave it at that and don't fill in the spare details, but he hasn't run away yet from all our other family oddities. "I've never met my mother," I say. "Well, I met her, but she left when I was one. She has a restless nature, guess it runs in the family."

He stops walking. "That's it? That's the explanation? For her leaving? And *never coming back*?"

Yes, it's nutso, but this Walker nutso has always made sense to me.

182

"Gram says she'll come back," I say, my stomach knotting up, thinking of her coming back right now. Thinking of Bailey trying so hard to find her. Thinking of slamming the door in her face if she did come back, of screaming, *You're too late*. Thinking of her never coming back. Thinking I'm not sure how to believe all this anymore without Bailey believing it with me. "Gram's Aunt Sylvie had it too," I add, feeling imbecilic. "She came back after twenty years away."

"Wow," Joe says. I've never seen his brow so furrowed.

"Look, I don't know my mother, so I don't miss her or anything…" I say, but I feel like I'm trying to convince myself more than Joe. "She's this intrepid, free-spirited woman who took off to traipse all around the globe alone. She's mysterious. It's cool." *It's cool?* God, I'm a ninny. But when did everything change? Because it did used to be cool, super-cool, in fact – she was our Magellan, our Marco Polo, one of the wayward Walker women whose restless boundless spirit propels her from place to place, love to love, moment to unpredictable moment.

Joe smiles, looks at me so warmly, I forget everything else. "You're cool," he says. "Forgiving. Unlike dickhead me." Forgiving? I take his hand, wondering from his reaction, and my own, if I'm cool and forgiving or totally delusional. And what about this dickhead him? Who is it? Is it the Joe that never talked to that violinist again? If so, I don't want to meet that guy, ever. We continue in silence, both of us soaring around in the sky of our minds for another mile or so and then we are there, and all thoughts of dickhead him and my mysterious missing mother are gone.

183

"Okay, close your eyes," I say. "I'll lead you." I reach up from behind him and cover my hands over his eyes and steer him down the path. "Okay, open them."

There is a bedroom. A whole bedroom in the middle of the forest.

"Wow, where's Sleeping Beauty?" Joe asks.

"That would be me," I say, and take a running leap onto the fluffy bed. It's like jumping into a cloud. He follows me. "You're too awake to be her, we've already covered this." He stands at the edge of the bed, looking around. "This is un-believable, how is this here?"

"There's an inn about a mile away on the river. It was a commune in the sixties, and the owner Sam's an old hippie. He set up this forest bedroom for his guests to happen upon if they hike up here, for surprise romance, I guess, but I've never seen a soul pass through and I've been coming forever. Actually, I did see someone here once: Sam, changing the sheets. He throws this tarp over when it rains. I write at that desk, read in that rocker, lie here on this bed and daydream. I've never brought a guy here before though."

He smiles, sits on the bed next to where I'm lying on my back and starts trailing his fingers over my belly.

"What do you daydream about?" he asks.

"This," I say as his hand spreads across my midriff under my shirt. My breathing's getting faster – I want his hands everywhere.

"John Lennon, can I ask you something?"

"Uh-oh, whenever people say that, something scary comes next."

184

"Are you a virgin?"

"You see – scary question came next," I mumble, mortified – what a mood-killer. I squirm out from under his hand. "Is it that obvious?"

"Sort of." Ugh. I want to crawl under the covers. He tries to backtrack. "No, I mean, I think it's cool that you are."

"It's decidedly uncool."

"For you maybe, but not for me, if…"

"If what?" My stomach is suddenly churning. Roiling.

Now he looks embarrassed – good. "Well, if sometime, not now, but sometime, you might not want to be one anymore, and I could be your first, that's where the cool part comes in, you know, for me." His expression is shy and sweet, but what he's saying makes me feel scared and excited and overwhelmed and like I'm going to burst into tears, which I do, and for once, I don't even know why.

"Oh, Lennie, I'm sorry, was that bad to say? Don't cry, there's no pressure at all, kissing you, being with you in any way is amazing—"

"No," I say, now laughing and crying at the same time. "I'm crying because … well, I don't know why I'm crying, but I'm happy, not sad…" I reach for his arm, and he lies down on his side next to me, his elbow resting by my head, our bodies touching length to length. He's peering into my eyes in a way that's making me tremble.

"Just looking into your eyes…" he whispers. "I've never felt anything like this."

I think about Genevieve. He'd said he was in love with her, does that mean…

185

"Me neither," I say, not able to stop the tears from spilling over again.

"Don't cry." His voice is weightless, mist. He kisses my eyes, gently grazes my lips.

He looks at me then so nakedly, it makes me lightheaded, like I need to lie down even though I'm lying down. "I know it hasn't been that long, Len, but I think … I don't know … I might be…"

He doesn't have to say it, I feel it too; it's not subtle – like every bell for miles and miles is ringing at once, loud, clanging, hungry ones, and tiny, happy, chiming ones, all of them sounding off in this moment. I put my hands around his neck, pull him to me, and then he's kissing me hard and so deep, and I am flying, sailing, soaring…

He murmurs into my hair, "Forget what I said earlier, let's stick with this, I might not survive anything more." I laugh. Then he jumps up, finds my wrists, and pins them over my head. "Yeah, right. Totally joking, I want to do *everything* with you, whenever you're ready, I'm the one, promise?" He's above me, batting and grinning like a total hooplehead.

"I promise," I say.

"Good. Glad that's decided." He raises an eyebrow. "I'm going to deflower you, John Lennon."

"Oh my God, so, so embarrassing, *quel, quel major dork*." I try to cover my face with my hands, but he won't let me. And then we are wrestling and laughing and it's many, many minutes before I remember that my sister has died.

24

*(Found on a candy wrapper half-buried by the roses,
Gram's garden)*

I see Toby's truck out front and a bolt of anger shoots through me. Why can't he just stay away from me for one freaking day even? I just want to hang on to this happiness. *Please*.

I find Gram in the art room, cleaning her brushes. Toby is nowhere in sight.

"Why is he always here?" I hiss at Gram.

She looks at me, surprised. "What's wrong with you, Lennie? I called him to help me fix the trellising around my garden and he said he would stop by after he was done at the ranch."

"Can't you call someone else?" My voice is seething with anger and exasperation, and I'm sure I sound completely bonkers to Gram. I am bonkers – I just want to be in love. I want to feel this joy. I don't want to deal with Toby, with sorrow and grief and guilt and DEATH. I'm so sick of DEATH.

Gram does not look pleased. "God, Len, have a heart, the guy's destroyed. It makes him feel better to be around us. We're the only ones who understand. He said as much last night." She is drying her brushes over the sink, snapping her wrist dramatically with each shake. "I asked you once if everything was all right between you two and you said yes. I believed you."

I take a deep breath and let it out slowly, trying to coerce Mr Hyde back into my body. "It's okay, it's fine, I'm sorry. I don't know what's wrong with me." Then I pull a Gram and walk right out of the room.

I go up to The Sanctum and put on the most obnoxious head-banging punk music I have, a San Francisco band called Filth. I know Toby hates any kind of punk because it was always a point of contention with Bailey, who loved it. He finally won her over to the alt-country he likes, and to Willie Nelson, Hank Williams and Johnny Cash, his holy trinity, but he never came around to punk.

The music is not helping. I'm jumping up and down on the blue dance rug, banging around to the incessant beat, but I'm too angry to even bang around BECAUSE I DON'T WANT TO DANCE IN THE INNER PUMP-KIN SANCTUM ALONE. In one instant, all the rage that I felt moments before for Toby has transferred to Bailey. I don't understand how she could have done this to me, left me here all alone. Especially because she promised me her whole life that she would never EVER disappear like Mom did, that we would always have each other, always, ALWAYS, ALWAYS. "It's the only pact that mattered, Bailey!" I cry out, taking the pillow and pounding it again and again into the bed, until finally, many songs later, I feel a little bit calmer.

I drop on my back on the bed, panting and sweating. How will I survive this missing? How do others do it? People die all the time. Every day. Every hour. There are families all over the world staring at beds that are no longer slept in, shoes that are no longer worn. Families that no longer have to buy a particular cereal, a kind of shampoo. There are people everywhere standing in line at the movies, buying curtains, walking dogs, while inside, their hearts are ripping to shreds. For years. For their whole lives. I don't believe time heals. I don't want it to. If I heal, doesn't that mean I've accepted the world without her?

I remember the notebook then. I get up, turn off Filth, put on a Chopin Nocturne to see if that'll settle me down, and go over to the desk. I take out the notebook, turn to the last page, where there are a few combinations that haven't yet been crossed out. The whole page is combinations of Mom's name with Dickens characters. Paige/Twist, Paige/ Fagan, Walker/ Havisham, Walker/Oliver/Paige, Pip/Paige.

I turn on the computer, plug in *Paige Twist* and then search through pages of docs, finding nothing that could relate to our mom, then I put in *Paige Dickens* and find some possibilities, but the documents are mostly from high school athletic teams and college alumni magazines, none that could have anything to do with her. I go through more Dickens combinations but don't find even the remotest possibility.

An hour's passed and I've just done a handful of searches. I look back over the pages and pages that Bailey did, and wonder again when she did it all and where she did it, maybe at the computer lab at the State, because how could I not have noticed her bleary-eyed at this computer for hours on end? It strikes me again how badly she wanted to find Mom, because why else would she have devoted all this time to it? What could have happened in February to take her down

190

this road? I wonder if that was when Toby asked her to marry him. Maybe she wanted Mom to come to the wedding. But Toby said he had asked her right before she died. I need to talk to him.

I go downstairs, apologize to Gram, tell her I've been emotional all day, which is true every freaking day lately. She looks at me, strokes my hair, says, "It's okay, sweet pea, maybe we could go on a walk together tomorrow, talk some—" When will she *get* it? I don't want to talk to her about Bailey, about anything.

When I come out of the house, Toby's standing on a ladder, working on the trellis in the front of the garden. Streamers of gold and pink peel across the sky. The whole yard is glowing with the setting sun, the roses look lit from within, like lanterns. He looks over at me, exhales dramatically, then climbs slowly down the ladder, leaning against it with arms crossed in front of his chest. "Wanted to say sorry ... again." He sighs.

"I'm half out of my mind lately." His eyes search mine. "You okay?"

"Yeah, except for the half out of my mind part," I say.

He smiles at that, his whole face alighting with kindness and understanding. I relax a little, feel bad for wanting to behead him an hour before.

"I found this notebook in Bailey's desk," I tell him, eager to find out if he knows anything and very eager not to talk or think about yesterday. "It's like she was looking for Mom, but feverishly, Toby, page after page of possible pseudonyms that she must have been putting in search en-

191

gines. She'd tried everything, must have done it around the clock. I don't know where she did it, don't know why she did it…"

"Don't know either," he says, his voice trembling slightly. He looks down. Is he hiding something from me?

"The notebook is dated. She started doing this at the end of February – did anything happen then that you know of?"

Toby's bones unhinge and he slides down the trellis, and drops his head into his hands and starts to cry.

What's going on?

I lower to him, kneel in front of him, put my hands on his arms. "Toby," I say gently. "It's okay." I'm stroking his hair with my hand. Fear prickles my neck and arms.

He shakes his head. "It's not okay." He can barely get the words out. "I wasn't ever going to tell you."

"What? What weren't you going to tell me?" My voice comes out shrill, crazy.

"It makes it worse, Len, and I didn't want it to be any harder for you."

"What?" Every hair on my body is on end. I'm really frightened now. What could possibly make Bailey's death any worse?

He reaches for my hand, holds it tight in his. "We were going to have a baby." I hear myself gasp. "She was pregnant when she died." No, I think, this can't be. "Maybe she was looking for your mom because of that. The end of February would have been around the time when we found out."

The idea begins to avalanche inside me, gaining speed and mass. My other hand has landed on his shoulder and although I'm looking at his face, I'm watching my sister hold their baby up in the air, making ferret faces at it, watching as she and Toby each take a hand of their child and walk him to the river. Or her. God. I can see in Toby's eyes all that he has been carrying alone, and for the first time since Bailey's death I feel more sorry for someone else than I do for myself. I close my arms around him and rock him. And then, when our eyes meet and we are again there in that helpless house of grief, a place where Bailey can never be and Joe Fontaine does not exist, a place where it's only Toby and me left behind, I kiss him. I kiss him to comfort him, to tell him how sorry I am, to show him I'm here and that I'm alive and so is he. I kiss him because I'm in way over my head and have been for months. I kiss him and keep kissing and holding and caressing him, because for whatever screwed-up reason, that is what I do.

The moment Toby's body stiffens in my arms, I know.

I know, but I don't know who it is.

At first, I think it's Gram, it must be. But it's not.

It's not Big either.

I turn around and there he is, a few yards away, motionless, a statue.

Our eyes hold, and then, he stumbles backward. I jump out of Toby's grasp, find my legs, and rush toward Joe, but he turns away, starts to run.

"Wait, please," I yell out. "Please."

193

He freezes, his back to me – a silhouette against a sky now burning up, a wildfire racing out of control toward the horizon. I feel like I'm falling down stairs, hurtling and tumbling with no ability to stop. Still, I force myself forward and go to him. I take his hand to try to turn him around, but he rips it away as if my touch disgusts him. Then he's turning, slowly, like he's moving underwater. I wait, scared out of my mind to look at him, to see what I've done. When he finally faces me, his eyes are lifeless, his face like stone. It's as if his marvelous spirit has evacuated his flesh.

Words fly out of my mouth. "It's not like us, I don't feel – it's something else, my sister…" *My sister was pregnant*, I'm about to say in explanation, but how would that explain anything? I'm desperate for him to get it, but I don't get it.

"It's not what you think," I say predictably, pathetically. I watch the rage and hurt erupt simultaneously in his face.

"Yes, it *is*. It's *exactly* what I think, it's exactly what I *thought*." He spits his words at me. "How could you… I thought you—"

"I do, I do." I'm crying hard now, tears streaming down my face. "You don't understand."

His face is a riot of disappointment. "You're right, I *don't*. Here."

He pulls a piece of paper out of his pocket. "This is what I came to give you." He crumples it up and throws it at me, then turns around and runs as fast as he can away into the falling night.

I bend over and grab the crumpled piece of paper, smooth it out. At the top it says *Part 2: Duet for aforementioned clarinettist and guitarist.* I fold it carefully, put it in my pocket, then sit down on the grass, a heap of bones. I realize I'm in the same exact spot Joe and I kissed last night in the rain. The sky's lost its fury, just some straggling gold wisps steadily being consumed by darkness. I try to hear the melody he wrote for me in my head, but can't. All I hear is him saying: *How could you?*

How could I?

Someone might as well roll up the whole sky, pack it away for good.

Soon, there's a hand on my shoulder. Toby. I reach up and rest my hand on his. He squats down on one knee next to me. "I'm sorry," he says quietly, and a moment later, "I'm going to go, Len." Then just the coldness on my shoulder where his hand had been. I hear his truck start and listen to the engine hum as it follows Joe down the road.

Just me. Or so I think until I look up at the house to see Gram silhouetted in the doorway like Toby was last night. I don't know how long she's been there, don't know what she's seen and what she hasn't. She swings open the door, walks to the end of the porch, leans on the railing with both hands.

"Come in, sweet pea."

I don't tell her what happened with Joe, just as I never told her what has been going on with Toby. Yet I can see in her mournful eyes as she looks into mine that she most likely already knows it all.

"One day, you'll talk to me again." She takes my hands. "I miss you, you know. So does Big."

195

"She was pregnant," I whisper.

Gram nods.

"She told you?"

"The autopsy."

"They were engaged," I say. This, I can tell from her face, she didn't know.

She encloses me in her arms and I stay in her safe and sound embrace and let the tears rise and rise and fall and fall until her dress is soaked with them and night has filled the house.

25

I do not go to the altar of the desk to talk to Bailey on the mountaintop. I do not even turn on the light. I go straight into bed with all my clothes on and pray for sleep. It doesn't come.

What comes is shame, weeks of it, waves of it, rushing through me in quick hot flashes like nausea, making me groan into my pillow. The lies and half-truths and abbreviations I told and didn't tell Joe tackle and hold me down until I can hardly breathe. How could I have hurt him like this, done to him just what Genevieve did? All the love I have for him clobbers around in my body. My chest aches. All of me aches. He looked like a completely different person. He is a different person. Not the one who loved me.

I see Joe's face, then Bailey's, the two of them looming above me with only three words on their lips: *How could you?*

I have no answer.

I'm sorry, I write with my finger on the sheets over and over until I can't stand it anymore and flip on the light.

But the light brings actual nausea and with it all the moments with my sister that will now remain unlived: holding her baby in my arms. Teaching her child to play the clarinet. Just getting older together day by day. All the future we will not have rips and retches out of me into the trash bin I am crouched over until there's nothing left inside, nothing but me in this ghastly orange room.

And that's when it hits.

Without the harbor and mayhem of Toby's arms, the sublime distraction of Joe's, there's only me.

Me, like a small seashell with the loneliness of the whole ocean roaring invisibly within.

Me.

Without.

Bailey.

Always.

I throw my head into my pillow and scream into it as if my soul itself is being ripped in half, because it is.

Bailey, do you love Gram more than me?

Nope.

Uncle Big?

Nope.

What about Toby?

I don't **love** anyone more than you, Lennie, okay?

Me, too.

That's settled then.

You'll never disappear like Mom?

Never.

Promise?

God, how many times do I have to say it:

I will **never** disappear like Mom. Now, go to sleep.

(Found on a takeaway cup, Rain River)

Bailey, do you love Gran more than me?

Nope.

Uncle Big?

Nope.

What about Toby?

I don't love anyone more than you, Lennie, okay?

Me, too.

That's settled then.

You'll never disappear like Mom?

Never.

Promise?

God, how many times do I have to say it:
I will never disappear like Mom. Now, go to sleep.

(Found scrawled on the branch of
a tree outside Clover High)

Bailey, do you love Gram more than me?
Nope.
Uncle Big?
Nope.
What about Toby?
I don't love anyone more than you, Lennie, Okay?
Me, too.
That's settled then.
You'll never disappear like Mom?
Never.
Promise?
God, how many times do I have to say it:
I will never disappear like Mom. Now, go to sleep.

(Found written on a desk, Clover Public Library)

Part 2

26

Len, where is she tonight?

I was sleeping.

C'mon, Len.

Okay, India climbing in the Himalayas.

We did that one last week.

You start then,

All right. She's in Spain. Barcelona. A scarf covering her head,
sitting by the water, drinking Sangria, with a man named Pablo.

Are they in love?

Yes.

But she will leave him come morning.

Yes.

She'll wake before dawn, sneak her suitcase out from under the bed
put on a red wig, a green scarf, a yellow dress, white pumps.

She'll catch the first train out.

Will she leave a note?

No.

She never does.

No.

She'll sit on the train and stare out the window at the sea.
A woman will sit next to her and they'll strike up a conversation.
The woman will ask her if she has any children, and she'll say, "No."
Wrong, Len. She'll say, "I'm on the way to see my girls right now."

*(Found on a piece of paper stuck
between two rocks at Flying Man's)*

I wake up later with my face mashed into the pillow. I lean up on my elbows and look out the window. The stars have bewitched the sky of darkness. It's a shimmery night. I open the window, and the sound of the river rides the rose-scented breeze right into our room. I'm shocked to realize that I feel a little better, like I've slept my way to a place with a little more air. I push away thoughts of Joe and Toby, take one more deep breath of the flowers, the river, the world, then I get up, take the trash bin into the bathroom, clean it and myself, and when I return head straight over to Bailey's desk.

I turn on the computer, pull out the notebook from the top desk drawer where I keep it now, and decide to continue from where I left off the other day. I need to do something for my sister and all I can think to do is to find our mother for her.

I start plugging in the remaining combinations in Bailey's notebook. I can understand why becoming a mother herself would have compelled Bailey to search for Mom like this. It makes sense to me somehow. But there is something else I suspect. In a far cramped corner of my mind, there is a dresser, and in that dresser there is a thought crammed into the back of the bottom-most drawer. I know it's there because I put it there where I wouldn't have to look at it. But tonight I open that creaky drawer and face what I've always believed and that is this: Bailey had it too. Restlessness stampeded through my sister her whole life, informing everything she did from running cross country to changing personas on stage. I've always thought that was the reason behind why she wanted to find our mother. And I know it was the reason I never wanted her to. I bet this is why she didn't tell me she was looking for Mom like this. She knew I'd try to stop her. I didn't want our mother to reveal to Bailey a way out of our lives.

One explorer is enough for any family.

But I can make up for that now by finding Mom. I put combination after combination into a mix of search engines. After an hour, however, I'm ready to toss the computer out the window. It's futile. I've gotten all the way to the end of Bailey's notebook and have started one of my own using words and symbols from Blake poems. I can see in the notebook that Bailey was working her way through Mom's box for clues to the pseudonym. She'd used references from *Oliver Twist*, *Siddhartha*, *On the Road*, but hadn't gotten to William Blake yet. I have his book of poems open and I'm combining words like *Tiger* or *Poison Tree* or *Devil* with *Paige* or *Walker* and the words chef, cook, restaurant, thinking as Gram did that that's how she might make money while traveling, but it's useless. After yet another hour of no possible matches, I tell the mountaintop Bailey in the explorer picture, I'm not giving up, I just need a break, and head downstairs to see if anyone is still awake.

Big's on the porch, sitting in the middle of the love seat like it's a throne. I squeeze in beside him.

"Unbelievable," he murmurs, goosing my knee. "Can't remember the last time you joined me for a nighttime chat. I was just thinking that I might play hooky tomorrow, see if a new lady-friend of mine wants to have lunch with me in a restaurant. I'm sick of dining in trees." He twirls his mustache a little too dreamily.

Uh-oh.

"Remember," I warn. "You're not allowed to ask anyone to marry you until you've been with her a whole year. Those were your rules after your last divorce." I reach over and tug on his mustache, add for effect, "Your fifth divorce."

"I know, I know," he says. "But boy do I miss proposing, nothing so romantic. Make sure you try it, at least once, Len – it's skydiving with your feet on the ground." He laughs in a tinkly way that might be called a giggle if he weren't thirty feet tall. He's told Bailey and me this our whole lives. In fact, until Sarah went into a diatribe about the inequities of marriage in sixth grade, I had no idea proposing wasn't always considered an equal-opportunity endeavor.

I look out over the small yard where hours before Joe left me, probably forever. I think for a minute about telling Big that Joe probably won't be around anymore, but I can't face breaking it to him. He's almost as attached to him as I am. And anyway, I want to talk to him about something else.

"Big?"

"Hmmm?"

"Do you really believe in this restless gene stuff?"

He looks at me, surprised, then says, "Sounds like a fine load of crap, doesn't it?"

I think about Joe's incredulous response today in the woods, about my own doubts, about everybody's, always. Even in this town where free-spiritedness is a fundamental family value, the few times I've ever told anyone my mother took off when I was one year old to live a life of freedom and itinerancy, they looked like they wanted to commit me to a nice rubber room somewhere. Even so, to me, this Walker family gospel never seemed all that unlikely. Anyone who's read a novel or walked down the street or stepped through the front door of my house knows that people are all kinds of weird, especially my people, I think, glancing at Big, who does God knows what in trees, marries perennially, tries to resurrect dead bugs, smokes more pot than the whole eleventh grade, and looks like he should reign over some fairy tale kingdom. So why wouldn't his sister be an adventurer, a blithe spirit? Why shouldn't my mother be like the hero in so many stories, the brave one who left? Like Luke Skywalker, Gulliver, Captain Kirk, Don Quixote, Odysseus. Not quite real to me, okay, but mythical and magical, not unlike my favorite saints or the characters in novels I hang on to perhaps a little too tightly.

"I don't know," I answer honestly. "Is it all crap?"

Big doesn't say anything for a long time, just twirls away at his mustache, thinking. "Nah, it's all about classification, know what I mean?" I don't, but won't interrupt. "Lots of things run through families, right? And this tendency, whatever it is, for whatever reason, runs through ours. Could be worse, we could have depression or alcoholism or bitterness. Our afflicted kin just hit the road—"

"I think Bailey had it, Big," I say, the words tumbling out of me before I can catch them, revealing just how much I might actually believe in it after all. "I've always thought so."

"Bailey?" His brow creases. "Nah, don't see it. In fact, I've never seen a girl so relieved as when she got rejected from that school in New York City."

"Relieved?" Now *this* is a fine load of crap! "Are you kidding? She *always* wanted to go to Juilliard. She worked sooooooooo hard. It was her dream!"

Big studies my burning face, then says gently. "Whose dream, Len?" He positions his hands like he's playing an invisible clarinet. "Because the only one I used to see working sooooooooo hard around here was you."

God.

Marguerite's trilling voice fills my head: *Your playing is ravishing. You work on the nerves, Lennie, you go to Juilliard.*

Instead, I quit.

Instead, I shoved and crammed myself into a jack-in-the box of my own making.

"C'mere." Big opens his arm like a giant wing and – closes it over me as I snuggle in beside him and try not to think about how terrified I'd felt each time Marguerite mentioned Juilliard, each time I'd imagine myself—

"Dreams change," Big says. "I think hers did."

Dreams change, yes, that makes sense, but I didn't know dreams could hide inside a person.

He wraps his other arm around me too and I sink into the bear of him, breathing in the thick scent of pot that infuses his clothes. He squeezes me tight, strokes my hair with his enormous hand. I'd forgotten how comforting Big is, a human furnace. I peek up at his face. A tear runs down his cheek.

After a few minutes, he says, "Bails might have had some ants in the pants, like most people do, but I think she was more like me, and you lately, for that matter – *a slave to love.*" He smiles at me like he's inducting me into a secret society. "Maybe it's those damn roses, and for the record, those I believe in: hook, line and sinker. They're deadly on the heart – I swear, we're like lab rats breathing in that aroma all season long…" He twirls his mustache, seems to have forgotten what he was saying. I wait, remembering that he's stoned. The rose scent ribbons through the air between us. I breathe it in, thinking of Joe, knowing full well that it's not the roses that have spurred this love in my heart, but the boy, such an amazing boy. *How could I?*

Far away, an owl calls – a hollow, lonesome sound that makes me feel the same.

Big continues talking as if no time has passed. "Nah, it wasn't Bails who had it—"

"What do you mean?" I ask, straightening up.

He stops twirling. His face has grown serious. "Gram was different when we were growing up," he says. "If any-one else had it, she did."

211

"Gram hardly leaves the neighborhood," I say, not following.

He chuckles. "I know. Guess that's how much I don't believe in the gene though. I always thought my mother had it. I thought she just bottled it up somehow, trapped herself in that art room for weeks on end, and threw it onto those canvases."

"Well, if that's the case, why didn't *my mother* just bottle it up, then?" I try to keep my voice down but I feel suddenly infuriated. "Why'd she have to leave if Gram just had to make some paintings?"

"I don't know, honey, maybe Paige had it worse."

"Had *what* worse?"

"I don't know!" And I can tell he doesn't know, that he's as frustrated and bewildered as I am. "Whatever makes a woman leave two little kids, her brother, and her mother, and not come back for sixteen years. That's what! I mean, we call it wanderlust, other families might not be so kind."

"What would other families call it?" I ask. He's never intimated anything like this before about Mom. Is it all a cover story for crazy? Was she really and truly out of her tree?

"Doesn't matter what anyone else would call it, Len," he says. "This is our story to tell."

This is our story to tell. He says it in his Ten Commandments way and it hits me that way: profoundly. You'd think for all the reading I do, I would have thought about this before, but I haven't. I've never once thought about the interpretative, the storytelling aspect of life, of my life. I

212

always felt like I was in a story, yes, but not like I was the author of it, or like I had any say in its telling whatsoever.

You can tell your story any way you damn well please.

It's your solo.

27

This is the secret I kept from you, Bails,
from myself, too:
I think I liked that Mom was gone,
that she could be anybody,
anywhere,
doing anything.
I liked that she was our invention,
a woman living
on the last page of the story
with only what we imagined
spread out before her.
I liked that she was ours, alone.

(Found on a page ripped out of Wuthering Heights,
spiked on a branch, in the woods)

Joelessness settles over the morning like a pall. Gram and I are slumped spineless over the kitchen table, staring off in opposite directions.

When I got back to The Sanctum last night, I put Bailey's notebook into the carton with the others and closed up the box. Then I returned St Anthony to the mantel in front of The Half Mom. I'm not sure how I'm going to find our mother, but I know it isn't going to be on the Internet. All night, I thought about what Big said. It's possible no one in this family is quite who I believed, especially me. I'm pretty sure he hit the jackpot with me.

And maybe with Bailey too. Maybe he's right and she didn't have it – whatever *it* is. Maybe what my sister wanted was to stay here and get married and have a family.

Maybe that was her color of extraordinary.

"Bailey had all these secrets," I say to Gram.

"Seems to run in the family," she replies with a tired sigh.

I want to ask her what she means, remembering what Big said about her too last night, but can't because he's just stomped in, dressed for work after all, a dead ringer for Paul Bunyan. He takes one look at us and says, "Who died?" Then stops midstep, shakes his head. "I *cannot* believe I just said that." He knocks on his head nobody-home-style.

Then he looks around. "Hey, where's Joe this morning?"

Gram and I both look down.

"What?" he asks.

"I don't think he'll be around anymore," I say.

"Really?" Big shrinks from Gulliver to Lilliputian before my eyes. "Why, honey?"

I feel tears brimming. "I don't know."

Thankfully, he lets it drop and leaves the kitchen to check on the bugs.

The whole way to the deli I think of the crazy French violinist Genevieve with whom Joe was in love and how he never spoke to her again. I think of his assessment of horn players as all-or-nothing types. I think how I had all of him and now I'm going to have none of him unless I can somehow make him understand what happened last night and all the other nights with Toby. But how? I already left two messages on his cell this morning and even called the Fontaine house once. It went like this:

Lennie (shaking in her flip-flops): Is Joe home?

Marcus: Wow, Lennie, shocker … brave girl.

Lennie (looks down to see scarlet letter emblazoned on her T-shirt): Is he around?

Marcus: Nope, left early.

Marcus and Lennie: Awkward Silence

Marcus: He's taking it pretty hard. I've never seen him so upset about a girl before, about anything, actually…

Lennie (close to tears): Will you tell him I called?

Marcus: Will do.

Marcus and Lennie: Awkward Silence

Marcus (tentative): Lennie, if you like him, well, don't give up.

Dial tone.

And that's the problem, I madly like him. I make an SOS call to Sarah to come down to the deli during my shift.

Normally, I am The Zen Lasagna Maker. After three and a half summers, four shifts a week, eight lasagnas a shift: 896 lasagnas to date – done the math – I have it down. It's my meditation.

I separate noodle after noodle from the glutinous lump that comes out of the refrigerator with the patience and precision of a surgeon. I plunge my hands into the ricotta and spices and fold the mixture until fluffy as a cloud. I slice the cheese into cuts as thin as paper. I spice the sauce until it sings. And then I layer it all together into a mountain of perfection. My lasagnas are sublime. Today, however, my lasagnas are not singing. After nearly chopping off a finger on the slicer, dropping the glutinous lump of noodles onto the floor, overcooking the new batch of pasta, dumping a truck-load of salt into the tomato sauce, Maria has me on moron-duty stuffing cannolis with a blunt object while she makes the lasagnas by my side. I'm cornered. It's too early for customers, so it's just us trapped inside the *National Enquirer* – Maria's the town crier, chatters nonstop about the lewd and lascivious goings-on in Clover, including, of course, the arboreal escapades of the town Romeo: my uncle Big.

"How's he doing?"

"You know."

"Everyone's been asking about him. He used to stop at The Saloon every night after he returned to earth from the treetops." Maria's stirring a vat of sauce beside me, a witch at her cauldron, as I try to cover the fact that I've broken yet another pastry shell. I'm a lovesick mess with a dead sister. "The place isn't the same without him. He holding up?" Maria turns to me, brushes a dark curl of hair from her perspiring brow, notes with irritation the growing pile of broken cannoli shells.

"He's just okay, like the rest of us," I say. "He's been coming home after work." I don't add, *and smoking three bowls of weed to numb the pain.* I keep looking up at the door, imagining Joe sailing through it.

"I did hear he had a treetop visitor the other day," Maria singsongs, back to everyone else's business.

"No way," I say, knowing full well that this is most likely the case.

"Yup. Dorothy Rodriguez, you know her, right? She teaches second grade. Last night at the bar, I heard that she rode up with him in the barrel high into the canopy, and *you know...*"

She winks at me. "They picnicked."

I groan. "Maria, it's my uncle, please."

She laughs, then blathers on about a dozen more Clover trysts until at last Sarah floats in dressed like a fabric shop specializing in paisley. She stands in the doorway, puts her arms up, and makes peace signs with both hands.

"Sarah! If you don't look like the spitting image of me

218

twenty years – sheesh, almost thirty years ago," Maria says, heading into the walk-in refrigerator. I hear the door thump behind her.

"Why the SOS?" Sarah says to me. The summer day has followed her in. Her hair is still wet from swimming. When I called earlier she and Luke were at Flying Man's "working" on some song. I can smell the river on her as she hugs me over the counter.

"Are you wearing toe rings?" I ask to postpone my confession a little longer.

"Of course." She lifts her kaleidoscopic pantalooned leg into the air to show me.

"Impressive."

She hops on the stool across the counter from where I'm working, throws down her book. It's by a Hélène Cixous. "Lennie, these French feminists are so much cooler than those stupid existentialists. I'm so into this concept of *jouissance*, it means transcendent rapture, which I'm sure you and Joe know all about—" She plays the air with invisible sticks.

"Knew." I take a deep breath. Prepare for the *I told you so* of the century.

Her face is stuck somewhere between disbelief and shock. "What do you mean, *knew*?"

"I mean, *knew*."

"But yesterday…" She's shaking her head, trying to catch up to the news. "You guys frolicked off from practice making the rest of us sick on account of the indisputable, irrefutable, unmistakable true love that was seeping out of every pore of your attached-at-the-hip bodies. Rachel nearly exploded. It was so beautiful." And then it dawns on her. "You didn't."

"Please don't have a cow or a horse or an aardvark or any other animal about it. No morality police, okay?"

"Okay, promise. Now tell me you didn't. I told you I had a bad feeling."

"I did." I cover my face with my hands. "Joe saw us kissing last night."

"You've got to be kidding?"

I shake my head.

As if on cue, a gang of miniature Toby skate rats whiz by on their boards, tearing apart the sidewalk, quiet as a 747.

"But why, Len? Why would you do that?" Her voice is surprisingly without judgment. She really wants to know. "You don't love Toby."

"No."

"And you're dementoid over Joe."

"Totally."

"Then why?" This is the million-dollar question.

I stuff two cannolis, deciding how to phrase it. "I think it has to do with how much we both love Bailey, as crazy as that sounds."

Sarah stares at me. "You're right, that does sound crazy. Bailey would kill you."

My heart races wild in my chest. "I know. But Bailey is dead, Sarah. And Toby and I don't know how to deal with it. And that's what happened. Okay?" I've never yelled at

220

Sarah in my life and that was definitely approaching a yell. But I'm furious at her for saying what I know is true. Bailey would kill me, and it just makes me want to yell at Sarah more, which I do. "What should I do? Penance? Should I mortify the flesh, soak my hands in lye, rub pepper into my face like St Rose? Wear a hair shirt?"

Her eyes bug out. "Yes, that's exactly what I think you should do!" she cries, but then her mouth twitches a little. "That's right, wear a hair shirt! A hair hat! A whole hair ensemble!" Her face is scrunching up. She bleats out, "St Lennie," and then folds in half in hysterics. Followed by me, all our anger morphing into uncontrollable spectacular laughter – we're both bent over trying to breathe and it feels so great even though I might die from lack of oxygen.

"I'm sorry," I say between gasps.

She manages, "No, me. I promised I wouldn't get like that. Felt good though to let you have it."

"Likewise," I squeal.

Maria sweeps back in, apron loaded with tomatoes, peppers, and onions, takes one look at us, and says, "You and your crazy cohort get out of here. Take a break."

Sarah and I drop onto our bench in front of the deli. The street's coming to life with sunburned couples from San Francisco stumbling out of B&Bs, swaddled in black, looking for pancakes or river rafts or weed.

Sarah shakes her head as she lights up. I've confounded her. A hard thing to do. I know she'd still like to holler: *What in flying foxes were you thinking, Lennie?* but she doesn't.

221

"Okay, the matter at hand is getting that Fontaine boy back," she says calmly.

"Exactly."

"Clearly making him jealous is out of the question."

"Clearly." I sink my chin into my palms, look up at the thousand-year-old redwood across the street – it's peering down at me in consternation. It wants to kick my sorry newbie-to-the-earth ass.

"I know!" Sarah exclaims. "You'll seduce him." She lowers her eyelids, puckers her lips into a pout around her cigarette, inhales deeply, and then exhales a perfect smoke blob. "Seduction always works. I can't even think of one movie where it doesn't work, can you?"

"You can't be serious. He's so hurt and pissed. He's not even speaking to me, I called three times today … and it's me, not you, remember? I don't know how to seduce anyone." I'm miserable – I keep seeing Joe's face, stony and lifeless, like it was last night. If ever there was a face impervious to seduction, it's that one.

Sarah twirls her scarf with one hand, smokes with the other. "You don't have to *do* anything, Len, just show up to band practice tomorrow looking F-I-N-E, looking *irresistible*." She says irresistible like it has ten syllables. "His raging hormones and wild passion for you will do the rest."

"Isn't that incredibly superficial, Ms French Feminist?"

"*Au contraire, ma petite*. These feminists are all about celebrating the body, its *langage*." She whips the scarf in the air. "Like I said, they're all after *jouissance*. As a means, of course, of subverting the dominant patriarchal paradigm and the white male literary canon, but we can get into that another time." She flicks her cigarette into the street. "Anyway, it can't hurt, Len. And it'll be fun. For me, that is…" A cloud of sadness crosses her face.

We exchange a glance that holds weeks of unsaid words.

"I just didn't think you could understand me anymore," I blurt out. I'd felt like a different person and Sarah had felt like the same old one, and I bet Bailey had felt similarly about me, and she was right to. Sometimes you just have to soldier through in your own private messy way.

"I couldn't understand," Sarah exclaims. "Not really. Felt—*feel* so useless, Lennie. And man, those grief books suck, so formulaic, total hundred percent garbage."

"Thanks," I say. "For reading them."

She looks down at her feet. "I miss her too." Until this moment, it hadn't occurred to me she might've read those books for herself also. But of course. She revered Bailey. I've left her to grieve all on her own. I don't know what to say, so I reach across the bench and hug her. Hard.

A car honks with a bunch of hooting doofuses from Clover High in it. Way to ruin the moment. We disengage, Sarah waving her feminist book at them like a religious zealot – it makes me laugh.

When they pass, she takes another cigarette out of her pack, then gently touches my knee with it. "This Toby thing, I just don't get it." She lights the smoke, keeps shaking the match after it's out, like a metronome. "Were you competitive with Bailey? You guys never seemed like those King Lear type of sisters. I never thought so anyway."

"No we weren't. No … but … I don't know, I ask myself the same thing—"

I've crashed head-on into that something Big said last night, that awfully huge something.

"Remember that time we watched the Kentucky Derby?" I ask Sarah, not sure if this will make sense to anyone but me.

She looks at me like I'm crazy. "Yeah, uh, why?"

"Did you notice the racehorses had these companion ponies that didn't leave their sides?"

"I guess."

"Well, I think that was us, me and Bails."

She pauses a minute, exhales a long plume of smoke, before she says, "You were both racehorses, Len." I can tell she doesn't believe it though, that she's just trying to be nice.

I shake my head. "C'mon, be real, I wasn't. God, no way. I'm not." And it's been no one's doing but my own. Bailey went as crazy as Gram when I quit my lessons.

"Do you want to be?" Sarah asks.

"Maybe," I say, unable to quite manage a yes.

She smiles, then in silence, we both watch car after car creep along, most of them filled with ridiculously bright rubber river gear: giraffe boats, elephant canoes and the like. Finally she says, "Being a companion pony must suck. Not metaphorically, I mean, you know, if you're a horse. Think about it. Self-sacrifice twenty-four/seven, no glory, no glamour … they should start a union, have their own Companion Pony Derby."

"A good new cause for you."

"No. My new cause is turning St Lennon into a femme fatale." She smirks. "C'mon, Len, say yes."

Her *C'mon, Len* reminds me of Bails, and the next thing I know, I hear myself saying, "Okay, fine."

"It'll be subtle, I promise."

"Your strong-suit."

She laughs. "Yeah, you're so screwed."

It's a hopeless idea, but I have no other. I have to do something, and Sarah's right, looking sexy, assuming I can look sexy, can't hurt, can it? I mean it is true that seduction hardly ever fails in movies, especially French ones. So I defer to Sarah's expertise, experience, to the concept of *jouissance*, and Operation Seduction is officially under way.

I have cleavage. Melons. Bazumbas. Bodacious tatas. Handfuls of bosom pouring out of a minuscule black dress that I'm going to wear in broad daylight to band practice. I can't stop looking down. I'm stacked, a buxom babe. My scrawny self is positively zaftig. How can a bra possibly do this? Note to the physicists: Matter can indeed be created. Not to mention that I'm in platforms, so I look nine feet tall, and my lips are red as pomegranates.

Sarah and I have ducked into a classroom next to the music room.

"Are you sure, Sarah?" I don't know how I got myself into this ridiculous *I Love Lucy* episode.

"Never been more sure of anything. No guy will be able to resist you. I'm a little worried Mr James won't survive it though."

"All right. Let's go," I say.

The way I get down the hallway is to pretend I'm someone else. Someone in a movie, a black-and-white French movie where everyone smokes and is mysterious and alluring. I'm a woman, not a girl, and I'm going to seduce a man. Who am I kidding? I freak out and run back to the classroom. Sarah follows, my bridesmaid.

"Lennie, c'mon." She's exasperated.

There it is again, *Lennie, c'mon*. I try again. This time I think of Bailey, the way she sashayed, making the ground work for her, and I glide effortlessly through the door of the music room.

I notice right away that Joe isn't there, but there's still time until rehearsal starts, like fifteen seconds, and he's always early, but maybe something held him up.

Fourteen seconds: Sarah was right, all the boys are staring at me like I've popped out of a centerfold. Rachel almost drops her clarinet.

Thirteen, Twelve, Eleven: Mr James throws his arms up in celebration. "Lennie, you look ravishing!" I make it to my seat.

Ten, Nine: I put my clarinet together but don't want to get lipstick all over my mouthpiece. I do anyway.

Eight, Seven: tuning.

Six, Five: tuning still.

Four, Three: I turn around. Sarah shakes her head, mouths *unfreakingbelievable*.

Two, One: the announcement I now am expecting. "Let's begin class. Sorry to say we've lost our only trumpet player for the festival. Joe's going to perform with his brothers instead. Take out your pencils, I have changes."

I drop my glamorous head into my hands, hear Rachel say, "I told you he was out of your league, Lennie."

28

There once was a girl who found herself dead.
She peered over the ledge of heaven
and saw that back on earth
her sister missed her too much,
was way too sad,
so she crossed some paths
that would not have crossed,
took some moments in her hand
shook them up
and spilled them like dice
over the living world.

It worked.
The boy with the guitar collided
with her sister.

"There you go, Len," she whispered.
        "The rest is up to you."

*(Found on a folded-up
flyer on the sidewalk,
Main Street)*

"May the force be with you," Sarah says, and sends me on my way, which is up the hill to the Fontaines' in aforementioned black cocktail dress, platforms and bodacious tatas. The whole way up I repeat a mantra: *I am the author of my story and I can tell it any way I want. I am a solo artist. I am a racehorse.* Yes, this puts me into the major freaker category of human, but it does the trick and gets me up the hill, because fifteen minutes later I am looking up at Maison Fontaine, the dry summer grass crackling all around me, humming with hidden insects, which reminds me: how in the world does Rachel know what happened with Joe?

When I get to the driveway, I see a man dressed all in black with a shuck of white hair, waving his arms around like a dervish, shouting in French at a stylish woman in a black dress (hers fits her), who looks equally peeved. She is hissing back at him in English. I definitely do not want to walk past those two panthers, so I sneak around the far side of the property and then duck under the enormous willow tree that reigns like a queen over the yard, the thick drapes of leaves falling like a shimmering green ball gown around the ancient trunk and branches, creating the perfect skulk den.

I need a moment to bolster my nerve, so I pace around

229

in my new glimmery green apartment trying to figure out what I'm going to actually say to Joe, a point both Sarah and I forgot to consider.

That's when I hear it: clarinet music drifting out from the house, the melody Joe wrote for me. My heart does a hopeful flip. I walk over to the side of Maison Fontaine that abuts the tree and, still concealed by a drape of leaves, I stand up on tiptoe and see through the open window a sliver of Joe playing a bass clarinet in the living room.

And thus begins my life as a spy.

I tell myself, after this song, I will ring the doorbell and literally face the music. But then, he plays the melody again and again and the next thing I know I'm lying on my back listening to the amazing music, reaching into Sarah's purse for a pen, which I find as well as a scrap of paper. I jot down a poem, spike it with a stick into the ground. The music is making me rapturous; I slip back into that kiss, again drinking the sweet rain off his lips—

To be rudely interrupted by DougFred's exasperated voice. "Dude, you're driving me berserk – this same song over and over again, for two days now, I can't deal. We're all going to jump off the bridge right after you. Why don't you just talk to her?" I jump up and scurry over to the window: Harriet the Spy in drag. *Please say you'll talk to her*, I mind-beam to Joe.

"No way," he says.

"Joe, it's pathetic … c'mon."

Joe's voice is pinched, tight. "I *am so* pathetic. She was lying to me the whole time … just like Genevieve, just like

Dad to Mom for that matter…"

Ugh. Ugh. Ugh. Boy, did I blow it.

"Whatever, already, with all of that – shit's complicated sometimes, man." *Hallelujah, DougFred.*

"Not for me."

"Just get your horn, we need to practice."

Still concealed under the tree, I listen to Joe, Marcus and DougFred practicing: it goes like this, three notes, then a cell phone rings: Marcus: *Hey Ami*, then five minutes later, another ring: Marcus: *Salut Sophie*, then Doug-Fred: *Hey Chloe*, then fifteen minutes later: *Hi Nicole*. These guys are Clover catnip. I remember how the phone rang pretty much continually the evening I spent here. Finally, Joe says: *Turn off the cell phones or we won't even get through a song* – but just as he finishes the sentence, his own cell goes off and his brothers laugh. I hear him say, *Hey Rachel.* And that's the end of me. *Hey Rachel* in a voice that sounds happy to hear from her, like he was expecting the call, waiting for it even.

I think of St Wilgefortis, who went to sleep beautiful and woke up with a full beard and mustache, and wish that fate on Rachel. Tonight.

Then I hear: *You were totally right. The Throat Singers of Tuva are awesome.*

Call 911.

Okay, calm down, Lennie. Stop pacing. Don't think about him batting his eyelashes at Rachel Brazile! Grinning at her, kissing her, making her feel like she's part sky… *What have I done?* I lie down on my back in the grass under

231

the umbrella of trembling sunlit leaves. I'm leveled by a phone call. How must it have been for him to actually see me kiss Toby?

I suck, there's no other way to put it.

There's also no other way to put this: I'm so freaking in love – it's just blaring every which way inside me, like some psycho opera.

But back to BITCHZILLA!?

Be rational, I tell myself, systematic, think of all the many innocuous unromantic reasons she could be calling him. I can't think of one, though I'm so consumed with trying I don't even hear the truck pull up, just a door slamming. I get up, peek out through the thick curtain of leaves, and almost pass out to see Toby walking toward the front door. WTF-asaurus? He hesitates before ringing the bell, takes a deep breath, then presses the button, waits, then presses it again. He steps back, looks toward the living room, where the music is now blasting, then knocks hard. The music stops and I hear the pounding of feet, then watch the door open and hear Toby say: "Is Joe here?"

Gulp.

Next, I hear Joe still in the living room: "What's his problem? I didn't want to talk to him yesterday and I don't want to talk to him today."

Marcus is back in the living room. "Just talk to the guy."

"No."

But Joe must have gone to the door, because I hear muffled words and see Toby's mouth moving, although he's quieted down too much for me to make out the words.

232

I don't plan what happens next. It just happens. I just happen to have that stupid it's-my-story-I'm-a-racehorse mantra back on repeat in my head and so I somehow decide that whatever is going to happen, good or bad, I don't want to be hiding in a tree when it does. I muster all my courage and part the curtain of leaves.

The first thing I notice is the sky, so full of blue and the kind of brilliant white clouds that make you ecstatic to have eyes. Nothing can go wrong under this sky, I think as I make my way across the lawn, trying not to wobble in my platforms. The Fontaine panther-parents are nowhere in sight; probably they took their hissing match into the barn. Toby must hear my footsteps; he turns around.

"Lennie?"

The door swings open and three Fontaines pile out like they've been stuffed in a car.

Marcus speaks first: "Va-va-voom."

Joe's mouth drops open.

Toby's too, for that matter.

"Holy shit" comes out of DougFred's perpetually de-ranged with-glee face. The four of them are like a row of dumbfounded ducks. I'm acutely aware of how short my dress is, how tight it is across my chest, how wild my hair is, how red my lips are. I might die. I want to wrap my arms around my body. For the rest of my life, I'm going to leave the femme fatale-ing to other femmes. All I want is to flee, but I don't want them to stare at my butt as I fly into the woods in this tiny piece of fabric masquerading as a dress. Wait a second here – one by one, I take in their idiotic

233

faces. Was Sarah right? Might this work? Could guys be this simple-minded?

Marcus is ebullient. "One hot tamale, John Lennon."

Joe glares at him. "Shut the hell up, Marcus." He has regained his composure and rage. Nope, Joe is definitely not this simpleminded. I know immediately this was a bad, bad move.

"What's wrong with you two?" he says to Toby and me, throwing up his arms in a perfect mimicry of his father's dervishness.

He pushes past his brothers and Toby, jumps off the stoop, comes up to me, so close that I can smell his fury. "Don't you get it? What you did? It's done, Lennie, we're done." Joe's beautiful lips, the ones that kissed me and whispered in my hair, they are twisting and contorting around words I hate. The ground beneath me begins to tilt. People don't really faint, do they? "Get it, because I mean it. It's ruined. *Everything* is."

I'm mortified. I'm going to kill Sarah. And what a total companion-pony move on my part. I knew this wouldn't work. There was no way he was going to toss aside this behemoth betrayal because I squeezed myself into this ridiculously small dress. How could I be so stupid?

And it's just dawned on me that I might be the author of my own story, but so is everyone else the author of their own stories, and sometimes, like now, there's no overlap.

He's walking away from me. I don't care that there are six pairs of eyes and ears on us. He can't leave before I have a chance to say something, have a chance to make him understand what happened, how I feel about him. I grab the bottom of his T-shirt. He snaps around, flings my hand away, meets my eyes. I don't know what he sees in them, but he softens a little. I watch some of the rage slip off of him as he looks at me. Without it, he looks unnerved and vulnerable, like a small disheartened boy. It makes me ache with tenderness. I want to touch his beautiful face. I look at his hands; they are shaking.

As is all of me.

He's waiting for me to speak. But I realize the perfect thing to say must be in another girl's mind, because it's not in mine. Nothing is in mine.

"I'm sorry," I manage out.

"I don't care," he says, his voice cracking a little. He looks down at the ground. I follow his gaze, see his bare feet sticking out of jeans; they are long and thin and monkey-toed. I've never seen his feet out of shoes and socks before. They're perfectly simian – toes so long he could play the piano with them.

"Your feet," I say, before I realize it. "I've never seen them before."

My moronic words drum in the air between us, and for a split second, I know he wants to laugh, wants to reach out and pull me to him, wants to tease me about saying something so ridiculous when he's about to murder me. I can see this in his face as if his thoughts were scribbled across it. But then all that gets wiped away as quickly as it came, and what's left is the unwieldy hurt in his unbatting eyes, his grinless mouth. He will never forgive me.

I took the joy out of the most joyful person on planet Earth.

"I'm so sorry," I say. "I—"

"God, stop saying that." His hands swoop around me like lunatic bats. I've reignited his rage. "It doesn't matter to me that you're sorry. You just don't get it." He whips around and bolts into the house before I can say another word.

Marcus shakes his head and sighs, then follows his brother inside with DougFred in tow.

I stand there with Joe's words still scorching my skin, thinking what a terrible idea it was to come up here, in this tiny dress, these skyscraping heels. I wipe the siren song off my lips. I'm disgusted with myself. I didn't ask for his forgiveness, didn't explain a thing, didn't tell him that he is the most amazing thing that's ever happened to me, that I love him, that he's the only one for me. Instead, I talked about his feet. *His feet.*

Talk about choking under pressure. And then I remember *Hey Rachel*, which explodes a Molotov cocktail of jealousy into my misery, completing the dismal picture.

I want to kick the postcard-perfect sky.

I'm so absorbed in my self-flagellation, I forget Toby's there until he says, "Emotional guy."

I look up. He's sitting on the stoop now, leaning back on his arms, his legs kicked out. He must have come straight from work; he's out of his usual skate rat rags and has on mud-splattered jeans and boots and button-down shirt and is only missing the Stetson to complete the Marlboro Man picture. He looks like he did the day he whisked my sister's heart away: Bailey's Revolutionary.

"He almost attacked me with his guitar yesterday. I think we're making progress," he adds.

"Toby, what're you doing here?"

"What are you doing hiding in trees?" he asks back, nodding at the willow behind me.

"Trying to make amends," I say.

"Me, too," he says quickly, jumping to his feet. "But to you. Been trying to tell him what's what." His words surprise me.

"I'll take you home," he says.

We both get into his truck. I can't seem to curb the nausea overwhelming me as a result of the hands-down worst seduction in love's history. Ugh. And on top of it, I'm sure Joe is watching us from a window, all his suspicions seething in his hot head as I drive off with Toby.

"So, what'd you say to him?" I ask when we've cleared Fontaine territory.

"Well, the three words I got to say yesterday and the ten I got in today added up to pretty much telling him he should give you a second chance, that there's nothing going on with us, that we were just wrecked…"

"Wow, that was nice. Busybody as you like, but nice."

He looks over at me for a moment before returning his eyes to the road. "I watched you guys that night in the rain … I saw it, how you feel."

His voice is full of emotion that I can't decipher and probably don't want to. "Thanks," I say quietly, touched that he did this despite everything, because of everything.

He doesn't respond, just looks straight ahead into the sun, which is obliterating everything in our path with unruly splendor. The truck blasts through the trees and I stick my hand out the window, trying to catch the wind in my palm like Bails used to, missing her, missing the girl I used to be around her, missing who we all used to be. We will never be those people again. She took them all with her.

I notice Toby's tapping his fingers nervously on the wheel. He keeps doing it. Tap. Tap. Tap.

"What is it?" I ask.

He grips the wheel tight with both hands.

"I really love her," he says, his voice breaking. "More than anything."

"Oh, Toby, I know that." That's the only thing I do understand about this whole mess: that somehow what happened between us happened because there's too much love for Bailey between us, not too little.

"I know," I repeat.

He nods.

Something occurs to me then: Bailey loved both Toby and me so much – he and I almost make up her whole heart, and maybe that's it, what we were trying to do by being together, maybe we were trying to put her heart back together again.

He stops the truck in front of the house. The sun streams into the cab, bathing us in light. I look out my window, can see Bails rushing out of the house, flying off the porch, to jump into this very truck I am sitting in. It's so strange. I spent forever resenting Toby for taking my sister away from me, and now it seems like I count on him to bring her back.

I open the door, put one of my platforms onto the ground.

"Len?"

I turn around.

"You'll wear him down." His smile is warm and genuine. He rests the side of his head on the steering wheel. "I'm going to leave you alone for a bit, but if you need me … for anything, okay?"

"Same," I say, my throat knotting up.

Our conjoined love for Bailey trembles between us; it's like a living thing, as delicate as a small bird, and as breathtaking in its hunger for flight. My heart hurts for both of us.

"Don't do anything stupid on that board," I say.

"Nope."

"Okay." Then I slide out, close the door, and head into the house.

29

Sometimes I'd see Sarah and her mom
share a look across a room
and I'd want
to have my life over like a table.
I'd tell myself not to feel that way
that I was lucky:
I had Bailey.
I had Gram and Big.
I had my clarinet, books, a river, the sky.
I'd tell myself that I had a mother too,
just not one anyone else could see
but Bailey and me.

(Found scribbled on the classified ads in The Clover Gazette
under the bench outside Maria's Deli)

Sarah's at State, since the symposium is this afternoon, so I have no one on which to blame the *Hey Rachel* seduction fiasco but myself. I leave her a message telling her I've been totally mortified like a good saint because of her *jouissance* and am now seeking a last-resort miracle.

The house is quiet. Gram must have gone out, which is too bad because for the first time in ages, I'd like nothing more than to sit at the kitchen table with her and drink tea.

I go up to The Sanctum to brood about Joe, but once there, my eyes keep settling on the boxes I packed the other night. I can't stand looking at them, so after I change out of my ridiculous outfit, I take them up to the attic.

I haven't been up here in years. I don't like the tombishness, the burned smell of the trapped heat, the lack of air. It always seems so sad too, full of everything abandoned and forgotten. I look around at the lifeless clutter, feel deflated at the idea of bringing Bailey's things up here. This is what I've been avoiding for months now. I take a deep breath, look around. There's only one window, so I decide, despite the fact that the area around it is packed in with boxes and mountains of bric-à-brac, that Bailey's things should go where the sun will at least seep in each day.

I make my way over there through an obstacle course of broken furniture, boxes, and old canvases. I move a few cartons immediately so I can crack open the window and hear the river. Hints of rose and jasmine blow in on the afternoon breeze. I open it wider, climb up on an old desk so I can lean out. The sky is still spectacular and I hope Joe is gazing up at it. No matter where I look inside myself, I come across more love for him, for everything about him, his anger as much as his tenderness – he's so alive, he makes me feel like I could take a bite out of the whole earth. If only words hadn't eluded me today, if only I yelled back at him: *I do get it! I get that as long as you live no one will ever love you as much as I do – I have a heart so I can give it to you alone!* That's exactly the way I feel – but unfortunately, people don't talk like that outside of Victorian novels.

I take my head out of the sky and bring it back into the stuffy attic. I wait for my eyes to readjust, and when they do, I'm still convinced this is the only possible spot for Bailey's things. I start moving all the junk that's already there to the shelves on the back wall. After many trips back and forth, I finally reach down to pick up the last of it, which is a shoebox, and the top flips open. It's full of letters, all addressed to Big, probably love letters. I peek at one postcard from an Edie. I decide against snooping further; my karma is about as bad as it's ever been right now. I slip the lid back on, place it on one of the lower shelves where there's still some space. Just behind it, I notice an old letter box, its wood polished and shiny. I wonder what an antique like this is doing up here instead of downstairs with all Gram's other treasures. It looks like a showcase piece too. I slide it out; the wood is mahogany and there's a ring of galloping horses engraved into the top. Why isn't it covered in dust like everything else on these shelves? I lift the lid, see that it's full of folded notes on Gram's mint-green stationery, so many of them, and lots of letters as well. I'm about to put it back when I see written on the outside of an envelope in Gram's careful script the name *Paige*. I flip through the other envelopes. Each and every one says *Paige* with the year next to her name. Gram writes letters to Mom? Every year? All the envelopes are sealed. I know that I should put the box back, that this is private, but I can't. Karma be damned. I open one of the folded notes. It says:

Darling,

The second the lilacs are in full bloom, I have to write you. I know I tell you this every year, but they haven't blossomed the same since you left. They're so stingy now. Maybe it's because no one comes close to loving them like you did – how could they? Each spring I wonder if I'm going to find the girls sleeping in the garden, like I'd find you, morning after morning. Did you know how I loved that, walking outside and seeing you asleep with my lilacs and roses all around you – I've never even tried to paint the image. I never will. I wouldn't want to ruin it for myself.

   Mom

Wow – my mother loves lilacs, *really* loves them. Yes, yes, it's true, most people love lilacs, but my mother is so gaga about them that she used to sleep in Gram's garden, night after night, all spring long, so gaga she couldn't bear

243

to be inside knowing all those flowers were raising hell outside her window. Did she bring her blankets out with her?
A sleeping bag? Nothing? Did she sneak out when everyone else was asleep? Did she do this when she was my age?
Did she like looking up at the sky as much as I do? I want
to know more. I feel jittery and lightheaded, like I'm meeting her for the first time. I sit down on a box, try to calm
down. I can't. I pick up another note. It says:

> Remember that pesto you made with walnuts instead
> of pine nuts? Well, I tried pecans, and you know
> what?
> Even better. The recipe:
> 2 cups packed fresh basil leaves
> 2/3 cup olive oil
> 1/2 cup pecans, toasted
> 1/3 cup freshly grated Parmesan
> 2 large garlic cloves, mashed
> 1/2 teaspoon salt

My mother makes pesto with walnuts! This is even
better than sleeping with lilacs. So normal. *So I think I'll
whip up some pasta with pesto for dinner.* My mother bangs
around a kitchen. She puts walnuts and basil and olive oil
in a food processor, and presses blend. She boils water for
pasta! I have to tell Bails. I want to scream out the window
at her: *Our mother boils water for pasta!* I'm going to. I'm going to tell Bailey. I make my way over to the window, climb
back up on the desk, put my head out, holler up at the sky,
and tell my sister everything I've just learned. I feel dizzy,
and yes, a bit out of my tree, when I climb back into the

attic, now hoping no one heard this girl screaming about pasta and lilacs at the top of her lungs. I take a deep breath. Open another one.

Paige,

I've been wearing the fragrance you wore for years. The one you thought smelled like sunshine. I've just found out they've discontinued it. I feel as though I've lost you now completely. I can't bear it.

Mom

Oh.

But why didn't Gram tell us our mother wore a perfume that smelled like sunshine? That she slept in the garden in the springtime? That she made pesto with walnuts? Why did she keep this real-life mother from us? But as soon as I ask the question, I know the answer, because suddenly there is not blood pumping in my veins, coursing all throughout my body, but longing for a mother who loves lilacs. Longing like I've never had for the Paige Walker who wanders the world. That Paige Walker never made me feel like a daughter, but a mother who boils water for pasta does. Except don't you need to be claimed to be a daughter? Don't you need to be loved?

And now there's something worse than longing flooding me, because how could a mother who boils water for pasta leave two little girls behind?

How could she?

I close the lid, slide the box back on a shelf, quickly stack Bailey's boxes by the window, and go down the stairs into the empty house.

The architecture
of my sister's thinking,
now phantom.
I fall
down stairs
that are nothing
but air.

(Found on a takeaway cup by a grove of old growth redwoods)

The next few days inch by miserably. I skip band practice and confine myself to The Sanctum. Joe Fontaine does not stop by, or call, or text, or e-mail, or skywrite, or send Morse code, or telepathically communicate with me. Nothing. I'm quite certain he and *Hey Rachel* have moved to Paris, where they live on chocolate, music and red wine, while I sit at this window, peering down the road where no one comes bouncing along, guitar in hand, like they used to.

As the days pass, Paige Walker's love of lilacs and ability to boil water have the singular effect of washing sixteen years of myth right off of her. And without it, all that's left is this: our mother abandoned us. There's no way around it. And what kind of person does that? Rip Van Lennie is right. I've been living in a dream world, totally brainwashed by Gram. My mother's freaking nuts, and I am too, because what kind of ignoramus swallows such a cockamamie story? Those hypothetical families that Big spoke of the other night would've been right not to be kind. My mother is neglectful and irresponsible and probably mentally deficient too. She's not a heroine at all. She's just a selfish woman who couldn't hack it and left two toddlers on her mother's porch and *never came back*. That's who she is. And that's who we are too, two kids, discarded, just left there. I'm glad Bailey never had to see it this way.

I don't go back up to the attic.

It's all right. I'm used to a mother who rides around on a magic carpet. I can get used to this mother too, can't I? But what I can't get used to is that I no longer think Joe, despite my compounding love for him, is ever going to forgive me. How to get used to no one calling you John Lennon? Or making you believe the sky begins at your feet? Or acting like a dork so you'll say *quel dork*? How to get used to being without a boy who turns you into brightness?

I can't.

And what's worse is that with each day that passes, The Sanctum gets quieter, even when I'm blasting the stereo, even when I'm talking to Sarah, who's still apologizing for the seduction fiasco, even when I'm practicing Stravinsky, it just gets quieter and quieter, until it is so quiet that what I hear, again and again, is the cranking sound of the casket lowering into the ground.

With each day that passes, there are longer stretches when I don't think I hear Bailey's heels clunking down the hallway, or glimpse her lying on her bed reading, or catch her in my periphery reciting lines into the mirror. I'm becoming accustomed to The Sanctum without her, and I hate it. Hate that when I stand in her closet fumbling from piece to piece, my face pressed into the fabrics, that I can't find one shirt or dress that still has her scent, and it's my fault. They all smell like me now.

Hate that her cell phone finally has been shut down.

With each day that passes, more traces of my sister

248

vanish, not only from the world, but from my very own mind, and there's nothing I can do about it, but sit in the soundless, scentless Sanctum and cry.

On the sixth day of this, Sarah declares me a state of emergency and makes me promise to go to the movies with her that night.

She picks me up in Ennui, wearing a black miniskirt, black minier tank top that shows off a lot of tanned midriff, three-foot black heels, all topped off with a black ski hat, which I'm supposing is her attempt at practicality, because a chill blew in and it's arctic cold. I'm wearing a brown suede coat, turtleneck, and jeans. We look like we are spliced together from different weather systems.

"Hi!" she says, taking the cigarette out of her mouth to kiss me as I get in. "This movie really is supposed to be good. Not like that last one I made you go to where the woman sat in a chair with her cat for the first half. I admit that one was problematico." Sarah and I have opposite movie-going philosophies. All I want out of celluloid is to sit in the dark with a huge bucket of popcorn. Give me car chases, girl gets boy, underdogs triumphing; let me swoon and scream and weep. Sarah on the other hand can't tolerate such pedestrian fare and complains the whole time about how we're rotting our minds and soon won't be able to think our own thoughts because our brains will be lost to the dominant paradigm. Sarah's preference is The Guild, where they show bleak foreign films where nothing happens, no one talks, everyone loves the one who will never love them back, and then the movie ends. On the program

249

tonight is some stultifyingly boring black-and-white film from Norway.

Her face drops as she studies mine. "You look miserable."

"Sucky week all around."

"It'll be fun tonight, promise." She takes one hand off the wheel and pulls a brown sack out of a backpack. "For the movie." She hands it to me. "Vodka."

"Hmm, then I'll for sure fall asleep in this action-packed, thrill-a-minute, black-and-white, silent movie from Norway."

She rolls her eyes. "It's not silent, Lennie."

While waiting in line, Sarah jumps around trying to keep warm. She's telling me how Luke held up remarkably well at the symposium despite being the only guy there, even made her ask a question about music, but then mid-sentence and mid-jump, her eyes bulge a little. I catch it, even though she's already resumed talking as if nothing has happened. I turn around and there's Joe across the street with Rachel.

They're so lost in conversation they don't even realize the light has changed.

Cross the street, I want to scream. *Cross the street before you fall in love.* Because that's what appears to be happening. I watch Joe lightly tug at her arm while he tells her something or other I'm sure about Paris. I can see the smile, all that radiance pouring over Rachel and I think I might fall like a tree.

"Let's go."

"Yup." Sarah's already walking toward the Jeep, fumbling in her bag for the keys. I follow her, but take one look back and meet Joe's eyes head on. Sarah disappears. Then Rachel. Then all the people waiting in line. Then the cars, the trees, the buildings, the ground, the sky until it is only Joe and me staring across empty space at each other. He does not smile. He antismiles. But I can't look away and he can't seem to either. Time has slowed so much that I wonder if when we stop staring at each other we will be old and our whole lives will be over with just a few measly kisses between us. I'm dizzy with missing him, dizzy with seeing him, dizzy with being just yards from him. I want to run across the street, I'm about to – I can feel my heart surge, pushing me toward him, but then he just shakes his head almost to himself and looks away from me and toward Rachel, who now comes back into focus. High-definition focus. Very deliberately, he puts his arm around her and together they cross the street and get in line for the movie. A searing pain claws through me. He doesn't look back, but Rachel does.

She salutes me, a triumphant smile on her face, then flips an insult of blond hair at me as she swings her arm around his waist and turns away.

My heart feels like it's been kicked into a dark corner of my body. *Okay I get it*, I want to holler at the sky. *This is how it feels*. Lesson learned. Come-uppance accepted. I watch them retreat into the theater arm in arm, wishing I had an eraser so I could wipe her out of this picture. Or a vacuum. A vacuum would be better, just suck her up, gone.

251

Out of his arms. Out of my chair. For good.

"C'mon Len, let's get out of here," a familiar voice says. I guess Sarah still exists and she's talking to me, so I must still exist too. I look down, see my legs, realize I'm still standing. I put one foot in front of the other and make my way to Ennui.

There is no moon, no stars, just a brightless, lightless gray bowl over our heads as we drive home.

"I'm going to challenge her for first chair," I say.

"Finally."

"Not because of this—"

"I know. Because you're a racehorse, not some stupid pony." There's no irony in her voice.

I roll down the window and let the cold air slap me silly.

31

Remember
how it was
when
we
kissed?
Armfuls
and
armfuls
of
light
thrown
right
at
us.
A
rope
dropping
down
from
the
sky.
How
can
the
word
love
the
word
life
even
fit
in
the
mouth?

(Found on a piece of paper under the big willow)

S arah and I are hanging half in, half out my bedroom window, passing the bottle of vodka back and forth.

"We could off her?" Sarah suggests, all her words slurring into one.

"How would we do it?" I ask, swigging a huge gulp of vodka.

"Poison. It's always the best choice, hard to trace."

"Let's poison him too, and all his stupid gorgeous brothers." I can feel the words sticking to the insides of my mouth. "He didn't even wait a week, Sarah."

"That doesn't mean anything. He's hurt."

"God, how can he like her?"

Sarah shakes her head. "I saw the way he looked at you in the street, like a crazy person, really out there, more demented than demented, holy Toledo tigers bonkers. You know what I think? I think he put his arm around her for your benefit."

"What if he has sex with her for my benefit?" Jealousy maddogs through me. Yet, that's not the worst part, neither is the remorse; the worst part is I keep thinking of the afternoon on the forest bed, how vulnerable I'd felt, how much I'd liked it, being that open, that *me*, with him. Had I ever felt so close to anyone?

254

"Can I have a cigarette?" I ask, taking one before she answers.

She cups a hand around the end of her smoke, lights it with the other, then hands it to me, takes mine, then lights it for herself. I drag on it, cough, don't care, take another and manage not to choke, blowing a gray trail of smoke into the night air.

"Bails would know what to do," I say.

"She would," Sarah agrees.

We smoke together quietly in the moonlight and I realize something I can never say to Sarah. There might've been another reason, a deeper one, why I didn't want to be around her. It's that she's not Bailey, and that's a bit unbearable for me – but I need to bear it. I concentrate on the music of the river, let myself drift along with it as it rushes steadily away.

After a few moments, I say, "You can revoke my free pass."

She tilts her head, smiles at me in a way that floods me with warmth. "Done deal."

She puts out her cigarette on the windowsill and slips back onto the bed. I put mine out too, but stay outside looking over Gram's lustrous garden, breathing it in and practically swooning from the bouquet that wafts up to me on the cool breeze.

And that's when I get the idea. The *brilliant* idea. I have to talk to Joe. I have to at least try to make him understand. But I could use a little help.

"Sarah," I say when I flop back onto the bed. "The roses, they're aphrodisiacal, remember?"

She gets it immediately. "Yes, Lennie! It's the last-re-sort miracle! Flying figs, yes!"

"Figs?"

"I couldn't think of an animal, I'm too wasted."

I'm on a mission. I've left Sarah sound asleep in Bailey's bed and I'm tiptoeing my thumping vodka head down the steps and out into the creeping morning light. The fog is thick and sad, the whole world an X-ray of itself. I have my weapon in hand and am about to begin my task. Gram is going to kill me, but this is the price I must pay.

I start at my favorite bush of all, the Magic Lanterns, roses with a symphony of color jammed into each petal. I snip the heads off the most extraordinary ones I can find. Then go to the Opening Nights and snip, snip, snip, merrily along to the Perfect Moments, the Sweet Surrenders, the Black Magics. My heart kicks around in my chest from both fear and excitement. I go from prize bush to bush, from the red velvet Lasting Loves to the pink Fragrant Clouds to the apricot Marilyn Monroes and end at the most beautiful orange-red rose on the planet, appropriately named: The Trumpeter. There I go for broke until I have at my feet a bundle of roses so ravishing that if God got married, there would be no other possible choice for the bouquet. I've cut so many I can't even fit the stems in one hand but have to carry them in both as I head down the road to find a place to stash them until later. I put them beside one of my favorite oaks, totally hidden from the house. Then I worry they'll wilt, so I run back to the house and prepare a basket with wet towels at the bottom and go back to the side of the road and wrap all the stems.

Later that morning, after Sarah leaves, Big goes off to the trees, and Gram retreats into the art room with her green women, I tiptoe out the door. I've convinced myself, despite all reason perhaps, that this is going to work. I keep thinking that Bails would be proud of this harebrained plan. *Extraordinary,* she'd say. In fact, maybe Bails would like that I fell in love with Joe so soon after she died. Maybe it's just the exact inappropriate way my sister would want to be mourned by me.

The flowers are still behind the oak where I left them. When I see them I am struck again by their extraordinary beauty. I've never seen a bouquet of them like this, never seen the explosive color of one bloom right beside another.

I walk up the hill to the Fontaines' in a cloud of exquisite fragrance. Who knows if it's the power of suggestion, or if the roses are truly charmed, but by the time I get to the house, I'm so in love with Joe, I can barely ring the bell. I have serious doubts if I'll be able to form a coherent sentence. If he answers I might just tackle him to the ground till he gives and be done with it.

But no such luck.

The same stylish woman who was in the yard squabbling the other day opens the door. "Don't tell me, you must be Lennie." It's immediately apparent that Fontaine spawn can't come close in the smile department to Mother Fontaine. I should tell Big – her smile has a better shot at reviving bugs than his pyramids.

"I am," I say. "Nice to meet you, Mrs Fontaine." She's being so friendly that I can't imagine she knows what's happened between her son and me. He probably talks to her about as much as I talk to Gram.

"And will you just look at those roses! I've never seen anything like them in my life. Where'd you pick them? The Garden of Eden?" Like mother, like son. I remember Joe said the same that first day.

"Something like that," I say. "My grandmother has a way with flowers. They're for Joe. Is he home?" All of a sudden, I'm nervous. Really nervous. My stomach seems to be hosting a symposium of bees.

"And the aroma! My God, what an aroma!" she cries. I think the flowers have hypnotized her. Wow. Maybe they do work. "Lucky Joe, what a gift, but I'm sorry, dear, he's not home. He said he'd be back soon though. I can put them in water and leave them for him in his room if you like."

I'm too disappointed to answer. I just nod and hand them over to her. I bet he's at Rachel's feeding her family chocolate croissants. I have a dreadful thought – what if the roses actually are love-inducing and Joe comes back here with Rachel and both of them fall under their spell? This was another disastrous idea, but I can't take the roses back now. Actually, I think it would take an automatic weapon to get them back from Mrs Fontaine, who is leaning farther into the bouquet with each passing second.

"Thank you," I say. "For giving them to him." Will she be able to separate herself from these flowers?

"It was very nice to meet you, Lennie. I'd been looking forward to it. I'm sure Joe will *really* appreciate these."

"Lennie," an exasperated voice says from behind me. That symposium in my belly just opened its doors to wasps and hornets too. This is it. I turn around and see Joe making his way up the path. There is no bounce in his walk. It's as if gravity has a hand on his shoulder that it never did before.

"Oh, honey!" Mrs Fontaine exclaims. "Look what Lennie brought you. Have you ever seen such roses. I sure haven't. My word." Mrs Fontaine is speaking directly to the roses now, taking in deep aromatic breaths. "Well, I'll just bring these in, find a nice place for them. You kids have fun…"

I watch her head disappear completely in the bouquet as the door closes behind her. I want to lunge at her, grab the flowers, shriek, *I need those roses more than you do, lady*, but I have a more pressing concern: Joe's silent fuming beside me.

As soon as the door clicks closed, he says, "You still don't get it, do you?" His voice is full of menace, not quite if a shark could talk, but close. He points at the door behind which dozens of aphrodisiacal roses are filling the air with promise. "You've got to be kidding. You think it's that easy?" His face is getting flushed, his eyes bulgy and wild. "I don't want tiny dresses or stupid fucking magic flowers!" He flails in place like a marionette. "I'm *already* in love with you, Lennie, don't you get it? But I can't be with you. Every time I close my eyes I see you with *him*."

I stand there dumbstruck – sure, there were some

259

discouraging things just said, but all of them seem to have fallen away. I'm left with six wonderful words: *I'm already in love with you*. Present tense, not past. Rachel Brazile be damned. A skyful of hope knocks into me.

"Let me explain," I say, intent on remembering my lines this time, intent on getting him to understand.

He makes a noise that's part groan, part roar, like *ahh-harrrrgh*, then says, "Nothing to explain. I saw you two. You lied to me over and over again."

"Toby and I were—"

He interrupts. "No way, I don't want to hear it. I told you what happened to me in France and you did this anyway. I can't forgive you. It's just the way I am. You have to leave me alone. I'm sorry."

My legs go weak as it sinks in that his hurt and anger, the sickness of having been deceived and betrayed, has already trumped his love.

He motions down the hill to where Toby and I were that night, and says, "What. Did. You. Expect?" What *did* I expect? One minute he's trying to tell me he loves me and the next he's watching me kiss another guy. Of course he feels this way.

I have to say something, so I say the only thing that makes sense in my mixed heart. "I'm so in love with you."

My words knock the wind out of him.

It's as if everything around us stops to see what's going to happen next – the trees lean in, birds hover, flowers hold their petals still. How could he not surrender to this crazy big love we both feel? He couldn't not, right?

I reach my hand out to touch him, but he moves his arm out of my reach.

He shakes his head, looks at the ground. "I can't be with someone who could do that to me." Then he looks right in my eyes, and says, "I can't be with someone who could do that to *her sister*."

The words have guillotine force. I stagger backward, splintering into pieces. His hand flies to his mouth. Maybe he's wishing his words back inside. Maybe he even thinks he went too far, but it doesn't matter. He wanted me to get it and I do.

I do the only thing I can. I turn around and run from him, hoping my trembling legs will keep me up until I can get away. Like Heathcliff and Cathy, I had the Big Bang, once-in-a-lifetime kind of love, and I destroyed it all.

All I want is to get up to The Sanctum so I can throw the covers over my head and disappear for several hundred years. Out of breath from racing down the hill, I push through the front door of the house. I blow past the kitchen, but backtrack when I glimpse Gram. She's sitting at the kitchen table, her arms folded in front of her chest, her face hard and stern. In front of her on the table are her garden shears and my copy of *Wuthering Heights*.

Uh-oh.

She jumps right in. "You have no idea how close I came to chopping your precious book to bits, but I have some self-control and respect for other people's things." She stands up. When Gram's mad, she practically doubles

261

in size and all twelve feet of her is bulldozing across the kitchen right at me.

"What were you thinking, Lennie? You come like the Grim Reaper and decimate my garden, my *roses*. How could you? You know how I feel about anyone but me touching my flowers. It's the one and only thing I ask. The one and only thing."

She's looming over me. "Well?"

"They'll grow back." I know this is the wrong thing to say, but holler-at-Lennie-day is taking its toll.

She throws her arms up, completely exasperated with me, and it strikes me how similar her expression and arm flailing resembles Joe's. "That is not the point and you know it." She points at me. "You've become very selfish, Lennie Walker."

This I was not expecting. No one's ever called me selfish in my life, least of all Gram – the never-ending fountain of praise and coddling. Are she and Joe testifying at the same trial?

Could this day get any worse?

Isn't the answer to that question always yes?

Gram's hands are on her hips now, face flushed, eyes blazing, double uh-oh – I lean back against the wall, brace myself for the impending assault. She leans in. "Yes, Lennie. You act like you're the only one in this house who has lost somebody. She was like my daughter, do you know what that's like? Do you? My *daughter*. No, you don't because you haven't once asked. Not once have you asked how I'm doing. Did it ever occur to you that I might need

262

to talk?" She is yelling now. "I know you're devastated, but, Lennie, you're not the only one."

All the air races out of the room, and I race out with it.

32

Bailey grabs my hand
and pulls me out of the window
into the sky,
pulls music out of my pockets.
"It's time you learned to fly,"
she says,

and vanishes.

I bolt down the hallway and out the door and jump all four porch steps. I want to run into the woods, veer off the path, find a spot where no one can find me, sit down under an old craggy oak and cry. I want to cry and cry and cry and cry until all the dirt in the whole forest floor has turned to mud. And this is exactly what I'm about to do except that when I hit the path, I realize I can't. I can't run away from Gram, especially not after everything she just said. Because I know she's right. She and Big have been like background noise to me since Bailey died.

I've hardly given any thought to what they're going through. I made Toby my ally in grief, like he and I had an exclusionary right to it, an exclusionary right to Bailey herself. I think of all the times Gram hovered at the door to The Sanctum trying to get me to talk about Bailey, asking me to come down and have a cup of tea, and how I just assumed she wanted to comfort me. It never once occurred to me that she needed to talk herself, that she needed *me*.

How could I have been so careless with her feelings? With Joe's? With everyone's?

I take a deep breath, turn around, and make my way back to the kitchen. I can't make things right with Joe, but at least I can try to make them right with Gram. She's in the same chair at the table. I stand across from her, rest my fingers on the table, wait for her to look up at me. Not one window is open, and the hot stuffy kitchen smells almost rotten.

"I'm sorry," I say. "Really." She nods, looks down at her hands. It occurs to me that I've disappointed or hurt or betrayed everyone I love in the last couple months: Gram, Bailey, Joe, Toby, Sarah, even Big. How did I manage that? Before Bailey died, I don't think I ever really disappointed anyone. Did Bailey just take care of everyone and everything for me? Or did no one expect anything of me before? Or did I just not do anything or want anything before, so I never had to deal with the consequences of my messed-up actions? Or have I become really selfish and self-absorbed? Or all of the above?

I look at the sickly Lennie houseplant on the counter and know that it's not me anymore. It's who I used to be, before, and that's why it's dying. That me is gone.

"I don't know who I am," I say, sitting down. "I can't be who I was, not without her, and who I'm becoming is a total screw-up."

Gram doesn't deny it. She's still mad, not twelve feet of mad, but plenty mad.

"We could go out to lunch in the city next week, spend the whole day together," I add, feeling puny, trying to make up for months of ignoring her with a lunch.

She nods, but that is not what's on her mind. "Just so you know, I don't know who I am without her either."

"Really?"

266

She shakes her head. "Nope. Every day, after you and Big leave, all I do is stand in front of a blank canvas thinking how much I despise the color green, how every single shade of it disgusts me or disappoints me or breaks my heart." Sadness fills me. I imagine all the green willowy women sliding out of their canvases and slinking their way out the front door.

"I get it," I say quietly.

Gram closes her eyes. Her hands are folded one on top of the other on the table. I reach out and put my hand over hers and she quickly sandwiches it.

"It's horrible," she whispers.

"It is," I say.

The early-afternoon light drains out the windows, zebraing the room with long dark shadows. Gram looks old and tired and it makes me feel desolate. Bailey, Uncle Big and I have been her whole life, except for a few generations of flowers and a lot of green paintings.

"You know what else I hate?" she says. "I hate that everyone keeps telling me that I carry Bailey in my heart. I want to holler at them: *I don't want her there*. I want her in the kitchen with Lennie and me. I want her at the river with Toby and their baby. I want her to be Juliet and Lady Macbeth, you stupid, stupid people. Bailey doesn't want to be trapped in my heart or anyone else's." Gram pounds her fist on the table. I squeeze it with my hands and nod *yes*, and feel *yes*, a giant, pulsing, angry yes that passes from her to me. I look down at our hands and catch sight of *Wuthering Heights* lying there silent and helpless and ornery as

267

ever. I think about all the wasted lives, all the wasted love crammed inside it.

"Gram, do it."

"What? Do what?" she asks.

I pick up the book and the shears, hold them out to her. "Just do it, chop it to bits. Here." I slip my fingers and thumb into the handle of the garden shears just like I did this morning, but this time I feel no fear, just that wild, pulsing, pissed off *yes* coursing through me as I take a cut of a book that I've underlined and annotated, a book that is creased and soiled with years of me, years of river water, and summer sun, and sand from the beach, and sweat from my palms, a book bent to the curves of my waking and sleeping body. I take another cut, slicing through chunks of paper at a time, through all the tiny words, cutting the passionate, hopeless story to pieces, slashing their lives, their impossible love, the whole mess and tragedy of it. I'm attacking it now, enjoying the swish of the blades, the metal scrape after each delicious cut. I cut into Heathcliff, poor, heartsick, embittered Heathcliff and stupid Cathy for her bad choices and unforgivable compromises. And while I'm at it, I take a swipe at Joe's jealousy and anger and judgment, at his *dickhead-him* inability to forgive. I hack away at his ridiculous all-or-nothing-horn-player bullshit, and then I lay into my own duplicity and deceptiveness and confusion and hurt and bad judgment and overwhelming, never-ending grief. I cut and cut and cut at everything I can think of that is keeping Joe and me from having this great big beautiful love while we can.

Gram is wide-eyed, mouth agape. But then I see a faint smile find her lips. She says, "Here, let me have a go." She takes the shears and starts cutting, tentatively at first, but then she gets carried away just as I had, and starts hacking at handfuls and handfuls of pages until words fly all around us like confetti.

Gram's laughing. "Well, that was unexpected." We are both out of breath, spent, and smiling giddily.

"I am related to you, aren't I?" I say.

"Oh, Lennie, I have missed you." She pulls me into her lap like I'm five years old. I think I'm forgiven.

"Sorry I hollered, sweet pea," she says, hugging me into her warmth.

I squeeze her back. "Should I make us some tea?" I ask.

"You better, we have lots of catching up to do. But first things first, you destroyed my whole garden, I have to know if it worked."

I hear again: *I can't be with someone who could do that to her sister*, and my heart squeezes so tight in my chest, I can barely breathe. "Not a chance. It's over."

Gram says quietly, "I saw what happened that night." I tense up even more, slide out of her lap and go over to fill the tea kettle. I suspected Gram saw Toby and me kiss, but the reality of her witnessing it sends shame shifting around within me. I can't look at her. "Lennie?" Her voice isn't incriminating. I relax a little. "Listen to me."

I turn around slowly and face her.

She waves her hand around her head like she's shooing a fly. "I won't say it didn't render me speechless

269

for a minute or two." She smiles. "But crazy things like that happen when people are this shocked and grief-stricken. I'm surprised we're all still standing."

I can't believe how readily Gram is pushing this aside, absolving me. I want to fall to her feet in gratitude. She definitely did not confer with Joe on the matter, but it makes his words sting less, and it gives me the courage to ask, "Do you think she'd ever forgive me?"

"Oh, sweet pea, trust me on this one, she already has." Gram wags her finger at me. "Now, Joe is another story. He'll need some time…"

"Like thirty years," I say.

"Woohoo – poor boy, that was an eyeful, Lennie Walker." Gram looks at me mischievously. She has snapped back into her sassy self. "Yes, Len, when you and Joe Fontaine are forty-seven—" She laughs. "We'll plan a beautiful, beautiful wedding—"

She stops mid-sentence because she must notice my face. I don't want to kill her cheer, so I'm using every muscle in it to hide my heartbreak, but I've lost the battle.

"Lennie." She comes over to me.

"He hates me," I tell her.

"No," she says warmly. "If ever there was a boy in love, sweet pea, it's Joe Fontaine."

33

Gram made me go to the doctor
to see if there was something wrong
with my heart.
After a bunch of tests, the doctor said:
Lennie, you _lucked_ out.
I wanted to punch him in the face,
but instead I started to cry
in a drowning kind of way.

I couldn't believe

I had a lucky heart

when what I wanted

was the same kind of heart

as Bailey.

I didn't hear Gram come in,
or come up behind me,
just felt her arms slip around my shaking frame,
then the press of both her hands hard
against my chest, holding it all in,

holding me together.
Thank God, she whispered,
before the doctor or I could utter a word.
How could she have possibly known
that I'd gotten good news?

*(Found on the back of an envelope on the trail
to the forest bedroom)*

When the tea is in the mugs, the window's opened, and Gram and I have relaxed into the waning light, I say quietly, "I want to talk to you about something."

"Anything, sweet pea."

"I want to talk about Mom."

She sighs, leans back in her chair. "I know." She crosses her arms, holding both elbows, cradling herself. "I was up in the attic. You put the box back on a different shelf—"

"I didn't read much … sorry."

"No, I'm the one who's sorry. I've wanted to talk to you about Paige these last few months, but…"

"I wouldn't let you talk to me about anything."

She nods slightly. Her face is about as serious as I've ever seen it. She says, "Bailey shouldn't have died knowing so little about her mother."

I drop my eyes. It's true – I was wrong to think Bailey wouldn't want to know everything that I do, whether it hurts or not. I rake my fingers around in the remains of *Wuthering Heights*, waiting for Gram to speak.

When she does, her voice is strained, tight. "I thought I was protecting you girls, but now I'm pretty sure I was just protecting myself." I lift my gaze to meet hers. "It's so hard for me to speak about her. I told myself the better

272

you girls knew her, the more it would hurt." She sweeps some of the book to herself. "I focused on the restlessness, so you girls wouldn't feel so abandoned, wouldn't blame her, or worse, blame yourselves. I wanted you to admire her. That's it."

That's it? Heat rushes up my body. Gram reaches her hand to mine. I slip it away from her.

I say, "You just made up a story so we wouldn't feel abandoned..." I raise my eyes to hers, continue despite the pain in her face. "But we *were* abandoned, Gram, and we didn't know why, don't know anything about her except some crazy story." I feel like scooping up a fistful of *Wuthering Heights* and hurling it at her. "Why not just tell us she's crazy if she is? Why not tell the truth whatever it is? Wouldn't that have been better?"

She grabs my wrist, harder than I think she intended. "But there's not just one truth, Lennie, there never is. What I told you wasn't some story I made up." She's trying to be calm, but I can tell she's moments away from doubling in size. "Yes, it's true that Paige wasn't a stable girl. I mean, who in their proper tree leaves two little girls and doesn't come back?" She lets go of my wrist now that she has my full attention. She looks wildly around the room as if the words she needs might be on the walls. After a moment, she says, "Your mother was an irresponsible tornado of a girl and I'm sure she's an irresponsible tornado of a woman. But it's also true that she's not the first tornado to blast through this family, not the first one who's disappeared like this either. Sylvie swung back into town in that beat-up yellow

Cadillac after twenty years' drifting around. Twenty years!" She bangs her fist on the table, hard, the piles of *Wuthering Heights* jump with the impact. "Yes, maybe some doctor could give it a name, a diagnosis, but what difference does it make what we call it, it still is what it is, we call it the restless gene, so what? It's as true as anything else."

She takes a sip of her tea, burns her tongue. "Ow," she exclaims uncharacteristically, fanning her mouth.

"Big thinks you have it too," I say. "The restless gene." I'm rearranging words into new sentences on the table. I peek up at her, afraid by her silence that this admission might not have gone over very well.

Her brow's furrowed. "He said that?" Gram's joined me in mixing the words around on the table. I see she's put *under that benign sky* next to *so eternally secluded*.

"He thinks you just bottle it up," I say.

She's stopped shuffling words. There's something very un-Gram in her face, something darting and skittish. She won't meet my eyes, and then I recognize what it is because I've become quite familiar with it myself recently – it's shame.

"What, Gram?"

She's pressing her lips together so tightly, they've gone white; it's like she's trying to seal them, to make sure no words come out.

"What?"

She gets up, walks over to the counter, cradles up against it, looks out the window at a passing kingdom of clouds. I watch her back and wait. "I've been hiding inside

274

that story, Lennie, and I made you girls, and Big, for that matter, hide in it with me."

"But you just said—"

"I know – it's not that it isn't true, but it's also true that blaming things on destiny and genes is a helluva lot easier than blaming them on myself."

"On yourself?"

She nods, doesn't say anything else, just continues to stare out the window.

I feel a chill creep up my spine. "Gram?"

She's turned away from me so I can't see the expression on her face. I don't know why, but I feel afraid of her, like she's slipped into the skin of someone else. Even the way she's holding her body is different, crumpled almost. When she finally speaks, her voice is too deep and calm. "I remember everything about that night..." she says, then pauses, and I think about running out of the room, away from this crumpled Gram who talks like she's in a trance. "I remember how cold it was, unseasonably so, how the kitchen was full of lilacs – I'd filled all the vases earlier in the day because she was coming." I can tell by Gram's voice she's smiling now and I relax a little. "She was wearing this long green dress, more like a giant scarf really, totally inappropriate, which was Paige – it's like she had her own weather around her always." I've never heard any of this about my mother, never heard about anything as real as a green dress, a kitchen full of flowers. But then Gram's tone changes again. "She was so upset that night, pacing around the kitchen, no not pacing, billowing back and forth in that

275

scarf. I remember thinking she's like a trapped wind, a wild gale imprisoned in this kitchen with me, like if I opened a window she'd be gone."

Gram turns toward me as if finally remembering I'm in the room. "Your mother was at the end of her rope and she never was someone with a lot of rope on hand. She'd come for the weekend so I could see you girls. At least that's why I'd thought she'd come, until she began asking me what I'd do if she left. 'Left?' I said to her, 'Where? For how long?' which is when I found out she had a plane ticket to God knows where, she wouldn't say, and planned on using it — a one-way ticket. She told me she couldn't do it, that she didn't have it right inside to be a mother. I told her that her insides were right enough, that she couldn't leave, that you girls were her responsibility. I told her that she had to buck up like every other mother on this earth. I told her that you could all live here, that'd I'd help her, but she couldn't just up and go like those others in this crazy family, I wouldn't have it. 'But if I did leave,' she kept insisting, 'what would you do?' Over and over she asked it. I remember I kept trying to hold her by her arms, to get her to snap out of it, like I'd do when she was young and would get wound up, but she kept slipping out of my grasp like she was made of air." Gram takes a deep breath. "At this point, I was very upset myself, and you know how I get when I blow. I started shouting. I do have my share of the tornado inside, that's for sure, especially when I was younger, Big's right." She sighs. "I lost it, really lost it. 'What do you think I'd do if you left?' I hollered. 'They're my granddaughters, but, Paige, if you leave you can

276

never come back. Never. You'll be dead to them, dead in their hearts, and dead to me. Dead. To all of us.' My exact despicable words. Then I locked myself in my art room for the rest of the night. The next morning – she was gone."

I've fallen back into my chair, boneless. Gram stands across the room in a prison of shadows. "I told your mother to never come back."

She'll be back, girls.

A prayer, never a promise.

Her voice is barely above a whisper. "I'm sorry."

Her words have moved through me like fast-moving storm clouds, transforming the landscape. I look around at her framed green ladies, three of them in the kitchen alone, women caught somewhere between here and there – each one Paige, all of them Paige in a billowy green dress, I'm sure of it now. I think about the ways Gram made sure our mother never died in our hearts, made sure Paige Walker never bore any blame for leaving her children. I think about how, unbeknownst to us, Gram culled that blame for herself.

I remember the ugly thing I'd thought that night at the top of the stairs when I overheard her apologizing to The Half Mom. I'd blamed her too. For things even the almighty Gram can't control.

"It's not your fault," I say, with a certainty in my voice I've never heard before. "It never was, Gram. *She* left. *She* didn't come back – her choice, not yours, no matter what you said to her."

Gram exhales like she's been holding her breath for sixteen years.

277

"Oh, Lennie," she cries. "I think you just opened the window" – she touches her chest – "and let her out."

I rise from my chair and walk over to her, realizing for the first time that she's lost two daughters – I don't know how she bears it. I realize something else too. I don't share this double grief. I have a mother and I'm standing so close to her, I can see the years weighing down her skin, can smell her tea-scented breath. I wonder if Bailey's search for Mom would have led her here too, right back to Gram. I hope so. I gently put my hand on her arm wondering how such a huge love for someone can fit in my tiny body. "Bailey and I are so lucky we got you," I say. "We scored."

She closes her eyes for a moment, and then the next thing I know I'm in her arms and she's squeezing me so as to crush every bone. "I'm the one who lucked out," she says into my hair. "And now I think we need to drink our tea. Enough of this."

As I make my way back to the table, something becomes clear: life's a freaking mess. In fact, I'm going to tell Sarah we need to start a new philosophical movement: messessentialism instead of existentialism: for those who revel in the essential mess that is life. Because Gram's right, there's not one truth ever, just a whole bunch of stories, all going on at once, in our heads, in our hearts, all getting in the way of each other. It's all a beautiful calamitous mess. It's like the day Mr James took us into the woods and cried triumphantly, "That's it! That's it!" to the dizzying cacophony of soloing instruments trying to make music together. That is it.

I look down at the piles of words that used to be my favorite book. I want to put the story back together again so Cathy and Heathcliff can make different choices, can stop getting in the way of themselves at every turn, can follow their raging, volcanic hearts right into each other's arms. But I can't. I go to the sink, pull out the trash can, and sweep Cathy and Heathcliff and the rest of their unhappy lot into it.

Later that evening, I'm playing Joe's melody over and over on the porch, trying to think of books where love actually triumphs in the end. There's Lizzie Bennet and Darcy, and Jane Eyre ends up with Mr Rochester, that's good, but he had that wife locked up for a while, which freaks me out. There's Florentino Aziza in *Love in the Time of Cholera*, but he had to wait over fifty years for Fermina, only for them to end up on a ship going nowhere. Ugh. I'd say there's slim literary pickings on this front, which depresses me; how could true love so infrequently prevail in the classics? And more importantly, how can I make it prevail for Joe and me? If only I could convert him to messessentialism … *If only I had wheels on my ass, I'd be a trolley cart.* After all that he said today, I think that about covers my chances.

I'm playing his song for probably the fiftieth time when I realize Gram's in the doorway listening to me. I thought she was locked away in the art room recovering from the emotional tumult of our afternoon. I stop mid-note, suddenly self-conscious. She opens the door, strides out with the mahogany box from the attic in her hands. "What a lovely melody. Bet I could play it myself at this point," she says, rolling her eyes as she puts the box on the table and drops into the love seat. "Though it's very nice to hear you playing again."

I decide to tell her. "I'm going to try for first chair again this fall."

"Oh, sweet pea," she sings. Literally. "Music to my tin ears."

I smile, but inside, my stomach is roiling. I'm planning on telling Rachel next practice. It'd be so much easier if I could just pour a bucket of water on her like the Wicked Witch of the West.

"Come sit down." Gram taps the cushion next to her. I join her, resting my clarinet across my knees. She puts her hand on the box. "Everything in here is yours to read. Open all the envelopes. Read my notes, the letters. Just be prepared, it's not all pretty, especially the earlier letters."

I nod. "Thank you."

"All right." She removes her hand from the box. "I'm going to take a walk to town, meet Big at The Saloon. I need a stiff drink." She ruffles my hair, then leaves the box and me to ourselves.

After putting my clarinet away, I sit with the box on my lap, trailing circles around the ring of galloping horses with my fingers. Around and around. I want to open it, and I also don't want to. It's probably the closest I'll ever get to knowing my mother, whoever she is – adventurer or wack job, heroine or villain, probably just a very troubled, complicated woman.

I look out at the gang of oaks across the road, at the Spanish moss hanging over their stooped shoulders like decrepit shawls, the gray, gnarled lot of them like a band of wise old men pondering a verdict—

The door squeaks. I turn to see that Gram has put on a bright pink floral no-clue-what – a coat? A cape? A shower curtain? – over an even brighter purple flowered frock. Her hair is down and wild; it looks like it conducts electricity. She has make-up on, an eggplant-color lipstick, cowboy boots to house her Big Foot feet. She looks beautiful and insane. It's the first time she's gone out at night since Bailey died. She waves at me, winks, then heads down the steps. I watch her stroll across the yard. Right as she hits the road, she turns back, holds her hair so the breeze doesn't blow it back into her eyes.

"Hey, I give Big one month, you?"

"Are you kidding? Two weeks, tops."

"It's your turn to be best man."

"That's fine," I say, smiling.

She smiles back at me, humor peeking out of her queenly face. Even though we pretend otherwise, nothing quite raises Walker spirits like the thought of another wedding for Uncle Big.

"Be okay, sweet pea," she says. "You know where we are…"

"I'll be fine," I say, feeling the weight of the box on my legs.

As soon as she's gone, I open the lid. I'm ready. All these notes, all these letters, sixteen years' worth. I think about Gram jotting down a recipe, a thought, a silly or not-so-pretty something she wanted to share with her daughter, or just remember herself, maybe stuffing it in her pocket all day, and then sneaking up to the attic before bed, to put it in this box, this mailbox with no pickup, year after year, not knowing if her daughter would ever read them, not knowing if anyone would—

I gasp, because isn't that just exactly what I've been doing too: writing poems and scattering them to the winds with the same hope as Gram that someone, someday, somewhere might understand who I am, who my sister was, and what happened to us.

I take out the envelopes, count them – fifteen, all with the name *Paige* and the year. I find the first one, written sixteen years ago by Gram to her daughter. Slipping my finger under the seal, I imagine Bailey sitting beside me. *Okay*, I tell her, taking out the letter, *Let's meet our mother*.

Okay to everything. I'm a messessentialist – okay to it all.

34

The Shaw Ranch presides over Clover. Its acreage rolls in green and gold majesty from the ridge all the way down to town. I walk through the iron gate and make my way to the stables, where I find Toby inside talking to a beautiful black mare as he takes her saddle off.

"Don't mean to interrupt," I say, walking over to him.

He turns around. "Wow, Lennie."

We're smiling at each other like idiots. I thought it might be weird to see him, but we both seem to be acting pretty much thrilled. It embarrasses me, so I drop my gaze to the mare between us and stroke her warm moist coat. Heat radiates off her body.

Toby flicks the end of the reins lightly across my hand. "I've missed you."

"Me too, you." But, I realize with some relief that my stomach isn't fluttering, even with our eyes locked as they now are. Not even a twitter. Is the spell broken? The horse snorts – perfect: thanks, Black Beauty.

"Want to go for a ride?" he asks. "We could go up on the ridge. I was just up there. There's a massive herd of elk roaming."

"Actually, Toby … I thought maybe we could visit Bailey."

"Okay," he says, without thinking, like I asked him to get an ice cream. Strange.

I told myself I would never go back to the cemetery. No one talks about decaying flesh and maggots and skeletons, but how can you not think of those things? I've done everything in my power to keep those thoughts out of my mind, and staying away from Bailey's grave has been crucial to that end. But last night, I was fingering all the things on her dresser like I always do before I go to sleep, and I realized that she wouldn't want me clinging to the black hair webbed in her hairbrush or the rank laundry I still refuse to wash. She'd think it was totally gross: Lady-Havisham-and-her-wedding-dress gross and dismal. I got an image of her then sitting on the hill at the Clover cemetery with its ancient oaks, firs and redwoods like a queen holding court, and I knew it was time.

Even though the cemetery is close enough to walk, when Toby's finished, we jump in his truck. He puts the key in the ignition, but doesn't turn it. He stares straight through the windshield at the golden meadows, tapping on the wheel with two fingers in a staccato rhythm. I can tell he's revving up to say something. I rest my head on the passenger window and look out at the fields, imagining his life here, how solitary it must be. A minute or two later, he starts talking in his low lulling bass. "I've always hated being an only child. Used to envy you guys. You were just so tight."

He grips his hands on the wheel, stares straight ahead. "I was so psyched to marry Bails, to have this baby ... I was psyched to be part of your family. It's going to sound so lame now, but I thought I could help you through this.

I wanted to. I know Bailey would've wanted me to." He shakes his head. "Sure screwed it all up. I just … I don't know. You understood… It's like you were the only one who did. I started to feel so close to you, too close. It got all mixed up in my head—"

"But you did help me," I interrupt. "You were the only one who could even find me. I felt that same closeness even if I didn't understand it. I don't know what I would have done without you."

He turns to me. "Yeah?"

"Yeah, Toby."

He smiles his squintiest, sweetest smile. "Well, I'm pretty sure I can keep my hands off you now. I don't know about your frisky self though…" He raises his eyebrows, gives me a look, then laughs an unburdened free laugh. I punch his arm. He goes on, "So, maybe we'll be able to hang out a little – I don't think I can keep saying no to Gram's dinner invitations without her sending out the National Guard."

"I can't believe you just made two jokes in one sentence. Amazing."

"I'm not a total doorknob, you know?"

"Guess not. There must have been some reason my sister wanted to spend the rest of her life with you!" And just like that, it feels right between us, finally.

"Well," he says, starting the truck. "Shall we cheer ourselves up with a trip to the cemetery?"

"Three jokes, unbelievable."

However, that was probably Toby's word allotment for

the year, I'm thinking as we drive along now in silence. A silence that is full of jitters. Mine. I'm nervous. I'm not sure what I'm afraid of really. I keep telling myself, it's just a stone, it's just a pretty piece of land with gorgeous stately trees overlooking the falls. It's just a place where my beautiful sister's body is in a box decaying in a sexy black dress and sandals. Ugh. I can't help it. Everything I haven't allowed myself to imagine rushes me: I think about airless empty lungs. Lipstick on her unmoving mouth. The silver bracelet that Toby had given her on her pulseless wrist. Her belly ring. Hair and nails growing in the dark. Her body with no thoughts in it. No time in it. No love in it. Six feet of earth crushing down on her. I think about the phone ringing in the kitchen, the thump of Gram collapsing, then the inhuman sound sirening out of her, through the floorboards, up to our room.

I look over at Toby. He doesn't look nervous at all. Something occurs to me.

"Have you been?" I ask.

"Course," he answers. "Almost every day."

"Really?"

He looks over at me, the realization dawning on him. "You mean you haven't been since?"

"No." I look out the window. I'm a terrible sister. Good sisters visit graves despite gruesome thoughts.

"Gram goes," he says. "She planted a few rosebushes, a bunch of other flowers too. The grounds people told her she had to get rid of them, but every time they pulled out her plants, she just replanted more. They finally gave up."

286

I can't believe everyone's been going to Bailey's grave but me. I can't believe how left out it makes me feel.

"What about Big?" I ask.

"I find roaches from his joints a lot. We hung out there a couple times." He looks over at me, studies my face for what feels like forever. "It'll be okay, Len. Easier than you think. I was really scared the first time I went."

Something occurs to me then. "Toby," I say, tentatively, mustering my nerve. "You must be pretty used to being an only child…" My voice starts to shake. "But I'm really new at it." I look out the window. "Maybe we…" I feel too shy all of a sudden to finish my thought, but he knows what I'm getting at.

"I've always wanted a sister," he says as he swerves into a spot in the tiny parking lot.

"Good," I say, every inch of me relieved. I lean over and give him the world's most sexless peck on the cheek. "C'mon," I say. "Let's go tell her we're sorry."

35

There once was a girl who found herself dead.
She spent her days peering
over the ledge of heaven,
her chin in her palm.
She was bored as a brick,
hadn't adjusted yet
to the slower pace of ~~the~~ heavenly life.

Her sister would look up at her
and wave,
and the dead girl would wave back
but she was too far away
for her sister to see.
The dead girl thought her sister

might be writing her notes,
but it was too long a trip to make
for a few scattered notes here and there
so she let them be.
And then, one day, her earthbound sister finally realized

she could hear music up there in heaven,
so after that, everything her sister needed to tell her
she did through her clarinet

and each time she played, the dead girl

jumped up (no matter what else she was doing),
and danced.

*(Found on a piece of paper in the stacks, B section,
Clover Public Library)*

I have a plan. I'm going to write Joe a poem, but first things first.

When I walk into the music room, I see that Rachel's already there unpacking her instrument. This is it. My hand is so clammy I'm afraid the handle on my case will slip out of it as I cross the room and stand in front of her.

"If it isn't John Lennon," she says without looking up. Could she be so awful as to rub Joe's nickname in my face? Obviously, yes. Well, good, because fury seems to calm my nerves. Race on.

"I'm challenging you for first chair," I say, and wild applause bursts from a spontaneous standing ovation in my brain. Never have words felt so good coming out of my mouth! Hmm. Even if Rachel doesn't appear to have heard them. She's still messing with her reed and ligature like the bell didn't go off, like the starting gate didn't just swing open.

I'm about to repeat myself, when she says, "There's nothing there, Lennie." She spits my name on the floor like it disgusts her. "He's so hung up on you. Who knows why?"

Could this moment get any better? No! I try to keep my cool. "This has nothing to do with him," I say, and nothing could be more true. It has nothing to do with her either, not really, though I don't say that. It's about me and my clarinet.

"Yeah, right," she says. "You're just doing this because you saw me with him."

"No." My voice surprises me again with its certainty. "I want the solos, Rachel." At that she stops fiddling with her clarinet, rests it on the stand, and looks up at me. "And I'm starting up again with Marguerite." This I decided on the way to rehearsal. I have her undivided totally freaked-out attention now. "I'm going to try for All-State too," I tell her. This, however, is news to me.

We stare at each other and for the first time I wonder if she's known all year that I threw the audition. I wonder if that's why she's been so horrible. Maybe she thought she could intimidate me into not challenging her. Maybe she thought that was the only way to keep her chair.

She bites her lip. "How about if I split the solos with you. And you can—"

I shake my head. I almost feel sorry for her. Almost.

"Come September," I say. "May the best clarinettist win."

Not just my ass, but every inch of me is in the wind as I fly out of the music room, away from school, and into the woods to go home and write the poem to Joe. Beside me, step for step, breath for breath, is the unbearable fact that I have a future and Bailey doesn't.

This is when I know it.

My sister will die over and over again for the rest of my

life. Grief is forever. It doesn't go away; it becomes part of you, step for step, breath for breath. I will never stop grieving Bailey because I will never stop loving her. That's just how it is. Grief and love are conjoined, you don't get one without the other. All I can do is love her and love the world, emulate her by living with daring and spirit and joy.

Without thinking, I veer onto the trail to the forest bedroom. All around me, the woods are in an uproar of beauty. Sunlight cascades through the trees, making the fern-covered floor look jeweled and incandescent. Rhododendron bushes sweep past me right and left like women in fabulous dresses. I want to wrap my arms around all of it.

When I get to the forest bedroom, I hop onto the bed and make myself comfortable. I'm going to take my time with this poem, not like all the others I scribbled and scattered. I take the pen out of my pocket, a piece of blank sheet music out of my bag, and start writing.

I tell him everything – everything he means to me, everything I felt with him that I never felt before, everything I hear in his music. I want him to trust me so I bare all. I tell him I belong to him, that my heart is his, and even if he never forgives me it will still be the case.

It's my story, after all, and this is how I choose to tell it.

When I'm done, I scoot off the bed and as I do, I notice a blue guitar pick lying on the white comforter. I must have been sitting on it all afternoon. I lean over and pick it up, and recognize it right away as Joe's. He must've come here to play – a good sign. I decide to leave the poem here for him instead of sneaking it inside the Fontaine mailbox like I had planned. I fold it, write his name on it, and place it on the bed under a rock to secure it from the wind. I tuck his pick under the rock as well.

Walking home, I realize it's the first time since Bailey died that I've written words for someone to read.

36

I'm too mortified to sleep. What was I thinking? I keep imagining Joe reading my ridiculous poem to his brothers, and worse to Rachel, all of them laughing at poor lovelorn Lennie, who knows nothing about romance except what she learned from Emily Brontë. I told him: *I belong to him*. I told him: *My heart is his*. I told him: *I hear his soul in his music*. I'm going to jump off of a building. Who says things like this in the twenty-first century? No one! How is it possible that something can seem like such a brilliant idea one day and such a bonehead one the next?

As soon as there's enough light, I throw a sweatshirt over my pajamas, put on some sneakers, and run through the dawn to the forest bedroom to retrieve the note, but when I get there, it's gone. I tell myself that the wind blew it away like all the other poems. I mean, how likely is it that Joe showed up yesterday afternoon after I left? Not likely at all.

Sarah is keeping me company, providing humiliation support while I make lasagnas.

She can't stop squealing. "You're going to be first clarinet, Lennie. For sure."

"We'll see."

"It'll really help you get into a conservatory. Juilliard even."

I take a deep breath. How like an imposter I'd felt every time Marguerite mentioned it, how like a traitor, conspiring to steal my sister's dream, just as it got swiped from her. Why didn't it occur to me then I could dream alongside her? Why wasn't I brave enough to have a dream at all?

"I'd love to go to Juilliard," I tell Sarah. There. Finally. "But any good conservatory would be okay." I just want to study music: what life, what living itself sounds like.

"We could go together," Sarah's saying, while shoveling into her mouth each slice of mozzarella as I cut it. I slap her hand. She continues, "Get an apartment together in New York City." I think Sarah might rocket into outer space at the idea – me too, though, I, pathetically, keep thinking: What about Joe? "Or Berklee in Boston," she says, her big blue eyes boinging out of her head. "Don't forget Berklee. Either way, we could drive there in Ennui, zigzag our way across. Hang out at the Grand Canyon, go to New Orleans, maybe—"

"Ughhhhhhhhhhhhhhhhhh," I groan.

"Not the poem again. What could be a better distraction than the divine goddesses Juilliard and Berklee. Sheesh. Unfreakingbelievable…"

"You have no idea how dildonic it was."

"*Nice* word, Len." She's flipping through a magazine someone left on the counter.

"*Lame* isn't lame enough of a word for this poem," I mutter. "Sarah, I told a guy that *I belong to him*."

"That's what happens when you read *Wuthering Heights* eighteen times."

"Twenty-three."

I'm layering away: sauce, noodles, *I belong to you*, cheese, sauce, *my heart is yours*, noodles, cheese, *I hear your soul in your music*, cheese, cheese, CHEESE…

She's smiling at me. "You know, it might be okay, he seems kind of the same way."

"What way?"

"You know, like you."

Bails?

Yeah.

Can you believe Cathy married Edgar Linton?

No.

I mean what she had with Heathcliff,

how could she have just thrown it away?

I don't know. What is it, Len?

What's what?

What's with you and that book already?

I don't know.

Yes you do. Tell me.

It's cornball.

c'mon, Len.

I guess I want it.

What?

To feel that kind of love.

You will.

How do you know?

Just do.

The toes knows?

The toes knows.

But if I find it,

     I don't want to screw it all up like they did.

You won't. The toes knows that, too.

Night, Bails.

Len, I was just thinking something . . .

What?

In the end Cathy and Heathcliff are together,

Love is stronger than anything, even death.

Hmm . . .

Night, Len.

*(Found on a folded-up piece of music paper,
in the parking lot, Clover High)*

I tell myself it's ridiculous to go all the way back to the forest bedroom, that there's no way in the world he's going to be there, that no New Age meets Victorian Age poem is going to make him trust me, that I'm sure he still hates me, and now thinks I'm dildonic on top of it.

But here I am, and of course, here he's not. I flop onto my back on the bed. I look up at the patches of blue sky through the trees, and adhering to the regularly scheduled programming, I think some more about Joe. There's so much I don't know about him. I don't know if he believes in God, or likes macaroni and cheese, or what sign he is, or if he dreams in English or French, or what it would feel like – uh-oh. I'm headed from PG to XXX because, oh God, I really wish Joe didn't hate me so much, because I want to do *everything* with him. I'm so fed up with my virginity. It's like the whole world is in on this ecstatic secret but me—

I hear something then: a strange, mournful, decidedly unforest-like sound. I pick my head up and rest on my elbows so I can listen harder and try to isolate the sound from the rustling leaves and the distant river roar and the birds chattering all around me. The sound trickles through the trees, getting louder by the minute, closer. I keep listening, and then I recognize what it is, the notes, clear and perfect now, winding and wending their way to me – the melody from Joe's duet. I close my eyes and hope I'm really hearing a clarinet and it's not just some auditory hallucination inside my lovesick head. It's not, because now I hear steps shuffling through the brush and within a couple minutes the music stops and then the steps.

I'm afraid to open my eyes, but I do, and he's standing at the edge of the bed looking down at me – an army of ninja-cupids who must have all been hiding out in the canopy draw their bows and release – arrows fly at me from every which way.

"I thought you might be here." I can't read his expression. Nervous? Angry? His face seems restless like it doesn't know what to emote. "I got your poem…"

I can hear the blood rumbling through my body, drumming in my ears. What's he going to say? I got your poem and I'm sorry, I just can't ever forgive you. I got your poem and I feel the same way – *my heart is yours, John Lennon*. I got your poem and I've already called the psych ward – I have a straitjacket in this backpack. Strange. I've never seen Joe wear a backpack.

He's biting his lip, tapping his clarinet on his leg. Definitely nervous. This can't be good.

"Lennie, I got *all* your poems." What's he talking about? What does he mean *all* my poems? He slides the clarinet between his thighs to hold it and takes off his backpack, unzips it. Then he takes a deep breath, pulls out a box, hands it to me. "Well, probably not all of them, but these."

I open the lid. Inside are scraps of paper, napkins, takeaway cups, all with my words on them. The bits and pieces of Bailey and me that I scattered and buried and hid. This is not possible.

"How?" I ask, bewildered, and starting to get uneasy thinking about Joe reading everything in this box. All these private desperate moments. This is worse than having someone read your journal. This is like having someone read the journal that you thought you'd burned. And how did he get them all? Has he been following me around? That would be perfect. I finally fall in love with someone and he's a total freaking maniac.

I look at him. He's smirking a little and I see the faintest: bat. bat. bat. "I know what you're thinking," he says. "That I'm the creepy stalker dude."

Bingo.

He's amused. "I'm not, Len. It just kept happening. At first I kept finding them, and then, well, I started looking. I just couldn't help it. It became like this weird-ass treasure hunt. Remember that first day in the tree?"

I nod. But something even more amazing than Joe being a crazy stalker and finding my poems has just occurred to me – he's not angry anymore. Was it the dildonic poem? Whatever it was I'm caught in such a ferocious uprising of joy I'm not even listening to him as he tries to explain how in the world these poems ended up in this shoebox and not in some trash heap or blowing through Death Valley on a gust of wind.

I try to tune in to what he's saying. "Remember in the tree I told you that I'd seen you up at The Great Meadow?

299

I told you that I'd watched you writing a note, watched you drop it as you walked away. But I didn't tell you that after you left, I went over and found the piece of paper caught in the fence. It was a poem about Bailey. I guess I shouldn't have kept it. I was going to give it back to you that day in the tree, I had it in my pocket, but then I thought you'd think it was strange that I took it in the first place, so I just kept it." He's biting his lip. I remember him telling me that day he saw me drop something I'd written, but it never occurred to me he would go *find* it and *read* it. He continues, "And then, while we were in the tree, I saw words scrawled on the branches, thought maybe you'd written something else, but I felt weird asking, so I went back another time and wrote it down in a notebook."

I can't believe this. I sit up, fish through the box, looking more closely this time. There are some scraps in his weirdo Unabomber handwriting – probably transcribed from walls or sides of barns or some of the other practical writing surfaces that I found. I'm not sure how to feel. He knows everything – I'm inside out.

His face is caught between worry and excitement, but excitement seems to be winning out. He's pretty much bursting to go on. "That first time I was at your house, I saw one sticking out from under a stone in Gram's garden, and then another one on the sole of your shoe, and then that day when we moved all the stuff, man … it's like your words were everywhere I looked. I went a little crazy, found myself looking for them all the time…" He shakes his head. "Even kept it up when I was so pissed at you.

300

But the strangest part is that I'd found a couple before I'd even met you, the first was just a few words on the back of a candy wrapper, found it on the trail to the river, had no idea who wrote it, well, until later…"

He's staring at me, tapping the clarinet on his leg. He looks nervous again. "Okay, say something. Don't feel weird. They just made me fall more in love with you." And then he smiles, and in all the places around the globe where it's night, day breaks. "Aren't you at least going to say *quel dork*?"

I would say a lot of things right now if I could get any words past the smile that has taken over my face. There it is again his *I'm in love with you* obliterating all else that comes out of his mouth with it.

He points to the box. "They helped me. I'm kind of an unforgiving doltwad, if you haven't noticed. I'd read them – read them over and over after you came that day with the roses – trying to understand what happened, why you were with him, and I think maybe I do now. I don't know, reading all the poems together, I started to *really* imagine what you've been going through, how horrible it must be…" He swallows, looks down, shuffles his foot in the pine needles. "For him too. I guess I can see how it happened."

How can it be I was writing to Joe all these months without knowing it? When he looks up, he's smiling. "And then yesterday…" He tosses the clarinet onto the bed. "Found out you belong to me." He points at me. "I own your ass."

I smile. "Making fun of me?"

"Yeah, but it doesn't matter because you own my ass too." He shakes his head and his hair flops into his eyes so that I might die. "Totally."

A flock of hysterically happy birds busts out of my chest and into the world. I'm glad he read the poems. I want him to know all the inside things about me. I want him to know my sister, and now, in some way, he does. Now he knows before as well as after.

He sits down on the edge of the bed, picks up a stick and draws on the ground with it, then tosses it, looks off into the trees. "I'm sorry," he says.

"Don't be. I'm glad—"

He turns around to face me. "No, not about the poems. I'm sorry, what I said that day, about Bailey. From reading all these, I knew how much it would hurt you—"

I put my finger over his lips. "It's okay."

He takes my hand, holds it to his mouth, kisses it. I close my eyes, feel shivers run through me – it's been so long since we've touched. He rests my hand back down. I open my eyes. His are on me, questioning. He smiles, but the vulnerability and hurt still in his face tears into me. "You're not going to do it to me again, are you?" he asks.

"Never," I blurt out. "I want to be with you forever!" Okay, lesson learned twice in as many days: you can chop the Victorian novel to shreds with garden shears but you can't take it out of the girl.

He beams at me. "You're crazier than me."

We stare at each other for a long moment and inside that moment I feel like we are kissing more passionately than we ever have even though we aren't touching.

I reach out and brush my fingers across his arm. "Can't help it. I'm in love."

"First time," he says. "For me."

"I thought in France—"

He shakes his head. "No way, nothing like this." He touches my cheek in that tender way that he does that makes me believe in God and Buddha and Mohammed and Ganesh and Mary et al. "No one's like you, for me," he whispers.

"Same," I say, right as our lips meet. He lowers me back onto the bed, aligns himself on top of me so we are legs to legs, hips to hips, stomach to stomach. I can feel the weight of him pressing into every inch of me. I rake my fingers through his dark silky curls.

"I missed you," he murmurs into my ears, my neck and hair, and each time he does I say, "Me too," and then we are kissing again and I can't believe there is anything in this uncertain world that can feel this right and real and true.

Later, after we've come up for oxygen, I reach for the box, and start flipping through the scraps. There are a lot of them, but not near as many as I wrote. I'm glad there are some still out there, tucked away between rocks, in trash bins, on walls, in the margins of books, some washed away by rain, erased by the sun, transported by the wind, some never to be found, some to be found in years to come.

"Hey, where's the one from yesterday?" I ask, letting my residual embarrassment get the better of me, thinking I might still be able to accidentally rip it up, now that it's done its job.

"Not in there. That one's mine." Oh well. He's lazily brushing his hand across my neck and down my back. I feel like a tuning fork, my whole body humming.

"You're not going to believe this," he says. "But I think the roses worked. On my parents – I swear, they can't keep their hands off each other. It's disgusting. Marcus and Fred have been going down to your place at night and stealing roses to give to girls so they'll sleep with them." Gram is going to love this. It's a good thing she's so smitten with the Fontaine boys.

I put down the box, scoot around so I'm facing him. "I don't think *any* of you guys need Gram's roses for that."

"John Lennon?"

Bat. Bat. Bat.

I run my finger over his lips, say, "I want to do everything with you too."

"Oh man," he says, pulling me down to him, and then we are kissing so far into the sky I don't think we're ever coming back.

If anyone asks where we are, just tell them to look up.

38

Bails?

Yeah?

Is it so dull being dead?

It was, not anymore.

What changed?

I stopped peering over the ledge...

What do you do now?

It's hard to explain — it's like swimming,
but not in water, in light.

Who do you swim with?

Mostly you and Toby, Gram, Big,
with Mom, too, sometimes.

How come I don't know it?

But you do, don't you?

I guess, like all those days we spent
at Flying Man's?

Exactly, only brighter.

(Written in Lennie's journal)

Gram and I are baking the day away in preparation for Big's wedding. All the windows and doors are open and we can hear the river and smell the roses and feel the heat of the sun streaming in. We're chirping about the kitchen like sparrows.

We do this every wedding, only this is the first time we're doing it without Bailey. Yet, oddly, I feel her presence more today in the kitchen with Gram than I have since she died. When I roll the dough out, she comes up to me and sticks her hand in the flour and flicks it into my face. When Gram and I lean against the counter and sip our tea, she storms into the kitchen and pours herself a cup. She sits in every chair, blows in and out the doors, whisks in between Gram and me humming under her breath and dipping her finger into our batters. She's in every thought I think, every word I say, and I let her be. I let her enchant me as I roll the dough and think my thoughts and say my words, as we bake and bake – both of us having finally dissuaded Joe of the necessity of an exploding wedding cake – and talk about inanities like what Gram is going to wear for the big party. She is quite concerned with her outfit.

"Maybe I'll wear pants for a change." The earth has just slid off its axis. Gram has a floral frock for every occasion –

I've never seen her out of one. "And I might straighten my hair." Okay, the earth has slid off its axis and is now hurtling toward a different galaxy. Imagine snake-haired Medusa with a blow-dryer. Straight hair is an impossibility for Gram or any Walker, even with thirty hours to go until party time.

"What gives?" I ask.

"I just want to look nice, no crime in that, is there? You know, sweet pea, it's not like I've lost my sex appeal." I can't believe Gram just said sex appeal. "Just a bit of a dry spell is all," she mutters under her breath. I turn to look at her. She's sugaring the raspberries and strawberries and flushing as crimson as they are.

"Oh my God, Gram! You have a crush."

"God no!"

"You're lying. I can see it."

Then she giggles in a wild cackley way. "I am lying! Well, what do you expect? With you so loopy all the time about Joe, and now Big and Dorothy … maybe I caught a little of it. Love is contagious, everyone knows that, Lennie."

She grins.

"So, who is it? Did you meet him at The Saloon that night?" That's the only time she's been out socializing in months. Gram is not the Internet dating type. At least I don't think she is.

I put my hands on my hips. "If you don't tell me, I'm just going to ask Maria tomorrow. There's nothing in Clover she doesn't know."

Gram squeals, "Mum's me, sweet pea."

No matter how I prod through hours more of pies,

cakes and even a few batches of berry pudding, her smiling lips remain sealed.

After we're done, I get my backpack, which I loaded up earlier, and take off for the cemetery. When I hit the trailhead, I start running. The sun is breaking through the canopy in isolated blocks, so I fly through light and dark and dark and light, through the blazing unapologetic sunlight, into the ghostliest loneliest shade, and back again, back and forth, from one to the next, and through the places where it all blends together into a leafy-lit emerald dream. I run and run and as I do the fabric of death that has clung to me for months begins to loosen and slip away. I run fast and free, suspended in a moment of private raucous happiness, my feet barely touching the ground as I fly forward to the next second, minute, hour, day, week, year of my life.

I break out of the woods on the road to the cemetery. The hot afternoon sunlight is lazing over everything, meandering through the trees, casting long shadows. It's warm and the scent of eucalyptus and pine is thick, overpowering. I walk the footpath that winds through the graves listening to the rush of the falls, remembering how important it was for me, despite all reason, that Bailey's grave be where she could see and hear and even smell the river.

I'm the only person in the small hilltop cemetery and I'm glad. I drop my backpack and sit down beside the gravestone, rest my head against it, wrap my hands and arms around it like I'm playing a cello. The stone is so warm against my body. We chose this one because it had a little cabinet in it, a kind of reliquary, with a metal door that has an engraving of a bird on it. It sits under the chiseled words. I run my fingers across my sister's name, her nineteen years, then across the words I wrote on a piece of paper months ago and handed to Gram in the funeral parlor: *The Color of Extraordinary*.

I reach for my pack, pull a small notebook out of it. I transcribed all the letters Gram wrote to our mom over the last sixteen years. I want Bailey to have those words. I want her to know that there will never be a story that she won't be a part of, that she's everywhere like sky. I open the door and slide the book in the little cabinet, and as I do, I hear something scrape. I reach in and pull out a ring. My stomach drops. It's gorgeous, an orange topaz, big as an acorn. Perfect for Bailey. Toby must have had it made especially for her. I hold it in my palm and the certainty that she never got to see it pierces me. I bet the ring is what they were waiting for to finally tell us about their marriage, the baby. How Bails would've showed it off when they made the grand announcements. I rest it on the edge of the stone where it catches a glint of sun and throws amber prismatic light over all the engraved words.

I try to fend off the oceanic sadness, but I can't. It's such a colossal effort not to be haunted by what's lost, but to be enchanted by what was.

I miss you, I tell her, *I can't stand that you're going to miss so much.*

I don't know how the heart withstands it.

I kiss the ring, put it back into the cabinet next to the notebook, and close the door with the bird on it. Then I reach into my pack and take out the houseplant. It's so decrepit, just a few blackened leaves left. I walk over to the edge of the cliff, so I'm right over the falls. I take the plant out of its pot, shake the dirt off the roots, get a good grip, reach my arm back, take one deep breath before I pitch my arm forward, and let go.

Epilogue

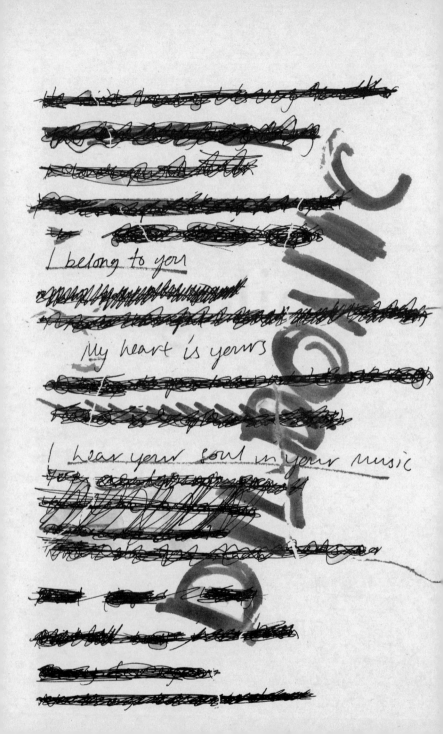

I belong to you

My heart is yours

I hear your soul in your music

(Found on the bed, in the forest bedroom)

*(Found again in the bombroom, in the trash can,
ripped into pieces by Lennie)*

*(Found again on Joe's desk, taped together, with the
word* dildonic *written over it)*

*(Found framed under glass in Joe's dresser drawer,
where it still is)*

Acknowledgements

In loving memory of Barbie Stein, who is everywhere like sky

I'd like to thank:

First and foremost, my parents, all four of them, for their boundless love and support: my awesome father and Carol, my huge-hearted mother and Ken. My whole family for their rollicking humor and steadfastness: my brothers Bruce, Bobby, and Andy, my sisters-in-law Patricia and Monica, my niece and nephews Adam, Lena, and Jake, my grandparents, particularly the inimitable Cele.

Mark Routhier for so much joy, belief, love.

My amazing friends, my other family, for every day, in every way: Ami Hooker, Anne Rosenthal, Becky MacDonald, Emily Rubin, Jeremy Quittner, Larry Dwyer, Maggie Jones, Sarah Michelson, Julie Regan, Stacy Doris, Maritza Perez, David Booth, Alexander Stadler, Rick Heredia, Patricia Irvine, James Faerron, Lisa Steindler, and James Assatly, who is so missed, also my extended families: the Routhier, Green, and Block clans … and many others, too many to name.

Patricia Nelson for around the clock laughs and legal expertise, Paul Feuerwerker for glorious eccentricity, revelry, and invaluable insights into the band room, Mark H for sublime musicality, first love.

The faculty, staff and student body of Vermont College of Fine Arts, particularly my miracle-working mentors: Deborah Wiles, Brent Hartinger, Julie Larios, Tim Wynne-Jones, Margaret Bechard, and visiting faculty Jane Yolen. And my classmates: the Cliff-hangers, especially Jill Santopolo, Carol Lynch Williams, Erik Talkin, and Mari Jorgensen. Also, the San Francisco VCFA crew.

And Marianna Baer – angel at the end of my keyboard.

My other incredible teachers and professors: Regina Wiegand, Bruce Boston, Will Erikson, Archie Ammons, Ken McClane, Phyllis Janowitz, C.D. Wright, among many others.

To those listed above who spirit in and out of this book – a special thank you.

Deepest appreciation and gratitude go to:

My clients at Manus & Associates Literary Agency, as well as my extraordinary colleagues: Stephanie Lee, Dena Fischer, Penny Nelson, Theresa van Eeghen, Janet and Justin Manus, and most especially, Jillian Manus, who doesn't walk, but dances on water.

Alisha Niehaus, my remarkable editor, for her ebullience, profundity, insight, kindness, sense of humor, and for making every part of the process a celebration. Everyone at Dial and Penguin Books for Young Readers for astounding me each jubilant step of the way.

Emily van Beek of Pippin Properties for being the best literary agent on earth! I am forever mesmerized by her joyfulness, brilliance, ferocity and grace. Holly McGhee for her enthusiasm, humor, savvy and soulfulness. Elena Mechlin for her behind-the-scenes magic and cheer. The Pippin Ladies are without peer. And Jason Dravis at Monteiro Rose Dravis Agency for his dazzling know-how.

In addition, I heartily thank:

At Walker UK, my wonderful editor, Helen Thomas, for her passion, astuteness, humor and all around delightfulness, who made 6,000 miles feel like none, and publisher Jane Winterbotham for her enthusiasm and vision. Jane and Helen took tremendously good care of this story and I am so grateful. I am now in the marvelous hands of Annalie Grainger, my new editor. Also, the incredible Katie Everson for her genius and creativity in making the book look more beautiful than in my wildest dreams. And of course, Vera the plant.

Much gratitude also goes to the amazing Alex Webb at Rights People.

And finally, an extra heartfelt double-whammy out-of-the-freaking-park thank you to my brother Bobby: True Believer.

An Interview with Jandy Nelson

Music plays a large role in Lennie's life. Why did you feel this was an important addition to her character? What made you want to include music in the book in the first place?

Well, the funny thing is I don't feel like I had that much to do with it! Lennie pretty much crashed into my psyche, clarinet in hand. So she was always a musician in my mind and I went from there, believing then that music would be an intrinsic factor in her growth, in the way she coped with her grief, in how she connected in a wordless way with Joe, in how she moved out of Bailey's shadow and into her own light. In the beginning of the story when Lennie's so shut down, she says, to express what she's feeling she'd need "a new alphabet, one made of falling, of tectonic plates shifting, of the deep devouring dark." I think over the course of the story, she realizes that, for her, music is this alphabet. She says, "What if music is what escapes when a heart breaks?" and I think this becomes true for her. More generally, I love music and wanted it to have a curative, aphrodisiacal, celebratory, and transformative role in this story. Like Jack Kerouac said, "The only truth is music." And Shakespeare: "If music be the food of love, play on." I wanted Lennie to play on.

You have an MFA in poetry. Is this why you decided to make Lennie a poet in the novel?

Before writing this book, I'd only written poetry, and *The Sky Is Everywhere* actually started as a novel in verse. I had this image in my mind of a grief-stricken girl scattering her poems all over a town – that was really the inciting image for the whole book and key right from the start to Lennie's character. I kept thinking of her, this bereft girl, who wanted so badly to communicate with someone who was no longer there that she just began writing her words on everything and anything she could, scattering her poems and thoughts and memories to the winds. In my mind, it was a way for Lennie to write her grief on the world, to mark it, to reach out to her sister and at the same time to make sure, in this strange way, that their story was part of everything. So it all began with Lennie's poems, but very early on, like after a couple weeks of writing, it became clear that Lennie's story needed to be told primarily in prose so I dived in and found myself falling in love with writing fiction – it was a total revelation! After that, I wrote both the prose and poems simultaneously, weaving the poems in as I went along.

Why did you want to tell Lennie's story? Did you ever imagine telling Bailey and Lennie's story from another point of view?

No, it was always Lennie's story I wanted to tell and always from her point of view. I wanted the immediacy of first person, to really be able to follow her closely, emotionally and psychologically, over the course of the story. That image I had of her scattering poems was incredibly persistent; it chased me everywhere until I sat down to write her story. I had lost someone very close to me years earlier and I wanted to write about that kind of catastrophic, transformational life event. I wanted to explore some of the intricacies and complexities of grief, but I wanted to explore them through a love story – or two really. I imagined a story where joy and sorrow cohabitated in really close quarters, where love could be almost as unwieldy as grief. James Baldwin said, "When you're writing you're trying to find out something which you don't know." I think there were things I wanted to explore and discover, and writing Lennie's story helped me do that. She really took me over. What's odd is that despite the subject matter, and even though many days I typed with tears falling onto the keyboard, writing this novel was an incredibly joyful experience, one of the happiest times of my life.

Was setting important to you in writing this story?

Absolutely. I very much wanted the setting to be a "character" in this story interplaying with the other characters. I love California, love writing about it. I'm very inspired by the landscape. The imagined town of Clover, where *The Sky Is Everywhere* takes place, has really dramatic natural elements: roaring rivers, skyscraping redwoods, thick old-growth forests. This landscape is in the DNA of the Walker family, and I wanted it to be instrumental in Lennie's recovery and awakening, as objective correlative, but also as almost a spiritual force in her life.

What do you want readers to take from this story?

It's funny there's a paragraph toward the end of the novel in Chapter 35. Lennie has just told Rachel she's going to challenge her for first chair and she's running through the woods on her way to write the poem for Joe. She's taking steps that will propel her into the future when she's suddenly clobbered (not for the first time) by the realization that she has a future and Bailey doesn't. It's agony for her and it occurs to her that grief is forever, that it will be with her always, step for step, breath for breath, but she also realizes in this moment that this is true because grief and love are conjoined and you can't have one without the other. Grief is always going to be a measure of the love lost. She thinks, "All I can do is love her [Bailey], and love the world, emulate her by living with daring and spirit and joy." Every time I come across this paragraph, I think to myself, Well there it is, the whole book crammed into one paragraph! So for me the ideas in that paragraph kind of ring out, but every reader will take something different from the novel and that's what I want, that's the magic of it all. Reading is such a wonderfully personal and private affair.

Jandy Nelson lives in San Francisco, where she, much like Lennie, divides her time between her proper tree and running loose through the park. Jandy is a published poet and perpetual academic with degrees from Brown, Cornell and Vermont College of Fine Arts. She's a superstitious sort and devout romantic who's madly in love with California – how it teeters on the edge of a continent.

The Sky Is Everywhere is Jandy's first novel. Her second book, *I'll Give You the Sun*, tells the story of twins and artists, Noah and Jude.

Follow Jandy on Twitter @jandynelson or visit her online at www.jandynelson.com.

Love is only half the story

I'll give you the sun

JANDY NELSON

Jude and her twin Noah were incredibly close –
until a tragedy drove them apart, and now they are
barely speaking. Then Jude meets a cocky, broken,
beautiful boy as well as a captivating new mentor,
both of whom may just need her as much as she
needs them. What the twins don't realize is that each
of them has only half the story and if they can just
find their way back to one another, they have
a chance to remake their world.

**This radiant book will leave you breathless,
crying and laughing – all at once.**

#IllGiveYoutheSun
@jandynelson @WalkerBooksUK

Praise for
I'll Give You the Sun

"Nelson's gifts in tackling huge subjects – death, grief,
all-consuming love – with humor and gravitas will draw
comparisons to ... John Green and Rainbow Rowell.
But the intensity of her writing stands alone."
Entertainment Weekly

"Be prepared with more tissues than you needed for *The
Fault in Our Stars*, a chunky notebook to scribble down all the
quotes and a handful of witty responses when people ask why
you're chuckling to yourself in the corner. Because this book
will make you realize how beautiful words can be."
The Guardian

"A gravity-defying, life-affirming experience."
San Francisco Magazine

"Readers are meant to feel big things, and they will –
Nelson's novel brims with emotion."
Publishers Weekly

"Electrifying." ***Chicago Tribune***

Also by Jandy Nelson

The Sky Is Everywhere

**WALKER
BOOKS**

JANDY
NELSON

For Dad and Carol

"Out beyond ideas of wrongdoing and rightdoing, there is a field.
I'll meet you there." – Rumi

"I believe in nothing but the holiness of the heart's affections and
the truth of the imagination." – John Keats

"Where there is great love, there are always miracles." – Willa Cather

"It takes courage to grow up and become who you really are."
– E.E. Cummings

First published in Great Britain 2015 by Walker Books Ltd
87 Vauxhall Walk, London SE11 5HJ

This edition published 2016

2 4 6 8 10 9 7 5 3 1

Text © 2015 Jandy Nelson
Illustrations © 2015 Sophie Heywood

The right of Jandy Nelson to be identified as author of this work has been asserted
by her in accordance with the Copyright, Designs and Patents Act 1988

This book has been typeset in Bembo

Printed and bound in Great Britain by Clays Ltd, St Ives plc

British Library Cataloguing in Publication Data: a catalogue record for this book
is available from the British Library

ISBN 978-1-4063-7640-1

www.walker.co.uk

Dear Reader,

I'm so excited for you to meet twins Noah and Jude. Noah is this flood in a paper cup. He has a mad desire to draw, to kiss the boy next door, to peel the blue off the sky, to *be* the blue in the sky. And Jude. She used to surf and cliff-dive and do the talking for both twins, but something's happened, and now she's gone quiet and is living with ghosts and following her grandmother's "bible" of superstitions. These twins became so real to me that one time while in the middle of writing the novel, I went to an art exhibit and my first thought was, "It's such a shame Noah and Jude couldn't come with me today."

This is a story about love, crazy complicated love of all kinds: between guys and girls, guys and guys, mothers and daughters, fathers and sons, artists and their art, the living and the dead, but mostly it's about the fierce, roller-coaster love between the twins themselves.

Writing Noah and Jude's story took three and a half years. It was the most exciting, exuberant and challenging creative experience of my life. These characters shook the ground beneath my feet. There's a moment in the novel when Jude's watching her stone-carving mentor Guillermo sculpt and she wonders if he's making the sculpture or if the sculpture is making him. That's what writing this novel felt like.

I so hope you enjoy!
Jandy

The
Invisible
Museum

Noah, Age 13

This is HOW it all Begins.

With Zephyr and Fry – reigning neighborhood sociopaths – torpedoing after me and the whole forest floor shaking under my feet as I blast through air, trees, this white-hot panic.

"You're going over, you pussy!" Fry shouts.

Then Zephyr's on me, has one, both of my arms behind my back, and Fry's grabbed my sketchpad. I lunge for it but I'm armless, helpless. I try to wriggle out of Zephyr's grasp. Can't. Try to blink them into moths. No. They're still themselves: fifteen-foot-tall, tenth-grade asshats who toss living, breathing thirteen-year-old people like me over cliffs for kicks.

Zephyr's got me in a headlock from behind and his chest's heaving into my back, my back into his chest. We're swimming in sweat. Fry starts leafing through the pad. "Whatcha been drawing, Bubble?" I imagine him getting run over by a truck. He holds up a page of sketches. "Zeph, look at all these naked dudes."

The blood in my body stops moving.

"They're not dudes. They're *David*," I get out, praying I won't sound like a gerbil, praying he won't turn to later drawings in the pad, drawings done today, when I was spying, drawings of *them*, rising out of the water, with their surfboards under arm, no wetsuits, no nothing, totally glistening, and, uh:

holding hands. I might have taken some artistic license. So they're going to think... They're going to kill me even before they kill me is what they're going to do. The world starts somersaulting. I fling words at Fry: "You know? Michelangelo? Ever heard of him?" I'm not going to act like me. *Act tough and you are tough,* as Dad has said and said and said – like I'm some kind of broken umbrella.

"Yeah, I've heard of him," Fry says out of the big bulgy mouth that clumps with the rest of his big bulgy features under the world's most massive forehead, making it very easy to mistake him for a hippopotamus. He rips the page out of the sketchpad. "Heard he was *gay*."

He *was* – my mom wrote a whole book about it – not that Fry knows. He calls everyone gay when he's not calling them homo and pussy. And me: homo and pussy *and* Bubble.

Zephyr laughs a dark demon laugh. It vibrates through me.

Fry holds up the next sketch. More *David*. The bottom half of him. A study in detail. I go cold.

They're both laughing now. It's echoing through the forest. It's coming out of birds.

Again, I try to break free of the lock Zephyr has me in so I can snatch the pad out of Fry's hands, but it only tightens Zephyr's hold. Zephyr, who's freaking Thor. One of his arms is choked around my neck, the other braced across my torso like a seat belt. He's bare-chested, straight off the beach, and the heat of him is seeping through my T-shirt. His coconut suntan lotion's filling my nose, my whole head – the strong smell of the ocean too, like he's carrying it on his back...

Zephyr dragging the tide along like a blanket behind him…
That would be good, that would be *it* (Portrait: *The Boy
Who Walked Off with the Sea*) – but not now, Noah, *so* not the
time to mind-paint this cretin. I snap back, taste the salt on
my lips, remind myself I'm about to die—

Zephyr's long seaweedy hair is wet and dripping down my
neck and shoulders. I notice we're breathing in synch, heavy,
bulky breaths. I try to unsynch with him. I try to unsynch with
the law of gravity and float up. Can't do either. Can't do anything. The wind's whipping pieces of my drawings – mostly
family portraits now – out of Fry's hands as he tears up one,
then another. He rips one of Jude and me down the middle,
cuts me right out of it.

I watch myself blow away.

I watch him getting closer and closer to the drawings that
are going to get me murdered.

My pulse is thundering in my ears.

Then Zephyr says, "Don't rip 'em up, Fry. His sister says he's
good." Because he likes Jude? They mostly all do now because
she can surf harder than any of them, likes to jump off cliffs,
and isn't afraid of anything, not even great white sharks or Dad.
And because of her hair – I use up all my yellows drawing it. It's
hundreds of miles long and everyone in Northern California
has to worry about getting tangled up in it, especially little kids
and poodles and now asshat surfers.

There's also the boobs, which arrived by overnight delivery,
I swear.

Unbelievably, Fry listens to Zephyr and drops the pad.

Jude peers up at me from it, sunny, knowing. *Thank you,* I tell her in my mind. She's always rescuing me, which usually is embarrassing, but not now. That was righteous.

(Portrait, Self-portrait: *Twins: Noah Looking in a Mirror, Jude out of It*)

"You know what we're going to do to you, don't you?" Zephyr rasps in my ear. He's back to the regularly scheduled homicidal programming. There's too much of him on his breath. There's too much of him on me.

"Please, you guys," I beg.

"Please, you guys," Fry mimics in a squeaky girly voice.

My stomach rolls. Devil's Drop, the second-highest jump on the hill, which they plan to throw me over, has the name for a reason. Beneath it is a jagged gang of rocks and a wicked whirlpool that pulls your dead bones down to the underworld.

I try to break Zephyr's hold again. And again.

"Get his legs, Fry!"

All six-thousand hippopotamus pounds of Fry dive for my ankles. Sorry, this is not happening. It just isn't. I hate the water, prone as I am to drowning and drifting to Asia. I need my skull in one piece. Crushing it would be like taking a wrecking ball to some secret museum before anyone ever got to see what's inside it.

So I grow. And grow, and grow, until I head-butt the sky. Then I count to three and go freaking *berserk*, thanking Dad in my mind for all the wrestling he's forced me to do on the deck, to-the-death matches where he could only use one arm and I could use everything and he'd still pin me down because he's thirty feet tall and made of truck parts.

But I'm his son, his *gargantuan* son. I'm a whirling, ass-kicking Goliath, a typhoon wrapped in skin, and then I'm writhing and thrashing and trying to break free and they're wrestling me back down, laughing and saying things like "what a crazy mother." And I think I hear respect even in Zephyr's voice as he says, "I can't pin him, he's like a frickin' eel," and that makes me fight harder – I love eels, they're *electric* – imagining myself a live wire now, fully loaded with my own private voltage, as I whip this way and that, feeling their bodies twisting around mine, warm and slick, both of them pinning me again and again, and me breaking their holds, all our limbs entwined and now Zephyr's head's pressed into my chest and Fry's behind me with what feels like a hundred hands, and it's just motion and confusion and I am lost in it, lost, lost, lost, when I begin to suspect … when I realize – I have a hard-on, a supernaturally hard hard-on, and it's jammed into Zephyr's stomach. High-octane dread courses through me. In my mind, I call up the bloodiest most hella gross machete massacre – my most effective boner-buster – but it's too late. Zephyr goes momentarily still, then jumps off me. "What the—?"

Fry rolls up onto his knees. "What happened?" he wheezes out in Zephyr's direction.

I've reeled away, landed in a sitting position, my knees to my chest. I can't stand up yet for fear of a tent, so I put all my effort in trying not to cry. A sickly ferret feeling is burrowing itself into every corner of my body as I pant my last breaths. And even if they don't kill me here and now, by tonight everyone on the hill will know what just happened. I might as well swallow a lit stick of dynamite and hurl myself off Devil's Drop. This is worse, so much worse, than them seeing some stupid drawings.

(Self-portrait: *Funeral in the Forest*)

But Zephyr's not saying anything, he's just standing there, looking like his Viking self, except all weird and mute. Why?

Did I disable him with my mind?

No. He gestures in the direction of the ocean, says to Fry, "Hell with this. Let's grab the slabs and head out."

Relief swallows me whole. Is it possible he didn't feel it? No, it isn't − it was steel and he jumped away totally freaked out. He's still freaked out. So why isn't he pussyhomoBubbling me? Is it because he likes Jude?

Fry twirls a finger by his ear as he says to Zephyr, "Someone's Frisbee is seriously on the roof, bro." Then to me: "When you least expect it, Bubble." He mimes my free-fall off Devil's Drop with his mitt of a hand.

It's over. They're headed back toward the beach.

Before they change their Neanderthal minds, I hustle over to my pad, slip it under my arm, and then, without looking back, I speed-walk into the trees like someone whose heart isn't shaking, whose eyes aren't filling up, someone who doesn't feel so newly minted as a human.

When I'm in the clear, I blast out of my skin like a cheetah − they go from zero to seventy-five mph in three seconds flat and I can too practically. I'm the fourth-fastest in the seventh grade. I can unzip the air and disappear inside it, and that's what I do until I'm far away from Zephyr and Fry and what happened. At least I'm not a mayfly. Male mayflies have two dicks to worry about. I already spend half my life in the shower because of my one, thinking about things I can't stop thinking about no matter how hard I try because I really, really, really like thinking about them. Man, I do.

At the creek, I jump rocks until I find a good cave where I can watch the sun swimming inside the rushing water for the next hundred years. There should be a horn or gong or something to wake God. Because I'd like to have a word with him. Three words actually: WHAT THE FUCK?!

After a while, having gotten no response as usual, I take out the charcoals from my back pocket. They somehow survived the ordeal intact. I sit down and open my sketchbook. I black out a whole blank page, then another, and another. I press so hard, I break stick after stick, using each one down to the very nub, so it's like the blackness is coming out of my finger, out of me, and onto the page. I fill up the whole rest of the pad. It takes hours.

(A Series: *Boy Inside a Box of Darkness*)

* * *

The next night at dinner, Mom announces that Grandma Sweetwine joined her for a ride in the car that afternoon with a message for Jude and me.

Only, Grandma's dead.

"Finally!" Jude exclaims, falling back in her chair. "She promised me!"

What Grandma promised Jude, right before she died in her sleep three months ago, is that if Jude ever really needed her, she'd be there in a flash. Jude was her favorite.

Mom smiles at Jude and puts her hands on the table. I put

mine on the table too, then realize I'm being a Mom-mirror and hide my hands in my lap. Mom's contagious.

And a blow-in – some people just aren't from here and she's one of them. I've been accumulating evidence for years. More on this later.

But now: Her face is all lit up and flickery as she sets the stage, telling us how first the car filled with Grandma's perfume. "You know how the scent used to walk into the room before she did?" Mom breathes in dramatically as if the kitchen's filling with Grandma's thick flowery smell. I breathe in dramatically. Jude breathes in dramatically. Everyone in California, the United States, on Earth, breathes in dramatically.

Except Dad. He clears his throat.

He's not buying it. Because he's an artichoke. This, according to his own mother, Grandma Sweetwine, who never understood how she birthed and raised such a thistle-head. Me neither.

A thistle-head who studies *parasites* for a living. No comment.

I glance at him with his lifeguard-like tan and muscles, with his glow-in-the-dark teeth, with all his glow-in-the-dark normal, and feel the curdling – because what would happen if he knew?

So far Zephyr hasn't blabbed a word. You probably don't know this, because I'm like the only one in the world who does, but a dork is the official name for a whale dick. And a blue whale's dork? Eight feet long. I repeat: EIGHT FEET LOOOOOOOONG! This is how I've felt since it happened yesterday:

(Self-portrait: *The Concrete Dork*)

Yeah.

But sometimes I think Dad suspects. Sometimes I think the toaster suspects.

Jude jostles my leg under the table with her foot to get my attention back from the salt shaker I realize I've been staring down. She nods toward Mom, whose eyes are now closed and whose hands are crossed over her heart. Then toward Dad, who's looking at Mom like her eyebrows have crawled down to her chin. We bulge our eyes at each other. I bite my cheek not to laugh. Jude does too – she and me, we share a laugh switch. Our feet press together under the table.

(Family Portrait: *Mom Communes with the Dead at Dinner*)

"Well?" Jude prods. "The message?"

Mom opens her eyes, winks at us, then closes them and continues in a séance-y woo-woo voice. "So, I breathed in the flowery air and there was a kind of shimmering…" She swirls her arms like scarves, milking the moment. This is why she gets the professor of the year award so much – everyone always wants to be in her movie with her. We lean in for her next words, for The Message from Upstairs, but then Dad interrupts, throwing a whole load of boring on the moment.

He's never gotten the professor of the year award. Not once. No comment.

"It's important to let the kids know you mean all this metaphorically, honey," he says, sitting straight up so that his head busts through the ceiling. In most of my drawings, he's so big, I can't fit all of him on the page, so I leave off the head.

Mom lifts her eyes, the amusement wiped off her face. "Except I don't mean it metaphorically, Benjamin." Dad used to make Mom's eyes shine; now he makes her grind her teeth. I don't know why. "What I meant quite literally," she says/ grinds, "is that the inimitable Grandma Sweetwine, dead and gone, was in the car, sitting next to me, plain as day." She smiles at Jude. "In fact, she was all dressed up in one of her Floating Dresses, looking *spectacular*." The Floating Dress was Grandma's dress line.

"Oh! Which one? The blue?" The way Jude asks this makes my chest pang for her.

"No, the one with the little orange flowers."

"Of course," Jude replies. "Perfect ghost-wear. We discussed what her afterlife attire would be." It occurs to me that Mom's making all this up because Jude can't stop missing Grandma. She hardly left her bedside at the end. When Mom found them that final morning, one asleep, one dead, they were holding hands. I thought this was supremely creepy but kept it to myself. "So…" Jude raises an eyebrow. "The message?"

"You know what I'd love?" Dad says, huffing and puffing himself back into the conversation so that we're never going to find out what the freaking message is. "What I'd love is if we could finally declare The Reign of Ridiculous over." This, again. The Reign he's referring to began when Grandma moved in. Dad, "a man of science," told us to take every bit of superstitious hogwash that came out of his mother's mouth with a grain of salt. Grandma told us not to listen to her artichoke of a son and to take those grains of salt and throw them right over our left shoulders to blind the devil.

Then she took out her "bible" – not The Bible but an

enormous leatherbound book stuffed with batshit ideas (aka: hogwash) – and started to preach the gospel. Mostly to Jude.

Dad lifts a slice of pizza off his plate. Cheese dives over the edges. He looks at me. "How about this, huh, Noah? Who's a little relieved we're not having one of Grandma's luck-infused stews?"

I remain silent. Sorry, Charlie. I *love* pizza, meaning: Even when I'm in the middle of eating pizza, I wish I were eating pizza, but I wouldn't jump on Dad's train even if Michelangelo were on it. He and I don't get on, though he tends to forget. I never forget. When I hear his big banging voice coming after me to watch football or some movie where everything gets blown up or to listen to jazz that makes me feel like my body's on backward, I open my bedroom window, jump out, and head for the trees.

Occasionally when no one's home, I go into his office and break his pencils. Once, after a particularly toilet-licking Noah the Broken Umbrella Talk (our version of the father–son chat), when he laughed and said if Jude weren't my twin he'd be sure I'd come about from parthenogenesis (looked it up: conception without a father), I snuck into the garage while everyone was sleeping and keyed his car.

Because I can see people's souls sometimes when I draw them, I know the following: Mom has a massive sunflower for a soul so big there's hardly any room in her for organs. Jude and me have one soul between us that we have to share: a tree with its leaves on fire. And Dad has a plate of maggots for his.

Jude says to him, "Do you think Grandma didn't just hear you insult her cooking?"

"That would be a resounding no," Dad replies, then hoovers into the slice. The grease makes his whole mouth gleam.

Jude stands. Her hair hangs all around her head like lighticicles. She looks up at the ceiling and declares, "*I* always loved your cooking, Grandma."

Mom reaches over and squeezes her hand, then says to the ceiling, "Me too, Cassandra."

Jude smiles from the inside out.

Dad finger-shoots himself in the head.

Mom frowns – it makes her look a hundred years old. "Embrace the mystery, Professor," she says. She's always telling Dad this, but she used to say it different. She used to say it like she was opening a door for him to walk through, not closing one in his face.

"I married the mystery, Professor," he answers like always, but it used to sound like a compliment.

We all eat pizza. It's not fun. Mom's and Dad's thoughts are turning the air black. I'm listening to myself chew, when Jude's foot finds mine under the table again. I press back.

"The message from Grandma?" she interjects into the tension, smiling hopefully.

Dad looks at her and his eyes go soft. She's his favorite too. Mom doesn't have a favorite, though, which means the spot is up for grabs.

"As I was saying." This time Mom's using her normal voice, husky, like a cave's talking to you. "I was driving by CSA, the fine arts high school, this afternoon and that's when Grandma swooped in to say what an absolutely perfect fit it would be for you two." She shakes her head, brightening and becoming her usual age again. "And it really is. I can't believe it never occurred to me. I keep thinking of that quote by Picasso: 'Every child is an artist. The problem is how to remain an artist once one grows up.'" She has the bananas look on her face that happens in museums, like she's going to steal the art. "But this. This is a chance of a lifetime, guys. I don't want your spirits to get all tamped down like…" She doesn't finish, combs a hand through her hair – black and way curly like mine – turns to Dad. "I really want this for them, Benjamin. I know it'll be expensive, but what an oppor—"

"That's it?" Jude interrupts. "That's all Grandma said? That was the message *from the afterlife*? It was about some *school*?" She looks like she might start crying.

Not me. Art school? I never imagined such a thing, never imagined I wouldn't have to go to Roosevelt, to Asshat High with everyone else. I'm pretty sure the blood just started glowing inside my body.

(Self-portrait: *A Window Flies Open in My Chest*)

Mom has the bananas look again. "Not just any school, Jude. A school that will let you shout from the rooftops every single day for four years. Don't you two want to shout from the rooftops?"

"Shout what?" Jude asks.

This makes Dad chuckle under his breath in a thistly way. "I don't know, Di," he says. "It's so focused. You forget that for the rest of us, art's just art, not religion." Mom picks up a knife and thrusts it into his gut, twists. Dad forges on, oblivious. "Anyway, they're in seventh grade. High school's still a ways away."

"I want to go!" I explode. "I don't want a tamped-down spirit!" I realize these are the first words I've uttered outside my head this entire meal. Mom beams at me. He can't talk her out of this. There are no surftards at art school, I know it. Probably only kids whose blood glows. Only revolutionaries.

Mom says to Dad, "It'll take them the year to prepare. It's one of the best fine arts high schools in the country, with top-notch academics as well, no problem there. And it's right in our backyard!" Her excitement is revving me up even more. I might start flapping my arms. "Really difficult to get in. But you two have it. Natural ability and you already know so much." She smiles at us with so much pride it's like the sun's rising over the table. It's true. Other kids had picture books, we had art books. "We'll start museum and gallery visits this weekend. It'll be great. You two can have drawing contests."

Jude barfs bright blue fluorescent barf all over the table, but I'm the only one who notices. She can draw okay, but it's different. For me, school only stopped being eight hours of daily stomach surgery when I realized everyone wanted me to sketch them more than they wanted to talk to me or bash my face in. No one ever wanted to bash Jude's face in. She's shiny and funny and normal – not a revolutionary – and talks to everybody. I talk to me. And Jude, of course, though mostly silently because that's how we do it. And Mom be-cause she's a blow-in. (Quickly, the evidence: So far she hasn't walked through a wall or picked up the house with her mind or stopped time or anything totally off-the-hook, but there've been things. One morning recently, for instance, she was out on the deck like usual drinking her tea and when I got closer I saw that she'd floated up into the air. At least that's how it looked to me. And the clincher: She doesn't have parents. She's a foundling! She was just left in some church in Reno, Nevada, as a baby. Hello? Left by *them*.) Oh, and I also talk to Rascal next door, who, for all intents and purposes, is a horse, but yeah right.

Hence, Bubble.

Really, most of the time, I feel like a hostage.

Dad puts his elbows on the table. "Dianna, take a few steps back. I really think you're projecting. Old dreams die—"

Mom doesn't let him say another word. The teeth are grinding like mad. She looks like she's holding in a dictionary of bad words or a nuclear war. "NoahandJude, take your plates and go into the den. I need to talk to your father."

We don't move. "NoahandJude, now."

"Jude, Noah," Dad says.

I grab my plate and I'm glued to Jude's heels out of there. She reaches a hand back for me and I take it. I notice then that her dress is as colorful as a clownfish. Grandma taught her to make her clothes. Oh! I hear our neighbor's new parrot, Prophet, through the open window. "Where the hell is Ralph?" he squawks. "Where the hell is Ralph?" It's the only thing he says, and he says it 24/7. No one knows who, forget where, Ralph is.

"Goddamn stupid parrot!" Dad shouts with so much force all our hair blows back.

"He doesn't mean it," I say to Prophet in my head only to realize I've said it out loud. Sometimes words fly out of my mouth like warty frogs. I begin to explain to Dad that I was talking to the bird but stop because that won't go over well, and instead, out of my mouth comes a weird bleating sound, which makes everyone except Jude look at me funny. We spring for the door.

A moment later we're on the couch. We don't turn on the TV, so we can eavesdrop, but they're speaking in angry whispers, impossible to decipher. After sharing my slice of pizza bite for bite because Jude forgot her plate, she says, "I thought Grandma would tell us something awesome in her message. Like if heaven has an ocean, you know?"

I lean back into the couch, relieved to be just with Jude. I never feel like I've been taken hostage when it's just us. "Oh yeah it does, most definitely it has an ocean, only it's purple, and the sand is blue and the sky is hella green."

She smiles, thinks for a moment, then says, "And when you're tired, you crawl into your flower and go to sleep. During the day, everyone talks in colors instead of sounds. It's so quiet." She closes her eyes, says slowly, "When people fall in love, they burst into flames." Jude loves that one – it was one of Grandma's favorites. We used to play this with her when we were little. "Take me away!" she'd say, or sometimes, "Get me the hell out of here, kids!"

When Jude opens her eyes, all the magic is gone from her face. She sighs.

"What?" I ask.

"I'm not going to that school. Only aliens go there."

"Aliens?"

"Yeah, freaks. California School of the Aliens, that's what people call it."

Oh man, oh man, thank you, Grandma. Dad has to cave. I have to get in. Freaks who make art! I'm so happy, I feel like I'm jumping on a trampoline, just boinging around inside myself.

Not Jude. She's all gloomy now. To make her feel better I say, "Maybe Grandma saw your flying women and that's why she wants us to go." Three coves down, Jude's been making them out of the wet sand. The same ones she's always doing out of mashed potatoes or Dad's shaving cream or whatever when she thinks no one's looking. From the bluff, I've been watching her build these bigger sand versions and know she's trying to talk to Grandma. I can always tell what's in Jude's head. It's not as easy for her to tell what's in mine, though, because I have shutters and I close them whenever I have to. Like lately.

(Self-portrait: *The Boy Hiding Inside the Boy Hiding Inside the Boy*)

"I don't think those are art. Those are..." She doesn't finish. "It's because of you, Noah. And you should stop following me down to the beach. What if I were kissing someone?"

"Who?" I'm only two hours thirty-seven minutes and thirteen seconds younger than Jude, but she always makes me feel like I'm her little brother. I hate it. "Who would you be kissing? Did you kiss someone?"

"I'll tell you if you tell me what happened yesterday. I know something did and that's why we couldn't walk to school the normal way this morning." I didn't want to see Zephyr or Fry. The high school is next to the middle school. I don't ever want to see them again. Jude touches my arm. "If someone did something to you or said something, tell me."

She's trying to get in my mind, so I close the shutters. Fast, slam them right down with me on one side, her on the other. This isn't like the other horror shows: The time she punched the boulder-come-to-life Michael Stein in the face last year during a soccer game for calling me a retard just because I got distracted by a supremely cool anthill. Or the time I got caught in a rip and she and Dad had to drag me out of the ocean in front of a whole beach of surftards. This is different. This secret is like having hot burning coals under my bare feet all the time. I rise up from the couch to get away from any potential telepathy – when the yelling reaches us.

It's loud, like the house might break in two. Same as the other times lately.

I sink back down. Jude looks at me. Her eyes are the lightest glacier blue; I use mostly white when I draw them. Normally they make you feel floaty and think of puffy clouds and hear harps, but right now they look just plain scared. Everything else has been forgotten.

(Portrait: *Mom and Dad with Screeching Tea Kettles for Heads*)

When Jude speaks, she sounds like she did when she was little, her voice made of tinsel. "Do you really think that's why Grandma wants us to go to that school? Because she saw my flying sand women?"

"I do," I say, lying. I think she was right the first time. I think it's because of me.

She scoots over so we're shoulder to shoulder. This is us. Our pose. The smush. It's even how we are in the ultrasound photo they took of us inside Mom and how I had us in the picture Fry ripped up yesterday. Unlike most everyone else on earth, from the very first cells of us, we were together, we came here together. This is why no one hardly notices that Jude does most of the talking for both of us, why we can only play piano with all four of our hands on the keyboard and not at all alone, why we can never do Rock, Paper, Scissors because not once in thirteen years have we chosen differently. It's always: two rocks, two papers, two scissors. When I don't draw us like this, I draw us as half-people.

The calm of the smush floods me. She breathes in and I join her. Maybe we're too old to still do this, but whatever. I can see her smiling even though I'm looking straight ahead. We exhale together, then inhale together, exhale, inhale, in and out, out and in, until not even the trees remember what happened in the woods yesterday, until Mom's and Dad's voices turn from mad to music, until we're not only one age, but one complete and whole person.

* * *

A week later, everything changes.

It's Saturday, and Mom, Jude, and I are in the city at the museum's rooftop café because Mom won the argument and we're both going to apply to CSA in a year.

Across the table, Jude's talking to Mom and at the same

...ng me secret silent death threats because she thinks ...ings came out better than hers and we're having a ... Mom's the judge. And fine, maybe I shouldn't have tried to fix Jude's for her. She's sure I was trying to ruin them. No comment.

She eye-rolls at me on the sly. It's a 6.3 on the Richter scale. I think about giving her a dead leg under the table but resist. Instead, I drink some hot chocolate and covertly spy on a group of older guys to my left. As far as my eight-foot concrete dork goes, still no fallout except in my mind: (Self-portrait: *Boy Gets Fed Piece by Piece to a Swarm of Fire Ants*). But maybe Zephyr's really not going to tell anyone.

The guys at the next table all have rubber plugs in their earlobes and studs in their eyebrows and are joking around with each other like otters. They probably go to CSA, I think, and the thought makes my whole body thrum. One of them has a moon face with blue saucer eyes and a bursting red mouth, the kind Renoir paints. I *love* those mouths. I'm doing a quick sketch of his face with my finger on my pants under the table when he catches me staring and instead of glaring at me so I'll mind my beeswax, he winks at me, slowly, so there's no mistaking it, then returns his attention to his friends as I go from solid to liquid mass.

He winked at me. Like he *knows*. But it doesn't feel bad. Not at all. In fact, I wish I could stop smiling, and now, oh wow – he's looking this way again and smiling too. My face is starting to boil.

I try to focus in on Mom and Jude. They're talking about

Grandma's batshit bible. Again. How it's like an encyclopedia of odd beliefs, Mom's saying. How Grandma collected ideas from everywhere, everyone, even left the bible open on the counter next to the cash register in her dress shop so all her customers could write in their batshit hogwash too.

"On the very last page," Mom tells Jude, "it says in case of her untimely death, it becomes yours."

"Mine?" She throws me her smuggest look. "*Just* mine?" She's all gift-wrapped now. Whatever. Like I even want some bible.

Mom says, "I quote, 'This good book is bequeathed to my granddaughter, Jude Sweetwine, the last remaining bearer of The Sweetwine Gift.'"

I barf bright green barf all over the table.

Grandma Sweetwine decided Jude had The Sweetwine Gift of Intuition when she discovered Jude could do the flower tongue. We were four years old. After, Jude spent days with me in front of a mirror, pressing her finger into my tongue, again and again, trying to teach me so I could have The Sweetwine Gift too. But it was useless. My tongue could flip and curl, but it couldn't blossom.

I look back over at the table of otters. They're packing up to leave. Winking Moon Face swings a backpack over his shoulder and then mouths *bye* to me.

I swallow and look down and burst into flames.

Then start mind-drawing him from memory.

When I tune back in minutes later, Mom's telling Jude that unlike Grandma Sweetwine, she'd haunt us flamboyantly and persistently, no quick visits in the car for her. "I'd be the kind of ghost that interferes with everything." She's laughing her rumbly laugh and her hands are twirling around in the air. "I'm too controlling. You'd never be rid of me! Never!" She bwah-ha-ha's at us.

What's weird is that she looks like she's in a windstorm all of a sudden. Her hair's blowing and her dress is slightly billowing. I check under the table to see if there's a vent or something, but there isn't. See? Other mothers don't have their own private weather. She's smiling at us so warmly, like we're puppies, and something catches in my chest.

I shutter myself in while they talk more specifically about what kind of ghost Mom would make. If Mom died, the sun would go out. Period.

Instead, I think about today.

How I went around from painting to painting asking each to eat me and each did.

How my skin fit the whole time, didn't once bunch up at my ankles or squeeze my head into a pin.

Mom's drum roll on the table brings me back. "So, let's see those sketchbooks," she says, excited.

I did four pastel drawings from the permanent collection – a Chagall, a Franz Marc, and two Picassos. I picked those because I could tell the paintings were looking at me as hard as I was looking at them. Mom'd said not to feel like we had to copy exactly. I didn't copy at all. I shook up the originals in my head and let them out all covered in me.

"I'll go first," I say, shoving my book into Mom's hands.

Jude's eye-roll is a 7.2 on the Richter this time, causing

the whole building to sway. I don't care, I can't wait. Something happened when I was drawing today. I think my eyes got swapped for better ones. I want Mom to notice.

I watch her page through slowly, then put on the granny glasses that hang around her neck and go through the drawings again, *and then again*. At one point she looks up at me like I've turned into a star-nosed mole and then goes back to it.

All the café sounds: The voices, the whirring of the espresso machine, the clink and clatter of glasses and dishes go silent as I watch her index finger hover over each part of the page. I'm seeing through her eyes and what I'm seeing is this: They're good. I start to get a rocket launch feeling. I'm totally going to get into CSA! And I still have a whole year to make sure of it. I already asked Mr. Grady, the art teacher, to teach me to mix oils after school and he said yes. When I think Mom's finally done, she goes back to the beginning and starts again. She can't stop! Her face is being swarmed by happiness. Oh, I'm reeling around in here.

Until I'm under siege. A psychic air raid discharging from Jude. (**Portrait:** *Green with Envy*) Skin: lime. Hair: chartreuse. Eyes: forest. All of her: green, green, green. I watch her open a packet of sugar, spill some on the table, then press a fingerprint of the crystals into the cover of her sketchbook. Some hogwash from Grandma's bible about sugar and good luck. I feel a coiling in my stomach. I should grab my sketchbook out of Mom's hands already, but I don't. I can't.

Every time Grandma S. read Jude's and my palms, she'd tell us that we have enough jealousy in our lines to ruin our lives ten times over. I know she's right about this. When I draw Jude and me with see-through skin, there are always rattlesnakes in our bellies. I only have a few. Jude had seventeen at last count.

Finally, Mom closes my book and hands it back to me. She says to us, "Contests are silly. Let's spend our Saturdays for the next year appreciating art and learning craft. Sound good, guys?"

Before even opening Jude's sketchbook, she says this.

Mom picks up her hot chocolate but doesn't drink. "Unbelievable," she says, shaking her head slowly. Has she forgotten Jude's book altogether? "I see a Chagall sensibility with a Gauguin palette, but the point of view seems wholly your own at the same time. And you're so young. It's extraordinary, Noah. Just extraordinary."

"Really?" I whisper.

"Really," she says seriously. "I'm stunned." Something in her face is different — it's like a curtain's been parted in the middle of it. I sneak a glance at Jude. I can tell she's crumpled up in a corner of herself, just like I do in emergencies. There's a crawlspace in me that no one can get to, no matter what. I had no idea she had one too.

Mom doesn't notice. Usually she notices everything. But she's sitting there not noticing anything, like she's dreaming right in front of us.

Finally she snaps out of it, but it's too late. "Jude, honey, let's see that book, can't wait to see what you've come up with."

"That's okay," Jude says in the tinsely voice, her book already buried deep in her bag.

Jude and I play a lot of games. Her favorites are How Would

You Rather Die? (Jude: freeze, me: burn) and The Drowning Game. The Drowning Game goes like this: If Mom and Dad were drowning, who would we save first? (Me: Mom, duh. Jude: depends on her mood.) And there's the other variation: If we were drowning, who would Dad save first? (Jude.) For thirteen years, Mom's stumped us. We had absolutely no idea who she'd dredge out of the water first.

Until now.

And without sharing a glance, we both know it.

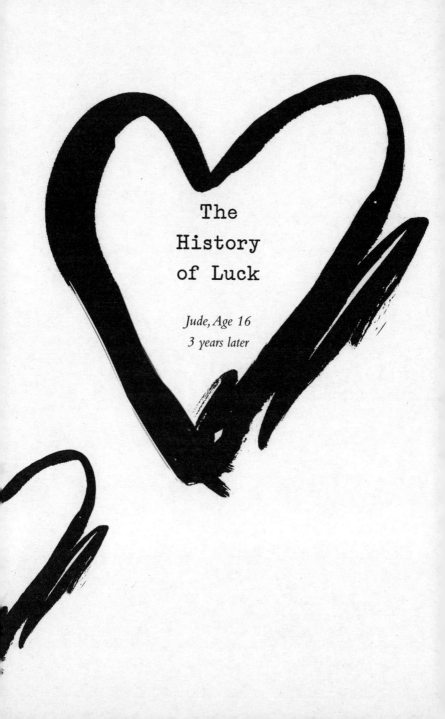

The History of Luck

Jude, Age 16
3 years later

Here I am.

Standing next to my sculpture in the studio at CSA with a four-leaf clover in my pocket. I spent all morning on hands and knees in a clover patch outside school, all for nothing – it was picked clean. But then, eureka! I super-glued a fourth leaf onto an ordinary old three-leafer, wrapped it in cellophane, and slipped it into my sweatshirt pocket right beside the onion.

I'm a bit of a bible thumper. Other people have the Gideon, I have Grandma Sweetwine's. Some sample passages:

A person in possession of a four-leaf clover
is able to thwart all sinister influences
*(Art school is rife with sinister influences. Especially today –
not only is it my critique day, I have a meeting with my advisor
and I might be expelled.)*

To avoid serious illness, keep an onion
in your pocket
(Check. Can't be too careful.)

If a boy gives a girl an orange,
her love for him will multiply
*(Jury's out.
No boy has ever given me an orange.)*

The feet of ghosts never touch the ground
(We'll get to this. Soon.)

The bell rings.

And there they are. The other clay second-years. Every last one of them ready to suffocate me with a pillow. Oops, I mean: staring dumbfounded at my sculpture. The assignment was to do another self-portrait. I went abstract, as in: blob. Degas had dancers, I have blobs. Broken, glued-together blobs. This is my eighth.

"What's working here?" asks Sandy Ellis, master ceramicist, clay instructor, and my advisor. The way he begins every critique.

No one says a word. The proper California School of the Aliens feedback sandwich starts and ends with praise − in between, people say the terrible things they really think.

I scan the room without moving my head. The sophomore clay crew is a pretty good sampling of the CSA student body: freak-flags of every variety flying proud and loud. Normal run-of-the-mill people like me − except for a few discreet tics, sure, who doesn't have something? − are the exception.

I know what you're thinking. It's Noah who belongs at this school, not me.

Sandy peers at the class over his round, tinted spectacles.

Usually everyone jumps right in, but the only sound in the studio is the electric hum of the fluorescent lights. I study the time on Mom's old watch − she was wearing it when her car sailed off the cliff two years ago, killing her on impact − as it ticks around my wrist.

Rain in December brings
with it an unforeseen funeral
(It rained most of the December before she died.)

"C'mon guys, positive impressions of *Broken Me-Blob No. 8*?"
Sandy slowly strokes his straggly beard. If we all morphed into
our mirror animals (a game Noah made me play constantly when
we were little), Sandy would poof into a billy goat. "We've been
talking about point of view," he says. "Let's discuss CJ's, shall we?"

CJ, short for Calamity Jane/Jude, is what everyone at school
calls me on account of my "bad luck." It's not just breakage in
the kiln. Last year, in pottery studio, some of my bowls alleg-
edly took flying leaps off the shelves at night when no one was
around, when the windows were all closed, when the closest
earthquake was in Indonesia. The night janitor was confounded.

Everyone was but me.

Caleb Cartwright raises both hands in a gesture that further
clinches his mime-artist thing: black turtleneck, black skinny
jeans, black eyeliner, black bowler hat. He's actually quite hot in
an arty cabaret kind of way, not that I've noticed. The boy boycott's on. I come fully equipped with boy-blinders and failsafe
invisibility uniform:

To disappear into thin air: Cut off three feet
of blond curls and shove remaining hair into a
black skullcap. Keep tattoo tucked away where no
one can see it. Wear only oversized hoodies,
oversized jeans, and sneakers. Stay quiet
(Occasionally, I write a bible passage of my own.)

Caleb scans the room. "I'll just say it for everyone, okay?" He pauses, taking great care to find the perfect words to throw me overboard. "It's impossible to critique CJ's work because it's *always* mangled, glued together like this. I mean, we're talking serious Humpty Dumpty every time."

I imagine myself in a meadow. This is what the school counselor told me to do when I feel mental, or as Grandma used to say: minus some buttons.

And if anyone was wondering: DIY four-leaf clovers have no juice.

"Well, what does that say in and of itself?" Sandy asks the class.

Randall "no offense, but" Brown starts to sputter. He's this all-star a-hole who believes he can say the most offensive things imaginable in critique if he precedes them with "No offense, but." I'd like to shoot him with a tranquilizer dart. "It would say a lot more, Sandy, if it were intentional." He looks at me. Here it comes. "I mean, CJ, *no offense, but* it's got to be that you're fundamentally careless. The only *rational* explanation for so much breakage in the kiln is that you don't knead your clay enough or let your work dry evenly."

Nail on the head. Bingo. Pop goes the weasel.

Sometimes explanations are *not* rational.

Strange things happen. And if we were allowed to talk when our work was being critiqued, and if I could get a signed affidavit from someone very high up, like God for instance, that I wouldn't be locked away for the rest of my life, then I'd say, "Doesn't anyone else have a dead mother angry enough at them to rise from the grave and break their artwork?"

Then they'd understand what I'm up against.

"Randall brings up a good point," Sandy says. "Does intentionality matter in our experience and appreciation of art? If CJ's final sculpture is in pieces, does her original conception of wholeness even matter? Is it about the journey or the destination, so to speak?"

The whole class hums like a happy hive at this and Sandy launches them into a theoretical discussion about whether the artist even matters after the art has been created.

I'd rather think about pickles.

"Me too – kosher dills, big fat juicy ones. Mmm. Mmm. Mmm," whispers Grandma Sweetwine in my head. She's dead like Mom, but unlike Mom, who just breaks things, Grandma's vocal and often visible. She's the good cop of my ghost world; Mom, the bad. I try to keep my face blank as she continues. "Ho, dee, hum, what a snooze. And really, that's a highly unattractive thing you've made. Why all this beating around the bush? Why don't they tell you better luck next time and move on to their next victim like that fella there with the bananas springing out of his head."

"Those are blond dreadlocks, Grandma," I tell her in my mind, careful not to move my mouth.

"I say you make a run for it, dear."

"I'm with you."

Those discreet tics? I confess, maybe not so discreet.

But, for the record: Twenty-two percent of the world's population sees ghosts – that's over one and a half billion people worldwide. (Professors as parents. Mad research skills.)

While the theoretical clone-drone continues, I amuse myself by playing: How Would You Rather Die? I'm the reigning champion of this game. It's not as simple as it seems, because making the deaths on either side of the equation comparably frightful takes enormous skill. For instance: eating fistful after fistful of crushed glass *or*—

I'm interrupted because to my surprise and everyone else's as well, Fish (no last name) has raised her hand. Fish's a mute like me, so this is something.

"CJ has good technique," she says, her tongue stud flashing like a star in her mouth. "I propose it's a ghost that's breaking her work." Everyone hardy-har-hars at this, including Sandy. I'm floored. She wasn't joking, I can tell. She meets my eyes, then lifts her wrist and gives it a subtle shake. On it is a cool punky charm bracelet that perfectly matches the rest of her: purple hair, tattoo sleeves, acid attitude. Then I recognize the charms: three pieces of ruby red sea glass, two four-leaf clovers in plastic, and a handful of sand-dollar birds, all strung together with black ratty leather. Wow. I hadn't realized I'd snuck so much luck into her bag, into her smock pockets. She just always seems so sad under all the ghoulish makeup. But how did she know it was me? Do the rest know too? Like that jittery new kid? Definitely minus some buttons. Been slipping him sand-dollar birds galore.

But Fish's dead ringer of a pronouncement and bracelet are the lone fireworks. For the rest of the hour, one by one, the others skewer *Broken Me-Blob No. 8* and I become more and more aware of my hands, which are in a white-knuckled clasp in front of me. They feel itchy. Very itchy. Finally, I unclasp them and try to examine them on the down low. No sign of a bite or rash. I search for a red spot that might indicate necrotizing fasciitis, more commonly referred to as flesh-eating disease, which I read *all* about in one of Dad's medical journals—

Okay, got it: How Would You Rather Die? Eating handful after handful of crushed glass, or a whopping case of necrotizing fasciitis?

The voice of Felicity Stiles – signifying the end is nigh! – pulls me out of this brain-squeezing conundrum where I'm leaning toward eating the glass.

"Can I do the closing, Sandy?" she asks like she always does. She has this gorgeous lilting South Carolinian accent that she uses to give a sermon at the end of every critique. She's like a flower that talks – an evangelical daffodil. Fish covertly mimes a dagger going into her chest. I smile at her and brace myself. "I just think it's sad," Felicity says, then pauses until the room is hers, which doesn't take more than a second because she doesn't only sound like a daffodil, she looks and acts like one too and we all become human sighs around her. She holds her hand out to my blob. "I can feel the pain of the *whole wide world* in this piece." It takes a full rotation of that world for her to drawl out all those *W*s. "Because we are all broken. I mean, aren't we now? I am. The *whole wide world* is. We try to do our best and this is what happens, time and time again. That's what all CJ's work says to me, and it makes me really, really sad." She faces me directly. "I understand how unhappy you are, CJ. I *really* do." Her eyes are huge, swallowing. Oh, how I hate art school. She raises a fisted hand and clutches it to her chest, then beats it three times, saying, "I. Understand. You."

I can't help it. I'm nodding back at her like a fellow flower, when the table beneath *Broken Me-Blob No. 8* gives way and my self-portrait tumbles to the floor and shatters into pieces. Again.

"That's cold," I tell Mom in my mind.

"You see," Fish declares. "A ghost."

This time nobody hardy-har-hars. Caleb shakes his head: "No way." Randall: "What the hell?" Tell me about it, countrymen. Unlike Casper and Grandma S., Mom is not a friendly ghost.

Sandy's under the table. "A screw fell out," he says in disbelief.

I get the broom I keep at my station for such occasions and sweep up broken *Broken Me-Blob No. 8* while everyone mutters about how unlucky I am. I empty the pieces into a trashcan. After the remains of my self-portrait, I toss in the useless DIY-clover.

I'm thinking maybe Sandy will feel sorry for me and postpone our big meeting until after winter break, which starts tomorrow, when he mouths at me *My office,* and gestures toward the door. I cross the studio.

```
Always walk right foot first to avert calamity,
         which comes at you from the left
```

* * *

I'm sunk into a giant plush leather chair across from Sandy. He's just apologized about the screw falling out and joked that maybe Fish was right about that ghost, eh, CJ?

Chuckling politely here at the absurd notion.

His fingers are piano-ing on the desk. Neither of us is speaking. I'm fine with this.

To his left is a life-size print of Michelangelo's *David*, so vivid in the fragile afternoon light that I keep expecting his chest to heave as he claims his first breath. Sandy follows my gaze over his shoulder to the magnificent stone man.

"Helluva biography your mother wrote," he says, breaking the silence. "Fearless in her examination of his sexuality. Deserved every bit of acclaim it got." He takes off his glasses and rests them on the desk. "Talk to me, CJ."

I glance out the window at the long stretch of beach buried in fog. "A white-out's coming for sure," I say. One of the town of Lost Cove's claims to fame is how often it disappears. "Do you know that some native peoples believe fog contains the restless spirits of the dead?" From Grandma's bible.

"Is that right?" He strokes his beard, transporting flecks of clay from his hand to it. "That's interesting, but right now we need to talk about you. This is a very serious situation."

I think I *was* talking about me.

Silence prevails once again … and I've decided to eat the crushed glass. Final answer.

Sandy sighs. Because I'm disturbing him? I disturb people, I've noticed. Didn't used to.

"Look, I know it's been an extraordinarily hard time for you, CJ." He's searching my face with his kind billy goat eyes. It's excruciating. "And we pretty much gave you a free pass last year because of the tragic circumstances." He has on The Poor Motherless Girl Look – all adults get it at some point when they talk to me, like I'm doomed, shoved out of the airplane without a parachute because mothers *are* the parachutes. I drop my gaze, notice a fatal melanoma on his arm, see his life pass before my eyes, then realize with relief it's a dot of clay. "But CSA is a tight ship," he says more sternly. "Not passing a studio is grounds for expulsion, and we decided to just put you on probation." He leans forward. "It's not all the breakage in the kiln. That happens. Granted, it seems to always happen to you, which calls into question your technique and focus, but it's the way you've isolated yourself and your clear lack of investment that deeply concern us. You must know there are young artists all around the country banging on our doors for a spot, for *your* very spot."

I think how much Noah deserves my spot. Isn't that what Mom's ghost is telling me by breaking everything I make?

I know it is.

I take a breath and then I say it. "Let them have my spot. Really, they deserve it. I don't." I lift my head, look in his stunned eyes. "I don't belong here, Sandy."

"I see," he says. "Well, you might feel that way, but the CSA faculty think differently. *I* think differently." He picks up his glasses, begins cleaning them with his clay-splattered shirt, making them dirtier. "There was something so unique in those women you made out of sand, the ones that were part of your admission portfolio."

Huh?

He closes his eyes for a moment like he's listening to distant music. "They were so joyful, so whimsical. So much motion, so much emotion."

What's he talking about?

"Sandy, I submitted dress patterns and sample dresses I made. I talked about the sand sculptures in my essay."

"Yes, I remember the essay. And I remember the dresses. Lovely. Too bad we don't have a fashion focus. But the reason you're sitting in that chair is because of the photographs of those wonderful sculptures."

There are no photographs of those sculptures.

Okay then, feeling a little light-headed here in this episode of *The Twilight Zone*.

Because no one ever even saw them. I made sure of it, always sneaking far down the beach to an isolated cove, the tide taking them away ... except Noah did tell me once, no, twice actually, that he followed me and watched me build. But did he take pictures? And send them to CSA? Nothing could seem less likely.

When he found out I got in and he didn't, he destroyed everything he'd ever made. Not even a doodle remains. He hasn't picked up a pencil, pastel, stick of charcoal, or paintbrush since.

I glance up at Sandy, who's rapping his knuckles on the desk. Wait, did he just say my sand sculptures were wonderful? I think he did. When he sees I'm listening again, he stops knuckle-rapping and continues. "I know we inundate you with lots of theory your first two years here, but let's you and me get back to basics. One simple question, CJ. Isn't there anything you want to make anymore? You've been through so much for someone so young. Isn't there something you want to say? Something you *need* to say?" He's gotten very serious and intense. "Because that's what all this is about. Nothing else.

We wish with our hands, that's what we do as artists."

His words are loosening something inside. I don't like it.

"Think about it," he says more gently. "I'm going to ask again. Is there something you need in the world that only your two hands can create?"

I feel a searing pain in my chest.

"Is there, CJ?" he insists.

There is. But it's off limits. Imagining that meadow now.

"No," I say.

He grimaces. "I don't believe you."

"There's nothing," I say, holding my hands together as tight as I can in my lap. "Nada. Zip."

He shakes his head, disappointed. "Okay then."

I gaze up at *David…*

"CJ, where are you?"

"Here, I'm here. Sorry." I turn my attention back to him.

He's clearly upset. Why? Why does he care so much? Like he said, there are young artists all around the country dying for my spot. "We need to talk to your father," he says. "You'd be giving up an opportunity of a lifetime. Is this really what you want?"

My eyes drift back to *David*. It's like he's made of light. What I want? I want only one thing—

Then it's as if *David*'s jumped off the wall and swooped me into his massive stone arms and is whispering into my ear.

He reminds me that Michelangelo made him over *five hundred* years ago.

"Do you really want to transfer out?"

"No!" The vehemence in my voice surprises us both. "I

need to work in stone." I point to *David*. An idea's exploding inside me. "There *is* something I need to make," I tell him. I feel wild, like I'm gulping for air. "Badly." I've wanted to make it since I got here, but I couldn't bear it if Mom broke it. Just couldn't bear it.

"This pleases me to no end," Sandy says, clasping his hands together.

"But it can't be built in clay. No kiln," I say. "It has to be stone."

"Much more resilient," he says, smiling. He gets it. Well, part of it.

"Exactly," I say. She will not be able to break this so easily! And more importantly, she's not going to want to. *I'm* going to dazzle her. I'm going to *communicate* with her. This is the way. "I'm so sorry, Jude," she'll whisper in my ear. "I had no idea you had it in you."

And then just maybe she'll forgive me.

I don't realize Sandy's been talking, oblivious of the music swelling, of the mother–daughter reconciliation that's occurring in my head. I try to focus.

"The problem is, with Ivan in Italy for the year, there's no one in the department to help you. If you wanted to work in clay and cast in bronze I could—"

"No, it's got to be stone, the harder the better, granite even." This is genius.

He laughs, back to his mellow goat-grazing-in-a-field self. "Maybe, hmm, maybe … if you're okay with being mentored by someone outside of school?"

"Sure." You kidding? Bonus.

Sandy's stroking his beard, thinking.

And thinking.

"What is it?" I ask.

"Well, there is someone." Sandy raises his eyebrows. "A master carver. One of the last ones standing perhaps. But no, I don't think it's possible." He pushes the idea away with his hand. "He doesn't teach anymore. Doesn't exhibit. Something happened to him. No one knows what the deal is, and even before all this, he wasn't the most ... hmm, how shall I put it?" He looks up at the ceiling, finds the word there: "Human." He laughs, starts digging around in a pile of magazines on his desk. "An extraordinary sculptor and a helluva speaker. I heard him when I was in grad school, amazing, he—"

"If not human, what?" I interrupt, intrigued.

"Actually..." He smiles at me. "I think your mother said it best."

"My mother?" I don't even need to have The Sweetwine Gift to know this is a sign.

"Yes, your mother wrote about him in *Art Tomorrow*. Funny. I was just looking at the interview the other day." He flips through a few issues of the magazine Mom used to write for, but doesn't find it. "Oh well," he says, giving up. He leans back in his chair. "Let me think ... what were her words? Oh yes, yes, she said, 'He was the kind of man who walks into a room and all the walls fall down.'"

A man who walks into a room and all the walls fall down?

"What's his name?" I ask, feeling a little breathless.

He presses his lips together for a long moment, studying me, then seems to make a decision. "I'll give him a call first. If it's a go, you can pay him a visit after winter break." He writes a name and address on a piece of paper and hands it to me.

Smiling, he says, "Don't say you weren't warned."

* * *

Grandma Sweetwine and I are lost in oblivion, unable to see anything in the fog as we make our way through the ground cloud to Day Street in the inland flats of Lost Cove where Guillermo Garcia's studio is. That's the name of the sculptor that was on the piece of paper Sandy gave me. I don't want to wait to *see* if it's a go, I just want to *go*.

Before leaving school I consorted with The Oracle: Google. Internet searches are better than tea leaves or a tarot deck. You put in your question: *Am I a bad person? Is this headache a symptom of an inoperable brain tumor? Why won't my mother's ghost speak to me? What should I do about Noah?* Then you sort through the results and determine the divination.

When I put in the question: *Should I ask Guillermo Garcia to be my mentor?,* up popped a link for the cover of *Interview Magazine*. I clicked on it. The photograph was of a dark, imposing man with radioactive green eyes wielding a baseball bat at Rodin's lovely romantic sculpture *The Kiss*. The caption read: *Guillermo Garcia: The Rock Star of the Sculpture World*. On the cover of *Interview*! I stopped there because of the cardiac symptoms.

"You look like a hoodlum in that getup," Grandma Sweetwine says, sweeping along beside me a good foot above the ground, twirling a magenta sun parasol, without a care for the dismal weather. She's dressed to the nines like always, in a color-splashed Floating Dress that makes her look like a billowy sunset, and enormous tortoiseshell movie-star sunglasses. She's barefoot. Not much need for shoes if you hover. She got lucky on the foot-front.

Some visitors from the beyond return with
their feet on backward
(Beyond disturbing. Thankfully, hers are on right.)

She continues. "You look like that fella, you know, whosama-callit, Reese's Pieces."

"Eminem?" I ask, with a smile. The fog's so thick, I have to walk with my arms out straight so I don't collide into any mail-boxes or telephone poles or trees.

"Yes!" She taps the sidewalk with the parasol. "I knew it was some kind of candy. Him." The parasol's pointing at me now. "All those dresses you make locked away in your bedroom. It's a travesty." She sighs one of her record-length sighs. "What about the suitors, Jude?"

"I don't have any suitors, Grandma."

"My point exactly, dear," she says, then cackles with delight at her own wit.

A woman passes us with two kids in fog harnesses, also known as leashes, not unusual in Lost Cove during a white-out.

I look down at my invisibility uniform. Grandma still doesn't get it. I tell her, "Being with boys is more dangerous for me than killing a cricket or having a bird fly into the house."

Other serious portents of death. "You know this."

"Nonsense. What I know is you have an enviable love-line on your palm, just like your brother, but even fate needs a goose in the rear sometimes. Best stop dressing like a life-size swede. And grow the hair back already, for Pete's sake."

"You're very superficial, Grandma."

She harrumphs at me.

I harrumph back, then turn the tables. "I don't want to alarm you, but I think your feet are starting to point the wrong way. You know what they say. Nothing ruins an ensemble like ass-backward feet."

She gasps, looking down. "How to give an old, dead woman a heart attack!"

By the time we get to Day Street, I'm damp through and shivering. I notice a small church at the end of the block, a perfect place to dry off, warm up, and strategize about how I'm going to convince this Guillermo Garcia to mentor me.

"I'll wait outside," Grandma tells me. "But please, take your time. Don't worry about me, all alone out here in the cold, wet fog." She wiggles her bare toes on both feet. "Shoeless, penniless, dead."

"Subtle," I say, heading down the path to the church.

"Regards to Clark Gable," she calls after me as I pull the ring to open the door. Clark Gable is her pet name for God. A blast of warmth and light embraces me the moment I step in. Mom was a church-hopper, always dragging Noah and me with her, except never when a service was going on. She said she just liked to sit in holy spaces. Me too now.

If you're in need of divine help, open a jar in a
place of worship and close it upon leaving
*(Mom told us she sometimes used to hide out from her foster
"situations" in nearby churches. I suspect she needed more than a
jar of help, though it was impossible to get her to talk much about
that time in her life.)*

This one is a beautiful boat-like room of dark wood and bright
stained-glass panels of, it looks like, yup, Noah building the ark,
Noah greeting the animals as they board, Noah, Noah, Noah.
I sigh.

In every set of twins,
there is one angel, one devil

I take a seat in the second row. While rubbing my arms furiously
to warm up, I think about what I'm going to say to Guillermo
Garcia. What does a Broken Me-Blob say to *The Rock Star of the
Sculpture World*? A man who walks into a room and all the walls
fall down? How am I going to convey to him that it's absolutely
dire that he mentor me? That making this sculpture will—

A loud clatter blasts me out of my thoughts, my seat, and
skin all at once.

"Oh bloody hell, you scared me!" The deep, whispery English-accented voice is coming out of a bent-over guy on the altar
picking up the candlestick he just knocked off. "Oh Christ! I
can't believe I just said bloody hell in church. And Christ, I just
said Christ! Jesus!" He stands up, rests the candlestick on the
table, then smiles the most crooked smile I've ever seen, like
Picasso made it. "Guess I'm damned." There's a scar zigzagging

In
Every
Set of
TWINS,
there is
one Angel,
one Devil

across his left cheek and one running from the base of his nose into his lip. "Well, doesn't matter," he continues in a stage whisper. "Always thought heaven would be crap anyway. All those preposterous puffy clouds. All that mind-numbing white. All those self-righteous, morally unambiguous goody two-shoes." The smile and accompanying crookedness hijack his whole face. It's an impatient, devil-may-care, chip-toothed smile on an off-kilter, asymmetrical face. He's totally wild-looking, hot, in a let's-break-the-law kind of way, not that I notice.

> Any marked peculiarity in the face indicates
> a similar peculiarity of disposition
> *(Hmm.)*

And where did he come from? England, it seems, but did he just teleport here mid-monologue?

"Sorry," he whispers, taking me in. I realize I'm still frozen with my hand plastered to my chest and my mouth open in surprise. I quickly rearrange myself. "Didn't mean to startle you," he says. "Didn't think anyone else was here. No one's ever here." He comes to this church often? To repent probably. He looks like he has sins, big juicy ones. He gestures at a door behind the altar. "I was just skulking about, taking photos." He pauses, tilts his head, studies me with curiosity. I notice a blue tattoo poking out of his collar.

"You know, you really ought to put a lid on it. Such a chatterbox, a guy can't get a word in."

I feel a smile maneuvering its way around my face that I resist as per the tenets of the boycott. He's charming, not that

I notice that either. Charming is bad luck. I also don't notice that his sinful self seems smart, nor how tall he is, nor the way his tangly brown hair falls over one eye, nor the black leather motorcycle jacket, perfectly worn in and ridiculously cool. He's carrying a beat-up messenger bag on one shoulder that's full of books – college books? Maybe, definitely a senior if still in high school. And he has a camera around his neck that is now pointing at me.

"No," I shriek loud enough to blow the roof as I duck behind the pew in front of me. I must look like a cold wet ferret. I don't want this guy having a picture of me looking like a cold wet ferret. And vanity aside:

> Every picture taken of you reduces your spirit
> and shortens your life

"Hmm, yes," he whispers. "You're one of those, afraid the camera will steal your soul or some such." I eye him. Is he versed in some such? "In any case, please keep your voice down. We are in church, after all." He grins in his chaotic way, then turns the camera up at the wooden ceiling, clicks. There's something else I'm not noticing: He seems familiar to me somehow, like we've met before, but I've no idea where or when.

I slip off my hat and start combing my fingers through the stubborn mat of neglected hair … like I'm not a girl with boy blinders! What am I thinking? I remind myself he's decaying like every other living thing. I remind myself I'm a bible-thumping Broken Me-Blob with hypochondriachal tendencies whose only friend is possibly a figment of her imagination. Sorry,

Grandma. I remind myself he's probably worse luck than all the world's black cats and broken mirrors combined. I remind myself some girls deserve to be alone.

Before I can get my skullcap back on, he says in a regular speaking voice, quite a deep, velvety one, not that I notice, "Change your mind? Please do. I'm going to have to insist on it." He's aiming the camera at me again.

I shake my head to indicate I am in no way changing my mind. I put my hat back on, pull it down low, practically over my eyes, but then I bring my index finger to my lips in a *shhh,* which might appear to be flirting to the casual viewer, but luckily there are no casual viewers present. I can't seem to help it. And it's not like I'll ever see him again.

"Right, forgot where we were for a minute," he says, smiling and bringing his voice down to a whisper again. He regards me for a long, unnerving moment. It's like being held in a spotlight. Actually, I'm not sure it's legal to be looked at like this. My chest starts humming. "Too bad about the photo," he says. "Hope you don't mind me saying, but you look like an angel sitting there." He presses his lips together as if considering this. "But in disguise, like you just fell down and then borrowed some bloke's clothes."

What do I say to that? Especially now that the humming in my chest has turned into jackhammering.

"In any case, can't blame you for wanting out of the angelic order." He's grinning again and I'm spinning. "Probably quite a bit more interesting to be among us screwed-up mortals, like I said before." He sure has the gift of the gab. I used to too, once, though you'd never know it. He must think my jaw's wired shut.

Oh boy. He's looking at me again in that way of his, like he's trying to see beneath the skin.

"Let me," he says, his hand circling the lens. It's more command than question. "Just one." There's something in his voice, in his gaze, in his whole being, something hungry and insistent, and it's untethering me.

I'm nodding. I can't believe it, but I'm nodding. To hell with my vanity, my spirit, my old age. "Okay," I say, my voice hoarse and strange. "Just one." It's possible he's put me in a trance. It happens. There are people who are mesmerists. It's in the bible.

He lands in a squat behind a pew in the front row, spins the lens a few times while looking through the camera. "Oh God," he says. "Yes. Perfect. Fucking perfect."

I know he's taking a hundred pictures, but I don't care anymore. A hot series of shivers is running through me as he continues clicking and saying: *Yes, thank you, this is totally bloody it, perfect, yes, yes, sodding hell, God, look at you.* It's like we're kissing, way more than kissing. I can't imagine what my face must look like.

"You're her," he says finally, putting the cover over the lens. "I'm sure of it."

"Who?" I ask.

But he doesn't answer, just walks down the aisle toward me, a lazy, lanky walk that makes me think of summer. He's completely unwound now, went from high gear to no gear the moment he covered the lens. As he approaches, I see that he has one green eye and one brown eye, like he's two people in one, two very intense people in one.

"Well," he says when he's by my side. He pauses there as if he's going to say something more, like, I'm hoping what he meant by "You're her," but instead he just adds, "I'll leave you to it," and points up at Clark Gable.

Looking at this totally unbelievable guy from such close range, it strikes me now with certainty that it's not the first time I've laid eyes on him.

Okay, I effing noticed.

I think he's going to shake my hand or touch my shoulder or something, but he just continues down the aisle. I turn around and watch him stroll along like he should have a piece of hay in his mouth. He picks up a tripod I didn't notice when I came in and swings it over his shoulder. As he goes out the door, he doesn't turn around, but raises his free hand in the air and waves slightly like he knows I'm watching him.

Which I am.

* * *

I leave the church a few minutes later feeling warmer, drier, and like I narrowly escaped something. Grandma Sweetwine's nowhere in sight.

I press down the street looking for the address of the sculpture studio.

To be clear, when you're me, guys like him are kryptonite, not that I've ever met a guy like him before, one who makes you feel like you're being kissed, no, *ravished,* from across a room. He didn't seem to notice I was roped off either. Well, I am and must remain that way. I can't let my guard down. My mother was right after all. I don't want to be *that girl*. I can't be.

> **What someone says to you right**
> **before they die will come true**
> *(I was on my way to a party and she said to me:*
> *"Do you really want to be that girl?" and pointed to my*
> *reflection in the mirror. It was the night before she died.)*

It wasn't the first time she'd said it either. *Do you really want to be* that girl, *Jude?*

Well, yeah, I did, because *that girl* got her attention. *That girl* got everyone's attention.

Especially the attention of the older guys on the hill, like Michael Ravens, aka Zephyr, who made me feel faint every time he spoke to me, every time he let me jump the line to catch a wave, every time he texted or messaged me at night, every time he casually touched me in conversation – above all, the time he looped his finger through the plastic ring of my bikini bottoms and pulled me to him so he could whisper in my ear: *Come with me.*

I went.

You can say no, he said.

His breath was ragged, his giant hands all over me, his fingers in me, the sand burning into my back, my brand-new cherub tattoo burning into my belly. The sun burning up the sky. *You can totally say no, Jude.* That's what he said, but it seemed like he meant the opposite. It seemed like he weighed as much as the ocean, like my bikini bottoms were already bunched in his hand, like I was being sucked into that wave you hope never finds you, the one that takes you under, takes your breath, your bearings, disorients you completely and never brings you back to the surface again. *You can say no.* The words rumbled between us. Why didn't I? It seemed like my mouth was filling with sand. Then the whole world filled with it. I didn't say a thing. Not aloud anyway.

It'd all happened so quickly. We were a few coves down from everyone else, hidden from the beach traffic by rocks. Minutes before we'd been talking about the surf, talking about his friend who'd done my tattoo, talking about the party we went to the previous night, where I'd sat on his lap and drank the first beer of my life. I'd just turned fourteen. He was almost four years older than me.

Then we stopped talking and he kissed me. Our first kiss.

I kissed him back. His lips tasted salty. He smelled like coconut suntan lotion. In between kisses, he started saying my name like it was this scalding thing in his mouth. Then he slipped the cups of my yellow bikini top to the sides and swallowed hard as he looked at me. I moved the fabric back in place, not because I didn't want him to stare at me like that, but because I did and it embarrassed me. It was the first time any guy had ever seen me without a bra or anything and my cheeks flamed. He smiled. His pupils were big and black, his eyes so dark as he lowered me onto my back in the sand and slowly pushed the fabric of my top again to the sides. This time I let him. I let him look at me. I let my cheeks flame. I could hear his breathing in my own body. He started to kiss my breasts. I wasn't sure I liked it. Then his mouth was on mine so hard I could barely breathe. That's when his eyes got unseeing and his hands and hands and hands were everywhere at once. That's when he started telling me I could say no and that's when I didn't. Then his whole body was pressing me into the hot sand, burying me in it. I kept thinking, it's okay, I can handle this. I can. It's okay, okay, okay. But it wasn't and I couldn't.

I didn't know you could get buried in your own silence.

And then it was over.

And then everything was.

There's more, but I'm not going to get into it now. Just know: I cut off three feet of blond hair and swore off boys forever because after this happened with Zephyr, my mother died. *Right* after. It was me. I brought the bad luck to us.

This boycott isn't whimsy. To me, boys don't smell like soap or shampoo or cut grass or sweat from soccer practice or suntan lotion or the ocean from hours spent in the green curl of a wave anymore, they smell like death.

I exhale, shove all that out the door of my mind with a swift kick, take a deep breath of the wet pulsing air, and start looking for Guillermo Garcia's studio. It's Mom I need to think about, and making this sculpture. I'm going to wish with my hands. I'm going to wish hard.

A few moments later I'm standing in front of a big brick warehouse: 225 Day Street.

The fog's barely lifted and the volume of the world's down way low – just me in the hush.

There's no bell by the door, or there was a bell, but it's been dismantled, or chewed up by a wild animal, only a bunch of ravaged wires sticking out. How very neighborly. Sandy wasn't kidding. I cross the fingers of my left hand for luck and knock on the door with my right.

Nothing.

I look around for Grandma – I wish she'd print out her daily schedule and give it to me – and try again.

Then I knock a third time, but more tentatively, because maybe this isn't a good idea. Sandy said this sculptor wasn't human, um, what does that mean anyway? And what my mother said about the walls? That doesn't sound, well, safe, now does it? Actually, what the hell am I thinking stopping in like this? Before Sandy's even talked to him to see if he's of sound mind. And in this fog, which is totally creepy and cold and foreboding. I cast around, jump down the step, ready to leap into the mist and disappear, when I hear the door creak open.

Horror movie creak.

There's a large man who's been sleeping for several centuries framed in the doorway. Igor, I think; if he/it had a name, it would be Igor. Hair crawls all over his head, culminating in a black wiry beard uncoiling in every direction at once.

An abundance of facial hair indicates a man
of an ungovernable nature
(*No question.*)

His palms are practically blue with thick calluses, like he's spent his life walking on his hands. This can't be the same guy in the photograph. This can't be Guillermo Garcia:

The Rock Star of the Sculpture World.

"Sorry," I say quickly. "I didn't mean to disturb you." I have to get out of here. Whoever this is, *no offense, but* he eats puppies.

He brushes hair out of his eyes and color jumps from them – a light green that is near fluorescent like in the picture. It *is* him. Everything's telling me to turn and run, but I can't seem to look away, and I guess, like the English guy, no one ever taught Igor it's not polite to stare, because we're in a deadlock – our gazes have glued themselves together – until he trips on absolutely nothing and almost falls, grabbing on to the door to keep himself up. Is he drunk? I inhale deeply, and yes, smell faintly the sweet acrid smell of alcohol.

Something happened to him, Sandy had said. *No one knows what the deal is.*

"Are you okay?" I ask, my voice barely audible. It's like he's fallen out of time.

"No," he answers firmly. "I am not." A Hispanic accent breaks through the words.

I'm surprised by his answer, find myself thinking: *Oh me neither, I'm not okay at all, haven't been in forever,* and I feel like saying it aloud for some reason to this crazy man. Maybe I've fallen out of time right along with him.

He looks me over as if inventorying my whole being. Sandy and Mom were right. This is not a normal dude. His gaze lands back in my eyes – it's like an electro-shock, a jolt straight to my core.

"Go away," he says forcefully, his voice as big as the whole block. "Whoever you are, whatever you want, do not come back here." Then he turns unsteadily, grabs the doorknob for balance, and shuts the door.

I stand there for a long time letting the fog erase me piece by piece.

Then, I knock again. Hard. I'm not going away. I can't. I need to make this sculpture.

"That's right." It's Grandma in my head. "That's my girl."

But it isn't Igor who opens the door this time, it's the English guy from the church.

Holy effing hell.

Surprise sparks in his mismatched eyes as he recognizes me. I hear banging and clattering and breaking from within the studio, like some super-humans are having a furniture-throwing contest. "Not a good time," he says. Then I hear Igor's voice erupt in Spanish as he throws a car across the room, from the way it sounds. The English guy looks over his shoulder, then back to me, his wild face wild with worry now. All his cocky confidence, his cheerfulness, his flirtatiousness have vanished. "I'm very sorry," he says politely, like an English butler in a movie, then closes the door in my face without another word.

* * *

A half hour later, Grandma and I are hidden in the brush above the beach waiting, if necessary, to save Noah's life. On the way home from Drunken Igor's, while already plotting my return visit, I received an emergency text from Heather, my informant: NOAH AT DEVIL'S DROP IN 15.

I don't take chances when it comes to Noah and the ocean.

The last time I stepped foot in the water was to drag him

out of it. Two years ago, a couple weeks after Mom died, he jumped off this same Devil's Drop, got caught in a rip, and almost drowned. When I finally got his body – twice my size, chest still as stone, eyes slung back – to shore, and to revive, I was so furious at him I almost rolled him back into the surf.

> When twins are separated, their spirits steal
> away to find the other

The fog's mostly burned off down here. Surrounded by water on three sides and forest everywhere else, Lost Cove is the end, the farthest point west you can go before falling off the world. I scan the bluff for our red house, one of many ramshackles up there, clinging to the edge of the continent. I used to love living on the cliffs – surfed and swam so much that even when I was out of the water, I could feel the ground rocking under my feet like a moored boat.

I check the ledge again. Still no Noah.

Grandma's peering at me over her sunglasses. "Quite the pair, those two foreign fellas. The older one doesn't have a button left on him."

"You're telling me," I say, digging my fingers into the cold sand. How am I ever going to convince that hairy, drunken, furniture-throwing, scary-ass Igor to mentor me? And if I do, how will I steer clear of that unremarkable, plain-faced, dull-witted English guy who turned boycotting-me into a molten mess in a matter of minutes – and in a church!

A flock of gulls swoops down to the breakers, wings outspread, crying.

And for some reason, I keep wishing I'd told Drunken Igor that I wasn't okay either.

Grandma releases her parasol into the air. I look up, see the pink disc whirling off into the steely sky. Beautiful. Like something Noah would've drawn when he used to draw. "You have to do something about him," she says. "You know you do. He was supposed to be the next Chagall, not the next doorstop. You are your brother's keeper, dear."

This is one of her refrains. She's like my conscience or something. That's what the counselor at school said anyway about Grandma's and Mom's ghosts, which was pretty astute considering I hardly told her anything.

One time, she made me do this guided meditation where I had to imagine myself walking in the woods and tell her what I saw. I saw woods. But then, a house appeared, only there was no way to get in it. No doors or windows. Major heebie-jeebies. She told me the house was me. Guilt is a prison, she said. I stopped going to see her.

I don't realize I'm checking my palms for creeping lesions, eruptions called cutaneous larva migrans, until Grandma gives me The Eye-Roll. It's dizzying. I'm pretty sure I acquired this skill from her.

"Hookworm," I say sheepishly.

"Do us all a favor, morbid one," she chides. "Stay out of your father's medical journals."

Though she's been dead for over three years, Grandma didn't start visiting me like this until two years ago. Just days after Mom died, I hauled the old Singer out of the closet and the moment I flipped the switch and the familiar hummingbird heartbeat of her sewing machine filled my bedroom, there she was in the chair beside me, pins in her mouth like always, saying, "The zigzag stitch is all the rage. Makes such a glamorous hem. Wait until you see."

We were partners in sewing. And partners in luck-hunting: four-leaf clovers, sand-dollar birds, red sea glass, clouds shaped like hearts, the first daffodils of spring, ladybugs, ladies in over-sized hats. *Best to bet on all the horses, dear,* she'd say. *Quick, make a wish,* she'd say. I bet. I wished. I was her disciple. I still am.

"They're here," I tell her, and my heart begins pacing around inside my chest in anticipation for the jump.

Noah and Heather are standing on the ledge gazing out over the whitecaps. He's in swimming trunks, she in a long blue coat. Heather's a great informant because she's never more than a shout away from my brother. She's like his spirit animal, a gentle, odd, spritely being who I'm pretty sure has a storage space somewhere full of fairy dust. We've had this secret Keep Noah from Drowning Treaty for a while now. The only problem is she's not lifeguard material herself. She never goes in the water.

A moment later, Noah's flying through the air, arms out-stretched like he's on the cross. I feel a surge of adrenaline.

And then what always happens: *He slows down.* I can't explain it, but it takes my brother forever to hit the surface of the water. I blink a few times at him suspended there midair as if on a tight rope. I've come to think either he has a way with gravity or I'm seriously missing more than a few buttons. I did read once that anxiety can significantly alter space–time perception.

Usually Noah faces the horizon not the shore when he jumps, so I've never before had a full frontal, tip-to-toe view of my brother dropping through space. His neck's arched, his chest's thrust forward, and I can tell, even from this distance, that his face is blown open, like it used to be, and now his arms are reaching upward like he's trying to hold up the whole sorry sky with his fingertips.

"Look at that," Grandma says, her voice tinged with wonder. "There he is. Our boy has returned. He's in the sky."

"He's like one of his drawings," I whisper.

Is this why he keeps jumping, then? To become for the briefest moment who he used to be? Because the worst thing that could ever happen to Noah has happened. He's become normal. He has the proper amount of buttons.

Except for this. This fixation with jumping Devil's Drop.

At last, Noah hits the water without a splash as if he's gathered no momentum on his way down, as if he's been placed gently on the surface by a kindly giant. And then he's under. I tell him: *Come in,* but our twin-telepathy is long gone. When Mom died, he hung up on me. And now, because of all that's happened, we avoid each other – worse, repel each other.

I see his arms flail once. Is he struggling? The water must be freezing. He's not wearing the trunks I sewed protective herbs into either. Okay, he's swimming hard now, through the chaos of currents that surround the cliffs … and then, he's out of danger. I exhale loudly, not realizing until I do that I'd been holding my breath.

I watch him scramble up the beach, then the bluff, with his head down, shoulders hunched, thinking about Clark Gable knows what. No traces of what I just saw in his face, in his very being, remain. His soul has crawled back into its trench.

This is what I want: I want to grab my brother's hand and run back through time, losing years like coats falling from our shoulders.

Things don't really turn out like you think.

To reverse destiny, stand in a field with a knife
pointed in the direction of the wind

The
Invisible
Museum

Noah, Age 13½

The NEIGHBORHOOD TERROR threat level

drops as I pan with Dad's binoculars from the forest and street on the front side of our house to the bluff and ocean in the back. I'm on the roof, the best surveillance spot, and Fry and Zephyr are paddling through the break on their surfboards. I can tell it's them because of the sign flashing over their heads that reads: *Itchy Blistering Brain-Boiled Sociopathic Onion-Eyed Asshats.* Good. I have to be down the hill at CSA in an hour and now I can take the streets, for once, instead of tearing through the woods, trying to give Fry the slip. Zephyr, for some reason (Into Jude? The concrete dork?), leaves me alone now, but everywhere I go, there's Fry, like some mad dog on meat. Throwing me over Devil's Drop is his obsession this summer.

I mentally send a school of famished great white sharks their way, then find Jude on the beach and zoom in. She's surrounded by the same bunch of girls she's been hanging around with all spring and so far this summer instead of me. Pretty hornet-girls in bright bikinis with suntans that glimmer for miles. I know all about hornets: If one sends out a distress signal, it can trigger a whole nest attack. This can be deadly to people like me.

Mom says Jude acts the way she does now on account of hormones, but I know it's on account of her hating me. She stopped going to museums with us ages ago, which is probably a good thing, because when she did, her shadow kept trying to strangle mine. I'd see it happening on the walls or on the floor. Sometimes lately, I catch her shadow creeping around my bed at night trying to pull the dreams out of my head. I have a good idea what she does instead of coming to the museum, though. Three times now, I've seen hickeys on her neck. Bug bites, she said. Sure. I heard while spying that she and Courtney Barrett have been riding bikes down to the boardwalk on weekends, where they see who can kiss more boys.

(Portrait: *Jude Braiding Boy After Boy into Her Hair*)

Truth is: Jude doesn't have to send her shadow after me. It's not like she can't take Mom down to the beach and show her one of her flying sand women before the tide wipes it out. It would change everything. Not that I want that.

Not one bit.

The other day, I was watching her make one from the bluff. She was at her place, three coves away. This time it was a big round woman, done bas relief, like always, except she was halfway turned into a bird – so incredible it made my head vibrate. I snapped a picture with Dad's camera, but then something really horrible and maggoty came over me and as soon as Jude had walked off and was out of sight and earshot, I slid down the whole cliff, raced through the sand, and, roaring like a howler monkey – its roar is epic – knocked into the awesome bird-woman with my whole body, toppling and kicking it to nothing. I couldn't even wait for the tide to take it out this time. I got sand everywhere, in my eyes and ears and down my throat.

I kept finding it on me days after, in my bed, in my clothes, under my nails. But I had to do it. It was too good.

What if Mom had gone for a walk and seen it?

Because what if it's Jude who has it? Why wouldn't that be the case? She surfs waves as big as houses and jumps off anything. She has skin that fits and friends and Dad and The Sweetwine Gift and gills and fins in addition to lungs and feet.

She gives off light. I give off dark.

(Portrait, Self-portrait: *Twins: The Flashlight and the Flashdark*)

Oh, my body's tightening into a wrung towel from thinking like this.

And all the color's spiraling off everything.

(Self-portrait: *Gray Noah Eating Gray Apples on Gray Grass*)

I pan back up the now colorless hill to the now colorless moving van parked in front of the now colorless house two doors down—

"Where the hell is Ralph? Where the hell is Ralph?" Prophet the parrot next door cries.

"Don't know, buddy. Nobody seems to know," I say under my breath, while I focus on the movers, the same two guys as yesterday – *not* colorless, oh man, so not colorless – horses, both of them, I already decided, one chestnut, one palomino. They're hulking a black piano into the house. I zoom in until I can see the sweat on their flushed foreheads, dripping down their necks, leaving wet transparent patches on their white shirts, which stick to them like skin… These binoculars are so awesome. A tan swath of the chestnut guy's smooth stomach slides out each time he raises his arms. He's more ripped than *David* even. I sit down, rest my elbows on my bent knees, and watch and watch, the swimming, thirsty feeling taking me over. Now they're lifting a couch up the front stairs—

But then I drop the binoculars because on the roof of the house I'm casing, there's a boy pointing a telescope right *at me*. How long has he been there? I peek up at him through my hair. He's wearing a weird hat, one of those old gangster movie ones, and there's white surfer hair sticking out every which way under it. Great, another surftard. Even without the binoculars, I can see he's grinning. Is he laughing at me? Already? Does he know I was watching the movers? Does he think…? He must, he must. I clench up, dread rising in my throat. But maybe not. Maybe he's just grinning in a hello-I'm-new kind of way? Maybe he thinks I was checking out the piano? And asshats usually don't have telescopes, do they? And that hat?

I stand, watching as he takes something out of his pocket, winds his arm back, and then lobs whatever it is into the air over the house between us. Whoa. I stick out my palm and as I do, something slaps hard in the center of it. I think it's burned a hole in my hand and broken my wrist, but I don't flinch.

"Nice catch," he yells.

Ha! It's the first time anyone has said those words to me in my life. I wish Dad heard. I wish a reporter for the *Lost Cove Gazette* heard. I have an allergy to catching and throwing and kicking and dribbling of any kind. *Noah is not a team player.* Well, duh. Revolutionaries aren't team players.

I examine the flat black rock in my hand. It's about the size of a quarter and has cracks all over it. What am I supposed to do with it? I look back at him. He's redirecting the telescope upward. I can't tell what animal he is. Maybe a white Bengal tiger with that hair? And what's he looking at? It's never occurred to me that the stars are still up there shining even in the daytime when we can't see them. He doesn't turn my way again. I slip the rock into my pocket.

"Where the hell is Ralph?" I hear as I quickly climb down the ladder at the side of the house. Maybe *he's* Ralph, I think. Finally. That would be *it*.

I whip across the street to take the woods down the hill to CSA after all, because I'm too embarrassed to pass the new kid. Plus, now that color has refastened itself to everything, it's supernaturally amazing to be in the trees.

People think people are in charge, but they're wrong; it's the trees.

I start to run, start to turn into air, the blue careening off the sky, careening after me, as I sink into green, shades and shades of it, blending and spinning into yellow, freaking yellow, then head-on colliding into the punk-hair purple of lupine: everywhere. I vacuum it in, all of it, in, in − (Self-portrait: *Boy Detonates Grenade of Awesome*) − getting happy now, the gulpy, out-of-breath kind that makes you feel you have a thousand lives crammed inside your measly one, and then before I know it, I'm at CSA.

When school got out two weeks ago, I started doing recon down here, peering in the studio windows when no one was around. I had to see the student artwork, had to find out if it was better than mine, had to know if I really had a shot. For the last six months, I've stayed after school almost every day oil painting with Mr. Grady. I think he wants me to get into CSA as much as Mom and I do.

The artwork must be stowed away, though, because in all my spying I didn't see one painting. I did, however, stumble onto a life drawing class being taught in one of the studio buildings off the main campus – a building with one whole side of it tucked into thick old-growth trees. A freaking miracle. Because what could stop me from taking this class? Covertly, you know, from outside the open window?

So here I am. Both classes so far, there's been a real live naked girl with missile boobs sitting on a platform. We do speed drawings of her every three minutes. Totally cool, even if I have to stand on tiptoe to see in and then bend down to draw, but so what. The most important part is that I can hear the teacher and I already learned this totally new way to hold the charcoal so it's like drawing with a motor.

Today I'm the first to arrive, so I wait for class to start, my back against the warm building, the sun smothering me through a hole in the trees. I take the black stone out of my pocket. Why did the kid on the roof give me this? Why was he smiling at me like that? It didn't seem mean, it really didn't, it seemed – a sound breaks into my thoughts, a very human sound, branches cracking: footsteps.

I'm about to bolt back into the woods, when, in my periphery, I catch some kind of movement on the other side of the building, then hear the same crunching noises as the foot-steps retreat. Where there was nothing, a brown bag's lying on the ground. Weird. I wait a bit, then sneak to the other side of the building and peek around the corner: no one. I go back to the bag wishing I had X-ray eyes, then crouch down and with one hand, shake it open. There's a bottle inside. I take it out: Sapphire gin, half full. Someone's stash. I quickly stuff it back in the bag, place it on the ground, and return to my side of the building. Hello? I'm not getting busted with it and blacklisted from going to CSA.

Peering through the window, I see that everyone's there now. The teacher, who has a white beard and holds his balloon belly when he talks, is by the door with a student. The rest of the class is setting up their pads on their stands. I was right too. They don't even need to turn on the overhead lights at the school. All the students have glowing blood. All revolutionaries. A room of Bubbles. There's not an asshat or surftard or hornet among them.

The curtain around the model's dressing area opens and a tall guy in a blue robe walks out. *A guy.* He undoes the robe, hangs it on a hook, walks naked to the platform, jumps the step, almost falls, then makes some joke that causes everyone to laugh. I don't hear it because of the heat storm roaring through my body. He's *so* naked, way more naked than the girl model was. And unlike the girl, who sat and covered parts of herself with her bony arms, this guy's standing on the platform, in a hand-on-hip pose, like a dare. God. I can't breathe. Then some-one says something I don't catch, but it makes the model smile and when he does, it's like all his features shift and scramble into the most disordered face I've ever seen. A face in a broken mirror. Whoa.

I wedge my pad against the wall, holding it in place with my right hand and knee. When my left hand finally stops shaking, I start to draw. I keep my eyes clamped on him, not looking at what I'm doing. I work on his body, feeling the lines and curves, muscle and bone, feeling every last bit of him travel through my eyes to my fingers. The teacher's voice sounds like waves on the shore. I hear nothing … until the model speaks. I don't know if it's ten minutes or an hour later. "How about a break, then?" he says. I catch an English accent. He shakes his arm out, then his legs. I do the same, realizing how cramped I've been, how my right arm has gone dead, how I've been balancing on one leg, how my knee is aching and numb from being jammed into the wall. I watch him cross to the dressing room, wobbling a little, and that's when it occurs to me the brown bag is his.

A minute later, he lazes across the classroom in his robe toward the door – he moves like glue. I wonder if he's in college around here like the teacher said the girl model was. He looks younger than she did. I'm certain he's coming for the bag even before I smell the cigarette smoke and hear the footsteps. I think about hightailing it into the woods, but I'm frozen.

He rounds the corner and immediately lowers to the ground, his back sliding down the building, not noticing me standing just yards away. His blue robe glitters in the sun like a king's. He stubs the cigarette out in the dirt, then drops his head into his hands – wait, what? And then I see it. This is the real pose, head in hands with sadness leaping off of him all the way to me.

(Portrait: *Boy Blows into Dust*)

He reaches for the bag, takes the bottle out and uncaps it, then starts chugging with his eyes closed. There's no way you're supposed to drink alcohol like this, like it's orange juice. I know I shouldn't be watching, know this is a no-trespassing zone. I don't move a muscle, afraid he'll sense me and realize he has a witness. Several seconds pass with him holding the bottle to his face like a compress, his eyes still closed, the sun streaming down on him like he's being chosen. He takes another sip, then opens his eyes and turns his head my way.

My arms fly up to block his gaze as he scoots back, startled. "Jesus!" he says. "Where the hell did you come from?"

I can't find any words anywhere.

He composes himself quickly. "You scared the life out of me, mate," he says. Then he laughs and hiccups at the same time. He looks from me to my pad resting against the wall, the sketch of him facing out. He recaps the bottle.

"Cat got your tongue? Or wait – do you Americans even say that?"

I nod.

"Right, then. Good to know. Only been here a few months." He gets up, using the wall as support. "So let's have a look," he says, walking unsteadily over to me. He fumbles a cigarette out of a pack that was in his robe pocket. The sadness seems to have evaporated right off him. I notice something remarkable.

"Your eyes are two different colors," I blurt out. Like a Siberian husky's!

"Brilliant. He speaks!" he says, smiling so that a riot breaks out in his face again. He lights the cigarette, inhales deeply, then makes the smoke come out his nose like a dragon. He points to his eyes, says, "Heterochromia iridum, would've had me burned at the stake with the witches, I'm afraid." I want to say how supremely cool it is, but of course I don't. All I can think about now is that I've seen him naked, I've seen *him*. I pray my cheeks aren't as red as they are hot. He nods toward my pad. "Can I?"

I hesitate, worried to have him look at it. "Go on, then," he says, motioning for me to get it. It's like singing the way he talks. I pick up the pad and hand it to him, wanting to explain the octopus-like position I had to be in on account of not having a stand, how I hardly looked down as I was drawing, how I suck. How my blood doesn't glow at all. I swallow it all, say nothing.

"Well done," he says with enthusiasm. "Very well done, you." He seems like he means it. "Couldn't afford the summer class, then?" he asks.

"I'm not a student here."

"You should be," he says, which makes my hot cheeks even hotter. He puts his cigarette out on the building, causing a shower of red sparks. He's definitely not from here. This is fire season. Everything's waiting to go up.

"I'll see if I can smuggle you out a stand on my next break." He stashes the bag by a rock. Then he holds up his hand, points his index finger at me. "You don't tell, I won't tell," he says, like we're allies now. I nod, smiling. English people are so not asshats! I'm going to move there. William Blake was English. Frances freaking-the-most-awesome-painter Bacon too. I watch him walking away, which takes forever on account of his sloth pace, and want to say something more to him, but I don't know what. Before he turns the corner, I think of something. "Are you an artist?"

"I'm a mess is what I am," he says, holding on to the building for support. "A bloody mess. You're the artist, mate." Then he's gone.

I pick up the pad and look at the drawing I did of him, his broad shoulders, his narrow waist, long legs, the trail of hair on his navel going down, down, down. "I'm a bloody mess," I say out loud with his bubbling accent, feeling giddy. "I'm a bloody artist, mate. A bloody mess." I say it a few more times, louder and with more and more gusto, then realize I'm talking with an English accent to a bunch of trees and go back to my spot.

A couple times in the following session, he looks right at me and winks because we're conspirators now! And on the next break, he brings me a stand *and* a footstool so I can really see in. I set it up – it's perfect – then lean against the wall next to him while he sips from the bottle and smokes. I feel way cool, like I'm wearing sunglasses even though I'm not. We're buds, we're *mates*, except he doesn't say anything to me this time, nothing at all, and his eyes have turned cloudy and dim. And it's like he's melting into a puddle of himself.

"Are you okay?" I ask.

"No," he answers. "Not okay at all." Then he throws the burning cigarette into a dry patch of grass before he gets up and stumbles away, not even turning around or saying good-bye.

I stomp out the fire he's started until it's dead, feeling as gloomy as I felt giddy before.

With the new footstool, I can see everything, so I witness what happens next in perfect detail. The teacher meets the model at the door and motions for him to go out into the hall. When the English guy comes back in, his head's down. He crosses the classroom to the dressing area, and when he emerges in clothes, he seems even more lost and out of it than he did on the last break. He never once looks up at the students or at me on his way out.

The teacher explains that he'd been under the influence and won't be modeling at CSA anymore, that CSA has zero tolerance, blah blah blah. He tells us to finish our drawings from memory. I wait a bit to see if the English guy's going to come back, at least for the bottle. When he doesn't, I hide the stand and stool in some bushes for next week and head back into the woods toward home.

* * *

A few steps into the walk, I see the kid from the roof, leaning against a tree, the same grin, the same dark green hat spinning now on his hand. His hair's a bonfire of white light.

I blink because sometimes I see things.

Blinking still. Then to further confirm his existence, he speaks.

"How was class?" he says like it's not the strangest thing in the world that he's here, not the strangest thing that I take drawing outside rather than inside a classroom, not the strangest thing that we don't know each other, and yet, he's smiling at me like we do, and mostly, not the strangest thing that he followed me, because there's no other explanation for him standing here in front of me. As if he heard me thinking, he says, "Yeah, dude, I followed you, wanted to check out the woods, but I've been busy with my own stuff." He points to an open suitcase full of rocks. He collects rocks? And carries them around in a suitcase? "My meteorite bag's still packed," he says, and I nod like this explains something. Aren't meteors in the sky, not on the ground? I look at him more closely. He's a bit older than me, taller and bigger anyway. I realize I have no idea what color I'd use for his eyes. None at all. Today is definitely the day of the supremely excellent-eyed people. His are such a light brown, practically yellow, or copper maybe, and all splintered with green. But you can only see flashes of the color because he squints, which is cool on a face. Maybe not a Bengal tiger after all…

"Stare much?" he says.

I drop my gaze, embarrassed, a total whale dick dork, my neck prickling and hot. I start shuffling some pine needles into a pyramid with the toe of my shoe.

He says, "Well, you're probably just used to it from staring at that drunk guy for so long today." I look up. Was he spying on me the whole time? He's eyeing my pad curiously. "He was naked?" He breathes in as he says it and it makes my stomach drop to the ground floor. I try to keep my face calm. I think about him watching me watch the removal men, about him following me down here. He glances at my pad again. Does he want me to show him the naked drawings of the English guy? I think he does. And I want to. Bad. A heat storm, way more intense than the one before, is whipping through me. I'm pretty sure I've been hijacked and am no longer at the brain controls. It's his weird squinting copper-colored eyes. They're hypnotizing me. Then he smiles but only with half his mouth, and I notice he has a space between his front teeth, also supremely cool on a face. He says with a laugh in his voice, "Look, dude, I have no idea how to get home. I tried and ended up back here. I've been waiting for you to lead the way." He puts on his hat.

I point in the direction we need to go and make my hijacked body start walking. He latches the suitcase full of rocks (hello?), picks it up by the handle, and follows. I try not to look at him as we walk. I want to be rid of him. I think. I keep my eyes on the trees. Trees are safe.

And quiet.

And don't want me to show them the naked pictures in my pad!

It's a long way, mostly uphill, and more daylight's seeping out of the woods every minute. Next to me, even with the suitcase of rocks, which must be heavy, because he keeps switching it from arm to arm, the guy bounces along under his hat, like his legs have springs in them.

After a while, the trees settle me back into my skin.

Or maybe he has.

Because it's actually not awful or anything walking with him.

He might even have some kind of Realm of Calm thing going on around him – maybe he emits it from a finger – because yeah, I feel relaxed now, I mean supernaturally relaxed, like I'm left-out butter. This is highly weird.

He keeps stopping to pick up rocks, examining them, and then either tossing them back or stuffing them in his sweatshirt pocket, which is starting to sag with the weight. I stand by when he does this, wanting to ask what he's searching for. Wanting to ask why he followed me. Wanting to ask about the telescope and if he can see the stars during the daytime. Wanting to ask where he's from and what his name is and if he surfs and how old he is and what school he's going to next fall. A few times I try to form a question so it sounds casual and normal, but each time the words get caught somewhere in my throat and never make it out. Finally, I give up and take out my invisible brushes and just start painting in my head. That's when it occurs to me that maybe the rocks are weighing him down so he doesn't rise into the air...

We walk and walk through the gray ashy dusk and the forest starts to fall asleep. The trees lie down side by side by side, the creek halts, the plants sink back into the earth, the animals switch places with their shadows, and then, so do we.

When we break out of the woods onto our road, he spins around. "Holy hella shit! That's the longest I've gone without talking. Like in my life! It was like holding my breath! I was having a contest with myself. Are you always like this?"

"Like what?" I say, my voice hoarse.

"Dude!" he cries. "Do you know those are the first words you've said?" I didn't. "Man. You're like the Buddha or some-thing. My mom's a Buddhist. She goes to these silent retreats. She should just hang out with you instead. Oh, oh, not counting, of course, 'I'm a bloody artist, a bloody mess, mate.'" He says this last part with a heavy English accent, then cracks up.

He heard me! Talking to the trees! So much blood's rushing and gushing to my head it might blow straight off my neck. All the silence of our walk is gurgling madly out of him now and I can tell he's someone who laughs a lot, the way it's taking him over so easily and lighting him all up, and even though he's laughing at me, it's making me feel okay, accepted, and making me feel a little bubble-headed as laughter starts to fizz up in me too. I mean, it was supremely funny, me yammering away in an English accent all alone like that, and then he says it again, his accent super-thick, "I'm a bloody artist," and then I say, "A bloody mess, mate," and something gives way and I'm laughing outright, and he says it again, and I do, and then we're both really laughing, then the doubled-over kind, and it's ages before we calm down, because each time one of us does, the other says, "I'm a bloody mess, mate," and the whole thing starts all over again.

When we finally get it back together, I realize I have no idea what just happened to me. Nothing like that has ever happened before. I feel like I just flew or something.

He points to my pad. "So I guess you just talk in there, is that it?"

"Pretty much," I say. We're under a streetlamp and I'm trying not to stare but it's hard. I wish the world would stick like a clock so I could look at him for as long as I want. There's something going on in his face right now, something very bright trying to get out — a dam keeping back a wall of light. His soul might be a sun. I've never met anyone who had the sun for a soul.

I want to say more so he doesn't leave. I feel *so* good, the freaking green leafy kind of good. "I paint in my head," I tell him. "I was the whole time." I've never told anyone I do this, not even Jude, and I have no idea why I'm telling him. I've never let anyone into the invisible museum before.

"What were you painting?"

"You."

The surprise opens his eyes wide. I shouldn't have said it. I didn't mean to, it just popped out. The air feels all crackly now and his smile's vanished. Just yards away, my house is a lighthouse. Before I even realize, I'm darting across the street, a queasy feeling in my stomach like I ruined everything – that last brushstroke that *always* destroys the painting. He'll probably try to throw me off Devil's Drop tomorrow with Fry. He'll probably take those rocks and—

As I reach the front step, I hear, "How'd I come out? In the painting." Curiosity in his voice, not a smidge of asshat.

I turn around. He's moved out of the light. I can only see a shadowy shape in the road. This is how he came out: He floated into the air high above the sleeping forest, his green hat spinning a few feet above his head. In his hand was the open suitcase and out of it spilled a whole sky of stars.

I can't tell him, though – how could I? – so I turn back around, jump the steps, open the door, and go inside without looking back.

* * *

The next morning, Jude calls my name from the hallway, meaning she's a moment away from barging into my room. I flip the page of my sketchpad, not wanting her to see what I've been working on: the third version of the copper-eyed, rock-collecting, star-gazing, out-of-control-laughing new kid floating in the sky with his green hat and suitcase full of stars. I finally got the color so perfect, the squint just right, that looking at his eyes in the picture gives me the same hijacked feeling the real ones did. I got so excited when I nailed it I had to walk around my chair about fifty times before I could calm down.

I pick up a pastel and pretend to work on a portrait of the naked English guy that I finished last night. I did it cubist so his face looks even more like it's in a smashed mirror. Jude teeters in wearing high heels and a tiny blue dress. Mom and she can't stop fighting about what she wants to wear now, which is not much. Her hair's snaky and swinging. When it's wet like this, it usually takes the fluff and fairy tale off her, making her seem more ordinary, more like the rest of us, but not today. She has makeup all over her face. They fight about this too. And about her breaking curfew, talking back, slamming doors, texting boys not from school, surfing with the older surftards, jumping off Dead Man's Dive – the highest, scariest jump on the hill – wanting to sleep at one of the hornet's houses practically every night, spending her allowance on some lipstick called Boiling Point, sneaking out her bedroom window. Basically, everything. No one asks me, but I think she's become BeelzeJude and wants every guy in Lost Cove to kiss her now because Mom forgot to look at her sketchbook that first day at the museum.

And because we left her. It was the Jackson Pollock exhibit. Mom and I had spent forever in front of the painting *One: Number 31* – because holy shit! – and when we walked out of the museum, Pollock's bright spidery paint was still all over us, all over the people on the sidewalk, all over the buildings, all over our endless conversation in the car about his technique, and we didn't realize Jude wasn't with us until we were halfway over the bridge.

Mom said, "Ohmygod, ohmygod, ohmygod," the whole speeding way back. All my organs were out of my body. When we screeched up to the museum, Jude was sitting on the sidewalk, her head tucked into her knees. She looked like a crumpled-up piece of paper.

Truth is: I think Mom and I had gotten used to not noticing her when the three of us were together.

She's carrying a box, which she puts on the bed, then comes up behind me, where I'm sitting at my desk and peers over my shoulder. A damp rope of hair lands on my neck. I flick it off.

The naked English guy's face stares up at us from the pad. I wanted to catch the unglued schizo way he looked before he got run over by misery, so I went way more abstract than usual. He probably wouldn't recognize himself, but it came out all right.

"Who's that?" she asks.

"No one."

"Really, who is he?" she insists.

"Just someone I made up," I say, pushing another wet squirrel tail of her hair off my neck.

"Nah-uh. He's real. I can tell you're lying."

"I'm not, Jude. Swear." I don't want to tell her. I don't want her to get any ideas. What if she starts sneaking down to stealth-take classes at CSA too?

She comes around to my side and leans in to better study the drawing.

"I wish he were real," she says. "He's *so* cool-looking. He's so … I don't know… There's something…" This is weird. She never responds like this when she sees my stuff anymore. She usually looks like she has a turd in her mouth. She folds her arms across her chest, which is so full of boobs now, it's like the clash of the titans. "Can I have it?"

This shocks me. She's never asked for a drawing before. I'm horrible at giving them away. "For the sun, stars, oceans, and all the trees, I'll consider it," I say, knowing she'll never agree. She knows how badly I want the sun and trees. We've been dividing up the world since we were five. I'm kicking butt at the moment – universe domination is within my grasp for the first time.

"Are you kidding?" she says, standing up straight. It annoys me how tall she's getting. It's like she's being stretched at night. "That leaves me just the flowers, Noah."

Fine, I think. She'll never do it. It's settled, but it isn't. She reaches over and props up the pad, gazing at the portrait like she's expecting the English guy to speak to her.

"Okay," she says. "Trees, stars, oceans. Fine."

"And the sun, Jude."

"Oh, all right," she says, totally surprising me. "I'll give you the sun."

"I practically have everything now!" I say. "You're crazy!"

"But I have *him*." She carefully rips the naked English guy out of my sketchbook, thankfully not noticing the drawing beneath it, and carries him with her over to the bed and sits down.

She says, "Have you seen the new kid? He's *such* a freak." I look down at my sketchpad, where the freak is exploding into the room in a burst of color. "He wears this green hat with a feather in it. *So* lame." She laughs in her new awful buzzy way. "Yeah. He's weirder than you even." She pauses. I wait, hoping she'll turn back into my sister, the way she used to be, not this new hornet version. "Well, probably not weirder than you." I turn around. The antennae are waving back and forth on her forehead. She's here to sting me to death. "*No one's* weirder than you."

I saw this show about these Malaysian ants that internally combust under threat. They wait until their enemies (like hornets) are close enough, then detonate themselves into a poison bomb.

"I don't know, Noah. Buzz. Buzz. Buzz."

She's on a roll. I begin countdown to detonation. Ten, nine, eight, seven—

"Do you have to be so, buzz, buzz, buzz, so *you,* all the time. It's…" She doesn't finish.

"It's what?" I ask, breaking my pastel in two, snapping it, like a neck.

She throws her hands up. "It's *embarrassing,* okay?"

"At least I'm still me."

"What's that supposed to mean?" Then more defensively, she says, "There's nothing wrong with me. There's nothing wrong with having other friends. Friends who aren't you."

"I have other friends too," I say, glancing down at the sketchpad.

"Oh yeah, who? Who's your friend? Imaginary ones don't count. Neither do the ones you draw."

Six, five, four – what I don't know is if the Malaysian ants kill themselves in the process of annihilating their enemies.

"Well, the new kid for one," I tell her. I reach into my pocket and wrap my fingers around the rock he gave me. "And he's not weird." Though he is! He has a suitcase of rocks!

"He's your friend? Sure he is," she says. "What's his name, if you're such good friends?"

Well, this is a problem.

"That's what I thought," she snips. I can't stand her. I'm *allergic* to her. I look at the Chagall print on the wall in front of me and try to dive into the swirly dream of it. Real life blows. I'm allergic to it too. Laughing with the new kid didn't feel like real life. Not one bit. Being with Jude didn't used to feel like real life either. Now it feels like the very worst strangling, toilet-licking kind. When Jude speaks again a moment later, her voice is sharp and tight. "And what did you expect? I had to make other friends. All you do is hole up making your lame drawings and obsessing about that stupid school with Mom."

Lame drawings?

Here I go. Three, two, one: I detonate with the only thing I have. "You're just jealous, Jude," I say. "All the time now, you're so jealous."

I flip the pad to a blank page, pick up a pencil to start on (Portrait: *My Hornet Sister*), no: (Portrait: *My Spider Sister*), that's better, full of poison and skittering around in the dark on her eight hairy legs.

When the silence between us has just about broken my ears, I turn around to look at her. Her big blue eyes are shining on me. All the hornet's buzzed out of her. And there's no spider to her at all.

I put the pencil down.

So quietly I can barely make out the words, she says, "She's my mom too. Why can't you share?"

The kick of guilt goes straight to my gut. I turn back to the Chagall, begging it to suck me in, please, just as Dad fills up the doorway. He has a towel around his neck, his suntanned chest is bare. His hair's wet too – he and Jude must've swum together. They do everything together now.

He tilts his head in a questioning way, like he can see the body parts and bug guts all around the room. "Everything okay in here, guys?"

We both nod. Dad puts one hand on either side of the frame, filling the entire doorway, filling the Continental United States. How can I hate him and wish I were more like him at the same time?

I didn't always want a building to land on him, though. When we were little, Jude and I used to sit on the beach like two ducklings, *his* ducklings, waiting and waiting for him to finish his swim, to rise out of the white spray like Poseidon. He'd stand in front of us, so colossal he eclipsed the sun, shaking his head so droplets would shower down on us like salty rain. He'd reach for me first, sit me up on one shoulder, then heave-ho Jude onto the other. He'd walk us up the bluff like that, making every other kid on the beach with their flimsy fathers out of their minds with jealousy.

But that was before he realized I was me. This happened the day he did a U-ey on the beach and instead of heading up the bluff, he took the two of us, perched there on his shoulders, back into the ocean. The water was rough and white-capped and waves were hitting us from all sides as we walked deeper and deeper in. I held on to his arm, which was belted securely around me, feeling safe because Dad was in charge and it was his hand that pulled the sun up each morning and down at night.

He told us to jump.

I thought I heard wrong until with an excited yelp, Jude flew off the shelf of his shoulder into the air, smiling crazily all the way down until the ocean swallowed her, still smiling like that when she broke through the surface of the water, where she bobbed like a happy apple, treading her legs, remembering everything we'd learned in our swimming class, while I, feeling Dad's arm unfastening around me, grabbed at his head, his hair, his ear, the slippery slope of his back, but was unable to get a grip anywhere on him.

"It's a sink-or-swim world, Noah," he said very seriously, and then the secure belt of his arm became a sling that flung me into the water.

I sank.

All.

The.

Way.

Down.

(Self-portrait: *Noah and the Sea Cucumbers*)

The first Broken Umbrella Talk happened that night. You need to be brave even when you're afraid, that's what it means to be a man. More talks followed: You need to act tough, sit up, stand straight, fight hard, play ball, look me in the eye, think before you speak. If it weren't for Jude being your twin, I'd think you came about by partheno-whatever. If it weren't for Jude, you'd be mincemeat on that soccer field. If it weren't for Jude. If it weren't for Jude. Doesn't it bother you to have a girl fight your battles for you? Doesn't it bother you to be picked last for every team? Doesn't it bother you to be alone all the time? Doesn't it bother you, Noah? Doesn't it? Doesn't it?

Okay already. Shut up! It does.

Do you have to be so you all the time, Noah?

They're the team now, not Jude and me. So too bad. Why should I share Mom?

"This afternoon, for sure," Jude's saying to Dad. He smiles at her like she's a rainbow, then fee-fi-fo-fums across the room, tapping me affectionately on the head and giving me a concussion. Outside, Prophet squawks, "Where the hell is Ralph? Where the hell is Ralph?"

Dad mimes strangling Prophet with his bare hands, then says to me, "How about that haircut? Looking pretty pre-Raphaelite there with all those long, dark locks." Because of Mom's contagiousness, even Dad, for all his asshatness, knows a lot about art, enough to insult me with anyway.

"I love pre-Raphaelite paintings," I mumble.

"Loving them and looking like a model for one are two

99

different things, huh, chief?" Another swipe to my head, another concussion.

After he's gone, Jude says, "I like your hair long." And it somehow vacuums up all the ick and yuck between us, all my mean cockroachy thoughts too. In a tentatively cheerful voice, she says, "Want to play?"

I turn around, remembering again that we got made together, cell for cell. We were keeping each other company when we didn't have any eyes or hands. Before our soul even got delivered.

She's taking some kind of board out of the box she brought in.

"What is it?" I ask.

"Where the hell is Ralph? Where the hell is Ralph?" Prophet demands again, still in a tizzy. Jude leans out the window by the bed, hollers, "Sorry, Prophet, nobody knows!" I didn't know she talks to Prophet too. I smile.

"A Ouija Board," she says. "Found it in Grandma's room. She and I did it once. We can ask it stuff and it gets the answers."

"From who?" I ask, though I think I've seen one before in some movie.

"You know. The spirits." She smiles and raises her eyebrows up and down and up and down in an exaggerated way. I feel my lips curving into a grin. I so want to be on a team with Jude again! I want things to be like they used to be with us.

"Okay," I say, "sure."

Her face lights up. "Come on." And it's like the whole horrible sticky stupid conversation didn't even happen, like we weren't just both in bits. How can everything change so quickly?

She teaches me how to do it, how to hold the pointer just

barely so the hands of the spirits can push it through my hands to the letters or to the "yes" and "no" written on the board.

"I'm going to ask a question now," she says, closing her eyes and putting her arms out like she's being crucified.

I start to laugh. "And I'm the weirdo? Really?"

She opens one eye. "This is how you have to do it, I swear. Grandma taught me." She closes the eye. "Okay, spirits. This is my question for you: Does M. love me?"

"Who's M.?" I say.

"Just someone."

"Michael Stein?"

"Uck, no way!"

"Not Max Fracker!"

"God no!"

"Then who?"

"Noah, the spirits aren't going to come if you keep interrupting. I'm not going to say who."

"Fine," I say.

She spreads her arms and asks the spirits again, then puts her hands on the pointer.

I put mine on too. It beelines to *No*. I'm pretty sure I pushed it there.

"You're cheating!" she cries.

The next time I don't cheat and it still goes to *No*.

Jude's supremely perturbed. "Let's try again."

This time I can tell she's moving it to *Yes*. "Now *you're* cheating," I say.

"Okay, once more."

It goes to *No*.

"Last try," she says.

It goes to *No*.

She sighs. "Okay, you ask a question."

I close my eyes and ask silently: Will I get into CSA next year?

"Out loud," she says, exasperated.

"Why?"

"Because the spirits can't hear inside your head."

"How do you know?"

"I just do. Now spill. And don't forget the arms."

"Fine." I put my arms out like I'm on the cross and ask, "Will I get into CSA next year?"

"That's a wasted question. Of course you're getting in."

"I need to know for sure."

I make her do it over ten times. Each time it goes to *No*. Finally, she flips the board. "It's just a stupid thing," she says, but I know she doesn't believe it. M. doesn't love her and I'm not going to CSA.

"Let's ask if you're going," I say.

"That's dumb. No way I'm getting in. Who knows if I'm even going to apply? I want to go to Roosevelt like everyone else. They have a swim team."

"C'mon," I say.

It goes to *Yes*.

Again.

And again.

And again.

* * *

I can't lie awake in bed for another minute, so I put on some clothes and climb onto the roof to see if the new kid's on his. He's not, which isn't totally surprising since it's not even six in the morning and barely light yet, but I kept thinking while I was tossing around in bed like a caught fish, that he was awake too, that he was up on his roof shooting electric bolts out of his fingers through the ceiling and into me and that's why I couldn't sleep. But I was wrong. It's just me up here with the fading fathead moon and every screaming seagull from far and wide visiting Lost Cove for a dawn concert. I've never been outside this early, didn't realize it was so loud. And so dreary, I think, taking in all the gray huddled-up old men disguised as trees.

I sit down, open my pad to a blank page and try to draw, but I can't concentrate, can't even make a decent line. It's the Ouija Board. What if it's right and Jude gets into CSA and I don't? What if I have to go to Roosevelt High School with 3,000 toilet-licking Franklyn Fry clones? If I suck at painting? If Mom and Mr. Grady just feel sorry for me? Because I'm so *embarrassing*, as Jude says. And Dad thinks. I drop my head in my hands, feel the heat of my cheeks on my palms, reliving what happened in the woods with Fry and Zephyr last winter.

(Self-portrait, Series: *Broken Umbrella No. 88*)

I lift my head, look over at the new kid's roof again. What if he realizes I'm me? A cold wind blows through me like I'm an empty room and I suddenly know everything's going to be terrible and I'm doomed; not only me, but the whole gloomy grubby gray world too.

I lie down on my back, stretch out my arms as wide as I can, and whisper, "Help."

Some time later, I wake to the sound of a garage opening. I get up on my elbows. The sky's gone blue: azure, the ocean bluer: cerulean, the trees are swirls of every hella freaking green on earth and bright thick eggy yellow is spilling over everything. Awesome. Doomsday's most definitely been cancelled.

(Landscape: *When God Paints Outside the Lines*)

I sit up, noticing then which garage it was that opened – *his*.

Several seconds that feel like several years later, he cruises down the driveway. Across his chest is a duffel-like black sack. The meteorite bag? He has a bag for *meteorites*. He carries pieces of the galaxy around in a bag. Oh man. I try to prick the balloon that's lifting me into the air by telling myself I shouldn't be this excited to see a guy I only met a day ago. Even if that guy carries the galaxy around in a bag!

(Self-portrait: *Last Sighting of Boy and Balloon Blowing West Over Pacific*)

He crosses the street to the trailhead, then stops where we had our laughing fit, hesitating for a moment there before he turns around and looks right at me, like he's known I've been here all along, like he knows I've been waiting for him since dawn. Our eyes lock and electricity rides up my spine. I'm pretty sure he's telepathically telling me to follow him. After a minute of the kind of mind-meld I've only ever had with Jude, he turns and heads into the grove.

I'd like to follow him. A lot, very much, so much, except I can't, because my feet are cemented to the roof. But why?

What's the big deal? He followed me all the way to CSA yesterday! People make friends. Everyone does it. I can too. I mean, we already are — we laughed together like hyenas. Okay. I'm going. I slide my sketchpad into my backpack, climb down the ladder, and take off for the trailhead.

He's nowhere on the trail. I listen for footsteps, hear nothing but my pulse hammering in my ears. I continue down the path, clearing the first bend to find him on his knees, hunched over the ground. He's examining something in his hand with a magnifying glass. What a toilet-licking idea this is. I won't know what to say to him. I won't know what to do with my hands. I need to get home. Immediately. I'm edging backward when he turns his head and looks up at me.

"Oh, hey," he says casually, standing and dropping whatever was in his hand to the ground. Most of the time people look less like you remember when you see them again. Not him. He's shimmering in the air exactly like he's been in my mind. He's a light show. He starts walking toward me. "I don't know the woods. Was hoping…" He doesn't finish, half smiles. This guy is just not an asshat. "What's your name, anyway?" He's close enough to touch, close enough to count his freckles. I'm having a hand problem. How come everyone else seems to know what to do with them? Pockets, I remember with relief, pockets, I love pockets! I slip the hands to safety, avoiding his eyes. There's that thing about them. I'll look at his mouth if I have to look somewhere.

His eyes are lingering on me. I can tell this even with my undivided attention on his mouth. Did he ask me something?

I think he did. The IQ's plummeting.

"Suppose I could guess," he says. "I'll go for Van, no got it, Miles, yeah, you totally look like a Miles."

"Noah," I blurt, sounding like the knowledge just flew into my head. "I'm Noah. Noah Sweetwine." God. Lord. Dorkhead.

"Sure?"

"Yup, definitely," I say, sounding chirpy and weird. My hands are totally and completely trapped now. Pockets are hand jails. I free them, only to clap them together like they're cymbals. Jesus. "Oh, what's yours?" I ask his mouth, remembering, despite the fact that my IQ is approaching the vegetal range, that he too must have a name.

"Brian," he says, and that's all he says because he functions.

Looking at his mouth is a bad idea too, especially when he speaks. Again and again his tongue returns to that space between his front teeth. I'll look at this tree instead.

"How old are you?" I ask the tree.

"Fourteen. You?"

"Same," I say. Uh-oh.

He nods, believing me, of course, because why would I lie? I have no idea!

"I go to boarding school back east," he says. "I'll be a sophomore next year." He must see the confused look I'm giving the tree, because he adds, "Skipped kindergarten."

"I go to California School of the Arts." The words blasting out of my mouth without my consent.

I sneak a look at him. His brow's creasing up and then I remember: It says California School of the Arts on practically every freaking wall of that freaking place. He saw me outside the building, not in it. He probably heard me tell the naked English guy I don't go there.

I have two choices: Run home and then don't come out of the house for the next two months until he leaves for boarding school, or—

"I don't really go there," I spill to the tree, really afraid to look at him now. "Not yet, anyway. I just want to. Like badly. It's all I think about, and I'm thirteen still. Almost fourteen. Well, in five months. November twenty-first. It's the painter Magritte's birthday too, that day. He did that one with the green apple smack in front of that guy's face. You've probably seen it. And the one where another guy has a birdcage instead of a body. Supremely cool and twisted. Oh, and there's this one of a bird flying but the clouds are inside the bird, not outside of it. Really awesome—" I stop myself because, whoa – and I could go on too. There isn't a painting I suddenly don't want to tell this oak tree about in great detail.

I slowly turn to Brian, who's staring at me with his squinting eyes, not saying anything. Why isn't he saying anything? Maybe I used up all the words? Maybe he's too freaked out that I lied, then unlied, then started a psychotic art history lesson? Why didn't I stay on the roof? I need to sit down. Making friends is supremely stressful. I swallow a few hundred times.

Finally, he just shrugs. "Cool." His lips curve into a half smile. "You are *a bloody mess*, dude," he says, throwing in the English accent.

"Tell me about it."

Then our eyes meet and we both crack up like we're made of the same air.

After that, the forest, which had stayed out of it, joins in. I take a deep breath of pine and eucalyptus, hear mockingbirds and seagulls and the rumbling surf in the distance. I spot three deer munching on leaves just yards from where Brian is now rummaging through the meteorite bag with both hands.

"There are mountain lions around here," I say. "They sleep in trees."

"Awesome," he says, still searching. "Seen one?"

"No, a bobcat, though. Twice."

"I've seen a bear," he mumbles into the bag. What's he looking for?

"A bear! Wow. I love bears! Brown or black?"

"Black," he answers. "A mother with two cubs. At Yosemite."

I want to know everything about this and I'm about to launch into a series of questions, wondering if he likes animal shows too, when it appears he's found what he's been looking for. He holds up an ordinary rock. The expression on his face is like he's showing me a frill-necked lizard or a leafy seadragon, not a plain old hunk of nothing. "Here," he says, putting it in my hand. It's so heavy it bends my wrist back. I reinforce with my other hand so I don't drop it. "This one's for sure. Magnetized nickel – an exploded star." He points to my backpack with the sketchpad sticking out. "You can draw it." I look at the black lump in my hand – this is a star? – and think there's nothing I can imagine less interesting to draw on earth, but say, "Okay. Sure."

"Excellent," he says, and turns around. I stand there with the star in my hand not sure what to do until he turns back around and says, "You coming or what? I brought an extra magnifying glass for you."

This makes the ground tilt. He knew I was going to come even before he left his house. He knew. And I knew. We both *knew*.

(Self-portrait: *I'm Standing on My Own Head!*)

He takes the extra magnifying glass out of his back pocket and holds it out to me.

"Cool," I say, catching up with him and taking the glass by the handle.

"You can classify too in the pad," he says. "Or draw what we find. Actually, that'd be totally stellar."

"What are we looking for?" I ask.

"Space garbage," he answers like it's obvious. "The sky's always falling. Always. You'll see. People have no idea."

No, people don't, because they're not revolutionaries like us.

Hours later, however, we haven't found one meteorite, not one piece of sky litter, but I so don't care. Instead of classifying, whatever that means, I've spent most of the morning in a belly flop, using the magnifying glass to look at slugs and beetles, all the time getting my head stuffed with intergalactic gobble-dygook by Brian, who traipsed around me scouring the forest floor with his magnet rake – yes, a magnet rake, which he made. He's the coolest person ever.

He's a blow-in too, no question. Not from another realm like Mom, but probably from some exoplanet (I just learned this word) with six suns. It explains everything: the telescope, this mad search for pieces of his homeland, the Einstein talk about Red Giants and White and Yellow Dwarfs (!!!!), which I immediately started drawing, not to mention the hypnotizing eyes and the way he keeps cracking me up like I'm some skin-fitting someone who has tons of friends and knows the perfect place in every sentence to say *dude* or *bro*. Also: The Realm of Calm is real. Hummingbirds laze around him. Fruit falls out of trees right into his open palms. Not to mention the drooping redwoods, I think, looking up. And me. I've never felt this relaxed in my life. I keep forgetting my body and then have to go back and get it.

(Portrait, Self-portrait: *The Boy Who Watched the Boy Hypnotize the World*)

I share this blow-in theory with him while we're sitting on a slate slide at the edge of the creek, water lulling slowly by us like we're on a rock boat.

"They've done a really good job in preparing you to pass as an earthling," I say.

He half smiles. I notice a dimple I hadn't before, at the top of his cheek. "No doubt," he says. "They've prepared me well. I even play baseball." He throws a pebble into the water. I watch it drown. He raises an eyebrow at me. "You, on the other hand…"

I pick up a stone and toss it in the same spot where his disappeared. "Yeah, no preparation whatsoever. They just threw me in. That's why I'm so clueless." I mean it as a joke, but it comes out serious. It comes out true. Because it is. I so totally missed class the day all the required information was passed out. Brian licks his bottom lip and doesn't respond.

The mood's changed and I don't know why.

From underneath my hair, I study him. I know from doing portraits that you have to look at someone a really long time to see what they're covering up, to see their inside face, and when you do see it and get it down, that's the thing that makes people freak out about how much a drawing looks like them.

Brian's inside face is worried.

"So, that picture…" he says hesitantly. He pauses, then licks his bottom lip again. Is he nervous? He seems to be, suddenly, though until this moment I didn't think it possible. It makes me nervous thinking he's nervous. He does it again, the tongue sweep across the bottom lip. Is that what he does when he's nervous? I swallow. Now I'm waiting for him to do it again, willing it. Is he staring at my mouth too? I can't help it. I sweep my tongue across my bottom lip.

He turns away, throws a few pebbles rapid-fire with some kind of bionic wrist movement that causes the stones to skip effortlessly across the surface of the water. I watch the vein in his neck pulse. I watch him convert oxygen to carbon dioxide. I watch him existing and existing and existing. Is he going to finish his sentence? Ever? Several more centuries of silence pass where the air gets more and more jumpy and alive, like all the molecules he previously put to sleep are waking up. And then it occurs to me he means the naked pictures from yesterday. Is that what he means? The thought's a bolt.

"Of the English guy?" I squeak. Argh, I sound like a mite. I wish my voice would stop cracking and change already.

He swallows and turns toward me. "No, I was wondering if you ever actually make the drawings you do in your head?"

"Sometimes," I answer.

"Well, did you make it?" His eyes catch me off guard, capturing me completely in some kind of net. I want to say his name.

"Make what?" I ask, stalling. My heart's kicking around in my chest. I know what picture he means now.

"The one" – he licks his bottom lip – "of me?"

I feel possessed as I lunge for the pad and flip the pages until I find him, that final version. I place it in his hands, watch his eyes dart up and down, down and up. I'm spiking a fever trying to tell if he likes it or not. I can't tell. Then I try to see the picture through his eyes and an uh-oh-kill-me-now feeling overtakes me. The Brian I made is him colliding at top speed into a wall of magic. It's nothing like the drawings of people I do at school. I realize with horror it's not a drawing of a friend. I'm getting dizzy. Every line and angle and color screams just how much I like him. I feel like I'm wrapped and trapped in plastic. And he's still not saying a thing. Not one thing!

I wish I were a horse.

"You don't have to like it or anything," I say finally, trying to get the pad back. My mind's bursting. "It's not a big deal. I draw everyone." I can't stop talking. "I draw everything. Even dung beetles and potatoes and driftwood and mounds of dirt and redwood stumps and—"

"Are you kidding?" he interrupts, not letting me take the pad away. It's his turn to go red. "I totally like it." He pauses. I watch him breathe. He's breathing fast. "I look like the freaking aurora borealis." I don't know what this is, but I can tell from his voice it's a very cool thing.

A circuit flips in my chest. One I didn't know I had.

"I'm so happy I'm not a horse!" I realize I've said it aloud only when Brian says, "What?"

"Nothing," I say. "Nothing." I try to calm down, try to stop smiling. Was the sky always this shade of magenta?

He's laughing for real like yesterday. "Dude, you are the strangest person ever. Did you actually just say you're so happy you're not a horse?"

"No," I say, trying not to laugh and failing. "I said—"

But before I can get another word out, a voice crashes into all this perfect. "Oh how romantic!" I freeze, knowing immediately whose hippo-head the sneering asshat words are coming out of. I swear the guy's installed a tracking device on me – it's the only explanation.

With him is a great ape: Big Foot. At least no Zephyr.

"Time for a dip, Bubble?" Fry says.

This is my cue to hightail it to the other side of the world. WE NEED TO RUN, I tell Brian telepathically.

Except when I glance at him, I see that his face has bricked up and I can tell running away is not part of his modus operandi. Which *really* sucks. I swallow.

Then holler, "Fuck off, you toilet-licking sociopaths!" only it comes out as complete silence. So I heave a mountain range at them. They don't budge.

My whole being focuses into one wish: *Please don't let me be humiliated in front of Brian.*

Fry's attention has shifted from me to Brian. He's smirking. "Nice hat."

"Thanks," Brian replies coolly, like he owns the air in the Northern Hemisphere. He's no broken umbrella, this is clear. He doesn't seem one bit afraid of these garbage-headed scum-suckers. Fry raises an eyebrow, which turns his gigantic greasy forehead into a relief map. Brian's piqued his psychopathic interest. Great. I appraise Big Foot. He's a slab of concrete in a Giants baseball cap. His hands are pushed deep into his sweatshirt pockets. They look like grenades through the fabric. I note the width of his right wrist, note that his fist is probably as large as my whole face. I've never actually been punched before, only shoved around. I imagine it, imagine all the paintings bursting out of my skull at impact.

(Self-portrait: *Pow*)

"So did you homos pack a picnic?" Fry says to Brian. My muscles tighten.

Brian slowly stands. "I'll give you a chance to apologize," he says to Fry, his voice icy and calm, his eyes the opposite. The rock-boat has given him a few extra feet, so he's looking down on all of us. His meteorite bag hangs heavy on his side. I need to stand but have no legs.

"Apologize for what?" Fry says. "For calling you homos homos?"

Big Foot laughs. It shakes the ground. In Taipei.

I can see Fry's exhilarated – no one challenges him around here, especially not any of us younger losers he's been calling homos and pussies and whatevers since we got ears.

"You think that's funny?" Brian says. "'Cuz I don't." He moves a step backward so he's even higher on the rock now. He's becoming someone else. Darth Vader, I think. The Realm of Calm's been sucked back into his index finger and now he looks like he eats human livers. Sautéed with eyeballs and toe-tips.

Hatred's rising off him in waves.

I want to run away with the circus but take a deep breath and stand, crossing my arms, which have grown skinnier in the past few moments, against my newly sunken chest. I do this as threateningly as I can, thinking of crocodiles, sharks, black piranhas for courage. Not working. Then I remember the honey badger – pound for pound the most powerful creature on earth! An unlikely furry little killer. I narrow my eyes, clamp my mouth shut.

Then the worst thing happens. Fry and Big Foot start to laugh at me.

"Ooooo, so scary, Bubble," Fry coos. Big Foot crosses his arms in an imitation of me, which Fry finds so hilarious, he does it too.

I hold my breath so I don't collapse into a heap.

"I really think it's time you two apologized and were on your way," I hear from behind me. "If not, I can't be responsible for what happens next."

I spin around. Is he freaking crazy? Does he not realize he's half Fry's size and a third of Big Foot's? And I'm me? Is he packing an Uzi?

But above us, poised on the rock, he seems unconcerned. He's tossing a stone from hand to hand, a stone like the one that's still in my pocket. We all watch as it pops between his palms, his hands hardly moving, as if he's making it jump with his mind.

"I guess you're not leaving?" he says to his hands, then looks up at Fry and Big Foot, somehow without breaking the rhythm of the skipping stone. It's incredible. "I just want to know one thing then." Brian smiles a slow careful smile, but the vein in his neck's pulsing furiously and it seems likely that whatever's about to come out of his mouth next is going to get us killed.

Fry glances at Big Foot and the two of them seem to come to a quick, silent understanding about what to do with our earthly remains.

I'm holding my breath again. All of us are waiting for Brian to speak, watching the dancing stone, mesmerized by it, as the air sizzles with coming violence. It's the real kind too. The lying in a hospital bed with only a straw sticking out of your bandaged head kind. The sick pounding kind of violence that I have to mute the TV to get through, unless Dad's around and then I have to endure it. I hope Mr. Grady gives the paintings I left in the art room to Mom. They can show my stuff at the memorial — my first and last art exhibit.

(Portrait, Self-portrait: *Brian and Noah Buried Side by Side*)

I make a fist but can't remember if you're supposed to keep your thumb inside or outside of it when you punch. Why did Dad teach me to wrestle? Who on earth wrestles? He should've taught me how to make a freaking fist. And what about my fingers? Will I still be able to draw after this is over? Picasso must've gotten in fights. Van Gogh and Gauguin fought each other. It'll be okay. Sure it will. And black eyes are cool, colorful.

Then all of a sudden Brian snatches the dancing stone into

one of his fists, stopping time.

"What I want to know," he says, drawling out each word, "is who the hell let you out of your cages?"

"Do you believe this guy?" Fry says to Big Foot, who grunts out an incomprehensible something in Big Footese. They lunge—

I'm telling Grandma Sweetwine I will be joining her shortly when I catch the whipping movement of Brian's arm a second before Fry cries out, his fingers flying to his ear, "What the hell?" Then Big Foot yelps and covers his head. I whirl around, see Brian's hand in the bag. Now Fry's ducking, and so is Big Foot, because meteorites are wailing at them, raining on them, hailing down on them, zooming past their skulls at the speed of sound, faster, at the speed of light, each time whooshing close enough to shave hairs, a millimeter away from ending their brain activity permanently. "Stop it!" Big Foot screams. Both of them are twisting and hopping and trying to shield their heads with their arms as more bits and pieces of fallen sky race through the air at warp speed. Brian's a machine, a machine gun, two at a time, three, four, underhand, overhand, both hands. His arm's a blur, he's a blur – each rock – each *star* – just barely missing, barely sparing Fry and Big Foot until they're both balled up on the ground, hands over their heads, saying, "Please, dude, stop."

"I'm sorry, I didn't hear that apology," Brian says, whipping one so close to Fry's head it makes me wince. Then another few for good measure. "Two apologies, actually. One to Noah. And one to me. Like you mean it."

"Sorry," Fry says, completely stunned. Maybe one did hit him in the head. "Now stop."

"Not good enough."

An additional series of meteorites rocket at their skulls at a billion miles per hour.

Fry cries out, "Sorry, Noah. Sorry, I don't know your name."

"Brian."

"Sorry, Brian!"

"Do you accept their apology, Noah?"

I nod. God and his son have been demoted.

"Now, get the hell out of here," Brian says to them. "Next time I won't miss your thick skulls on purpose."

And then they're fleeing in a second rain of meteorites, their arms helmetting their heads, as *they* run away from *us*.

"The pitcher?" I ask him as I grab my pad.

He nods. I catch the half smile breaking through the wall of his face. He hops off the rock-slide and starts picking up the meteorites and loading them back into his bag. I grab the magnet rake, lying there like a sword. This guy's so totally more magic-headed than anyone, even Picasso or Pollock or Mom. We jump the creek and then we're tearing through the trees together in the opposite direction of home. He's as fast as I am, fast like we could run down jumbo jets, comets.

"You know we're dead, right?" I shout, thinking of the coming payback.

"Don't count on it," Brian shouts back.

Yeah, I think, we're *invincible*.

We're sprinting at the speed of light when the ground gives way and we rise into the air as if racing up stairs.

* * *

I give up on the sketch, close my eyes, lean back in my desk chair. In my mind, I can draw Brian with lightning.

"What?" I hear. "You meditating now? Swami Sweetwine has a certain ring."

I keep my eyes shut. "Go away, Jude."

"Where've you been all week?"

"Nowhere."

"What have you been doing?"

"Nothing."

Each morning since he hurled those meteorites at Fry and Big Foot, five mornings so far to be exact, I've waited on the roof, totally deranged, my head a few feet above my neck, for his garage to open so we can plunge into the woods again and become imaginary – that's the only way I can describe it.

(Portrait, Self-portrait: *Two Boys Jump and Stay Up*)

"So is Brian nice?" I open my eyes. She knows his name now. He's no longer *such a freak*? She's leaning against the doorframe in lime-green pajama bottoms and a fuchsia tank top, looking like one of those color-swirled lollipops you get on the boardwalk. If you squint your eyes, lots of girls look like those lollipops.

Jude holds out her hand in front of her, examines five shiny purple nails. "Everyone's talking about him like he's this baseball god, like he's headed for the major leagues. Fry's cousin – he's here for the summer – his little brother goes to the same school back east. They call him The Ax or something."

I burst out laughing. The Ax. Brian is called The Ax! I flip the page and start drawing it.

Is this why there's been no retaliation? Why Fry passed me

the other day while I was having a discussion with Rascal the horse and before I could even think of peeling away to Oregon, he pointed at me and said, "Dude." And that was it.

"So is he?" she repeats. Her hair's particularly bloodthirsty tonight, snaking all around the room, swarming the furniture, vining up the legs of chairs, stretching over the walls. I'm next.

"Is he what?"

"Nice, Bubble, is Brian, your new best friend, nice?"

"He's fine," I say, ignoring the Bubble, whatever. "Like anyone."

"But you don't like *anyone*." I hear the jealousy now. "What animal is he, then?" She's twirling a string of hair around her index finger so tightly the tip's ballooning red and bulbous like it might burst.

"A hamster," I say.

She laughs. "Yeah, right. The Ax is a hamster."

I have to get her off Brian. Forget shutters, if I could put the Great Wall of China around him and me, I would. "So who's M.?" I ask, remembering the asshat Ouija board.

"He's no one."

Fine. I turn back around to *The Ax* drawing—

I hear, "How would you rather die? Drinking gasoline and then lighting a match in your mouth or getting buried alive?"

"The explosion," I say, trying to hide my smile because after all these months of ignoring me, she's sucking up. "Duh. Obviously."

"Yeah, yeah. Just warming you up. It's been a while. How about—"

There's a tapping at the window.

"Is that him? At the window?" I hate the excitement in her voice.

Is it, though? At night? I did casually mention to him which room was mine – right on the street with easy access – a few dozen times because, well, I have my reasons. I get up from my desk and walk over to the window and flip the shade. It *is* him. Real and everything. Sometimes I wonder if I'm making the whole thing up and if someone were looking down from above they'd see me alone all day, talking and laughing by myself in the middle of a forest.

He's framed in the light from the room, looking like he stuck his toe in a socket. He's not wearing his hat, and his hair's amped out all over his head. His eyes are all sparked up too. I open the window.

"I totally want to meet him," I hear Jude say from behind me.

I do not want that. Do not. I want her to fall in a hole.

I bend down and stick my head and shoulders out, spreading myself as much as I can across the windowsill so Jude can't see out or Brian in. The air is cool, feathery on my face.

"Hey," I say, like he always knocks at my window at night and I'm not gunning inside at top speed.

"You gotta come up," he says. "Got to. It's clear finally. And no moon. It's an intergalactic gorge fest up there."

Really, if someone told me I could hang out in da Vinci's studio while he painted the *Mona Lisa* or go up on Brian's roof with him at night – I'm on the roof. The other day he mentioned us going to some movie about an alien invasion and

I almost blacked out thinking of it. I'd rather sit next to Brian for two hours in a dark theater than have a wall-painting party with Jackson Pollock. The only problem with spending time with him in the woods all day is that there's so much space in there. The trunk of a car would be better, or a thimble.

Despite my efforts at hogging the window, I feel myself getting shoved aside as Jude squeezes her head and then her shoulders out beside mine until we're a two-headed hydra. I watch Brian's face light up at the sight of her and get seasick.

(Portrait: *Jude: Drawn and Quartered*)

"Hi, Brian Connelly," she says in a flirty bouncy way that makes my body temperature drop several degrees. When did she learn to talk like that?

"Wow, you guys look nothing alike," Brian exclaims. "I thought you'd look like Noah except—"

"With boobs?" Jude interjects. She said *boobs* to him!

And why was he thinking about what she'd look like anyway?

Brian cracks *the* half smile. I need to throw a bag over his head before Jude comes under the spell of his strange, squinting eyes. Do they have those burka things for guys? At least he hasn't licked his lips, I think. "Well, yeah. Exactly," he says to her, and licks his lips. "Though I'm pretty sure I would've phrased it differently."

It's over. His eyes are squinting. My sister's a lollipop – everyone loves lollipops. And my head's been replaced by a cabbage.

"You should come up too," he says to her. "I was going to show your brother Gemini – the Twins, you know – so it's perfect." *Your brother?* I'm her brother now?

(Portrait: *Jude in Her New Home in Timbuktu*)

She's about to speak, to say, "Cool!" or "Awesome!" or "I love you!" so I ram her with my elbow. It's the only practical solution. She returns the ram with a jab to my ribs. We're used to concealing battles under tables at restaurants or at home, so keeping Brian out of this particular scuffle is a piece of cake until I blurt out, "She can't come. She has to go to ubudowasow for sodojiokoa—" I'm just making sounds, throwing syllables together, hoping they'll collide and find a meaning in Brian's head, as I, in one spectacularly idiotic motion, hoist myself up and then frog-leap out the window, only narrowly landing on my feet and not tumbling headfirst into Brian. I right myself, brush the hair out of my eyes, noting the dampness of my forehead, then turn around and place my hand on the bottom of the window and start pulling down, only at the last minute deciding not to decapitate my sister, even though it really seems like a good idea. Instead, I push on her shoulder to get her and her yellow strangling sweep of hair and purple nails and shimmery blue eyes and bouncing bobbling boobs back inside—

"Jesus, Noah. Got the hint. Nice to meet you," she manages before I slam down the window.

"You too," he says, rapping on the glass with his knuckles. She raps back two confident knowing raps that match the confident knowing smile on her face. It's like they've been rapping back and forth like this their whole lives and have their own special Bengal Tiger to Lollipop Morse code.

Brian and I walk down the road in silence. I've broken into a full body sweat. I feel exactly the way I do when I wake up from the dream where I'm naked in the school cafeteria and only have those flimsy pathetic napkin squares to cover myself up.

Brian speaks to what just happened succinctly. "Dude," he says. "Mental."

I sigh, mumble, "Thanks, Einstein."

And then to my surprise and relief, he starts to laugh. Fountainous, mountainous laughter. "*So* mental." He karate-chops the air. "I mean, I thought you were going to slice her in half with the window!" This sends him on a rollicking ride of hysterics that I soon find myself on too. Further fueled when Prophet starts in, "Where the hell is Ralph? Where the hell is Ralph?"

"Oh my God. That freaking bird." Brian holds his head with both his hands. "We have to find Ralph, man. We have to. It's a national emergency."

He doesn't seem to care a bit that Jude didn't come with us. Maybe I imagined it all? Maybe his face didn't light up at the sight of her? Maybe he didn't blush at her words? Maybe he doesn't even like lollipops?

"The Ax?" I say, feeling loads better.

"Oh man." He groans. "That was fast." There's both embarrassment and pride in his voice. He holds up his right arm. "No one messes with The Ax." The Ax comes down on my shoulder and jostles me. We're under a streetlamp and I pray my face isn't revealing what's happened inside me at this contact. It's the first time he's touched me.

I follow him up the ladder to the roof, my shoulder still tingling, wishing the ladder went for miles and miles. (Portrait,

Self-portrait: *The Two Boys Breaking Out of the Two Boys* As we climb, I can hear plants growing in the dark, can feel the blood speeding around inside me.

And then the scent of jasmine engulfs us.

Grandma Sweetwine used to tell us to hold our breath around the scent of night-blooming jasmine if we didn't want to give away all our secrets. She'd say the police would do much better handing out vines of the white trumpet flowers to the accused than hooking them up to a lie detector. I really hope this one bit of hogwash is true. I want to know Brian's secrets.

Once up, he takes a flashlight from his sweatshirt pocket and shines our way to the telescope. The light from it is red, not white, he explains, so we don't lose our night vision. Our night vision!

While he's crouched over a bag at the foot of the telescope, I listen to the crashing sea, imagining all the fish swimming through the endless freezing darkness.

"I could never be a fish," I say.

"Me neither," he replies, his words obstructed by the end of the flashlight, which he's holding in his mouth so he can use both hands to rifle through the bag.

"Maybe an eel, though," I say, still amazed how I say aloud so many things I'd normally just say to myself. "It'd be cool to have electric body parts, you know? Like your hair."

I hear his muffled laugh through the flashlight and it shoots me dead with happiness. I'm thinking the reason I've been so quiet all these years is only because Brian wasn't around yet for me to tell everything to. He takes a book out of the bag, then standing, flips through it until he finds what he's looking for. He passes the open book to me, then steps real close so he can shine the flashlight – back in his hand now – on the page. "Here," he says. "The Twins."

I feel his hair on my cheek, on my neck.

I have the same feeling I get right before I start crying.

"That star," he says, pointing, "is Castor, that one Pollux. They're the heads of the Twins." He takes a pen out of his pocket and starts drawing – it's a glow-in-the-dark pen. Cool. He makes light-lines between stars until two stick figures appear.

I can smell his shampoo, his sweat. I breathe in deeply, silently.

"They're both dudes," he says. "Castor was mortal. Pollux, immortal."

Do guys normally stand so close to other guys? I wish I'd paid more attention to these kinds of things before. I notice my fingers are trembling and I can't be one hundred percent sure they won't reach across the air and touch his bare wrist or neck, so I slip them in the hand jails to be safe. I close my fingers around the rock he gave me.

"When Castor died," he says, "Pollux missed him too much, so he made a deal to share his immortality with him and that's how they both ended up in the sky."

"I'd do that," I say. "Totally."

"Yeah? Must be a twin thing," he says, misunderstanding. "Though you'd never know it from that Death by Window Maneuver." I feel my face flush because I'd meant him, duh, I'd share my immortality with him. *I meant you,* I want to holler.

Brian's bent over the telescope adjusting something. "The

Twins are thought to be responsible for shipwrecks, said to appear to sailors as St. Elmo's Fire. Know what that is?" He doesn't wait for an answer, just plows on in his Einstein mode. "It's an electrical weather phenomenon where a luminous plasma's created because charged particles separate and create electric fields that in turn create this corona discharge—"

"Whoa," I say.

He laughs, but continues on just as incomprehensibly. I get the gist: The Twins cause things to burst into flames. He turns around, shines the flashlight in my face. "It's crazy that it happens," he says. "But it does, all the time too."

He's like a bag of selves. This Einstein one. The fearless meteor-hurling god. The crazy laughing guy. The Ax! There's more too, I know it. Hidden ones. Truer ones. Because why is his inside face so worried?

I grab the flashlight out of his hand and shine it on him. The wind's billowing his shirt against his chest. I want to flatten the ripples with my hand, want to so bad my mouth goes dry.

It's not just me that's staring this time.

"The smell of jasmine makes people tell their secrets," I say to him, my voice low.

"Is that jasmine?" he asks, swirling the air with his hand.

I nod. The flashlight's bright on his face. It's an inquisition.

"Why do you think I have secrets?" He crosses his arms.

"Who doesn't?"

"Tell me one of yours, then?"

I pull out a fairly harmless one, though juicy enough to get him to reveal something good. "I spy on people."

"Who?"

"Well, basically, everyone. Usually I'm drawing, but sometimes not. I hide in trees, bushes, on my roof with the binoculars, wherever."

"Ever get caught?"

"Yeah, twice. Both times by you."

He laughs a little. "So … ever spy on me?" The question makes my breath catch in my throat. The truth is, after an in-depth investigation, I've determined his room spy-proof.

"No. Your go."

"Okay." He motions toward the ocean. "I can't swim."

"Really?"

"Yeah. Hate the water. Don't even like hearing it. Baths freak me out. Sharks freak me out. Living here freaks me out. You go."

"I hate sports."

"But you're fast."

I shrug. "Go."

"Okay." He licks his lip, then exhales slowly. "I'm claustrophobic." He frowns. "I can't be an astronaut now. It blows."

"You weren't always?"

"No." He looks away and for a split second I see his inside face again. "Your turn."

I flick off the flashlight.

My turn. My turn. My turn. *I want to put my hands on your chest. I want to be in a thimble with you.*

"I keyed my father's car once," I say.

"I stole a telescope from school."

It's easier with the flashlight off. The words falling in the dark, like apples from trees.

"Rascal, the horse across the street, talks to me."

I can tell he's smiling, then not. "My dad left."

I pause. "I wish my dad would."

"No, you don't," he says, his voice serious. "It sucks. My mom spends all her time on this website LostConnections writing him notes he's never even going to see. Totally pathetic." There's a silence. "Oh, still my go? I do math problems in my head, like all the time. Even on the pitcher's mound."

"Right now?"

"Right now."

"Like I mind-paint."

"Yeah, probably."

"I'm scared I suck," I say.

He laughs. "Me too."

"I mean suck bad."

"Me too," he insists.

We're quiet for a second. The ocean rumbles beneath us.

I close my eyes, take a breath. "I've never kissed anyone."

"No one?" he says. "No one meaning no one?" Does this mean something?

"No one."

The moment stretches and stretches and stretches—

Then snaps. He says, "A friend of my mom's came on to me."

Whoa. I turn the flashlight back on his face. He's blinking, looking uneasy, embarrassed. I watch his Adam's apple as he swallows once, then again.

"How old? How much on?" I ask, instead of what I want to ask, wishing he'd used a pronoun. Was it a boyfriend?

"Not that old. On enough. Just one time. No big deal." He takes the flashlight out of my hand and goes back to the telescope, ending the conversation. Clearly it was a big deal. I have a googleplex of questions about *on enough,* which I keep to myself.

I wait in the cold air where his body was.

"Okay," he says a little while later. "All set up."

I go behind the telescope, peer into the eyepiece, and all the stars crash down on my head. It's like taking a shower in the cosmos. I gasp.

"Knew you'd freak," he says.

"Oh man. Poor van Gogh," I say. "*Starry Night* could've been so much cooler."

"I totally knew it!" he exclaims. "If I were an artist, I'd go crazy." I need something to hold on to, besides him. I grab one of the legs of the telescope with my hand. No one has ever been this excited to show me something, not even Mom. And he kind of just called me an artist.

(Self-portrait: *Throwing Armfuls of Air into the Air*)

He comes up behind me. "Okay, now check this out. You're going to lose your mind." He leans over my shoulder and pulls down some lever and the stars rush even closer and he's right, I am losing my mind, but not because of the stars this time. "Can you see the Twins?" he asks. "They're in the upper right quadrant." I can't see a thing because my eyes are closed. All I care about the cosmos is happening here on this roof. I think how to respond so his hand stays on that lever, so he remains this close to me, so close I can feel his breathing on the back of my neck. If I say yes, he'll probably step backward. If I say no, maybe he'll adjust the telescope again and we can stay like this a minute longer. "I don't think I see them," I say, my voice rough, unsteady. This was the right answer, because he says, "Okay, here," and he does something that brings not only the stars but him a breath closer.

My heart stops beating.

My back is to his front and if I move an inch backward I'd fall into him and then if it were a movie, not one I've ever seen, mind you, he'd put his hands all over me, I know he would, and then I'd twist around and we'd melt together like hot wax. I can see it happening in my head. I don't move.

"Well?" He breathes the word more than says it, and that's when I know he feels it too. I think about those two guys in the sky causing shipwrecks, causing things to burst into flames, just like that with no warning. "It's crazy that it happens," he'd said about them. "But it just does."

It just does.

It's happening to us.

"I have to go," I say, helpless.

What makes you say the opposite of what every cell in your body wants you to say?

"Yeah," he replies. "Okay."

* * *

The Hornet Girls: Courtney Barrett, Clementine Cohen, Lulu Mendes, and Heather somebody are propped on the big rock beside the trailhead when Brian and I come out of the woods the next afternoon. At the sight of us, Courtney leaps from her perch, lands with hands on hips, creating a pink-bikini-clad human roadblock in our path, thereby cutting short my diatribe about the genius of the blobfish, the world's most underrated waste-of-space animal, forever in the shadow of the three-toed sloth. This followed Brian's breaking news about a boy in Croatia he read about on the web who's magnetic. His family and friends throw coins at him, which stick. As do frying pans. He says this is indeed possible for a gobbledygook reason I didn't follow.

"Hey," Courtney says. She's a year older than the other hornets, going to high school next year, so the same age as Brian. Her smile's all scarlet lips, sparkling white teeth, and menace. The antennae on her head are pointing right at him. "Wow!" she exclaims. "Who knew you were hiding *those* eyes under that silly hat?" Her bikini top, two pink strips and a string, covers very little of her. She plucks the string, revealing a secret line of white skin that wraps around her neck. She's plucking it like a guitar string.

I watch Brian watch this. Then I watch Brian being watched by her, knowing Courtney's registering the way his T-shirt falls like water over his broad chest, registering his tanned strong baseball arms, registering the totally cool space between the teeth, the squint, the freckles, registering that there's no word in her hornet head to describe the particular color of his eyes.

"Think I take offense on behalf of my lucky hat," Brian replies with a smoothness and coolness that drive spikes into my eardrums. Another Brian's emerging, I can tell. One I'm certain I'm not going to like at all.

It occurs to me that Jude does this too, changes who she is depending on who she's with. They're like toads changing their skin color. How come I'm always just me?

Courtney fake pouts. "No offense intended." She lets go of the bikini string and flicks the rim of his hat with two long fingers. Her nails are the same purple color as Jude's. "Why lucky?" she says, tilting her head, tilting the whole world so everything flows in her direction. Without a doubt, this is the girl who's been giving Jude flirting lessons. Hey, where *is* Jude? How come she skipped this ambush?

"It's lucky," he says, "because good things happen when I wear it." It's possible Brian glances at me for a nanosecond when he says this, but lots of things are possible and extremely unlikely, like world peace and summer snowstorms and blue dandelions and what I think happened on the roof last night. Did I imagine it? Each time I think of it, every ten seconds or so all day long, I faint inside.

Clementine, posed on the rock not unlike the girl model from CSA – her body in three triangles – says in the same hornet dialect as Courtney, "Fry's cousin from LA says he wishes the rocks you threw at him didn't miss so he could've charged people to see the scar when you're in the major leagues." She tells all this to the purple-polished nails on one of her hands. Jesus. How blown away must Fry and Big Foot have been by The Ax and his bionic arm to admit defeat like this to a bunch of hornets.

"Good to know," Brian replies. "Next time he acts like a jerkoff I'll aim to maim."

A wave of awe at Brian's comment ripples from girl to girl.

Barf. Barf. Barf. Something alarming's occurring to me, more alarming than the fact that Jude's joined this purple polish cult. It's that this Brian is cool. His alien kin have not only prepared him to pass but to surpass. He's probably supernaturally popular at that boarding school. A jock *and* popular! How could I not have noticed? I must've gotten thrown off by the endless geek rants about globular clusters orbiting galactic cores, rants that I see are being kept under wraps in present company. Doesn't he know popular people are covered in flame retardant? Doesn't he know popular people aren't revolutionaries?

I want to grab him by the wrist and head back into the woods, tell these guys, sorry but I found him first. But then I think, no, that's not true: He found me. He *tracked* me like a Bengal tiger. I wish he'd choose that self and stick to it.

Clementine, still talking to her nails, says, "Should we call you The Ax? Or maybe just Ax? Ooooo." She squeals exactly like a warthog. "I like that."

"I'd prefer Brian," he says. "It's the off-season."

"Okay, *Brian*," Courtney says like she invented his name. "You guys should totally come hang out at The Spot." She looks at me. "Jude does."

I'm shocked to be acknowledged. My cabbagehead nods without my consent.

She smiles at me in a way that could just as easily be a scowl. "Your sister says you're some kind of prodigy." She plucks on the bikini string. "Maybe I'll let you draw me sometime."

Brian crosses his arms in front of his chest. "Ah, no. You'd be lucky if *he* lets *you* pose for him sometime."

I grow sixty thousand feet taller.

But then Courtney slaps her own wrist, mewing at Brian. "Bad girl. Got it."

Okay, time to torch the neighborhood. And the worst part is, her lameness breaks out his half smile, which she's mirroring back at him with one of her radiant own.

(Self-portrait: *Boy in Plastic Bag Turning Blue*)

A few sandpipers skitter down the road toward Rascal's stable. I do wish I were a horse.

Several moments pass and then Lulu slides off the rock and stands beside Courtney. Clementine follows, slipping in next to Lulu. The hornets are swarming. Only Heather remains on the rock.

"You surf?" Lulu asks Brian.

"I'm not much into the beach," he replies.

"Not into the beach?" Lulu and Courtney cry at once, but this inconceivability is eclipsed by Clementine, who says, "Can I try on your hat?"

"No, let me," Courtney says.

"I want to!" says Lulu.

I roll my eyes and then hear someone laugh without a trace of hornet hum. I look over at Heather, who's looking back at me sympathetically like she alone can see the cabbage on my neck. I've hardly noticed her over there. Or ever. Even though she's the only one of the hornets who goes to the public middle school like we do. A mess of black curls, similar to mine, falls around her small face. No antennae. And she looks more like a frog than a lollipop, a chachi tree frog. She's the one I'd draw, perched in an oak, hidden away. I check her nails: They're light blue.

Brian's taken his hat off his head. "Hmm."

"You choose," Courtney says, confident she'll be chosen.

"I couldn't," Brian says. He starts spinning the hat on his finger. "Unless..." With a quick flick of his wrist, he tosses the hat onto my head. And I'm soaring. I take back everything. He is a revolutionary.

Until I realize they're all laughing, including him, like this is the funniest thing ever.

"Cop-out," Courtney says. She takes the hat off my head like I'm a hat rack and hands it back to Brian. "Now, choose."

Brian smiles fully at Courtney, showcasing the space between his teeth, then cocks his hat over her brow, like she knew he would. The look on her face is unmistakably mission accomplished.

He leans back and regards her. "Suits you."

I want to kick him in the head.

Instead, I let the wind at my back scoop me up and toss me over the cliff into the sea.

"Gotta bounce," I say, remembering that's what I heard someone say to someone sometime somewhere, at school or maybe it was on TV, or in a movie, probably not even from this decade, but who cares, all I know is I have to get away before I evaporate or crumple or cry. I think for a hopeful moment that Brian might follow me across the street but he just says, "Later."

My heart leaves, hitchhikes right out of my body, heads north, catches a ferry across the Bering Sea and plants itself in Siberia with the polar bears and ibex and long-horned goats until it turns into a teeny-tiny glacier.

Because I imagined it. Last night, this is what happened: He adjusted a lever on the telescope, that's it. I just happened to be standing in the way. *Noah has an overactive imagination,* written on every school report I've ever gotten. To which Mom would laugh and say, "A leopard can't change its spots, now can it?"

When I get inside the house, I go immediately to the front window that frames the street to watch them. The sky's over-flowing with orange clouds and each time one floats down, Brian bats it back up like a balloon. I watch him hypnotize the girls as he does the fruit in the trees, the clouds in the sky, as he did me. Only Heather seems immune. She's lying on the rock, looking at the orange paradise above instead of in his direction.

I tell myself: He didn't find me, didn't track me. He's not a Bengal tiger. He's just some new kid who saw someone around his age and mistakenly befriended him before the cool kids came along and saved him.

Reality is crushing. The world is a wrong-sized shoe. How can anyone stand it?

(Self-portrait: *Keep Out*)

I hear Mom's footsteps only a moment before I feel the warm press of her hands on my shoulders. "Beautiful sky, huh?" I breathe in her perfume. She's changed kinds. This one smells like the forest, like wood and earth, with her mixed in. I close my eyes. A sob's rising in me as if it's being pulled up by her hands. I keep it down by saying, "Only six months now until the application's due."

She squeezes my shoulders. "So proud of you." Her voice is

calm and deep and safe. "Do you know how proud I am?" This I know. Nothing else. I nod and she wraps her arms around me. "You're my inspiration," she says, and we rise together into the air. She's become my real eyes. It's like I haven't even drawn or painted anything until she sees it, like it's all invisible until she gets that look on her face and says, "You're remaking the world, Noah. Drawing by drawing." I want to show her the ones of Brian so bad. But I can't. As if he heard me thinking about him, he turns in my direction, all silhouette in the firelight, a perfect painting, so good it makes my fingers flit at my side. But I'm not going to draw him anymore. "It's okay to be addicted to beauty," Mom says, all dreamy. "Emerson said 'Beauty is God's handwriting.'" There's something about her voice when she talks about being an artist that always makes me feel like the whole sky is in my chest. "I'm addicted to it too," she whispers. "Most artists are."

"But you're not an artist," I whisper back.

She doesn't respond and her body has tensed up. I don't know why.

"Where the hell is Ralph? Where the hell is Ralph?"

This untenses her and she laughs. "I have a feeling Ralph is on his way," she says. "The Second Coming is at hand." She kisses the back of my head. "Everything's going to be okay, sweetheart," she says because she's a people-mechanic and always knows when I'm malfunctioning. At least that's why I think she says it, until she adds, "It's going to be okay for all of us, I promise."

Before we even land back on the rug, she's gone. I stay, staring out the window until darkness fills the room, until the five of them walk off in the direction of The Spot, Brian's lucky hat on Courtney's lucky head.

Paces behind the rest, Heather glides along, still looking up. I watch her raise her arms swanlike and then lower them. A bird, I think. Of course. Not a frog at all. I was wrong.

About everything.

*   *   *

The next morning, I do not go up on the roof at dawn because I'm not leaving my bedroom until Brian's back at boarding school three thousand miles from here. It's only seven weeks away. I'll drink the plant water if I get thirsty. I'm lying on the bed staring at a print on the ceiling of Munch's *The Scream*, an off-the-hook painting I wish I made of a guy blowing a gasket.

Like I am.

Jude and Mom are bickering on the other side of the wall. It's getting loud. I think she hates Mom even more than she hates me now.

Mom: You'll have plenty of time to be twenty-five when you're twenty-five, Jude.

Jude: It's just lipstick.

Mom: Lipstick you're not wearing, and while I'm on your bad side, that skirt is way too short.

Jude: Do you like it? I made it.

Mom: Well, you should've made more of it. Look in the mirror. Do you really want to be *that girl*?

Jude: Who else am I going to be? For the record, *that girl* in the mirror is me!

Mom: It's really scaring me how wild you're getting. I don't recognize you.

Jude: Well, I don't recognize you either, Mother.

Mom has been acting a little strange. I've noticed things too. Like how she sits lobotomized at red lights long after they turn green and doesn't hit the gas until everyone starts honking at her. Or how she says she's working in her office, but spying reveals that she's really going through boxes of old photographs she got down from the attic.

And there are horses galloping inside her now. I can hear them.

Today, she and Jude are going to the city together for a mother–daughter day to see if it can make them get along. Not a good start. Dad used to try to get me to go to ball games when they did this, but he doesn't bother anymore, not since I spent a whole football game facing the crowd instead of the field, sketching faces on napkins. Or maybe it was a baseball game?

Baseball. The Ax. The Axhat.

Jude rapid-fire knocks, doesn't wait for me to say come in, just swings open the door. I guess Mom won, because she's lipstick-free and wearing a colorful sundress that goes to her knees, one of Grandma's designs. She looks like a peacock tail. Her hair is calm, a placid yellow lake around her.

"You're home for once." She seems genuinely happy to see me. She leans against the doorframe. "If Brian and I were drowning, who'd you save first?"

"You," I tell her, glad she didn't ask me this yesterday.

"Dad and me?"

"Please. You."

"Mom and me?"

I pause, then say, "You."

"You paused."

"I didn't pause."

"You so did, but it's okay. I deserve it. Ask me."

"Mom or me?"

"You, Noah. I'd always save you first." Her eyes are clear blue skies. "Even though you almost beheaded me the other night." She grins. "It's okay. I admit it. I've been awful, huh?"

"Totally rabid."

She makes an eye-bulging crazy face that cracks me up even in my mood. "You know," she says, "those girls are okay but they're so *normal*. It's boring." She does a goofy, fake ballerina leap across the room, lands on the bed, and shoulders up to me. I close my eyes. "Been a while," she whispers.

"So long."

We breathe and breathe and breathe together. She takes my hand and I think how otters sleep floating on their backs in water, holding hands exactly like this, so they don't drift apart in the night.

After a while, she picks up her fist. I do the same.

"One two three," we say at the same time.

Rock/Rock

Scissors/Scissors

Rock/Rock

Paper/Paper

Scissors/Scissors

"Yes!" she cries. "We still got it, yes we do!" She jumps to her feet. "We can watch the Animal Channel tonight. Or a movie? You can pick."

"Okay."

"I want to—"

"Me too," I reply, knowing what she was going to say. I want to be us again too.

(Portrait, Self-portrait: *Brother and Sister on a Seesaw, Blindfolded*)

She smiles, touches my arm. "Don't be sad." She says it so warmly, it makes the air change color. "It came right through the wall last night." This was worse when we were younger. If one cried, the other cried even if we were on different sides of Lost Cove. I didn't think it happened anymore.

"I'm fine," I say.

She nods. "See you tonight then if Mom and I don't kill each other." She gives a salute and is off.

I don't know how this can be but it can: A painting is both exactly the same and entirely different every single time you look at it. That's the way it is between Jude and me now.

* * *

A little while later, I remember that it's Thursday, which means life drawing at CSA, which means I'm ending my house arrest. Anyway, why should I stay locked up just because Brian's a popular axhat jock covered in flame retardant who likes toilet-licking hornet girls like Courtney Barrett?

My stand and footstool are where I left them last week. I set them up, telling myself that nothing matters but getting into CSA and I can hang out with Jude for the rest of the summer. And Rascal. And go to the museum with Mom. I don't need Brian.

The teacher begins class – a different girl model today – lecturing about positive and negative space, about drawing the space around a form to reveal a form. I've never done this before and get lost in the exercise, concentrating on finding the model by drawing what is not her.

But during the second part of class, I sit down with my back against the wall and begin drawing Brian in this outside-in way, even though I said I'd never draw him again. I can't help it. He's in me and needs to get out. I do sketch after sketch.

I'm concentrating so hard that I don't sense anyone approaching until my light gets blocked. I spring back in surprise and an embarrassing garbled sound flies out of my mouth as my brain catches up to the fact that it's *him,* that Brian's standing in front of me. He has no meteorite bag, no magnet rake, which means he came all the way down here to find me. *Again.* I attempt to keep the joy behind my face, not on it.

"Waited this morning," he says, and then licks his bottom lip so nervously, so perfectly, it causes pain deep in my chest. He glances at my pad. I flip it over before he can see himself, then get up, motioning for him to go back into the woods so no one inside hears us. I stow the stool and stand, hoping my knees don't give out, or alternatively, that I don't start dancing a jig.

He's waiting by the same tree as last time.

"So the English guy," he says as we start walking. "He there today?"

If there's one thing I know how to read in a voice, thanks to Jude, it's jealousy. I take a supremely happy breath. "He got booted last week."

"The drinking?"

"Yeah."

The woods are quiet except for our crunching footsteps and a crooning mockingbird somewhere in the trees.

"Noah?"

I suck in air. How can someone just saying your name make you feel like this? "Yeah?" There's a lot of emotion running around his face, but I don't know what kind it is. I focus on my sneakers instead.

Minute after silent minute ticks by.

"It's like this," he says eventually. He's stopped walking and is picking bark off an oak tree's trunk. "There are all these planets that get ejected from the planetary systems that they first belonged in and they just wander on their own through deep space, going their lonely way across the universe without a sun, you know, forever…"

His eyes are begging me to understand something. I think about what he just said. He's talked about this before, these lonely, drifting, sunless planets. So, what? Is he saying he doesn't want to be an outsider like me? Well, fine. I turn to go.

"No." He grabs my sleeve. *He grabbed my sleeve.*

The Earth pauses on its axis.

"Oh, fuck it." He licks his lip, looks at me desperately. "Just…" he says. "Just…"

He's stammering?

"Just what?" I ask.

"Just don't worry, okay?" The words fly out of his mouth and loop around my heart and fling it right out of my chest. I know what he's saying.

"Worry about what?" I say to mess with him.

He half smiles. "About getting hit in the head by an asteroid. It's extremely unlikely."

"Cool," I say. "I won't."

And so, I stop worrying.

I don't worry when a few seconds later he says with a full-on grin, "I totally saw what you were drawing back there, dude."

I don't worry that I blow off Jude that night and every single night that follows. I don't worry when she comes home and finds Brian and the hornets on the deck, all of the hornets posing for me like some photo they saw in a magazine. I don't worry that night when she says, "So Mom wasn't enough? You have to steal all my *friends* too?"

I don't worry that those are the last words she says to me all summer.

I don't worry that I seem to become cool by association, *me!*, that I hang out at The Spot with Brian and countless surf-tards and asshats and hornets encased in his Realm of Calm, hardly ever feeling like a hostage, mostly knowing what to do with my hands, and no one tries to chuck me off a cliff, or calls me anything but Picasso, a nickname started by Franklyn Fry of all asshats.

I don't worry that it's not as hard as I thought to pretend to be like everyone else, to change your skin color like a toad. To wear a little flame retardant.

I don't worry that when Brian and I are alone in the woods or up on his roof or in his living room watching baseball (whatever), he puts up an electrical fence between us, and never once do I risk death by brushing against it, but when we're in public, like at The Spot, the fence vanishes, and we become clumsy magnets, bumping and knocking into each other, grazing hands, arms, legs, shoulders, tapping the other on the back, even occasionally the leg, for no good reason except that it's like swallowing lightning.

I don't worry that all through the movie about the alien invasion, our legs microscopically drift: his, right, right, right, mine, left, left, left, until halfway through, they find each other and press so hard against each other for one, two, three, four, five, six, seven, eight delirious seconds, that I have to get up and run to the bathroom because I'm exploding. I don't worry that when I get back to my seat, it all starts again, but this time our legs find each other immediately and he grabs my hand beneath the armrest and squeezes it and we electrocute and die.

I don't worry that when all that happened, Heather was on my other side and Courtney on his.

I don't worry that Courtney still hasn't given Brian his hat back or that Heather doesn't take her ancient gray eyes off me.

I don't worry that Brian and I never kiss, not once, no matter how much mind control I exert on him, no matter how much I beg God, the trees, every molecule I come across.

And most important, I don't worry when I come home one

day and find a note on the kitchen table written by Jude asking Mom to come down to the beach to see a sculpture she's building out of sand. I don't worry that I take the note and bury it at the bottom of the garbage can. I don't worry, not really, even though it makes my stomach hurt to do it, no not my stomach, it makes my soul hurt that I could do it, that I actually did it.

I should've been worrying.

I should've been worrying a lot.

* * *

Brian's leaving tomorrow morning to go back to boarding school for the fall, and tonight I'm in the underworld looking for him. I've never been to a party before, didn't know it was like being miles and miles underground, where demons walk around with their hair on fire. I'm pretty certain no one here can see me. It must be because I'm too young or skinny or something. Courtney's parents are out of town and she decided we'd use her older sister's party as a going away bash for Brian. I don't want to be at a going away party for Brian. I want to be going away with Brian, like on a plane to the Serengeti to watch the blue wildebeests migrate.

I head down a smoky crowded hall, where everyone's pressed to the walls in clumps like people-sculptures. No one's face is arranged right. In the next room, it's their bodies. People are dancing, and after I make sure Brian's not here yet, I lean against the wall and take in the whole mob of sweating gleaming people with their piercings and plumage and windmilling arms as they jump and sway and spin and lift off into the air. I'm staring and staring, getting eaten by the music, getting new eyes – when I feel a hand, or maybe it's a bird talon clawing into my shoulder. I turn to see an older girl with tons of springy red hair. She's wearing a short shimmery brown dress and is way taller than me. Winding around her entire arm is an off-the-hook tattoo of a red-and-orange fire-breathing dragon. "Lost?" she asks loudly over the music, like she's talking to a five-year-old.

I guess I'm not invisible after all. Her whole face is sparkling, especially the emerald-green wings around her icy blue eyes. Her pupils are huge black caves where bats live. "You're so cute," she shouts into my ear. She has a strange accent, kind of like Dracula's, and looks like one of the ladies Klimt paints. "Your hair." She pulls one of my curls until it's perfectly straight. I can't look away from her because that's what happens with demons. "Such big, dark, soulful eyes," she says slowly in her thick accent, like she's making a meal of each word. The music has quieted down and thankfully so has her voice. "Bet all the little girls are after you." I shake my head. "They will be, trust me." She smiles and there's a gash of red lipstick on one of her fangs. "Ever kiss a girl?" I shake my head again. I can't seem to lie to her or break the demon spell in any way. And then with no warning, her crackly lips are pushing against mine, in between mine, and I can taste her, all smoky and the gross kind of too sweet like an orange that's been in the sun all day. My eyes are open, so I can see the black spidery eyelashes sleeping on her cheeks. She's really kissing me! Why? She pulls back, opens her eyes, and laughs when she sees the expression on my face. Putting one of her talons on my shoulder again, she leans in and whispers in my ear, "See you in a few years." Then she turns and walks away on long bare legs, her devil tail swishing back and forth. I watch the fire-breathing dragon tattoo on her arm slither all the way up her shoulder and wrap around her neck.

Did that really just happen to me? Did I imagine it? Um, don't think so, because I certainly wouldn't have picked her if my imagination were in charge. I bring my hand to my mouth and wipe my lips. Red comes off on my fingers, her lipstick. It did happen. Do all people taste like sun-rancid oranges on the inside? Do I? Does Brian?

Brian.

I start toward the front door. I'll wait for him outside and convince him to go up to the roof instead for his last night, like I wanted to anyway, so all the stars can fall on our heads one final time, so maybe what hasn't happened all summer might finally happen, but as I enter the front hallway, I spot him following Courtney up a staircase, watch him as he razors through the crowd, nodding his head to guys, returning the smiles of girls, like he belongs. How is it he belongs everywhere?

(Portrait: *The Boy with All the Keys in the World with All the Locks*)

When he reaches the top of the stairs, he turns around. His hands are on the banister and he's leaning forward, surveying the room – is he looking for me? Yes, I know he is and it shape-shifts me into a waterfall. Can you die of this feeling? I'm thinking yes. I can't even draw or paint it out of me anymore. When it comes on, and it comes on all the time now, I just have to lie down on my back and let it wash me away.

Courtney tugs on his arm and he slips off behind her

without having found me and so I turn back into a person.

I squeeze up the steps after them with my head down. I don't want to make eye contact, don't want anyone talking to me, kissing me! Do people at parties just kiss other people for no reason? I know nothing. When I've almost reached the top of the stairs, I feel a hand on my arm. Not again. A small girl who looks like a gothed-out chipmunk hands me a red plastic cup full of beer. "Here," she says, smiling. "You seem like you need one." I say thanks and continue up. Maybe I do need one. I hear her say, "Isn't he a little hottie?" to someone who replies, "Cradle robber." God. So much for my secret garage workouts with Dad's weights. Everyone here thinks I'm in kindergarten. But am I hot? It's not possible, is it? I always assume girls look at me because they think I'm strange, not because they think I'm cute. Mom tells me I'm so handsomeadorablegorgeous, but that's her job. How do you know if you're hot? The redheaded kissing demon did say that my eyes were soulful.

Does Brian think I'm hot?

The idea goes straight to my groin and jerks me awake. *He grabbed my hand under the armrest at the movie.* More than awake. I stop, breathe, try to get under control, take a sip of the beer, well more like a giant gulp. It's not horrible. I continue up the stairs.

The second floor is the opposite of the first, as it's in heaven. I'm standing in a long, white-carpeted, white-walled cloud of a hallway with a bunch of closed doors on either side.

Which room did Brian and Courtney go into? What if they're alone? What if they're kissing? Or worse? Maybe she already has her shirt off. I take another drink of beer. What if he's licking her boobs? Guys are really into that. *He told me not to worry. He told me not to worry. He told me not to worry.* Which was code, wasn't it? Code for: *I will not lick Courtney Barrett's boobs,* right? I take a huge gulp of the beer, worrying a real real lot.

In movies, terrible haywire things always happen on people's last night places.

I go left down the hall, where it looks like some of the doors might be open a crack. In an alcove, I spot two people in a frenzy of red-hot making out. I slip back to watch. The guy has an incredible back that narrows just so into his jeans and the girl's sandwiched between his body and the wall. His head's moving like he can't kiss her hard enough or fast enough. I tell myself to move on already, but then something catches my eye. The girl's hands reaching around the guy's back aren't girls' hands at all – no, there's no way in hell those hands are anything but another guy's. My chest starts to vibrate. I lean to the left and then I see flashes of both faces, strong-boned male faces, eyes closed like moons, smashed noses, mouths crushing together, their bodies climbing up each other and falling down each other at the same time. My legs start to shake, every part of me starts to shake. (Self-portrait: *Earthquake*) I've never seen two guys kiss like this, like the world's ending, except in my own head and it wasn't half this good. Not even close. They're so *hungry*.

I step back and steady myself against the wall out of sight.

I'm not sad, far far from it, so I don't know why tears are busting out of my eyes.

Then I hear the squeak of a door opening on the other side of the hall. I wipe my face with the back of my hand and turn in the direction of the sound. Heather's stepping out of a room – everything in me stills. It's horrible to see her, like walking out of the best movie ever into some same old afternoon.

"Oh!" she cries, her face beaming. "I was coming to look for you." I give my head a shake so hair curtains my face as much as possible. She's walking toward me, getting closer and closer to the three of us. I kick into gear, rushing to intercept her. Her smile grows bigger and more welcoming and I realize she's misinterpreted my leap across the hall as excitement to see her when all I want is to protect the kissing guys from her, from the whole world.

(Portrait: *Adam and Adam in the Garden*)

When I reach her, I try to turn my mouth into a smile. It's hard. I hear a hushed gruff laugh behind me, muffled words. Heather peers over my shoulder.

"Where is everyone?" I ask to get her attention back. I realize I'm still shaking. I bury my free hand deep in my pocket.

"You okay?" she asks, tilting her head. "You seem strange." Her steady gray eyes are studying me. "More so than usual, I should say." She smiles warmly and I relax a little. Heather and I have a secret but I have no idea what it is.

I wish I could tell her what just happened to me because even though I wasn't technically part of that kiss, I feel like it happened to me, unlike the demon kiss downstairs, which technically happened to me but feels like it didn't. But what would I tell her anyway? When I draw it, I'm going to make my skin see-through and what you'll see is that all the animals in the zoo of me have broken out of their cages.

"Maybe it's the beer," I say.

She giggles, lifts a red plastic cup and taps mine. "Me too."

Her giggling takes me aback. There's nothing giggly about Heather usually. She's the opposite; hanging out with her is like sitting in an empty church. That's why I like her. She's quiet and serious and a thousand years old and seems like she can talk to the wind. I always draw her with arms up like she's about to take flight or with her hands together like she's praying. She's not a giggler.

"C'mon," she says. "Everyone's in here already." She points toward the door. "We've been waiting for you. Well, I have." She giggles again, then blushes like a geyser went off inside her. I have a supremely bad feeling.

We walk into some kind of den. I see Brian right away across the room talking to Courtney. All I want is to blink us into the bodies of the guys in the alcove. I try to, just in case. Then I think how many fingers I'd give up for one minute like that with him and decide seven. Or eight even. I could totally still draw with two fingers if one was a thumb.

I look around. It's the same crew of hornets and surftards that hang out at The Spot, minus the older guys like Fry and Zephyr and Big Foot, who're probably downstairs. I'm used to these people by now, and them me. There's also a bunch of kids I don't recognize that must go to Courtney's private school. Everyone's standing around in awkward shuffling bunches like they're waiting for something. The air is full of breathing. The air's full of Jude too. She's leaning on a windowsill talking to like five hundred guys at once, wearing the tight red ruffly dress she made that Mom forbade her from ever wearing out of the house. I'm totally surprised to see her. She's been giving me a wide angry berth all summer and knew I'd be here. I wonder what she told Mom. I just said I was going to say good-bye to Brian. We're definitely not allowed to be at a party like this.

I catch her eye as Heather and I cross the room. She throws me a look that says: *Nothing, not even a world where it rains light, where snow is purple, where frogs talk, where sunsets last a full year — could make up for the fact that you're the worst mother-stealing, friend-pillaging twin brother on earth,* and resumes her conversation with her harem.

My bad feeling is compounding.

I return my attention to Brian, who's leaning against a bookcase, still talking to Courtney. About what? I try to hear as we approach them, then realize Heather's speaking to me.

"It's totally stupid. We haven't played this kind of game since fifth grade, but whatever. We're playing with a sense of irony, right?" Has she been talking this whole time?

"What game?" I ask.

Courtney turns around at the sound of our voices. "Oh, good." She nudges Heather, who giggles again. Courtney turns to me. "It's your lucky night, Picasso. You like games?"

"Not really," I say. "Not at all, actually."

"You'll like this one. Promise. It's a blast from the past. Heather and Jude and I were talking the other day about the parties we used to go to. Simple premise. Put two people of the opposite sex in a closet for seven minutes. See what happens." Brian won't meet my eyes. "Don't worry, Picasso," she says. "It's fixed, of course." Heather's ears go red at this. They lock arms and then burst out laughing. My stomach goes watery. "Face it, dude," Courtney says to me. "You could use a little help."

I sure could.

I sure could because suddenly coils and coils of Jude's hair are slithering in my direction like an army of serpents. *Jude was there*, Courtney said. Was this Jude's idea, then? Because she knows I threw out that note she left for Mom? Because she knows how I feel about Brian?

(Portrait, Self-portrait: *Twins: Jude with Rattlesnake Hair, Noah with Rattlesnake Arms*)

I'm getting a metal taste in my mouth. Brian's reading the titles on the spines of books on the shelves like he's going to be tested on it.

"I love you," I say to him, only it comes out, "Hey."

"So damn much," he says back, only it comes out, "Dude."

He still won't meet my eyes.

Courtney picks up Brian's hat, which has been resting on a small table. It's full of folded-up pieces of paper. "All the guys' names are already in, including yours," she says to me. "Girls pick."

She and Heather walk away. As soon as they're out of earshot, I say to Brian, "Let's go." He doesn't respond, so I say it again. "Let's get out of here. Let's climb out this window." I'm checking the one beside us and there's a landing that leads to a supremely climbable tree. We could totally make it. "C'mon," I say. "Brian."

"I don't want to go, okay?" There's irritation in his voice. "It's just a stupid game. Whatever. No big deal."

I study him. Does he want to play? He does. He must.

He wants to be with Courtney because if it's fixed and Courtney's doing the fixing, that's what's going to happen. That's why he won't meet my eyes. The realization drains the blood out of me. But why did he tell me not to worry? Why did he grab my hand? Why everything?

All the empty cages begin to rattle inside me.

I stumble over to an ugly beige chair in the middle of this ugly beige room. I fall onto it, only to discover it's hard as stone and it breaks my spine in two. I sit there, broken in half, chugging the rest of my beer like it's orange juice, remembering the English guy downing the gin that day. Then I grab another cup of beer that someone left and drink what's in that one too. Purgatory, I think. If hell is downstairs and heaven is the hallway, then this must be purgatory – what happens in purgatory again? I've seen paintings of it but can't remember. I feel supremely woozy. Am I drunk?

The lights start flashing on and off. Courtney's at the switch, Heather by her side. "Ladies and gentlemen, the moment you've all been waiting for."

Clementine reaches in first and chooses a guy named Dexter. Some tall kid I've never seen before with a cool haircut and clothes ten times too big for him. Everyone jeers and cheers and generally acts lame as they get up and walk into the closet with we-are-so-beyond-this looks on their faces. Courtney makes a display of setting the egg-timer. All I can think about is how much I hate her, how much I want her to get stampeded by a herd of pissed-off snapping turtles before she can get in that closet with Brian.

I stand with the help of the armrest, then bushwhack through an impossible thicket of Jude's blond hair to a bathroom, where I splash cold water on my face. Beer sucks. I lift my head. It's still me in the mirror. It's still me in me, right? I'm not sure. And I'm certainly not hot, I can see that. I look like a skinny pathetic coward too afraid to jump off his dad's shoulder into the water. *It's a sink-or-swim world, Noah.*

The second I walk back into the room, I'm assaulted by, "You've been chosen, dude," and "Heather picked you," and "Your turn, Picasso."

I swallow. Brian's still studying those spines of books, his back to me as Heather takes my hand and leads me toward the closet, her arm pulled tight as if forcing an unwilling dog on a leash.

What I notice right away about the walk-in closet is that there are tons of dark suits hanging everywhere, looking like rows of men at a funeral.

Heather switches off the light, then says softly, shyly, "Help me find you, okay?" I think about escaping into the hanging suits, joining the men in mourning until the egg-timer goes off, but then Heather bumps into me and laughs. Her hands quickly find my arms. Her touch is so light, like two leaves have fallen on me.

"We don't have to," she whispers. Then, "Do you want to?"

I can feel her breath on my face. Her hair smells like sad flowers.

"Okay," I say, but don't move a muscle.

Time passes. It feels like lots and lots of it, so much that when we walk out of this closet, it'll be time for us to go to college or die even. Except, because I'm counting in my head,

I know that not even seven seconds of the seven minutes have passed. I'm calculating how many seconds are in seven minutes when I feel her small cool hands leave my arms and land on my cheeks, then feel her lips brush across mine, once, then again, the second time staying there. It's like being kissed by a feather, no, smoother, a petal. So soft. Too soft. We're petal people. I think about the earthquake kiss in the alcove and want to cry again. This time because I *am* sad. And scared. And because my skin has never fit this badly before.

(Self-portrait: *Boy in a Blender*)

I realize my arms are lying limp at my sides. I should do something with them, shouldn't I? I rest a hand on her waist, which totally feels like the wrong place for it, so I move it to her back, which also feels entirely wrong, but before I can reposition it, her lips open, so I open my mine too – it's not disgusting. She doesn't taste like a rancid orange but like mint, like she had a mint right before. I'm wondering what I taste like as her tongue slips into my mouth. It shocks me how wet it is. And warm. And tongue-y. My tongue's going nowhere. I'm telling it to move and enter her mouth, but it won't listen to me. I figure it out: There's 420 seconds in seven minutes. Maybe twenty seconds have passed, which means we still have 400 seconds left of this. Oh fucking fuck.

And then it happens. Brian rises out of the darkness of my mind and takes my hand like he did in the movie theater and pulls me to him. I can smell his sweat, can hear his voice. *Noah,* he says in that bone-melting way and my hands are in Heather's hair, and I'm pressing my body against hers hard, drawing her closer to me, pushing my tongue deep inside her mouth…

We must not hear the ding of the timer, because all of a sudden the light switches on and the mourning men are all around us again, not to mention Courtney in the doorway tapping an invisible watch on her wrist. "C'mon, lovebirds. Time's up." I blink a few hundred times at the invasion of light. At the invasion of the truth. Heather looks dizzy, dreamy. Heather looks one hundred percent like Heather. I've done a bad thing. To her, to me. To Brian, even if he doesn't care, it still feels that way. Maybe the girl downstairs turned me into a demon like her with that kiss.

"Wow," Heather whispers. "I've never… No one's ever… Wow. That was incredible."

She can barely walk. I look down to make sure I don't have a tent in my pants as she takes my hand and we emerge from the closet like two unsteady cubs from a hibernation den. Everyone starts whistling and saying lame things like, "Bedroom's down the hall."

I scan the room for Brian, expecting him to be examining the spines of books still, but he's not. His face is like I've seen it only once before, all bricked up with fury, like he wants to hurl a meteorite at my head and he's not going to miss.

But?

Heather runs off to join the hornets. The whole room's been engulfed by Jude's hair. The whole universe has. I fall into a recliner. Nothing makes sense. *It's just a stupid game,* he said. *No big deal.* But then, he said it was *No big deal* when his mother's friend (boyfriend?) came on to him too and that

159

seemed like it was a big deal to him. Maybe *No big deal* is code for: This is Supernaturally Screwed Up. *I'm sorry,* I tell him in my mind. *It was you,* I tell him. *I kissed you.*

I drop my head in my hands, start involuntarily eavesdropping on a group of guys behind me, who must be having a contest to see how many times they can say how *gay* this or that is in one conversation, when someone touches my shoulder. It's Heather.

I nod at her, then try to hide in my hair and mind-control her to go away, like to the Amazon… I feel her stiffening beside me, probably not understanding why I've sent her six thousand miles away to the jungle after a kiss like that. I hate being like this to her, but I don't know what else to do. When I peek up through my hair moments later, she's gone. I hadn't realized I'd been holding my breath. I'm mid-exhale when I see Brian being escorted into the closet, not by Courtney, but *by my sister.*

My sister.

* * *

How is this happening? This can't be happening. I blink and blink, but it's still happening. I look over at Courtney, who has her hand in Brian's hat. She's opening the folded pieces of paper wondering what went wrong. *Jude* is what went wrong. I can't believe she'd go this far.

I have to do something.

"No!" I shout, jumping up from the chair. "No!"

Only I don't do that.

I run to the egg-timer, grab it off the table, and ring it and ring it and ring it.

Only I don't do that either.

I don't do anything.

I can't do anything.

I've been eviscerated.

(Self-portrait: *Gutted Fish*)

Brian and Jude are going to kiss each other.

They're probably kissing each other right this second.

Somehow I manage to get up from the chair, out of that room, down the stairs, and out the door of the house. I stagger across the porch, feeling like I'm falling off my feet with every step. Blurs of people are blurring around the yard. I stumble through them, through the black back-stabbing air toward the road. In my daze, I realize I'm scanning the crowd for the crazy-in-love, making-out guys from the alcove, but they're nowhere. I bet I imagined them.

I bet they don't exist.

I look toward the woods, watch all the trees crash down.

(Group Portrait: *All the Glass Boys Shatter*)

From behind me, I hear someone with a slurring English accent say, "If it isn't the clandestine artist." I turn to see the naked English guy, except he's dressed in a leather jacket and jeans and boots. He has the same mental smile on his same mental face. The same eyes that don't match. I remember how Jude gave up the sun and stars and oceans for my drawing of him. I'm going to steal it back from her. I'm going to take *everything* from her.

If she were drowning, I'd hold her head under.

"I know you, mate," he says, teetering on his feet, pointing at me with a bottle of some kind of alcohol.

"No you don't," I say. "No one does."

His eyes clear for a second. "You're right about that."

We stare at each other for a moment without saying anything. I remember how he looked naked and don't even care because I'm dead. I'm going to move underground with the moles and breathe dirt.

"What are you called anyway?" he asks.

What am I called? What a strange question. Bubble, I think. I'm called freaking Bubble.

"Picasso," I say.

His eyebrows arch. "You taking the piss?"

What does that mean?

He slurs on, throwing words into the air all around us. "Well, that must keep the bar nice and low, no problem filling those shoes, like naming your kid Shakespeare. What were they thinking, your parents?" He takes a swig.

I pray to the forest of fallen trees that Brian looks out the window and sees me here with the naked English guy. Jude too.

"You're like from a movie," I think and say at the same time.

He laughs and his face kaleidoscopes. "A crap movie, then. Been sleeping in the park for weeks now. Except for the night I slept behind bars, of course."

Jail? He's an outlaw? He looks like one. "Why?" I ask.

"Drunk and disorderly. Disturbing the peace. Whoever heard of getting arrested for being disorderly?" I struggle to decipher his sloshed words. "Are you orderly, Picasso? Is anyone?" I shake my head and he nods. "That's what I said. There's no peace to disturb. I kept telling the cop: No. Peace. To. Disturb.

Man." Putting two cigarettes in his mouth, he lights one, the other, then sucks on them both. I've never seen someone smoke two at once. Gray plumes of smoke come out his nose and mouth at the same time. He hands me one of the cigarettes, which I take because what else am I going to do? "Got myself chucked from that posh art school you don't go to." He puts a hand on my shoulder to steady himself. "Doesn't matter, would've gotten chucked anyway when they found out I wasn't really eighteen." I feel how wobbly he is and plant my feet into the ground. Then I remember the cigarette in my hand and bring it to my lips, only to suck in and immediately cough it out. He doesn't notice. He might be as drunk as one of those guys who talks to lampposts and I'm the lamppost. I want to take the bottle from him and pour it out.

"I gotta go," I say, because I've started imagining Brian and Jude touching each other in the dark. All over. Can't stop imagining it.

"Right," he says, not looking at me. "Right."

"Maybe you should go home," I say, then remember about the park, about jail.

He nods, despair stuck to every part of his face.

I start walking off, ditching the cigarette first thing. After a few steps, I hear, "Picasso," and turn.

He points the bottle at me. "I modeled a couple times for this barking maniac of a sculptor called Guillermo Garcia. He has loads of students. I'm sure he wouldn't even notice if you showed up one afternoon. You could actually be in a room with a model, like that other Picasso bloke."

"Where?" I ask, and when he tells me, I repeat the address a few times in my head so I'll remember. Not that I'll go, because I'll be in prison myself for the murder of my twin sister.

Jude planned this. I'm sure of it. I know it was her idea. She's been pissed at me for so long about Mom. About the hornets. And she must've found the note she wrote to Mom buried in the garbage. This is her revenge. She probably had a piece of paper with Brian's name on it right in her hand.

Without any of the hornets realizing it, she triggered a nest attack on me.

I walk down the hill toward home, getting carpet-bombed with images of Brian and Jude, him all tangled up in her hair, in her light, in her normal. That's what he wants. That's why he erected the fence between us. Then electrified it for double protection against me, stupid weirdo me. I think how full-on I kissed Heather. Oh God. Is Brian kissing Jude like that? Is she him? A horrible flailing monster of a noise comes out of me and then the whole disgusting night wants to come out of me too. I run to the side of the road and throw up each grain of beer and that disgusting drag of a cigarette, every last lying, revolting kiss, until I'm just a bag of clattering bones.

When I get home, I see that there are lights on in the living room, so I climb through my window, always open a crack, in case Brian decided to break and enter one night, like I'd imagine before falling asleep, all summer long. I cringe at myself. At what I wanted.

(Landscape: *The Collapsed World*)

I turn on the lamp in my bedroom and beeline for Dad's

camera, but it's not where I always leave it under my bed. I tear the room apart with my eyes, exhaling only when I spot it on my desk, sitting there like a live grenade. Who moved it? Who freaking moved it? Did I leave it there? Maybe I did. I don't know. I lunge for it and call up the photos. The first one that comes up is from last year when Grandma died. A big round laughing sand lady with her arms open to the sky like she's about to lift off. It's freaking amazing. I put my finger on the delete button and press hard, press murderously. I call the rest up, each one more awesome and strange and cool than the next, and wipe them out, one by one, until every trace of my sister's talent is gone from the world and only mine is left.

Then, after I sneak by the living room – Mom and Dad have fallen asleep in front of some war movie – I go into Jude's room, take the portrait of the naked English guy off the wall, rip it to shreds and spread it like confetti all over the floor. Next, I return to my room and start on the drawings of Brian – it takes forever to tear them all to pieces, there are so many. When I'm done, I stuff his remains into three large black plastic bags and stow them under the bed. Tomorrow I'm going to throw him, every last bit of him, over Devil's Drop.

Because he can't swim.

Even after all that, Jude's still not home! It's an hour past our summer curfew now. I can only imagine. I have to stop imagining.

I have to stop holding this rock and praying he's going to come to the window.

He doesn't.

The
History
of Luck

Jude, Age 16

I'm going to WISH with my HANDS

like Sandy said.

I'm going to use The Oracle.

I'm going to sit here at my desk and use it – in the traditional way – to find out everything I can about Guillermo Garcia aka Drunken Igor aka The Rock Star of the Sculpture World. I have to make this sculpture and it has to be in stone and he's the only one who can help me do that. This is the way to get through to Mom. I feel it.

However, before I do all this, I'm going to suck the living hell out of this lemon – the mortal enemy of the aphrodisiacal orange:

> Nothing curdles love in the heart
> like lemon on the tongue

Because I *have* to nip this in the bud.

Grandma pipes in. "Ah yes, Him with a capital H and I don't mean Mr. Gable. A certain big ... bad ... British ... wolf?" She milks the last bit for all its worth.

"I don't know what it was about him," I tell her in my head. "Oh man. Besides *everything,*" I tell her outside my head.

And then I can't help it. Giving it my best English accent, I say,

169

"Such a chatterbox, a guy can't get a word in." The smile I denied him in church overtakes my face until I'm beaming at the wall.

Oh Clark Gable, stop.

I shove the half-lemon in, shove Grandma out, tell myself the English bloke has glandular fever, cold sores, and tooth decay, the trifecta of unkissability, like every other hot male in Lost Cove.

Cooties. Major cooties. English cooties.

With sour making my whole head pucker, with the boy boycott back in full swing, I boot up my laptop and type into The Oracle: *Guillermo Garcia* and *Art Tomorrow*, hoping to find Mom's interview. But no luck. The magazine doesn't archive online. I input his name again and do an image search.

And it's Invasion of the Granite Giants.

Massive rock-beings. Walking mountains. Expression explosions. I love them instantly. Igor told me he wasn't okay. Well, neither is his art. I start bookmarking reviews and pieces, choose a work that makes my heart sink and swell at the same time as a new screensaver, then grab my sculpture textbook off the shelf, certain he's in it. His work is too amazing for him not to be.

He is, and I'm on the second read of his bona fide bonkers biography, one that belongs in Grandma's bible, not a textbook, so I've ripped it out and clipped it into the over-stuffed leather-bound book, when I hear the front door open, followed by a flurry of voices and a stampede of footsteps coming down the hall.

Noah.

I wish I'd shut my door. Dive under the bed? Before I can make the move, they're barreling by, peering in at me like I'm

The Bearded Lady. And somewhere in that happy humming hive of athletic, preternaturally normal teenagers is my brother.

Best sit down for it:

Noah's joined a sports team at Roosevelt High.

Granted, it's cross-country, not football, and Heather's on the team, but still. He's a member of a *gang*.

To my surprise, a moment later, he doubles back and enters my room, and it's as if Mom's standing before me. It's always been the case, me fair like Dad, him dark like Mom, but his resemblance to her has become uncanny, therefore: heart-snatching. Whereas there's not a hint of Mom on me, never was. When people used to see us alone, I'm sure they assumed I was adopted.

It's unusual, Noah in my room, and my stomach's clenching up. I hate how nervous it makes me to be near him now. Also — what Sandy said today. How, unbeknownst to me, someone took pictures of my flying sand women and sent them in to CSA. It had to have been Noah, which means: He got me in only to end up having to go to Roosevelt himself.

I taste guilt right through the citrus.

"So, hey," he says, shuffling back and forth on a pair of running mud-cakes, driving dirt deeper and deeper into my plush white carpet. I say nothing about it. He could chop off my ear and I'd say nothing about it. His face is the opposite of how it looked in the sky earlier today. It's padlocked. "You know how Dad's going away for the week? We—" He nods at his room, where music and laughter and uniformity resounds. "We thought it'd be cool to have a party here. You okay with that?"

I stare at him, beseeching the aliens or Clark Gable or

whoever's in charge of soul abductions to bring back my brother. Because in addition to joining dangerous gangs and having parties, this Noah also goes out with girls, keeps his hair buzzed and tidy, hangs at The Spot, watches sports with Dad. For all other sixteen-year-old boys: fine. For Noah, it signifies one thing: death of the spirit. A book with the wrong story in it. My brother, the revolutionary weirdo, has covered himself in flame retardant, to use his terminology. Dad's thrilled, of course, thinks Noah and Heather are a couple – they're not. I'm the only one who seems to know how dire the situation is.

"Um, Jude, do you know there's a lemon wrapped around your teeth?"

"Of course I know," I say, though it sounds like garble for obvious reasons. Ah, lightbulb! Taking advantage of the sudden language barrier, I look right at him and add, "What have you done with my brother? If you see him, tell him I miss him. Tell him I'm—"

"Hello? Can't understand you with the voodoo lemon in your mouth." He shakes his head in a dismissive Dad kind of way and I can tell he's about to get on my case. My interests disturb him, which I guess makes us even. "You know, I borrowed your laptop the other day to do a paper when Heather was using mine. I saw your search history." Uh-oh. "Jesus, Jude. How many diseases can you think you have in one night? And all those freaking obituaries you read – like from every county in California." Now seems like a good time to imagine the meadow. He points to the bible outspread on my lap. "And maybe you could give that totally lame book a rest for a while, and, I don't know, get out. Talk to someone besides our dead grandmother. Think about things besides dying. It's so—"

I take out the lemon. "What? *Embarrassing?*" I remember saying this to him once – how embarrassing he was – and cringe at the former me. Is it possible our personalities have swapped bodies? In third grade, Mrs. Michaels, the art teacher, told us we were to do self-portraits. We were across the room from each other and without so much as sharing a glance, I drew him, and he me. Sometimes, now, it feels like that.

"I wasn't going to say embarrassing," he says, brushing a hand through his bushel of hair, only to find that it's no longer there. He touches the back of his neck instead.

"Yes you were."

"Okay I was, because, it *is* totally embarrassing. I go to pay for my lunch today and pull out these." He reaches in his pocket and shows me the assortment of extremely protective beans and seeds I stowed there.

"I'm just looking out for you, Noah, even if you're a card-carrying artichoke."

"Totally freaking mental, Jude."

"You know what I think is mental? Having a party on the second anniversary of your mother's death."

His face cracks for a second, then just as quickly seals up. "I know you're in there!" I want to scream. It's true; I do know it. This is how:

1) His weird obsession with jumping Devil's Drop and the sublime way he looked in the sky today.

2) There are times when he's slumped in a chair, lying on his

bed, curled up on the couch, and I wave my hand across his face and he doesn't even blink. It's as if he's gone blind. Where is he during those times? What's he doing in there? Because I suspect he's painting. I suspect that inside the impenetrable fortress of conventionality he's become, there's one crazy-ass museum.

And most significantly: 3) I've discovered (search-history snooping is a two-way street) that Noah, who hardly ever goes online, who's probably the only teenager in America indifferent to virtual reality and all social media, posts a message on a site called LostConnections.com, always the same one and pretty much every week.

I check – he's never gotten a response. I'm certain the message is for Brian, who I haven't seen since Mom's funeral, and who, as far as I know, hasn't been back to Lost Cove since his mother moved away.

For the record, I knew what was going on between Brian and Noah even if no one else did. All that summer when Noah came home at night from hanging out with him, he'd draw pictures of NoahandBrian until his fingers were so raw and swollen he'd have to take trips from his room to the freezer, where he'd bury his hand in the ice tray. He didn't know I was watching him from the hallway, how he'd collapse against the refrigerator, his forehead pressed against the cold door, his eyes closed, his dreams outside of his body.

He didn't know the moment he left in the morning, I'd go through the secret sketchpads he hid under his bed. It was like he'd discovered a whole new color spectrum. It was like he'd found another galaxy of imagery. It was like he'd replaced me.

To be clear: More than anything, I wish I hadn't gone into that closet with Brian. But their story wasn't over that night.

I wish I hadn't done a lot of things I did back then.

I wish going into that closet with Brian was the worst of it.

The right-handed twin tells the truth,
the left-handed twin tells lies
(Noah and I are both left-handed.)

He's looking down at his feet. Intently. I don't know what he's thinking and it makes my bones feel hollow. He lifts his head. "We're not going to have the party on the anniversary. It'll be the day before," he says quietly, his dark eyes soft, just like Mom's.

Even though the last thing I want is a bunch of Hideaway Hill surfers like Zephyr Ravens anywhere near me, I say, "Have it." I say this instead of what I'd say to him if I still had the voodoo lemon in: *I'm sorry. For everything.*

"Come for once?" He gestures toward the wall. "Wear one of those?" Unlike me, my room is one big blast of girl, with all the dresses I make – floating and not – hanging all over the walls. It's like having friends.

I shrug. "Don't do social events. Don't wear the dresses."

"You used to."

I don't say, "And you used to make art and like boys and talk to horses and pull the moon through the window for my birthday present."

If Mom came back, she wouldn't be able to pick either of us out of a police lineup.

Or Dad, for that matter, who's just materialized in the

doorway. *Benjamin Sweetwine: The Sequel* has skin the color and texture of gray earthenware clay. His pants are always too big and belted awkwardly so he looks like a scarecrow, like if someone pulled the belt he'd turn into a pile of straw. This might be my fault. Grandma and I have largely taken over the kitchen, using the bible as cookbook:

> To bring joy back to a grieving family,
> sprinkle three tablespoons of crushed
> eggshells over every meal

Dad seems to always appear like this now too, without the foreshadowing of say, footsteps? My eyes migrate to his shoes, which are indeed on his feet, which are indeed on the ground *and* pointing in the right direction – good. Well, you start to wonder who's the specter in the family. You start to wonder why your dead parent is more present and accounted for than the living one. Most of the time, I only know Dad's home because I hear a toilet flush or the TV turn on. He never listens to jazz or swims anymore. He mostly just stares off with a faraway perplexed look on his face, like he's trying to work through an impenetrable mathematical equation.

And he goes for walks.

The walking started a day after the funeral when all Mom's friends and colleagues still filled the house. "Going for a walk," he'd said to me, bowing out the back door, leaving me (Noah was nowhere to be found), and not returning home until after everyone had left. The next day was the same: "Going for a walk," and so were the days and weeks and months and years that followed, with everyone always telling me they saw my dad up on Old Mine Road, which is fifteen miles from here, or at Bandit Beach, which is even farther. I imagine him getting hit by cars, washed away by rogue waves, attacked by mountain lions. I imagine him not coming back. I used to ambush him on his way out, asking if I could walk with him, to which he'd reply, "Just need some time to think, honey."

While he's thinking, I wait for the phone to ring with the news that there's been an accident.

That's what they tell you: *There's been an accident.*

Mom was on her way to see Dad when it happened. They'd been separated for about a month and he was staying at a hotel.

She told Noah before she left that afternoon that she was going to ask Dad to come home so we could be a family again.

But she died instead.

To lighten the mood in my head, I ask, "Dad, isn't there a disease where the flesh calcifies until the poor afflicted person is trapped within their own body like it's a stone prison? I'm pretty sure I read about it in one of your journals."

He and Noah share one of their "glances" at my expense. Oh Clark Gable, groan.

Dad says, "It's called FOP and it's extremely rare, Jude. Extremely, extremely rare."

"Oh, I don't think I have it or anything." Not literally, anyway. I don't share that I think the three of us all might have it metaphorically. Our real selves buried so deep in these imposter ones. Dad's medical journals can be just as illuminating as Grandma's bible.

"Where the hell is Ralph? Where the hell is Ralph?" And a moment of family bonding ensues! We all roll our eyes in unison with dramatic Grandma Sweetwine flair. But then Dad's forehead creases. "Honey, is there a reason why there's a very large onion in your pocket?"

I look down at my illness deflector yawning open my sweatshirt pocket. I'd forgotten about it. Did the English guy see it too? Oh dear.

Dad says, "Jude, you really—" But what I'm certain is to be another artichoke lecture about my bible-thumping tendencies or my long-distance relationship with Grandma (he doesn't know about Mom) is cut short because he's been shot with a stun gun.

"Dad?" His face has gone pale – well, paler. "Dad?" I repeat, following his distraught gaze to the computer screen. Is it *Family of Mourners*? It was my favorite of the Guillermo Garcia works I saw, very upsetting, though. Three massive grief-stricken rock-giants who reminded me of us, the way Dad, Noah, and I must've looked standing over Mom's grave as if we might topple in after her. It must remind Dad too.

I look at Noah and find him in the same condition, also staring intently at the screen. The padlock is gone. A red glow of emotion has taken over his face and neck, even his hands. This is promising. He's actually reacting to art.

"I know," I say to both of them. "Incredible work, right?"

Neither of them responds. I'm not sure if either of them even heard me.

Then Dad says brusquely, "Going for a walk," and Noah says equally brusquely, "My friends," and they're gone.

And I'm the only bat in this belfry?

The thing is: I know I've slipped. I see my buttons popping off and flying in all directions on a daily basis. What worries me about Dad and Noah is that they seem to think they're okay.

I go to the window, open it, and in come the eerie moans and caws of the loons, the thunder of the winter waves, *stellar* waves, I see. For a moment I'm back on my board, busting through the break zone, cold briny air in my lungs – except then, I'm dragging Noah in to shore and it's again that day two years ago when he almost drowned and the weight of him is pulling us both under with each stroke – no.

No.

I close the window, yank down the shade.

If one twin is cut, the other will bleed

Later that night when I get on the computer to learn more about Guillermo Garcia, I find that the bookmarks I saved have been deleted.

The *Family of Mourners* screensaver has been changed to a single purple tulip.

When I question Noah about it, he says he doesn't know what I'm talking about, but I don't believe him.

* * *

Noah's party's raging all around me. Dad's off at his parasite conference for the week. Christmas was a bust. And I just made an early New Year's resolution, no, it's a New Year's *revolution,* and this is it: to return to Guillermo Garcia's studio tonight and ask him to mentor me. So far since winter break began, I've chickened out. Because what if he says no? What if he says yes? What if he bludgeons me with a chisel? What if the English guy is there? What if he isn't? What if *he* bludgeons me with a chisel? What if my mother breaks stone as easily as clay? What if this rash on my arm is leprosy?

Etc.

I put all such questions into The Oracle a moment ago and the results were conclusive. No time like the present, it was decided, egged on by the fact that people from Noah's party – Zephyr included – kept knocking on my door, which was locked with a dresser in front of it. So out the window I went, sweeping the twelve sand-dollar birds I keep on the sill into my sweatshirt pocket. They're not as lucky as four-leaf clovers or even red sea glass, but they'll have to do.

I follow the yellow reflectors in the middle of the road down the hill, listening for cars and serial killers. It's another white-out. It's way spooky. And this is a really bad idea. But I'm committed to it now, so I start to run through the cold wet nothingness and pray to Clark Gable that Guillermo Garcia is just a regular sort of maniac and not a girl-murdering one and try not to wonder if the English guy will be there. Try not to think about his different-colored eyes and the intensity that crackled off him and how familiar he looked and how he called me a fallen angel and said, "You're her," and before too long all that not-thinking has gotten me to the studio door and light is pouring out from beneath it.

Drunken Igor must be inside. An image of him with his greasy hair and wiry black beard and blue calloused fingers fills my head.

A very itchy image. He probably has lice. I mean, if I were a louse I'd choose him to colonize. All that hair. *No offense, but* ick.

I take a few steps back, see a bank of windows on the side of the building, all lit up – the studio space must be back there. An idea begins to take shape. A great idea. Because maybe there's a way to spy inside his studio undetected … yes, like from that fire escape in back, I think, spotting it. I want to see the giants. I want to see Drunken Igor too, and from behind glass seems perfect. Brilliant, really. Before I know it, I'm over the fence, and hustling down a pitch-dark alley, one in which girls get bludgeoned with chisels.

`It is very unlucky to fall on your face`
(This is an honest-to-goodness entry.
The wisdom of Grandma's bible knows no bounds.)

I reach the fire escape – alive – and start climbing, mouse-quiet, toward the light blaring from the landing.

What am I doing?

Well, I'm doing it. At the top of the stairs, I squat down and scoot like a crab under the windows. Once I've cleared them, I stand back up, hugging the wall as I peer into a huge brightly lit space—

And there they are. Giants. *Giant* giants. But different from the ones in the photographs. These are all couples. Across the room, enormous rock-beings are embracing as if on a dance floor, as if they've all frozen mid-move. No, not embracing, actually. Not yet. It's like each "man" and "woman" were hurling themselves at each other passionately, *desperately*, and then time stopped before they could make it into each other's arms.

Adrenaline courses through me. No wonder *Interview* had him taking a baseball bat to Rodin's *The Kiss*. It's so polite and, well, boring, in comparison—

My train of thought's interrupted because bounding into the large space as if his skin can't contain the uproar of blood within is Drunken Igor, but utterly transformed. He's shaved, washed his hair, and put on a smock, which is spattered with clay, as is the water bottle he's holding to his lips. There was no mention in his bio that he worked in clay. He guzzles from the bottle like he's been wandering the desert with Moses, drains it, then tosses it into a trash can.

Someone's plugged him in.

To a nuclear reactor.

Ladies and gentlemen: The Rock Star of the Sculpture World.

He moves toward a clay work-in-progress in the center of the room and when he's within a few feet of it, he begins circling it slowly, like predator on prey, speaking in a deep rumble of a voice I can hear through the window. I look at the door, assuming someone's about to follow him in, someone immersed in this conversation with him, like the English guy, I think with a flutter, but no one joins him. I can't make out a word of what he's saying. It sounds like Spanish.

Maybe he has ghosts too. Good. Something in common then.

All at once, he seizes on the sculpture and the suddenness of the action makes my breath catch. He's a downed power line, the way he moves. Except now the power's been cut and he's pressing his forehead into the belly of the sculpture. No offense (again), but what a freak. He has his large open hands on each side of the work, and he's just staying like that, unmoving, as if he's praying or listening for a pulse or totally off his rocker. Then I see his hands begin to move slowly up and down and across the surface of the piece, dragging clay off, bit by bit, throwing fistfuls onto the floor, but as he does this, he never once lifts his head to look at what he's doing. He's sculpting *blind*. Oh wow.

I wish Noah could see this. And Mom.

Eventually, he steps back in a stumbling kind of way as if pulling himself out of a trance, takes a cigarette pack out of a pocket in his smock, lights up, and, leaning against a nearby table, he smokes and stares at the sculpture, tilting his head from left to right. I'm recalling his bonkers biography. How he came from a long line of gravestone cutters in Colombia and began carving at the age of five. How no one had ever seen angels as magnificent as his, and people who lived near the cemeteries where his statues watched over the dead swore they heard them singing at night, swore that their heavenly voices carried into their homes, their sleep, their dreams. How it was rumored that the boy carver was enchanted or possibly possessed.

I'm going with the latter.

He's the kind of man who walks into a room and all the walls fall down. Agreed, Mom, which puts me back at square one. How am I going to ask *him* to mentor *me*? This him is far more frightening than Igor.

He flicks his cigarette on the floor, takes a long sip of water from a glass on the table, then spits it from his mouth onto the clay — ah, gross! — then he works the moistened section furiously with his fingers, his eyes now glued to what he's doing. He's lost in it, drinking and spitting and molding, drinking and spitting and molding, sculpting like he's trying to pull something he needs out of the clay, needs badly. As time passes and passes, I begin to see a man and a woman take shape — two bodies tangled up like branches.

This is wishing with your hands.

I don't know how much time goes by as I and a handful of enormous stone couples watch him work, watch him rake his hands, dripping with wet clay, through his hair, over and over again, until it's not clear if he's making the sculpture or if the sculpture is making him.

* * *

It's dawn and I'm sneaking back up Guillermo Garcia's fire escape.

Once on the landing, I again crawl along under the sill until I'm at the same vantage point as last night, then rise just enough to see into the studio… He's still there. I somehow knew he would be. He's sitting on the platform, his back to me, head hung down, his whole body limp. He hasn't changed his clothes. Has he slept at all? The clay sculpture beside him appears to be finished now — he must've worked all night — but it's nothing like it was when I left. No longer are the lovers entwined in each other's arms. The male figure's on his back now and it looks like the female figure's wrenching herself out of him, climbing right out of his chest.

It's awful.

I notice then that Guillermo Garcia's shoulders are rising and falling. Because he's crying? As if by osmosis, a dark swell of emotion rises in me. I swallow hard, accordion my shoulders tight. Not that I ever cry.

Tears of mourning should be collected
and then ingested to heal the soul
*(I've never cried about Mom. I had to fake
it at the funeral. I kept sneaking into the bathroom
to pinch my cheeks and rub my eyes so I'd look right.
I knew if I cried, even one tear: Judemageddon. Not Noah.
For months, it was like living with a monsoon.)*

I can hear the sculptor through the window – a deep dark moaning that's sucking the air out of the air. I have to get out of here. Tucking down to leave, I remember the lucky sand-dollar birds still in my pocket from last night. He needs them. I'm lining them up on the windowsill, when out of the corner of my eye, I catch a quick flash of motion. His arm's whipped back and is starting to reel forward—

"No!" I shout, not thinking and slamming my own hand into the window to stop his from making contact and sending the anguished lovers tumbling to their death.

Before I fly down the fire escape, I see him staring up at me, the expression on his face turning from shock to rage.

* * *

I'm halfway over the fence when I hear the door horror-movie-squeak open like it did the other day and see in my periphery his immense frame emerge from it. I have two choices. I retreat back into the alley and get ambushed or I jump onto the sidewalk and make a run for it. Not much of a choice really, I think, as I land feet first – *whew* – but then stumble forward into what would've been an extremely unlucky face-flop had a very large hand not reached out and iron-gripped my arm, restoring my balance.

"Thank you," I hear myself say. *Thank you?* "That would've been a bad fall," I explain to his feet, quickly adding, "You can't imagine how many brain injuries happen from falling and if it's frontal lobe, well, forget it, you can just kiss your personality good-bye, which really makes you wonder what a person is if they can just become someone else if they bonk their heads, you know?" Whew – on a roll, off to the races, put on this earth solely to soliloquize to his ginormous clay-covered shoes. "If it were up to me," I go on, kicked into some heretofore unknown gear, "which of course nothing is, and if it didn't present such a total fashion conundrum, I'd have us all in titanium helmets from womb to grave. I mean, *anything* can fall on your head at *any* time. Have you ever thought about that? An air conditioner for instance, one could just drop out of a second-story window and crush you while you're minding your own business shopping for bagels on Main Street." I take a breath. "Or a brick. Of course there's the flying brick to worry about."

"The flying brick?" The timbre of his voice has a lot in common with thunder.

"Yes, the flying brick."

"A flying brick?"

What, is he dense? "Sure. Or a coconut, I suppose, if you live in the tropics."

"You are off the rocker."

"*Your* rocker," I say quietly. I still haven't raised my head, think that's best.

A lot of Spanish is coming out of his mouth now. I recognize the word *loca* quite a few times. On the exasperation scale, I'd say he's at a ten. His smell's very strong, *no offense, but* we're talking total sweaty ape. Not a whiff of alcohol on him, though. Igor's not here, this maniac's all Rock Star.

I remain committed to my eyes-on-the-shoes strategy, so I'm not sure but believe he's released his grip on my arm so he can accompany the ranting in Spanish with flailing hand gestures. That or birds are swooping around above my head. When the movement stills and the irate Spanish peters out, I gather my nerve and raise my head to take a gander at what I'm up against here. Not good. He's a skyscraper, impossibly imposing with his arms crossed now against his chest in a battle stance, studying me like I'm a new life form. Which really is pot meet kettle, because, wow, up close he looks like he just emerged from a pit of quicksand – a total swamp thing. He's completely covered in clay except for the streaks on his cheeks from crying and the hellfire green eyes that are drilling into me.

"Well?" he says with impatience, like he's already asked me a question I didn't answer.

I swallow. "I'm sorry," I say. "I didn't mean to..." Um, what comes next? I didn't mean to jump a fence, climb a fire escape, and watch you have a nervous breakdown.

I try again. "I came last night—"

"You've been up there watching me all night?" he roars.

"I tell you go away the other day and you come back and watch me all night?"

Not only puppies, this man eats adorable bouncing babies.

"No. Not *all* night…" I say, and then before I know it, I'm at it again. "I wanted to ask you to mentor me, you know, I'd work as an intern, do whatever, clean up, anything, because I have to make this sculpture." I meet his eyes. "Just *have* to make it and it has to be in stone for many reasons, ones you wouldn't even believe, and my teacher Sandy said you're the only one who carves anymore, like practically in the world" – did he just smile ever so faintly? – "but when I came you seemed so … I don't know what, and of course, you told me to go away, which I did, but then I came back last night thinking I'd try to ask again, but chickened out, because, okay, you're a little scary, I mean frankly, whoa – you are like *totally* scary…" His eyebrows rise at that, cracking the clay on his forehead. "But last night, the way you sculpted that piece blind, it was…" I try to think of what it was, but can't come up with anything to do it justice. "I just couldn't believe it, *could not believe it,* and then I've been thinking that you might be, I don't know, maybe a little magical or something because in my sculpture textbook it talked all about those angels you used to carve as a kid, and it said you were believed to be enchanted, or possessed even, no offense, and this sculpture, the one I have to make, well, I need help, *that* kind of help, because I have this idea that I can make things right, like if I make it, maybe someone will understand something finally and that is very important to me, very, very important, because she never understood me, not really, and she's very mad about something I did…" I take a breath, add, "And I'm sad too." I sigh. "I'm not okay either. Not at all. I wanted to tell you that the last time I came. Sandy even made me go to the school counselor, but she just told me to imagine a meadow…" I realize I'm done, so I close my mouth and stand there waiting for the paramedics, or whoever comes with the straightjacket.

It's more than I've talked in the last two years combined.

He brings his hand to his mouth and begins examining me less like I'm a space alien and more like he did that sculpture last night. When he finally speaks, to my great surprise and relief, he doesn't say, "I'm calling the authorities," but, "We will have a cup of coffee. Yes? I could use a break."

* * *

I follow Guillermo Garcia down a dark dusty hallway with many closed doors leading to rooms where all the other sixteen-year-old art students are kept chained up. It occurs to me that no one knows I'm here. Suddenly the whole gravestone-cutter thing doesn't seem like such a plus.

For courage, say your name three times
into your closed hand
(How about a can of pepper spray instead, Grandma?)

I say my name three times into my closed hand. Six times. Nine times and counting…

He turns around, smiles, points with his finger into the air. "No one makes coffee as good as Guillermo Garcia."

I smile back. So that didn't seem particularly homicidal, but maybe he's trying to relax me, ease me into his lair, like the witch in Hansel and Gretel.

Health Alert: A respirator is in order. Whole civilizations of motes are caught in the thick stripes of light beaming down from two high windows. I look at the floor, jeez, it's *so* dusty I'm making footprints. I wish I could hover like Grandma S. so as not to stir it all up. And this dankness – there's got to be toxic black mold spores creeping all over these cement walls.

We enter a bigger area.

"The mailroom," Guillermo says.

He's not kidding. There are tables, chairs, couches, landsliding with months, maybe years of mail, all unopened, falling to the floor in piles. There's a kitchen area to my right teeming with botulism, another closed door, surely where some bound and gagged hostages are, a staircase leading to a loft area – I can see an unmade bed – and on my left, oh Clark Gable yes, to my great happiness, there is: a life-size stone angel that looks like it lived outside long before it moved in here.

It's one of *them*. It has to be. Jackpot! In his biography, it said that to this day, in Colombia, people come from far and wide to whisper their wishes into the cold stone ears of a Guillermo Garcia angel. This one is spectacular, as tall as me, with hair that falls down her back in long loose locks that appear to be made of silk, not stone. Her wide oval face is cast downward like she's gazing lovingly over a child, and her wings rise from her back like freedom. She looks like *David* did in Sandy's office, one breath away from life. I want to hug her or start squealing but instead ask calmly, "Does she sing to you at night?"

"I am afraid, the angels, they do not sing to me," he says.

"Yeah, me neither," I say, which for some reason makes him turn around and smile at me.

When his back is to me again, I make a hard left and tiptoe across the room. I can't help it. I have to get my wish in that angel's ear immediately.

He waves an arm in the air. "Yes, yes, everyone does that. If only it work."

I ignore his skepticism and wish my heart out into the perfect shell-like ear of the angel – *Best to bet on all the horses, dear* – noticing, when I've finished, that the wall behind the angel is covered in sketches, mostly of bodies, lovers, blank-faced men and women embracing or rather exploding in each other's arms. Studies, I suppose, for the giants in the other room? I survey the mailroom again, see that most of the walls are similarly covered. The only break in the cave art is where a large painting hangs without a frame. It's of a woman and a man kissing on a cliff by the sea while the whole world around them spins into a tornado of color – the palette is bold and bright like Kandinsky's or my Mom's favorite Franz Marc's.

I didn't know he painted too.

I walk over to the canvas, or maybe it's the other way around. Some paintings stay on a wall; not this one. It's color-flooding out of two dimensions, so I'm smack in the middle of it, smack in the middle of a kiss that could make a girl, one not on a boycott, wonder where a certain English guy might be...

"It saves paper," Guillermo Garcia says. I didn't realize I'd started tracing my hand over one of the wall-sketches by the painting. He's leaning against a large industrial sink watching me. "I like the trees very much."

"Trees are cool," I say absently, a bit overwhelmed by all the naked bodies, all the love, the lust everywhere around me. "But they're my brother's, not mine," I add without thinking. I glance at his hand for a wedding ring. None. And no feeling that a woman's been here for ages. But what about the giant couples? And the woman wrenching out of the male form in the sculpture he made last night? And this painting of a kiss? And all these lusty cave drawings? And Drunken Igor? And the sobbing I witnessed? Sandy said something happened to him – what was it? What is it? There's definitely the feeling here that something's gone terribly wrong.

The clay on Guillermo's forehead has crinkled up with his confusion. I realize what I just said about the trees. "Oh, my brother and I divvied up the world when we were younger," I tell him. "I had to give him the trees and the sun and some other stuff for an incredible cubist portrait he made that I wanted."

The remains of the portrait are still in a plastic bag under my bed. When I got home from Brian's going away party that night, I saw that Noah had ripped it up and scattered it all over my bedroom. I thought: That's right, I don't deserve a love story. Not anymore. Love stories aren't written for girls who could do what I just did to my brother, for girls with black hearts.

Still, I gathered up every last piece of the guy. I've tried to put him back together so many times, but it's impossible. I can't even remember what he looked like now, but I'll never forget the reaction I had when I first saw him in Noah's drawing pad. I *had* to have him. I would've given up the real sun, so giving him an imaginary one was nothing.

"I see," Guillermo Garcia says. "So how long did these negotiations last? To divide the world?"

"They were ongoing."

He crosses his arms, again in that battle stance. It seems to be his preferred pose. "You are very powerful, you and your brother. Like gods," he says. "But honestly, I do not think you make a good trade." He shakes his head. "You say you are so sad, maybe this is why. No sun. No trees."

"I lost the stars and the oceans too," I tell him.

"This is terrible," he says, his eyes widening inside the clay mask of his face. "You are a terrible negotiator. You need a lawyer next time." There's amusement in his voice.

I smile at him. "I got to keep the flowers."

"Thank God," he says.

Something strange is going on, something so strange I can't quite believe it. I feel at ease. Of all places, here, with him.

Alas, that's what I'm thinking when I notice the cat, the *black* cat. Guillermo leans down, takes the black bundle of bad luck into his arms. He nuzzles his head into its neck, cooing to it in Spanish. Most serial killers are animal lovers, I read that once.

"This is Frida Kahlo." He turns around. "You know Kahlo?"

"Of course." Mom's book on her and Diego Rivera is called *Count the Ways*. I've read it cover to cover.

"Wonderful artist ... so tormented." He holds up the cat so she's facing him. "Like you," he says to the cat, then lowers her to the floor. She slinks right back to him, rubbing herself against his legs, oblivious to the years of rotten luck she's filling our lives with.

"Did you know that toxoplasmosis and campylobacteriosis are transmitted to humans from the fecal matter of cats?" I ask Guillermo.

He knits his brow, making the clay on his forehead break into fissures. "No, I did not know. And I do not want to know that."

He's spinning a pot in the air with his hands. "I've erased it from my mind already. Gone. Poof. You should too. Flying bricks and now this. I never even hear of those things."

"You could go blind or worse. It happens. People have no idea how dangerous having pets is."

"This is what you think? That it is dangerous to have a little kitty cat?"

"Most definitely. Especially a *black* one, but that's a whole other bunch of bananas."

"Okay," he says. "That is what you think. You know what I think? I think you are crazy." He throws his head back and laughs. It warms up the entire world. "Totally *loca*." He turns around and starts talking in Spanish, saying Clark Gable knows what as he takes off his smock, hangs it on a hook. Underneath he's wearing jeans and a black T-shirt like a normal guy. He pulls a notepad out of the front pocket of the smock and slips it into the back pocket of his jeans. I wonder if it's an idea pad. At CSA, we're encouraged to keep an idea pad on our person at all times. Mine's empty. He turns both faucets on full blast, puts one arm underneath, then the other, scrubbing both with industrial soap. Brown water runs off him in muddy streams. Next he puts his whole head under the faucet. This is going to take a while.

I bend down to make friends with bad-luck Frida, who's still circling Guillermo's feet. Keep your enemies close, as they say. What's so odd is that even with Frida and the toxoplasmosis and this man who should terrify me for so many reasons, I feel more at home than I have anywhere for so long. I scratch my fingers on the floor, trying to get the cat's attention. "Frida," I say softly.

The title of Mom's book *Count the Ways* on Kahlo and Rivera is a line taken from her favorite poem by Elizabeth Barrett Browning. "Do you know it by heart?" I'd asked her one day when we were walking in the woods together, just us, a rarity.

"Of course I do." She did a joyful little skip and pulled me close to her so that every inch of me felt happy and leaping. "'How do I love thee?'" she said, her big dark eyes shining on me, our hair whipping around our heads, blending and twisting together in the wind. I knew it was a romantic poem, but that day, it felt about us, our private mother–daughter thing. "'Let me count the ways,'" she sang out ... wait, she *is* singing out! "'I love thee to the depth and breadth and height my soul can reach—'"

It's her, here, now – her deep gravelly voice is reciting the poem to me!

"'I love thee with the breath, smiles, tears, of all my life; and, if God choose, I shall but love thee better after death.'"

"Mom?" I whisper. "I hear you."

Every single night before I go to bed, I read this poem aloud to her, wishing for this.

"Okay down there?" I peer up into the unmasked face of Guillermo Garcia, who now looks like he just got out of the ocean, his black hair slicked back and dripping, a towel thrown over his shoulder.

"I'm fine," I say to him, but I'm far from it. My mother's ghost spoke to me. She recited the poem back to me. She told me she loves me. Still.

I get to my feet. What must I have looked like? Squatting there on the floor, no cat in sight, totally lost, whispering to my dead mother.

Guillermo's face now resembles the photos I saw online. Any one of his features would be dramatic, but all of them together, it's a turf war, a rumble for territory, nose against mouth against flashing eyes. I can't tell if he's grotesque or gorgeous.

He's examining me too.

"Your bones" – he touches his own cheek – "are very delicate. You have the bird bones." His eyes drop, sweeping past my breasts, landing with confusion somewhere in the middle of me. I look down, expecting the onion to be in plain view or something else I forgot I was carrying for luck today, but it's not that. My T-shirt has risen up under my unzipped sweatshirt and he's staring at my exposed midriff, my tattoo. He takes a step toward me, and without asking, lifts my shirt so he can see the whole image. Oh boy. Ohboyohboy. His hand's holding up the fabric. I can feel the heat of his fingertips on my belly. My heart speeds up. This is inappropriate, right? I mean, he's old. A dad's age. Except he sure doesn't seem like a dad.

Then I see in his face that my stomach's about as interesting to him as stretched canvas. He's mesmerized by my tattoo, not me. Not sure if I'm relieved or insulted.

He meets my eyes, nods approval. "Raphael on the belly," he says. "Very nice." I can't help but smile. He does too. A week before Mom died, I spent every penny I'd ever saved on it. Zephyr knew this guy who'd tattoo underage kids. I chose Raphael's cherubs because they reminded me of NoahandJude – more one than two. Plus they can fly. Mostly now I think I did it to piss off Mom, but I never even got to show it to her… How can people die when you're in a fight with them? When you're smack in the middle of hating them? When absolutely nothing between you has been worked out?

To reconcile with a family member, hold a bowl
out in the rain until full, then drink the
rainwater the first moment the sun shines again
*(Months before she died, Mom and I went on a
mother-daughter day to the city to see if it could improve
our relationship. Over lunch, she told me she felt like she was
always, in her mind, looking for the mother who abandoned her.
I wanted to tell her: Yeah, me too.)*

Guillermo motions for me to follow him, then stops at the entrance to the grand studio space, which unlike the rest of the place is sunny and fairly tidy. He holds his hand up to the room of giants. "My rocks, though I suppose you've already met."

I suppose I have met them, but not like this, towering above us like titans.

"I feel so puny," I say.

"Me too," he says. "Like an ant."

"But you're their creator."

"Perhaps," he says. "I don't know. Who knows…" He's muttering something I can't hear and conducting a symphony with his hands as he walks away from me toward a counter that has a hot plate with a kettle on it.

"Hey maybe you have Alice in Wonderland Syndrome!" I call after him, the idea taking hold of me. He turns. "That's this totally cool neurological condition where the scale of things gets distorted in the mind. Usually people who have it see everything teeny-tiny – miniature people driving around in Matchbox cars, that sort of thing – but it can happen like this too." I hold my hands out to the room as proof of my diagnosis.

He does not seem to think he has Alice in Wonderland Syndrome. I can tell because the *loca* tirade in Spanish has begun again as he bangs around the cabinets. While he makes coffee and rants, good-naturedly, I believe, this time – it's possible I'm amusing him – I circle the pair of lovers closest to me, brushing my fingers over their gritty granular flesh, then step between them and reach my hands up, wanting to climb up their giant lovelorn bodies.

Maybe he's suffering from a different kind of syndrome after all. Lovesickness, it would seem, if the repeating motif around this place is any indication.

I keep my new diagnosis to myself as I join him at the counter. He's pouring water from the kettle through two filters poised over mugs and has begun singing to himself in Spanish. It occurs to me what the unfamiliar feeling is that's overtaking me: well-being. At ease has graduated to a full-on sense of well-being. And maybe he's experiencing it too, what with the singing and all.

Perhaps I could move in? I'd bring my sewing machine and that's it. I'd just have to dodge the English guy … who maybe is Guillermo's son … a love child he didn't know about until recently, who grew up in England. Yes!

And … I'm looking around for a lemon.

"As promised, nectar of the gods," he says, placing the two steaming mugs on a table. I sit down on the red sofa beside it. "Now, we talk, yes?" He joins me on the couch, as does his ape-man smell. But I don't even care. I don't even care that the sun's going to burn out in a matter of years, ending all life on Earth, well, five billion years, but still, guess what? I don't care. Well-being is a wonderful thing.

He picks up a box of sugar on the table and proceeds to pour a ton into his mug, spilling as much.

"That's lucky," I say.

"What is?"

"Spilling sugar. Spilling salt is bad luck, but sugar…"

"I've heard that one before." He smiles, then whacks the box with the back of his hand so that it falls over and its contents spill onto the floor. "There."

I feel a surge of delight. "I don't know if it counts if you do it on purpose."

"Of course it counts," he says, tapping a cigarette out of a crumpled pack left on the table, next to another one of those notepads. He leans back, lights up, inhales deeply. The smoke curls in the air between us. He's examining me again. "I want you to know I hear what you say outside. About this." He places his hand on his chest. "You were honest with me, so I be honest with you." He's looking into my eyes. It's dizzying. "When you came the other day, I was not in good shape. I am not in good shape sometimes … I know I told you go away. I don't know what else I say to you. I don't remember much … that whole week." He waves the cigarette in the air. "But I tell you, I am not teaching anymore for a reason. I don't have it, the thing you need. I just don't have." He takes a drag, exhales a long gray stream of smoke, then gestures at the giants. "I am like them. Every day I think to myself, it happen, finally I become the rock I carve."

"Me too," I blurt out. "I'm made of stone too. I thought that exact thing the other day. I think my whole family is. There's this disease called FOP—"

"No, no, no, you are not made of the stone," he interrupts. "You do not have this disease called FOP. Or any disease called anything." He touches my cheek tenderly with his calloused fingers, leaves them there. "Trust me," he says. "If anyone knows this, it is me."

His eyes have become gentle. I'm swimming in them.

It's suddenly so quiet inside me.

I nod and he smiles and takes his hand away. I place mine where his was, not understanding what's going on. Why all I want is his hand back on my face. All I want is for him to touch my cheek like that and tell me I'm fine again and again until I am.

He stamps out the cigarette. "I, however, am a different story. I have not taught in years. I will not. Probably not ever again. So…"

Oh. I wrap my arms around myself. I've been terribly mistaken. I thought when he invited me in for coffee he was saying yes. I thought he was going to help me. My lungs feel like they're closing up.

"I only want to work now." A shadow has darkened his face. "It is all I have. It is all I can do to…" He doesn't finish, just stares off at the giants. "They are the only ones I want to think about or care about, understand? That's it." His voice has grown solemn, leaden.

I stare down at my hands, disappointment pooling inside me, black and thick and hopeless.

"So," he continues. "I think about this, assume you are at CSA because you mention Sandy, yes?" I nod. "There is someone there, no? Ivan something, he is in that department, he can surely help you with this piece?"

"He's in Italy," I say, my voice cracking. Oh no. How can this be? Now? Oh not now, please. But it is now. For the first time in two years, tears are streaming down my cheeks. I wipe them away quickly, again and again. "I understand," I say, getting up. "Really. It's fine. It was a dumb idea. Thank you for the coffee." I have to get out of here. I have to stop crying. There's a sob building inside me so immense and powerful it's going to break all my bird bones. It's Judemageddon. I keep my arms tightly fastened around my ribs as I make my trembling legs move across the bright sunny studio, through the mailroom, and down the dark musty hallway, completely blinded from the contrast, when his baritone voice stops me.

"This sculpture needs to be made so much you cry like this?"

I turn around. He's leaning against the wall by the painting of the kiss, his arms crossed.

"Yes," I gasp out, then say more calmly, "Yes." Is he changing his mind? The sob begins to retreat.

He's stroking his chin. His expression softens. "You need to make this sculpture so badly, you will risk your young life by sharing space with a disease-carrying cat?"

"Yes. Totally, yes. Please."

"You are sure you want to forsake the warm, moist breath of clay for the cold, unforgiving eternity of stone."

"I am sure." Whatever that means.

"Come back tomorrow afternoon. Bring your portfolio and a sketchpad. And tell your brother to give you back the sun, trees, stars, all of it already. I think you need."

"You're saying yes?"

"I am. I do not know why but I am."

I'm about to leap across the room and hug him.

"Oh no." He wags a finger at me. "Do not look so happy. I tell you ahead of time. All my students despise me."

* * *

I click Guillermo's front door shut, lean against it, not sure what happened to me in there. I feel disoriented like I've been watching a movie or like I've just woken up from a dream. I thank and rethank the beautiful stone angel inside who granted my wish. There is the problem of my portfolio being full of broken bowls and blobs. There is also the problem that he said to bring a sketchpad and I can't sketch. I got a C in life drawing last year. Drawing is Noah's thing.

Doesn't matter. He said yes.

I look around, taking in Day Street, wide and tree-lined, with a combination of dilapidated Victorians where college students live, warehouses, the occasional business, and *the* church.

I'm letting the first sun we've seen this winter soak into my bones, when I hear the screech of a motorcycle. I watch the adrenaline-happy driver, who thinks he's at the Indy 500, boomerang a turn at such an extreme angle the side of the bike scrapes the street. Jeez, *no offense, but* what a stupid reckless idiot.

Evel Knievel screeches once again, but to a halt this time, not fifteen feet from me, and takes off his helmet.

Oh.

Of course.

And in sunglasses. Someone call medevac.

"Well, hello there," he says. "The fallen angel has returned."

He doesn't talk, he lilts, his words taking to the air like birds. And why do English people sound smarter than the rest of us? Like they should be awarded the Nobel Prize for a simple greeting?

I zip up my sweatshirt to my neck.

But can't seem to get the boy blinders on.

Still a reckless idiot, yes, but damn, he looks fine, sitting on that bike on this sunny winter day. Guys like him really shouldn't be allowed on motorcycles. They should have to bounce around on pogo sticks, or better: Hippity Hops. And no hot guy should be allowed to have an English accent *and* drive a motorcycle.

Not to mention wear the leather jacket or sport the cool shades. Hot guys should be forced into footie pajamas.

Yes, yes, the boycott, the boycott.

Still, I'd like to say something this time so he doesn't think I'm a mute.

"Well, hello there," I offer, mimicking him exactly, *English accent and all!* Oh no. I feel my face flushing. Losing the accent,

I quickly add, "Nice turn back there."

"Ah yes," he says, dismounting. "I have a problem with impulse control. Or so I'm quite frequently told."

Great. Six feet of bad luck and impulse-control issues. I cross my arms like Guillermo. "You probably have an underdeveloped frontal lobe. That's where self-control comes from."

This cracks him up. It makes his face go everywhere at once. "Well, thank you for the medical opinion. Much appreciated."

I like that I made him laugh. A nice laugh, easy and friendly, lovely really, not that I notice. Frankly, I also believe *I* have impulse-control issues, well, used to. Now I'm very much in control of things. "So what kind of impulses can't you control?"

"Not one, I'm afraid," he says. "That's the problem."

That *is* the problem. He's tailor-made to torture. I'm betting he's at least eighteen, betting he stands alone at parties leaning against walls, knocking back shots while long-legged girls in fire-engine red mini-dresses slink up to him. Granted, I haven't been to a lot of parties lately, but I have seen a lot of movies and he's that guy: the lawless, solitary, hurricane-hearted one who wreaks havoc, blowing through towns, through girls, through his own tragic misunderstood life. A real bad boy, not like the fake ones at my art school, with their ink and piercings and trust funds and cigarettes from France.

I bet he just got out of jail.

I decide to pursue his "condition" as it falls under medical research, not because I'm fascinated by him or flirting with him or anything like that. I say, "Meaning if you were in the room with The Button, you know, *the end of the world nuclear bomb button,* just you and it, man and button, you'd press it? Just like that."

He laughs that wonderful easy laugh again. "Kapow," he says, illustrating the explosion with his hands.

Kapow is right.

I watch as he locks his helmet on the back of his bike, then detaches a camera bag from the handlebars. The camera. I have an instant Pavlovian response to it, remembering how I'd felt sitting in church with him looking at me through it. I drop my gaze to the ground, wishing my pale skin didn't blush so easily.

"So what's your business with The Rock Star?" he asks. "Let me guess. You want him to mentor you like every other female art student from The Institute."

Okay, that was snide. And does he think I go to The Institute in the city? That I'm in college?

"He's *agreed* to mentor me," I reply triumphantly, not appreciating the innuendo. No other art student, female or not, needs his help like I do, to make things right with their dead mother. This is a very unique situation.

"Is that right?" He's out of his head pleased. "Well done." I'm back in the spotlight of his gaze and having the same sense of vertigo I did in church. "I just can't believe it. Well done, you. It's been a very, very long time since he's taken on a student." This makes me nervous. As does he. Kapow, kaboom, kaput. Time to go. Which involves moving the legs. Move the legs, Jude.

"Got lucky," I say, trying not to trip over my own feet as I pass him, my hands deep in my sweatshirt pockets, one wrapped around the onion, the other around a bag of herbs that promise protection. I say, "You should really trade in that thing for a

Hippity Hop. Much safer." For the female gender, I don't add.

"What's a Hippity Hop?" he says to my retreating back. I don't notice how incredibly cute the words *Hippity Hop* sound coming out of his mouth with that accent.

Without turning around, I reply, "A large, round rubber animal you bounce around on. You hold on to the ears."

"Oh, of course, a Space Hopper, then." He laughs. "We call them Space Hoppers in England. I had a green one," he yells after me. "A dinosaur I named Godzilla. I was a very original thinker." Mine was a purple horse I named Pony. I was also an original thinker. "Well, nice seeing you again, whoever you are. The photos of you are brilliant. I stopped by the church a few times looking for you. Thought you might want to see them."

He was looking for me?

I don't turn around; my cheeks are burning up. *A few times?* Be cool. Keep cool. I take a breath and with my back still to him, I raise my hand and wave bye exactly like he did that day in church. He laughs again. Oh Clark Gable. Then I hear, "Hey, wait a minute."

I consider ignoring this, but can't resist the impulse (you see?) and turn around.

"Just realized I have an extra," he says, pulling an orange out of the pocket of his leather jacket. He tosses it to me.

He's got to be kidding. Is this really happening? *The orange!* As in, the anti-lemon:

> If a boy gives a girl an orange,
> her love for him will multiply

I catch it in my open palm.

"Oh no you don't," I say, tossing it right back to him.

"Odd response," he says, catching it. "Definitely an odd response. Think I'll try again. Would you like an orange? I have an extra."

"I'd like to give *you* the orange, actually."

One of his eyebrows arches. "Well, yes, that's fine and good, but it's not yours to bloody give." He holds it up, smiling. "This is *my* orange."

Is it possible I've found the only two people in Lost Cove I amuse rather than disturb?

"How about this," I say. "You give it to me and I'll give it back to you. Sound acceptable?"

And yes, I'm flirting, but this is necessary. And wow, it's like riding a bicycle.

"All right then." He walks up to me, close, so close I could reach up and trace his scars with my finger if I wanted to. They're like two hastily sewn seams. And I see that his brown eye has a splash of green in it and the green one a splash of brown. Like Cezanne painted them. Impressionist eyes. And his lashes are black as soot, exquisite. He's so close I could run my fingers through his shiny, tangly brown hair, run them across the faint spidery wrinkles that fan out at his temples, across the dark worrying shadows beneath. Across his red satiny lips. I don't think other guys' lips are this red. And I know their faces aren't this colorful, this vivid, this lived-in, this superbly off-kilter, this brimming with dark, unpredictable music.

NOT THAT I EFFING NOTICE.

Nor do I notice that he's regarding my face with the same intensity I am his. We're two paintings staring at each other across a room. A painting I've seen before, I'm sure of it. But where and when? If I'd met this guy, I'd remember. Maybe he looks like an actor I've seen in a movie? Or some musician? He definitely has that sexy musician hair. Bass player hair.

For the record, breathing is overrated. The brain can go six whole minutes without oxygen. I'm at three airless minutes when he says, "Well, then. The matter at hand." He holds up the orange. "Would you like an orange, whoever you are?"

"Yes, thank you," I reply, taking it, then say, "And now I'd like to give you an orange, whoever you are."

"No thank you," he says, slipping his hands in his pockets. "I have another." All holy hell breaks loose on his face as it erupts into a smile and then in a flash he's up the path, the steps, and in the studio.

Not so fast, buddy.

I walk over to his motorcycle, slip the orange into the helmet.

Then I use all my self-control not to burst into song – he went to the church looking for me! A few times! Probably to tell me what he meant that day when he said, "You're her." I head home, kicking myself because I got so flustered I didn't even think to ask what *his* relationship to The Rock Star is. Or his name. Or how old he is. Or who his favorite photographer is. Or—

Snap.

Out.

Of.

It.

I stop walking. Remembering. The boycott is no lark. It's a necessity. I can't forget that. I can't. Especially not today on the anniversary of the accident.

Not any day.

> If bad luck knows who you are,
> become someone else

What I need to do is make this sculpture and try to make things right with my mother.

What I need to do is wish with my hands.

What I must do is eat every last lemon in Lost Cove by morning.

* * *

It's the next afternoon and I'm hurrying down the grimy fungal hallway in Guillermo Garcia's studio because no one came to the door when I knocked. I'm sweating and nervous and reconsidering the last sixteen years. Under my arm is my CSA portfolio of broken blobs and bowls. The only reason I even have a portfolio is because we're required to take a progression of pictures of every piece we make. My progressions are insane, certainly not an advertisement of ability – more like an accounting of a ceramic shop after an earthquake.

Right before I enter the mailroom, I hear the English-accented voice and a whole percussion section bursts to life in my chest. I back against the wall, try to silence the pounding. I was hoping he wouldn't be here. And hoping he would be. And hoping I'd stop hoping he would be. However, I've come prepared.

If bad
LUCK knows
who you are
Become
SOMEONE
Else.

Carrying a burnt candle stub will extinguish
feelings of love should they arise
(Front left pocket.)

Soak a mirror in vinegar to deflect
unwanted attention
(Back pocket.)

To change the leanings of the heart,
wear a wasp nest on the head
(Not this desperate. Yet.)

Alas, perhaps I'm not prepared for this: sex noises. Unmistakable
sex noises. Moaning and groaning and obscene murmurings.
Is this why nobody answered the door? In an English accent,
I hear: "Holy Christ, so good. God, *soooooo* damn good. Better
than any drug, I mean any. Better than *any*thing." Followed by
a long drawl of a moan.

Then a deeper groan, which must be Guillermo's. Because
they're lovers! Of course. How stupid could I be? The English
guy is Guillermo's boyfriend, not his long-lost son. But he sure
seemed straight when he was taking pictures of me in church
and when he was talking to me outside the studio yesterday too.
So attentive. Did I misread him? Or maybe he's bi? And what
about all Guillermo's hyper-heterosexual artwork?

And not to judge, but cradle-rob much? There's probably a
quarter century between them.

Should I leave? They seem to have settled down and are
now just bantering back and forth. I listen closely. The English
guy is trying to convince Guillermo to go to some type of sauna

with him later this afternoon. Definitely gay. Good. This is great news, actually. The boycott will be a snap to maintain, oranges or no oranges.

I make a bunch of noise, stamping on the floor, clearing my throat several times, a few more stomps, then step around the corner.

In front of me is a fully clothed Guillermo and a fully clothed English guy on opposite sides of a chessboard. There's no indication they were just in the throes of passion. Each has a half-eaten donut in his hand.

"Very clever, aren't we?" the English guy says to me at once. "Never would've suspected you of such subterfuge, whoever you are." With his free hand, he reaches into the messenger bag resting beside him and pulls out *the orange*. In a flash it's airborne, then in my hand, and his face has broken into five million pieces of happiness. "Nice catch," he says.

Victorious, he takes a bite of donut, then moans theatrically.

Okay. Not gay. Not lovers, they both just appear to like donuts more than your average bear. And what am I going to do now? Because my invisibility uniform doesn't seem to work with this guy. And ditto the vinegar-soaked mirror and extinguished candle stub.

I stuff the orange in with the onion and pull my cap down.

Guillermo gives me a curious look. "So you've already met the resident guru? Oscar is trying to enlighten me as usual." Oscar. He has a name and it's Oscar, not that I care, though I do like the way Guillermo says it: *Oscore!* Guillermo continues. "Every day, something else. Today it is Bikram yoga." Ah, the sauna. "You know this yoga?" he asks me.

"I know that's a real lot of bacteria in one hot sweaty room," I tell Guillermo.

He drops his head back and laughs heartily. "She is so crazy with the germs, *Oscore*! She think Frida Kahlo is going to kill me." This relaxes me. *He* relaxes me. Who would've thought Guillermo Garcia, The Rock Star of the Sculpture World, would have this soothing effect on me? Maybe *he's* the meadow!

A surprised look has crossed Oscar's face as he studies Guillermo, then me. "So how did the two of you meet?" he asks.

I rest my portfolio and bag against an easy chair that's smothered in unopened mail. "He caught me on the fire escape spying on him."

Oscar's eyes widen but his attention's back on the chessboard. He moves a piece. "And you're still sentient? Impressive." He pops the remaining piece of donut in his mouth and closes his eyes as he slowly chews. I can see the rapture taking him over. Jesus. That must be some donut. I tear my eyes off him, hard to do.

"She win me over," Guillermo says while studying Oscar's move. "Like you win me over, Oscore. Long time ago." His face darkens. *"Ay, cabrón."* He starts muttering in Spanish as he nudges a piece forward.

"G. saved my life," Oscar says with affection. "And checkmate, mate." He leans back on his chair, balancing on the rear legs, says, "I hear they're giving lessons down at the senior center."

Guillermo groans, for the first time not donut-related, and flips the board so pieces go flying in every direction. "I kill you in your sleep," he says, which makes Oscar laugh, then Guillermo picks up a white bakery bag and holds it out to me.

I decline, way too nervous to eat.

"'The road of excess leads to the palace of wisdom,'" Oscar says to me, still balancing on the back legs of his chair. "William Blake."

Guillermo says to him, "Yes, very good, one of your twelve steps, Oscore?" I look at Oscore. Is he in AA? I didn't know you could be an alcoholic if you weren't old. Or maybe he's in NA? Didn't he just say something about no drug being as good as that donut? Is he a drug addict? He did say he has impulse-control issues.

"Indeed," Oscar says with a smile. "The step known only to the in crowd."

"How did you save his life?" I ask Guillermo, dying to know.

But it's Oscar who answers. "He found me half dead from pills and booze in the park and somehow recognized me. According to him: 'I hoist Oscore over my shoulders like a deer'" – he's slipped into a perfect Guillermo Garcia impersonation that includes hand gestures – "'and I carry him across town like Superman and deposit him in the loft.'" He turns back into himself. "All *I* know is I woke up with G.'s monstrous face in mine" – he laughs his god-awful laugh – "and had no idea how it had gotten there. It was mad. He started barking orders at me right away. Told me I could stay here if I got clean. Ordered me to go to 'two meetings a day, understand, Oscore? The NA in the morning, the AA in the evening.' Then, maybe because I'm English, I don't know, he quoted Winston Churchill: 'If you're going through hell, *keep going*.' Understand, Oscore? Morning, noon, and night he said this to me: 'If you're going through hell, keep going,' so I did. I kept going and going and now I'm at university and not dead in a ditch somewhere and that is how he saved my life. Highly abridged and sanitized. It *was* hell."

And that is why there are several lifetimes in Oscar's face.

And he is in college.

I glance down at my sneakers, thinking about that Churchill quote. What if there was a time when I was going through hell too, but I didn't have the courage to keep going? So I just stopped. Pressed pause. What if I'm still on pause?

Guillermo says, "And to thank me for saving his life, he beat me at chess every single day since."

I look at the two of them mirroring each other across the table and realize: They *are* father and son, just not by blood. I didn't know that family members could just find each other, choose each other like they have. I love the idea. And I'd like to trade in Dad and Noah for these two.

Guillermo shakes the bag at me. "Your first lesson: My studio is not a democracy. Have a donut."

I walk over and peek into the bag. The smell almost makes my knees give out – they weren't exaggerating. "Wow," I hear myself say. They both smile. I choose one. It's not covered in chocolate but drowned in it. And it's still warm.

"Ten dollars says you can't eat that donut without moaning," Oscar says. "Or closing your eyes." He looks at me in a way that causes a minor cerebral hemorrhage. "Actually, let's say twenty. I remember how you got in front of the camera." He knew how I'd felt that day in church?

He holds out his hand to seal the bet.

I shake it — and experience close to a lethal dose of electricity. I'm in trouble.

No time to dwell, though. Guillermo and Oscar are giving the show before them — me — their undivided attention. How did I get into this? Tentatively, I lift the donut to my mouth. I take a small bite and despite the fact that all I want to do is close my eyes and moan a porn soundtrack, I resist.

Oh… It's harder than I thought! The second bite is bigger and brings joy to each cell in my body. This is the kind of thing you should only do in private, not with a Guillermo and an Oscore staring you down, both of them with arms crossed and very superior expressions on their faces.

I'm going to have to up the ante. I mean, I have a bevy of horrific diseases to choose from, don't I? Diseases to imagine in vivid moan-repressing detail. Skin conditions are the worst.

"So there's this disease," I tell them, taking a bite, "called tungiasis where fleas burrow and lay eggs beneath your skin and you can see them hatching and moving around under there, *all over your body*."

I take in their appalled expressions. Ha! Three bites down.

"Remarkable, even with the fleas," Guillermo says to Oscar.

"She doesn't have a prayer," he replies.

I bring out the heavy artillery.

"There was this Indonesian fisherman," I tell them. "He's called The Tree Man because he had such a severe case of human papillomavirus of the skin that thirteen pounds of horn-like warts had to be removed from his body." I make eye contact with one, then the other, repeat, *"Thirteen pounds of warts."*

I relate the way the poor Tree Man's extremities hung from him like gnarled trunks, and with that disturbing image firmly planted in my head, I'm pumped, confident, and take a bigger bite. But it's the wrong move. The rich warm chocolate overtakes my mouth, erases my mind, spinning me into a state of transcendence. Tree Man or not, I'm defenseless and the next thing I know, my eyes are closed and out of my mouth explodes, "Oh my fucking God! What's in this?" I take another bite and then unleash a moan so obscene I can't believe it came out of me.

Oscar laughs. Guillermo, equally pleased, says, "There it is. The government should use Dwyer's donuts to control our minds."

I dredge a crumpled twenty-dollar bill from my jeans pocket, but Oscar holds up a hand. "First loss on the house."

Guillermo pulls up a chair for me – it feels like being admitted into a club – then holds the bag out. We each take another donut, and then the three of us proceed to visit with Clark Gable.

After, Guillermo slaps his thighs with his hands and says, "Okay, CJ, now we get to it. I leave a message for Sandy this morning on his voicemail. I tell him I agree to do a studio credit for your winter term." He stands.

"Thank you. This is so amazing." I stand too, feeling jittery, wishing we could just sit around and eat donuts all afternoon. "But how..." I realized last night I hadn't yet told him my name.

He registers my surprise. "Oh. Sandy leave a message on the machine, a garbled message – I kick that old machine one too many times – said a CJ wanted to work in stone. That is all I understand. Days ago, he call. I did not check until today."

"CJ," Oscar says like it's a revelation.

I'm about to tell them my real name, then decide not to. Maybe for once I don't have to be Dianna Sweetwine's poor motherless daughter.

Frida Kahlo slinks into the room and pads over to Oscar, curling around his leg. He picks her up and she nuzzles her nose into his neck, purring like a turbine. "I have a way with the ladies," he says to me, stroking Frida under her chin with his index finger.

"I wouldn't notice," I say. "I'm on a boycott."

He lifts his green and brown Cezanne eyes. His eyelashes are so black they look wet. "A boycott?" he asks.

"A *boy* boycott."

"Really?" he says with a grin. "I'll take that as a challenge." Help.

"Behave, Oscore," Guillermo berates. "Okay," he says to me. "Now we find out what you are made of. Ready?" My legs go weak. I'm made of fraud. And Guillermo's about to realize.

He puts a hand on Oscar's shoulder.

"I have to meet Sophia in two hours," Oscar says. "That work?" Sophia? Who's Sophia?

Not that I care. In the slightest.

But who is she?

And work for what?

Oscar starts taking off his clothes.

I repeat: Oscar is taking off his clothes!

My mind's racing and my hands are swampy and Oscar's

218

cool violet bowling shirt is now strewn across the back of a chair and his chest is sinewy and beautiful, his muscles long and taut and defined, his skin smooth and tanned, *not that I notice*! There's a tattoo of Sagittarius on his left bicep and what looks like a Franz Marc blue horse on his right shoulder that twists all the way up his neck.

Now he's unfastening the button of his jeans.

"What are you *doing*?" I ask, panicking. Imagining the meadow. Imagining the relaxing effing meadow!

"Getting ready," he says matter-of-factly.

"Getting ready for *what*?" I ask his *bare* butt as he struts in that slow summer way of his across the room and grabs a blue robe from a hook on the wall next to the smocks. He swings it over his shoulder and heads down the hall to the studio.

Oh, duh. Got it.

Guillermo tries to hold back a smile, fails. He shrugs. "All models, they are the exhibitionists," he says lightly. I nod, flushing. "We have to put up with them. Oscore is very good. Very graceful. Much expression." He frames his own face with his hand. "We are going to draw together, but first I see the portfolio."

When Guillermo said to bring my sketchpad, I thought he'd have me work on the studies of the sculpture I want to make, not sketch *with him*. And in front of Oscar. Sketching Oscore!

"Drawing is critical," Guillermo says. "Many sculptors do not know this."

Terrific. I follow him down the hall, portfolio in hand, stomach in turmoil.

I spot Oscar's leather jacket hanging on a hook – yes. I slip the orange into the pocket without Guillermo noticing.

Guillermo opens one of the doors that line the hallway, flicks on the light. It's a jail cell of a room with a table and a couple chairs. In one corner are bags of clay stacked on shelves. In the other, hunks of stone, all different colors and sizes. There's a shelf full of tools, only some familiar to me. He takes the portfolio case from me, unzips it, and opens it on the table.

The thought of his eyes on my work is making my toes curl.

He flips through quickly at first. Photos of bowls in every size in various stages of development, then the final photo of the piece broken and glued together. His forehead creases in confusion more and more with each passing page. Then he comes to the blobs. It's the same. Each blob whole and then all broken and glued together in the final photo.

"Why?" he asks.

I go with the truth.

"It's my mother. She breaks everything I make."

He's horrified. "Your mother breaks your artwork?"

"Oh no," I say, understanding what he's thinking. "She's not mean or crazy or anything. She's dead."

I see the earthquake in his expression, the concern for my safety turn into concern for my sanity. Well, whatever. There's no other explanation.

"Okay," he says, adjusting. "Why would your dead mother want to do this?"

"She's mad at me."

"She's mad at you," he repeats. "This is what you think?"

"This is what I know," I say.

"Everyone in your family is very powerful. Your brother and you divide the world between you. Your mother come back to life to break your bowls."

I shrug.

"This sculpture you have to make, it is for your mother then?" he asks. "She is the one you mention yesterday? You think if you make this sculpture she will not be mad at you anymore and she will stop breaking your bowls? This is why you cry when you think I do not help you?"

"Yes," I say.

He strokes an imaginary beard, studying me for a very long time, then returns his attention to *Broken Me-Blob No. 6*. "Okay. But that is not the problem here. Your mother is not the problem. The best part, the most interesting part of this work is the breaks." He touches the final photo with his index finger. "The problem here is that *you* are not here. Some other girl make it all maybe, I don't know." He looks at several more blobs. "Well?" he says. I glance up at him. I didn't realize he was waiting for a response.

I don't know what to say.

I resist the impulse to step back so I don't get swatted by his hands. "I do not see the girl who climbed up my fire escape, who thinks spilled sugar will change her life, who believe she is in mortal danger because of a cat, who cries because I will not help her. I do not see the girl who told me she was as sad as me, who says her angry dead mother break her bowls. Where is that girl?" *That girl?* His eyes are blazing into mine. Does he expect an answer? "She is not making this work. She is not in this work, so why do you waste your time and everyone else's?"

He sure doesn't mince words.

I take a deep breath. "I don't know."

"That is obvious." He closes the portfolio. "You will put *that girl* in the sculpture you make with me, understand?"

"I understand," I say, except I have no clue how to do that. Have I ever done it? Certainly I haven't at CSA. I think about my sand sculptures. How hard I used to work to get them to look like they did in my head. Never getting it. But maybe then. Maybe that's why I was so afraid Mom wouldn't like them.

He smiles at me. "Good. We will have fun then. I am Colombian. I cannot resist a good ghost story."

He taps his hand on the case. "I am not sure you are ready for stone. Clay is kind – it can do anything, though you do not know this yet. Stone can be stingy, ungenerous, like the unrequited lover."

"It will be more difficult for my mother to break it if it's in stone."

Understanding crosses his face. "She will not break this sculpture no matter what it is made of. You will have to trust me on that. You will learn to carve first on a practice rock. Then together we will figure out the best material for this sculpture after I see the studies. Will it be of your mother?"

"Yes. I don't usually do realistic, but…" Then, before I know I'm going to, I'm telling him. "Sandy asked me if there was something I needed in the world that only my two hands could create." I swallow, meet his eyes. "My mom, she was really beautiful. My dad used to say she could make trees bloom just by looking at them." Guillermo smiles. I go on. "Every morning she used to stand on the deck staring out at the water. The wind would stream through her hair, her robe would billow behind her. It was like she was at the helm of a ship, you know? It was like she was steering us across the sky. Every day it was like that. Every day I thought that. The image is always somewhere in my mind. Always." Guillermo's listening so intently and I'm thinking maybe he's the kind of man who makes all the walls in people fall down too, not just rooms, because like yesterday, I want to tell him more. "I've tried everything to get through to her, Guillermo. Absolutely everything. I have this weird book and I scour it for ideas nonstop. I've done it all. I've slept with her jewelry under my pillow. I've stood on the beach at midnight, holding up a picture of the two of us to a blue moon. I've written letters to her and put them in her coat pockets, in red mailboxes. I've thrown messages into storms. I recite her favorite poem to her every night before I go bed. And all she does is break what I make. That's how angry she is." I've started to sweat. "It would kill me if she broke this." My lips are trembling. Covering my mouth, I add, "It's the one thing I have."

He puts a hand on my shoulder. I can't believe how much I want him to hug me. "She will not break," he says gently. "I promise you. You will make it. You will have this. I will help you. And, CJ, this is the girl you need to let into your artwork."

I nod.

Then he walks over to the shelf, grabs some charcoal. "Now we draw."

Unbelievably, I'd forgotten about Oscar *naked* in the next room.

We walk over to a corner of the studio where there's a platform with one chair pulled up to it. I'm feeling unsteady – I didn't even tell the counselor at CSA the things I just told Guillermo. And so much for not being a poor motherless girl in his eyes.

Oscar, wearing the blue robe, is sitting reading, his feet propped up on the platform. It looks like a textbook, but he closes it too fast for me to catch what sort.

Guillermo pulls another chair over, then gestures for me to sit.

"Oscore is my favorite model," he says. "He has a very strange face. I don't know if you notice. God was very drunk when he made him. A little bit of this. A little bit of that. Brown eye. Green eye. Crooked nose, crooked mouth. Lunatic smile. Chipped tooth. Scar here, scar there. It is a puzzle."

Oscar shakes his head at the ribbing. "I thought you didn't believe in God," he says.

For the record, I'm in the midst of a penis panic attack.

At CSA, I'm fairly penis-neutral in life class, but not at the moment, no siree.

"You misunderstand," Guillermo says. "I believe in everything."

Oscar slips off the robe.

"Me too. You wouldn't believe the things I believe in," I interject, sounding frantic, wanting to join in their repartee so I don't stare at *it*. Too late. Oh my effing Clark Gable – what was that again about a dinosaur he named Godzilla?

"Do tell," Oscar says to me. Ha! Not telling what I'm thinking! "Tell us one thing you believe in, CJ, that we wouldn't believe."

"Okay," I say, trying to regain some semblance of composure

and maturity. "I believe that if a guy gives a girl an orange, her love for him will multiply." I couldn't resist.

He cracks up, falling out of the pose Guillermo just positioned him in. "Oh, I absolutely believe you believe that. I have evidence to support you believe it quite fervently."

Guillermo taps his foot impatiently. Oscar winks at me, sending my stomach on an elevator ride. "To be continued," he says.

To be continued…

Wait. Who's Sophia? His little sister? His great-aunt? The plumber?

"Quick sketches, CJ," Guillermo says to me, and a brand-new set of nerves kicks in. Then to Oscar, "Change position every three minutes." He sits down in the chair next to me and starts to draw. I'm aware of his hand flying across the page. It's stirring the air. I take a breath and begin, telling myself it's going to be okay. Five minutes or so pass. Oscar's new pose is stunning. His spine's arched and his head's hanging backward.

"You go too slow," Guillermo says quietly.

I try to sketch more quickly.

Guillermo gets up and stands behind me, looking over my shoulder at my work, which, I see through his eyes, is dreadful.

I hear:

"Faster."

Then:

"Pay attention to where the light source is."

Then, touching a spot on my drawing:

"That is not a shadow, that is a cave."

Then:

"You hold the charcoal too tight."

Then:

"Do not take the charcoal off the paper so much."

Then:

"Eyes off the page, on the model."

Then:

"Oscore is in your eyes, in your hands, your eyes, your hands, he travels through you, do you understand that?"

Then:

"No, all wrong, everything. What are they teaching you at that school? Nothing, I think!"

He squats by my side and his smell overwhelms me, a sign at least that I haven't died of mortification. "Listen, it is not the charcoal that draws the picture. It is you. It is your hand, which is attached to your body, and in that body is a beating heart, okay. You are not ready for this." He takes the stick of charcoal out of my hand and throws it onto the floor. "Draw him without it. Use only your hand. See it, feel it, draw it. All one thing, not three things. Don't take your eyes off of him. See, feel, draw. One verb, go now. Do not think. Above all else: *Do not think so much*. Picasso, he say, 'If only we could pull out our brain and use only our eyes.' Pull out your brain, CJ, use only your eyes!"

I'm embarrassed. I want an eject button. At least, mercifully, Oscar's eyes are fixed to the opposite corner of the room. He hasn't looked over at us once.

Guillermo is back in his chair. "Do not worry about Oscore. Do not be self-conscious because of him," he says. Is he telepathic? "Now draw like you mean it. Like it means something. Because it does, you understand this, CJ? It has to mean something. You hop a fence and climb up on my fire escape in the middle of the night. It means something to you!"

He begins to sketch again next to me. I watch how ferociously he's attacking the paper, the lines so bold and certain, how quickly he flips the page, like every ten seconds. We do thirty-second drawings at school. But he's lightning.

"Go," he says. "Go!"

And then I'm paddling through the break, watching a big wave swelling, coming toward me, knowing that in a moment it will sweep me up into something enormous and powerful. I would count down like I'm doing now for some reason:

Three, two, one:

I go. With no charcoal in my hand, I go.

"Faster," he says. "Faster."

I am flipping the pages like him every ten seconds, drawing absolutely nothing and not caring, feeling Oscar come alive in my hand.

"Better," he says.

Then again:

"Better."

See feel draw: one verb.

"Good. That is it. You will see with your hands, I promise you.

Now I contradict myself. Picasso he do too. He say pull out your brain, yes, he also say, 'Painting is a blind man's profession' and 'To draw you must close your eyes and sing.' And Michelangelo, he say he sculpts with his brains, *not* his eyes. Yes. Everything is true at once. Life is contradiction. We take in every lesson. We find what works. Okay, now pick up the charcoal and draw."

After a few minutes, he takes the scarf from around his neck, wraps it around my eyes, and blinds me.

"Understand?"

I do.

* * *

Later, I'm in the jail cell room, fetching my portfolio, waiting for Guillermo, who needed to run an errand, when Oscar, once again buttoned and zipped, with camera at the ready, sticks his head in.

He leans against the doorframe. Some guys are born to lean. He's definitely one of them. James Dean was another. "Bravo," he says.

"Be serious," I say, but in truth, I feel electrified, jangly, *awake*. I've never felt this way at CSA.

"I'm quite serious." He's fiddling with the camera and his dark hair's fallen into his face. I want to push it back.

I zip up my portfolio to busy my hands. "Have we met before, Oscar?" I ask at long last. "I'm pretty sure we have. You look *so* familiar."

He lifts his eyes. "She says after she's seen me naked."

"Oh God… No, I didn't mean… You know what I mean…" Heat's radiating off of every inch of me.

"Whatever you say." He's amused. "But not a chance. Never forget a face, especially not one like yours—" I hear the click before I realize I've even been shot. It's weird how he maneuvers the camera without even looking through the viewfinder. "Did you ever go back to the church after we met?"

I shake my head. "No, why?"

"I left something for you. A photo." Did a flash of shyness cross his face? "With a note on the back." Not breathing. "It's gone. I went back to check. Someone else must've taken it. Probably for the best. Too Much Information, as you lot say."

"What kind of Information?" It's amazing one can speak and be stone-cold passed out at the same time.

He doesn't answer, lifts the camera instead. "Can you tilt your head like you just did. Yes, that's it." He moves away from the wall, bends his knees, angles the camera. "Yes, perfect, God, *so* damn perfect." What happened to me in church is happening again. When glaciers break up due to rising world temperatures, it's called calving. I'm calving. "Your eyes are so ethereal, your whole face is. I stared at pictures of you for hours last night. You give me chills."

And you give me *global warming*!

But there's something else, something beyond chills and calving and global warming, something I felt from that first moment in church. This guy makes me feel like I'm actually here, unhidden, seen. And this is not just because of his camera. I do not know what this is because of.

Plus, he's different than the boys I know. He's *exciting*. If I made a sculpture of him, I'd want it to look like an explosion. Like kapow.

I take a long deep breath, remembering what happened the last time I liked a guy.

229

That done, WHAT KIND OF INFORMATION WAS IN THE NOTE AND WHAT PHOTO?

"So can I take pictures of you sometime?" he asks.

"You *are* taking pictures of me, *Oscore!*" I say it like Guill-ermo, packed with exasperation.

He laughs. "Not here. Not like this. At this abandoned build-ing I just discovered by the beach. At sunset. I have an idea." He peeks around the side of the camera. "And not with your clothes on. Only fair." His eyes are bright as the devil's. "Say yes."

"No!" I cry. "Are you kidding? So creepy. Ax-murderer Avoidance Rule Number One: Don't go to the abandoned building with the total stranger and take off your clothes under any circumstance. Jeez. Does that line usually work for you?"

"Yes," he says. "It *always* works."

I laugh, can't help it. "You're *such* bad news."

"You have no idea."

"I think I do. I think they should arrest you and lock you up as a community service."

"Yes, they tried that once." I feel my mouth drop. He really has been in jail. He reads my shock, says, "It's true. You've defi-nitely fallen in with the wrong crowd."

Except I feel the opposite. I feel like Goldilocks. Everything is just as right here as it is wrong at home.

"What did they arrest you for?" I ask.

"I'll tell you if you say yes to my invitation."

"To be ax-murdered?"

"To live a little dangerously."

I practically choke on his words. "Ha! Wrong girl," I say.

"Beg to differ."

"*You* have no idea." Our rapport is so easy. Why is it so easy?

Grandma answers, sing-songing in my head, "Because love is in the air, my blind little bat. Now get a strand of your hair into his pocket. Immediately."

> As long as a man has a lock of your hair on
> his person, you will be in his heart
> *(Thanks, but no thanks. I did this with Zephyr.)*

I pretend she's a normal dead person: silent.

There's a tap-tapping of heels on the cement floor. Oscar glances out the door. "Sophia! In here." Definitely not the plumber, unless the plumber wears stilettos. He turns to me. I can tell he wants to say something before we're interrupted. "Look, bad news I may be, but I'm not a stranger. You said so yourself. 'I'm *so* familiar to you.'" He mimics me with perfect beach girl inflection, then snaps the cover on his lens. "I'm certain I've never met you until that day in the church, but I'm also certain I was *meant* to meet you. Don't think me a nutter, but it's been prophesized."

"Prophesized?" I say. Is this the Information? It must be. "By whom?"

"My mum. On her deathbed. Her very last words were about you."

> What someone says to you right before they
> die will come true?

* * *

Sophia – definitely not his little sister nor his great-aunt – and her comet of red hair streaks into the room. She has on a fuchsia fifties swing dress with a neckline that plunges to the equator. Green-and-gold sparkling sweeps wing her pale blue eyes.

She glitters like she walked out of a Klimt painting.

"Hello my darling," she says to Oscar in a thick accent, I swear, identical to Count Dracula's.

She kisses his left cheek, right cheek, then presses her lips to his in a long, lingering finale. Very long and lingering. My chest caves in.

Still lingering…

Friends do not greet each other like this. Under any circumstances.

"Hello there," Oscar says warmly. Her magenta lipstick is smudged all over his lips. I have to put my hand in my sweatshirt pocket so I don't reach over and wipe it off.

I take back all that Goldilocks garbage.

"Sophia, this is CJ, Garcia's new disciple from The Institute." So he does think I go there. He thinks I'm their age. And a good enough artist to get into The Institute.

I don't clear up any of it.

Sophia reaches out a hand to me. "I've come to suck your blood," she says in her Transylvanian accent, but perhaps I misheard, perhaps she said, "You must be a very good sculptor."

I mumble some gibberish in reply, feeling like a sixteen-year-old darkness-eating troll with leprosy.

And she, with her flaming hair and bright pink dress, is an exotic orchid. Of course he loves her. They're two exotic orchids together. It's perfect. They're perfect. Her sweater's fallen off her shoulder and a magnificent tattoo is twisting out of her dress and around her entire arm, a red-and-orange fire-breathing dragon. Oscar notices the sweater and adjusts it like he's done it a hundred times. A dark surge of jealousy rises in my chest.

What about the prophecy, whatever it is?

"We should go," she says, taking his hand, and a moment later, they're gone.

When I'm certain they've left the building, I run at a full sprint – thankfully Guillermo's still not back – down the hallway to the front window.

They're already on the motorcycle. I watch her wrap her arms around his waist and I know just how it feels, how he feels, from sketching him today. I imagine it: gliding my hands up his long oblique muscles, lingering over the grooves of his abdomen, feeling the heat of his skin in my hands.

I press my hand against the cold glass. I actually do this.

He kick-starts the bike, revs the throttle, and then they're ripping down the street, her red hair crackling like a wildfire behind them. When he kamikazis the corner at 500 mph, at an absolutely fatal angle, she raises both hands in the air and whoops in delight.

Because she's fearless. *She* lives dangerously. Which is the worst part of all.

* * *

Walking back through the mailroom feeling dismal, I notice that a door I could've sworn was closed when I ran past a moment ago is now ajar. Did the wind open it? A ghost? Peering in, I find it hard to imagine one of mine would want to lure me in here, but who knows? Opening doors is not Grandma's thing.

"Mom?" I whisper. I say a few lines of the poem, hoping she might recite them back to me again. Not this time.

I open the door wider, then step into a room that was once an office. Before a cyclone hit it. I quickly close the door behind me. There are overturned bookcases and books toppled everywhere. There are drifts of paper and sketchbooks and notepads that have been swept off the desk and other surfaces. There are ashtrays full of cigarette butts, an empty bottle of tequila on its side, another one smashed in a corner. There are punch marks in the walls, a shattered window. And in the center of the floor, there's a large stone angel facedown on the ground, her back broken.

The room has been taken apart in a rage. I'm thinking maybe the one that was going on the first time I came here, the one that sounded like a furniture-throwing contest. I look around at the physical manifestation of Guillermo's trouble, whatever it is, and a mixture of excitement and fear weaves through me. I know I shouldn't snoop, but curiosity quickly overrides my conscience as it often does – snoop-control issues – and I'm bending down and randomly perusing some of the papers on the floor: mostly old letters. There's one from an art student in Detroit wanting to work with him. Another handwritten from a woman in New York promising him anything (underlined three times) if only he'd mentor her – jeez. There are consignment forms from galleries, a proposal from a museum about a commission. Press releases from past shows. I pick up a notepad like the one he keeps in his pocket and leaf through it, wondering if there might be some clue in it, in this room, as to what happened to him. The small pad is full of sketches, some lists and notes too, all in Spanish. Maybe material lists? Notes on sculptures? Ideas? Feeling guilty, I toss it back onto the heap, but then I can't help myself and pick up another one, flip through it, find more of the same, until I come to a page where there are some words in English:

Dearest,
I have gone mad. I do not want to eat or drink, or I will lose the taste of you in my mouth, do not want to open my eyes if not to see you, do not want to breathe any air that you have not breathe, that has not been inside your body, deep inside your beautiful body. I must

I turn to the next page, but it doesn't continue. I must – *what?* I whip through the rest of the pad, but the remaining pages are blank. I search through a few more notepads scattered around, but find no more words in English, no more words for Dearest. The skin on my arms is prickling. Dearest is her. It has to be. The woman in the painting. The clay woman climbing out of the clay man's chest. The female giant. All the female giants.

I read the note again. It's so steamy, so desperate, *so* romantic.

If a man doesn't give his beloved the letter
he writes, his love is true

That's what happened to him then: love. Tragic, impossible love. And Guillermo's so perfectly cast. No woman can resist a man who has tidal waves and earthquakes beneath the skin.

Oscar seems like he has natural disasters under the skin too. But give me a break. Male leads in love stories need to be devoted, need to chase trains, cross continents, give up fortunes and thrones, defy convention, face persecution, take apart rooms and break the backs of angels, sketch the beloved all over the cement walls of their studios, build sculptures of giants as homages.

They don't flirt shamelessly with the likes of me when they have Transylvanian girlfriends. What an effing jerk.

I separate the page with the love note from the rest of the notepad, and as I'm pressing it into the safety of my jeans pocket, I hear the front door to the studio do its horror-creak. Oh no. My pulse speeds as I tiptoe over to the door and tuck behind it so I'll be hidden should Guillermo decide to come in. I'm definitely not supposed to be in here. This is a most private kind of chaos, like the contents of his mind all spilled out. I hear a chair scrape across the floor, then smell smoke. Great. He's having a cigarette right outside the door.

I wait. And stare down at all the art books piled everywhere, recognizing a lot of them from school, recognizing my mother. Half of her face is staring back at me from one of the stacks. It's the author photo on the back of her Michelangelo biography, *Angel in the Marble*. It gives me a start. But of course it's here. He has every art book in here. I squat down and reach for it, careful not to make a sound as I pull it out of the stack. I open to the title page, wondering if she signed it when they met. She did.

To Guillermo Garcia,
" I saw the angel in the marble and carved until
I set him free." Thank you for the interview – a
tremendous honor.

    Yours with admiration,
    Dianna Sweetwine

Mom. I close the book quickly, quickly, keeping it shut with my hands so it doesn't fly open, so I don't. My knuckles are white with the effort. She always signed with that Michelangelo quote. It was her favorite. I hug the book to my chest tight, so tight, wanting to jump inside it.

Then I secure it inside the waistband of my jeans and cover it with my sweatshirt.

"CJ," Guillermo calls. I hear his retreating footsteps. When I'm certain he's gone, I slip soundlessly out of the room, shutting the door behind me. I cross the mailroom swiftly, quietly, and enter the jail cell room, where I hide Mom's book in my portfolio case, aware, oh, yes, I am, that I'm acting like a super-kook, buttons flying everywhere today. Though it's not my first bout of larceny. I've stolen quite a few copies of Mom's books from the school library too – every time they replace them, in fact. And the town library. And several bookstores. I do not know why I do it. I do not know why I stole the love note. I do not know why I do much of anything.

I find Guillermo in the studio, squatting, petting a blissed-out

Frida Kahlo's belly. His note to Dearest is burning up my pocket. I want to know more. What happened to them?

He nods at me. "Are you ready?" He rises. "Are you ready for your life to change?"

"And how," I say.

The rest of the afternoon consists of my choosing a practice rock — I fall in love with an amber-colored alabaster one that looks like a fire's burning inside it — and listening to Guillermo, who has become Moses, recite commandments about carving:

Thou shalt be bold and courageous.

Thou shalt take chances.

Thou shalt wear protective gear.

(BECAUSE THERE'S ASBESTOS IN THE DUST!)

Thou shalt have no preconceptions about what is inside the practice rock but shall wait for the rock to tell thee directly.

After this one, he touches my solar plexus with his outspread hand, adding, "What slumbers in the heart is what slumbers in the stone, understand?"

Then he bestows the final commandment onto me:

Thou shalt remake the world.

This is something I would very much like to do, though no clue how carving a rock will achieve it.

When I get home after hours and hours of practice carving — I'm spectacularly horrible at it — with my wrist muscles aching, thumbs bruised from hundreds of hammer mishaps, asbestosis disease already spreading through my lung tissue despite the face mask, I open my bag and find three big round oranges looking up at me. I'm stupid-struck with love for

Oscar for a moment, then remember Sophia.

What duplicity! Seriously, what a major asshat, as Noah used to say when he was Noah.

I bet he told Sophia his mother prophesized about her too.

I bet his mother's not even dead.

I take the oranges to the kitchen and make juice.

* * *

On returning to my bedroom after The Great Orange Massacre hoping to sew for a bit, I find Noah squatting over the bag I left on the floor, flipping through a sketchpad that had been tucked safely inside the bag only moments before. Instant payback from the universe for going through Guillermo's papers?

"Noah? What're you doing?"

He jumps up, exclaims, "Oh! Hey! Nothing!" Then proceeds to put his hands on his waist only to move them to his pockets, then back to his waist. "I was just … nothing. Sorry." He laughs too loud, then claps his hands together.

"Why are you going through my stuff?"

"Wasn't…" He laughs again, well, more like whinnies. "I mean, I guess I was." He looks at the window like he wants to jump out of it.

"But why?" I ask, giggling a little myself – he hasn't acted like such a certifiable weirdo in forever.

He smiles at me as if he heard me thinking. It does something wonderful inside my chest. "Guess I just wanted to see what you were working on."

"Really?" I ask, surprised.

"Yup," he says, shifting back and forth on his feet. "Yeah."

"Okay." I hear the eagerness in my voice.

He gestures toward the pad. "I saw the sketches of Mom. Are you doing some kind of sculpture of her?"

"Yes," I say, excited by his curiosity, not caring at all about the sketchpad spying – how often did I used to do the same to him? "But those studies in there aren't even close to being finished. I just started them last night."

"Clay?" he asks.

A sudden powerful how-dare-I-talk-to-him-about-my-artwork feeling is overtaking me, but it's been so long since we've connected about anything, so I go on. "Not clay, *stone*," I tell him. "Marble, granite, don't know yet. I'm working with this totally cool sculptor now. He's *amazing*, Noah." I walk over and pick the pad up off the floor. Holding it in front of both of us, I point to the most completed sketch, a frontal view. "I was thinking of doing it realistic. Not at all bulbous-y like usual. I want it to be elegant, a little willowy, but wild somehow too, you know, like her. I want people to see the wind in her hair, in her clothes – oh, it'll be a Floating Dress for sure, but only we'll get that. I hope, well, you know how she used to stand on the deck every—" I stop because he's taken a phone out of his pocket. It must've vibrated. "Hey dude," he says, and then starts talking about some trail-run and mileage and other cross-country mumbo jumbo. He makes an apologetic face at me like it's going to be a while and leaves the room.

I tiptoe to the door, wanting to hear him talk to his friend. Sometimes I stand outside his room when he and Heather are hanging out and listen to them gossip, laugh, be goofy. A few times on weekends, I've sat reading by the front door, thinking they might ask me to go with them on one of their zoo trips or after-running pancake extravaganzas, but they never do.

Halfway down the hallway, Noah abruptly stops talking mid-sentence and puts the phone back into his pocket. Wait. So he faked the call and was pretend-talking to no one just to get away from me? Just to stop me blathering on like that? My throat constricts.

We're never going to be okay. We're never going to be us again.

I walk over to the window, flip the shade so I can see the ocean.

I stare it down.

There are times when surfing where you'll take on a wave only to realize the bottom's dropped out of it and so suddenly without warning you're free-falling down the entire face.

It feels like this.

* * *

When I arrive at Guillermo's studio the next afternoon at the scheduled time – he doesn't seem to care it's winter break and there's nowhere I'd rather be, so – I find a piece of paper thumb-tacked to the door that says: *Be back soon – GG.*

All morning, while sucking on anti-Oscar lemons, I listened from across town, hoping my practice rock would tell me what was inside it. So far, not a peep. Not a peep between Noah and me since yesterday either, and this morning he was gone before I woke up. As was all of the cash Dad left us for emergencies. Effing whatever.

Back to the clear and present danger: Oscar. I'm ready.

241

In addition to the lemons, in preparation for a possible encounter, I did some catch-up reading on a myriad particularly raunchy venereal diseases. Followed by some bible study:

> People with two different-colored eyes
> are duplicitous cads
> *(Yes, I wrote this passage.)*

The Oscar case is closed.

I slip quickly down the hallway, thrilled to find Grandma and no one else in the mailroom. She's in a splendid outfit. A striped straight skirt. Vintage floral sweater. Red leather belt. Paisley scarf championed with attitude around her neck. All topped off with black felt beret and John Lennon sunglasses. Exactly what I'd wear to the studio if I weren't bound to the root vegetable look.

"Perfect," I tell her. "Very shabby chic."

"Chic would suffice. Shabby as a label offends my sensibilities. I was going for Summer of Love with more than a smidgeon of Beatnik. All this art, the mess and disorder, these mysterious foreign men are making me feel very free-spirited, very throw caution to the wind, very daring, very—"

I laugh. "I get it."

"No, I don't think you do. I was going to say very Jude Sweetwine. Remember that intrepid girl?" She points to my pocket. I pull out the extinguished candle. She tsk tsks at me. "Don't use my bible to forward your dreary agenda."

"He has a girlfriend."

"You don't know that for sure. He's European. They have different mores."

"Haven't you read Jane Austen? English people are *more* uptight than us, not less."

"One thing that boy doesn't seem is uptight." Her whole face contorts with the effort of a wink. She's not a subtle winker, not a subtle anything.

"He has trichomoniasis," I grumble at her.

"Nobody has that. Nobody but you even knows what it is."

"He's too old."

"Only I'm too old."

"Well, he's too hot. *Way* too hot. And he knows it. Did you see the way he leans?"

"The way he what?"

"Leans against a wall like James Dean, *leans*." I do a quick demonstration against a pillar. "And he drives that motorcycle. And has that accent and those different-color eyes—"

"David Bowie has different-color eyes!" She throws up her arms, exasperated. Grandma has a great passion for David Bowie. "It's good luck when a boy's mother prophesizes about you." Her face goes soft. "And he said you give him chills, honey."

"I have a feeling his *girlfriend* gives him chills too."

"How can you judge a fella until you picnic with him?" She opens her arms as if to embrace the whole world. "Pack a basket, pick a spot, and go. Simple as that."

"*So* corny," I say, spotting one of Guillermo's notepads on a stack of mail. I quickly leaf through it for notes to Dearest. None.

"Who with a beating heart in her chest scoffs at a picnic?" she exclaims. "You have to see the miracles for there to be miracles, Jude." She used to say this a lot. It's the very first passage she wrote in the bible. I'm not a miracle-seer. The very last passage she wrote in the bible was: *A broken heart is an open heart.* I somehow know she wrote it for me, to help me after she died, but it didn't help.

```
        Throw a handful of rice into the air,
     and the number of kernels that land back
      in your hand are the amount of people you
                   will love in your life
```
(Grandma would put up the closed sign for my sewing lessons.
At the table in the back of her shop, I'd sit on her lap and
breathe in her flowery scent while learning to cut and drape
and stitch. "Everyone gets a one-and-only and you're mine,"
she'd tell me. "Why me?" I'd always ask, and she'd nudge
her elbow into my ribs and say something silly like,
"Because you have such long toes, of course.")

A knot's forming in my throat. I walk over to the angel and when I'm finished wishing my second wish – you always get three wishes, right? – I join Grandma in front of the painting. Not Grandma. Grandma's ghost. There's a difference. Grandma's ghost only knows things about her life that I know. Questions about Grandpa Sweetwine – he left when Grandma was pregnant with Dad and never came back – go unanswered like they did when she was alive. Lots of questions go unanswered. Mom used to say when you look at art, it's half seeing, half dreaming. Same with ghosts, maybe.

"Meanwhile, this is one hell of a kiss," she says.

"Sure is."

We both sigh into our own thoughts, mine, much to my distress, becoming R-rated, Oscar-rated. I really don't want to be thinking about him, but I am…

"What's it like to be kissed like that?" I ask her. Even though I've kissed a bunch of boys, it never ever felt like this painting looks.

Before she can answer me, I hear, "I'd be more than happy to show you. If you'd break the boycott, that is. Give it a go, anyway. Even if you are barking mad." I pull my hand away from my mouth – when had it crept up to my lips as a substitute for his? – and inch around to see that Oscar has jumped out of my mind and is standing in full flesh form on the landing of the loft. He's leaning (a sexy lanky front forward one this time) on the railing with his camera focused on me. "Thought it only fair I pipe in before things went any further with that hand of yours."

No.

I flail in place, suddenly finding my skin extremely confining. "I didn't know anyone was here!"

"Quite apparent," he says, trying not to laugh. "Quite, quite apparent."

Oh no. How crazy must I have looked chattering away with the air? Heat pours into my face. How much of that conversation did he hear? Well, conversation, so to speak. Oh oh oh. And how long had I been making out with the *hand*? Does he know I was thinking about him? Kissing him? He continues. "Very fortunate for me. These zoom lenses. They miss nothing. Hell, oranges – who knew? Could've saved a bundle on cologne, candlelit dinners, et cetera, et cetera." He knows.

"You're assuming I was thinking about you," I say.

"Indeed."

I roll my eyes at the absurdity.

He puts both hands on the rail. "Who were you talking to, CJ?"

"Oh that," I say. How to respond? I don't know why, but like with Guillermo yesterday, I go with the truth. "Just Grandma popping in for a spell."

He makes a weird choking-coughing sound.

I have no idea what's happening on his face because I don't dare look his way. "Twenty-two percent of the world's population sees ghosts," I tell him via the wall. "It's not unusual. About one in four. And it's not like I'm some ghost-whisperer. I don't see ghosts per se. Just my grandmother and my mother, but my mom, she doesn't talk or appear to me, she just breaks things. Except for the other day when she recited a poem to me." I exhale. My cheeks are on fire. Probably less was more.

"What poem?" I hear. Not the response I expected.

"Just a poem," I answer. Telling him which poem somehow feels too personal to share even after the admission that I converse with dead relatives.

There's a moment of silence during which I listen intently for beeps indicating a 911 call. "I'm very sorry they're both gone, CJ," he says, his voice sincere and serious. I peer up at him, expecting to see The Poor Motherless Girl Look, but that's not what I see on his face.

I think his mom's dead after all. I turn away.

The good news is that he seems to have forgotten I was

hooking up with my hand. The bad news is that now I'm running through the conversation that he might've overheard. Writing a *love letter* to him would've been less revealing. Nothing to do but cover the eyes with the hands. Desperate times call for ostrich measures. "How much did you hear, Oscar?"

"Hey, no worries about that," he says. "I couldn't make out much. I was sleeping when your voice started trickling into my dream."

Is he telling the truth? Or just being kind? I do speak quietly. I fan my fingers. In time for his languid descent down the steps. Why does he move so slowly? Seriously. It's impossible not to watch him, to hang on his every move, to wait for him to arrive...

He slinks in behind me, close as a shadow.

Not sure the Oscar case is entirely closed, actually. I didn't account for proximity. And didn't he just say he'd be more than happy to kiss me like in the painting? I'm remembering specifically how he said he'd: *Give it a go, anyway.*

"So what'd you wish for, then?" he asks. "I saw you communing with the angel as well as your grandmother." His voice is low and silken and intimate and I don't trust myself to answer this question.

He's looking at me in that way of his that should be illegal or patented, and it's affecting my ability to remember things like my name and species and all the reasons a girl might go on a boy strike. Why don't I care one iota about the bad luck that might befall me? All I want is to comb my fingers through his tousled brown hair, to cup my hand around the blue horse on his neck, to press my lips against his like Sophia did.

Sophia.

I completely forgot about Sophia. It seems he did too, from the way he's *still* looking at me. What a louse. A lousy louse. Such a scalawag rake bounder miscreant scamp playboy player guyslut!

"I made orange juice out of the oranges you planted in my bag," I tell him, coming to my senses. "Pulverized them to pulp."

"Ouch."

"How come you're doing this?"

"What?"

"I don't know, this thing, this act. That voice. Looking at me like I'm this … this … donut. Standing so close. I mean, you don't even know me. Not to mention your girlfriend, remember her?" I'm talking too loud. I'm barking. What's gotten into me?

"But I'm not doing anything." He holds up his hands like he's surrendering. "Not acting. This is my voice – just woke up. I don't think you're in any way, shape, or form a donut, trust me on that. I'm not chatting you up. I respect the boycott."

"Good, because I'm not interested."

"Good, because my intentions are honorable." He pauses, then says, "Haven't you read Jane Austen? We English are more uptight than you lot, isn't that so?"

I gasp. "I thought you didn't hear anything!"

"I was being polite. We English are *very* polite, you know." He's grinning crazily, kind of like he's brainless. "Heard every word, I believe."

"It wasn't about you—"

"No? About the other bloke who rides a motorcycle and

has two different-colored eyes and leans like James Dean. Thank you, by the way. No one's ever commented on the lean."

I have no idea how else to navigate this moment except to make a run for it. I turn and head toward the jail cell room.

"What's more," he says, laughing his breezy laugh. "You think I'm hot. *Too* hot, in fact. *Way too hot,* I believe were the exact words." I close the door, hear through it, "And I don't have a girlfriend, CJ."

Is he effing kidding me? "Does Sophia know that?" I'm shouting like a maniac.

"As a matter of fact, she does!" he replies, equally maniacally. "We broke up."

"When?" We're yelling on either side of the door.

"Oh. Over two years ago." Two years ago? But that kiss. Was it not as long and lingering as I thought? Anxiety can alter perception; I know that. "Met at a party and I believe we lasted five days."

"Was that a record for you?"

"The record is nine days, actually. And I didn't realize you were on the Morality Police Force!"

I lie on the cold cement floor and let all the contaminated dust and microbes and toxic black mold spores do with me what they will. I'm racing inside. If I'm not mistaken, Oscar and I just got into a fight. I haven't fought with anyone since Mom. It doesn't feel entirely bad.

Nine days is his record. OMFCG. He's *that guy*.

I'm trying to get a grip, wondering when Guillermo's going to return, trying to focus on the reason I'm here, the sculpture I need to make, trying to make myself think about what could possibly be hiding inside my practice rock and not the revelation that Sophia and Oscar are not a couple! – when the door opens and in comes Oscar, waving a clay-covered towel.

He raises an eyebrow when he sees I'm lying on the floor like a corpse but doesn't comment. "White flag," he says, holding the mostly unwhite towel up. "I come in peace." I hoist myself onto my elbows. "Look, you were right," he says. "Well, partially. It is an act. *I* am an act. Totally full of it. About ninety-eight percent of the time anyway. My intentions are rarely honorable. It's not terrible to be called out for once." He walks over to the wall. "Watching? Ladies and gents: The Lean." He presses one shoulder into the wall, crosses his arms, cocks his head, squints his eyes, mugging James Dean better than James Dean. I can't help but laugh, which was the point. He smiles. "All right then. Moving on." He breaks the pose and begins pacing the small room, trial lawyer style. "I need to talk to you about those oranges *and* the red ribbon around your wrist *and* that unbelievably large onion you've been carrying around for days now…" He gives me a *gotcha* look, then reaches into his front jeans pocket and pulls out a chipped conch-shaped shell. "I wanted to let you know I don't go anywhere without my mum's magic seashell because if I do I will die, probably within minutes." This makes me laugh again. It's alarming how charming he can be. He tosses it to me. "Furthermore, I have conversations in my dreams with my mother, who passed away three years ago. Sometimes," he says, "I go to sleep in the middle of the afternoon, like I did today, just to see if she'll talk to me. You're the only person I've ever told this, but I owe you for eavesdropping before." He walks over, snatches the seashell out of my hands, grinning boyishly, adorably. "I *knew* you'd want to pinch my shell. Not happening. It's my most beloved possession." He slips it back into his pocket, stands over me, his eyes glinting, his smile headlong, anarchic, utterly irresistible.

Lord. Have. Mercy. On. My. Boycotting. Soul.

The next thing I know, he's at eye level and then lying down on the filthy floor next to me. Yes. A sound comes out of me that could only be described as a squeal of delight. He's crossed his arms over his chest and shut his eyes as mine were when he walked through the door. "Not bad," he says. "It's like we're at the beach."

I resume the position beside him. "Or in our coffins."

"What I like about you is how you always look on the bright side."

Laughing, again. "I do like that you came down on the floor with me," I say, looking on the bright side, feeling on the bright side, knowing there's no one in my life who'd lie on the floor with me like this. Or who carries a shell in their pocket so they don't die. Or who goes to sleep so they can talk to their dead mother.

A comfortable quiet falls over us. Really comfortable, like we've lain on filthy floors corpselike together for several lifetimes now.

"The poem was by Elizabeth Barrett Browning," I tell him.

"'How do I love thee?'" he croons. "'Let me count the ways.'"

"That's the one," I say, thinking: *He's* the one. And some thoughts once thought are very hard to unthink. "It *is* kind of like being on the beach," I say, growing more and more elated. I roll onto my side, cradle my head in my hand, and secretly stare at Oscar's madhouse face. Until he pops open an eye and catches me admiring him – you are so busted, his smile says. He closes the eye. "Shame you're not interested."

"I'm not!" I cry, falling back down on the sandy beach. "Artistic curiosity is all. You have an unusual face."

"And you have a mind-blowingly beautiful one."

"You're such a flirt," I say, effervescing.

"It's been said."

"What else has been said?"

"Hmm. Well, unfortunately, it's been said very recently I stay away from you or I get castrated." He sits up and spins his hands in the air like Guillermo. *"Castration, Oscore! Understand? You have seen me use the circular saw, yes?"* He relaxes into being himself again. "Which is actually why I've come in here waving the white flag. I have this way of ruining things and I don't want to ruin this. You're the first person besides me who's made G. laugh in years. That he's teaching again is a miracle. We're talking loaves and fishes, CJ. You've no idea." A miracle? "It's like you've cast this spell on him. Around you … I don't know … he's *okay* again. The guy's been bloody ferocious for a very long time." Is it possible I'm Guillermo's meadow like he's mine? "Plus we now know you *both* converse with invisible mates." He winks. "So" – he presses his hands together – "per your request and his, this is how it's going to be from now on. When I want to ask you to abandoned buildings or kiss those lips of yours or stare into your otherworldly eyes or imagine what you look like under all those baggy drab clothes you're always hiding in or ravish you on some grimy floor like I'm desperate to this very minute, I'll just bugger off on my Hippity Hop. Deal?" He holds out his hand. "Friends. *Just* friends."

Talk about mixed signals; he's like a roller coaster that talks.

No deal, no way. "Deal," I say, and take his hand but only because I want to touch him.

Moments tick by, our hands clasped, electricity jolting wildly through me. And then he's pulling me slowly toward him, looking into my eyes even as he just swore he wouldn't and heat's bursting in my belly, radiating everywhere. I feel my body opening. Is he going to kiss me? Is he?

"Oh man," he says, letting go of my hand. "I should probably go."

"No, don't. Please don't go." The words are out of my mouth before I can stop them.

"How about I sit over here, then, where it's safer," he says, scooting a few feet away from me. "Did I mention I have impulse-control issues?" He smiles. "I'm having a particularly strong impulse, CJ."

"Let's just talk," I say, my heart rate off the charts. "Remember the circular saw?" His laugh cartwheels across the room. "You have this great laugh," I blurt out. "It's like wow, it's—"

"You're not helping things. Please keep all compliments to yourself. Oh!" He's coming toward me again. "I know! An idea." He pulls my hat down so it covers my entire face and half my neck. "There," he says. "Perfect. Let's talk."

Except I'm laughing now inside my hat and he's laughing outside of it and we're getting carried away, far away, and I don't think I've been this happy maybe ever.

It's very hot and steamy to laugh out of control inside a wool hat, so after a time I lift it up and see him there, his face splotchy and eyes watering from truly losing it, and I'm filled with something I can only describe as recognition. Not because he looks familiar on the outside this time, but because he feels familiar on the inside.

Meeting your soul mate is like walking into a house you've been in before - you will recognize the furniture, the pictures on the wall, the books on the shelves, the contents of drawers. You could find your way around in the dark if you had to

"So if you're full of it ninety-eight percent of the time," I say, collecting myself. "What about the other two percent?"

The question seems to suck all the residual laughter out of his face and I'm immediately sorry I asked. "Yeah, no one meets that guy," he says.

"Why?"

He shrugs. "Perhaps you're not the only one in hiding."

"How come you think I'm in hiding?"

"Just do." He pauses, then says, "Maybe it's because I've spent a fair bit of time with your photos now. They speak volumes." He looks curiously at me. "But you could tell me *why* you're in hiding."

I consider it, consider him. "Now that we're friends, *just* friends. Are you the friend I call if I find myself in possession of a dead body and a bloody knife in my hand?"

He smiles. "Yes. I would not turn you in. No matter what."

"I trust you," I say, surprising myself, and from the expression on his face, him as well. Why I trust someone who's just told me he's full of it ninety-eight percent of the time I don't know. "I wouldn't turn you in either," I tell him. "No matter what."

"You might," he says. "I've done some pretty terrible things."

"Me too," I say, and suddenly I want more than anything to confide in him.

Write your sins on apples still hanging on
the tree; when they fall away so do your burdens
(There are no apple trees in Lost Cove.
I've tried this with a plum tree, an apricot tree,
and an avocado tree so far. Still burdened.)

"Well," he says, staring at his hands steepled in front of him. "If it's any comfort, I'm pretty sure the things I've done are far worse than whatever it is you've done."

I'm about to speak, to refute this, but the uneasy look in his eyes silences me. "When my mum was sick," he says slowly. "We could only afford this day nurse. My mother wouldn't go to hospital anymore and NHS wouldn't cover it. So at night, I watched after her. Except I started gobbling down her pain meds by the handful. I was off my face all the time, I mean, all the time." His voice has grown strange, tight, lilt-less. "It was just me and her, always, no other family." He pauses, takes a deep breath. "One night, she took a tumble out of bed, probably she needed the bedpan, but then after she fell, she couldn't get herself up. She was too weak, too sick." He swallows. There's perspiration on his forehead. "She spent fifteen hours on the floor, shivering, hungry, in excruciating pain, *calling for me*, while I was passed out cold in the next room." He breathes out slowly. "And that's just a starter anecdote. I have enough for a book."

The starter anecdote has practically strangled him. And me too. We're both breathing too fast and I can feel his desperation taking me over like it's my own. "I'm so sorry, Oscar."

That prison of guilt the counselor at school talked about, he's in one too.

"Jesus." He's pressing his palms to his forehead. "I can't believe I told you that. I never talk about that. Not with anyone, not even G., not even at meetings." His face is in a whole different kind of turmoil than usual. "You see? Better when I'm full of it, isn't it?"

"No," I say. "I want to know all of you. One hundred per cent."

This unsettles him further. He does not want to be known one hundred percent by me, if his face is any indication. Why did I say that? I look down, embarrassed, and when I look back up I see that he's rising to his feet. He won't make eye contact.

"I need to do some work upstairs before my shift at La Lune," he says, already at the door. He can't get away from me fast enough.

"You work at that café?" I ask, when what I want to say is: I understand. Not the circumstances, but the shame. I understand the quicksand of shame.

He nods and then unable to help myself, I ask, "You said I was her, that first day in church. Who did you mean? And how could your mother have prophesized about me?"

But he just shakes his head and ducks out of the room.

I remember then I still have Guillermo's note to Dearest on me. I scrolled it up and tied it in a lucky red ribbon. No idea why, until now.

```
       To win his heart, slip the most passionate love
            note ever written into his jacket pocket
```
(Writing scripture on the fly here. Should I do this? Should I?)

"Hey one sec, Oscar." I catch him outside the door and brush a layer of dust off the back of his jacket. "That's one dirty floor," I say as I slip the hot burning words into his pocket. As I press play on my life.

Then I pace around the small room waiting for Guillermo to return so I can start carving, waiting for Oscar to get the love note and run to me or away from me. A valve has loosened inside me and some kind of something is escaping, making me feel entirely different from the boycotting girl who walked into this studio with a burnt candle in her pocket to extinguish feelings of love. I think of that counselor telling me I was the house in the woods with no doors or windows. No way to get in or out, she said. But she was wrong, because: Walls fall down.

And then at once, from across the studio, it's as if my practice rock has gotten on a loudspeaker to inform me what's inside it.

What slumbers in the heart, slumbers in the stone.

There is a sculpture I need to make first, and it's not of my mother.

* * *

I'm surrounded by giants.

In the center of the outdoor work area is one of Guillermo's massive couples but unfinished, and against the far fence is another mammoth work called *Three Brothers*. I'm trying not to make eye contact with them as Guillermo demonstrates different techniques on my practice rock. Let's just say, they're not the jolliest of giants, those three stone brothers. I'm wearing every piece of protective gear I could find: a plastic suit, goggles, and face mask, because I did some research on the health risks of carving stone last night and I'm surprised any stone sculptor lives past thirty. While Guillermo instructs me on how not to bruise the surface of the rock, how to use the rasp, how to do something called cross-hatch, how to choose the right chisel for each task and what angles are best suited for what kind of carving, I try unsuccessfully not to dwell on Oscar and the stolen love note I gave him. Probably not my best idea, both the stealing of the note and the giving of it. Impulse-control issues, clearly. Trying to be subtle, I manage a few questions about Oscar in between others on chisel position and model building. I find out the following: He's nineteen. He dropped out of high school in England and took the exams here and now is a freshman at Lost Cove University, studying mostly literature, art history, and photography. He has a dorm room but still sometimes stays in the loft.

However, I realize I'm not being as subtle as I think with my questions when Guillermo puts his hand under my chin, lifts my face so our eyes meet, and says, "Oscore? He is like my—" He brings his fist to his chest to finish the sentence. Like his heart? His son? "He fall in my nest when he was very young, very troubled. He have no one." His face is full of warmth. "It is very strange with Oscore. When I get sick of every last person, I am not sick of him. I do not know why this is. And he is so good at chess." He holds his head like he has a headache. "I mean *so so* good. It make me crazy." He looks at me. "But listen carefully. If I have a daughter, I keep her in another state from him. Understand?" Um? Loud and clear. "When Oscore breathe in, the girls come rushing to him from everywhere, and when he exhale—" He makes a gesture with his hand to indicate all the girls being literally blown away, blown off, in other words: blown to bits. "He is too young, too dumb, too careless. I was the same once. I have no idea about women, about love, until much later. Understand?"

"Understood," I tell him, trying to hide the sinking disappointment in my gut. "I will bathe in vinegar, down some raw eggs, and start looking for a wasp nest ASAP to put on my head."

"I do not understand this," he says.

"To reverse the leanings of the heart. Ancient family wisdom."

He laughs. "Ah. Very good. In my family, we just suffer."

Then he drops a bag of earthenware clay on my table and commands me to make the model, first thing, now that I know what hides inside the practice rock.

The sculpture I'm seeing is two round bubble bodies, shoulder to shoulder, every part of the figures, spherical and full, curved bulging chests pregnant with the same breath, heads tilting upward, gazes sky-bound. The whole thing about a foot across and high. As soon as Guillermo leaves, I start building, and before long, I forget Oscar the Girl-Exhaler and the heartbreaking story he told me and the way I'd felt in that jail cell room with him and the note I put in his pocket, until finally it's just me and NoahandJude.

This is the sculpture I need to make first.

When I finish the model, hours later, Guillermo inspects it and then uses it to pencil different reference points on my practice rock that mark where I'll cut in for "shoulders" and "heads." We decide the boy's outer shoulder is the first point of entry and then he leaves me to it.

It happens right away.

The very moment I put hammer to chisel with the intention of finding NoahandJude, my mind goes to the day Noah almost drowned.

Mom had just died. I was at the sewing machine with Grandma Sweetwine, one of her very first visits. I was working on the seam of a dress, when it's like the room shook me, that's the only way I can describe it. Grandma said: *Go,* only it was more like a tornado blowing the word at me. I flew out of my chair, out of the window, slid all the way down the bluff, my feet touching the sand as Noah hit the water. He didn't come up. I knew he wasn't going to. I've never been scared like that before, not even when Mom died. There was boiling liquid in my veins.

I ram the chisel with the hammer, watch a corner of the stone break off, watching myself rush into the surf that winter day. I swam fast as a shark despite my clothes, then started diving down where he sank, gripping armful after armful of water, trying to think about currents and riptides and maelstroms and everything Dad had ever taught me. I let the rip take me, dove down again, up and down, until there was Noah floating faceup, alive, but not conscious. I dragged him to shore, swimming one-armed, sinking more every stroke with the weight of him, both our lives pounding inside me, and then on the beach, I beat his sternum with shaking hands, blew breath after terrified breath into his cold clammy mouth, and when he revived, the second I knew he was okay, I slapped him as hard as I could across the face.

Because how could he have done this?

How could he have chosen to leave me here all alone?

He told me he hadn't been trying to kill himself, but I didn't believe him. That first jump was different than all the others that followed. That time he was trying to fling himself off the earth for good. I know he was. He wanted out. He'd chosen to leave. To leave me. And he would have had I not dragged him back.

I think the valve inside me that loosened during the conversation with Oscar has popped its gasket. I'm whacking the chisel with such force now my whole body's vibrating, the whole world is.

Noah had stopped breathing. So there were these moments when I was in life without him.

For the first time. Not even in the womb were we apart. Terror doesn't come close to describing it. Fury doesn't come close. Heartbreak, no. There is no way to describe it.

He wasn't there. He wasn't with me anymore.

I'm starting to sweat in the plastic jumpsuit as I slam the hammer into the chisel with all the power in me, forgetting proper angles now, not caring about anything Guillermo just taught me, remembering only how my anger toward Noah

wouldn't go away after that. I couldn't get rid of it and everything he did seemed to compound it. I went to Grandma's bible,
desperate, but it didn't matter how many rosehips I put in my
tea, how much lapis lazuli I hid under my pillow, I couldn't get
rid of the rage.

And I'm feeling it again, as I cut into the rock, as I drag
Noah out of the ocean, as I rip into the stone, wanting us out,
out of the treacherous water, out of this suffocating rock, wanting us free, when I hear, "So that's why you did it?" It's Mom
and Grandma in unison. When did they become a team? A
chorus? They say it again, their voices a duet of accusation in
my head. "So is that why? Because it was right after that. We
watched you do it. You didn't think anyone saw. But we did."
I position the chisel on the other side of the stone and try to
hammer away their voices but I can't. "Leave me alone," I hiss
under my breath, peeling off the plastic suit, ripping off the face
mask and goggles. "You're not real," I tell them.

I stumble into the studio, feeling rudderless, hoping their
voices won't follow me, not sure if I make them up or not, not
sure of anything.

Inside, Guillermo is absorbed in another clay piece – so far,
a man, all huddled up.

But something's wrong in here too.

Guillermo's bent over the bent-over clay man. His hands
are working the face from behind and he's talking in Spanish,
his words growing more and more hostile. I watch in disbelief
as he raises a fist and heaves it into the back of the clay man,
leaving a hollow that I feel on my own spine. The blows come

fast after that. *The guy's bloody ferocious,* Oscar had said. I think of the punched-in walls of the cyclone room, the smashed window, the broken angel. He steps aside to inspect the damage he just inflicted, and as he does, he catches a glimpse of me and the violence in his fists is now in his eyes and directed at me. He puts his hand up and motions me out.

I back into the mailroom, my heart slamming inside my chest. No, it's not like this at CSA.

If this is what he meant about putting yourself into your art, if this is what it takes, I don't know, I really don't know if I'm up to it.

* * *

There's no way I'm going back into the studio where bloody ferocious Guillermo is beating up on an innocent clay man or out on the patio where bloody ferocious Grandma and Mom are wanting to beat up on me, so I head upstairs. I know Oscar's gone because I heard his motorcycle peel away over an hour ago.

The loft's smaller than I'd imagined. Just a guy's bedroom really. There are nails and thumbtack holes all over the walls where pictures and posters have been removed. The bookshelves have been ransacked. Only a few shirts hang in the closet. There's a table with a computer and some kind of printer, maybe for photos. A desk. I walk over to the unmade bed, where he was hoping to dream about his mother earlier today.

It's a tangle of brown sheets, one lone swirl of a Mexican blanket, a sad flat pillow in a faded pillowcase. A lonely-looking boy bed. I can't help it; despite warnings and ghosts and shaky boycotts and cataclysmic girl-destroying exhalations, I lie down, rest my head on Oscar's pillow, and breathe in the faint scent of him: peppery, sunny, wonderful.

Oscar does not smell like death.

I cover myself to the shoulders with his blanket and close my eyes, seeing his face, the desperate way it looked today when he told me what happened with his mother. He was so alone in that story. I breathe him in, all cocooned up in the place he dreams, tenderness crushing into me. And I understand why he shut down like that. Of course I do.

Opening my eyes, I see that on the bedside table, there's a framed picture of a woman with long gray hair in a floppy white hat. She's seated in a chair in a garden, a drink in her hand. There's sweat on the glass. Her face is leathery from the sun and jam-packed with Oscar. She's laughing and I somehow know she had the same breezy laugh he does.

"Forgive him," I say to his mother, sitting up. I touch her face with my finger. "He needs you to forgive him already."

She doesn't answer. Unlike my dead relatives. Speaking of which, what happened to me outside? Like taking a chisel to my own psyche. That counselor said ghosts — she used finger quotes around the word — are often manifestations of a guilty conscience. Check. Or sometimes of a deep inner longing. Check. She said the heart overcomes the mind. Hope or fear overcomes reason.

After a loved one dies, you must cover every
mirror in the house so the spirit of the departed
can rise – otherwise they will be stuck forever
among the living

(I've never told anyone this, but when Mom died, not only didn't I cover the mirrors, I went to the drugstore and bought dozens of pocket ones. I left them all over the house, wanting her spirit to get stuck with us, wanting it so bad.)

I don't know if I make up the ghosts or not, I only know I don't want to think about what they just said to me, so I start perusing the titles of books stacked by Oscar's bed. Mostly art history, some religion, novels. There's an essay sticking out of one of the books. I remove it. It's titled "The Ecstatic Impulse of the Artist," and in the corner of the page it says: *Oscar Ralph, Professor Hendricks, AH 105, Lost Cove University.*

I hug the paper to my chest. My mother used to teach AH 105. It's the introductory art history course for freshmen. Had she not died, she would've met Oscar, read this paper, graded it, talked to him during her office hours. She would've loved his topic: "The Ecstatic Impulse of the Artist." It makes me think of Noah. He sure had an ecstatic impulse. It didn't used to feel safe how much he could love a color or a squirrel or brushing his teeth even. I turn to the last page of the paper, where a big fat A is circled in red with the line: *Entirely compelling argument, Mr. Ralph!* It's then that Oscar's last name crashes into my consciousness. Oscar *Ralph.* Last name, first name, who cares? Oscar is Ralph! *I found Ralph.* I start to laugh. This is a sign. This is destiny. This is a miracle, Grandma! This is Clark Gable being very funny.

I get up, feeling worlds better – I found Ralph! – and peek over the railing of the loft to make sure Guillermo isn't in the mailroom listening to me giggling up here all alone. Then I walk over to the desk because hanging on the chair is Oscar's leather jacket. I reach in the pocket and … no note. Which means he got it. Which makes my stomach whirl.

I put on the jacket; it's like climbing right into his arms and I'm luxuriating in its heavy embrace, its scent, when I glance down at the desk and see *me*. All over it. Photograph after photograph arranged in a row, some with yellow sticky notes on them, some not. The air starts to vibrate.

Above the whole thing on a yellow sticky note, it says: *The Prophecy*.

The first photo is of an empty pew in the church where we met. A sticky note on it says: *She said I'd meet you in church. Granted, she probably said this so I'd go to church. I kept coming back to this one to photograph the empty pews.*

The second photo is of me sitting in the same pew as the previous shot. The note says: *Then one day they weren't empty.* Except I hardly recognize myself. I look, I don't know, hopeful. And I don't remember smiling at him like that at all. I don't remember smiling at anyone like that in my whole life.

The next photo is also from that day. The sticky says: *She said I'd know you right away because you'd glow like an angel. Yes, she was high as hell on pain meds, as was I – like I told you – but you glow. Look at you.* I look at the me he saw through his camera and again I hardly recognize her. I see a girl looking very swoony. I don't understand. I'd only met him moments before.

The third photo is of me, taken the same day but before I said he could take photos of me. He must've been stealth shooting. It's the moment when I put my finger to my lips to shush him and my grin's as law-breaking as his. The sticky says: *She said you'd be a bit odd.* He made a smiley face. *Forgive me, don't mean to offend, but you are bizarre.*

Ha! He *no offense, but*-ed me, English-style.

It's like his camera has found this other girl, one I wish I could be.

The next photo is of me taken today in the mailroom talking to Grandma Sweetwine, talking to no one. There's no denying how completely empty the room is, how alone I am, how ma-rooned. I swallow.

But the sticky note says: *She said you would feel like family.*

So he came up here to print photos and write these mes-sages after he left me downstairs? He must've wanted to tell me these things even as he fled like his feet were on fire.

If you dream you're taking a bath,
you will fall in love

If you stumble going upstairs,
you will fall in love

If you walk into someone's room and find
countless pictures of yourself with lovely notes
attached to them, you will fall in love

I sit down, not quite believing any of this, that he might really like me too.

I pick up the last photo in the series. It's of us kissing. Yes, kissing. He blurred out the background and added wild swirling color to everything around us so that we're … exactly like the couple in the painting! How'd he do it? He must've used a photo he took of me kissing my hand and then manipulated one of himself into the image.

The sticky on this one reads: *You asked what it would be like. This is what it ~~would~~ will be like. I don't want to be just friends.*

I don't either.

Meeting your soul mate *is* like walking into a familiar house. I *do* recognize everything. I *could* find my way around in the dark. The bible rules.

I pick up the photograph of the kiss. I'm going to take it to La Lune and tell him I don't want to be just friends either—

Then footsteps clomping up the steps, loud and hurried, mixed with laughter. I hear Oscar say, "Love when they over-staff. The extra helmet is right up here. And you can wear my jacket. It's going to be cold on the bike."

"So glad we finally get to hang out." It's a girl's voice. Not Sophia's from Transylvania either. Oh no, please. Something in my chest is collapsing. And I have about one second to make a decision. I choose the bad movie option, diving for the closet and shutting myself in before Oscar's boots are stomping across the room. I do not like the way this girl said *hang out*. Not one bit. It was definitely code for *hook up*. Definitely code for kissing his lips, his closed eyelids, his scars, the tattoo of the beautiful blue horse.

Oscar: I could've sworn I left my jacket here.

Girl: Who's she? She's pretty.

Shuffling, shuffling. Is he sweeping the photos of me from sight?

Girl (voice tight): Is she your girlfriend?

Oscar: No, no. She's nobody. It's just a project for school.

Knife stab, center chest.

Girl: You sure? That's a lot of pictures of one girl.

Oscar: Really, she's nobody at all. Hey, come here. Sit on my lap.

Come here, sit on my lap?

Did I say knife? It's an ice pick.

This time I'm certain no donuts are involved in the intimate sounds I'm hearing. This time I'm also certain I'm not misconstruing friendship for romance like I did with Sophia. I don't understand. I don't. How can the same guy who took those photos of me and wrote those notes to me be making out with another girl on the other side of this door? I hear him say the name Brooke in between heavy breaths. This is hell. This has to be karmic retribution for the last time I was in a closet I shouldn't have been in.

I can't stay in here.

Nobody-at-all pushes open the closet door. The girl springs out of Oscar's lap like a crazed cat. She has long tumbling brown hair and almond-shaped eyes that are popping out of her head at the sight of me. She's buttoning her shirt with frenzied fingers.

"CJ?" Oscar exclaims. There's lipstick all over the bottom of his face. Again. "What're you doing up here? In there?" Definitely a valid question. Unfortunately, I've lost the capacity for speech. And, I believe, for movement as well. I feel pinned to this awful moment like a dead insect. His eyes have landed on my chest. I realize I'm hugging the photograph of the kiss to me. "You saw," he says.

"Nobody at all, huh?" the girl named Brooke says, picking up her bag from the floor and slinging it over her shoulder in preparation, it seems, for a quick, angry exit.

"Wait," he says to her, but then his eyes dart back to me. "G.'s note?" he says, something dawning in his face. "You put it in my jacket?"

It hadn't occurred to me he'd recognize Guillermo's handwriting, but of course.

"What note?" I squeak out. Then I tell the girl, "I'm sorry. Really. I was just, oh I don't know what I was doing in there, but there's nothing between us. Nothing at all." I find my legs are working enough to get me down the stairs.

I'm halfway across the mailroom when I hear Oscar from the stairs. "Check the other pockets." I don't turn around, just push down the hallway, through the door, then down the path, landing on the sidewalk, panting, sick to my stomach. I forge up the street on legs so weak and wobbly I can't believe they're carrying me. Then when I'm about a block away, throwing all dignity to the wind, I start checking the pockets of the jacket, finding nothing but a film canister, candy wrappers, a pen. Unless… I run my hands over the inside lining and there's a zipper. I unzip it, reach in and pull out a piece of paper, carefully folded up. It looks like it's been there a while. I open it. It's a color copy of one of the photos of me in the church. The one with the law-breaking grin. He keeps me with him?

But wait. How can it matter? It can't. It can't matter if he chose to be with someone else anyway, to be with her right after writing those amazing notes to me, right after what happened between us on the floor of the jail cell room – not that I know what happened, but something did, something real, the laughing as well as the very intense rest of it when I had this sense there might be a key somewhere somehow that could set us both free. I really did.

And then: *Nobody at all.* And: *Come here, sit on my lap.*

I imagine him inhaling Brooke, inhaling girl after girl, like Guillermo said, like he's done to me, so now he can exhale and blow me to smithereens.

I am so stupid.

They do make love stories for girls with black hearts after all. They go like this.

I'm not even a block away – the picture balled up in my hand – when I hear someone behind me. I turn around, certain that it's Oscar, hating the fountaining of hope in my chest, only to find Noah: wild-eyed, unhinged, no padlocks anywhere on him, looking petrified, looking like he has something to tell me.

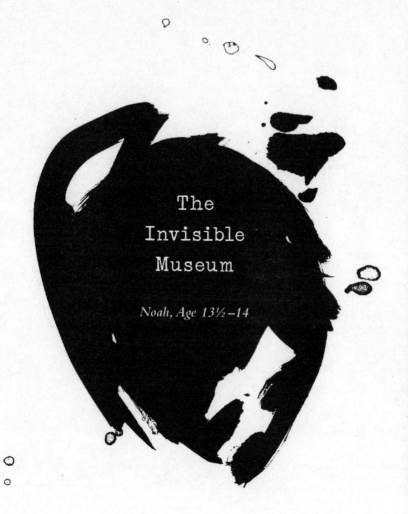

The
Invisible
Museum

Noah, Age 13½–14

The DAY after Brian leaves

for boarding school, I sneak into Jude's room while she's in the shower and see a chat on the computer.

Spaceboy: *Thinking about you*

Rapunzel: *Me too*

Spaceboy: *Come here right this minute*

Rapunzel: *Haven't perfected my teleporting*

Spaceboy: *I'll get on it*

I blow up the entire country. No one freaking notices.

They're in love. Like black vultures. And termites. Yes, turtle doves and swans aren't the only animals that mate for life. Ugly, toilet-licking termites and death-eating vultures do too.

How could she do this? How could he?

It's like having explosives on board 24/7, the way I feel. I can't believe when I touch things they don't blow to bits. I can't believe I was so way off.

I thought, I don't know, I thought wrong.

So wrong.

I do what I can. I turn each of Jude's doodles I find around the house into a murder scene. I use the most hideous deaths from her stupid How Would You Rather Die? game. A girl being shoved out a window, knifed, drowned, buried alive, strangled by her own hands. I spare no detail.

I also put slugs in her socks.

Dip her toothbrush in the toilet bowl. Every morning.

Pour white vinegar into the glass of water by her bed.

But the worst part is that for the few minutes every hour when I'm not psychopathic, I know that to be with Brian: *I would give all ten fingers. I would give anything.*

(Self-portrait: *Boy Rowing Madly Back Through Time*)

A week passes. Two. The house gets so big it takes hours for me to walk from my bedroom to the kitchen and back, so big that even with binoculars, I can't make out Jude across a table or room. I don't think our paths will ever cross again. When she tries to talk to me over the miles and miles of betrayal between us, I put in ear buds like I'm listening to music, when really, the other end is attached to my hand in my pocket.

I never want to speak to her again and make this very clear. Her voice is static. She is static.

I keep thinking Mom will realize that we're at war and act like the United Nations as she's done in the past, but she doesn't.

(Portrait: *Disappearing Mother*)

Then one morning, I hear voices in the hallway: Dad talking to a girl who isn't Jude, who I quickly realize is *Heather*. I've barely given a speck of brain space to her, even after what happened between us in the closet. That horrible lie of a kiss. *I'm sorry, Heather,* I say in my head as I pad silently over to the window, *sorry, so sorry,* as I lift it as quietly as possible. I climb out, falling to safety below the sill as I hear the knock on the door and Dad saying my name. It's all I can think to do.

Halfway down the hill, a car peels by me and I want to stick out my thumb. Because I should hitchhike to Mexico or Rio like a real artist. Or to Connecticut. Yes. Just show up where Brian is in that dorm – *in a shower full of wet naked guys*. The thought comes out of nowhere and all the explosives on board detonate at once. It's worse than thinking about him and Jude in the closet. And better. And much worse.

When I emerge out of the nuclear mushroom of this thinking, burnt to a crisp, I'm at CSA. My feet somehow got here on their own. Summer classes have been over for more than two weeks and lots of the students who board are returning. They look like highly functioning graffiti. I watch them lug suitcases and portfolios and boxes out of car trunks, hug parents who are peering at each other with eyes that say, *Maybe this wasn't such a good idea*. I vacuum it all in. The girls with blue green red purple hair shrieking into each other's arms. A couple of tall weedy guys leaning against a wall smoking and laughing and radiating cool. A ragtag group with dreads who look like they just tumbled out of a dryer. A guy walking past me with a mustache on one side of his face and a beard on the other. *So* awesome. They not only make art, they *are* art.

I remember then the conversation I had with the naked English guy at the party and decide to take my burnt remains on a recon mission to the inland flats of Lost Cove, where he said that barking mad sculptor had a studio.

Before too long, a few seconds later maybe – because trying not to think about Brian turns me into a superhuman speed-walker – I'm standing in front of 225 Day Street. It's a big warehouse and the door's half-open, but there's no way I can walk on in, can I? No. I don't even have my sketchpad. I want to, though, want to do something, have to do something. *Like kiss Brian.* The idea snags me and then I can't get out of it. I totally should've tried. But what if he'd punched me? Cracked my head open with a meteorite? Oh, but what if he hadn't? What if he'd kissed me back? Because I'd catch him staring at me sometimes when he didn't think I was paying attention to him. I was always paying attention to him.

I blew it. I did. I should've kissed him. One kiss, then I could die. Well, wait, no freaking way, if I'm going to die, I want to do more than kiss. Way way more. I'm sweating. And hard. I sit on the sidewalk, try to breathe, just breathe.

I pick up a stone and toss it into the street, trying to mimic his bionic wrist movement and after three pathetic tries, my whole thinking flips over. There was an electric fence between us. He put it up. Kept it up. He wanted Courtney. And he wanted *Jude* from the first moment he saw her. I just didn't want to believe it. He's a popular douchebag jock who likes girls. He's the red giant. I'm the yellow dwarf. The end.

(Self-portrait: *Everyone Lives Happily Ever After Except for the Yellow Dwarf*)

I shake it off, all of it. All that matters are the worlds I can make, not this toilet-licking one I have to live in. In the worlds I make, anything can happen. *Anything.* And if – when – I get into CSA I'll learn how to make it all come out half as decent on paper as it is in my head.

I stand, suddenly realizing I could totally climb the fire escape that scales the side of the warehouse. It leads to a landing where there's a bank of windows, which must look down on something.

All I'd have to do is hop the outside fence without anyone seeing me. Well, why not? Jude and I used to sneak over tons of fences so we could visit various horses or cows or goats or a certain madrone tree we both married when we were five (Jude was also the minister).

I glance up and down the quiet street. See in the distance the back of an old-looking woman in a bright-colored dress ... who actually may be floating. I blink – she's still floating and it looks like she's barefoot for some reason. She's entering a small church. Whatever. Once she's inside, I cross to the other side of the street, then easily and quickly monkey up and over the fence. I bolt down the alley, climb carefully up the stairs of the escape, trying not to creak the old metal, grateful there's some kind of construction going on nearby to cover up any sound I may be making. I scoot across the landing and peer around the side of the building, realizing the ear-splitting sound I'm hearing is not coming from a construction site, but the courtyard below, where I believe the apocalypse has just occurred, because whoa: It's the scene after the aliens have launched a chemical attack on Earth. All over the yard, there are rescue workers in hazmat suits and face masks and goggles, wielding power drills and circular saws, emerging from and disappearing into white billowing clouds as they attack hunks of rock. This is a stone studio? These are stone sculptors? What would Michelangelo think? I watch and watch and when the dust settles, I see that three massive pairs of eyes are boring into me.

My breath catches. From across the yard, three enormous stone men-monsters are staring at me.

And they're *breathing*. I swear it.

My ex-sister Jude would freak. Mom too.

I need to get closer to them, I'm thinking, when a tall, dark-haired man walks out of the building through an entire wall that's pulled halfway up like a garage door. He's talking with some kind of accent into a phone. I watch him throw his head back in supreme happiness, like he's hearing that he gets to choose the colors for all the sunsets from now on or that Brian's waiting for him in his bedroom naked. He's practically dancing around with the phone now, then he laughs a laugh so happy it blasts about a billion balloons into the air. This must be the barking mad artist and the scary-ass granite men-monsters across from me must be his barking mad art.

"Hurry," he says, his voice as big as he is. "Hurry, my love." Then he kisses two of his own fingers and touches the phone, before slipping it in his pocket. Total whale dork move, right? But not when he did it, trust me. Now he has his back to the courtyard and is facing a pillar, his forehead touching it. He's smiling at the concrete like a total whack job, but I'm the only one who knows, due to my stellar vantage point. He looks like he would give all ten fingers too. After a few minutes, he pivots out of his delirium and I get the first clear shot of his face. His nose is like a capsized ship, his mouth the size of three, his jaw and cheekbones hefty as armor, and his eyes are iridescent. His face is a room overstuffed with massive furniture. I want to draw it immediately. I watch as he surveys the apocalyptic scene before him, then raises his arms like a conductor and in an instant every power tool goes silent.

As do the birds, the passing cars. In fact, I can't hear a rustle of wind, the buzz of a fly, a word of conversation. I can't hear *anything*. It's like someone pressed mute on the whole world because this man is about to speak.

Is he God?

"I talk very much about bravery," he says. "I say to you carving is not for cowards. Cowards stick to clay, yes?"

All the rescue workers laugh.

He pauses, swipes a matchstick on a column. It bursts into flame. "I tell you, you must take risks in my studio." He finds a cigarette behind his ear and lights it. "I tell you not to be timid. I tell you to make the choices, make the mistakes, big, terrible, reckless mistakes, really screw it all up. I tell you it is the only way."

An affirmative murmur.

"I say this, yes, but I still see so many of you afraid to cut in." He begins to pace, slowly like a wolf, which is definitely his mirror animal. "I see what you are doing. When you leave yesterday, I go from work to work. You feel like Rambo maybe with the drills, the saws. You make lots of noise, lots of dust, but very few of you have found even this much" – he pinches two fingers together – "of your sculptures. Today this changes."

He walks over to a short blond-haired girl. "May I, Melinda?"

"Please," she says. I can see how much she's blushing even from up here. She's totally in love with him. I look at the faces of the others who have gathered around them and realize they all are, male and female both.

(Portrait, Landscape: *A Man on a Geographic Scale*)

He takes a long drag on the cigarette, then tosses it barely smoked onto the ground and steps on it. He smiles at Melinda. "We find your woman, yes?"

He studies the clay model beside the large rock, then closes his eyes and combs the surface with his fingers. He does the same with the hunk of stone next to it, examining it with his hands while his eyes are closed. "Okay," he says, taking a power drill off the table. I can feel the excitement of the students, as he, without any hesitation, plows straight into the rock. Before long, a dust cloud forms and I can't see any more. I need to get closer. I mean really close. I think I need to live on this man's shoulder like a parrot.

When the noise stops and the dust clears, all the students start clapping. There in the rock is the curved back of a woman identical to the one on the clay model. It's unbelievable.

"Please," he says. "Back to your own work." He hands Melinda the drill. "You will find the rest of her now."

He goes from student to student, sometimes not saying a thing, sometimes exploding into praise. "Yes!" he cries to one of them. "You did it. Look at that breast. The most beautiful breast I ever see!" The kid cracks up and the artist cuffs him on the head like a proud father might. It makes something pull in my chest.

To another student, he says, "Very good. Now it's time to forget everything I just say. Now you go slow. So, so slow. You caress the stone. You make love to it but gently, gently, gently, understand? Use the chisels, nothing else. One wrong move and you ruin everything. No pressure." Same head cuff for him.

When he seems to determine that no one needs him, he goes back inside. I follow him, walking to the other side of the landing where the windows are, standing to the side so I can see in without being seen. Inside, there are more rock giants. And on the far side of the studio, three naked women, with thin red scarves veiling their bodies, are modeling on a platform surrounded by a group of students sketching.

No naked English guy.

I watch the artist as he goes from student to student, standing behind each one and peering down at their work with a cold hard stare. I tense up as if he's looking at my sketches. He's not pleased. All at once, he claps his hands and everyone stops drawing. Through the window I hear muffled words as he becomes increasingly animated and his hands begin to glide around like Malaysian flying frogs. I want to know what he's telling them. I *need* to know.

Finally, they resume drawing. He grabs a pencil and pad off a table and joins them, saying the following so loudly and with so much rocket fuel in his voice I hear it through the window, "Sketch like it matters, people. No time to waste, nothing to lose. We are remaking the world, nothing less, understand?"

Just like Mom says. And yes, I do understand. My heart is speeding. I *totally* understand.

(Self-portrait: *Boy Remakes World Before World Remakes Boy*)

He sits down and begins sketching with the group. I've never seen anything like the way his hand races back and forth across the pad, the way his eyes seem to suck in every morsel of the models posing before him. My stomach's in my throat as I try to figure out what he's doing, as I study the way he holds the pencil, the way he *is* the pencil. I don't even need to see his sketchpad to know the genius that's on it.

Until this moment, I didn't realize how badly I sucked. How far I have to go. I really might not get in to CSA. The Ouija Board was right.

I stumble down the fire escape, lightheaded, unsteady. In one split second I saw everything I could be, everything I want to be. And all that I'm not.

The sidewalk has risen up and I'm sliding down it. I'm not even fourteen, I tell myself. I have years and years to get good. But I bet Picasso was already hella good at my age. What have I been thinking? I totally freaking blow. I'm never going to get in to CSA. I'm so stuck in this toilet-licking conversation in my head, I almost fly past the red car parked out front that looks just like Mom's car. But it couldn't be. What in the world would she be doing all the way over here? I glance at the plates – it *is* Mom's car. I swivel around. Not only is it Mom's car, but Mom's in it, bent over the passenger seat. What's she doing?

I knock on the window.

She springs up, but doesn't seem as surprised to see me as I am to see her. She doesn't seem surprised at all, in fact.

She rolls down the window, says, "You scared me, honey."

"What were you doing bent over like that?" I ask instead of the more obvious question: What are you doing here?

"I dropped something." She looks strange. Her eyes are too bright. There's sweat on her lip. And she's dressed like a fortune-teller, with a glittery purple scarf around her neck and a yellow river of a dress with a red sash. On her wrists are color bangles. Except the times when she wears one of Grandma's Floating Dresses, she usually dresses like a black-and-white movie, not a circus.

"What?" I ask.

"What what?" she asks back, confused.

"What did you drop?"

"Oh, my earring."

Both her ears have earrings in them. She sees me see this. "Another earring, I wanted to change pairs."

I nod, pretty sure she's lying to me, pretty sure she saw me and was hiding from me and that's why she didn't seem surprised to see me. But why would she hide from me?

"Why?" I ask.

"Why what?"

"Why did you want to change pairs?"

We need a translator. I've never needed a translator with Mom before.

She sighs. "I don't know, I just did. Get in, honey." She says this like we had a plan all along for her to pick me up here. This is so weird.

On the way home, the car is a box of tension and I don't know why. It takes me two blocks to ask her what she was doing in that part of town. She tells me there's a very good dry cleaner on Day Street. And there are about five closer to our house, I don't say. But she hears anyway because she explains further, "It was one of the dresses Grandma made for me. My favorite. I wanted to make sure it was in very good hands, the best hands, and this cleaner is the best." I look for the pink receipt, which she usually clips to the dash. Not there. But maybe it's in her purse? I guess this could be true.

It takes another two blocks for her to say what she should've said immediately. "You're a long way from home."

I tell her I went for a walk and ended up there, not wanting to tell her I hopped a fence, climbed a fire escape, and stalked some genius, who made it very clear she's wrong about me and my talent.

She's about to question me further, I can tell, but then her phone vibrates on her lap. She looks at the number and presses the button to ignore it. "Work," she says, glancing my way. I've never known her to perspire like this. There are darkened circles in the yellow fabric under her arms like she's a construction worker.

She squeezes my knee with her hand when we pass the CSA studio buildings, now so familiar to me. "Soon," she says.

Then it all becomes clear. She followed me. She's worried about me because I've been such a hermit crab. There's no other explanation that makes sense. And she hid and lied to me about the dry cleaner because she didn't want me to freak out about her spying on me and invading my privacy. I relax into this explanation.

Until she takes the second instead of the third left up the hill, and near the top, pulls into a driveway. I stare in disbelief as she gets out, saying, "Well, aren't you coming in?" She's almost to the door, keys in hand, when she realizes she's on her way into some other house, where some other family lives.

(Portrait: *Mom Sleepwalking into Another Life*)

"Where's my head?" she says, when she gets back in the car. This could be funny, it should be, but it's not. Something's not right. I can feel it in every bone, but I don't know what it is. She doesn't start up the engine either. We stay in this other family's driveway in silence, staring out at the ocean, where the sun has made its gleaming road to the horizon. It looks like there are stars on the water and I want to take a walk on it. It totally sucks that only Jesus gets to walk on water. I'm about to say this to Mom when I realize the car has filled up with the thickest, heaviest kind of sadness and it's not mine. I had no idea she was so sad. Maybe that's why she hasn't noticed Jude and I have gotten a divorce.

"Mom?" I say, my throat suddenly so dry it comes out like a croak.

"Everything's going to work out," she says quickly, quietly, and starts the engine. "Don't worry, honey."

I think about all the horrible things that happened the last time someone told me not to worry, but nod, just the same.

* * *

The end of the world begins with rain.

September washes away, then October. By November, even Dad can't stay on top of it, which means it's pretty much raining inside as well as outside the house. There are pans and pots and buckets everywhere. "Who knew we needed a new roof?" Dad mumbles to himself again and again like a mantra.

(Portrait: *Dad Balancing the House on His Head*)

This, after a lifetime of replacing batteries before flashlights conk out, lightbulbs before they go dark: *Can't be too prepared, son*.

However, after much observation, I've concluded that it's not raining on Mom. I find her on the deck smoking (she's not a smoker) as if under an invisible umbrella, always with the phone to her ear, not saying anything, just swaying and smiling like someone's playing her music on the other end. I find her humming (she's not a hummer) and jingling (she's not a jingler) through the house, down the street, up the bluff in her new circus clothes and bangles, her own private sunbeam enclosing her while the rest of us grip the walls and furniture so we don't wash away.

I find her at her computer where's she's supposed to be writing a book but instead is staring up at the ceiling like it's full of stars.

I find her and find her and find her but I can't find *her*.

I have to say her name three times before she hears it. I have to bang on the wall with my fist when I walk into her office or kick a chair across the kitchen before she even notices someone's joined her in the room.

It occurs to me with rising concern that a blow-in can also blow away.

The only way I can snap her out of it is to talk about my CSA portfolio, but because she and I have already chosen the five drawings I'm painting in oils with Mr. Grady, there's not much to discuss until the great unveiling and I'm not ready. I don't want her to see them until they're done. They're close. I've worked on them every single day at lunch and after school all fall long. There's no interview or anything, getting in is based pretty much only on your artwork. But after seeing that sculptor sketch, my eyes got swapped again. Sometimes now, I swear I can see sound, the dark green howling wind, the crimson crush of rain – all these sound-colors swirling around my room while I lie on my bed thinking about Brian. His name, when I say it aloud: azul.

In other news, I've grown over three inches since the summer. If anyone still messed with me, I could kick them off the planet. No problem. And my voice has dropped so low most humans can't register it. I hardly use it, except occasionally with Heather. She and me, we're sort of getting along again now that she likes some other boy. A couple times, I even went running with her and her runner friends. It was okay. No one cares if you don't talk much when you're running.

I've turned into a very quiet King Kong.

Today, a very worried, very quiet King Kong. I'm trudging up the hill from school in torrential rain with one thing on my mind: What am I going to do when Brian comes back for Christmas break and he's with Jude?

(Self-portrait: *Drinking the Dark out of My Own Cupped Hands*)

When I get home, I see no one's here, as usual. Jude's hardly ever home for very long these days – she's taken to surfing in the rain after school with the diehard surftards – and when she is home she's on the computer chatting with Brian, aka Spaceboy. I saw a couple more of their exchanges. In one he talked about the movie – the one we were watching when he grabbed my hand under the armrest! I almost threw up on the spot.

Sometimes at night, I sit on the other side of the wall wanting to pull off my ears so I don't hear the ding of yet another message from him over the hum of her stupid sewing machine.

(Portrait: *Sister in the Guillotine*)

I drip through the house, a raincloud, dutifully kicking over a bucket by Jude's bedroom so the dirty water soaks into her fluffy white carpet and hopefully mildews it, then enter my room, where I'm surprised to find Dad sitting on my bed.

I don't cringe or anything. For some reason, he doesn't bug me so much lately. It's like he drank a potion, or maybe I did. Or maybe it's because I'm taller. Or maybe it's because we're both all messed up. I don't think he can find Mom either.

"Storm catch you?" he asks. "I've never seen anything like this rain. Time for you to build that ark, eh?"

This is a popular joke at school too. I don't mind. I love Bible Noah. He was nearly 950 years old when he died. He got to leave with the animals. He started the whole world over: blank canvas and endless tubes of paint. Freaking the coolest.

"Totally got me," I say, grabbing a towel off my desk chair. I start drying my head, waiting for the inevitable comment about the length of my hair, but it doesn't come.

What comes is this: "You're going to be bigger than me."

"You think?" The idea's an instant mood-lifter. I'm going to take up more space in a room than my father.

(Portrait, Self-portrait: *Boy Hops from Continent to Continent with Dad on Shoulders*)

He nods, raises both eyebrows. "At the rate you're going lately, sure seems like it." He surveys the room as if taking an inventory, museum print to museum print – they pretty much cover every inch of wall and ceiling – then he looks back at me and slaps his hands on his thighs. "So, I thought we could get some dinner. Have some father–son time."

He must register the horror on my face. "No" – he makes fingers quotes – "*talks*. Promise. Just some grub. I need some mano a mano."

"With me?" I ask.

"Who else?" He smiles and there's absolutely no asshat anywhere in his face. "You're my son."

He gets up and walks to the door. I'm reeling from the way he said: *You're my son.* It makes me feel like his son.

"I'm going to wear a jacket," he says, meaning a suit jacket, I guess. "Want to?"

"If you want me to," I say, bewildered.

Who knew the first date of my life would be with my father?

Only I realize as I put on my one jacket – I last wore it at Grandma Sweetwine's funeral – that the sleeves come closer to my elbows than my wrists. Holy Jesus, I really am King Kong! I walk to Mom and Dad's bedroom with the evidence of my gigantism still on my back.

"Ah," Dad says, grinning. He opens his closet and pulls out a dark blue blazer. "This should do it, just a little snug on me." He taps his non-existent belly.

I take off my jacket and slip his on. It fits perfectly. I can't stop smiling.

"Told you," he says. "Wouldn't even think of wrestling you now, tough guy."

Tough guy.

On my way out the door, I ask, "Where's Mom?"

"Got me."

Dad and I go to a restaurant on the water and sit by the window. The rain makes rivulets, distorting the view. My fingers twitch to draw it. We eat steaks. He orders a scotch, then another, and lets me have sips. We both get dessert. He doesn't talk about sports or bad movies or loading the dishwasher properly or weird jazz. He talks about me. The whole time. He tells me that Mom showed him some of my sketchpads, he hoped that was all right, and he was blown away. He tells me he's so excited I'm applying to CSA and that they'd be idiots not to take me. He said he can't believe his one and only son is so talented and that he can't wait to see my final portfolio. He said he's so proud of me.

I'm not lying about any of this.

"Your mother thinks you're both shoo-ins."

I nod, wondering if I heard wrong. Last I knew, Jude wasn't applying. I must've heard wrong. What would she even submit?

"You're really lucky," he says. "Your mom has so much passion for art. It's contagious, isn't it?" He smiles, but I can see his inside face and it isn't smiling at all. "Ready to switch?"

I reluctantly lift my chocolate decadence to trade for his tiramisu.

"Nah, forget it," he says. "Let's get two more. How often do we do this?"

Over our second dessert, I gear up to say that the parasites and bacteria and viruses he studies are as cool as the art Mom studies, but then decide it'll sound lame and phony, so I motor through the cake instead. I start to imagine people around us thinking to themselves, "Look at that father and son having dinner together, isn't that nice?" It blows me up with pride. Dad and me. Buddies now. Chums. *Bros*. Oh, I'm feeling supernaturally good for once – it's been so long – so good I start blabbing like I haven't since Brian left. I tell Dad about these basilisk lizards I just found out about that can move so fast across the surface of water, they can go sixty-five feet without sinking. So Jesus isn't the only one after all.

He tells me how the peregrine falcon hits speeds of 200 miles per hour in a dive. I raise my eyebrows in a wow to be polite, but hello, who doesn't know that?

I tell him how giraffes eat up to seventy-five pounds of food a day, sleep for only thirty minutes a day, are not only the tallest animal on earth, but have the longest tail of any land mammal and tongues that are twenty inches long.

He tells me about these tiny microscopic water bears they're thinking about sending into space because they can survive temperatures ranging from minus-328 Fahrenheit to 303 Fahrenheit, can cope with 1,000 times the radiation it would take to kill a human, and can be revived after being dried out for ten years.

For a moment, I want to kick the table over because I can't tell Brian about the water bears in space, but then I climb right out of it by making Dad guess what the most deadly animal is to humans and totally stumping him after he goes for all the usual suspects: hippos, lions, crocs, etc. It's the malaria-carrying mosquito.

We go back and forth exchanging facts about animals until the bill comes. It's the most fun we've ever had together.

When he's paying the check, I blurt out, "I didn't know you like animal shows!"

"What do you mean? Why do you think *you* like them? That's all you and I did together when you were little. Don't you remember?"

I. Don't. Remember.

I remember, *It's a sink-or-swim world, Noah.* I remember, *Act tough and you are tough.* I remember every heart-stomping look of disappointment, of embarrassment, of bewilderment from him. I remember: *If your twin sister wasn't my spitting image I'd swear you came about from parthenogenesis.* I remember the 49ers, the Miami Heat, the Giants, the World Cup. I do not remember *Animal Planet.*

When he pulls into the garage, I see Mom's car's still not there. He sighs. I sigh too. Like I'm catching him now.

"I had this dream last night," he says, turning off the engine. He makes no move to get out of the car. I settle into my seat. We are so totally buddies now! "Your mother was walking through the house, and as she did, everything fell off the shelves and from the walls: books, pictures, knick-knacks, everything. All I could do was follow her around the house trying to put everything back in its place."

"Did you?" I ask. He looks at me, confused. I clarify, "Did you get everything back where it belonged?"

"Don't know," he says, shrugging. "Woke up." He glides a finger around the steering wheel. "Sometimes you think you know things, know things very deeply, only to realize you don't know a damn thing."

"I totally get what you mean, Dad," I say, thinking about what happened with Brian.

"You do? Already?"

I nod.

"Guess we have lots of catching up to do."

I feel a springing in my chest. Could Dad and I be close? Like a real father and son? Like it could've been all along if I'd flown off his shoulder that day like Jude did? If I'd swum instead of sunk?

"Where the hell is Ralph? Where the hell is Ralph?" we hear and both laugh a little. Then he surprises me by saying, "You think we'll ever find out where the hell Ralph is, kid?"

"I hope so," I say.

"Me too." A comfortable silence follows and I'm marveling at how supernaturally cool Dad's being when he says, "So, you still seeing that Heather?" He nudges me. "Cute girl." He gives my shoulder a squeeze of approval.

This sucks.

"Kind of," I say, then add with more conviction because I have no choice, "Yeah, she's my girlfriend."

He gives me that dumb you-sly-dog expression. "We're going to have to have a little talk, me and you, aren't we, son? Fourteen years old." He cuffs me on the head just like that sculptor did his students. And that gesture, plus the word *son* again, the way he keeps saying it: Yeah, I had no choice about Heather.

Once inside, I go to my room, noting that Jude knocked over a water bucket on my floor in retaliation. Whatever. I throw a towel down on the puddle and as I do, glance at the clock on my desk, which has the date as well as the time.

Oh.

Later, I find Dad sunk into the couch in front of a college football game. I went through all my sketchpads and couldn't find one drawing of him with his head still on, so I took out my best pastels and did a new one of the two of us on the back of a blue wildebeest. On the bottom, I wrote, *Happy Birthday*.

He looks right in my eyes. "Thanks." The word comes out all scrunched up like it was hard to get out. No one remembered. Not even Mom. What's her problem? How could she not remember Dad's birthday? Maybe she's not a blow-in after all.

"She forgot the turkey on Thanksgiving too," I say, trying to make him feel better, only realizing after I say it how lame it is to compare him to a turkey.

He laughs though, which is something. "Is that a blue wildebeest?" he asks, pointing to the drawing.

When we're done with the world's longest conversation on the blue wildebeest, he pats the couch and I sit down next to him. He puts his hand on my shoulder, leaves it there like it fits, and we watch the rest of the game together. It's pretty boring, but the athletes, well, you know.

The lie I told him about Heather is a stone in my belly.

I ignore it.

＊ ＊ ＊

A week after Dad's forgotten birthday, with the rain beating the crap out of the house, Mom and Dad seat Jude and me in the frozen part of the living room no one ever sits in to inform us that Dad's temporarily moving down to the Lost Cove Hotel.

They, well actually, Mom tells us he'll be renting a studio apartment by the week until they can work out some issues they're having.

Even though we haven't spoken in forever, I can feel Jude's heart clenching and unclenching inside my chest with mine.

"What issues?" she asks, but after that the rain gets so loud I can't hear what anyone's saying anymore. I'm convinced the storm's going to bust down the walls. Then it does and I'm remembering Dad's dream because it's happening. I watch as the wind sweeps everything off the shelves: knick-knacks, books, a vase of purple flowers. No one else notices. I grip the armrests of the chair tight.

(Family Portrait: *Assume the Crash Position*)

I can hear Mom's voice again. It's calm, too calm, yellow fluttering birds that don't belong in this life-bucking tempest. "We still love each other very much," she says. "We just both need some space right now." She looks at Dad. "Benjamin?"

At the mention of Dad's name, all the paintings, mirrors, family photographs come crashing down from the walls. Again, only I notice. I glance at Jude. Tears suspend in her eyelashes. Dad seems like he's going to say something, but when he opens his mouth, no words come out. He drops his head into his hands, his teeny-tiny hands, like raccoon paws — when did that happen? They're too little to cover up what's happening on his face, how his features have all squeezed shut. My stomach churns and churns. I hear pots and pans in the kitchen plummeting out of the cupboards now. I close my eyes for a second, see the roof whip off the house, reel across the sky.

Jude explodes, "I'm going with Dad."

"Me too," I say, shocking myself.

Dad lifts his head. Pain's leaking out of every part of his face. "You'll stay here with your mother, kids. It's temporary." His voice is so flimsy and I notice for the first time how thin his hair's getting as he stands and leaves the room.

Jude gets up and walks over to Mom, looking down on her like she's a beady little beetle. "How could you?" she says out of clenched teeth and makes her own exit, her hair twisting and winding angrily across the floor behind her. I hear her calling for Dad.

"Are you leaving us?" I say/think, rising to my feet. Because even though Dad's leaving now, Mom's already left. She's been AWOL for months. I know this and I can't look at her.

"Never," she says, grabbing my shoulders. I'm surprised by the strength of her grip. "You hear me, Noah? I will never leave you and your sister. This is between your father and me. It has nothing to do with you kids."

I melt into her arms like the traitor that I am.

She strokes my hair. It feels so good. "My boy. My tender boy. My dream boy. Everything's going to be okay." She repeats how okay everything's going to be again and again like a chant, but I can tell she doesn't believe it. Neither do I.

Later that evening, Jude and I are shoulder to shoulder at the window. Dad's walking to his car carrying a suitcase. The rain's wailing down on him, stooping him more and more with every step.

"I don't think there's anything in it," I say, watching him toss the piece of luggage into the trunk like it's filled with feathers.

"There is," she says. "I checked. One thing. A drawing of you and him on some weird animal. Nothing else. Not even a toothbrush."

These are the first words we've exchanged in months. I can't believe the only thing Dad took with him is me.

That night, I'm in bed unable to sleep, wondering if I'm staring at the darkness or it's staring at me, when Jude opens the door, crosses the room, and gets in bed next to me. I flip the pillow so it won't be wet. We're lying on our backs.

"I wished for it," I whisper, telling her what's been tearing me up for hours. "Three times. Three different birthdays. I wished he would leave."

She turns on her side, touches my arm, whispers back, "I once wished for Mom to die."

"Take it back," I say, turning onto my side. I can feel her breathing on my face. "I didn't take it back in time."

"How?"

"I don't know."

"Grandma would know how," she says.

"That's a load of help," I say, and then out of nowhere and at the exact same moment, we both burst out laughing and can't stop and it's the gasping snorting kind and we have to put the pillow over our faces so Mom doesn't hear and decide we think Dad being kicked out of the family is the funniest thing that's ever happened to us.

When we settle back into our selves, everything feels different, like if I turned on the light we'd be bears.

The next thing I know, there's a shuffling of motion and Jude's sitting on me. I'm so surprised I do nothing. She takes a deep breath. "Okay, now that I have your undivided attention. Are you ready?" She bounces a few times.

"Get off me," I say, but she's talking over me.

"Nothing happened. You hear me? I've tried to tell you so many times but you wouldn't listen." She spells it out. "N–O–T–H–I–N–G."

She goes on, "Brian is *your* friend, I get it. In the closet, he told me about something called a globular cluster, I think. He talked about how amazing your drawings are, for Pete's sake! It's true I was so mad at you because of Mom and because you totally stole *all* my friends too and because you threw away that note – I know you did that and it really sucked, Noah, because that was like the only sand sculpture I ever made that I thought was maybe good enough for Mom to see. So I might've had Brian's name on a piece of paper in my hand at that party but NOTHING HAPPENED, okay? I did not steal your—" She pauses. "Your best friend, okay?"

"Okay," I say. "Now get off me." It comes out gruffer than I intend on account of my spanking new voice. She doesn't move. I can't let on what this information is doing to me. My mind is speeding around, rearranging that night, the last few months, rearranging everything. All the times she tried to talk to me, how I walked away, slammed the door, blasted the TV, unable to look at her, forget listen to her, how I even ripped up a card she gave me without reading it, until she gave up trying. *Nothing happened.* They're not in love. Brian isn't going to come back in a few weeks and escape with her into her bedroom like I kept imagining. They're not going to be watching movies on the couch when I come home or looking for meteorites in the woods. Nothing happened. Nothing happened!

(Self-portrait: *Boy Hitches Ride on Passing Comet*)

But wait. "Who's Spaceboy then?" I was so sure it was Brian. I mean: outer space, hello?

"Huh?"

"Spaceboy, on the computer."

"Spy much? Jeez." She sighs. "That's Michael, you know, Zephyr. 'Spaceboy' is the name of some song he's into."

Oh.

OH!

And I guess other people – probably millions of them – besides Brian and me have seen that alien movie. Or might joke with her about teleporting. Or might use the name Spaceboy!

Now I'm remembering the Ouija Board. "Zephyr's M.? You like Zephyr?"

"Maybe," she says coyly. "I don't know yet."

This is news but *Nothing Happened* steamrolls right over it. I forget she's in the room, not to mention sitting on me, until she says, "So are you and Brian like in love with each other or something?"

"What? No!" The words fly out of my mouth. "God, Jude. Can't I have a friend? I totally hooked up with Heather, if you didn't notice." I don't know why I say all this. I push her off me. I feel the stone in my stomach get bigger.

"Okay, fine. It's just—"

"What?" Did Zephyr tell her what happened that day in the woods?

"Nothing."

She gets back in bed and we shoulder up again into the smush. She says quietly, "So you can stop hating me now."

"I never hated you," I say, which is a total lie. "I'm really—"

"Me too. *So* sorry." She holds my hand.

We start to breathe together in the dark.

"Jude, I've—"

"So much," she finishes.

I laugh. I'd forgotten this.

"I know, me too," she says, giggling.

My next sentence, however, she will not be able to mind-read.

I tell her, "I've probably seen all of your sand sculptures." I feel a stab of guilt. I wish I didn't destroy the photographs now. I could've shown them to her. She could've gotten into CSA with them. She could've had them forever. She could've shown Mom. This will have to do. "They're freaking amazing."

"Noah?" I've caught her completely off guard. "Really?"

I know she's smiling because my face is too. I want to tell her how scared I am that she's better than me. Instead, I say, "I can't stand the ocean washing them away."

"But that's the best part."

I listen to the waves pounding away at the shore outside, and think about all those incredible sand women being swept off before anyone can see them and I'm wondering how in the world that could possibly be the best part, tumbling that around and around in my head, when she says very quietly, "Thank you."

And everything in me goes quiet and peaceful and right.

We breathe and drift. I'm imagining us swimming through the night sky to the bright moon and hoping I remember the image in the morning so I can make it and give it to her. Before I'm all the way gone, I hear her say, "I still love you the most," and I say, "Me too," but in the morning I'm not sure if we said it or if I just thought it or dreamt it.

Not that it matters.

* * *

It's the beginning of winter break, otherwise known as The Return of Brian, and the off-the-hook smell wafting out of the kitchen has brain-commanded me out of my chair and down the hallway. "Is that you?" Jude yells from her room. "C'mere, please."

I walk into her room, where she's reading Grandma's bible in bed. She's been trying to find some hogwash in it that will bring Dad back.

She hands me a scarf. "Here," she says. "Tie me to the bedpost."

"What?"

"It's the only solution. I need a little reminder not to be weak and go in the kitchen. I'm not giving Mom the satisfaction of eating one bite. How come she decides to become Julia Child now? You shouldn't eat anything she makes either. I know you got into that chicken pot pie after we came home from Dad's last night. I saw." She gives me a hard look. "Promise not one morsel?" I nod, but there's not a chance in hell I'm not having whatever it is that's filling the house with this supernaturally awesome smell. "I mean it, Noah."

"Okay," I say.

"Only one wrist so I can turn the pages." As I tie her wrist to the bedpost, she goes on. "It smells like pie, apple or pear, or maybe turnovers, or a crumble. God, I love crumbles. Of all unfairness. Who knew she even knew how to bake?" She turns the page of Grandma's bible. "Be strong," she says after me as I head for the door.

I salute her. "Aye, Captain."

I've become a double agent. This is how it's been since Dad left: After eating takeout with Jude and Dad in his dead-body blue hotel studio, I, on arriving home, wait for the moment Jude locks herself in her room to chat with Spaceboy, who is Zephyr! Not Brian! and then head for the kitchen to feast with Mom. But whether I'm sitting with Dad watching *Animal Planet*, breathing gray air, pretending not to notice he's all folded up like a chair, or with Mr. Grady in the art room making the final touches on my CSA portfolio paintings, or learning salsa dancing in the kitchen with Mom while soufflés rise, or playing How Would You Rather Die? with Jude while she sews, I'm really only doing one thing. I'm a human hourglass: Waiting, waiting, waiting for Brian Connelly to come home.

Any day, hour, minute, second now.

Jude's right. On the kitchen counter this morning is indeed an apple pie with a golden roof over it *and* a plate of turnovers.

Mom's at the counter kneading dough, her face spotted in flour.

"Oh good," she says. "Scratch my nose, will you? I've been going crazy."

I walk over to her and scratch her nose. "Harder," she says. "That's it. Thanks."

"It's weird to scratch someone else's nose," I tell her.

"Just wait until you're a parent."

"It's much squishier than it looks," I say. She smiles at me and it sends a warm summer breeze around the room.

"You're happy," I say, but only meant to think it. My new trombone of a voice makes it sound like an accusation, which I guess it is. Not only is she happier since Dad's been gone, she's actually in a room when she's in a room. She's returned from the Milky Way. She even got drenched along with Jude and me in a downpour the other day.

She stops kneading.

"How come you didn't cook like this when Dad lived here?" I ask, instead of what I want to ask: How come you don't miss him? How come he had to leave for you to become normal again?

She sighs. "I don't know." She traces her finger through a mound of flour, starts spelling her name. Her face is closing up.

"It smells incredible," I say, wanting her happiness back, needing it and hating it at the same time.

She smiles faintly. "Have a piece of pie *and* a turnover. I won't tell your sister."

I nod, grab a knife and cut an enormous slice, a quarter of the pan practically, and put it on a dinner plate. Then I take a turnover. Since I've become King Kong, I can't get enough food in me ever. I'm heading over to the table with my full plate, the smell making me want to walk on my hands, when Jude's bad mood ambles in.

The eye-roll is a 10.5 on the Richter. The Big One. California has slipped into the ocean. She puts her hands on her hips, exasperated. "What's your problem, Noah?"

"How'd you get free anyway," I say, my mouth full of turnover.

"Free?" Mom asks.

"I tied her up so she wouldn't be tempted to come in here and eat."

Mom laughs. "Jude, I know you're furious with me. It doesn't mean you can't have a turnover for breakfast."

"Never!" She walks across the room and takes a box of Cheerios from a cabinet and pours some into a sad old bowl.

"I think I used up all the milk," Mom says.

"Of course you did!" Jude cries, sounding a lot like a braying donkey. She sits down next to me, crunching and martyring her way through the bowl of dry cereal, eyeing my plate the whole time. When Mom's back is turned, I slide it over to her with the fork and she shovels pastry in until her mouth is stuffed, then slides it back over.

It's at this moment that Brian Connelly comes through the door.

"I knocked," he says nervously. He's older, taller, hatless, and he's cut his hair – the white bonfire is gone.

I involuntarily jump up, then sit down, then jump up again, because this is what normal people do when someone walks into a room, right? Jude kicks me under the table, gives me a look that says: *Stop being a freak,* then tries to smile at Brian, but her mouth is too stuffed with pie, so she makes a weird disfigured chipmunk face at him. I certainly can't talk because I'm too busy jumping up and down.

Fortunately, there's Mom.

"Well, hello." She wipes her hands on her apron, walks over, and shakes his hand. "Welcome back."

"Thank you," he replies. "Good to be back." He takes a deep breath. "We can smell what you're baking all the way down at our house. We were salivating over our cornflakes."

"Please," Mom says. "Help yourself. I'm going through a little cooking phase. And certainly bring something back for your mother."

Brian looks at the counter with longing. "Maybe later." His eyes travel to me. He licks his bottom lip and the gesture, so familiar, makes my heart lurch.

Somewhere in between up and down, I've frozen: humpbacked, arms swinging monkey-like. I register how crazy I look in the puzzled expression on his face. I choose up. Whew. Up was the right move! I'm standing. I'm a person on legs, which are designed for this purpose. And he's five feet away, now four, three, two—

He's in front of me.

Brian Connelly is standing in front of me.

What's left of his hair is a deep buttery yellow. His eyes, his eyes, his amazing squinting eyes! are going to make me lose consciousness. There's nothing hiding them anymore. I'm surprised all the passengers didn't follow him off the plane and aren't waiting outside the door. I want to draw him. *Now.* I want to do everything. *Now.* (Portrait, Self-portrait: *Two Boys Racing into Brightness*)

I try to calm myself by counting his freckles to see if there are any that are new.

"Stare much?" he says quietly so only I hear. Practically the first words he ever said to me, all those months ago. His lips curl into the half smile. I catch his tongue poised on the precipice between his front teeth.

"You look different," I say, wishing it didn't come out so dreamily.

"Me? Dude, you're huge. I think you're bigger than me. How'd that happen?"

I glance down. "Yeah, super far from the toes now." This is something I've been thinking a lot about. My toes are pretty much in another time zone.

He cracks up and then I do, and the sound of our laughter getting all mixed up together is like a time machine and we're instantly back to last summer, the days in the woods, the nights on his roof. We haven't talked in five months and we both look like different people, but it's the same, same, same. I notice Mom watching us curiously, intently, not totally comprehending what she's seeing, like we're some foreign movie with no subtitles.

Brian turns to Jude, who's finally managed to get her food down. "Hey," he says.

She waves, then goes back to her dry Cheerios. It's true. There's nothing between them. It was probably like being in an elevator with a stranger in that closet. I get a pang of guilt over what *I* did in that closet.

"Where the hell is Ralph? Where the hell is Ralph?"

"Oh my God," Brian exclaims. "I forgot! I can't believe I've gone months without thinking about the whereabouts of Ralph!"

"Quite an existential dilemma that parrot has put us all in," Mom says, smiling at him.

He returns her smile, then meets my eyes. "Ready?" he says, like we have some plan.

I notice he doesn't have his meteorite bag and see out the window it's probably going to pour any minute, but we need to get out of here. Immediately. "We're going to search for meteorites," I say, like that's what most people do on winter mornings. I never really told either of them too much about last summer, which is reflected in both of their flummoxed faces. But who freaking cares?

Not us.

In a flash, we're through the door, across the street and into the woods, running for no reason and laughing for no reason and totally out of breath and out of our minds when Brian catches me by my shirt, whips me around, and with one strong hand flat against my chest, he pushes me against a tree and kisses me so hard I go blind.

* * *

The blindness lasts just a second, then the colors start flooding into me: not through my eyes but right through my skin, replacing blood and bone, muscle and sinew, until I am

redorangebluegreenpurpleyellowredorangebluegreenpurple
yellow. Brian pulls away and looks at me. "Fuck," he says. "I've
wanted to do that for so long." His breath's on my face. "So long.
You're just…" He doesn't finish, instead he brushes my cheek
with the back of his hand. The gesture is startling, atom-splitting,
because it's so unexpected, so *tender*. As is the look in his eyes. It
makes my chest ache with joy, horses-plunging-into-rivers joy.

"God," I whisper. "It's happening."

"Yeah, it is."

I think the heart of every living thing on earth is beating
in my body.

I run my hands through his hair, finally, finally, then bring
his head to mine and kiss him so hard our teeth collide, planets
collide, kissing him now for each and every time we didn't all
summer long. I know absolutely everything about how to kiss
him too, how to make his whole body tremble just from biting his lip, how to make him moan right inside my mouth by
whispering his name, how to make his head fall back, his spine
arch, how to make him groan through his teeth. It's like I've
taken every class there is on the subject. And even as I'm kissing
him and kissing him and kissing him, I wish I were kissing him,
wanting more, more, more, more, like I can't get enough, never
will be able to get enough.

"We're them," I think/say, stopping for a moment to catch
my breath, my life, our mouths inches apart, our foreheads
pressed together now.

"Who?" His voice is a rasp. It creates an immediate riot in
my blood, so I can't tell him about the guys in the alcove at the

party. Instead, I place my hands under his shirt, because I can now, I can do everything I've thought and thought and thought about. I touch the river of his stomach, his chest and shoulders. He whispers the word *yeah* under his breath, which makes me shudder, which makes him shudder, and then his hands travel under my shirt and the demanding hungry feel of them on my skin burns me to the ground.

Love, I think and think and think and think and don't say. Don't say it.

Don't say it. Don't tell him you love him.

But I do. I love him more than anything.

I close my eyes and drown in color, open them and drown in light because billions and billions of buckets of light are being emptied on our heads from above.

This is *it*. This is freaking *everything*. This is the painting painting itself.

And that's what I'm thinking when the asteroid comes crashing into us.

"No one can know," he says. "Ever."

I step back, look at him. In an instant, he's turned into a siren. The whole forest goes mum. It doesn't want anything to do with what he just said either.

He says more calmly, "It'd be the end. Of everything. My athletic scholarship at Forrester. I'm the assistant captain of the varsity team as a sophomore and—"

I want him to be quiet. I want him back with me. I want his face to look the way it did a minute ago when I touched his stomach, his chest, when he brushed my cheek with his hand. I lift

up his shirt, slip it over his talking head, then take off my own, and
step into him so we're all lined up, legs to legs, groin to groin, bare
chest to bare chest. His breath hitches. We fit perfectly. I kiss him
slowly and deeply until the only word he can manage is my name.

He says it again.

And again.

Until we're two lit candles melting into one.

"No one's gonna find out. Don't worry," I whisper, not
caring if everyone in the whole world knows, not caring about
anything except more now him and me under the open sky as
thunder cracks and the rain comes down.

* * *

I'm propped on my bed drawing Brian, who's a few feet away
at my desk watching a meteor shower on some astronomy site
he's addicted to. In the drawing, the stars and planets are storming out of the computer screen and into the room. This is the
first time we've seen each other since the woods except for
the kabillion times I've seen him in my mind over the last few
days, which included Christmas. What happened between us has
colonized every last brain cell. I can barely tie my shoelaces. I
forgot how to chew this morning.

I thought maybe he'd hide from me for the rest of our
lives, but a few minutes after I heard his mom's car pull into
the garage today, signaling their return from some Buddhist
center up north, he was at my window. I've listened to an
endless state of the intergalactic union and now we're fighting about whose Christmas was worse. He's acting like what
happened between us didn't happen, so I am too. Well, trying

to. My heart's bigger than a blue whale's, which needs its own parking spot. Not to mention my eight feet of concrete, which has kept me perpetually in the shower. I am so clean. If there's a drought, blame me.

In fact, I just happen to be thinking about the shower, him and me in it, thinking about hot water sliding down our naked bodies, thinking about pressing him against the wall, about gliding my hands all over him, thinking about the sounds he'd make, how he'd throw his head back and say *yeah* like he did in the woods, thinking all this, as I tell him in an even, controlled voice how Jude and I spent Christmas in Dad's hotel room eating takeout Chinese food and breathing gray air. It's amazing how many things you can do at once. It's amazing how what goes on in the head stays in the head.

(Self-portrait: *Do Not Disturb*)

"Give it up," he says. "No way you can beat this. I had to go to an all-day sit with my mom and then sleep on the floor on a mat and eat gross gruel for Christmas dinner. I got a prayer from the monks as my only present. A prayer for peace! I repeat: an all-day sit, *me!* I couldn't say anything. Or do anything. For eight hours. And then gruel and a prayer!" He starts laughing and I catch it immediately. "And I had to wear a robe. A fricken dress." He turns around, lit up like a lantern. "And what's worse is the whole time, I couldn't stop thinking about..."

I see him tremble. Oh God.

"It was *so* painful, dude. Luckily we had these weird pillow things on our laps so no one knew. Sucked." He's staring at my mouth. "And didn't suck too." He turns back to the stars.

I see him shudder again.

My hand goes limp and I drop my pencil. He can't stop thinking about it either.

He swivels around. "So, who were the 'them' you mentioned, anyway?"

It takes me a second but then I understand. "I saw these guys making out at that party."

His brow furrows. "The party where you hooked up with Heather?"

For months, I've been so pissed at him and Jude about something that didn't happen, it never occurred to me that he could be mad at me about what actually did. Is he still? Is that why he never called or emailed? I want to tell him what really happened. I want to say sorry. Because I am. Instead, I just say, "Yeah, that party. They were…"

"What?"

"I don't know, amazing or something…"

"Why?" His talking is turning into breathing. There's no answer. Really, they were amazing only because they were guys kissing.

I tell him, "I decided I'd give up all my fingers, if…"

"If what?" he presses.

I realize I can't possibly say it aloud but don't have to because he does. "If it could've been us, right? I saw them too."

It's a thousand degrees inside me.

"It'd be hard to draw with no fingers," he says.

"I'd manage."

I close my eyes, unable to contain the feeling inside me and when I open them a second later, it's like he's gotten hitched on a hook and I'm the hook. I follow his gaze to my bare stomach – my shirt's ridden up – then lower to where there's no hiding how I'm feeling. I think he's Tasering me or something, because I can't move.

He swallows, swivels back around to face the computer, and puts a hand on the mouse but doesn't click the screensaver away. I watch his other hand travel down.

Still looking at the screen, he asks, "Want to?" and I'm a flood in a paper cup.

"Totally," I say, knowing without a doubt what he means, and then our hands are on our belts, unbuckling. From across the room, I watch his back, unable to see much, but then his neck arches, and I can see his face, his eyes all swimming and wild, locking with mine, and it's like we're kissing again, but from across the room this time, kissing even more intensely than in the woods, where our pants stayed on. I didn't know you could kiss with your eyes. I didn't know anything. And then the colors are forcing down the walls of the room, the walls of me—

Then, the impossible.

My mother as in *my mother* bursts in, waving a magazine. I thought I'd locked the door. I could've sworn I locked it!

"This is the best essay I've ever read on Picasso, you're going—" Her confused gaze darts from me to Brian. His hands, my hands, fumbling, shoving, zipping.

"Oh," she says. "Oh. Oh."

Then the door's closed and she's gone, like she was never there, like she hadn't seen a thing.

* * *

She doesn't pretend it didn't happen.

An hour after Brian's frantic dive-bomb out the window, there's a knock at my bedroom door. I say nothing, just flip on my desk light so she doesn't find me sitting in the dark, where I've been since he left. I grab a pencil, start to draw, but my hand won't stop shaking, so I can't make a decent line.

"Noah, I'm coming in."

All the blood in my body mad-dashes to my face as the door slowly opens. I want to die.

"I'd like to talk to you, honey," she says in the same voice she uses when talking to Crazy Charlie, the town loon.

Whatever. Whatever. *Whatever,* I chant in my head, drilling the pencil into the pad. I'm hunched over the paper now, hugging it practically, so I don't have to see her. Whole forests are burning out of control inside me. How come she doesn't know to leave me alone for the next fifty years after what just happened?

Her hand touches my shoulder as she passes. I cringe.

From the bed where she's sat down, she says, "Love's so complicated, Noah, isn't it?"

I go rigid. Why did she say that? Why is she using the word *love*?

I throw the pencil down.

"It's okay, what you're feeling. It's *natural.*"

A giant *No* slams through me. How does she know what I'm feeling? How does she know anything about anything? She doesn't. She can't. She can't just barge into my most secret world and then try to show me around it. Get out, I want to holler at

her. Get out of my room. Get out of my life. Get out of my paintings. Get out of everything! Blow back to your realm already and
leave me alone. How can you take this experience away from me
before I've even gotten to experience it? I want to say all these
things but can't make any words. I can hardly breathe.

Brian couldn't either. He was hyperventilating after she left
the room. His hands covering his face, his body all contorted,
repeating, "Oh God! Oh God! Oh God!" I was wishing he'd
say something besides "Oh God!" but when he started talking,
I changed my mind.

I'd never seen anyone act like that. He was sweating and
pacing and his hands were in his hair like he was going to rip it
all out. I thought he was going to take apart the walls, or me. I
really thought he might kill me.

"So at my old school," he said. "There was this kid on the
baseball team. People thought, I don't know. They saw that he
went to some website or something." His inside face had become his outside face and it was all knotted up. "They made it
impossible for him to play. Every day, they found another way
to mess with him. Then one Friday after school, they locked
him in the storage closet." He winced, as if remembering and
I knew. I knew then. "All night long and the whole next day.
A tiny, dark, disgusting airless space. His parents thought he was
at the away game and someone told the coaches he was sick, so
no one even looked for him. No one knew he was trapped in
there." His chest was heaving and I was remembering how he
told me he didn't used to have claustrophobia and now he did.
"He was really good too, probably the best player on the team

or could have been. And he didn't even *do* anything. The guy just went to these sites and someone saw. Do you get it? Do you get what it would mean for me? The assistant captain? I want to be captain next year so maybe I can graduate early. No scholarship. No *nothing*. These guys aren't" – he made finger quotes – "*evolved*. They're not from Northern California. They don't do all-day sits or draw pictures." The dagger went straight in. "It's brutal in a locker room."

"No one will find out," I said.

"You don't know that. You remember that idiot cousin of Fry's I nearly decapitated last summer, the one who looks like an ape? His little brother goes to my school. I thought I was hallucinating. He looks exactly like him." He licked his bottom lip. "Anyone could've seen us the other day, Noah. Anyone. Fry could've and then... I didn't even think about it I was so..." He shook his head. "I can't get forced off this team. Can't lose my athletic scholarship. We have no money. And this high school – the physics teacher's an astrophysicist... I just can't. I need to get a baseball scholarship for college. Have to."

He came over to where I was standing. His face was crazy red and his eyes were too intense and he seemed about twelve feet tall and I didn't know if he was going to kiss me or punch me. He took me by the T-shirt again except this time he balled a piece of it up in his fist and said, "It's done with us. It has to be. Okay?"

I nodded and something really big and bright in me crushed to nothing in an instant. I'm pretty sure it was my soul.

"And it's all your fault!" I spit out at my mother.

"What is, honey?" she says, alarmed.

"Everything! Don't you see? You've crushed Dad. You banished him like a leper. He loves you! How do you think he feels all alone in that dying room breathing gray air and eating cold stale pizza and watching shows about aardvarks while you cook feasts and wear circus clothes and hum all the time and have the sun follow you around in the pouring rain? How do you think that makes him feel?" I can see I've hurt her and don't care. She deserves it. "Who knows if he even has a soul left thanks to you?"

"What do you mean by that? I don't understand."

"Maybe you stomped it to nothing and now he's hollow and empty, a shell with no turtle inside."

Mom pauses. "Why would you say that? Do you feel that way sometimes?"

"I'm not talking about me. And you know what else? You're not special. You're just like everyone else. You don't float or walk through walls and you never will!"

"Noah?"

"I always thought that you blew in from somewhere so cool, but you're just regular. And you don't make anyone happy anymore like you used to. You make everyone miserable."

"Noah, are you done?"

"Mom." I say it like bugs live in the word. "I am."

"Listen to me." The sudden sternness of her voice jars me. "I didn't come in here to talk about me or about me and Dad. We can have those conversations, I promise, but not now."

If I don't look at her, she'll drop it, she'll disappear, and what she saw Brian and me doing will disappear with her. "You didn't see anything," I yell, completely out of control now. "Guys do that. They do. Whole baseball teams do it. Circle jerks, that's what it's called, you know?" I drop my head in my hands, filling them with tears.

She gets up, walks over to me, puts her hand under my chin, and lifts my face so I'm forced into the earnest hold of her eyes. "Listen to me. It takes a lot of courage to be true to yourself, true to your heart. You always have been very brave that way and I pray you always will be. It's your responsibility, Noah. Remember that."

* * *

The next morning, I wake at dawn in a stark raving panic. Because she can't tell Dad. She has to promise me that. After fourteen years, I have a father, I like it. No, I *love* it. He finally thinks I'm a fully functioning umbrella. I prowl through the dark house like a thief. The kitchen's empty. I tiptoe to Mom's bedroom door and sit down with my ear to it and wait for her to stir. It's possible she already told Dad, though it was late when she left my room last night. Could she ruin my life anymore? First she destroyed everything with Brian. Now she's going to do the same with Dad.

I'm falling back asleep, Brian's lips on mine, his hands on my chest, all over me, when the sound of Mom's voice jolts me. I shake off the phantom embrace. She must be on the phone. I cup both hands around my ear and place it against the door – does this actually work? It actually does. I can hear better. Her voice sounds strained like it gets when she talks to Dad now. "I need to see you," she says. "It can't wait. I've been up all night thinking. Something happened with Noah yesterday." She *is* going to tell him! I knew it. Dad must be talking now, because it's silent until she says, "Okay, not the studio, at The Wooden Bird. Yes, one hour's perfect." I don't think she's ever even been to his studio. She just leaves him at that hotel to rot.

I knock and then swing open the door after I hear her say come in. She's in her peach robe, cradling the phone to her chest. Mascara's smudged all around her eyes like she's been crying all night. Because of me? My stomach rolls over. Because she doesn't want a gay son? Because no one does, not even someone as open-minded as her. Her face looks old, like she's aged hundreds of years overnight. Look what I've done to her. Her disappointed skin is hanging all over her disappointed bones. So she just said what she did last night to make me feel better?

"Morning, sweetheart," she says, sounding fake. She tosses the phone on the bed and walks over to the window, opening the curtains. The sky has barely woken up yet. It's a gray, homely morning. I think about breaking my own fingers, I don't know why. One by one. In front of her.

"Where're you going?" I manage to get out.

"I have a doctor's appointment." What a liar! And she lies so easily too. Has she been lying to me my whole life? "How'd you know I was going out?"

Think of something, Noah. "I just assumed because you weren't up early baking."

This works. She smiles, walks over to her dressing table, and sits down in front of the mirror. The Kandinsky biography she's reading is facedown beside her silver brush. She starts rubbing cream around her eyes, then takes cotton and wipes off darkness.

(Portrait: *Mom Replacing Her Face with Another*)

When she's finished doing her makeup, she starts sweeping her hair up into a clip, then changes her mind, shakes it back out, picks up the brush. "I'm going to make a red velvet cake later..." I zone out. I just have to say it. I'm the expert blurter too. Why can't I get the words out?

"You look so upset, Noah." She's staring at me through the mirror.

(Portrait, Self-portrait: *Trapped in a Mirror with Mom*)

I'll tell the Mom in the mirror. It'll be easier. "I don't want you to mention to Dad what you saw. Not that you saw anything. Because there was nothing to see. Not that it means anything anyway..." Mayday, mayday.

She puts her brush down. "Okay."

"Okay?"

"Absolutely okay. It's your private business. If you want to tell your father what I didn't see, you will. If what I didn't see ever actually does mean something, then I encourage you to. He's not really the way he seems sometimes. You underestimate him. You always have."

"I underestimate him? Are you serious? He underestimates me."

"No he doesn't." She holds my eyes in the mirror. "He's just a little afraid of you, always has been."

"Afraid of me? Sure. Dad's afraid of me." What's she saying?

"He thinks you don't like him."

"He doesn't like *me*!"

Well, he didn't. Now he does for some reason and I want to keep it this way.

She shakes her head. "You two will figure it out. I know you will." Maybe we will, maybe we are, but not if she tells him. "You're very much alike. You both feel things very deeply, too deeply sometimes." What? "Jude and I have quite a bit of armor on us," she continues. "It takes a lot to break through it. Not you and Dad." This is news. I never thought I was anything like Dad. But what she's really saying is that we're both wusses. That's what Brian thinks too. I'm just someone who "draws pictures." And it burns in my chest that she thinks Jude's like her and I'm not. How come everything I think about our family keeps changing? How come the teams keep switching? Is this how all families are? And most importantly, how do I know she's not lying to me about not telling Dad? She just lied about the doctor's appointment. Why is she meeting him then? And hello? She said: *Something happened with Noah last night.*

She absolutely is going to tell him. That's why they're going to The Wooden Bird. I can't trust her anymore.

She walks over to her closet. "We can talk more about this later, but I really do have to get ready. My doctor's appointment's in less than an hour." Pinocchio! Pants on Fire!

As I turn to leave, she says, "Everything's going to be okay, Noah. Don't worry."

"You know what?" I say, bunching my fingers into fists. "I really wish you'd stop saying that, Mom."

Of course I'm going to follow her. When I hear the car back

out of the driveway, I make a run for it. On the trails, I can get to The Wooden Bird almost as fast as she can by car.

* * *

No one knows who made The Wooden Bird. The artist carved it out of a humongous redwood stump, wooden feather by wooden feather. It must've taken years, ten or twenty even. It's huge and each feather is unique. Now there's a trail to it from the road and a bench by it that overlooks the ocean, but when the artist carved it, there was none of that. He was like Jude, doing it because he liked to, not really caring if anyone ever saw it. Or maybe he did care and liked the idea of strangers stumbling on it and wondering.

I'm hidden in the brush, yards away from Mom, who's sitting on the bench staring out at the sea. The sun's broken a hole in the fog and light's reeling around in the trees. It's going to be hot, one of those weird warm winter days. Dad's not here yet. I close my eyes, find Brian; he's everywhere inside me now, always swimming up my body. How can he shut this off? Will he change his mind? I'm reaching into my pocket for the rock when I hear footsteps.

I open my eyes expecting to see Dad; instead there's a strange man strolling down the trail. He stops at the tree line and stares at my mother, who doesn't seem to sense his presence at all. I pick up a stick. Is he a psycho? Then he turns his head slightly and I recognize him – that face, its geographic scale. It's the artist from Day Street. Here! I drop my sword, relieved. He's probably making a sculpture of her in his head, like I do with paintings. Is he out walking, I'm wondering, when all of a sudden, the sky comes crashing down in shards because my mother has flown to her feet, dashed over to him, and fallen into his open arms. I feel myself ignite.

I shake my head. Oh, it's not Mom, of course, that's it. The barking maniac sculptor has a wife who looks like my mother.

But it *is* her in his arms. I know my own mother.

What. Is. Going. On?

What. The. Hell. Is. Going. On?

Things start coming together. Fast. Why she was in front of his studio that day, her kicking Dad out, her phone conversations (his phone conversation! *Hurry, my darling*), her happiness, her unhappiness, her spaciness, her cooking and baking and stopping at green lights, her salsa dancing, her bangles and circus clothes! Everything clicking madly into place. Them, there, so clearly *together*.

The howling in my head is so loud I can't believe they can't hear it.

She's having an affair. She's cheating on Dad. She's a two-timer. A toilet-licking asshat liar. Mom! How could this not have occurred to me? But it didn't occur to me exactly because she's Mom. My mother would never do anything like this. She brings donuts – the best donuts I ever tasted – for the toll collectors. She doesn't have affairs.

Does Dad even know?

Affair. I whisper it aloud to the trees, but they've all run away. I know it's my father she's betraying, but it feels like it's me too. And Jude. And every single day of our lives.

(Family Portrait: *And Then We All Blew Away*)

They're kissing now and I'm watching and can't stop watching. I've never seen her and Dad kiss like this. Parents aren't allowed to kiss like this! Now Mom's taken his hand and is leading him to the edge of the cliff. She looks *so* happy and it cuts into me. I have no idea who this lady is spinning around in this stranger's arms, spinning and spinning, like they're in some lame movie until they lose their footing and fall to the ground.

(Portrait: *Mother in Blinding Color*)

What did she say this morning? It takes a lot to break through her armor. This man has broken through her armor.

I pick up the stick. I need to defend my father. I need to fight this asshat artist. I should throw a meteorite at his head. I should shove him off the cliff. Because my poor artichoke of a father doesn't have a chance. And he knows it. I understand now that what is shrinking him, what is turning the air around him that awful gray, is defeat.

He's a broken umbrella. Has he always been one? We both are. Like father, like son.

Because I know it too. I don't have a chance either. *"It's done with us. It has to be. Okay?"*

No, it is not okay. Nothing is okay! They're kissing again. I think my eyes are going to fly from their sockets, my hands from my arms, my feet from my legs. I don't know what do. I don't know what to do. I need to do something.

So I run.

I run and run and run and run and run and when I reach one of the last bends before the trailhead onto our street, I see Brian walking with Courtney.

His meteorite bag is wrapped around his shoulder and their arms are crisscrossed behind them, his hand in the back pocket of her jeans and hers in the back pocket of his. Like they're together. There's a smudge of bright color on his lips, which confuses me for a second until I realize it's her lipstick. Because he kissed her.

He kissed her.

It starts as a tremor deep inside, growing quickly into a quaking, and then it's all erupting together, what happened at The Wooden Bird, what happened in my bedroom last night, what's happening right now, all the rage and confusion, the hurt and helplessness, the betrayal, it's a blowing volcano inside me and out of my mouth flies, "He's gay, Courtney! Brian Connelly is gay!"

The words ricochet around in the air. I instantly want them back.

Brian's face slides off and there's loathing underneath it. Courtney's mouth drops open. She believes me, I can see it. She steps away from him. "Are you, Brian? I thought—" She doesn't finish her sentence because she sees his expression.

This is what his face must've looked like when he was inside that storage closet all alone hour after hour. This is what a face looks like when all the dreams get sucked out of it.

And I did it to him this time. Me.

* * *

I can't stop seeing Brian's face hating me as I bolt across the street. I'd do anything to take my words back, to put them again in the safe silent vault inside me where they belong. Anything.

My stomach feels like I've eaten nails. How could I have done that after what he told me?

I'd do anything to not have seen what I saw at The Wooden Bird too.

Once in the house, I go straight to my room, open a sketchpad, and start drawing. First things first. I need to get Mom to stop this and I only know one way to do that. It takes a long time to get the picture right, but eventually I do.

When I finish, I leave the drawing on her bed, and then go look for Jude. I need Jude.

Fry tells me she went off with Zephyr, but I can't find them anywhere.

I can't find Brian either.

There's only Prophet, who as usual won't shut up about Ralph.

At the top of my lungs, I yell, "There is no Ralph, you stupid bird. Ralph does not exist!"

* * *

When I get back home, Mom's waiting for me in my room, the picture I made on her lap. It's of her and the sculptor kissing by The Wooden Bird in the foreground and Dad, Jude, and me as one blur making up the background.

Her mascara's making black tears. "You followed me," she says. "I really wish you hadn't, Noah. I'm so sorry. You shouldn't have seen that."

"You shouldn't have been *doing* that!"

She looks down. "I know, which is why—"

"I thought you were going to tell Dad about me," I blurt.

"That's why I followed you."

"I told you I wasn't going to."

"I heard you say on the phone 'something happened with Noah last night.' I thought you were talking to Dad, not your *boyfriend*."

Her face stiffens at the word. "I said that because when I heard myself telling you last night that it was your responsibility to be true to your heart, I realized I was being a hypocrite and I needed to take my own advice. I needed to be brave like my son." Wait, did she just use me to justify her traitorous actions? She stands, hands me the drawing. "Noah, I'm asking Dad for a divorce. I'm going to tell him today. And I want to tell your sister myself."

A divorce. Today. Now. "No!" This is my fault. If I hadn't followed her. If I hadn't seen. If I hadn't drawn the picture. "Don't you love us?" I meant to say *don't you love Dad,* but that's what came out.

"I love nothing more than you and your sister. Nothing. And your dad is a wonderful, wonderful man…"

But now I can't focus on what she's saying because a thought's taken over my entire brain. "Is he going to live here?" I ask her, interrupting whatever she was saying. "That man? With us? Is he going to sleep on Dad's side of the bed? Drink out of his coffee cup? Shave in his mirror? Is he? Are you going to marry him? Is that why you want a divorce?"

"Sweetheart…" She touches my shoulder, trying to comfort me. I pull away from her, hating her for the first time in my life, real live squawking hatred.

"You are," I say in disbelief. "You're going to marry him, aren't you? That's what you want."

She doesn't say no. Her eyes are saying yes. I can't believe this.

"So you're just going to forget about Dad? You're going to pretend everything you had with him is nothing." Like Brian's doing to me. "He won't survive it, Mom. You don't see him at that hotel. He's not like he used to be. He broke." And me too. And what if I, in turn, broke Brian? How can love be such a wrecking ball?

"We tried, Dad and I," she says. "We've been trying very hard for a very long time. All I ever wanted for you kids was the stability I didn't have growing up. I never wanted this to happen." She sits back down. "But I'm in love with another man." Her face slides off her face – no one can keep their faces on today – and the one underneath is desperate. "I just am. I wish things were different but they're not. It's not right to live a lie. It never is, Noah." There's begging in her voice. "You can't help who you love, can you?"

This silences the racket in me for a moment. I can't help it, that's for sure, and I suddenly want to tell her everything. I want to tell her that I'm in love too and I can't help it either and that I just did the worst thing I could've possibly done to him and I don't know how I could've done it and can't believe how much I wish I could take it back.

But instead I walk out of the room.

The History of Luck

Jude, Age 16

I'm lying in bed UNABLE to sleep

thinking about Oscar kissing brown-haired Brooke while I karmically fermented in the closet. Thinking about Grandma's and Mom's ghosts uniting against me. Thinking mostly about Noah. What was he doing down by Guillermo's studio today? And why did he look so frightened, so worried? He said he'd gone running and was totally fine and it was a coincidence we ran into each other on Day Street. But I didn't believe him, like I didn't believe him when he said he didn't know how all the files I bookmarked about Guillermo got deleted. He must've followed me down there. But why? I had the strongest sense there was something he wanted to tell me. But like maybe he was too afraid.

Is he keeping something from me?

And why *was* he going through my stuff the other day? Maybe it wasn't just curiosity. Also, the emergency money – what did he use it for? I looked all over his room when he went out tonight, found absolutely nothing new.

I sit up, hearing a suspicious noise. Ax-murderers. They always try to break in at night when Dad's away at his conferences. I push off the blankets, get out of bed, grab the baseball bat I keep underneath it for such occasions, and do a quick walk-through of the house to make sure Noah and I will live another day. I end my patrol in the doorway of Mom and Dad's bedroom thinking what I always do: The room's still waiting for her to come back.

The dressing table's still decorated with her antique atomizers, French perfume bottles, bowls shaped like shells filled with eye shadows, lipsticks, pencils. Black hair's still webbed in the silver hairbrush. The biography of Wassily Kandinsky still rests facedown on it as if she's going to pick it up and resume reading from where she left off.

But it's the photograph that draws me in tonight. Dad keeps it on his night table, I imagine, so it's the first thing he sees when he wakes up. Neither Noah nor I had ever seen this picture until after Mom died. Now I can't seem to get enough of it, of Mom and Dad in this moment. She's wearing an orange tie-dye hippie dress and her blustery black hair's blowing into her face. Her eyes are painted dramatically with kohl like Cleopatra's. She's laughing, it seems, at Dad, who's next to her on top of a unicycle, his arms out to the sides for balance. His grin is gleeful. On his head is a Mad Hatter–style black top hat and the sun-bleached blond hair beneath it goes halfway down his back. (The silent exchange between Dad and Noah when Noah saw the hair: Oh my Clark Gable.) There's a satchel around Dad's torso filled with a stack of vinyl. Matching wedding rings glint on their tan hands. Mom looks exactly like Mom but Dad looks like another person entirely, someone who might actually have been raised by Grandma Sweetwine. Apparently, this unicycle-riding super-kook asked Mom to marry him after knowing her for only three days. They were both in graduate school, he, eleven years older.

He said he couldn't risk her getting away. No other woman had ever made him feel so damn happy to be alive.

She said no other man had ever made her feel so safe. This super-kook made her feel safe!

I put down the photograph, wondering what would've happened had Mom lived and Dad moved back in with us like she'd decided. The mother I knew didn't seem so interested in safety. The mother I knew had a glove compartment full of speeding tickets. She mesmerized lecture halls of students with her drama and passion, with ideas that critics called daring and groundbreaking. She wore capes! Went skydiving on her fortieth birthday! And this: She'd secretly, regularly make plane reservations for one passenger to cities all over the world (I'd overhear her doing it), only to let them expire a day later – why? And for as long as I can remember, when she thought no one was looking, she played chicken with the stove, seeing how long she could keep her hand over the flame.

Noah once told me he could hear horses galloping inside her. I got it.

But I know so little about her life before all of us. Only that she was, in her words: *a hellion,* who was shuttled from one unhappy foster situation to another. She told us art books in the town libraries saved her life and taught her to dream and made her want to go to college. That's it really. She always promised she was going to tell me everything when I was a little bit older.

I'm a little bit older and I want her to tell me everything.

I sit down at the makeup table in front of the long oval wood-framed mirror. Dad and I boxed up all the clothes, but neither of us could bear touching the dressing table. It felt sacrilegious. This was her altar.

```
    When you talk to someone through a mirror,
            your souls switch bodies
```

I dab her perfume on my neck and wrists, and then I'm remembering being thirteen years old, sitting right here before school, methodically putting on all the makeup of hers I wasn't allowed to wear to school: the darkest red lipstick she had called Secret Embrace, black kohl eyeliner, bright blue and green shadows, glittery powders. Mom and I were enemy combatants then. I'd just stopped going to museums with her and Noah. She came up behind me but instead of getting mad, she picked up the silver-plaited hairbrush and started brushing my hair like she used to do when I was little. We were framed in the glass together. I noticed our hair was twining together in the hairbrush, light and dark, dark and light. Through the mirror, I looked at her and she at me. "It'd be easier with us and I'd worry less," she said gently, "if you didn't remind me so much of myself, Jude."

I pick up the same brush she used that day, three years ago, and comb it through my hair until every gnarl and knot is freed, until there's as much of my hair webbed in the brush as hers.

```
    If your hair tangles with someone's in a
        hairbrush, your lives will forever tangle
                    outside of it
```

No one tells you how gone gone really is, or how long it lasts.

Back in my bedroom, I have to stop myself from taking the baseball bat to everything, the missing's so bad. If only there was something in the bible to really help us. If only there was something to unflip the car (five times, according to the eyewitness), unshatter the windshield, uncrinkle the guardrail, unspin the wheels, unslick the road. Something to unbreak the twenty-two bones in her body including the seven in her neck, uncollapse her lungs, unstop her heart, and unhemorrhage her brilliant brain.

But there isn't.

There isn't.

I want to heave the stupid useless bible at stupid useless Clark Gable.

Instead, I put my ear to the wall between our rooms to see if I can hear Noah. For months after Mom died when he used to cry in his sleep, I would get up at the first sound of it and go into his room and sit on his bed until he stopped. He never once woke up and found me there sitting in the dark with him.

I put both hands on the wall between us, wanting to push it down—

That's when I get the idea. An idea so obvious I can't believe it's taken so long for it to occur to me. A moment later, I'm at my desk booting up the laptop.

I go straight to LostConnections.com.

There's Noah's post to Brian, his plea, like always:

I'd give ten fingers, both arms. I'd give anything. I'm sorry. I'm so sorry. Meet me 5 p.m. Thursday. You know where. I'll be there every week at that time for the rest of my life.

No responses.

But what if there were a response? My pulse quickens. How could I not have thought of this before? I ask The Oracle: *What if I contact Brian Connelly?*

To my amazement, the divination is bountiful. Link after link about Brian has appeared: *Scouts Descend on Forrester Academy Eyeing Gay Pitcher "The Ax" for Third-Round Draft Pick*

Connelly Dodges Draft and Opts for Free Ride to Stanford to Pitch for the Cardinal

And the one I click on: *The Bravest Man in Baseball Is Seventeen Years Old*

The other links were fairly recent ones from his school's paper, *The Forrester Daily*, or the local town paper, the *Westwood Weekly*, but the one I click is linked everywhere.

I read the article three times. It describes how Brian came out to his entire school at a pep rally the spring of his sophomore year. The baseball team was in the middle of a winning streak where he'd pitched two no hitters and his fastball was coming in consistently at eighty-nine mph. On the field everything was going great, but off it there'd been rumors about Brian's sexual orientation and the locker room had become a war zone. It says Brian realized he had two choices: Quit the team as he'd done in a similar situation when he was younger or think of something else quick. At the pep rally, in front of the Forrester student body, he got up and said his piece about all those past and present who've been forced off the field because of prejudice. He got a standing ovation. Key teammates rallied around him, and in time, the harassment abated. The Tigers won the league championship that spring. He became team captain as a junior and at the end of that year he was offered a minor-league contract, which he didn't accept because he got a baseball scholarship to Stanford. The article concludes by saying the fact that MLB is now trying to recruit openly gay players is a sign that history is in the making.

Clark effing Gable! But none of it surprises me, just confirms what I already knew: Brian is a way cool person and he and my brother were in love.

The most eye-popping piece of information in this article, however, next to the fact that Brian might be changing history and all, is that he's at Stanford. Now. Not even two hours away! It would mean he skipped his last year of high school, but that's entirely possible considering how he spoke in incomprehensible scientific paragraphs when he got going. I find the Stanford University newspaper online and search for his name but nothing comes up. Then I do another search for "The Ax." Nothing still. I return to the article. Maybe I misread and he didn't skip a grade and is coming next fall? But no, I didn't misread. Then I remember that baseball is a spring sport! The season hasn't begun. That's why he's not in the newspaper. I go to the Stanford website, find a directory of undergraduates and lickety-split, I find his email. Should I do this? Should I? Is it wrong to meddle?

No. I have to do it for Noah.

Before I change my mind, I copy the URL for Noah's post on LostConnections and email it to Brian Connelly from an anonymous email account I make up.

It'll be up to him. If he wants to respond to Noah he can. At least he'll see it – who knows if he has? I know things didn't end well between them. Nothing to do with me. Brian could barely look Noah in the eye at Mom's funeral. He didn't even come to the house after. Not once. And yet, it's Noah who's been apologizing for years on that website. The article says Brian came out at that pep rally the spring of his sophomore year, which followed his last winter break here. After that, his mother moved farther north and he never returned. But the timing is suspicious. Were the rumors about him and Noah then? Is that what ended their relationship? Did Noah start the rumors? Could that be what he's apologizing for? Oh, who knows?

I get back in bed, thinking how happy Noah will be if he finally gets a response to his post. For the first time, in a very long time, my heart feels light. I fall asleep immediately.

And dream of birds.

If you dream of birds, a great change in your
life is about to take place

* * *

When I wake the next morning, I check to see if Brian's responded to Noah's post (nope), check to see if Noah's already gone like yesterday (yup), and then, despite bone-deep disappointment about Oscar the Girl-Exhaler and uneasiness about both bloody ferocious Guillermo and the vigilante ghost squad, I'm out the door.

I need to get NoahandJude out of that rock.

I'm a few steps down the hallway at Guillermo's, when I hear raised voices coming from the mailroom. Guillermo and

Oscar are arguing intently about something. I hear Oscar say, "You couldn't possibly understand! How could you?" Then Guillermo, with an unfamiliar hardness in his voice: "I understand very well. You take risks on that motorcycle, but that is it. You are a coward in a tough leather jacket, Oscore. You let no one in. Not since your mother die. You hurt before you can be hurt. You are afraid of the shadow." I about-face and am almost to the door and out of there, when Oscar says, "I let *you* in, G. You're … like a father … the only one I've had."

Something in his voice stops me, sears me.

I rest my forehead against the cold wall, their voices quieter now, unintelligible, not understanding how it can be that even after everything that happened yesterday with Brooke, all I want to do is run to the motherless boy in the next room who is afraid of the shadow.

I do not.

* * *

Instead, I go to church. And when I return to the studio an hour or so later, all's quiet. I spent my time with Mr. Gable trying not to be a compassionate person. Trying not to think about a scared grieving boy in a tough leather jacket. Wasn't too hard. I sat in the pew, the same one I was in when Oscar and I met, and repeated the mantra: *Come here, sit on my lap,* ad infinitum.

Guillermo greets me in the mailroom with safety goggles on his head. There's nothing in his expression to indicate he's recently taken a circular saw to Oscar. He does look different, though. His black hair's powdered with dust like Ben Franklin. And a large paisley scarf, also dusted with white powder, is wrapped a few times around his neck. Has he been carving? I glance up at the loft – no sign of Oscar. He must've left. Not surprising. Guillermo sure wasn't holding back on the tough love. I can't even remember the last time Dad went at Noah or me like that. I can't remember the last time Dad was really a dad.

"I was afraid we scare you away," Guillermo says, examining me a little too closely. The examining and the "we" make me wonder what Oscar might've told him. And that makes me wonder if what I overheard before might've had something to do with me. "Oscore say you leave very upset yesterday."

I shrug, feeling heat in my face. "It's not like I wasn't warned."

He nods. "If only the heart listen to reason, right?" He puts an arm around me. "C'mon, what is bad for the heart is good for art. The terrible irony of our lives as artists." *Our* lives as artists. I smile at him and he squeezes my shoulder the way I've seen him squeeze Oscar's, and instantly, my mood brightens. How did I ever find this guy? How did I get so *lucky*?

When I pass the stone angel, I reach out my hand and touch hers.

"The rocks call me back," he says, brushing dust off his smock. "I am outside with you today." I notice how dingy and graying his smock is, like all the others that hang on hooks around the studio. I should make him a better one, a colorful one that suits him. A Floating Smock.

When we pass by, I see that the clay man survived yesterday's battery, more than survived. He's no longer huddled and defeated but unfurling like a frond. He's finished, drying, and beautiful.

"So I look at your practice rock and model last night," Guillermo says. "I think you are ready for some electricity. You have a lot of stone to remove before you can even begin to find the brother and sister, understand? This afternoon I teach you to use the power tools. With these you must be so, so careful. The chisel, like life, allows for second chances. With the saws and drills, often there is no second chance."

I stop walking. "You believe that? About second chances? In life, I mean." I know I sound like an *Oprah* episode, but I want to know. Because to me, life feels more like realizing you're on the wrong train barreling off in the wrong direction and there's nothing you can do about it.

"Of course, why not? Even God, he have to make the world twice." His hands take to the air. "He make the first world, decide it is a very terrible world he made, so he destroy with the flood. Then he try again, start it all over with—"

"With Noah," I say, finishing his sentence.

"Yes, so if God can have two tries, why not us? Or three or three hundred tries." He laughs under his breath. "You will see, only with the diamond blade circular saw do you have one chance." He strokes his chin. "But even then sometimes you make a catastrophic mistake, you think I am going to kill myself because the sculpture is ruined, but in the end it come out more incredible than had you not made the mistake. This is why I love the rocks. When I sculpt with clay, it feel like cheating. It is too easy. It has no will of its own. The rocks are formidable. They stand up to you. It is a fair fight. Sometimes you win. Sometimes they win. Sometimes when they win, you win."

Outside, sunlight has gathered from all corners of the earth. It's a gorgeous day.

I watch Guillermo climb the ladder up to the female giant's head. He pauses for a moment, pressing his forehead to her massive stone one, before rising above her. Then he lowers the safety goggles, lifts his scarf to cover his mouth – oh, I see, he's too cool for a face mask – picks up the diamond blade circular saw that's resting on top of the ladder, and wraps the cord around his shoulder. A loud jack-hammer-like noise fills the air, quickly followed by the shriek of granite, as Guillermo, without any hesitation, takes his one chance and slices into Dearest's head, and then is lost in a cloud of dust.

It's crowded in the yard today. In addition to Guillermo and the unfinished couple, *The Three* (extremely frightening) *Brothers,* and me, there's Oscar's motorcycle, for some reason. Also, Grandma and Mom are at the ready, I sense it. And I keep thinking someone's watching me from the fire escape, but each time I look up, there's only Frida Kahlo basking in the sun.

I forget everything else and work on freeing NoahandJude.

Slowly I chip, chip, chip away at the stone, and as I do, like yesterday, time begins to rewind, and I start to think and can't stop thinking about things I don't normally let myself think about, like how I wasn't home when Mom left that afternoon to reconcile with Dad. I wasn't there to hear her say that we were going to be a family again.

I wasn't there because I'd run off with Zephyr.

I think about how she died believing I hated her because

that's all I'd been telling her since she kicked Dad out. Since before that.

I drive the chisel into a groove and hit it hard with the hammer, taking off a big chunk of rock, then another. Had I been at home that afternoon and not with Zephyr raining down bad luck, I know everything would've been different.

I take off another hunk, a whole corner, and the force of the hit sprays granules onto my goggles, into my exposed cheeks. I do it again on the other side, hit after hit, the misses bloodying my fingers, hitting and missing, hacking away at the stone, at my fingers, and then I'm remembering the moment Dad told me about the accident and how I threw my hands over Noah's ears to protect him from what I was hearing. My first reaction. Not over my own ears but over Noah's. I'd forgotten I'd done that. How could I have forgotten that?

What happened to that instinct to protect him? Where'd it go?

I take the hammer and crush it into the chisel.

I have to get him out of here.

I have to get both of us out of this fucking rock.

I slam into the stone again and again, remembering how Noah's grief filled the whole house, every corner, every crevice. How there was no room left for mine or Dad's. Maybe that's why Dad started walking, to find some place where Noah's heartbreak didn't reach. I'd see Noah all curled up in his room and when I'd try to comfort him, he'd tell me how I didn't understand. How I didn't know Mom like he did. How I couldn't possibly comprehend what he was feeling. Like I hadn't just lost my mother too! How could he have said those things to me? I'm beating on the stone now, taking off more and more rock. Because I couldn't believe he was hogging her in death, just like he had in life. Making me believe I had no right to grieve, to miss her, to love her, like he did. And the thing is I believed him. Maybe that's why I never cried. I didn't feel entitled to.

Then he threw himself off Devil's Drop and almost drowned that day, almost *died*, and my anger toward him got wild and thrashing, monstrous and dangerous.

So maybe you're right, I yell at Mom and Grandma in my mind. *Maybe that's why I did it.*

I'm pounding on the stone now, cracking into it, opening it all up.

Opening it all up.

Noah's application to CSA had been sitting on the kitchen counter radiating genius since the week before Mom died. He and Mom had sealed the envelope together for luck. They didn't know I was watching from the door.

Three weeks after Mom's accident, a week after Noah jumped off the cliff, the night before the CSA application was due, I wrote the application essays, stapled them to a couple dress patterns, added two sample dresses. What else did I have to submit? My sand women had all washed away.

Dad drove us to the post office to mail off the applications. We couldn't find a parking spot so Dad and Noah waited in the car while I went in. That's when I did it. I just did it.

I only mailed mine.

I took from my brother the thing he wanted most in the

world. What kind of person does that?

Not that it matters, but I went back to the post office the next day, ran all the way there, but the garbage had been emptied. All his dreams got taken out with the trash. Mine went straight to CSA.

I kept telling myself I would tell Noah and Dad. I would tell them at breakfast, after school, at dinner, tomorrow, on Wednesday. I would tell Noah in time so he could reapply, but I didn't. I was so ashamed – the kind that feels like suffocating – and the longer I waited, the more the shame grew and the more impossible it got to admit what I'd done. Guilt grew too, like a disease, like every disease. There weren't enough diseases in Dad's library. Days kept passing, then weeks, and then, it was too late. I was too scared if I confessed, I'd lose Dad and Noah forever, too cowardly to face it, to fix it, to make it right.

This is why my mother destroys everything I make. This is why she can't forgive me.

When CSA announced the freshmen class on their website, his name wasn't on the list. Mine was. When my acceptance letter came, I waited for him to ask about his rejection letter, but he didn't. He'd already destroyed all his artwork by then. And sometime before this, he must've sent in pictures of my sand sculptures and gotten me in.

The world has gone dark. Guillermo's standing in front of me blocking the sun. He takes the hammer and chisel out of my hands, which have long ago stopped carving. He takes off his scarf, shakes it out, and wipes the stripe of brow between my hat and goggles. "I don't think you are okay," he says. "Sometimes you work the stone, sometimes the stone works you. I think today the rock win."

I slip down my face mask, and say, "So this is what you meant when you said what slumbers in here" — I touch my chest — "slumbers in here." I touch the rock.

"This is what I meant," he says. "I think we have a coffee?"

"No," I say quickly. "I mean, thank you, but I need to keep working."

And that's what I do. I work for hours, obsessively, frenetically, unable to stop cutting into the stone, Grandma and Mom chanting at me with every hit: *You crushed his dreams. You crushed his dreams. You crushed his dreams.* Until for the first time since she died, Mom materializes and is standing before me, her hair a blaze of black fire, her eyes damning me.

"And you crushed mine!" I yell at her in my head before she vanishes again into thin air.

Because isn't that also true? Isn't it? Over and over again, day after day, all I wanted was for her to see me, to really see me. Not to forget me at the museum, like I didn't exist, and go home without me. Not to call off a contest, certain of my failure, before she even looked at my drawings. Not to keep reaching inside me to turn down the light while at the same time reaching into Noah to turn his to full brightness. Always as if I were nothing but some stupid slutty girl named *that girl*. Invisible to her in every other way!

But what if I don't need her permission, her approval, her praise to be who I want to be and do what I love? What if I'm in charge of my own damn light switch?

I put down the tools, take off the goggles, the mask, the plastic suit. I peel off my hat and toss it on the table. I'm so sick of being invisible. Sunshine tosses its giddy greedy fingers through my hair. Off comes my sweatshirt and I have arms again. The breeze welcomes them, skidding over the surface of my skin, raising hair after hair, tingling, awakening every exposed inch of me. What if my reasons for not sending Noah's application had more to do with Mom and me than it did him and me?

To awaken your spirit, throw a stone into your
reflection in still water

(I never believed Noah and I shared a soul, that mine was half a tree with its leaves on fire, like he said. I never felt like my soul was something that could be seen. It felt like motion, like taking off, like swimming toward the horizon or diving off a cliff or making flying women out of sand, out of anything.)

I close my eyes for a moment and then it's as if *I've* woken from the deepest slumber, as if someone has extricated me from granite. Because I realize: It doesn't matter if Noah hates me, if he never forgives me. It doesn't matter if I lose him and Dad forever. It just doesn't. I have to uncrush his dream. That's all that matters.

I go into the studio and climb the stairs to Oscar's room, where there's a computer. I turn it on, log onto my account, and write an email to Sandy at CSA asking if we can meet before school on Wednesday, the first day back after break. I tell him it's urgent and that my brother will be coming to the meeting too with a painting portfolio that will blow his mind.

To
awaken
your spirit,
throw a stone
into your
Reflection
in still
WATER

I'm going to give up my spot. It's what I should've done every single day for the last two years.

I press send and the feeling is unmistakable: I'm free.

I'm *me*.

I text Noah: WE NEED TO TALK. IT'S IMPORTANT! Because he better get painting. He has four days to put a portfolio together. I lean back in the chair, feeling like I've emerged from the darkest cave into bountiful blinding sunlight. Only then do I look around the loft. At Oscar's bed, his books, his shirts. Disappointment takes hold of me – but there's nothing to do about it. The coward in the tough leather jacket has made it very clear how he feels about the coward in the invisibility uniform.

As I get up to leave, I spot Guillermo's note that I gave Oscar on the bedside table by the photograph of his mother. I take it with me downstairs, and once I put it back in the notepad in Guillermo's cyclone room where it belongs, I go outside and ask him to teach me how to use the diamond blade circular saw. He does.

It's time for second chances. It's time to remake the world.

Knowing I only have one shot to get it right with this tool, I wrap the cord around my shoulder, position the circular saw between Noah's shoulder and my own, and turn on the power. The tool roars to life. My whole body vibrates with electricity as I split the rock in two.

So that NoahandJude becomes Noah and Jude.

"You kill them?" Guillermo says in disbelief.

"No, I saved them."

Finally.

* * *

I walk home in moonlight, feeling absolutely incredible, like I'm standing in a clearing, in a river, in the most awesome shoes, high-heeled even. I know I still have to tell Noah and Dad about Noah's CSA application, but that's okay because no matter what happens, Noah will paint again. I know he will. Noah will be Noah again. And I can be someone I can stand to see in a mirror, in an art studio, in a Floating Dress, in good health, in a love story, in the world. It is bizarre, however, that Noah hasn't responded to my texts. I tried several times too, each time with more urgency and more exclamation points. He usually gets back to me right away. I guess if he's still out when I get home, I'll just wait up.

I raise my arms to the bright bursting moon, thinking how I haven't had a terminal illness in hours and how all's quiet on the vigilante ghost front too, and what a relief both these things are when the text comes in from Heather:

AT THE SPOT. NOAH VERY DRUNK. ACTING CRAZY. WANTS TO JUMP DEAD MAN'S! I HAVE TO LEAVE IN 5. PLEASE COME NOW! NO IDEA WHAT'S WRONG W/HIM. WORRIED.

* * *

I'm at the edge of the world looking for my brother.

The wind's pummeling me, the salty spray nicking my hot face, the ocean below drumming as ferociously in my head as out of it. Steeped in sweat from the sprint up the hill and with the full moon showering down so much light it could be daytime, I look up at Devil's Drop and Dead Man's Dive and see that both ledges are deserted. I thank Clark Gable profusely, catch my breath, and then even though she said she had to leave,

I text Heather, then Noah again, trying to convince myself he's come to his senses. I can't.

I have a bad feeling.

I acted too late.

I turn around and head into the mayhem. In all directions, loud partying brigades from public and private high schools, from Lost Cove Uni, are gathered around kegs, bonfires, picnic tables, drum circles, car hoods. Every kind of music is blaring out of every kind of car.

Welcome to The Spot on a turbo-moonlit Saturday night.

I recognize no one until I return to the far side of the parking lot and spot Franklyn Fry, resident douchebag of epic proportions, with some older Hideaway surfers, all of them at least a year out of high school by now. Zephyr's crew. They're sitting on the flatbed of Franklyn's truck, illuminated eerily in the headlights like jack-o'-lanterns.

At least Zephyr's sun-blaze of long straggly surfer hair is nowhere in sight.

I want to get my invisibility sweatshirt and skullcap out of my bag and put them on. But I don't. I want to believe the red ribbon around my wrist will keep me safe always. But it won't. I want to play How Would You Rather Die? instead of figuring out how to live. But I can't. I'm over being a coward. I'm sick of being on pause, of being buried and hidden, of being petrified, in both senses of the word.

I don't want to imagine meadows, I want to run through them.

I approach the enemy. Franklyn Fry and I have bad blood.

My strategy is to offer no greeting and ask him calmly and

politely if he's seen Noah.

His strategy is to sing the opening lyrics of "Hey Jude" – why didn't my parents think of this when they named me? – then to eye me slowly, stickily, up and down, down and up, making sure not to miss an inch before pit-spotting at my breasts. Make no mistake, there are advantages to an invisibility uniform. "Slumming it?" he says directly to my chest, then takes a slug of beer, wiping his mouth sloppily with the back of his hand. Noah was right; he looks exactly like a hippopotamus. "Come to apologize? Taken you long enough."

Apologize? He's got to be kidding.

"Have you seen my brother?" I repeat, louder this time, articulating every syllable, like he doesn't speak the language.

"He took off," a voice says from behind me, immediately silencing all music, all chatter, the wind and the sea. The same parched sandpapery voice that at one time made me melt into my surfboard. Michael Ravens, aka Zephyr, is standing behind me.

At least Noah decided against jumping, I tell myself, and then I turn around.

It's been a very long time. The taillights from Franklyn's truck are in Zephyr's eyes and his hand's cupped over them like a visor. Good. I don't want to see his narrow green hawk eyes, see them enough in my mind.

This is what happened right after I lost my virginity to him two years ago: I sat up, pulled my knees to my chest, and gasped at the salty air as quietly as possible. I thought of my mother. Her disappointment blooming inside me like a black flower. Tears burned my eyes. I forbade them to fall and they didn't. I was caked in sand. Zephyr handed me my bikini bottoms. It occurred to me to shove them down his throat. I saw a used condom dotted with blood splayed on a rock. That's me, I thought: disgusting. I didn't even know he'd put it on. I hadn't even thought about condoms! Everything in my stomach was rising up, but I forbade that too. I put on my bathing suit, tried to hide the shaking as I did. Zephyr smiled at me like everything was fine. Like everything that had just happened was FINE! I smiled back like everything was. Does he know how old I am? I remember thinking. I remember thinking he must've forgot.

Franklyn saw Zephyr and me walking up the beach after. It had started to rain softly. I wished I was in my wetsuit, a thousand wetsuits. Zephyr's arm was a lead weight on my shoulders, pushing me down into the sand. The night before, at the party he took me to, he kept telling everyone what an awesome surfer I was and how I'd been known not to jump but dive off Devil's Drop. He kept saying I was *such a badass,* and I'd felt like one.

That had been less than twenty-four hours earlier.

Somehow Franklyn knew what we'd done. When we reached him, he took my arm and whispered in my ear so Zephyr couldn't hear: "Now it's my turn," he said. "Then Buzzy, then Mike, then Ryder, right? That's how it works, just so you know. You don't think Zeph actually likes you, do you?" That's exactly what I'd thought. I had to wipe Franklyn's words off my ear because they were covered in spit, and after I did that, I spun out of his grip, hollering, "No!", finally finding the godforsaken word, way too late, and in front of everyone, I kneed Franklyn Fry in the balls, hard, like Dad taught me in case of an emergency.

Then the mad dash home, with tears biting my cheeks, my skin crawling, my stomach in shambles, heading straight for Mom. I'd made the biggest mistake of my life.

I needed my mother.

I needed my mother.

There's been an accident, that's what Dad told me the moment I burst into the house.

There'd been an accident.

That's when I threw my hands over Noah's ears.

Dad took them off and held them in his.

So even as the police officer told us these unimaginable, world-breaking things, I was still crawling around in the wrongness of what I'd just done. It was caked along with sand in every pore of my body. The horrible wrong scent of it was still in my hair, on my skin, inside my nose, so every inhalation carried it deeper inside me. For weeks afterward, no matter how many times I showered, no matter how hard I scrubbed, no matter what kind of soap I used – I tried lavender and grapefruit and honeysuckle and rose – I couldn't get it off me, couldn't get Zephyr off me. Once, I went to a department store and used every single tester perfume on the counter, but it was still there. It's always there. It's *still* there. The smell of that afternoon with Zephyr, the smell of my mother's death, one and the same.

Zephyr steps out of the glare of Franklyn's headlights. This is how I think of him: like his namesake, the raven, a harbinger of death and doom. He's a human hex, a tall blond column of darkness. Zephyr Ravens is an eclipse.

"So Noah went home?" I ask. "How long ago?"

He shakes his head. "No. Not home. He took off up there, Jude." He points to the very top of the bluff to a ledge that doesn't even have a name, because who would dare it? The hang-gliders use it occasionally, but that's it. It's too high to jump, probably double Dead Man's, and below it there's a shelf that juts out so if you don't leap far enough and clear it, you slam into that before you ever hit water. I've only heard of one kid who's ever jumped it. He didn't make it.

My internal organs are failing, falling, one by one.

Zephyr says, "Got a text. They're playing some drinking game. Loser jumps and apparently your brother's losing on purpose. I was heading up there to try and stop it."

Next thing, I'm diving through the crowd, knocking over drinks, people, not caring about anything except getting to the cliff path, the quickest way up the bluff. I hear Grandma's voice blowing like wind at my back. She's right behind me on the trail. Branches are cracking, her heavy footsteps hitting the path moments after mine, then I remember she doesn't have footsteps. I stop and Zephyr barrels into me, grabbing my shoulders so I don't careen face forward into the ground.

"Jesus," I say, jumping quickly out of his grip, away from the smell of him, again so close.

"Oh man, sorry."

"Stop following me, Zephyr. Go back, please." I sound as desperate as I feel. The last thing I need in this moment is him.

"I'm on this trail every day. I know it so—"

"Like I don't."

"You're going to need help."

This is true. However, not from him. Anyone but him. Except it's too late, he's already brushed past me and is forging ahead into the moonlit dark.

After Mom died, he came over a few times, tried to get me back on my board, but the ocean had dried up as far as I was concerned. He also tried to be with me again in the guise of comforting me. Two words: as if. And not just him. So did Fry and Ryder and Buzzy and the rest of them, but not in the guise of anything except harassment. Incessantly. They'd all become jerks overnight, especially Franklyn, who was pissed and posted obscene things about me on the Hideaway message board and graffitied *Slutever Sweetwine* in the beach bathroom, rewriting it every time someone – Noah? – crossed it out.

Do you really want to be *that girl*? Mom had asked me over and over that summer and fall as my skirts got shorter, my heels higher, my lipstick darker, my heart angrier and angrier at her. Do you really want to be *that girl*? she asked me the night before she died – the last words she ever said to me – when she saw what I was wearing to go to the party with Zephyr (not that she knew I was going to a party with Zephyr).

Then she was dead and I was really and truly *that girl*.

Zephyr's setting a fast pace. My breath's tumbling around in my chest as we climb and climb and climb in silence.

Until he says, "I still got his back like I promised you."

Once, long before we did what we did, I asked Zephyr to look out for Noah. Hideaway Hill can be very *Lord of the Flies* and in my seventh-grade mind, Zephyr was like the sheriff, so I asked for his help.

"Got your back too, Jude."

I ignore this, then can't. The words come out shrill and accusatory, sharp as darts. "I was too young!"

I think I hear him suck in air, but it's hard to know because of the waves, loud and relentless, crashing into the rocks, eroding the continent.

As am I, kicking up dirt, kicking the shit out of the continent, driving my feet into the ground with every step. I was in eighth grade, he in eleventh − a whole year older than I even am now. Not that he should treat any girl at any age like that, like a dishrag. And then in the lightning bolt to the head kind of way, it occurs to me that Zephyr Ravens is not a harbinger of anything at all. He's not bad luck − he's a terminal burnout dimwit loser asshole, *offense intended*.

And what we did didn't cause bad luck either − it caused *endless inner-ick* and *regret* and *anger* and—

I spit on him. Not metaphorically. I hit his jacket, his ass, then shoot one right in the back of his mongrel head. That one he feels, but thinks it's some kind of bug he can shoo off with his hand. I nail him again. He turns around.

"What the—? Are you spitting at me?" he asks, incredulous, his fingers in his hair.

"Don't do it again," I say. "To anyone."

"Jude, I always thought you—"

"I don't care what you thought then or what you think now," I say. "Just don't do it again."

I blow past him and double our speed. Now I feel like a badass, thank you very much.

Maybe Mom was wrong about *that girl* after all. Because *that girl* spits on guys who treat her badly. Maybe it's *that girl* who's been missing. Maybe it's *that girl* breaking her way out of that rock at Guillermo's. Maybe it's *that girl* who can see it's not my fault that a car with my mother in it lost control no matter what I did with this jerkoff beforehand. I didn't bring the bad luck to us, no matter how much it felt that way. It brought itself. It brings itself.

And maybe it's *that girl* who's now brave enough to admit to Noah what I did.

If he doesn't die first.

As we get closer to the ledge, I begin to hear something strange. At first I think it's the wind howling spookily in the trees, then realize it's a human sound. Singing maybe? Or chanting? A moment later I realize what's being chanted is my last name and my heart catapults out of my body. I think Zephyr realizes it at the same moment because we've both broken into a sprint.

Sweetwine, Sweetwine, Sweetwine.

Please, please, please, I think as we crest the last hill and reach the flat sandy area, where a bunch of people are in a semicircle like they're at a sporting event. Zephyr and I elbow our way through, parting the curtain of bodies, until we have a front-row seat for the suicidal game that's being played. On one side of a raging bonfire is a noodly guy with a bottle of tequila in his hand, swaying back and forth like a reed. He's about twenty feet from the edge of the cliff. On the other side of the fire is Noah, ten feet from the edge, the crowd favorite to end his life. A half-empty bottle is on its side at his feet. He has his arms out like wings and is turning around and around, the wind rippling his clothes, the glow of the fire lighting him up like a phoenix.

I can feel his desire to jump as if it were in my own body.

A kid on a rock nearby shouts, "Okay, Round Five! Let's roll!" He's the master of ceremonies, and, it appears, as drunk as the contestants.

"You grab Noah," Zephyr says, his voice all business now. At least he's good for something. "I'll get Jared. They're so wasted, it'll be easy."

"On three," I say.

We plunge forward, emerging in the center of the circle. From on top of the rock, the announcer slurs, "Hey, there appears to be some kind of interruption in The Death Match."

My rage is meteoric. "Sorry to ruin the show," I shout up at him. "But I have a really great idea. Next time why don't you have *your* brother jump dead drunk off this cliff instead of mine?" Oh wow. *That girl* has many uses. I think I underutilized her in the past. I will not make that mistake again.

I grab Noah's arm, hard, expecting a fight, but he melts into me, saying, "Hey, don't cry. I wasn't gonna jump." Am I crying?

"I don't believe you," I say, looking into the open blooming face of the old Noah. So much love is filling my chest, it may explode.

"You're right," he laughs, then hiccups. "I'm totally gonna jump. Sorry, Jude."

In a sudden swift movement that seems impossible considering how drunk he is, he spins out of my arms, casting me backward in slow, torturous motion. "No!" I reach for him as he dashes to the edge, raising his arms again.

It's the last image I see before my head hits the ground and the crowd collectively gasps.

* * *

The ledge is now empty. But no one's racing down the cliff path, the quickest way to the beach. No one's even looking over the edge to see if Noah survived. The crowd's in a mass exodus toward the street.

And I need to stop hallucinating.

I must've suffered some kind of brain trauma, because no matter how many times I blink or shake my head, they're still there.

Belly-flopped on my brother not two feet from me is Oscar.

Oscar, who came out of absolutely nowhere to tackle Noah before he reached the edge.

"Hey, it's you," Noah says in wonderment as Oscar rolls off him and onto his back. Oscar's panting like he just raced up Everest, and in motorcycle boots, I note. His arms are outspread, his hair wet with sweat. Thanks to the moon and the bonfire, my hallucination's practically in high def. Noah's sitting up now, gazing down at him.

"Picasso?" I hear Oscar say, still trying to catch his breath. It's been ages since I've heard anyone call Noah that. "All grown up I see, and with a buzz cut."

Now they're fist-bumping. Yes, Noah and Oscar. The two

I vote least likely to fist-bump. I have to be imagining this. Oscar's sitting up now and has put a hand on Noah's shoulder. "What the hell, mate?" He's reprimanding Noah? "And what's with the drinking? Following in my footsteps? This isn't you, Picasso."

How does Oscar know who Noah is to know who Noah isn't?

"It isn't me," Noah slurs. "I'm not me anymore."

"Know the feeling," Oscar replies. Still seated, he holds out a hand to me.

I ask, "How are you here—"

But Noah interrupts, garbles at me, "You kept texting me, so I kept drinking 'cause I thought you knew…"

"Knew what?" I ask him. "This is all because of my texts?" I try to recall what I wrote, just that I had to speak with him and it was urgent. What did he think I wanted to talk about? What did he think I knew? There is definitely something he's been keeping from me. "Knew what?" I ask him again.

He smiles stupidly at me, swiping the air with his hand. "Knew what," he repeats like an imbecile. Okay, he's drunk out of his gourd. I don't think he ever has more than a beer or two. "My sister," he says to Oscar. "She used to have hair that followed us around like a river of light, remember?" At least that's what I believe he said. He's speaking Swahili.

"Your *sister*!" Oscar cries. He falls onto his back again. Noah flops happily down next to him, a loony smile on his face. "That's brilliant," Oscar says. "Who's Dad? Archangel Gabriel? And hair like a river of light, huh?" He lifts his head so he can see me. "You sure you're okay? You seem a bit stunned. And you look great without your hat and that giant vegetable-stuffed sweatshirt. Great, but like you might be cold. You know what? I'd offer you my leather jacket, but someone stole it." He's back in fighting form, I see, recovered from this morning. Except I sort of feel like I've read his diary.

Still. "Don't flirt with me," I say. "I'm immune to your charms. I've been inoculated by one not–girlfriend too many." For the record, *that girl* rocks.

I'm expecting a snappy retort but instead he looks at me in a completely unguarded way and says, "I'm so sorry about yesterday. I can't tell you how sorry."

I'm taken aback, have no idea how to respond. I'm not sure what he's apologizing for either. For me seeing what I saw or for him doing what he did?

"Thank you for saving my brother's life," I say, ignoring the apology for now, and really, I'm just brimming with gratitude because: What in the world? "No clue how you appeared like this, like some superhero. Or how you two know each other…"

Oscar gets up on his elbows. "Proud to say, I've taken off my clothes for the both of you."

This is strange. When would Oscar have modeled for Noah? Noah gets up on his elbows too because it appears he's playing Follow the Leader with Oscar. His face is flushing. "I remember your eyes," he says to Oscar. "But not those scars. They're new."

"Yeah, well, you should see the other guy, as they say. Or in this case the pavement along Highway 5."

They're chattering to each other, both flat on their backs

again, batting words back and forth, English and Swahili, gazing up at the glowing night sky. It makes me smile; I can't help it. It's like when Oscar and I were on the floor of the jail cell room. I remember that sticky note: *She said you would feel like family.* Why does he? And what about that apology? What was that? He sounded earnest, real. So not full of it.

I smell weed and turn around. Zephyr and the noodly kid named Jared and a handful of others are smoking up as they leave, all walking in the direction of the street, probably on their way back to The Spot. Some help he was. If Oscar hadn't dropped out of the sky, Noah would be dead. A loud bomb of a wave crashes into the shore below as if to confirm this. It's some kind of miracle, I think, it has to be. Maybe Grandma's right: *You have to see the miracles for there to be miracles.* Maybe I've been looking at the world, living in the world, in too much of a stingy cowardly way to see much at all.

"Do you realize Oscar saved your life?" I say to Noah. "Do you have any idea how high this cliff is?"

"Oscar," Noah repeats, then wobbles to a sitting position and points at me, saying, "He didn't save my life and it doesn't matter how high it is." He's getting drunker by the minute, talking with two tongues now. "It's Mom who keeps me up. It's like I have a parachute on. Like I can practically fly." He makes a slow swoosh with his hand through the air. "I sail all the way down so incredibly slowly. Every time."

My mouth falls open. Yes, he does. I've seen it.

This is why he keeps jumping then, so Mom will break his fall? Isn't that what I always think when I get The Poor

Motherless Girl Look? Like I've been shoved out of the airplane without a parachute because *mothers are the parachutes*. I'm remembering the last time I watched him jump Devil's. How he seemed to stay up forever. He could've had his nails done.

Oscar sits up. "That's completely daft," he says to Noah, his voice distressed. "Are you mad? You jump off that cliff in your present condition, you die. I don't care who you have in your pocket on the other side." He combs a hand through his hair. "You know, Picasso, I bet your mother would prefer it if you lived your life rather than risked it." I'm surprised to hear these words out of Oscar's mouth, wonder if they might've come out of Guillermo's this morning.

Noah looks down at the ground, says quietly, "But it's the only time she forgives me."

Forgives *him*? "For what?" I ask.

He's grown grave. "It's all a big lie," he says.

"What is?" I ask. Is he talking about liking girls? Or not doing art? Or wearing flame retardant? Or something else? Something that would make him jump off a cliff at night while drunk because he thought from my texts I might know what it is?

He looks up, stunned, like he realizes he's been talking, not thinking. I wish I could tell him the truth about CSA right now, but I can't. He needs to be sober for that conversation. "You're going to be okay," I tell him. "I promise. Everything's about to get better."

He shakes his head. "No, it's about to get worse. You just don't know it yet." A chill runs through me. What does he mean?

I'm about to press him further when he rises to his feet and immediately falls over.

"Let's get you home," Oscar says, securing an arm around him. "So where's home? I'd offer to ride him, but I'm on foot. G. stole my motorcycle in case I ended up like this tonight. We got in a big row this morning." So that's why the motorcycle was in the yard. I feel like maybe I should tell him I heard some of that row, but now's not the time.

"G.?" Noah asks and then seems to forget he said anything.

"It's close," I tell Oscar. "Thank you," I say. "Really, thank you."

He smiles. "I'm the one you call, remember? Dead body, bloody knife."

"She said you would feel like family," I say to him, only realizing too late I probably should've kept this to myself. How corny.

But again he doesn't react like I think. He breaks out the most genuine smile I've ever seen on him, one that starts in his eyes and doesn't seem to end anywhere on his face. "She did and you do."

While Oscar and Noah fumble along like they're in a three-legged race, I try to calm the electrical storm in my head. *She did and you do.* And now I'm remembering how he had that picture of me in his jacket. And Brooke in his arms, Jude, please. Yeah, well, he just saved Noah's life. And what about the way he said: *I can't tell you how sorry.* And how he was this morning with Guillermo. And it's not like he and I were really together. Oh boy. Lather. Rinse. Repeat.

When we get to the road, Noah shakes free of Oscar's hold and pushes ahead of us. I keep an eye on him as he hobbles along on his own.

Oscar and I walk side by side. A few times, our hands brush. I wonder if he's doing it on purpose, if I am.

When we're about halfway to the house, he says, "So this is how I'm here. I was at The Spot. I was very upset – G. said some things that really got to me. He has a way of holding up a mirror and what I saw in it was pretty horrifying. All I wanted was to get pissed, really smashed. I was contemplating taking my first drink in 234 days 10 hours – my last slip-up. I was calculating the minutes actually, had my eyes on my wristwatch, when this whirling dervish, who had a striking resemblance to you, came speeding out of nowhere and knocked the pint of gin out of my hand. It was incredible. A sign, right? My mum? A miracle? I didn't know. Only, I didn't get to contemplate the sublime or even divine nature of the occurrence, because I became immediately, frantically, and wrongly convinced you were being chased into the forest by some Nordic giant. So, I ask, who saved whose life tonight?"

I look up at the shining silvery coin of a moon rolling around in the sky and think I might be seeing the miracles.

Oscar takes something out of his pocket and holds it up. There's enough light for me to make out that he's mounted his mother's seashell and strung it on a red ribbon that looks like the very same one I wrapped around Guillermo's note to Dearest. The next thing I know, every part of him is so close to every part of me because he's tying it around my neck.

"But you'll die within minutes without it," I whisper.

"I want you to have it."

I'm too moved to say another word.

We continue walking. The next time our hands touch, I catch and hold his in mine.

* * *

I'm at my desk finishing up the studies for Mom's sculpture, really working for a likeness. I'm going to show them to Guillermo tomorrow. Noah's sleeping it off. Oscar's long gone. I'm certain the magic seashell – his most beloved possession, he'd said! – around my neck radiates joy. I thought about calling Fish from school, dying to tell someone – someone among the living, for a change – about the seashell, about the photographs and sticky notes too, about everything that's going on, but then I remembered it's winter break and the dorms are closed (I'm one of a few people who don't board), it's the middle of the night, and we're not really friends. But maybe we should be, I'm thinking. Maybe I need an alive friend badly. Sorry, Grandma. Someone to discuss how when Oscar and I were outside on the front step, just now, the two of us breathing and pulsing inches from each other, I thought for sure he was going to kiss me, but he didn't, and I don't know why. He didn't even come in, which I guess is good, because he probably would've figured out that I'm still in high school. He was surprised I lived at home. He said, "Oh, I assumed you lived on campus. Did you stay to take care of your little brother after your mother died?"

I changed the subject. But I know I have to tell him and

I will. About overhearing some of the fight with Guillermo too. Very shortly, I will be a girl without *any* secrets.

Feeling okay about the sketches, I close the pad and sit down at the sewing table. There's no way I can sleep, not after everything that happened today and tonight, with Oscar, with Noah, with Zephyr, with the ghosts, and anyway, I want to get started on the smock I'm going to make for Guillermo out of floating dress scraps. I rummage through my bag for the old smock of his I swiped to use for a pattern. I start blocking it out on the table, and as I do, I feel something in the front pocket. I reach in and pull out a couple notepads. I leaf through one. Just notes and lists in Spanish, sketches, the usual. Nothing in English, nothing for Dearest. I flip through the second, much of the same, except then, in English and most definitely for Dearest, three drafts of the same note, each with slight variations, like he was intent on getting it right. Maybe he was going to send it as an email? Or in a card? Or with a black velvet box with a ring inside it. The one with the least cross-outs:

I can no longer do this. ~~I have to know~~
I need to know an answer. I cannot live
without you. I am half a man, with
half a body, half a heart, half a soul.
There is only one answer, ~~I hope~~ you know
this. You must know ~~by what~~ this
by now. How can you not know?
Marry me, my love   Say yes.

I fall into my chair. She said no. Or maybe he never asked her. Either way, poor Guillermo. What did he say today? *What is bad for the heart is good for art.* Clearly, this was very bad for his heart and very good for his art. Well, I'm going to make him the most beautiful smock to make his art in. I sort through my bag of scraps for reds, oranges, purples, heart colors.

I start sewing the pieces together.

I have no idea how long the knocking's been going on when it dawns on me that the noise I'm hearing isn't coming from my sewing machine acting up but from someone at the window. Oscar? Did he take a risk on the only lit-up window in the house? It has to be him. A second later, I'm at the mirror, shaking my head a little to wake up my hair, then a lot to make it wild. I reach into the top drawer of my dresser and grab the reddest lipstick I have. Yes, I want to. I also want to take one of the prize dresses off the wall and put it on – The Gravity Dress maybe? – and then, that's exactly what I'm doing.

"One sec," I holler at the window.

I hear Oscar say, "Rightio."

Rightio!

I'm standing before the full-length mirror in The Gravity Dress, my response to The Floating Dress. It's a coral-colored, tight-fitting mermaid shape that flares and ruffles at the bottom. No one has ever seen me in it or in any of the dresses I've made over the last couple years. Including me. I make them all to fit my form but envision them for another girl, always thinking if someone opened my closet, they'd be certain there were two of us living in this room and they'd want to be friends with the other one.

There you are, I think, and it hits me. So she's the one I've been designing for all along without realizing it. If I ever have a line of dresses like Grandma, I'm calling it: *That Girl*.

I cross the room, part the curtains, and slide open the window.

He does a double take. "Oh my God," he exclaims. "Look at you. Bloody look at you. You're stunning. And this is how you dress when you're all alone in the middle of the night? And in potato sacks when you're out in broad daylight?" He smiles his haywire smile. "I think you might very well be the most eccentric person I've ever met." He puts his hands on the windowsill. "But that's not what I've come to say. I was halfway home and I remembered something very important I needed to tell you."

He gestures with his index finger for me to come closer. I bend down and lean out the window into the night. I feel the soft breeze in my hair.

His face has grown serious.

"What is it?" I ask.

"This." So quickly I don't see it coming he reaches both his hands around my head and kisses me.

I pull back for a moment, wondering if I can trust him, because I'd be crazy to. But what if I do? What if I just do? And you know, if he exhales me to kingdom come, so be it—

This is when it happens. Perhaps it's the moonlight spilling down, alighting his features from above that does it, or maybe it's the glow of my bedroom light on his face just so, or maybe it's that I'm finally ready to see it, what's been eluding me since the moment we first met.

He modeled for Noah.

Oscar's the guy in the portrait.

He's him.

And this is exactly like I always imagined it.

I lean back out again into the night. "I gave up practically the whole world for you," I tell him, walking through the front door of my own love story. "The sun, stars, ocean, trees, everything, I gave it all up for you."

Bafflement crosses his face, quickly followed by delight. Quickly followed by both of my hands reaching for him, pulling him to me, because *he's him,* and all the years of not noticing and not doing and not *living* are breaking through the dam of the moment until I'm kissing him hungrily, wanting my hands on his body, and I'm reaching for him, and he me, and his fingers are knotting in my hair and before I know it I'm all the way out the window and toppling him to the ground.

"Man overboard," he murmurs, wrapping me up in his arms and we're laughing and then the laughing dies out because who knew kissing could be like this, could so alter the landscape within, tipping over oceans, sending rivers up mountains, unpouring the rain.

He rolls us over so his body is pressing into mine, the weight of him, the weight of that other day, and Zephyr begins elbowing his way between us. My muscles tense. I open my eyes, afraid of the unseeing stranger I'll find this time, but I don't find a stranger. It's Oscar, present, so present, with love in his face.

That's how come I trust him. You can see love. It looks like this face. To me, it has always looked like this crazy mismatched face.

He touches my cheek with his thumb, says, "It's okay." Like he somehow knows what happened.

"You sure?"

Around us the trees rustle softly.

"One hundred percent sure." He gently tugs at the seashell. "Promise."

The night's warm, shy, barely touching our skin. It envelops us, entwines us. He kisses me slowly, tenderly, so that my heart creaks open, so that all those moments on the beach from that horrid, horrid day wash away, so that, just like that, the boycott comes to an end.

* * *

It's extremely difficult to concentrate on Oscar in my bedroom because: Oscar is in my bedroom! Oscar, who's the guy in the portrait!

He's flipped out that the dresses on the walls and the one on my body were made by me and has now picked up a framed photograph of me surfing. He's excavating me, just without hammer and chisel. "Pornography for an English bloke," he says, waving the picture at me.

"Haven't surfed in years," I tell him.

"Shame." He taps the *Physician's Desk Reference*. "Now this I expected." He picks up another photo. A jump off Devil's. He studies it. "So you used to be a daredevil?"

"Guess so. I didn't think about it. I just loved doing that kind of stuff then." He looks up like he's expecting me to say more.

"When my mom died … I don't know, I got scared. Of pretty much everything."

He nods like he gets it, says, "It's like a hand at your throat all the time, isn't it? Nothing's inevitable anymore. Not the next heartbeat, not anything." More than gets it. He sits down on my sewing chair, regards the photo again. "Though I went the other way. Started using all that fear as a punching bag. Nearly got myself killed on a daily basis." He frowns, puts down the picture. "That's partly what the row with G. was about. He thinks I take ridiculous risks on the bike or in the past with drugs but won't—" He stops when he sees my face. "What is it?"

"Oscar, I overheard some of that fight this morning. As soon as I realized you guys were arguing, I left, but—" I stifle the confession because I'm thinking his organs may have caught fire.

Not sure what's happening, except that he's on his feet and bounding toward me at a breakneck un-Oscar-like pace. "Then you know," he says. "You must, CJ."

"Know what?"

He takes me by the arms. "That I'm fucking terrified of you. That I can't seem to keep you out like I can everyone else. That I think you could devastate me."

Our breathing's loud, fast, in synch. "I didn't know," I whisper, barely getting the words out before his mouth lands hard and urgent on mine. I feel the unrestrained emotion in his lips, feel it unburying, unleashing something in me, something daring and fearless and winged.

Ka-effing-pow.

"I'm so dead," he says into my hair, "so dead," into my neck, then pulls back, his eyes shining. "You're going to obliterate me, aren't you? I know it." He laughs in an even more tumbling, cascading way than usual and there's something new in his face, an openness, a freedom maybe. "You already have. Look at me. Who is this guy? I assure you no one's ever met this tempest before. *I* haven't met him before. And none of what I just told you was really even part of the fight with G., for Christ's sake! I just had to tell you. You have to know I've never" – he waves his hand in the air – "flipped the lid before. Not even close. Not a lid flipper." He's saying he's never been in love? I remember Guillermo telling him how he hurts before he can be hurt, how he lets no one in. But he can't keep me out?

"Oscar," I say.

He puts his palms on my cheeks. "Nothing happened with Brooke after you left. Nothing. After I told you that stuff about my mother and me, I totally freaked out and was this total wanker. A coward – you probably heard that fine praise this morning on G.'s lips. I think I tried to ruin this before…" I follow his gaze to the window, to the black world outside this room. "I kept thinking now that you had a glimpse of the underbelly, of who I really was, you'd—"

"No," I say, understanding. "It was the opposite. It made me feel closer to you. But I get it, I think the same way, like if people really knew me, they could never—"

"*I* could," he says.

It kicks the breath out of me, kicks bright light into me.

At the same time, we reach for each other and then we're in each other's arms, joined together, pressed together, but this time not kissing, not moving, just holding each other so tightly. Moments pass, lots and lots of them, with us holding on, it feels like for dear life, or maybe holding on *to* dear life. So dear.

"Now that you have the seashell," he says, "I'm thinking this is about as much distance I can safely be away from you at all times."

"*That's* why you gave it to me, then!"

"My entirely sinister plan."

I didn't think it possible, but he draws me even closer into him. "We're Brancusi's *The Kiss*," I whisper. One of the most romantic sculptures ever made: a man and a woman pressed together into one.

"Yes!" he says. "Just like it." He steps back, brushes a strand of hair out of my face.

"A perfect fit like we're split-aparts."

"Split-aparts?"

His face brightens. "So Plato talked about these beings that used to exist that had four legs and four arms and two heads. They were totally self-contained and ecstatic and powerful. Too powerful, so Zeus cut them all in half and scattered all the halves around the world so that humans were doomed to forever look for their other half, the one who shared their very soul. Only the luckiest humans find their split-apart, you see."

I think about the latest note to Dearest. How Guillermo

said he was half a man with half a soul, half a mind... "I found another note Guillermo wrote. It was in one of those notepads he has everywhere, a marriage proposal—"

"Yeah, I'm going to have to take the Fifth, isn't that what you Americans say? He'll tell you all about it one day, I'm sure. I've promised him—"

I nod. "I understand."

"Those two were split-aparts, though, that's certain," he says. His hands find my waist. "I have a brilliant idea," he says, his face whirring with emotion. Not any percent of him seems full of it anymore. "Let's do it. Let's flip our bloody lids together. Here it is, the rest of it: I was a mess at The Spot because I thought I blew it with you. I don't care that G. has added a beheading to the list of barbaric punishments for my coming near you. I think my mother's prophecy is real. I look everywhere. I search crowds. I take so many pictures. But I recognized you, only you. In all these years." The most ridiculous grin has taken over his face. "So how about it? We'll pop around on Hippity Hops. And talk to ghosts. And think we have the Ebola virus and not the common cold. And carry onions in our pockets until they sprout. And miss our mums. And make beautiful things—"

Completely swept up, I say, "And ride around on motorcycles. And go to abandoned buildings and take off our clothes. And maybe even teach an English bloke how to surf. Except I don't know who just said all that."

"I do," he says.

"I feel so happy," I say, overwhelmed. "I have to show you

something." I unclasp myself from him and reach under the bed for the plastic bag.

"So, Noah drew you. Not sure how—"

"You don't know? He used to camp outside the window at that arts high school and draw the models."

I cover my mouth with my hand.

"What?" Oscar says. "Did I say something wrong?"

I shake my head, try to make this image of Noah peering into a CSA classroom go away. He would have done anything. But then I take a deep breath, tell myself, it's all right, because by next week he'll be at CSA and that calms me enough to rummage around for the plastic bag. A moment later, I sit back down next to Oscar with it on my lap. "Okay. So once upon a time, I saw this cubist portrait my brother did of you and had to have it." I look at him. "*Had* to have it. It was love at first sight." He smiles. "He and I were always playing this game where we'd swap parts of the world for others in a quest for universe domination. He was winning. We're ... competitive, that's the nice way of putting it. Anyway, he didn't want me to have you. I had to give up almost everything. But it was worth it. I kept you here." I show him the spot where the picture hung by my bed. "I would stare and stare at you and wish you were real and imagine you coming to that window, just like you did tonight."

He bursts out laughing. "That's incredible! We're absolutely split-aparts."

"I don't know if I want a split-apart," I say honestly. "I think I need my own soul."

"That's fair. Maybe we can be occasional split-aparts. On occasions like these, for instance." He runs a finger slowly down the side of my neck, crossing over my collarbone, then down, down. What was I thinking with this plunging neckline? I wouldn't say no to a fainting couch. I wouldn't say no to anything. "But why rip me up and stuff me in a bag?" he asks.

"Oh, my brother did that. He was angry at me. I tried to put you back together many times."

"Thank you," he says, but then something across the room catches his attention and in a flash he's up and walking toward my dresser. He picks up a photograph of my family and studies it. I'm watching him in the mirror. His face has turned ashen. What? He turns around and stares right through me. "You're not his older sister," he says more to himself than me. "You're twins." I can see the wheels spinning in his head. He must know how old Noah is and now he knows how old I am.

"I was going to tell you," I say. "I guess I was afraid to. I was afraid you'd—"

"Holy hell." He's springing for the window. "Guillermo doesn't know." He's halfway over the ledge. I don't know what's going on.

"Wait," I say. "Wait. Oscar. Of course he does. Why would he care? Why is it that big of a deal?" I run to the window, yell out, "My father was eleven years older than my mother! It doesn't matter."

But he's already gone.

I go to the dresser, pick up the photograph. It's my favorite family portrait. Noah and I are about eight and dressed in matching sailor outfits looking totally daffy. But it's because of my parents that I love it.

My mother and father are gazing at each other like they have the best secret.

The
Invisible
Museum

Noah, Age 14

One by One

I empty each tube of paint into the laundry sink.

I need color, rich, bright, fuck-you, fuck-off, fuck-everything color, mounds and mounds of it. I need the gleam of new paint. I need to sink my fingers, my hands, into chartreuse, into magenta, into turquoise, into cadmium yellow. I wish I could eat it. I wish I could drown my whole body in it. That's what I want, I think, mixing and swirling, making green, making purple, making brown, spiraling one into the next, sinking my hands, my arms into the cold slippery shining mush until my eyes are dancing.

About an hour ago, I watched Mom get into her car from the window.

The second she turned on the engine, I ran out after her. It had started to drizzle.

That's when I screamed it: *I hate you. I hate you so much.*

She looked at me, shocked, her eyes huge, tears running down her cheeks. She mouthed: *I love you,* then put her hand to her heart and pointed at me like I was deaf.

A second later, she peeled out of the driveway to go tell Dad she wanted a divorce so she could marry that other man.

"I don't care," I say out loud to no one. I don't care about her and Dad. About Brian and Courtney. Not even CSA. I don't care about anything but color, color and more brightness. I add a tube of cornflower blue to the growing mountain—

That's when the phone rings.

And rings.

And rings. She must've forgotten to turn on the machine. Ringing, still. I find the phone in the living room, wipe my hands on my shirt but still get paint all over the phone.

A man with a gruff voice says, "Is this the residence of Dianna Sweetwine?"

"That's my mom."

"Is your father home, son?"

"No, he doesn't live here now." A current zips through me – something's wrong. I can hear it in his voice. "Who is this?" I ask, though I know it's the police before he even confirms it. I don't know how, but I know everything in that moment.

(Self-portrait: *The Boy Inside the Boy Stops Breathing*)

He doesn't tell me there's been an accident. That a car's spun out of control on Highway 1. He doesn't tell me anything. But somehow I know.

"Is my mother okay?" I demand, running to the window. The police radio crackles in the background. I see several surfers paddling out, none of them Jude. Where is she? Fry said she took off with Zephyr. Where did they go? "Did something happen?" I ask the man, watching as the ocean disappears, then the horizon. "Please tell me." Mom was so upset when she left. Because of me. Because I told her I hated her. Because I followed her to The Wooden Bird. Because I made that picture. All the endless love I have for her fountains up, up, up, up. "Is she okay?" I ask again. "Please tell me she's okay."

"Can I have your father's cell phone number, son?" I want him to stop calling me *son*. I want him to tell me my mother's okay. I want my sister home.

I give him Dad's cell.

"How old are you?" he asks. "Is anyone with you?"

"It's only me here," I say, panic flipping me over. "I'm fourteen. Is my mom okay? You can tell me what happened." But as soon as I say it out loud, I know I don't want him to tell me. I don't want to ever know. I see now paint has dripped all over the floor like multicolored blood. I've tracked it everywhere. There are handprints all over the window, the back of the couch, the curtains, lampshades.

"I'm going to call your dad now," he says quietly, then hangs up.

I'm too scared to try Mom's cell. I call Dad. It goes straight to voicemail. I'm sure he's talking to the cop, who's telling him everything he didn't tell me. I get the binoculars and go to the roof. It's still drizzling. And way too warm. Everything's wrong. I don't see Jude on the beach or the street or anywhere on the cliffs. Where'd she and Zephyr go? I tell her telepathically to come home.

I look over at Brian's house, wishing he were on his roof, wishing he knew how sorry I was, wishing he'd come over and talk about planetary orbits and solar flares. I reach in my pocket for the rock and close my hand around it. Then I hear a car skid into the driveway. I run to the other side of the roof. It's Dad, who *never* skids. Behind him is a police car. My skin falls off. I fall off.

(Self-portrait: *Boy Careens Off World*)

I climb down the ladder at the side of the house, go through the sliding doors into the living room. I'm a statue in the hallway when Dad's key turns in the lock.

He doesn't have to say a word. We crash together, falling to the ground, to our knees. He holds my head to his chest with both hands. "Oh Noah. I'm so sorry. Oh God, Noah. We have to get your sister. This is not happening. This is not happening. Oh God."

I don't plan it. The panic's coursing out of him and into me, out of me and into him, and the words just fly out. "She was going to ask you to come home so we could all be a family again. She was on her way to tell you that."

He pulls away, looks into my burning face. "She was?"

I nod. "Before she left she said that you were the love of her life."

* * *

There's something I have to do. The house is still full of mourners and misery and food, so much food spoiling on all the counters and tables. The funeral was yesterday. I walk through the red-eyed people, past the hunching walls, the graying paint, the collapsing furniture, the darkening windows, the moth-eaten air. I see I'm crying when I pass a mirror. I don't know how to stop. It's become like breathing. An always thing. I tell Dad I'll be right back. Jude – who cut off all her hair so I hardly recognize her – tries to come with me, but I say no. She won't let me out of her sight. She thinks I'm going to die too now. Last night I found dirt-covered hogwash roots in my bed. And when I had a coughing fit in the car on the way home from the cemetery, she went ballistic, yelling at Dad to go to the emergency room because I could have pertussis, whatever that is. Dad, being an expert on disease, talked her down.

Somehow I make it to the sculptor's studio. Then I sit down on the sidewalk and wait, whipping pebbles at the asphalt. Eventually he'll have to come out. At least he had the decency not to come to the funeral. I looked for him the whole time.

Brian came. He sat in the last row with his mother, Courtney, and Heather. He didn't find me after.

What does it matter? All the color's gone. There's only darkness in the sky-buckets now, spilling out over everything and everybody.

Ages later, the sculptor crumbles out of the doorway and up to the mailbox. He opens the little door, pulls out a bunch of letters. I see the crying all over his face.

And he sees me.

He's staring and I'm staring and I can tell how much he loves her in the way he's looking at me, a tsunami of feeling rolling out of him to me. I don't care.

"You look just like her," he whispers. "Your hair."

There's one thought in my head, the thought that's been there for days: *If it weren't for him, she'd be alive.*

I stand but have been sitting so long lumped up there, my legs give. "Hey," he says, catching me and settling me back onto the sidewalk, right next to him. Heat's rising off his skin and an overpowering man smell too. I hear a wail, the kind that comes out of jackals, and realize it's coming out of me. The next thing I know, his arms are around me and I can feel him shaking, both of us are, like we're in sub-arctic conditions. He pulls me closer, then he pulls me onto his lap, cradling me so that his sobs land on my neck and mine on his arms. I want to crawl down his throat. I want to live in the pocket of his smock. I want him to rock me like this forever, like I'm a small boy, the smallest boy who ever was. He knows just how to do it too. Like Mom's inside of him telling him how to comfort me. How come he's the only one who knows how? How come he's the only one she's inside of?

No.

Birds screech in the trees above us.

This is not right.

I didn't come here for this. I came for the opposite of this. He can't hold me like we're in this together, like he understands. He's not my father. He's not my friend.

If it weren't for him, she'd be alive.

And then I'm twisting and wriggling out of his embrace, returning to my full-grown size and person, my full-grown knowledge and revulsion and hatred. I stand over him and say what I came to. "It's your fault she's dead." His face wrecks. I go on. "I blame you." I'm the wrecking ball now. "She didn't love you. She told me she didn't." Wrecking and wrecking him and I don't care. "She wasn't going to marry you." I slow down so every word sinks in. "She wasn't going to ask my father for a divorce. She was on her way to ask him to come home."

Then I enter the crawlspace deep inside me and shut the hatch. Because I'm not coming back out. Ever.

(Self-portrait: *Untitled*)

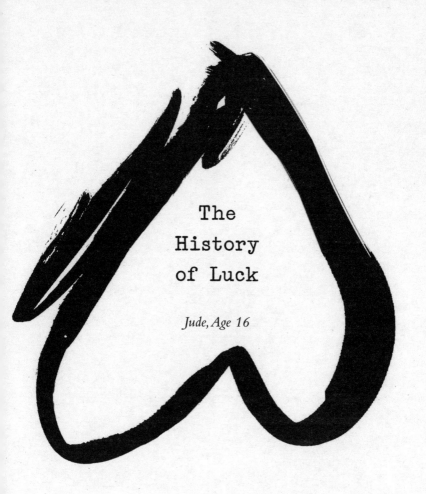

The
History
of Luck

Jude, Age 16

when I WAKE UP

Noah's already gone, like usual these days, so I can't tell him what I need to or ask him all that I want to. The irony of this is not lost on me. Now that I want more than anything to confess about CSA, I can't. I check LostConnections.com, where there's still no response from Brian, then grab Oscar's leather jacket, my sketchpad, and head down the hill.

Soon after I arrive, I'm tapping my foot nervously on the floor as Guillermo opens my sketchpad on the large white drafting table in the center of the studio. I want him to like the studies of Mom's sculpture and I want him to agree to the piece being done in stone, preferably marble or granite. He flips through the first studies quickly, back views. I'm watching him and can't tell what he's thinking, but then he stops at the frontal view and inhales sharply as he raises a hand to his mouth. That bad? Now he's trailing a finger over my mother's face. Oh yes, of course. I'd forgotten that they met. I guess I nailed the likeness. He turns to me and his expression causes me to jerk backward.

"Dianna is your mother." He doesn't so much speak the words as becomes them.

"Yes," I say.

His breathing has gone volcanic. No idea what's happening

here. He returns his gaze to the sketches, touching them now like he wants to peel them off the page.

"Well," he says. The skin under his left eye won't stop twitching.

"Well?" I ask, confused and getting frightened.

He closes the pad. "I don't think I can help you after all. I will call Sandy back, recommend someone else."

"What?"

In a cold, closed voice I've never heard before, he says, "I am sorry. I am too busy. I was wrong. It is too distracting to have someone here so much." He won't look at me.

"Guillermo?" My heart's shaking inside my chest.

"No, please go. Now. You must. I have things to do." I'm too stunned to argue. I take my pad and start for the door, hear, "Do not come back to my studio."

I turn around but he's facing the opposite direction. I don't know why I glance up at the window to the fire escape, maybe the same sense that someone's watching me that I had while working outside yesterday. And I'm right, someone is watching.

Looking down on us with one hand pressed to the glass is Noah.

Guillermo turns to see what I'm looking at and by the time we both look back at each other, Oscar has walked through the studio door, his face shining with fear.

A moment later, Noah blasts into the studio like a lit stick of dynamite, then freezes as he scans the room. Guillermo's face is unrecognizable – he's scared, I think. *Guillermo* is scared. *Everyone's* scared, I realize. We are four points in a rectangle and three of those points have these wild panicked eyes on me. No one's saying a word. It's clear everyone knows something I don't and if their expressions are any indication, I'm not sure I want to know what it is. My eyes dart from one of them to the next and back again, not understanding, because, what – or more accurately, whom – it seems, each one of them is afraid of is: me.

"What?" I ask finally. "What's going on? Someone tell me, please. Noah? Is it about Mom?"

It's mayhem.

* * *

"He killed her." Noah's finger is pointed at Guillermo, his voice trembling with anger. "If it wasn't for him, we'd still have her." The studio begins to pulse, to rock beneath my feet, to tip over.

Oscar turns to Noah. "Killed her? Are you crazy? Look around you. No man has ever loved a woman more than he loved her."

Guillermo says softly, "Oscore, be quiet."

The room's really swaying now, swinging, so I find the only thing near me and lean against it, the leg of a giant, but immediately lurch back because I swear it shuddered – it *moved* – and then I'm seeing it. The giants are stomping and roaring to life, hurling their colossal bodies into each other's arms, fed up with spending eternity frozen, always a breath away from their heart's desire. Split-aparts, all of them, now throwing themselves together. Each couple spinning across the floor, arm in arm, turning and turning, causing tremor after tremor inside me, as things start adding up. It wasn't my age that freaked Oscar out last night. It surely wasn't. It was the family photograph. And what turned Guillermo into Drunken Igor was nothing but the anniversary of my mother's death.

Because she is Dearest.

I turn to Noah, try to speak. "But you said…" is all I can get out before my voice gets sucked back in. I try again. "You told us…" I still can't finish and then all I can say is, "Noah?"

This is what he's been keeping from me.

"I'm sorry, Jude," he cries. And then it's as if Noah really and truly is busting through stone, as if his spirit's rising up as his back arches, his arms suspend behind him and he says, "She was on her way to ask Dad for a divorce so she could marry …" He turns to Guillermo, meets his eyes. "… you."

Guillermo's mouth has fallen open. And now my words are coming out of it. "But Noah, you said…" His stare could burn a hole in granite. "You told me…" Oh, Noah – what did you do? I can tell Guillermo's trying to tamp down the emotion in his face, hide from us what is swelling from the very core of him, but it's starting to seep out of him anyway: joy, no matter how belated.

Her answer was yes.

I need to get out of here, away from all of them. It's too much. Too, too much. Mom is Dearest. She's the clay woman climbing out of the clay man's chest. She's the stone woman he makes again and again and again. She's the color-drenched faceless woman in the painting of the kiss. Her body turns and twists and bends and arches facelessly over every inch of the walls in the studio. They were in love. They were split-aparts! She was never going to ask Dad to come home. We were never going to be a family again. And Noah's known this. And Dad doesn't! Finally my father's perpetually perplexed preoccupied expression makes sense. Of course he doesn't understand. For years, he's been trying to compute a mathematical problem in his head that does not compute. No wonder he walks the soles off all his shoes!

I'm staggering down the sidewalk, sun blinding my eyes, careening from car to telephone pole, trying to get away from the truth, from the frenzy of emotions chasing me down. How could she have done this to Dad? To us? She's *an adulterer. She's* that girl! And not in the good way, not in the badass way! And then, something occurs to me. This is why, after she died, Noah kept telling me I didn't understand how he was feeling, that I didn't know Mom like he did. Now I get it. He was right. I had no idea who Mom was. He wasn't being cruel. He wasn't hogging her. He was protecting her. And Dad and me. He was protecting our family.

I hear quick frantic footsteps gaining on me. I pivot around, knowing they're his. "You were protecting us? That's why you lied?"

He reaches for me but doesn't touch me. His hands are manic birds. "I don't know why I did it, maybe I wanted to protect you and Dad or maybe I just didn't want it to be this way. I didn't want her to be this way." His face is flushed, his dark eyes storming. "I knew she didn't want me to lie about her life. She wanted me to tell the truth, but I couldn't. I couldn't tell the truth about *anything*." He looks at me so apologetically. "That's why I couldn't be around you, Jude." How did Noah and I ever get so locked up in secrets and lies? "It was so much easier just to blend in than to be me, to face…" He's stopped talking, but there's definitely more and I can tell he's gearing up to say it. I'm seeing him again like I did in the studio, like a figure busting out of rock. It's a jailbreak. "I think I lied because I didn't want it to be my fault," he says. "I saw them together that day. I followed her and I saw them. And that's why she got in the car. That's why." He's starting to cry. "It's not Garcia's fault. I want it to be his so it doesn't have to be mine, but I *know* it's mine." He's holding his head like he's trying to keep it from exploding. "I told her I hated her before she left, Jude, right before she drove away. She was crying. She shouldn't have been driving. I was so angry at her—"

I take him by the shoulders. "Noah." My voice has returned. "It wasn't your fault. It wasn't." I repeat the words until I'm sure he's heard them, believes them. "It wasn't anyone's. It just happened. This terrible thing happened to her. This terrible thing happened to us."

And then it's my turn. I'm being shoved forward, shoved right out of my skin with just how terrible – Mom ripped out of my life the very moment I needed her the most, the bottomless unconditional shielding sheltering love she had for me taken forever. I let myself feel the terrible, surrender to it finally instead of running from it, instead of telling myself it all belongs to Noah and not to me, instead of putting an index of fears and superstitions between me and it, instead of mummifying myself in layers of clothing to protect myself from it, and I'm falling forward with the force of two years of buried grief, the sorrow of ten thousand oceans finally breaking inside me—

I let it. I let my heart break.

And Noah is there, strong and sturdy, to catch me, to hold me through it, to make sure I'm safe.

* * *

We take a long winding way home through the woods, tears streaming down my face, words out of his mouth. Grandma was right: A broken heart is an open heart. "So much was going on then," Noah's saying. "More even than—" He flicks his wrist in the direction of Guillermo's studio. "Stuff with me."

"And Brian?" I ask.

He looks at me. "Yeah." This is the first time he's admitted it. "Mom caught us…" How could so much have happened to both of us in one week, on one day?

"But Mom was okay with it, wasn't she?" I ask.

"That's just it. She was totally okay with it. One of the last things she said to me was how wrong it is to live a lie. How it's my responsibility to be true to my heart. And then I go and turn her life into a lie." He pauses. "And my own too." He grabs a stick off the ground and breaks it in half. "And I totally ruined Brian's life." He breaks the stick into smaller and smaller pieces. There's torment in his face, shame.

"No you didn't."

"What do you mean?"

"Ever heard of Google?"

"I did that once, twice actually."

"When?" Twice. OMCG, only Noah. He's probably never been on a social network in his life.

He shrugs. "There wasn't anything."

"Well, there is now."

His eyes widen but he doesn't ask me what I know, so I don't offer, figuring he wants to find out for himself. He's increased his pace, though. Okay, he's speed-walking now to The Oracle.

I stop. "Noah, I have something to tell you too." He turns around and I start talking — it's the only way. "I have a feeling after I tell you this, you'll never speak to me again, so first I want to say how sorry I am. I should've told you ages ago, but I was too afraid I'd lose you forever if I did." I look down. "I still love you the most. I always will."

"What is it?" he says.

I am my brother's keeper, I tell myself, and then I just say it. "You didn't not get into CSA. What I mean is you didn't apply. That day?" I take a breath and blow out the words from the darkest place in me: "I never mailed your application."

He blinks. And blinks. And blinks some more. His face is blank and I don't know what's happening inside him, when all of a sudden he throws up his arms and jumps into the air and his face is awash in rip-roaring joy — no, ecstasy: This is ecstasy.

"Did you hear me right?"

"Yes!" he cries. Now he's laughing wildly and I'm sure he's lost all his buttons until out of his mouth flies, "I thought I sucked! I thought I sucked! For so long. I thought it was only Mom seeing them that made them any good." He arches his neck back. "And then … I realized, it doesn't matter."

"What doesn't?" I look for anger or hatred in his face, but there's none. It's like the betrayal hasn't registered. He's only elated.

"Come with me," he says.

Fifteen minutes later, we're on an abandoned construction site looking at a crumbling cement wall. On it, in a rage of colors, is ... *everything*.

There's NoahandJude spray-painted from behind, shoulder to shoulder, our hair braided together into a river of light and dark that wraps around the whole mural. There's Brian in the sky opening up a suitcase full of stars. There's Mom and Guillermo kissing into a tornado of color at The Wooden Bird. There's Dad emerging from the ocean like a sun god and morphing into a body made of ashes. There's me in my invisibility uniform blending into a wall. There's Noah crouched in a tiny space inside his own body. There's Mom's car bursting into flames as it busts through the sky. There's Heather and Noah riding a giraffe. There's Noah and Brian climbing a ladder that goes on forever. There are buckets and buckets of light pouring over two shirtless boys kissing. There's Noah swinging a baseball bat at Brian who shatters into pieces. There's Noah and Dad under a big bright red umbrella waiting out a storm. There's Noah and me walking along the path the sun makes on the ocean but in opposite directions. There's Noah being held midair in the palm of a giant and that giant is Mom. There's already me surrounded by Guillermo's stone giants working on NoahandJude.

There is the world, remade.

I take out my phone and start snapping pictures. "So gorgeous, Noah. So, so gorgeous. And it will get you into CSA immediately! I'm giving up my spot for you. I've already sent an email to Sandy about it. We three have a meeting Wednesday morning. He's going to die. It doesn't even look like spray paint. I don't know what it looks like except incredible, so, so incredible—"

"Don't." He grabs my phone to stop me from taking any more pictures. "I don't want your spot. I don't want to go to CSA."

"You don't?"

He shakes his head.

"Since when?"

"Since right this minute, I guess."

"Noah?"

He kicks his foot into the ground. "It's like I forgot how awesome it was before I cared if I was any good or good enough to get into some stupid art school. I mean, seriously, like *who fucking cares?*" The sun's hitting his face. He looks clear, self-possessed, older, and for some reason, I think: We're going to be okay. "It's so not about that," he continues. "It's about *magic*." He shakes his head. "How could I have forgotten that?" His smile's as loopy as it was when he was drunk last night. I can't believe he's smiling at me like this. Why isn't he furious with me? He goes on. "When I figured out you were going to Garcia's" – Is that why he was going through my sketches that day? – "I knew everything was about to blow up, all my lies. And it's like *I* blew up. *Finally*. I couldn't just paint in my head anymore." Aha! "I had to tell the truth out loud, somewhere, somehow. I had to let Mom know I heard her that day. I had to apologize to her, to Brian, to you and Dad, even to Garcia. I used the emergency money Dad left, bought all this spray paint, remembered this wall from running. I think I watched every video ever made on spray painting. First attempts have been painted over and over and – hey…" He tugs at my sleeve. "I'm not mad at you, Jude. I'm not going to be either."

I can't believe this. "Why? You should be. How can you not be?"

He shrugs. "I don't know. I'm just not."

He reaches for my hands, takes them in his. Our eyes meet and hold, and the world starts to fall away, time does, years rolling up like rugs, until everything that's happened unhappens, and for a moment, it's us again, more one than two.

"Wow," Noah whispers. "IV Jude."

"Yeah," I say, the enchantment of him feeding my very cells. I feel a smile sweep across my face, remembering all the light showers, the dark showers, picking up rocks and finding spinning planets, days with thousands of pockets, grabbing moments like apples, hopping fences into forever.

"I forgot *this*," I say, and remembering practically lifts me off my feet, lifts us both off our feet.

We. Are. Off. Our. Feet.

I look up. The air's shimmering with light. The world is.

Or I'm imagining this. Of course I am.

"Feel that?" Noah says.

Mothers are the parachutes.

I did not imagine it.

For the record, woohoo! Not just art, but life – *magic*.

"Let's go," Noah says, and we're running together into the woods like we used to, and I can see how he'll draw it later, with the redwoods bowing, the flowers opening like houses for us to enter, the creek following behind us in winding wending color, our feet inches above the ground.

Or maybe he'll do it like this: the forest a blur of green over our heads while we lie on our backs, playing Rock, Paper, Scissors.

He picks rock. I pick scissors.

I pick paper. He picks scissors.

He picks rock. I pick paper.

We give up, happily. It's a new age.

Noah's looking up at the sky. "I'm not mad, because I could've just as easily done it to you," he says. "I *did* do it to you. Just in smaller ways. Over and over again. I knew how you were feeling at the museum all those weekends with Mom and me. I knew how left out you felt all the time. And I know how much I didn't want Mom to see your sculptures. I made sure she didn't. I was always afraid you were better than me and she'd realize." He sighs. "We got all messed up. *Both* of us."

"Still, CSA was your—"

He interrupts. "Sometimes it felt like there wasn't enough of Mom to go around."

This thought silences me and we're quiet for a long time after that, breathing in the scent of eucalyptus, watching the leaves fluttering all around us. I think about how Mom told Noah it was his responsibility to be true to his heart. Neither of us has been. Why is it so hard? Why is it so hard to know what that truth is?

"Does Heather know you're gay?" I ask.

"Yeah, but no one else."

I roll on my side to face him. "So can you believe how weird I've gotten and how normal you've gotten?"

"It's astounding," he says, which cracks us both up. "Except most of the time," he adds, "I feel like I'm undercover."

"Me too." I pick up a stick, start digging with it. "Or maybe a person is just made up of a lot of people," I say. "Maybe we're accumulating these new selves all the time." Hauling them in as we make choices, good and bad, as we screw up, step up, lose our minds, find our minds, fall apart, fall in love, as we grieve, grow, retreat from the world, dive into the world, as we make things, as we break things.

He grins. "Each new self standing on the last one's shoulders until we're these wobbly people poles?"

I die of delight. "Yes, exactly! We're all just wobbly people poles!"

The sun's setting and the sky's filling with pink wispy clouds. We should be getting home. Dad returns tonight. I'm about to say so when Noah speaks.

"That painting in the hallway of his studio. The one of the kiss, I just saw it for a second, but I think Mom made it."

"You do? I didn't know Mom painted."

"Neither did I."

Was that her secret? Another secret? "Like you," I say, and something clicks into place, perfectly into place. Noah was Mom's *muse*. I feel certain of it, and unbelievably without jealousy, understand it.

I flop onto my back again, dig my fingers into the loamy

soil and imagine Mom making that incredible painting, wishing with her hands, being that in love. How can I be mad at her for that? How can I be mad at her for finding her split-apart and wanting to be with him? As Guillermo said, the heart doesn't listen to reason. It doesn't abide by laws or conventions or other people's expectations either. At least her heart was full when she died. At least she was living her life, busting out of its seams, letting the horses gallop, before she had to leave.

Except, no.

Sorry.

How could it have been okay for her to break Dad's heart like that? To break all the promises she made to him? To break up our family? Then again, how could it not be okay if she was being true to herself? Argh. It was right and wrong both. Love does as it undoes. It goes after, with equal tenacity: joy and heartbreak.

Her happiness was his unhappiness and that's the unfair way it was.

But he still has life and time to fill it with more happiness.

"Noah, you have to tell Dad. Right away."

"Tell Dad what?" And there is our footstep-less father looking down on us. "This is a sight for sore eyes, sore, tired, traveling eyes. I saw you two running into the woods hand in hand when I drove by in the cab. It was like a time warp."

He joins us on the forest floor. I squeeze Noah's hand.

"What is it, son? What do you need to tell me?" Dad asks, and my heart spills over with love.

* * *

Later that evening, I'm sitting in a chair as Noah and Dad move swiftly around the kitchen making dinner. They won't let me help even though I've promised to retire the bible. Noah and I made a deal. He'll stop jumping off cliffs if I stop bible-thumping and suspend all medical research, effective immediately. I'm going to make a giant-size, paper flying woman sculpture out of each and every bible passage. Grandma's going to love it. It's the first idea I put in that blank idea pad I've been carrying around since I started CSA. I'm going to call the piece: *The History of Luck*.

When Noah told Dad the truth about Mom and Guillermo hours ago in the forest, Dad simply said, "Okay, yes. That makes more sense." He didn't burst out of granite like Noah or have oceans break inside him like I did, but I can see that the storm in his face has quelled. He's a man of science and the unsolvable problem is solved. Things finally make sense. And sense to Dad is everything.

Or so I thought.

"Kids, I've been thinking about something." He looks up from the tomato he's chopping. "How do you feel about moving? Not out of Lost Cove but to another house. Well, not to just any old house…" His smile is ridiculous. I have no idea what he's going to say. "A house*boat*." I can't decide what's more amazing: the words coming out of Dad's mouth or the expression on his face. He looks like the unicycle-riding super-kook. "I think we need an adventure. The three of us together."

"You want us to live on a boat?" I ask.

"He wants us to live on an *ark*," Noah answers, awe in his voice.

"I do!" Dad laughs. "That's exactly right. I've always wanted to do this." Really? News to me. Um, who is this man? "I just did some research and you will not believe what's for sale down by the marina." He goes to his briefcase and pulls out some pictures he must've printed from the Internet.

"Oh wow," I say. This is no rowboat. It *is* an ark.

"An architect owned it previously," Dad tells us. "Renovated the whole thing, did all the woodwork and stained glass herself. Incredible, isn't it? Two stories, three bedrooms, two baths, great kitchen, skylights, wraparound decks on both floors. It's a floating paradise."

Noah and I must register the name of the floating paradise at the exact same moment, because we both blurt out, imitating Mom, "Embrace the mystery, Professor."

The name of this houseboat is *The Mystery*.

"I know. Was hoping you wouldn't catch that. And yes, if I weren't me, if I were you, for instance, Jude, I'd be certain it was a sign."

"It *is* a sign," I say. "I'm in and I'm not even going to mention one of the thousand potential hazards of houseboat living that have flown into my head."

"What kind of Noah would I be?" Noah says to Dad.

"It's time," Dad says, nodding at us.

Then, unbelievably, he puts on some jazz. The excitement in the room is palpable as Noah and Dad continue chopping and dicing. I can tell Noah's painting in his head while Dad rhapsodizes about what it will be like to dive off the deck for a swim and what an inspiring place it would be to live if only anyone in the family had artistic inclinations.

Somehow it's us again, with a few motley additions to our wobbly people poles, but us. The imposters have left the premises.

When we returned from the woods, I found Dad in his office and told him about Noah's CSA application. Let's just say, I'd rather spend the remainder of my life in a medieval torture chamber rotating from Head Crusher to Knee Splitter to The Rack than see that look on Dad's face again. I didn't think he was ever going to forgive me, but an hour or so later, after he talked to Noah, he asked me to go for a swim with him, our first in years. At one point when we were stroke for stroke in the setting sun's glinting path, I felt his hand squeeze my shoulder, and as soon as I concluded he wasn't trying to drown me, I realized he wanted me to stop.

Treading there in the middle of the ocean, he said, "I haven't exactly been there for—"

"No, Dad," I said, not wanting him to apologize for anything.

"Please let me say this, honey. I'm sorry I haven't been better. I think I got a little lost. Like for a decade." He laughed and took a mouthful of salt water in the process, then continued. "I think you can sort of slip out of your life and it can be hard to find a way back in. But you kids are my way back in." His smile was full of sadness. "I know how crushed you've been. And what happened with Noah and CSA … well, sometimes a good person makes a bad decision."

It felt like grace.

It felt like a way back in.

Because, as corny as it may be: I want to be a wobbly people pole that tries to bring joy into the world, not one that takes joy from it.

Bobbing there like buoys, Dad and I talked and talked about so many things, hard things, and after, we swam even farther toward the horizon.

"I'd like to help cook," I tell the chefs. "I promise I'll add nothing bible-y."

Dad looks at Noah. "What do you think?"

Noah throws me a pepper.

But that's the beginning and end of my culinary contribution, because Oscar has walked into the kitchen in his black leather jacket, hair more unruly than usual, face full of weather. "Sorry to interrupt," he says. "I knocked, no one answered. The door was open…" I'm having déjà vu to the time Brian walked into the kitchen when Mom was baking. I look at Noah and know he's having it too. Brian still hasn't responded. Noah spent all afternoon with The Oracle, though. He knows Brian's at Stanford. I can feel all the news roiling inside him, the possibilities.

"It's okay. We never hear the door," I say to Oscar, walking over to him and taking his arm. He stiffens at my touch. Or maybe I imagined it? "Dad, this is Oscar."

Dad's once-over is not subtle or generous.

"Hello, Dr. Sweetwine," Oscar says, back to being the English butler. "Oscar Ralph." He's holding out his hand, which Dad shakes, tapping him on the back with the other.

"Hello, young man," my father says like it's the 1950s. "And

I'm emphasizing the *man* part intentionally." Noah laughs into his hand and then tries to pass it off as a cough. Oh boy. Dad's back. Present and accounted for.

"About that." Oscar looks at me. "Can we talk for a moment?"

I did not imagine it.

When I reach the doorway, I turn around because I'm hearing odd strangled noises. Dad and Noah are both doubled over behind the counter in hysterics. "What?" I ask.

"You found Ralph!" Noah croaks out and then doubles over again. Dad's wheezing-laughing so hard he's succumbed to the floor.

How I'd rather join my ark-mates than hear what I'm about to hear.

* * *

I follow an uncharacteristically grim Oscar out onto the front stoop.

I want to put my arms around him but don't dare. This is a good-bye visit. It's engraved all over his face. He sits down on the step and puts his hand on the space beside him so I'll join him. I don't want to join him, don't want to hear what he's going to say. "Let's sit on the bluff," I say, also not wanting Dad and Noah spying on us.

He follows me around to the back of the house. We sit, but so our legs don't touch.

The sea is calm, the breakers shuffling into shore without conviction.

"So," he says, smiling a cautious smile, which doesn't suit him. "I don't know if it's okay to talk about this, so stop me if

415

it's not." I nod slowly, unsure of what's coming. "I knew your mother well. I felt like she and Guillermo…" He trails off, regards me.

"It's all right, Oscar," I say. "I want to know."

"Your mum was around when I was at my worst, jonesing all the time, bouncing off the walls, afraid to leave the studio because I'd use if I did, afraid of the grief that was leveling me without the booze and drugs to mask it. The studio was different then. G. had tons of students. She used to paint there and I'd model for her just so she'd talk with me." So Noah was right. Mom was a secret painter.

"Was she Guillermo's student?"

He exhales slowly. "No, she was never his student."

"They met when she interviewed him?" I ask. He nods and then is quiet. "Go on."

"You sure?"

"Yes, please."

He smiles a truly madhouse smile. "I loved her. It was she more than G. who got me into photography. The strange thing is we used to sit and talk in that church where you and I first met. That's why I go there so much, it reminds me of her." This makes the hair on my arms rise up. "We'd sit in the pew and she'd go on and on about her twins." He laughs. "I mean *on and on and on*. Especially about you."

"Really?"

"Oh yes. I know so much about you, you have no idea. I've been trying to reconcile the two girls in my mind. The Jude your mother talked about and the CJ I was falling in love with." The past tense hitches on my heart. "She always joked that I wasn't to meet you until I'd been sober for three years and you were at least twenty-five because she was certain we'd fall head over heels in love and that would be that for both of us. She thought we were kindred spirits." He takes my hand and kisses the back of it, then rests it back on my lap. "She was right, I think."

"But what? Because the *but* here is killing me, Oscar."

He looks away from me. "But it's not our time. Not yet."

"No," I say. "It is our time. It's absolutely most definitely our time. I know you know it is too. It's Guillermo making you do this."

"No. It's *your mother* making me do this."

"You're not that much older than me."

"I'm three years older than you, which is a lot now but won't always be." I think how much less the three years between him and me seem than the years between Zephyr and me seemed when I was fourteen. I feel like Oscar and I are the same age.

"But you'll fall in love with someone else," I say.

"It's much more likely you will."

"Not possible. You're the guy in the portrait."

"And you're the girl in the prophecy."

"*My* mother's prophecy too, it seems," I say, taking his arm, thinking how strange it is that I gave Oscar a note Guillermo meant for my mother, like the words had fallen through time from them to us. Like a blessing.

"You're still in high school," Oscar's saying. "You're not even sodding legal, which didn't occur to me until Guillermo pointed it out a few hundred times last night. We can be great friends. We can bounce around on Hippity Hops and play chess and I don't know what." There's hesitation, frustration in his voice, but then he smiles. "I'll wait for you. I'll live in a cave. Or become a monk for a few years, wear a robe, shave the head, the whole bit. I don't know, I just really need to do the right thing here."

This is not happening. If ever there was a moment to press play, it's this one. Words start tumbling out of me. "And the right thing is turning our backs on what might be the love story of our lives? The right thing is denying destiny, denying all the forces that have conspired to bring us together, forces that have been at work for years now? No way." I feel the spirits of both Sweetwine women who came before me uprising inside me. Hear the sound of horses galloping through generations. I go on. "My mother, who was about to upend her life for love, and my grandmother, who calls God himself Clark Gable, do not want us to run away from this, they want us to run toward it." My hands are getting involved in the soliloquy thanks to Guillermo's tutelage. "I ended the boycott for you. I gave up practically the entire world for you. And for the record, a sixteen-year-old girl and a nineteen-year-old guy are probably at the exact same maturity level. Furthermore Oscar, *no offense, but* you're frightfully immature."

He laughs at that and before he knows what's happening I push him down and climb over and straddle him, holding his hands over his head so he's helpless.

"Jude."

"You know my name," I say, smiling.

"Jude is my favorite of all the saints," he says. "Patron saint of lost causes. The saint to call on when all hope is gone. The one in charge of miracles."

"You're kidding," I say, letting go of his hands.

"I kid you not."

So much better than traitorous Judas. "My new role model, then."

He inches up my tank top and there's just enough light from the house so that he can see the cherubs. His fingers trace their shapes. He holds my gaze, watching what his touch is doing to me, watching how it's making me free-fall. My breathing's getting faster and his eyes have gotten wavy with desire. "I thought you had impulse-control issues," I whisper.

"Totally in control here."

"Is that so?" I slip my hands under his shirt, let them wander, feel him tremble. He closes his eyes.

"Oh man, I bloody tried." He swings his hand around my back and in one swift move he's leaning over me, and then he's kissing me and the joy I feel and the desire I feel and the love I feel and feel and feel—

"I'm crazy about you," he says breathlessly, the bedlam in his face at an all-time peak.

"Me too," I answer.

"And I'm going to be crazy about you for a very long time."

"Me too."

"I'm going to tell you the things I'm afraid to tell anyone else."

"Me too."

He leans back, smiles, touches my nose. "I think that Oscar is the most brilliant bloke I've ever met, not to mention, way hot, and ladies and gentlemen, what a lean he has."

"Me too."

"Where the hell is Ralph?" Prophet squawks.

Right effing here.

* * *

Noah and I are outside Guillermo's studio. He wanted to come with me, but now he's fidgeting. "I feel like we're betraying Dad."

"We asked Dad."

"I know. But I still feel like we're supposed to challenge Garcia to a duel in Dad's honor."

"That would be funny."

Noah grins and shoulder-bumps me. "Yeah, it would."

I get it, though. My feelings about Guillermo kaleidoscope from hating him one minute for destroying our family, for breaking my father's heart, for a future that's never going to happen – and, what would've happened? Would he have lived with us? Would I have moved in with Dad? – to adoring him the next moment, like I have from the very first time I laid eyes on him as Drunken Igor and he said he wasn't okay. I keep thinking how strange it is that I would've met Guillermo and Oscar if Mom had lived too. We were all heading for each other on a collision course, no matter what. Maybe some people are just meant to be in the same story.

Guillermo's not answering the door, so Noah and I let

ourselves in and make our way together down the hallway. Something's different, I notice, but only realize when we get into the mailroom what it is. The floors have been mopped, and unbelievably, the mail's been cleared out. The door to the cyclone room is open and inside is an office again. I go to the doorway. In the center of the room, the broken angel is upright, with a stunning crack zigzagging across her back beneath her wings. I remember Guillermo saying the cracks and breaks were the best and most interesting parts of the work in my portfolio. Perhaps it's the same with people and their cracks and breaks.

I look around the mail-less, dustless space and wonder if Guillermo's opening up the studio again for students. Noah's standing in front of the painting of the kiss. "That's where I saw them that day," he says. His hand touches a dark shadow. "This is The Wooden Bird, you see it? Maybe they went there a lot."

"We did," Guillermo says, coming down the stairs with a broom and dustpan.

"My mother painted this," Noah says to him, no question in his voice.

"Yes," Guillermo replies.

"She was good," Noah says, still facing the painting.

Guillermo puts down the broom and dustpan. "Yes."

"She wanted to be a painter?"

"Yes. Deep down, I think so."

"Why didn't she tell us?" Noah turns around. There are tears in his eyes. "Why didn't she show us anything?

Guillermo says, "She was going to. She was not happy with anything she make. She wanted to show you something, I do not know, perfect maybe." He studies me, crosses his arms. "Maybe for the same reason you did not tell her about your sand women."

"My sand women?"

"I bring from home to show you." He walks over to the table where a laptop sits. He clicks the pad and a spread of photos appears on the screen.

I walk over to the computer. There they are. My flying sand ladies washed ashore after years at sea. How can it be? I turn to Guillermo, realize something remarkable. "It was you. You sent in the photos to CSA?"

He nods. "I did, anonymously. I feel that is what your mother want me to do. She was so worried you would not apply. She tell me she was going to send herself. So I do it." He points to the computer. "She love them very much, how carefree and crazy they are. Me too."

"She took these pictures?"

"No, I did," Noah says. "She must've found them on Dad's camera and downloaded them before I deleted them all." He looks at me. "The night of that party at Courtney's."

I'm trying to take all this in. Mostly that Mom knew something about the inside of me that I didn't think she did. It's making me feel weightless again. I look down. My feet are still touching the floor. People die, I think, but your relationship with them doesn't. It continues and is ever-changing.

I realize Guillermo's talking. "Your mother was so proud of both of you. I never know a mother so proud."

I glance around the room, sensing Mom so much, certain

this is what she wanted. She knew we each held an essential part of the story that needed to be shared. She wanted me to know she saw the sculptures and only Guillermo could tell me that. She wanted Guillermo and Dad to hear the truth from Noah. She wanted me to tell Noah about CSA and maybe I wouldn't have found the courage if I hadn't come to Guillermo, if I hadn't picked up a chisel and hammer. She wanted us in Guillermo's life, and he in ours, because we are, each one of us for the other, a key to a door that otherwise would've remained locked forever.

I think of the image in my mind that got me here in the first place: Mom, at the helm, steering us across the sky, keeping the course. Somehow, she did it.

"What am I, chopped liver?" It's Grandma!

"Of course not," I tell her without moving my lips, thrilled she's back and back to normal. "You're the bee's knees."

"Damn straight. And *for the record,* as you're so fond of saying, missy, *you,* young lady, do not make me up. How presumptuous. No idea where you picked up that thankless trait."

"No idea, Grandma."

Later, after he sets up Noah with canvases and paint – Noah couldn't resist when Guillermo offered – Guillermo finds me in the yard, where I've started on the clay model for Mom's sculpture. "I never see anyone paint like him," he says. "He is an Olympian. It is incredible to watch. Picasso, he once paint forty canvases in a month. I think Noah might in a day. It is like they are already finished and he is just delivering them."

"My brother has the ecstatic impulse," I say, remembering Oscar's essay.

"I think maybe your brother *is* the ecstatic impulse." He leans against the worktable. "I see a few pictures of you two when this small." He lowers a hand to the ground. "And Dianna, she always talk about Jude and her hair. I would never know, never ever would I think that you…" He shakes his head. "But now I think to myself of course you are her daughter. Noah, he look exactly like her, it hurt me to look at him, but you. You look nothing, nothing like her, but are so, so much like her. Everyone is afraid of me. Not your mother. Not you. You both just jump right in." He touches his chest. "You make me feel better from the very first instant I catch you on my fire escape and you talk about the flying brick." He covers his brow with his hand and when he lifts it, his eyes are red-rimmed. "But I understand if…" He falters, his face clouding with emotion. "I want very much for you to keep working with me, Jude, but I understand if you do not want or if your father do not want you to."

"You would've been my stepfather, Guillermo," I say as my answer. "And I would've made your life mis-er-a-ble."

He drops his head back and laughs. "Yes, I can see it. You would have been the holy terror."

I smile. Our connection is still so natural, though now, for me, it's tinged with guilt because of Dad. I turn back to my clay model, start caressing my mother's shoulder into shape, her upper arm. "It's like some part of me knew," I tell him, working the bend of her elbow. "I don't know what I knew, but I knew I was supposed to be here. You made me feel better too. So much better. I was so locked in."

"This is what I think," he says. "I think maybe Dianna, she

break your bowls, so you come find a stone carver."

I look at him. "Yeah," I say, the back of my neck tingling. "Me too."

Because who knows? Who knows anything? Who knows who's pulling the strings? Or what is? Or how? Who knows if destiny is just how you tell yourself the story of your life? Another son might not have heard his mother's last words as a prophecy but as drug-induced gibberish, forgotten soon after. Another girl might not have told herself a love story about a drawing her brother made. Who knows if Grandma really thought the first daffodils of spring were lucky or if she just wanted to go on walks with me through the woods? Who knows if she even believed in her bible at all or if she just preferred a world where hope and creativity and faith trump reason? Who knows if there are ghosts (sorry, Grandma) or just the living, breathing memories of your loved ones inside you, speaking to you, trying to get your attention by any means necessary? Who knows where the hell Ralph is? (Sorry, Oscar.) No one knows.

So we grapple with the mysteries, each in our own way.

And some of us get to float around on one of them and call it home. We visited *The Mystery* this morning and Dad hit it off with the owner, Melanie – I mean *really* hit it off. They're having drinks this evening on the deck of the ark. To discuss the sale, he told us, trying to hide the super-kook grin.

I wipe my hands clean on a nearby towel, reach in my bag and take out Guillermo's copy of Mom's book on Michelangelo.

"I stole it. I don't know why. I'm sorry."

He takes it from me, looks down at Mom's picture. "She call

me that day from the car. She sound so upset, so very upset. She say she need to see me later to talk. So when Noah come here and tell me… I am sure this is what she was going to say to me: that she change her mind."

On my way out, I stop to visit with the angel and make my last wish. For Noah and Brian.

Best to bet on all the horses, dear.

* * *

It's Thursday, two weeks later, and Dad and I are on the front stoop, peeling off our wetsuits. He swam, I surfed, or more accurately, I got rag-dolled wave after wave – totally amazing. As I dry off, I'm keeping my eyes glued to the trailhead across the street because I feel fairly certain the five p.m. rendezvous spot is in the woods where Noah and Brian spent all their time that summer.

Noah told me he found Brian's address online and sent him a series of drawings he did – around the clock like a maniac – called *The Invisible Museum*. A few days later, there was a response to his post on LostConnections. It said: *I'll be there.*

Last week, Noah received an invitation to attend CSA, based on the photos of his mural I took. I told Sandy I'd give up my spot for him if necessary. It wasn't. Noah hasn't decided what he's going to do.

The sunset has turned the sky into a carnival of color as Noah and Brian walk out of the forest, hand in hand. Brian notices Dad and me first and shrugs his hand away, but Noah immediately finds it again. At this, Brian's eyes squint up and his face cracks open in a heart-crushing smile. Noah, like always around Brian, can barely keep his head on his neck, he's so happy.

"Oh," Dad says. "Oh, I see. Okay. I didn't realize. I thought, Heather, you know? But this makes more sense."

"It does," I say, noticing a ladybug has landed on my hand.

Quick, make a wish.

Take a (second or third or fourth) chance.

Remake the world.

Acknowledgements

Writing this novel took a lot of time, way too much of it away from the people I adore the very most. My deepest heartfelt gratitude goes to them – I named names last time; it's the exact same names this time, so I'll just say: my friends, my family, my dd – thanks to all of you for bending the days and weeks and years toward joy, for squeezing in with me under the umbrella during storms, for understanding when I'm in writing lockdown and celebrating with me when I'm not. Like Jude says: Some people are just meant to be in the same story. I'm so happy I get to be in the same story with you wonderful people.

For the earliest reads when I was still at VCFA and this story was nothing but a nascent mess of first pages in a packet, thanks go to my wondrous mentors: Julie Larios and Tim Wynne Jones. For her passionate, intimate, dazzling discourse with me and this work during my VCFA post graduate semester, a big thank-you: Louise Hawes. For early reads that must've felt like bushwhacking, thank you so very much: Brent Hartinger, Margaret Bechard, Patricia Nelson, Emily Rubin, my amazing mother, Edie Block, who is my heart and ballast, and for later reads: Larry Dwyer and Marianna Baer. For all the phone calls and emails about writing emergencies and revelries, thank you again and to the moon: Marianna. For teaching me how to carve stone, thank you to the terrific stone sculptor: Barry Baldwin. For help with everything surfing, thank you: Melanie Sliwka. For science queries, thanks go to my mad scientist brother: Bruce. For Paris, *merci beaucoup*, Monica. For their constant support and daily check-ins while writing this one, special thanks go to: my brother Bobby, my mom, Annie, and especially specially: my darling Paul. Almost all of Jude's "bible entries" I made up but a few may be frankensteined from the fantastic 1903 *Encyclopaedia of Superstitions, Folklore and the Occult Sciences of the World* edited by Cora Linn Daniels and C. M. Stevens.

I am so lucky to have Holly McGhee of Pippin Properties as my literary agent. I'm grateful every day for her brilliance, her savvy, her support, her humor, her passionate devotion to art and writing. Her joy. She offered profound, insightful feedback on this story along with wild enthusiasm. Really, more often than not she makes me feel airborne with excitement! Endless thanks also go to the other Pippins: Elena Giovinazzo (for so very much) and Courtney Stevenson (who also read and gave excellent notes on the manuscript, plus much more). I'm absolutely indebted to my editor Jessica Garrison at Dial who had keen, perfect instincts for this story and whose superb feedback was spot on, revelatory, and invaluable. Plus she's patient, funny, and kind to boot: a delight. I deeply thank everyone else at Dial and Penguin Young Readers Group too, particularly: Lauri Hornik, Heather Alexander, copy editor Regina Castillo, designer Jenny Kelly, and Theresa Evangelista, who designed this kickass cover I so adore. In addition, many thanks go to everyone at Walker Books UK, especially Jane Winterbotham and my terrific editor, Annalie Grainger, who is a joy to work with. I'm thrilled with this stunning edition and so appreciative of all the hard work and beautiful design that went into creating it. Finally, I'm so grateful for my foreign rights agents, Alex Webb, Allison Hellegers, Alexandra Devlin, Harim Yim, and Rachel Richardson at Rights People in the UK as well as for my film agent Jason Dravis of Monteiro Rose Dravis Agency. It takes a village and I have an extraordinary one!

My dear friend: the fierce, gracious, beautiful, ridiculously brilliant and talented poet Stacy Doris died while I was writing this book. This story about artistic passion and pleasure, about the ecstatic impulse, about split-aparts, is also dedicated to her.

Lennie Walker, seventeen, *Wuthering Heights*
obsessed, clarinet player, band geek. Also hopeless
romantic, prone to scattering poems all over town
and, as of four weeks ago, sisterless...

**A heart-breaking, heart-lifting, utterly
compelling and completely unforgettable
novel about first love and first loss.**

#TheSkyIsEverywhere
@jandynelson @WalkerBooksUK